WHAT BIG EYES YOU HAVE

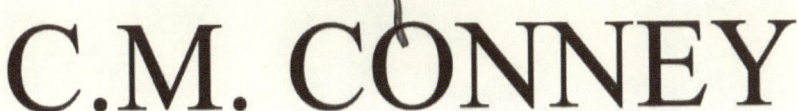

C.M. CONNEY

Published by
Ace Lyon Books
2025

Published by
Ace Lyon Books
Acelyonbooks.com
First Edition
Cover Design by S. M. Savoy
What Big Eyes You Have, C. M. Conney
ISBN 978-1-947122-60-4

Contents

ONE

I reluctantly turned off the lathe to let Howard finish sweeping. Howard, Jace, and I were the only ones still in the machine shop. Everyone else had called it quits hours ago. I was sure Howard wanted to get out of here, but I was also certain he'd be horrified if I offered to clean up. Which was silly when my father wouldn't notice or care.

I began neatening the mess I'd made, stacking the remaining wood into a neat pile and tossing the finished pieces of trim into a box to take with me, then using a shop vac to vacuum the sawdust.

I hoped my pile of supplies wasn't in the way here because Howard wouldn't tell me to move it unless my dad came in and ordered it moved, which wasn't likely as he rarely came to this shop. Still, I should get this all out before my father saw it and thought to ask what it was doing here.

I figured it would take another two to four weeks for me to finish.

I still needed ten spindles to finish the stairs, sixteen table legs, thirty corbels, and too many odds and ends to count.

"Kate!" Jace called. "If you're going, park this beast for me."

He tossed me the keys to my mother's vintage silver Aston Martin DB5.

"Why is it in here anyway," I asked as I snagged the keys.

"I had to fabricate a new frame for the taillight."

I walked around the car to examine it. To my eye the two lights were an exact match.

"Did you make two new ones?"

"Nah. Just the one."

"Great job!"

He shrugged, but I could see he was pleased.

I wished I could think of something—anything else to say, but as usual, I came up with nothing.

You'd think after all these months of drooling over him I'd have thought of something wittier than great job...

Howard yelled from the driveway, "Turn off the lights, will you? I'm starving."

Jace nodded, waving agreement, muttering, "Me too."

And without thinking, I said, "Wanna get something to eat?"

"With you?"

I immediately felt like a fool.

"I do eat too, you know."

My flush felt like fire.

I forced a laugh, dangling the keys, "I'll let you drive."

"*Ha!* Your mother would kill us."

But his eyes had lit.

Excitement made me really laugh—I had him now, all six-foot-two of muscled gorgeousness and wavy brown hair.

"Don't be a baby," I said teasingly.

"Don't be a tease. You know I can't risk this job—for a stupid car ride."

My heart thudded. I hoped I wasn't reading him wrong because I thought he was implying he would risk it for dinner with me.

I grinned at him as I took out my phone to call my mother.

"Yes, Kate," she said in her usual brisk way.

"Your car is fixed. Can I take it to—"

"Don't be too late, dear."

"Go commit a murder?"

His mouth dropped open and I laughed as I waggled my phone at him. "Dial tone. She doesn't care where I take it. Let's go."

He laughed, making my pulse pound again as he held out his hand, saying, "I'm driving, remember?"

I tossed the keys back to him.

"I got the door," I said as I hit the switch.

The garage door rumbled up. It took a good minute because it was a large door.

He drove out and I turned off the lights, set the alarm, and hit the switch to close the door.

"Brush yourself off, fool," he said when I opened the car door.

Another hot flush scalded my cheeks as I glanced down at my filthy jeans.

I hastily brushed sawdust from my shirt and pants and pulled the elastic from my hair to finger comb it. *I must be a hot mess*, I thought in rising dismay.

I was sorry I'd asked him now—sort of.

Better to get it over with, I told myself. Maybe I could get more work done if I stopped mooning over him. Of course, if this went as badly as I thought it was going to, I wouldn't dare show my face again...

While I was thinking of the billions of stupid ways I could mess this up, he was driving us down our long private drive past the three other garages and the house.

He kept to the speed limit when we reached the road, which sort of surprised me.

I was glad he was driving because I'd have been speeding, trying to impress him.

I made a mental note of his causal pose, not that I thought I could mimic it, at least not without hours of practice, but at least I wouldn't look like a spaz the next time I tried to impress a boy with my mad driving skills, *which would be never...*

"So, where do you want to eat?" he asked.

"McDonalds?"

He rolled his eyes at me, saying, "I might not be as rich as you, but I can afford a pizza..."

I said, "I'm not rich. I have twenty bucks to spend on dinner, and since I invited you..."

He snorted with laughter.

"What the hell do you spend it on? It certainly isn't clothes and makeup."

One part of me was thrilled that he'd noticed me enough to know I didn't care about clothes and makeup, but the bigger part was angry — and hurt—even though I *didn't* care about clothes or makeup.

I said, "What? You think I cut those trees down myself to get that wood?"

It came out angrier than I'd intended.

"I guess I thought your dad bought it for you."

I snorted and was surprised when he winced.

"Not every girl spends all their money on shoes," I said tartly.

"Just every Avery girl," he said laughingly.

That really pissed me off.

I said nothing.

"Sorry," he said a second later. "That was uncalled for. You're nothing like Everly."

That was true—and not what I wanted to hear from him or any boy because boys *loved* my sister.

I shrugged.

He said, "So what do you do with all your dough? Besides buy wood. And what do you do with all of that wood anyway?"

"I'm not telling you."

"*Aww*, don't be like that. I meant that Everly thing as a compliment. No offense or anything but I think your sister is a—ditz."

That made me snort with laughter, although ditz wouldn't have been my adjective of choice.

I said, "I'm not telling because no one knows, except Grayson."

"Now you *have* to tell me!"

"We can go halves on the pizza," I said grudgingly because I hadn't been kidding about the twenty dollars and I needed to buy more wood stain.

"Nope. You don't get to eat till you tell me."

"And if I tell and then you tell, it'll be ruined."

He drove in silence for a few minutes before saying thoughtfully, "You mean that, don't you?"

"Yes."

"Fine. Don't tell me then. But I *can* keep a secret."

He'd said that last bit angrily, which made me think someone had blamed him for telling a secret when he hadn't. I knew intimately how awful it felt being blamed for shit that you hadn't done.

I said, "I'm building a house."

He gaped at me.

I burst into laughter.

He frowned, turning back to the road, placing two hands on the wheel.

"To hide your corpses, no doubt," he said sarcastically.

That made me laugh so hard it made my eyes water.

"Exactly."

"Funny," he said dryly like he thought I was a bigger bitch than Everly. My stomach sank.

"Seriously. I'll show you. It's the old place on Briarwood."

He turned to gape at me again, but surprised relief lit his eyes.

It occurred to me that he maybe thought I was just like Everly after all. And she liked nothing better than to make people look stupid—to feel small. Or maybe that was just me because no one else seemed to mind her stupid tricks. Or maybe they pretended not to just like I did because reacting made her happy, which made her try harder to get a reaction.

While I was musing on why anyone in the world hung out with my sister, he was driving us to my house.

I said absently, "I should've brought that finished trim with me."

"You're seriously rebuilding it—yourself?"

"Yep. Remember you promised not to say anything. I'm going to be seriously pissed if you mention this to anyone!"

"Your brother Grayson knows though?"

"I needed an adult to buy it for me."

"Jesus, how much did it cost! And whatever it was, you were robbed! It's falling down. How the hell did you talk him into it?"

"I have a solid plan."

"Which is?"

"I'm going to open a hotel—a gothic mystery getaway. Briarwood Manor will open in three, maybe four years."

"How the hell..." he shook his head, his lips pursing and both hands on the wheel again.

"My mom thought I was crazy too," I said bitterly.

Thinking about her laugh still hurt. That she hadn't even glanced at me as I poured out my dream, hadn't looked at my sketches or lists or read my prospectus, hadn't even *glanced* at it, hurt more.

I said, "My grandfather left me enough to buy it, and you're right, they weren't asking much at all because it's so rundown. So I signed that money over to Grayson and he bought it for me, and loaned me enough to get the roof fixed and a new fuse box put in. The rest I'll fix a little at a time. I pay all the bills on it. The taxes aren't bad at all. My goal is to have one functioning bathroom by August."

"What happens in August?"

"I turn eighteen and can move in."

"I thought you were going to Princeton?"

"*Ha!* That's my father's plan for me."

But I was thrilled he was paying enough attention to me to know that.

"You're not going... does he know that?"

"I've said it often enough, but I haven't *argued* about it. He assumes I'm going, but that's his fault! I never even applied. He did."

"Oh boy..."

I nodded.

"Yep. It's going to be awful, which is why I'm moving out the minute I can. I hope my mom will give me my college fund when she sees I'm serious about this."

"And if she doesn't?"

"Then it takes me longer."

"So why the hell did you take the college prep classes if you didn't want to go to college?"

"How did you know I did?"

He flushed.

Excited tingles made my skin feel tight.

I said, "Kenya and Grayson both got really nice cars when they graduated with honors. I'm no dummy..."

He snorted with laughter.

"I'm going to sell mine though..."

He gaped at me again, which made me snort with laughter.

"I'll have to. I figure I can live off that car for a year."

"How will you afford the supplies you need to repair the place?"

"I can get a part time job, although that's a last resort. I'm hoping my You Tube channel will supply enough, or I might rent rooms dirt cheap so I don't have to let them use the rest of the house."

"What You Tube channel?"

"The one I'm going to start once I move out. I've been filming my project."

"Yeah... you're pretty enough to get people to watch just about anything."

That pleased me and angered me in equal measure. On one hand, I was glad—thrilled—he thought I was pretty. It wasn't a compliment I heard much. On the other hand, it was bullshit of him to assume I had nothing fun or interesting to show anyone. I didn't know how to respond, so I didn't.

He slowed to pull into my driveway.

A tall, crumbling brick wall covered with vines and scrub brush ran along the front of the property. I hadn't decided yet if I intended to tear that wall down or rebuild it. I was definitely keeping the massive pillars that were on either side of the driveway entrance though.

I said, "Someday I'll get a new gate. I've drawn out exactly what I want it to look like. It'll say Briarwood in really fancy script with roses with big thorns intertwined. I'll keep the drive gravel for the nice crunchy effect when you pull in and add in a formal garden, the kind with hedges and paths. I'll let it be sort of overgrown with lots of roses and stuff to keep it a bit creepy. If everything goes as planned, I'll start it next year so it has time to grow a bit before I open. Eventually, I'll build a conservatory behind the house, the kind with fancy windows and exotic plants.

I figure I can grow some of the plants I'll need in it but mostly I want it for atmosphere."

"The kind of place an artist would dig," he said thoughtfully, and I nodded pleased approval.

He continued, "Sort of mysterious and sort of romantic with just a hint of practical."

I was thrilled he got me so well.

I said, "I'll put in another garden with paths and arbors leading into the woods, and I'll put in hedges around a pool and some fountains. I hope to rent it out for weddings and stuff."

He said, "It would be a great spot for a wedding what with the view of the river if you cleared the scrub out."

I nodded eagerly. "It's going to be themed but *tastefully* themed.

The driveway and yard were completely overgrown, except for a few trampled paths from the workmen who'd put on the new roof and a swath I'd cleared so I wouldn't scratch my dad's truck.

Jace parked at the end of the driveway right passed the pillars.

I said, "Watch your step. I only slapped some boards on the porch so I don't fall through. This whole porch needs to be replaced.

"Cha Ching."

I nodded—it was going to be a huge expense.

I said, "I planned to make it go all around the house and add in wooden trim like it should've had—and maybe some secret passages. I haven't decided yet because they'd have to be small tunnels to fit and I wasn't sure if anyone would bother use something like that, although maybe a really short one…

"Welcome to Briarwood," I said as I unlocked the door.

"It's *uh* charming."

I snickered.

I'd been removing the old wallpaper in the front hall in between other projects, so the walls were best described as patchy. I'd taken down all of the light fixtures, leaving just a few bare bulbs. I'd begun repairing the spindles of the staircase, stripping the paint from the molding, and had begun removing the old tile in the hallway. My plan called for an old-fashioned bell-pull system in all the rooms, which I'd already run piping for through the ceilings beside the water pipes for the sprinkler system that building codes required, but I hadn't covered the holes yet. It was a mess.

I said, "I never have enough cash to finish a project, so I work on the refinishing while waiting on my allowance. Luckily, there's plenty of things that just need elbow grease that I can do while waiting. I have one room finished, except for the doors."

I pointed to the pocket doors that I was in the process of stripping of a hundred years of old paint.

He stepped closer to examine the drawing I'd tapped up beside the door.

"Is this how it was or will be?"

"In this case, it's how it is. I've been drawing this place for as long as I can remember. I know just how I want each room to look. They all have a drawing."

I slid the door open, watching his face. I really really wanted him to like it—to be impressed.

"Briarwood," I said with what I felt was justifiable pride.

To my eyes, the room was beautiful.

The painstakingly sanded and refinished wood floor gleamed. I'd added paneling going three quarters of the way up the walls and stained it a dark brown, replastered and painted the fireplace, adding built-in shelves on either side that held old books that I'd gotten over the years from flea markets and tag sales, vintage games, playing cards, and a few knickknacks that I thought matched the tone of the room. I'd put in two new stained-glass windows that I'd made myself on either side of the fireplace, which was how the fireplace would've been originally. Both of the windows had been made at summer camp when I was sixteen. I'd had to backlight them because of a latter addition to the house that had made the fireplace on an interior wall.

I laughed to myself as he examined the windows, remembering begging my mother to attend that camp. I'd chosen it more to escape Everly, it being the sort of thing she'd never do, but had really loved it. Someday, I wanted to build my own glass studio, but it would need to wait until the house was making money.

I'd re-glazed the original leaded glass windows and there were seven of them, all of them nine-feet-tall with fancy metal work, four in the bowed curve of the far wall opposite the doorway and three on the front wall. All of the windows were framed with dark blue velvet curtains that pooled on the floor. I'd made them myself from material I'd thrifted.

An almost life-size painting of my grandmother as I imagined her to be when she was young, beautiful, and haughty, wearing a ball gown in matching blue colors, holding her cat Trixie who wore a sparkling diamond collar, hung above the fireplace. It had taken me a week to get the knack of making the eyes appear to follow you.

The room was furnished with a dark blue velvet couch, which sat on an oriental rug bracketed by two upholstered chairs, one with a footstool. I planned to add pillows once I'd painted the rest of the walls down here so I could match the colors better. I'd made the small end table on one side of the couch myself. The other, my inspiration piece, I'd saved from the dump and refinished. It held a bronze table lamp with a real Tiffany shade with pink roses, teal-green leaves, and a blue bird, which I'd gotten from my grandmother. She'd called it old trash, but a little elbow grease had shone the bronze right up.

The couch was far enough from the wall that you could walk all the way around it.

A floor lamp that I'd made myself from a crystal chandelier I'd gotten from a thrift store sat in the corner of the room with a few potted plants in planters I'd made with faux marble finishes and two vintage wood chairs that I'd bought at a tag sale and refinished. I'd made them simple cushions that matched the drapes.

In front of the couch, to one side of the hearth, there was a small table and two chairs, also from thrift stores and refinished, with a fake tree and an old bird cage. An upholstered Queen Anne chair with a floor-length mirror behind it was on the other side. I'd made the mirror frame from scrap wood that I'd painted to resemble aged gold. It was sort of clunky and uneven but I liked the overall effect.

A few smaller paintings, one of my grandmother's cat, two of my grandmother as she'd aged, and a garden scene with Briarwood as it would be hung on the walls. Candelabra sconces bracketed the fireplace. A bear head rug lay on the floor in front of the hearth. But the *piece de resistance* was hidden in the hearth.

He whistled softly as he gazed about. "Holy cow!"

My face heated from nervous excitement because I thought he really was impressed.

"*Ta da,*" I said proudly as I pulled the right candelabra.

The hearth slid aside with the faintest creak, revealing narrow steep stairs.

"I dare you," I said laughingly.

"Was that here all along? How did you find it?"

"I put it in. Every room will have at least one secret. This one has three."

He leaned past me, so close I could feel the heat from his body and smell his aftershave, which even after a hard day at work still smelled amazing.

"Where's it go?"

"Go see."

"It's not going to collapse or anything, is it?"

I laughed in delight, shaking my head.

"I considered adding that but didn't want anyone suing me. Stairs are always just stairs."

He took out his phone to turn his flashlight on.

"Cheater," I whispered.

He turned to me laughing as he took the first step, which put us eye-to-eye.

I don't think he noticed the red light that lit the stairs from the foot of them when he'd stepped on the stair because his gaze was locked on me.

I stopped breathing when he leaned in to kiss me.

His lips on mine filled me with lightness, leaving me feeling buoyant as if I could just float away—or to him. The warmth of him was like gravity pulling me closer.

"What took you so long?" I asked breathlessly when we parted.

"I have no idea..."

He kissed me again, pulling me even closer.

The heat of him lit a fire in my stomach.

I never wanted him to stop.

I slid my hands under his t-shirt, which I knew was too much too soon, but I couldn't stop myself. He was pressed so hard against me I could feel his erection against my leg, which was all the encouragement I needed.

I'm crazy, I thought in one corner of my mind.

My mother's warnings about how boys never respected a girl who was easy were ringing in my ears.

Everly never seemed to have a problem with boys calling her back, I told myself when those cautions might have made me hesitate—because more than anything, I wanted him to call me back, which reminded me that he hadn't called me this time. I had no idea why he'd agreed to dinner and almost didn't care if he was just seeing how far I'd go.

The heat of his palm branded the skin of my waist.

I'd never forget the feeling if I lived to be a hundred.

His hand slid upward with maddening slowness.

I wished we were both naked.

I wished we'd been lovers for years so there'd be no awkwardness, so I'd know just what to do, which reminded me I hadn't a clue and hadn't prepared and was acting like a complete slut. But I didn't stop him when his hand cupped my breast. His thumb grazed my nipple, making me moan.

He dropped his hand, pulling back, breathing hard, muttering, "What am I doing?"

A pit formed in my stomach.

"I remember now why I never asked."

His grip on me tightened as I jerked away, but he released me a second later.

I'd never felt so humiliated—so awful—so meaningless—in my life.

"You're way out of my league, Kate."

"Which league is that?" I tried to say lightly, but my voice trembled, which pissed me off.

"You know exactly what I mean," he said angrily.

"I wasn't playing in any league," I said with as much dignity as I could muster when I wanted to burst into tears.

He tossed his phone to the rug to frame my face with his hands. "You're going to break my heart."

Hope left me breathless.

I shook my head.

"No one like you seriously falls for a guy like me."

I quirked a brow saying, "A smoking hot guy who likes to work with his hands like she does?"

He gazed around the room as if he was surprised to find himself there.

"Look at this place, Kate! This is serious money. *You're* serious money. I'm beer and potatoes."

"Most of this room budget was on the rug and couch. I bought a huge stack of used wood panels from this guy online. I think it might've been hot, but beggars can't be choosers. I got another even bigger stack of wood pallets that didn't cost me anything, except the gas and time to move them all. I pick up furniture people toss out at the dump, from the side of the road, and thrift shops and then fix it up. Some of it I use and some I sell.

"It cost me almost two thousand dollars to do this room, which was four hundred over budget, but the secret stairs were a learning curve, so I forgive myself."

"No way."

"Yes way. And what difference does that make?"

"Your father will hate me."

"*Pfft*. He likes you more than he likes me!"

He frowned at me, searching my face.

"You know that's not true. He might like me just fine for working on his cars, but for his daughter... I don't think so."

"I think I was perfectly clear that I'm not following the path he's laid out for me."

"And I don't want to be the guy you use to dick him over."

I headed to the door too angry to speak, not that I knew what to say to that.

TWO

"Kate..."

"You're not interested. Fine. Whatever. Let's get pizza."

"You're being ridiculous!"

I turned to yell at him, "No one ever sees me! I tell them and they don't hear me! It's like I don't exist at all! I'm just an image of a girl floating around. Everyone sees me however the hell they imagine I am! Except Grayson..."

My unexpected outburst shocked us both. I never ever yelled. Never. I had no idea why I'd decided tonight of all nights I'd be a crazy bitch.

We stared at each other for a minute before he said, "I'm sorry. You're right, but to be fair, I was trying not to see you at all!"

I shrugged.

He stepped from the stairs, and despite how angry and hurt I was, I was still pleased to see the hearth slide closed just like it was supposed to.

He crouched to examine it as he said, "I really like my job, Kate. Messing with his daughters is sure to get me fired."

"You don't need to *mess* with *them*."

"You really made this yourself?"

"That, the paintings, the tables, the windows..."

"How long did it take?"

"Greyson bought the house a year and a half ago. It took six months to do the roof and electric. He wouldn't let me work inside until it was done or while they were here."

"So a year for one room..."

I tried not to let that hurt. It *was* taking me a long time, but I had to teach myself how to do almost everything as well as having to work on it in secret after school.

I said, "I've demo'd all the rooms and started other projects here and there, and like I said, I've been working as I can afford the parts. I knew it would take me years to do it."

He grabbed his phone and stuffed it into his pocket, then toured the room slowly, pausing in front of the painting over the hearth.

"You did this?"

"Yeah."

"It's beautiful," he said so doubtfully that I giggled.

"I'm not lying."

"I didn't think you were. I've seen you painting on the back deck. I just never imagined... this is really good."

"Thanks..."

"Are you supposed to go study art?"

"*Ha*! Art isn't a real job. It isn't for grownups! It's for flakes and losers and people who don't know how to work."

He winced at me.

I shrugged, wondering what the hell was wrong with me with these crazy outbursts.

"I bought the frame from a thrift store and repainted it to make it look like antique metal."

"It's wood?"

"Yeah. I'd like to learn to make wood filigree like that someday, but old frames are a lot cheaper than new wood. I've got a bunch now ready to hang."

"With paintings?"

I nodded. "I still have paintings to finish. Plus, I've decided to paint the hall instead of papering it. I've learned to do this really cool special effect to make writing appear when I change the light color. I'll use paint I can write on that I can add my messages to and then erase it. It'll look like wallpaper when I'm done. That hall will take me a month or so to paint. I think I'll sand the floor in the dining and drawing rooms next— after a bathroom, I mean. I'd like to get that done before I move in just to keep the dust down, plus it won't cost me much to rent the sander. I haven't decided yet if I'll put a wood floor in the hall or retile it or maybe I'll do a mix of both. A wood inlay floor would look nice, and I might be able to use my pallets for it."

He continued his slow examination of the room, tugging lightly on the other candelabra as he said, "Will you stay in this room?"

"No. I'll seal this room off with plastic."

He turned, putting his hands on his hips as he said, "Okay, I give up. Where are the other two secrets?"

"There's a safe behind the painting, and the light in the corner opens the window."

He tugged the frame.

I said, "It's *secret*, not obvious."

He began removing books, reading the titles before putting them back.

He laughed when he lifted the old Clue board game and the frame released with a loud click.

"I made it loud on purpose, which took me a few days of searching the web to learn how to do."

"I think I love you."

My breath caught. I was glad he wasn't looking at me because the room clouded with my tears.

I'd regained my cool by the time he'd turned from examining the safe.

He joined me, surprising me by taking my hand, twining his fingers with mine. "No bullshit, Kate. I'm going to be more than pissed if you're playing with me. I don't want to be a chump."

"I'm *not* Everly. I'm Kate."

My breath left me in a hard sigh as he kissed me.

We kissed long enough to leave me breathless and unsteady.

The automatic exterior lights came on, and he jumped, laughing nervously.

I went to close the velvet drapes on the front windows as I said, "My brother insisted. He put in the security because I work late here a lot. The lights in the other rooms go on and off randomly so people think there's people here."

"I don't think that's working. I hadn't heard this place was being restored."

I sat on the rug. "Come sit a minute. Take in the vibe."

He sat beside me.

"Does the fireplace work?"

"In theory. Grayson had them all checked for cracks and cleaned when the roof was done, but I haven't checked the dampers."

"Checked them for what?"

"I have no idea... I'll Google it someday..."

15

He snorted with laughter.

I said, "Maybe I'll try one of the fireplaces in the other rooms first. I'd hate to get this room all smokey."

His fingers grazed my neck as he tucked a loose strand of my hair back.

That small touch made my breasts ache.

The books on the farther shelf slid out a bit.

He didn't seem to notice, and I didn't care enough to interrupt him by pointing it out.

He continued to fuss with my hair, missing the flickering light behind him. I'd sat here purposefully to trigger the effects that I'd painstakingly worked out. I'd been dying to show them off but watching his eyes darken and lips part was much more interesting than spooky books and lights.

For over a year now I'd been daydreaming of running my hands through his hair and it felt like a dream as I did it.

The entire night suddenly felt surreal.

"Am I dreaming?" I whispered as I leaned in to kiss him.

"We both are."

He lay back taking me with him.

The heat of his kiss traveled through my body. I let my hands wander under his shirt, down his sides, across his back and then his sides again and over his chest.

We both laughed in giddy excitement as he stripped off his shirt.

I pulled mine off too and helped him with my bra.

My bare breasts against his chest was terrifying and perfect.

"God, you're so beautiful," he said as he sat back to watch himself cup my breast.

He leaned down to kiss it.

I slipped my hands under the waistband of his jeans, caressing his ass and was a bit disappointed when he stopped kissing my breasts to kiss my lips until I realized he was undoing his pants.

Conflicting desires made me dizzy. I *wanted* to continue but *knew* I was being a fool.

He undid his pants, then mine.

In minutes we were both naked.

I wished I was more experienced—any experience would've given me more confidence, not that he seemed put off by my tentative caresses.

His fingers and lips kept distracting me from my explorations of him.

My entire body felt flushed.

Jace Blake was going to make love to me.

It felt like one of my fantasies, like I'd wake any minute in my bedroom at home.

I was touching his naked body. That thought would've made me laugh in amazement if I had breath to laugh.

He kissed me for another long minute, resting his forehead on mine to say, "You're sure."

"God, yes."

He laughed and rolled us over to kneel between my legs— and someone pounded on the front door.

"They'll go away," I said hopefully because no one ever knocked.

He groaned but reached for his pants.

"I'll get it," I said resignedly.

I dressed hurriedly, not bothering with my bra or shoes.

Whoever it was pounded twice more before I reached the door.

I yanked the door open, saying, "What the hell—"

"Kate?" my father said in surprise.

"What are you doing here?" we both said.

I laughed nervously.

"I saw my car," he said.

"Mom's car."

"Don't be pedantic.

"Whatever."

"Why are you answering the door? Whose house is this?"

"Grayson's."

Not technically a lie as it *was* his until my eighteenth birthday.

"What?"

"Grayson—your son. Surely you remember him."

"*Ha.* Get him down here."

"He isn't here."

"Then why are *you* here.

"I'm going to be painting."

"Oh—well good. Do something useful with that hobby thing. Why do you have your *mother's* car though?"

"She said I could use it. I won't be late."

"In the future, use the Toyota or Ford when coming here—or anywhere. That's too much car for you."

"Sure thing, Dad."

His eyes narrowed.

I saluted.

He huffed in annoyance and stomped away.

I called Grayson.

"Hey," he said as greeting.

"I'm at the house and Dad was just here. I told him it was your house, and that I was painting."

"I didn't say a word to him, I swear."

"I know. It was my fault. I'd borrowed Mom's car and he saw it."

"He saw it...what the hell was he doing on that street?"

"I didn't think to ask him."

"I know I said I'd keep it secret, but I'm not going to lie."

"You don't have to lie. If he asks, tell him the truth. It's an investment."

"Kate..."

"Please, Gray! If you tell him, God knows what he'll do, but whatever it is, I'm the one who'll be stuck there listening to it! It's just a few more months. And it *isn't* a lie. It *is* an investment!"

"Fine. But if he presses..."

"Why would he? He doesn't care what we do."

"Kate..."

"Don't Kate me. You know he doesn't."

"Just...be careful. I don't like you going there alone at night."

"As opposed to being alone in the expensive looking house?"

"You're not alone there."

I snorted.

"Sure, "Felicity and Wolfgang are going to be great bodyguards. Or maybe I could send Hannah and Harley out? Or did you imagine Everly would fight off a burglar?"

"If you go..."

"We aren't arguing about this again. I love them. I really really do, but I'm not giving up my dream to babysit. The kids could stay here with me whenever they want to, but I'm not staying in the house with her one day longer than I have to."

"Mom is going to freak."

"That's her problem. Besides, I was younger than Everly when I began watching them and they were just babies, much harder to watch than they are now."

"I know, I know, it's just... I hate the idea of them stuck with our bitch of a sister too..."

"Then say something—but not till I go cause she's going to be unbearable."

"I should say something now. You shouldn't be chased from your own home."

"*This* is my home."

"You can come stay with me or Kenya, you know that, right?"

"Are you crazy! He'd freak. Neither of you need that."

"Like he isn't going to freak the minute he realizes I encouraged you?"

"You didn't. Well, you did, but not like you mean. You've been great. The best big brother anyone ever had."

"I love you too."

He hung up.

I pocketed my phone.

"Sorry," I said ruefully to Jace.

My heart sunk when I saw he'd dressed completely, shoes and all.

"I should've got the door," he said.

"Don't be silly. I'd never ask you to lie. Besides, he'd have been pissed as shit if you'd taken the car out."

He said worriedly, "I don't know what to do here, I really want to ask you out again—well, for the first time, but it will piss him off, maybe enough to fire me."

"I'd say yes."

He rolled his eyes at me.

I giggled and his tense expression eased.

He stepped forward to hug me.

I said, "Don't take this wrong, but the mood was ruined for me. Besides, I should wait at least until the second date. I don't want you to think I'm easy."

He snorted with laughter.

"Yeah, your dad is anti-Viagra. It's like a superpower."

He kissed me, running his fingers through my hair, which left me heated enough that I said thoughtfully, "On the other hand, he isn't likely to come back here tonight..."

"Don't tempt me," he said primly as he stepped away. "I didn't come prepared. Your superpower is making me lose every spec of common sense. Unless... are you prepared?"

I flushed to my toes.

He snickered for a moment before he flushed too, looking away, then turning away to head back to the parlor, saying oh so casually, "Are you a virgin, Kate?"

"Of course I am," I said angrily. "Who's bothering with gawky Kate?"

"As opposed to everyone can have Everly Avery?" He turned back and I could see from his flush that he was embarrassed too. "Look, I didn't mean to embarrass either of us. It's just I never saw you with anyone and you never flirt or anything but then tonight... and I didn't want to just assume, but it's a big deal for a nice girl like you, *and* for me, and I don't want to be an ass."

"I hear that," I said grudgingly.

He snickered again.

I said, "I won't mention us to anyone—if there's going to be an us. You can tell whoever you want whatever you want."

He headed into the parlor where he grabbed my shoes and bra. He tossed me the shoes then held up my bra, which for some reason was way more embarrassing than letting him touch my naked breasts.

"Nice," he said and handed it over.

I rolled my eyes at him.

"Like I need to ask if you're a virgin," I muttered.

He shrugged, laughing an uneasy laugh.

I rolled my eyes at him again, huffing in amusement.

That made him really laugh, which made me laugh too.

We hugged again.

He kissed me a soft, sweet kiss when we parted.

I sat on the couch to put on my sneakers. I was putting on my bra, without removing my shirt, when he exclaimed in surprise, jerking back from the bookshelf, shooting me a wounded look when I burst into laughter.

"*Ha ha,* very funny," he said laughingly. "How'd you get the books to do that?"

"It's been going off since we sat on the rug."

He flipped the rug back.

"Examine it later," I said. "I'm still deciding on how often it should go off. I'm going to add it to every bookcase or something like it. Want to see the rest of the place?"

"Sure. What other special effects will you add?"

"I'm working on a ghost for the front stairs and one for the windows. You ever hear of a Pepper's Ghost?"

He shook his head as he stopped by the next room to examine the drawing tacked to the wall.

"It's a special effect like they use in the Haunted Mansion at Disney."

I explained how a Pepper's Ghost worked and where I thought I could put one while he sifted through the stack of drawings tacked to the wall.

"A library billiards room?"

"Yeah. It'll have a television, a game table, a few smaller tables, a bar and the shelves and stuff. It'll be the main hangout. It's a big room. Someone added it on. It'll need lots of work to make it match the rest of the house so it looks original."

We entered the future library, which was now my workroom. Piles of plywood, two-by-fours, sheetrock, and paint cans were stacked along the back wall, blocking the boarded-up windows. Only two windows were unboarded, one of which had a fan in it. I planned to put in French doors leading to the back garden on the far wall. I wasn't sure how I'd make the rest of the windows match the old ones.

My camera equipment was set up to face the saw at the moment. I'd need to move it tomorrow if I was going to start on the bathroom, which I *should* do instead of going to the garage at home or he'd be sure I was stalking him.

While he was looking around, I straightened up my tool bench that held my saws, which was in the middle of the room with a rolling toolbox beneath it.

He stopped to examine the two tables made from plywood and sawhorses that held an assortment of half-finished projects, everything from lights to a headboard.

We exited through the door at the end of the room, passing a large box beside the door holding my cleaning products and a few cans of paint thinner. A box on the opposite side held rags with eight gallons of water beside that and a half empty case of drinking water.

I said, "This door will be hidden behind shelves on this side and a glass-fronted hutch on the dining room side. The closet there will be hidden by the paneled wall. There's a trap door in the ceiling with a ladder that goes up into the attic. I debated having it open into the bedroom it passes through, but I didn't want to infringe on the guests' private spaces, so I'll add another ladder from the attic into the hall up there instead. I can have it exit in the laundry closet. Someday, I'd like to connect it to a tunnel that leads to the conservatory that I want to build and the carriage house."

"There's a carriage house?"

"It's an old barn that was badly converted into a four-car garage. It was a real carriage house—a building to house carriages. My goal is to make that upper floor a separate apartment for the maid."

"You want a live-in maid?"

"Eventually I'd need one to take over so I could move on to another house and fix that up. I want to do a chain of these—assuming this one is a success."

He wrinkled his nose at me.

"A maid to take over...like a housekeeper, you mean?"

"Sure, or butler, but I was planning to wear a maid costume to welcome the guests."

His eyes gained a heated look that made my body flush.

"Not that kind of maid costume, dolt."

"I'd sure hope not," he said, but he looked disappointed.

I wasn't sure if I should be flattered or worried that he thought maids were sexy because *maybe* he thought it was *me* who was sexy.

Just thinking it made me flush in embarrassment because I had no idea how to be sexy, but I really wished I did.

I wonder if I can Google that?

I said, "I want to host mystery weekends. I haven't worked out all the details yet, but I know I'll need a person—me—to clean up and serve and keep the game going, but I want it to stay in character. I want the guests to feel like guests visiting a manor house for a weekend in the country like they used to do, not like they're in a hotel, so I'll greet them like a house servant."

"Sounds fun if the people aren't dicks."

I shrugged.

"If I hate it, I'll just rent the rooms."

I stopped in the cabinet-lined corridor that connected the kitchen to the dining room and another short hall that led to the old butler and maid quarters.

"This is the butler pantry. It's the only room I haven't thought of anything extra to add to yet. The bathroom for the guests is behind this wall, and I want to do something to the mirror in there, but it'll be a real bathroom, so I need to be careful about privacy. Maybe I'll put another Pepper's ghost in there..."

I also haven't decided on the kitchen layout other than generalities. It needs to be really practical so I can host large events. I'm hoping I get some good recommendations on designs for it once I start my You Tube channel.

"This hall leads to my rooms and will be off limits to guests."

We peeked down the hall but there wasn't much to see because I'd torn out all of the non-load bearing walls.

As we were talking, we returned to the dining room to enter the hallway. I led him past a gutted bathroom, having to tug his hand a bit because he kept stopping to look at my drawings, through the empty room that would one day be the kitchen, then into the small drawing room across from the parlor that held my finished paintings, an easel, and a stack of unused frames and canvases.

I took his hand to tug him back to the hall.

"Can I see them?"

"Sure, but I'm hungry. Think of it as incentive to ask me out again."

I was hoping he would right then, but he didn't say anything.

It made butterfly's dance in my stomach and my face feel hot.

We went upstairs and peeked into the rooms, which were all empty and down to bare studs in spots.

"I'm changing the layout to add a bathroom to each room so there'll be six bedrooms in total. Each with their own bathroom. One room will have a small connecting room with bunk beds built in and the penthouse suite will have a small balcony overlooking the back garden and a small sitting room."

"You're going to build a balcony?"

"It's there already behind that plywood. I'll repair it, replacing the floor and railing. It already has a new roof."

"Did you get it checked to be sure it was still solid?"

"Yep. This house was built like a truck. The only rotten bits are from water damage from the roof or previous tenants. The foundation is sound. Even the wiring isn't that old. It was redone in the eighties. But I'm checking it all as I go. I know the plumbing all needs work, but I can lay out the pipe and then get it inspected and have a real plumber do the hard connections."

"This is a hell of a project, Kate. I wish I'd thought of it first, not that I think I could do it..."

A sharp pang pierced me. I hadn't been expecting him to doubt me when he'd seen the parlor—or maybe I'd just been hoping he'd be as supportive as Grayson was, *or maybe I was just crazy thinking I could do this...*

He didn't notice that he'd hurt my feelings being too busy flipping through the stack of drawings tacked to the wall.

He said, "I can hardly wait to see it finished. What room are you doing next?"

Relief made me laugh giddily.

"My bathroom."

23

"So… no running water here?"

"Sort of. There's a hose out back that I use to clean my brushes and fill my water bottles."

"Did you get the water tested?"

"…You sound like Grayson. He lectures me like I'm an idiot too."

Jace flushed, saying, "Sorry, I didn't mean anything by it. It's just you can get really sick, even die from bad water, and people on city water never think to check it."

"You're right. I'm being a bitch. It's just I'm so tired of people thinking I can't do things…"

"Your dad, you mean?"

"My mom, my sister, everyone… although half the time I think my mom says it so I won't try and she'll lose her babysitter."

"She must know she's going to need a new sitter if she thinks you're going away to college?"

"She has Everly. My grandma knows I don't want to go. She hasn't said anything to me about it though, except to say that college isn't for everyone and sometimes a year or two makes all the difference."

"She's right. You might change your mind."

I thought my grandmother said it because she didn't think I could pass college classes because she told me all the time that my name wouldn't get me good grades in a real school, which always pissed me off because Everly had the same name and got terrible grades. But, of course, I never said anything to her and didn't say anything to him now.

I said, "And suddenly decide I want to be a lawyer—I don't think so."

"I don't think that either. You're obviously an artist at heart. But you might decide to go study that."

"I can't imagine I'd find it fun to have to write essays on the masters. I'd rather do this. This is the most… fun isn't the word; it's more than fun. I *love* this. I painted the top bit of the parlor five times before I got the exact shade of blue right. That room looks like it *should* look. People will be happy there and comfortable. I can see them here, playing cards, having a drink, talking, laughing, and all the while this house will be setting the mood, a mood I'll create."

"I can see it too. This place is perfectly you."

"It will be."

"It already is. You and it are just becoming this amazing perfect vision."

I was almost insulted until I realized, or at least hoped, he'd meant he was seeing us both for the first time and saw the potential in both of us.

Tears again clouded my eyes.

"Kate," he said gruffly.

I kissed him back hard.

"Let's go get that pizza," he said when we parted. "Tomorrow, we're going for Chinese."

His eyes lit when I laughed.

He continued, "You know what that butler pantry needs, one of those cabinets where you open it and the stuff in it is gone. And one of the cabinets should turn around completely so one side has food and the other poisons, or in this case cleaning supplies repackaged in brown glass bottles."

I laughed in delight.

"Tell me more," I said breathlessly.

THREE

The next morning, after I dropped the kids off, I headed right to planned parenthood.

An hour and a half later I left with an implant in my arm and a box of condoms to use for the next week until the implant kicked in.

I'd had to use my emergency funds, which for the first time in my life hadn't bothered me a whit. I was almost giddy with excitement, laughing at nothing, wearing a stupid grin that I *knew* was stupid, but I couldn't stop myself. It wasn't so much the idea of having sex, although that was exciting—and nerve wracking—but that Jace Blake was probably thinking about me now the same way I was about him.

It was a huge thought that kept making me laugh because I couldn't really picture him wondering how my hands would feel on his bare ass or if he'd be wondering how I'd want to be touched like I was wondering how he liked to be.

To keep my mind off of him, I spent the rest of the day putting film clips together, reading voiceovers, and making notes on the shots and graphics I needed to add.

My goal was a one hour show a week. I needed a minimum of a hundred and fifty-six shows and had thirty-six done, except for the animated intro I was still making. As soon as that was done, I'd upload and schedule the releases to begin the Friday after my birthday. I was getting better at splicing the recordings, adding the soundtracks and voice overs, and lining up my shots. I figured it wouldn't take me nearly as long to do the rest of the shows as these first ones had taken.

A door slamming downstairs and childish laughter followed by Everly yelling told me the kids had come home.

I slid my laptop under my bed.

Getting dressed for my date was going to be a problem, I realized.

I wanted to look good, but not like I was trying to look good. I especially didn't want the effort noticeable to my mother or Everly. I kept a makeup kit and my hair stuff at my house because that's where I usually filmed myself, but my mother had more makeup then a thousand women could use, and she wouldn't mind if I used it. I'd done it in the past to take pictures of the kids for my paintings.

So I used my little sisters, Hannah, and Felicity, as my stooges, dressing them up, doing their hair and makeup and taking some pictures all as an excuse to do my own.

Dressing was the bigger issue. I had no sexy clothes at all. I had a few cute dresses, gifts from my mom, but they'd notice for sure if I changed into a dress to go out.

I returned to my underwear drawer, which was thankfully full of nice things due to my mother's penchant for shopping Victoria's Secret. Everly and I both received the coupon items. My mom would buy a new nightie and get a coupon to buy three pairs of underwear for the price of one. She'd buy a robe and one of us would get a new bra. They were constantly sending coupons, so I had plenty of nice bras and underwear.

I picked a white set, then changed my mind for a blue one with little flowers. I debated a good ten minutes on whether to wear shorts or jeans and finally opted for jeans as appearing less desperate and less likely to arouse parental suspicion.

I had a relatively new v-neck t-shirt in a pretty blue color that matched the bra, which I'd bought as a business expense meaning to wear it while filming. I threw on a paint-stained flannel over it. It *was* a bit warm for flannel, but she'd buy I was wearing it to keep my shirt clean and it would get cooler later, especially if I really was going to be painting the night sky, which was my planned lie if I was asked.

I figured the chances she asked where eighty-twenty in my favor. I hoped my father wouldn't be there for dinner. The chances were about seventy-thirty in my favor that he wouldn't be. He'd be more likely to ask where I was going but only if he saw me actually heading for the door. If he was there, I'd eat with them and then go.

I escorted all four of the kids down to the dining room where my mother was setting a roast out on the table that the kids and I had set earlier, foresight being second nature when I planned to leave the kids for the night.

"My, don't you look nice," she said when she saw us.

Hannah, bless her heart, said, "Kate took pictures. She's going to paint me a princess!"

My mother kissed her nose and helped her into her chair.

"You are a princess. Mommy's princess."

Everly made gagging noises.

My mother ignored it, saying to Felicity, "You're as pretty as a picture."

Everly said to me, "At least you can paint yourself a figure."

"Girls," my mother said absently.

I said, "I'll do the dishes in the morning. Fell, you and Wolf can stack them in the sink for me?"

Felicity nodded, agreeing for both of them. "Sure, Kate. Where ya going?"

"I want to hit the paint sale tonight. I'll grab a bite out."

"Loser," Everly said.

"Don't be late," my mother said.

I gratefully escaped.

The Ford had the kiddos' booster seats but looked cooler than the Toyota. It was parked in the house garage with my mom's car while the Toyota was in the parking lot of the shop garage.

I grabbed the Toyota keys from the peg in the garage and went to get the Toyota.

Jace's truck was still parked at the second shop where most of the metal work was done.

Four large metal buildings lined the bottom drive. Three of them were for working on cars—the repair and upholstery shop—the paint shop—the fabrication shop, and the first one, the largest one, was for storing cars.

The Toyota wasn't deemed worthy of indoor space. It was always parked outside in the lot with the rest of the unworthy cars along with my dad's employees' cars.

All of the buildings had big roll-up garage doors and smaller people-size doors. Customers were rarely allowed here, but my mother liked things nice, so there were a few benches and flowerpots between the buildings and a small picnic area for the help to eat at.

There was a little kitchen in the second building and a small loft that had two offices and a room with a cot for the painters to use if they were staying late to spray another coat or were just catching a nap while waiting for a delivery. Building two—the repair shop where most car repairs and custom work happened also had a small reception area for the very infrequent customer.

Because they only worked on really high-end cars installing expensive custom modifications, that area was plushly appointed with a coffee machine, a small bar, four comfortable chairs, and a dinette set, which is where Jace was when I poked my head inside the people-sized door.

Howard and three of the other guys were with him. As an excuse for looking in, I said to Howard, "Can I use the lathe again tomorrow?"

"Sure. If you want, I can text you when we get a job that would need it so you'd know when it's free?"

"That would be great. One more thing, and you can say no if it's a problem. Can I get an order of wood delivered here? Someone would need to sign for it. It could be left anywhere out of the way. It doesn't need to be inside. I'll just leave a tarp to stack it on."

I figured there was an eighty-twenty chance my father wouldn't let me use the shops here once I moved out, so I needed to finish before I did. Since the chance he noticed me working here was forty-sixty, the odds were in my favor to get the delivery, which would save me a bit of money, a lot of effort, and a little time. It would also give me an excuse to see Jace every day, and an excuse to go to my house to drop off the parts I'd finished, if I could talk him into another dinner—which was my main goal.

"I don't see why not," Howard said.

"I promise it won't be here long."

I held my breath, but he didn't ask what I was doing with it.

"Night, all."

"Night, Kate," they all said.

Jace exited a minute later and pulled his truck up beside the Toyota.

"Smooth," he said.

I shrugged.

"Meet you there?" he asked.

"The place off main?"

I really want to kiss you," he said wistfully as he nodded agreement.

"We could get it to go..."

He laughed, shaking his head. "And have you think I'm just interested in one thing?"

"As long as you don't lose interest."

He cocked his head as if he couldn't decide if that were a joke or not.

"See you there," I said hurriedly and drove away.

"You are such a dork!"

I'd regained my cool, what there was of it, by the time I reached the restaurant, and had time to get all nervous again while he found a spot to park his truck.

I left my flannel shirt in the car thinking how pathetic it was to have your first date at eighteen, well *almost* eighteen. I didn't know what to do with my hands, a problem I'd never experienced before. I'd never noticed them before, but now I couldn't seem to stop worrying—*should I put them in my pockets? Front pockets? Back pockets? Cross my arms? Keep my hands flat or clenched?* The choices seemed endless and all of them wrong. The short walk to the door seemed to take a year as I imagined him wildly regretting asking a dork like me out.

He seemed so—normal, not at all nervous, *but why would he be...* He was probably used to girls throwing themselves at him. This was probably a pity date. I'd basically *forced* him to ask me.

"No purse?" he asked as he held the door for me—effortlessly as if he hadn't worried about the right way to do it at all, *which, of course, he probably hadn't.*

My interior litany of what I was doing wrong was distracting me enough that it took me a moment to realize what he'd meant.

I, of course, flushed like an idiot as I said, "My cash is in my pocket. I hardly ever carry a purse."

He frowned at me.

"That isn't what I meant. I don't expect you to pay for dinner... and you do so carry one. An enormous one!"

"No I don't."

"Yes you do."

"You must be mistaking me for someone else because I'd certainly know if I carried a purse!"

I held my hands up and twirled around.

"See! No purse."

A man approaching stopped to say suspiciously, "Did you lose it or..."

His gaze measured Jace as if debating if he was holding me up, which made me burst into giggles.

I said, "*Nah*, my date just thinks all girls carry big purses."

The man chuckled. "Most do." He cocked his head at an approaching woman who was rooting through a suitcase-sized purse, and we all laughed.

The man and woman disappeared into the restaurant.

I held out my phone, waggling it to show it had my ID, my prepaid credit card, a credit card my father had given me to use for gas, groceries, and kids' stuff, and my cash, which I'd had to take from my emergency fund.

Jace surprised me by kissing me.

I kissed him back, completely forgetting we'd been arguing and were blocking the door.

"I've been thinking about that all day," he said when we parted. He took my hand and led me inside. When we were seated, he said, "Not to beat a dead horse or anything, but I'm not crazy. I see you every day with a blue and white striped purse. And some days there's a pink one with white polka dots too.

I burst into laughter.

"The blue one is for the kiddos. The pink is my sketch bag."

"The kiddos...oh, right, you're dropping the kids off at school or whatever. You do that every day?"

"Yeah, I've been bringing them lately. Felicity and Wolfgang are in fifth grade. The little ones are in preschool. Felicity has allergies, bad ones, so I always have that bag with me when I have her."

"Poor thing..."

"She's a trooper about it. But occasionally something gets by us, or she develops a new one or something just plain doesn't agree with her, so we keep the clothes and wipes handy, which also makes a good excuse to carry her EPI pen because seeing that freaks her right the hell out."

"I bet."

"I haven't ever had to use it, thank God. Seeing my parents use it on her is terrifying! I'd probably faint if I had to do it..."

He laughed, shaking his head.

"*Nah*, you'd do fine. Afterwards maybe..."

I said, "Do you have any allergies?"

"Nope. You?"

"No—well, actually yes. Everly gives me hives."

He snickered.

I hadn't been joking. My sister could get me so upset I broke out in hives, but I laughed as if *were* joking.

"Do you have siblings?" I asked.

"An older sister who I haven't seen in four years or so. We don't get along. Actually, that's not really true, we just don't—anything. I don't know her well enough to really dislike her or anything. She's just disinterested."

"That's too bad. My older brother is great. My sister Kenya is... busy all the time. She's nice. I love her but we aren't close like me and Gray are."

"I don't think I've met her."

"Probably not. She isn't around the house much. Too many kids there for her. She visits the parents at work though, so you might've seen her there. You'd remember her. She's beautiful, very posh like she's always on her way to a photoshoot."

"I don't get to the car lot much."

"Kenya lives in a high rise, a really fancy place, and works in the city."

"Doing what?"

"Law like all good Avery's do." I realized that sounded snarky, so added hurriedly, "What's your sister do?"

"I've no earthly clue. Last I heard she was a dealer."

My jaw dropped open.

He snickered.

"Not that kind of a dealer, or at least I don't think so. A card dealer in Vegas."

"*Ahh*...that would be fun. I considered it."

It was my turn to snicker for shocking him.

"Are you pulling my leg?"

I slipped one of my credit cards out from the case and ran it through my fingers, flipping it from one to the other, then from one hand to the next, then made it disappear.

"Holy shit! Do that again!"

"It'll cost you."

He quirked an eyebrow.

"I don't turn tricks for free." I tapped the table. "Money on the table, pal. It's a buck a hand; ten if you want me to add a card—I pay double or nothing if I drop them."

For the first time in my life the phrase 'turning tricks' didn't make me simmer with anger. I was amused by it and wondered if someday I'd look back on all of Everly's taunts and find them amusing. I couldn't imagine it, but I'd never imagined finding that funny although I'd been pretending to for years.

Laughing, he laid a dollar on the table.

Making a production of it, I took both credit cards out and ran them through my fingers, going from one hand to the next then making them both disappear.

"Seriously, how are you doing that?"

I pocketed his dollar and tapped the table.

He snorted, shaking his head. "I can't afford you!"

I nodded approvingly as I put my cards back into the case.

"I made three hundred dollars the first week I did this and probably two thousand that first month. I bet I made over five thousand on sucker bets over the years on that one trick."

"You have more?"

I said in my sexiest breathiest voice, "I have a repertoire."

The waitress giggled as she said, "What'll it be?"

I would've been embarrassed, but he was obviously amused.

I winked at him as I tied our straws together then pulled them apart.

"How'd you do that?" the waitress asked.

Jace said, "Give her a free coke and she'll do it again slower."

The waitress nodded happily and hurried away.

Jace and I bumped fists.

FOUR

Jace and I exited the restaurant two hours later and held hands back to my car.

He kissed me a long minute, pressing me hard against the side of the car.

I wished we'd gotten takeout so I could do what I really wanted to do—slip my hands under his clothes to feel the real warmth of him.

He said a bit nervously, "I had a great time, Kate. Can we do this again?"

I was confused and disappointed because it sounded to me like a polite sort of brush off.

"Sure. You know where to find me."

"Speaking of that, you should know I work a lot."

I rolled my eyes at him.

"You drive right by my house... I can see your car from my back deck..."

"Right... it's just I don't want you to think I'm... not interested because between work and getting you in at a decent hour so your parents don't, *uh,* twig, our dates are going have to be short. I don't want you to lie to your folks, but I don't want to get fired either. And they're sure as shit going to wonder where you are if you come in late too many nights."

"Well, the good news is that if you pick me up, they won't even know I'm not home. They'll just think I'm out back painting the lake or something. Everly comes in at all hours and no one ever notices or says anything. Plus, I go for bike rides all the time. Trust me, she won't notice."

"Where does she think you are when you're at your house?"

"I have no idea."

"She's never asked?"

"No."

"That's weird."

"Is it? She never asks Everly either. If she sees me leave or I want to be sure she intends to be there for the kids, I tell her I'm going out shopping or for a bike ride or sometimes to Grayson's. My house *is* his until I'm eighteen and can legally own it, so I'm not *really* lying. Gray and I have dinner once a week or so. He brings me pizza there once in a while..."

"Still...I'm twenty-two and live by myself and my mom still asks where I'm going when I leave her house."

"As long as I can remember, I'd go out at night to paint. She probably thinks I'm still doing it, which I am, except maybe not where she thinks I'm doing it."

"Why not just tell her?"

"Because oh my god the drama... I don't want to sit through it—I don't want my kids to sit through it either. If I'm not there to yell at, she won't yell."

"*Your* kids?"

I shrugged. "They *are* my kids. My kid sisters and brothers. *The* kids sounds like I don't like them or something. Saying my siblings includes Everly, which ick. So they're my kids when I'm worried about them."

"That was perfectly Kate."

"I'm not sure if that was a compliment or put down..."

"Neither really. It was an observation. You're a lot different than I imagined you'd be."

I considered that for a minute. "You're pretty much like I imagined you'd be."

"I'm afraid to ask..."

"Me too."

He laughed and kissed me again. He kept hugging me, which was amazing.

Still hugging me, he finally said, "I never imagined a beautiful girl like you would be so practical. That you'd be so funny and sweet—so nice. It almost feels like a trick."

"I knew kids like that. Everly's friend Margo would pick one of the shy normal kids and make him think she was interested just to embarrass him by turning him away, loudly and publicly and usually by telling intimate details, most of which I'm sure were lies. But lie or not, having a pretty girl say your breath stinks or you can't get it up would be sooo embarrassing, never mind the jabs about their bedroom being babyish or their mom stupid and stuff… She was such a bitch I was always amazed she'd get another sucker to fall for it."

"Am I being a sucker?"

That shocked me.

"Am I?"

He drew away to stare at me as he shook his head.

I said, "In my experience, it's the guys who do that shit more than the girls. It was like a law or something in our school that every boy had to find some poor girl to kiss and tell on."

He lifted my hand to kiss it.

"What happens between us, stays between us."

I nodded agreement.

I gathered my courage and said, "Want to go back to my house?"

"Yes, but not tonight." He winked at me as he added, "I don't want you to think I'm easy."

That made me laugh although I was also embarrassed that he probably thought *I* was easy, *which I was for him*, so I supposed that was fair.

He ran his fingertips lightly across my hot cheek.

"I love your face."

I had no idea what one said to that, so I said the first thing that popped into my head.

"I love yours too."

He laughed.

I sighed wistfully. "I really wish I was smoother."

"Never change, Kate. You're perfect. When can I see you again?"

"You'll see me tomorrow at the garage making a million more spindles and table legs and stuff. I'm bringing it all to my house after dinner if you wanted to stop by…"

"It's a date."

His heated tone made my chest ache.

He said, "Text me when you get in so I know you're all safe and sound."

I nodded.

He kissed me lightly.

It was the most maddeningly frustrating kiss ever—I'd never forget it.

36

The next evening, I told my mom I was going to Grayson's, *not technically a lie,* and brought my date clothes with me, which was just a clean white t-shirt.

I really needed to go shopping but clothes just weren't in my budget. Since I'd thought of making a hotel years ago, I'd been saving every penny I made from Christmas gifts, birthdays, babysitting, my furniture flips, and the few short-term jobs I'd gotten over the years, but I knew I'd need way more to finish the house.

Maybe I could find some clothes at the flea market, or thrift store...

I applied a little makeup when I got to my house, not much because it felt silly to me to apply it *now* when he'd seen me on and off all day without it. I did fix my hair though, combing out the sawdust and then curling it a bit so it would look nice down, which he shouldn't think was too much since it'd been up in a messy bun most of the day, so he could have no idea I'd styled it just for him.

I even applied a spritz of perfume—a gift from Kenya. It smelled amazing, which it should for the cost of the bottle. And it was a beautiful bottle. I planned to add it to my collection of bottles and reuse it with something I could afford when it was empty.

I decided I'd start wearing makeup during the day, just a little at a time to get them used to me wearing it, so maybe my sister wouldn't notice, and my mother wouldn't think it was odd that I was wearing it if Everly made fun of me. My sister was much more likely to wonder why I was wearing it than my mother was, but we seldom saw each other.

While I was pondering how best to avoid Everly, I took measurements and began taping out the dimensions of the furniture I was planning in what would be my bedroom and bathroom while waiting for him to arrive.

Some of the dimensions were fixed like if I wanted to someday add a washing machine to my bathroom, I had to make the linen closet the dimensions of a standard model, but some I could customize like the end tables and chairs and the bathroom vanity, which I intended to make myself, and even the wall placement. There had been four rooms here. I wanted a bedroom, bathroom, and walk-in closet.

"Kate!"

I'd lost track of time completely, jumping up in surprise when I heard him.

"Sorry!" I called back. "I didn't hear you arrive. I'm back here!"

I ran to meet him.

He'd brought a pizza, which he held out awkwardly to kiss me.

I didn't kiss him as long as I wanted to because of the pizza.

I said, "Eat before it gets cold. I ate at home."

Which was a lie, but I was too nervous to eat.

"You should lock the door."

"I normally do but I knew you were coming."

"Still... lock it anyway and maybe get one of those alarms that beeps when it opens even when it's unlocked."

"Paranoid much?"

"Practical. Just do it, Kate. There's lots of crazies out there."

"You sound like Grayson. My next bit of spare cash, I promise."

"Where should we eat? I don't want to get your parlor all dirty."

"Don't be silly. It's made to eat and drink in. I didn't think to bring sodas or anything but there's bottled waters in the library. I won't be a minute. I just need to grab my notebook."

I ran back to my room.

He followed me.

"What all this?"

"The final layout of the room."

He took my notebook, handing me the pizza.

I headed back to the parlor and set the pizza on the table then closed all the curtains. I went to grab waters, paper towels, and locked the front door, more because I didn't want anyone else—like my father—just walking in than I was worried about burglars.

When I returned, he was there. I handed him a water and set the paper towels on the table.

I said, "This is a safe neighborhood. There's hardly any crime around here."

"Good. But why take chances?"

"I agree, I'm just saying..."

I took my notebook back to flip through to my projected expenses. Buying a door sensor was on my list. There was a small picture of it with the store information listed as twenty-three dollars with no price changes with a note that said: housing fabrication not designed. Which meant I hadn't decided how to hide the ugly plastic bits.

"What's the problem?" he asked.

"I didn't buy the alarm yet because I'm not sure how to hide the sensor."

"Let me see."

He took the book back and said, "That's easy. Take the guts out and put them right into the door. Just router out a hole, carefully mind so you don't break the facing. Make it as thin as you can, which should be pretty damned thin because you could put the chiming part right into the wall. Maybe put a decorative metal grill over it and don't forget to make it easy to remove to change batteries unless you're going to hardwire it, but batteries would be better so a power outage doesn't leave you defenseless. You could use an old-fashioned bell instead though, which would be a much quicker install."

"Which would be friendlier? I want this place to feel like a grand home you've been invited to visit, not a hotel-hotel."

"Do you have a smart watch?"

"Yes. My grandmother got us all watches for Christmas. I never use it, except when I'm going to see her, not that she ever seems to notice or care—I was thinking about selling it."

"Then get a door alarm that can be set to silent and will send notifications and wear your watch. That way you'd know if someone came in or out so you can keep track of who's in the building without it being super obvious."

"That's a great idea! It'll probably cost more than twenty bucks though... maybe I'll go with a bell for now."

He nodded agreement, offering me a slice of pizza, which I declined, making a mental note of the toppings he'd chosen.

I said, "It hadn't occurred to me to place the sensors *in* the windows. I'm going to Google that later and see how other people do it. These windows in this room don't open, except for the one I rigged, but almost all the rest of them are newer."

"I hate to say it, but I think you'll need to fix the windows to meet code for a hotel."

"No. I checked. They're grandfathered in as long as the room has two egresses."

"I don't think secret passages count."

"I guess I could make one of the other windows open..."

He stood to examine the window, frowning thoughtfully.

"Hinging it like a door like the other one would be easiest, but that would ruin the entire secret door thing cause why have a secret door next to a real one... you might as well put an exit sign over that door. Maybe you could put another door into the hall behind the chair there instead, or doesn't that count if they're on the same wall?"

"I don't know. I'll have to check."

"How crucial is your secret door?"

39

"Not hugely, I guess. It's more for fun than anything. My idea was I'd tell the villain about the secrets and let them plan out their own crime. Each game would need at least a few players. One villain, maybe a victim, or even all of the guests being thieves and trying to rob my safes by having to find the combinations, or any combination they wanted of villains and detectives. I have lots of ideas, lots of story lines I'm working on. The person who's hosting picks the sort of crime from my listings, or they can even use their own ideas and send me the guest list and I pick the villain and send them the plans of the house with a packet that has their crimes and story details and any props they'd need for the story.

"The rest of the guests would get a fancy invitation followed by a packet saying who their character was so they could prepare if they wanted to. I'd supply the necessary props like a gaudy necklace that had to be stolen or poison bottles, that sort of thing. So the more options the thieves have to sneak about with, the harder it would be for the others to figure out how the crime was committed. Another entrance to this room would be great for a thief because they could sneak into it without being seen by people in the dining room or library and once in it, they could cut through the dungeon to get to the back stairs and attic."

"So technically, they could do the reverse and come up through the dungeon?"

"Yeah. It'd be quicker though to nip in through the window and back out to the back door and come in from the kitchen. Anyone in the dining room can see the front door and the doorway to this room, so even if you left the table to go to the kitchen, they'd have to prove how you managed it. Plus, the hearth makes a little noise, and the window doesn't."

"You really thought all this out," he said approvingly.

"Except for the two egresses thing..."

"You could hinge the other window and put a loud obnoxious emergency exit alarm on it..."

"That's a great idea!"

"Plant a rose bush right in front of it—maybe one without thorns just in case anyone really does ever need to use it."

I snickered. "You have the best ideas."

"You ain't seen nothing yet."

I flushed to my toes.

He drew in a long breath, exhaling slowly as he leaned to kiss me. He tasted of pizza and uniquely undefinable him as if I were to kiss a million men, I could pick him from the taste and texture of his lips.

"We're really doing this?" he asked breathlessly.

"I sure hope so."

He laughed, saying, "I think that's my favorite thing about you."

"What, that I'm easy?"

He frowned shaking his head.

"I never thought that, Kate. I think you have a serious crush on me and are just being honest, not doing what you think you should, but what feels right without planning it all out—which is maybe naïve of me..."

"I'm a planner. I tried to plan this, but I have no frame of reference—so I'm winging it. Plus I don't want to miss my chance."

"Chance at what?"

"You—us. I do have a serious crush and it still feels sort of surreal that you're here now. I hope you like me, not just the idea of a willing girl but *me,* but I'll settle for the willing girl for now because, after all, you hardly know me. And like I said, I don't want to miss my chance. I've never felt anything like I feel when you kiss me. Your kiss heats my entire body..."

I realized I was babbling when he chuckled.

"Yours does the same to me. Kiss me again, Kate."

His hand rose to cup my breast through my shirt.

We undressed each other slowly, sharing long kisses between each piece of clothing we dropped on the floor.

When we were naked, I said, "I went to the clinic and got an implant in my arm, but it won't work for a week. They gave me condoms, but I'm not sure they'll fit you..."

He groaned then said huskily, "We should wait a week. I want to feel all of you our first time."

I said, "Let's compromise. Withdrawal is seventy-eight percent effective. I missed the immediate effectiveness date of the implant by only two days, so I'm probably not fertile anyway for another week at least. So if we start without a condom and end with one, the chance of pregnancy is probably less than ten percent, which is pretty good seeing as the only hundred percent method is to not have sex."

"You're frighteningly logical."

I shrugged, running my hand along the hard length of him.

"I'm in," he said hoarsely.

I kept stroking him, feeling out the shape of him, committing it to my memory.

I said, "Of course, if you come before we make love, there's less chance of an accident when you're ready again..."

"You're terrifying," he said approvingly.

I giggled and went to flip the room lights off, leaving just the candelabras lit.

He gathered me close, kissing my neck as he ran his hands over me.

His breath caught in a hard inhale as I kissed my way down his body to kneel and admire his erection.

"You're so beautiful. I'd love to paint you."

I licked him and he moaned.

"I'm going to last like two seconds," he said laughingly as he rested his hands on my head.

"See, it was a good idea."

"It's a fucking amazing idea, don't stop."

I obliged him for a minute. My position and low lighting made it difficult see his expression. I could hear his breath and feel the tension of his body.

"Do you want to lay down?" I asked.

"Do you want me to?"

"I want you to tell me, or show me, what you like because I don't really know what I'm doing."

I sank to me heels to lick the length of him.

He groaned loudly, burying his hands in my hair, thrusting in tiny jerks as if he couldn't help himself, which made the warmth in my chest spread lower.

"Oh god," he said, so I was ready and drew away just seconds after he began to come.

I sort of wished I'd left the light on to see better.

"Jesus..."

His breath left him in a hard exhale as I grasped him to slide my hand along him. I was careful to grasp lightly and rub slowly because I'd heard somewhere that some men became really sensitive. I probably should've backed right off but I wanted to feel all of him, to have this entire experience to reflect on. I wanted to feel the heat of him.

"You're so beautiful," I said again.

"Kate..."

He sank to his knees to hug me, and he hugged me a long time while catching his breath.

When he leaned back, I got to my feet and handed him a water and paper towel then wet another to clean my hands. I drank half a bottle of water, more so he wouldn't be grossed out then to lose the taste of him, then sat on the rug in front of the fireplace.

He settled beside me, absently finger combing my hair.

He said thoughtfully, "I'm going to learn how to make a fire in an indoor fireplace because I really want to see you naked in the firelight." He set his water down to lean closer and kiss me, running his thumb over my nipple as he whispered, "I want to watch you watch me come. I want to watch you come... I want to feel it."

He leaned away from me to grab his pants, pulled out a condom, ripped it open, but set it aside.

"I'll be careful," he said. "Lay back, Kate, and let me look at you."

He nudged my knees apart to kneel between them, sitting back on his heels like I had, running his hands down my side then back up to caress my breasts a minute.

My hips flexed without my will, and he leaned closer, sliding his hands down to my legs to pull them farther apart.

All thought left me head, all of my attention caught by his fingers and lips, which made me feel shivery and weak in the most amazing way. I stopped worrying about what he was thinking, what I should be doing, and just let my body react.

He'd found the perfect rhythm with his fingers, the perfect placement. I could feel—something, a tightness growing. "Oh..."

My very first orgasm made me scream. I screamed again when he slid inside me. The thick heat of him made my hips jerk hard without my control.

"Jace...oh god...Jace...."

He pulled me up so we're sitting face-to-face, my hips still twitching against him, my entire body shaking. It was perfect but *too* much perfect. I began to cry.

His hands stilled on my back.

"Don't stop. Don't stop..."

He laughed a low sexy breathless laugh as he thrust slowly.

"Don't stop," I said again.

He growled and rolled us, bracing his hands on the floor, pumping hard for a few minutes before withdrawing and grabbing for the condom, grunting in frustration as he applied it.

He said, "It has lube but it's plastic so..."

He slid slowly at first then faster until he was once again thrusting hard.

"I want to feel the heat of you," I said, and he groaned loudly.

"Kate..."

I love you, my soul screamed but I didn't dare say it. He'd for sure think I was nuts.

43

I said, "I'm counting down the days until we can do this without the condom."

We kissed for a long time, exploring each other, learning each other.

He finally pulled slowly away and carefully removed the condom, gathering it and the wrapper and folding it in a paper towel.

He wet another towel and placed it against me.

"How sore are you?"

"A bit. It's good though—an echo of you."

"You're…. amazing."

"I'm glad you think so, but really that was all you…"

"What time do you have to be home?"

"I am home," I said as I reached for him.

FIVE

3 WEEKS LATER

I'd brought a picnic basket and blanket as requested and drove to the address Jace had sent me, not knowing where we were going other than the obvious—a picnic.

I'd seen him every day over the last three weeks at the shop and most nights at my house for at least an hour or so. This was our second official date, and I was surprisingly nervous.

Our quiet flirtation at work was fun and easy—a smile, a quick stolen kiss, a simple hello or see you later, all of it made more exciting because I *knew* he'd drop by later. He'd mentioned pizza, or I'd say I was making the kids dinner or was making myself a sandwich, which he knew meant I was bringing food. I was living in a happy bubble where everything was us.

Our evenings were easy now too—mostly. I was comfortable with us as lovers. I could read his face, the small sounds he made, the tenseness of his body, the depth of his breaths. I hated the brevity of our encounters, but I didn't dare stay too late or my mother might notice—or worse, Everly might. She'd ruin this for me, I knew that. It was always a terrifying thought in the back of my head. So I tried to do nothing that might alert anyone that anything was different for me.

And there was the fact that I was pretty certain my father was having an affair with a woman who lived down the street. I saw his car there at least twice a week in the evenings and once in a while at lunchtime. He hadn't stopped in again. I'd no idea what I'd say if he did. Call him out on it? Pretend I didn't know?

I saw her outside gardening occasionally, mowing her lawn, tending her flowers, getting the mail, or bringing out trash, a pretty, petite, blond, curvy, not at all like my mother. She looked sweet, which had to be a lie because a sweet woman wouldn't steal a husband. Or maybe she didn't know he had a wife and eight kids, four of whom would be devastated to lose the father they loved and seldom got to see now when he lived with us. And then there was my poor mother… worrying about it though wouldn't help anyone.

It wasn't any of my business. Jace was my business.

This picnic date felt sort of like a test to me, one I hoped I could pass. *Could I keep his attention with my clothes on?* I knew the wild passion we shared would eventually fade, which made me sad when I considered it. But all relationships peeked and plateaued, settling into a rhythm of easy company or crashing and burning. I'd seen it countless times, the couples who couldn't get enough of each other one week and didn't speak three weeks later. Or if they were lucky, they were still together but holding hands or exchanging a quick kiss, not the long passionate ones they'd shared when they'd first met. I was both hoping for and dreading the latter.

It really worried me that I'd still be in the wanting the passionate kisses stage and he'd move on to the quick kisses in passing. But as long as I got that passion occasionally, I'd take it. I'd take him any way I could get him. I was hopelessly, terrifyingly, in love.

I arrived at a small parking lot of a bait shack that had a rickety dock with four sketchy looking rowboats tied to pylons.

Jace was waiting with fishing poles, a cooler, and a hopeful smile.

I parked, grabbed the picnic basket, and joined him.

"I should've brought my sketch book," I said.

We exchanged quick kisses that made me giggle nervously.

He said, "Can you swim? I assume you can because you have a pool but…"

"I can swim. I was a lifeguard at the kids' pool when I was fifteen. Just a two-hour shift in the mornings. I taught a beginner's class in the afternoon but spent most of my time there doing office work. Can you swim?"

"Yeah."

"Will we *need* to?"

He laughed, shaking his head, then he winked, saying, "You never know. Bob's boats look like crap but they're sound."

"Bob—a friend of yours?"

"Yeah, I guess."

"You guess?"

"He was a friend of my father's. My dad used to take me here. I haven't been back in ages. It's pretty though, and private, and I thought you'd like to see it. Why didn't you bring your sketchbook?"

"It didn't occur to me."

Small lines appeared by his eyes.

I could see that answer hadn't pleased him but wasn't sure why.

He turned away heading for the dock saying, "There's life vests under the seat if you're nervous."

"What are we fishing for?"

He shrugged. "Whatever we can catch. They won't really start biting until dusk. Have you ever rowed a boat before?"

"No. It doesn't look hard, though. Can I try?"

"Sure."

He put the poles, his cooler, and the basket and blanket in, then got in and offered me his hand.

The warmth of it flushed my entire body.

Without thinking I said, "I don't know how you do that."

He laughed the barest breath of sound, leaning forward awkwardly to kiss me a heated kiss that made that small fire flare.

"Sit here in the middle and try to pull the oars the same strength."

He sat facing me, and we laughed as I struggled to get the boat away from the dock, banging everything and going in a complete circle before I figured it out enough to go straight.

"Which way?'

"Either."

I began rowing.

He said, "You do the same thing to me when we kiss—hell, when I see you. I've never met anyone like you. I don't think I ever will again, which is terrifying. It's going to kill me when you move on. I love you so damned much, Kate."

I stopped rowing to gape at him.

"You love me?"

I was shocked and then something I didn't have a name for—it was hope and fear. I wanted it to be true but was afraid to believe it.

He said, "I love every single thing about you. If you were older, I'd be proposing right this second, but I know that it would be unfair right now. I'm damned tempted too though because I think I could convince you..."

"I love you too," I said breathlessly.

"I know you *think* you do. I hope it lasts… I hope this isn't just a first crush where you feel like you'll die if they don't call…"

His words hurt in a way I didn't have words for but also gave me hope that maybe he really meant it.

"Who broke your heart?" I asked.

He winced.

I began rowing again, my sweaty hands sliding on the slick wood of the oar.

He said, "I was sixteen and thought she was the one, but I realize now it wasn't her—it was me. *She* could've been anyone. I didn't even know her. I liked how she looked and how she made my body feel—I thought that was love."

"*Ahh*… you think my lust for you is blinding me."

"I love your lust. I adore it! I never ever want it to change. But you don't really know me…"

My heart fluttered. I wasn't sure if I believed him that he loved me and not the lust, but I wanted to. I'd never wanted anything more.

I said, "I think I know you; not all of you, but I like how you can make beautiful things with your hands and how you aren't afraid to work hard, that you have a dream and work for it. I like the way you talk about your mom and the way you don't trash talk anyone at all. I think you're honest, hardworking, kind, beautiful, sexy, smart—why would I change my mind about that?"

"I like to fish."

"Is that code?"

He laughed.

His eyes narrowed as he said challengingly, "I like to watch the games and drink beer at the bar."

"I'm not stopping you."

He huffed in annoyance.

"I never make my bed, but I *hate* a dirty bathroom. I hardly ever bother to cook for myself."

"I'm not sure what you want me to say? I'm not going to cook for you. Well, I probably am because I like to cook, but I'm not going to do it to wait on you or clean your bathroom or anything."

He laughed in relief, leaving me even more confused.

"Good. You should always be you."

I was mad now.

"Is this like a… a test to see what I'm willing to do to keep you?"

"What *are* you willing to do?"

48

"Probably just about anything unless you're a real dick about it."

He snorted with laughter, leaning forward to kiss me.

"I love you, Kate," he said when we parted. "I hope you can love a guy like me. I don't want us to just be all about the sex even though it's the most amazingly mind-blowing sex I've ever had. You should be comfortable enough to bring your sketchbook for crying out loud..."

"*Ahh...* I'm not sure I'll like fishing, but so what if I don't? I do like to sketch, which I could do here or anywhere and I'm sure drawing is quiet enough not to scare the fish away. Plus, I have like a million things I could do while you fish."

"That worries me a bit too. I like that you have all these interests, but I want to share some of it with you."

"And that's worrying, why?"

"You're a bit of a control freak."

"I have to be. I'm really pressed for time what with my kids and all—do you mind the kids?"

"I'm not sure. I don't think I do, but I'm hardly ever around them. I'm not wild about the idea of us babysitting all the time. I'm hoping we can compromise about it if it starts to be a problem."

"Okay."

"Okay?"

"Sure, I can compromise. They aren't *our* kids. I get you don't want them underfoot twenty-four seven. I can set a schedule. It needs to be flexible cause they *are* kids and need me sometimes, and I want to attend their big deal stuff."

"I love you."

I grinned at him, my heart as light and buoyant as a balloon.

"You said that already," I said happily, "Say it a lot. I love hearing it."

He began to tie a shiny little fish to the line on his pole, saying, "When you turn eighteen, we'll tell your parents about us."

"Okay. You should move in with me."

He drew in a sharp breath, shaking off his finger then sucking on it a second, his gaze weighing me.

"Maybe. We'll see. I don't want to rush you."

"What do you think about making that carriage house your garage?"

"... I think I'd drive you crazy so close."

"You absolutely would. I can barely keep my hands off you. But I can respect boundaries. You could do whatever you wanted in there and I wouldn't come grope you or anything unless you invited me in."

He snorted with laughter again.

I said wistfully, "I'd love for that house to be *our* house."

"What if I didn't want to do a hotel?"

"Then we could live somewhere else and I'd run it myself. But not for a while because I can't afford two places, so we'd have to live there until it was done at least and I could get a mortgage."

"You'd really be willing to live somewhere else?"

"Sure."

"And if I didn't want you to wear a maid uniform there?"

"Then I wouldn't. But it wasn't going to be the sexy kind."

"Still.... I absolutely hate the idea of you being the maid because sexy clothing or not, you're beautiful and they'd see the clothes and think they could take... liberties."

"If it bugs you when it's time, we'll find something that doesn't bug you."

"We should both think about this. It's a big step. I love all of these ideas but I'm really worried that you're too young and if I jump in like I want too and you change your mind, it's going to mess us both up."

"I'm totally cool with what we're doing now—for now."

He cast out the line and handed me the pole that I had to take awkwardly because of the oars. He helped me settle them, then turned away to bait the other pole saying," Just don't... lead me on. If you start to change your mind, let me know it. I really don't want to come home one day and find my stuff in the yard."

"Deal."

SIX

"Let me record you," I said as I smoothed Jace's hair back.

We were alone in the shop. Everyone else had left for the night an hour ago.

I'd finished too and had come to watch him work, which I *knew* was distracting him because he kept coming to the work bench that I was sitting on to kiss me. But I'd stay until he was ready to leave, or he asked me to go.

"What for? No one is doing this stuff."

"*You're* doing it."

"You know what I mean. It isn't the type of thing people want to learn to do."

"That's where you're wrong, but that isn't what I meant anyway. I meant, *you're* doing it, so I want the recording for me. I don't care if no one else watches it, although I think they will. I want to save this so when I'm old and gray I can look back and remember how utterly perfectly beautiful you are."

"You know, sometimes I think you mean that," he said in the deep husky tone that turned my knees to mush.

"I love you."

His eyes smiled into mine as he set aside the huge pliers that he used to grip the hot metal.

His kisses never sated me. They always left me wanting more of them. I pulled him back for another one that he laughingly obliged.

"We could always do this tomorrow night," I said cajolingly.

"That's what you said *last* night."

I slid my hands down his back onto his ass to press him against me.

"Of course, one more night won't hurt," he said breathlessly as he tugged off his thick work glove.

His palm on my breast even through my shirt made me moan.

He groaned as he glanced back at the forge.

"I've got that fire going just perfect, Kate."

"You sure do."

He chuckled as he stepped away to turn off the gas. "You win. Well, I win."

"What did you win?" Everly asked sweetly, making us both jump guiltily.

I hadn't heard the door open and hoped she hadn't been watching long.

"What do you want?" I asked.

"To save him from your pathetic stalking."

He put his gloves back on and picked up the pliers.

I ignored her. I always ignored her because I knew I couldn't win.

She sauntered closer, ignoring me to smile sweetly at him.

"It's sweet how nice you are to her, but you can tell her to go. My father would totally understand that she was bugging you while you were trying to work."

"Good. Then get the hell out."

Her mouth dropped open, snapping closed when I snickered.

She glared over her shoulder at me then smirked as she said, "You heard him, Kate. Get the hell out."

I rolled my eyes at her, snickering again when she flushed.

"You're making a fool of yourself, Everly," he said.

She said to me, "You're the fool, panting over him as if he'd give a shit if you weren't the boss's daughter."

Jace gaped at her a second before saying, "Jesus, you're a bitch."

"And you're pathetic. Even Kate will see through you—what a loser you are sooner or later. Sooner would be my guess. Linda told me you showed up alone at the Den last night and even scuzzy what's her name, the one with all those kids who lives in your shitty trailer park, slapped your face when you tried that lame come on. But she left with you when you gave her the tenner..." she turned to smirk at me. "Maybe you should try that, Kate? Slip him a fifty and maybe he'll let you suck his dick."

She flounced out.

"She's such a bitch!" he said as if he couldn't believe how big of a one.

"What girl?"

"Seriously?"

"She's a bitch. There's no doubt about that. But what girl?"

"You really believe that bullshit?"

"Not at all—well, part of it. I believe you went to the bar and there was a girl there… the rest, who knows. Everly lies *all* the time, but sometimes there's nuggets of truth in them, and since I have no idea where you live or go when you're not here or with me, I think it's a fair question. Although, I suppose you don't really have to answer it seeing as how we aren't exclusive or anything."

"Are you fucking kidding me right now?"

"Why does everyone get mad at *me* for what *she* says? It's like her superpower."

He tossed the pliers aside to put his hands on his hips, leaning really close to say tightly, "You and me are exclusive. We better fucking be, Kate! You're my girl, no one else's."

"How romantic."

He huffed in annoyance.

I slid from the workbench to hug him.

He returned my embrace.

I could feel his pulse pounding.

"Angering people speechless is her superpower," I said, which made him relax against me. "I love you."

"I love you too," he whispered and kissed my temple. "She's my cousin. And Everly's right. She's a bit of a ho, but I love her and all her damned kids. She's nice and a good mom ninety percent of the time, but when her current guy bails, she goes right out to pick up another loser. My mom called yesterday to say Crystal's latest baby daddy had beat feet and would I go bring her home. So I did."

"Stalling the inevitable?"

"Yep. But since it's the only thing I can do…"

"I have a better idea. Let's set her up with Howard."

He snickered then stepped back to search my face.

"You're serious?"

"Sure. Howard's a really nice guy with a good job, but we could make him look loser-ly for her if she digs that type. Invite them both over. Get her drunk and let her nature take its course. He'll thank you for it one day."

"He's thirty-two and probably a virgin."

"What's your point?"

"That you're right as usual."

He pulled out his cell and made a call.

"I need a favor. Can you come over... no don't worry about the kids, just come over. I know a girl who *loves* to babysit. Sure she will, she digs me."

I rolled my eyes at him.

He blew me a kiss that made me laugh.

"In an hour. Thanks Chris. Oh...is all you need to do is laugh at his jokes. He works with me, and if he doesn't cheer up soon, I'm gonna kill him. I'll pick up pizza. He just needs a night out with a pretty girl telling him he ain't so bad."

He waggled his phone at me. "One down."

"How many kids?"

"Four."

"Four!"

He winked at me as he dialed and then said, "Howard, hey pal, I need a favor. Can you stop by my place in an hour? Yeah, I know it's short notice. I'll owe you one."

He pocketed his phone, smiling smugly.

"He didn't ask what the favor was?"

"*Nah*, he'd assume it was work related."

He turned off the gas and began neatening his tools.

"Four kids, *huh*?"

"They're great kids, except for maybe Evan... but I'm sure you can handle him."

I grunted, making him laugh.

"Come on. Let me show you my humble abode."

"Really?"

He frowned at me.

I said, "I'm just surprised is all. It's been a month and you never mentioned your house at all."

The best month of my life.

"I live alone. My mom just remarried, and I didn't want to be a third wheel. I like Frank. He's a great guy. I'm happy for them and she didn't ask me to go or anything. My uncle on my dad's side owns the trailer park, so I got a great deal. It's only two hundred bucks a month and before you judge, keep in mind that I'm saving up for my own garage and tools are stupid expensive. Besides, I'm almost never there."

That was true. He worked twelve hours a day every day, except Sunday. Sundays he spent with his mom in the morning and the afternoons with me when I could get away.

I said, "This might be naïve of me, but I thought you worked these long hours because you liked it."

"I do. I'd just like it better if I was working for myself. But I'm still learning too, and this place is amazing for that. Your dad hires the best."

"He does," I agreed.

SEVEN

I'd never before even driven past the trailer park where Jace lived. I hadn't known it existed or that there even was a trailer park in town or even near our town, which in hindsight was really stupid when the kids at school were relentless with their trailer park jokes. I'd thought them all just assholes like Everly.

And they *were* assholes because the kids they picked on looked perfectly normal. None of them looked like I imagined trailer park trash people would look—like some of the men here looked with their stained, wife-beater t-shirts barely covering their beer belies, and the old ratty ball caps, dirty hair, cold eyes, bad tattoos and the desperate looking women sitting at the tables with them.

The park was huge with trailers of all sizes and in all different conditions from some that looked like regular houses with little picket fences, to run down rust heaps that were melting into the ground, and everything in between. There were even a few streets of trendy tiny homes.

Kids were everywhere. Almost every trailer had a table of some sort outside. I imagine it was horribly hot in those tin cans in the summer, which was why everyone was outside now, enjoying the cool spring air.

I wondered if I'd like it better than the cold imposing stone of my home. Our house was always cool with the stone floors and super high ceilings through the entire downstairs.

He slowed to a crawl as we passed a busy playground and a small herd of young teens on bikes.

I said wistfully, "They must have so much fun together."

I turned to watch them, trying to get a strong enough mental impression to draw the expressions, which were varied from angry, amused, bored, happy. I reached for my cell to snap a picture, but he turned a corner, and we headed down a row of similar looking double-wides with the little fences. Almost all of them were well kept with flowers and little decorations.

"My mom's place," he said challengingly as he pointed past my shoulder.

"Cute." The second I said it, I realized it sounded insulting, but it *was* cute. She'd put faux shutters around her windows the same color light blue as her tiny porch. A huge pot of purple pansies was beside the door that had a green wreath with the word welcome in blue and purple.

Her little table was dark purple with comfortable looking chairs with blue cushions. I could imagine him sitting there eating and laughing.

"Do you think she'd let me come paint it?"

He didn't answer.

We pulled up in front of another smaller trailer with about a hundred toys in the little yard.

"Crystal's."

Which I'd already figured.

He was angry. I wasn't sure if it was for my cute comment or asking to paint it—and had no idea how to fix it.

I followed him to the door where Crystal greeted me like we were friends, which eased the tension a bit. She was really pretty with bright blue eyes, curly blond hair, and a beautiful smile. And she was way too young to have a ten-year-old who glowered at me with his mother's beautiful eyes.

The other three kids were small blond replicas of her. Evan was tall at that gangly stage that I remembered so well with a creamy brown complexion and jet-black hair cut really short on the sides and just a bit longer on top. I imagined he'd be beautiful, as beautiful as Jace when he was a man.

He picked up the baby who was trying to climb his leg. She couldn't have been two. The boy and girl reminded me strongly of Hannah and Harley, both clambering for attention from Jace, their mom, their brother, and even me; trying to show all of us their toys, tell us what they were going to eat for dinner, share their life in a burst of sound and smiles.

The home smelled of a hundred past meals. Breads, cookies, sauce, it all lingered. I wished I could paint the feeling it evoked. This was a good place—a happy place. A bit messy but comfortable with happy kids.

Without being told or asked Evan took the baby to the small kitchen and placed her into the highchair there then began making her dinner while she banged her spoon yelling happily, Ev, Ev, Ev! Exactly the same way Harley had yelled Kate. It made my eyes cloud from the remembered emotion. He'd adored me—he still adored me and I him. I really hoped Jace would learn to love my brothers and sisters like I did.

Crystal began kissing their cheeks as she said, "I won't be late, darlings. Evan, you know how to reach me. He can tell you where things are."

I said, "Do they have any allergies?"

"No. Be good, darlings."

Jace kissed my cheek and they left.

That he hadn't said anything made my throat feel tight.

The baby stopped chanting as soon as Evan placed her bowl in front of her. She dropped the spoon to use her fingers.

He began taking frozen dinners from the freezer.

I said to the kiddos, "Bring me the dirty plates and cups. Let's get them sparkling."

They ran off eagerly.

I said to him, "Want to make brownies?"

He shrugged.

"Have any good cereal like Fruity Pebbles or Lucky Charms?"

His eyes narrowed but he brought me a box.

"I need a bowl and a stick of butter."

The kiddos returned with a few glasses and one plate as he set the required items on the counter.

I dumped the whole box of cereal into the bowl and handed it to the blond boy.

"You guys mash that up. Evan, melt the butter. Thirty seconds in the microwave."

I opened cabinets until I found her baking supplies. She was well stocked, which didn't surprise me. I took out the ingredients I needed, saying to the kiddos, "It needs to be smaller. Maybe use a can or something to smash it."

They giggled happily as they took turns smashing the cereal.

I handed the bowl of ingredients to Evan.

"Add three eggs if you have them, if not, add a cup of milk or even water with a sprinkle of vegetable oil. Mix it good."

He took the bowl.

I laid my hand on his arm as I said, "Anyone have any allergies?"

58

He shook his head, his eyes lighting as we shared a parents are so stupid, look.

I said, "Dump in raisins if you have them, nuts, dried fruit, even small candies are okay."

"How much?"

"Doesn't matter. These bars are always good. I make them all the time. They last about a week before getting stale and make a great breakfast if you're in a hurry."

"I'm not allowed to use the stove."

"I wasn't either, but these cook great in the microwave. You can use maple syrup instead of the Karo syrup I used, but the Karo is better. It makes the stuff nice and clumpy. Dump the cereal in and let them mix it up."

When it was mixed, which took a while because they kept adding more ingredients, dried figs I chopped for them, two colors of raisins, dried apricots that were expired but looked and smelled fine, peanut butter, and a package of salted peanuts that for some reason made them all laugh.

I said, "Now you decide if you want balls or bars or even shapes. Bars are easiest and easier to pack into a lunch, plus balls can get wasted if the kids will use them to throw. Which should we make?"

"Bars."

I showed them how to place the big glob into a large Ziplock and mash it into the desired shape. I cut it into bars right across the bag so the knife wouldn't stick then placed them on a plate.

"Make sure you check that no bag got stuck on them. Cook it for three minutes. Check it by letting it cool and tasting it. If it's still runny or whatever just put it in another minute or two. You have to get used to judging it but even overdone it's always good. You can eat it warm just wait at least three minutes so they don't burn their mouths."

I began cleaning the mess as I was talking.

They all happily watched the microwave and ate their microwave dinners, which gave me time to wash everything.

"What's the baby's name," I asked as I lifted her, holding her at arm's length to avoid the food splattered across her.

"Belle."

"Can you grab her pajamas? I'll wash her quick."

We had Belle cleaned up in pajamas with a bottle, settled in a portable crib beside us in no time.

I said, "I need four plastic cups and something small enough to fit under them."

By the time Crystal and Jace returned, Belle, Diana, and Bobby were asleep, tucked up in bed. Evan was in the kitchen with me still trying to master the magic tricks I'd shown him.

I said, "Remember, that one only works on stupid people—or drunk ones. But if you start with that one and they fall for it, you'll amaze them. I could make a good fifteen, twenty dollars at a party with that."

He laughed, nodding happily.

I handed him back all of the change the kids had given me.

"Practice makes perfect," I said and kissed the top of his head.

He gave me a hug.

Crystal said, "How'd it go?"

She'd sounded suspicious or surprised, but also hopeful.

"Kids are chumps," I said, and Evan and I bumped fists.

He grabbed the cups and ran to his bedroom, yelling, "Night, Mom. Night, Jace." He stopped in the doorway to say to me, "You going to babysit again?"

"You going to have some money worth taking?"

We both laughed.

He nodded eagerly and ran into his room.

"What on earth?" she said as if she wasn't sure if she should be amused or horrified.

I said, "It's nothing just a trick my brother showed me at that age. My parents had the most boring parties, but I could always find someone to pull it on." I winked at Jace as I said, "A real stupid mark will let me do it ten times or more at a dollar an attempt. It got me through middle school..."

I hated to remember middle school. I hated thinking about school at all. I hated school period. That it would be over in two days felt like a miracle.

I said, "Kids can be dicks, but they'll respect a well done con."

She nodded agreement.

I said, "We made breakfast bars and left them in the microwave. They look like crap but they taste good and are as nutritious as cereal with fruit. My kids love them for breakfast to go when I'm running late. I sometimes make it ahead of time and freeze it. Thirty seconds in the microwave and it's good as new."

"How many kids do you have," she asked, shooting Jace an amazed glance.

Judging by the glance, he'd been vocal in the past about raising another man's kids.

It made a pit form in my stomach.

"Four. None of them are mine. Call if you want to set up a play date or something. I have two Evan's age, an almost four-year-old and an almost five-year-old."

"How do you make the bars?"

"Evan knows the recipe."

Jace said to her, "Don't forget you promised to drop off lunch for us tomorrow, and no cheating. I want the homemade lasagna like grandma used to make."

She laughed and gave him a hug.

"Thanks," she said softly with a wealth of emotion.

We all knew she didn't mean for a night out or babysitting but just giving a crap.

"Night," I said.

We got into his truck, and I said, "How'd it go?"

"Good...you and Evan hit it off?"

"Yeah. He reminds me of me... I was always the odd one out too. You're going to think I'm retarded or something but I had no idea there was a trailer park in town."

He burst into laughter.

I said, "It isn't funny because my sister has been calling me—and everyone else she dislikes—trailer park trash for years. I think I probably offended a lot of people..."

"How so?"

His tone was too casual.

"By agreeing with her."

"You called people that too?"

I nodded. "She'd make fun of my hair or clothes being dirty, which they usually were with paint stains, and I'd say it's because the trailer didn't have a washer or something stupid. And then she'd say something lame and one of my friends would try to help and Everly would call her dirty white trash and I'd say she didn't have a washer in her trailer either, which always made all my friends laugh. Although when I say friends, I really mean acquaintances. I had no real friends."

"Come on, you had to have had at least one."

"Nope. No one was strong enough to withstand an Everly assault. She was brutal. I stopped trying to make any particular friends and learned to amuse everyone with the stupid magic tricks and jokes. I'd prank the teachers a lot. The kids all knew it and the teachers never suspected me because I was a nerd.

"She stopped bothering me sophomore year. I think because it was starting to make her look bad or maybe she just had better things to do, but by then my persona was firmly established. I was Kate Avery, nerd, good for a joke or help with a project but otherwise uninteresting. They weren't mean, except for Everly's crew. But she was mean to everyone except her crew, and even to them sometimes. I was just ignored because everyone knew talking to me made them a target to her and her friends."

"Your parents never did anything?"

I shook my head, saying, "I bet you were really popular in school."

"I guess... but probably not like you think. I had some good friends though."

"Had? You're not still friends?"

"Sure, but all except one has moved away."

"Are you lonely?"

"Not anymore."

EIGHT

From the top of the stairs, Everly said, "Don't trip, loser."

Neither of my parents reacted.

I finished buckling my heels, not giving her the satisfaction of glancing up.

Her tone gained a malicious edge as she added, "Those poor kids having to listen to you rattle on."

My father said, "You need to pick up your grades, young lady, if you expect to be the valedictorian."

"She hasn't a prayer," I said.

"Like I'd want to be a super geek like you!"

She flounced away.

My parents and I headed out to my dad's vintage Jaguar. It was a cool looking car but had a really cramped backseat.

Not that he'd care if I arrived looking a wrinkled mess as long as he looked good.

I knew it was a petty thought, but I was pissed that no one ever called Everly out for being such a jerk.

They dropped me off by the gymnasium with the rest of the kids.

"We're so proud of you, Kate," my mother said.

"She's an Avery," my father said like that was the reason I'd graduated head of my class.

My mother said, "It isn't too late to invite friends over."

They drove away before I had to say what friends.

I took my seat and didn't pay any attention at all to the speeches that no one was paying any attention to. Most of the audience had their phones out, ostensively to take pictures, but I thought most were just killing time scrolling the web or texting while waiting for us to throw our hats in the air.

My grandmother sat with my parents, Grayson, and Kenya. Jace had come too. He stood in the back with the rest of the people who didn't have tickets and a lot of the other kids from the school who'd wanted to see their friends—or enemies—graduate and get out of their hair.

Everly was there with her inner circle. I imagined she'd be truly awful next year without having to worry I'd tell our parents what she was up to. Not that I had told in years. There wasn't any point since it only got me yelled at.

The principal called my name, and I was surprised by the amount of applause. Our entire class and most of the kids watching clapped for me.

Everly yelled out, "Loser!"

My father's jaw tightened. He cast a furious glance over his shoulder at her.

He said something to my mother that made her flush and my grandmother smirk.

I stood to make my speech.

Jace gaped at me.

I shrugged, smiling back, saying, "Most of us will go on from here with a feeling of relief. We'll be able to reinvent ourselves, choosing our own paths, our own friends, our own careers without the social pressures of this closed community. A lot of us will pick the path that we think we should be on, but I say to hell with that! Follow your dreams. Be the you that you want to be, not the you that you felt like you had to be to fit in or please others. Choose what makes you happy!"

I sat.

My grandmother was saying something that was making my father turn red. But I thought it was about Everly, not me, because he kept glaring over his shoulder. I don't think either of them had even heard my speech, such as it was. Only my mother clapped. Kenya and Grayson were laughing along with a lot of the clapping audience.

The principle looked really annoyed.

My class stood to clap, which I thought was for the brevity of the speech, not the speech itself.

We threw our hats into the air, and I was free.

All around me kids laughed together and cried while exchanging hugs, disregarding the cliques that had been sacrosanct for years. People who to my knowledge hadn't spoken at all were hugging and calling goodbye as if they'd been friends the entire time.

I was surprised again by how many of them gave me hugs and invited me to their graduation parties.

When I finally got away, Jace was gone, which was good because I couldn't have spoken to him without Everly noticing, and maybe my father.

He was yelling at Everly, which made me snicker and her glare. She should've known he'd be pissed by such a public display because if there was anything my grandmother disapproved of it was public displays. And when she was pissed, she'd cut everyone, even the kiddos—and threatened to leave her money to charity, which pissed my father off royally.

My brother and sister were talking with one of the teachers who I knew had gone to school here with them years ago. My mother and grandmother were nowhere in sight.

I headed to the car.

My mother was yelling at my grandmother, furiously yelling, not loudly but red-faced and leaning in.

She *never* yelled at anyone, except me, that way.

I stopped to gape and was shocked when my grandmother hit her.

I ran forward and they stepped apart.

"What's going on?" I asked.

My grandmother said coldly, "Your mother is... nothing. Nothing at all. Let's just forget it ever happened, Alise."

My mother stared around, looking bewildered.

I gave her a quick hug.

"You okay, Mom?"

"What... you graduated! We're so proud, Kate."

She didn't look proud. She looked sick.

I said to my grandmother, "Don't you dare ever hit her again!"

"It's none of your business, young lady!"

She stomped away.

"Mom?"

"Will any of your friends be joining us? We're so proud of you, Kate."

I gave up.

"No. It's just us."

"Find your father or Grayson. We need to pick up the kids. We'll meet you at the restaurant. We're so proud of you, Kate."

I held in my sigh with effort and gave her another hug.

When I glanced back, she was crying. Whatever my grandmother had said had seriously upset her.

I found my father with Grayson and Kenya heading to the parking lot.

"Where's your mother?"

"At the car crying. Grandma was yelling at her."

He heaved an annoyed exasperated sigh.

"I'll take care of it."

"She was really upset... what's—"

"It's nothing for you to worry about. My mother was just embarrassed by Everly's outburst. I've sent your sister home to think about how her actions reflect on the rest of the family."

God forbid she had to think about how they affected me, I thought angrily.

He continued, "Grayson will give you a ride to the restaurant."

He stomped off.

Kenya said, "Grandma was glaring daggers, which is stupid. It's not Mom's fault Everly is such a bitch."

She gave me a hug and then handed me a small package.

"Your speech was great, Kate."

Grayson snickered. "I appreciated the brevity."

I laughed too, shrugging.

He handed me a gift card to the local hardware store.

Kenya said, "Way to put some effort in, bro. You could've at least got it at a store she actually shops at, not one you happened to be at."

I gave him a hard hug.

"Thanks. It's perfect. You're the best brother ever. Let's get this dinner over with."

I opened her gift, which was pretty gold bracelet with a graduation hat with the year on it.

"Thanks, Ken, it's beautiful."

She hugged me as she said, "My real gift will be helping you settle into your dorm. I'm going to bring you and spend the weekend. It'll be fun. I'll take you around to all of our old haunts."

I wasn't up to a fight with her, so just nodded while wondering if it was her idea because she knew our parents couldn't be bothered or if they'd asked her.

Grayson snorted softly.

The two of them began arguing over the best places to get food at Princeton while we drove to the restaurant in his Porsche Panamera—a gift from our parents when he'd graduated law school.

My grandmother didn't attend the dinner. My mother acted perfectly normal. No one mentioned Everly. My father gave me the keys to a brand-new Mercedes. My mother gave me a lecture on driving safely.

I couldn't wait for this day to end.

When we returned home, we found that Grandma had left a note saying that Everly was staying with her for a week.

My mother said to me, "Can you be home to get the kids off the bus?"

"Of course she can," my father said. "We'll be on our balcony enjoying an early evening in. Keep the noise down."

They headed upstairs.

I said to the kids, "Popcorn and a movie?"

Felicity came to the kitchen to help make it while Wolfgang and the kiddos went to find a movie we could all watch.

She said, "We don't need anyone to help us off the bus. The driver would just let us off with the kiddos if you have things to do."

I gave her a quick hug, saying, "I don't mind, Fell. You and Wolf can help me with my project."

"We making another chair?" she asked eagerly.

"A bench with a secret compartment."

It's weird how Everly doesn't like to build things when we all do..."

"That's because Everly is weird."

She snorted with laughter.

We took the popcorn and drinks to the playroom. I was glad Everly was gone, but pissed they'd let her go. She was going to be unbearable now that she knew she could get away with defying our father like this.

I wondered if she done it for just this reason although that was risky on her part. Grandma might've been pissed too—in fact, I was surprised she wasn't. That sort of public embarrassment was more likely to earn you the cold shoulder for a few months instead of a week of shopping, but I guess our grandmother blamed our mom for Everly's bad manners.

How the hell my sister always got others into trouble for her actions...

I was still musing on that, not paying much attention to the movie when Jace texted me.

You were beautiful and brilliant. You should've said you were going to be making the speech! I can't believe you're mine. You are still mine, aren't you?

I texted him back, *ALWAYS !!! Kids go to bed at eight. I'm taking my new car for a ride. Meet me?"*

I'll be waiting. Love you.

NINE

Three Weeks Later

The air was sticky with humidity, clinging to our sweaty skin. July in Georgia was always sticky. We'd had a few record setting days for both humidity and heat. I'd spent them here in the cool of my house's basement putting in the keypads in my dungeon room and felt bad for Jace who'd spent them in the sweltering shop.

Jace and I lay on the bare floorboards right inside the parlor to make the most of the fan in the hall. We'd been kissing and talking, laying there naked for an hour now, idly caressing each other.

We'd been coming here almost nightly for the last few weeks. It still amazed me that he seemed as caught up as I was in us.

I could feel the reluctance—or at least hoped I could when he sat.

"Don't stop."

"We should go."

"No."

"Kate…"

"Please," I whispered.

He groaned, tossing his shirt aside to resume kissing me.

I sighed in contentment, twining my leg over him.

I wasn't exactly sore, and I was more than ready for him, but it made me moan when he thrust.

"This is too much," he said but he didn't stop.

I shifted to give him a deeper angle, forgetting every thought in my head and didn't even realize I'd been speaking at all until my orgasm made me scream his name, which came out in a mangle of words.

"Kate! Kate…"

He fell forward, panting hard.

My body jerked against him with a mind of its own.

"You okay," he asked worriedly, and I realized I was crying.

"This is your fault. Maybe I wouldn't be so... desperate for you if we spent more than an hour together. Let's take a full day off here."

He shifted his hips and even spent he felt amazing.

"Desperate?" he said musingly and a bit smugly as he flexed his hips again, purposefully, while leaning up on his elbows to see my face.

"Yeah, you make me desperate," he whispered, flexing again.

His thumb against my nipple made me cry out and jerk faster.

I forgot myself completely again, reacting to the magic of his hands.

Hours later, he whispered drowsily, "I should bring you home."

"I am home."

I reluctantly released him though to reach for my discarded clothing.

He said, "We're putting the shower in and no arguments about me helping."

I nodded agreement because we were both dripping with sweat despite the industrial size fan roaring in the hallway. And I had some extra cash thanks to a generous graduation gift from my grandmother. She'd intended it to be spent on clothing appropriate for Princeton, making it perfectly clear I had nothing appropriate at all—and that she doubted I'd manage to buy anything she'd deem worthy. Since nothing I bought would ever please her, I'd been using it to please myself, upgrading my dungeon with it.

"Move in with me," I said.

He tossed me my shirt, taking his from me.

"I will as soon as your parents won't freak."

I didn't bother argue because I knew he hated the idea that people would think he was taking advantage as much as I hated the idea of taking advantage of his willingness to help me. Which was likely part of the problem. He wouldn't feel at home here if I never let him do anything.

I said, "A shower sounds amazing, unfortunately for you, it'll be just cold water until I sell the car."

"I could—"

"Maybe. Let's see how long the hot water heater takes to come in."

He grinned at me, resuming dressing.

I was dressed before him so took a second to gather my hair into a ponytail then a messy bun.

His hands stilled on his laces, his eyes taking on the lustful look that heated my insides as his gaze slid over me.

I love you," I said when his gaze reached my eyes.

He flushed, releasing his laces to stand and hug me.

"I love you—desperately."

I could feel his reluctance—which exactly matched my own—when he finally stepped away.

"Just another few weeks."

We left the house, stepping into the cooler summer air outside where he threw my bike into the back of his truck.

On the way back to my house, he said, "Don't they wonder why you never use the car?"

"I doubt they notice," I said absently, cuddling closer to press my lips to his neck.

"You should really wear your seatbelt," he said like he did every night.

I ignored it to kiss under his ear.

The truck swerved hard, surprising an eep out of me.

"I'm too tired, Kate. You're going to kill us. I closed my damned eyes..."

I giggled, sitting back saying primly, "My apologies, sir."

He took my hand to kiss it, keeping it in his for the rest of the way back, which only took a few minutes, but I was almost asleep myself when we got there.

He got out to take my bike from his truck, saying for the millionth time," Text me when you get inside."

"What do you imagine will happen to me as I peddle down my driveway?"

"Nothing—but text me anyway so I *know* you're safely inside."

I'd do it to make him happy. I'd do anything to make him happy. Plus I understood his paranoia because his neighborhood wouldn't be at all safe for anyone alone late at night. Criminal types came out like stars in the sky, growing bolder as it got later. Almost all of the crime that made into the paper happened on that side of town—at night.

He kissed my cheek and got back into his truck.

I waved and headed home. That small gesture of asking me to text him always made me *feel* loved in a way passionate declarations didn't. I loved hearing him say he loved me, but I really loved feeling that burst of unexpected warmth over the simple things he did that made me feel his love.

When I rounded the last curve of the long drive, I could see lights were on downstairs, which made me suddenly worry about the late hour.

I'd been thinking no one would notice when I came in because Everly came in at all hours and no one ever responded to the low beep of the house alarm—except me.

I'd get up and check that the kids hadn't slipped out of bed or that Wolfgang wasn't sleepwalking.

To my surprise, my mother was up. She stomped to the door when I came in, saying angrily, "Where were you?"

"At Grayson's."

Not technically a lie.

"Did you forget your phone?" she asked sarcastically.

I reached for it and realized I had, in fact, forgotten it.

"Sorry, I put it on the charger there and forgot to grab it."

She eyed me for a minute, then the anger drained from her face and she smiled tiredly.

"I don't want you on the bike at this hour and why take a bike all the way there for God's sake!"

For a moment I was shocked, confused, but touched by her display of concern.

She spun away saying over her shoulder, "Don't forget the kids need to be at the park at by nine-thirty."

It felt like a punch.

"I won't forget." I said as normally as I could through my suddenly tight throat.

I tiptoed into my dad's office to call Jace.

"Mr. Avery," he said breathlessly.

"No. It's just me."

"You scared twenty years off my life!"

"Sorry. I left my phone and didn't want you to worry."

"I thought you'd been run over or something for crying out loud!"

I was instantly relieved that his worry hadn't been *solely* because he'd though my dad had found out I was with him.

"Sorry," I repeated but this time I meant it.

"Thanks for calling. I would've worried..."

"See ya tomorrow?"

"You know it."

He hung up.

I went up to my room feeling much better.

I was making pancakes the next morning for Harley and Hannah when Wolfgang came into the kitchen.

"What are you doing home?" I asked in surprise.

I'd thought the twins would be gone until Sunday night.

"Grandma sent us home last night when Felicity got sick."

"Fell? Is she okay?"

"I'm fine," Felicity grumbled as she stomped in.

"Why are you both up so early?"

"I'm starving!"

"She woke me." Wolfgang shrugged, clearly not at all worried about her or being woken.

I tousled his hair and kissed his forehead then felt hers before doing the same.

She batted my hand away but grinned at me.

"Grandma made me eat the stupid banana pudding. I told her I was allergic, but she didn't believe me, said it wasn't on the list Mom sent, said I was gold bricking. What's that anyway?"

"Everly."

They both made a face that made me laugh.

"I'll call and give her the updated list," I said as I kissed Felicity's forehead again.

They both looked exhausted, which did nothing to reassure me that they were, in fact, fine.

"What time did you come home?"

"Dunno. Late. No one wanted to come get us. Where were you? I called like ten times!"

The last spec of hope that my mother had actually gotten up to check on me died.

I forced a light tone as I said, "Sorry. I forgot to charge my phone. I'll be more careful."

I debated giving them Jace's number as I poured out more pancake mix.

I shouldn't without speaking to him first, I told my guilty conscience as I whipped up more pancakes.

I called my grandmother.

"Hi, gram, hope I didn't wake you."

"Kate! We were worried."

"I forgot to charge my phone. I'll text you the updated list of her allergies."

"Your mother did already."

72

"She forgets to update the list. Go by mine—or trust that Fell knows what she can and can't eat."

"Lesson learned," Gram said dryly with a hint of disapproval, probably at my cheek for daring to correct her.

"So where were you so late?"

"Kate!" Hannah yelled as Felicity said, "Grab a towel, stupid."

"Milk emergency. I've got to go. Call you later."

I hung up, grateful for the interruption.

I cleaned the table while making the pancakes.

I made both the twins three before setting the plates on the table because long experience had shown that serving either of them first inevitably led to a mess and arguments as they shared the one plate.

"So what are you two up to today?" I asked as I sat with my plate and a delicious cup of hot fragrant coffee.

I'm going to miss this coffee, I thought wistfully as I took a long sip, nearly scalding my mouth. The beans were way out of my budget, but maybe I could make myself a thermos when I came to pick up the kids...

I was musing on that, not paying much attention to their whispered argument.

"They're staying inside and being as quiet as mice," Everly said as she meandered in. She thunked the top of Wolfgang's head as she passed. Not hard enough to be called a slap. She was a master at passive aggressive and hiding her physical taunts in fake affectionate gestures.

Wolfgang flushed angrily but kept eating his breakfast, stabbing the pancakes with the fork to show his displeasure.

I said to him, "Take the kiddos to get their shoes on. You can come with me if you want. I'm going to go to the flea market after I drop them off."

They brightened, exchanging relieved grins.

Everly smiled smugly at me.

I waited until they left the room then slapped her across the back of the head as she turned to pour herself a coffee from the pot I'd just made. It surprised an exclamation from her followed by a curse as her coffee spilled across the counter.

"You lay one fucking finger on them again, and I'll beat your ass bloody."

She gaped in astonishment.

I stomped away before I punched her stupid face.

I expected her to yell after me, threats, or taunts, but she said nothing.

She'd probably thought she'd won, I thought sourly as I helped tie laces. And she *had* won. Here I was taking the kids when she was supposed to be watching them, but there was no way I could leave them with her when I knew she'd be a bitch to them all day for the crime of existing. That, and I *knew* she'd get them all worked up. They'd be fighting with everyone, including the kiddos, which would make our mom mad, and then all four of them would be in trouble, which would make them cranky as anything when I had them Sunday.

My mood didn't improve one whit when I found the Ford had a flat and the spare was gone.

I stomped back into the house to call the garage, getting Howard.

"This is Kate. The Ford has a flat and I need to get the kiddos to their camp by nine-thirty. So either send someone with a new tire, or one of the cars and someone who knows how to move the dumb car seats."

"Sure thing, Kate. I'll be right there."

When I got back to the car, Wolfgang said, "Come on, Fell, let's go grab our stash. Maybe we'll find something good."

The two of them ran back into the house.

I peered after them with rising anxiety. That they hadn't dared ask me to wait a minute for them to grab their money made me realize how very much they didn't want to be left with Everly.

I was furious by the time Howard got there with Jace.

"What's up?" he asked worriedly.

"That goddamned bitch has been abusing my kids!"

Howard gaped at me.

"She means Everly," Jace said absently.

Hannah said cheerfully, "You said a bad word. Kate said a bad word. A bad bad word."

Jace snickered.

"She sure did, squirt," he said as he swung her into his arms, earning a happy squeal and a smacking kiss on his cheek.

I wished I could kiss him.

I drew in a long breath, holding for the count of ten before allowing myself to say as calmly as I could.

"You're right, Hannah banana. I shouldn't say those words. Neither should you."

"Ladies don't say those words," Jace said pompously, making her giggle. He kissed her cheek and set her down to pick up Harley. "Hey, pal. You swimming today?"

"Course."

"I'm swimming too!" Hannah said.

He kissed Harley on the cheek, getting a Harley hug in return, then set him down, crouching to be at eye level.

"No bad words," he said seriously.

They both nodded, beaming at him. They adored him as much as I did.

"Avery adoration is your superpower."

He winked at me.

"What am I going to do about her?" I asked.

"Give me a hand with this!" Howard called.

Jace wrinkled his nose at me and went to help Howard.

Felicity and Wolfgang returned a few minutes later. Both of them had their book bags with sweatshirts stuffed through the shoulder straps.

Anger simmered to life again at this simple proof—this hopeful planning.

I said, "I hope you guys brought the mosquito repellant. They'll be out like crazy at dusk in this humidity.

Wolfgang's smile was heartbreaking.

He thrust his bag at Felicity and ran back in, yelling, "I'll get it."

Tears of anger blurred my vision.

Jace said gruffly, "Let me get that for you, Fell." He leaned down to whisper to her, "What you really need is Everly repellent."

She giggled at him but cast a nervous glance over her shoulder.

I said, "She's got that. Me!" I frowned at her as I said, "Why didn't you say she was being such a cow?"

Tears sprang to Felicity's eyes. She turned again to peer worriedly over her shoulder.

I said hastily, "Never mind. We can talk later. I won't leave you guys with her again. I promise."

Her tears remained. Her terror was breaking my heart.

Jace muttered, "Jesus, Kate."

"I didn't *know*!" I said indignantly.

But I *should've* known. I hadn't been paying any attention to them though.

"Know what?" Felicity asked.

"What an idiot I was being."

"You got that right," Everly said.

I turned to see her leaning against the open door sipping her coffee with her silk robe gaping, exposing what I hoped was a bathing suit but was pretty sure was underwear, but I refused to give her the satisfaction of looking at her, which was so clearly what she wanted, so I'd only gotten a quick glimpse.

"Want some?" she asked sweetly. "It's delicious. My dad has the beans imported special."

I glanced over to see her holding out her cup to Jace.

If she'd been a nice person, I'd have been nervous because she was beautiful if you liked a bit of ho in your girl. If she hadn't been so blatantly skanky and just been sincerely offering coffee...but she *was* a skank, and she wasn't offering coffee, and he wasn't an idiot who'd fall for her stupid smug smile.

I turned away again to say to Howard, "We almost done here?"

"Yes, ma'am," he said cheerfully. "Two ticks and you're good to go."

"Wolf!"

He ran around from the side of the house.

Her smile at me sparkled with malice.

Jace grabbed my arm, shaking his head the smallest amount.

"Let's get you guys buckled in," he said as he opened the door to lift Hannah into her carseat.

Harley said, "Wolf, sit with me. You promised."

I took both bags from Felicity. "You're the co-pilot then, Fell."

"Dork," Everly said.

She laughed as she said, "Stop by after work, Jace. All my friends will be here. We're having a barbecue. It'll be a late night cause my mom and dad are both out of town."

"Where'd they go?" I asked.

"The auction. The same one they go to every year... you really are an idiot."

"I wouldn't come to one of your parties for a million bucks," Jace said as if the idea of it would make him vomit. Contempt dripped from his voice.

Howard turned to gape at him.

Jace crouched to check the lug nuts himself then snapped the hubcap back into place.

Howard said to me, "Stop by the garage when you get back and I'll put another spare in the back for you."

Everly flounced away.

I went to the back to toss their bags in.

Howard whispered to Jace, "You can't talk to her like that, man."

I said, "Thanks for coming to fix the tire."

"You're welcome," Howard said uncertainly. His worried gaze passed over all of us, lingering on the door.

"Is everything, *um*, okay?"

"Yeah. My sister's just being a bigger—"

Jace pointedly cleared his throat, interrupting me.

"You better get going," he said. "Stop and get your phone."

I shrugged at him.

"Stop and get it. You might need it if you get another flat."

His lips pursed as he examined me, then he handed me his phone. "Give me the key and I'll get yours. We can meet for lunch or something and switch back."

I handed him the house key.

"Thanks."

"We'll figure something out."

I knew he didn't mean the stupid phones.

Howard said, "I could run in and get it and drop it off if you're in that much of a hurry."

"*Nah*, it's all good. See you later, Kate." He slapped the hood of the car, stepping away.

Howard looked confused again.

I got into the driver seat, saying, "You guys all buckled in."

A chorus of yes's answered me.

I checked anyway.

Howard and Jace drove away while I was still checking seat belts.

We dropped the kiddos off at the park with the rest of the day campers and then headed to the flea market.

I said, "You guys can tell me anything. No matter what she said to you, I'd believe you over her. Not that you have to tell me. But I'd help if I could. You can come with me on weekends or any time. There isn't a thing she could ever say or do that would change that."

I debated adding that I knew she probably had something on them that they were afraid to tell me, or have our father find out, but they were already so obviously traumatized that I didn't have the heart.

I said, "Okay, we're looking for a feather mattress, pillows, quilts, maybe some kitchen stuff—"

"Boring," Wolfgang said in a put-upon tone.

"Are we still looking for peacocks?" Felicity asked.

I nodded as I added, "Any stuffed animals—real animals, not toys. I need some more gears too like the ones you found last time."

77

Wolfgang brightened. "When you going to show us what you're making?"

"Soon."

"We won't tell."

It occurred to me that maybe they were keeping the Everly shit on the down low because they thought I'd think they were snitches.

"I know. I just wanted to finish it before showing it because everyone will think it's stupid if it doesn't work."

He nodded like that made perfect sense.

I glanced over at Felicity, who was pursuing her lips at me.

She shrugged, turning away when I caught her eye.

I glanced back in the rearview.

"I'm good on frames unless you see really big ones like the kind I like."

He nodded.

I said, "What are you guys looking for?"

"Camping stuff."

"Wolf," Felicity said warningly, smiling a fake a smile at me.

"We want to build a treehouse," he said hurriedly.

Her smile eased to a more natural one as she nodded.

"Do you have a tree picked out?" I asked.

"No—do we need one?"

"Dolt," Felicity said without heat.

He said, "I meant right now, stupid. I know we need one."

I said, "You need the tree picked out so you can measure and plan because a house will need to be braced on the branches or have ground supports."

"You'll help us?" he asked eagerly.

"Of course. If Mom okays it."

"She won't care."

That was probably true.

I said, "It'll cost more than you're probably thinking it will."

"How much?"

"It depends on how big, but let's say it's eight-by-eight which is the size of Everly's closet. I'd say it'll be about four hundred dollars for the wood and shingles. We might be able to shave some of that off if we buy used wood."

"I have that."

"Then there's the rope and anything else it needs."

"We can do it," Felicity said.

"We'll look for a good tree tomorrow," Wolfgang said.

"Not tomorrow. Unless you want to come to," she said hopefully.

"Sure, we can look for the tree and figure out what we need."

I had no idea what to do—what they really needed. I knew it wasn't a treehouse, except that a treehouse would be a place to escape our sister.

TEN

I picked up the kiddos and took all the kids out for dinner. We didn't return to the house until almost bedtime.

The kiddos went upstairs to start a bath while the twins helped me set out stuff for breakfast the next day while I washed the dishes left from breakfast.

Felicity and Wolfgang hurried away when Everly entered the kitchen.

I called after them, "I'll be right up."

Everly grabbed a plastic shopping bag and began filling it with ice from the dispenser.

I said, "That bag is probably dirty."

"Your crush is pathetic."

I ignored her.

"Even you can do better."

I continued washing the dishes.

A girl's happy shriek from the backyard cut off in a loud splash followed by raucous laughter.

Margo, Everly's best friend, yelled laughingly, "That's one way to get her wet, I guess," which caused more laughter.

I was pretty sure Everly's friends were all drunk or stoned or both, but I wasn't up to the fight that would ensue if I kicked them out. They'd go, but she'd wake the kids and do god knew what to scare them even more.

I said, "Keep your scumbag friends quiet."

She didn't say anything because we both knew I could get her party shut down, which maybe I should or she was going to think I was afraid of her...

She said, "Why not come out and join us when the brats are asleep?"

As if I'd be stupid enough to fall for that!

"Just keep it down."

"Think you're too good for us?" she called after me. "You think you're fucking perfect?"

I turned to say, "I'm not even close to perfect but you're.... nothing at all."

Her face turned bright red. I smirked for a moment before heading upstairs.

I gave the kiddos a bath while Felicity and Harley took showers on their own.

By the time the kiddos were done splashing around, Felicity and Wolfgang were in their PJs and had made a bed on the floor of the girl's room. Harley was thrilled they were camping out. And Hannah was thrilled it was in her room.

I closed their curtains to mute the low sounds from the pool.

I didn't even try to talk them into going into their own rooms.

I said, "Where's my pillow? Wolf, grab my blanket. Fell, you can pick a story."

She didn't complain that she was too old for bedtime stories.

She and Hannah sorted through the books, finally handing me one.

Wolf returned with my blanket and pillow. The four of them lay on the floor, giggling and whispering through the first part of the book. I waited until they were all sound asleep to tiptoe to the bathroom and call Jace.

"Sorry about breaking our date, but they're totally freaked out."

"About what?"

"I have no idea, but they're hiding out in the kiddos' room, and I think they're planning to run away. I told them I wouldn't leave them alone with her. They want my help to build a treehouse... I have no idea what to do."

"Can't you tell your parents?"

"Sure, but it might make it worse."

"How could that make it worse?"

"My mom won't want to believe it. She's likely to yell at them, not her."

"What about your dad?"

"What about him?"

"Tell him."

I thought about that for a minute.

"I have no idea what he'd do..."

"Would it be worse than the kids too terrified to sleep in their own rooms? And I know it's none of my business, but what the hell, Kate? What's she doing to them?"

"My guess is she's convinced them that she can get them sent away, which if they were together, they might not mind, but they will absolutely lose their shit if my parents separate them! Which of course she'd know! She must have convinced them... she probably caught them doing something bad or just told them she'd lie and say she did."

"What the hell could she have caught them doing? They're just ten for crying out loud!"

"Who knows? She kept me terrified for a year at that age by saying she'd tell our father it was me who'd stained the seat of his Jag."

"Was it you?"

"Yes... but that's not the point. I was absolutely convinced that he'd throw me out on the street, I was bloody terrified!"

"Did she ever tell?"

"He sold the stupid car, and it isn't funny, Jace."

"You can't let her bully you like that."

"I don't anymore because I learned it makes no difference what I say or do. I'm not the problem though. She mostly leaves me alone. I didn't think she'd bother them! I mean, what would be the point!"

"What was the point of bothering you?"

"She's an ass! But you're right, she did it to get me to do all the chores and to steal all my toys and stuff. They'd have nothing she wants...or maybe they do. They started hiding their money. I wonder if she's stealing their allowance?"

"Ask them."

"I will."

"Tell your parents—both of them."

"Yeah..."

"Are you scared of them, Kate?"

"No. It's just so frustrating because I know my mom won't do a thing to help them. For the life of me I have no idea why she keeps having kids..."

"Is there anything I can do?"

"No. Thanks. *I* have no idea what to do. I can't leave them here like this though. Maybe I should make them a room at my house?"

"Will your mom let them stay there?"

"Maybe... but not if Everly causes a scene about it."

"What the actual hell?"

"My mom *hates* a scene. Everly could really embarrass her by telling my mom's friends that she sent the kids to live with me—not that she'd say it like that. She'd be all sweet and worried. I swear to God, I want to smack her senseless."

"That wouldn't help anyone."

"Except me. It would make me feel better, but of course I wouldn't. She'd probably love it if I lost control like that. Baiting me into yelling at her was a favorite pastime of hers for years!"

A hot flush of remembered anger heated my face. My mother had always blamed me, yelled at me, even when she'd heard Everly start it. Everly would gloat when I got lectured. The worse our mom yelled at me, the happier it made her.

"Where is she now?" he asked, bringing my attention back to him. I hated how even now Everly could get me mad and she wasn't even here.

"Outside with her skanky friends."

"Stay away from them."

"No duh."

"Your parents would freak if they knew..."

"Knew what?"

"The kind of people she hangs out with. Lock the doors, Kate."

"Oh the scene if I locked her out."

"Then lock the bedroom door and keep a phone on you. Or better yet, call your parents right now and tell them what's going on."

"I wish I knew what was going on... but maybe."

"Call them."

"Yeah..."

"I love you."

"I love you too."

I stared at my phone for a few minutes, working out what I'd say—if my mother stayed on the line long enough for me to say anything.

"Yes, Kate," she said when she answered.

"Felicity and Wolfgang are terrified of Everly," I blurted.

"Seriously, Kate, we go away so seldom, and you pull... this?"

"I'm not pulling anything. I'm telling you that your children are scared. They're afraid to sleep in their own rooms. Something needs to be done."

"Just tell them to go to bed for god's sake! Really, Kate, you're almost an adult. You should be able to handle two kids.

Four. I didn't say that though.

"They're sleeping. They aren't the problem!"

"Don't take that tone with me, young lady."

"I saw her hit him, Mom."

"She hit him?"

"I'm telling you, they're both scared!"

"I'll speak to them when I come home."

Which wouldn't do a spec of good.

"Mother, the kids aren't the problem. Everly is the problem."

"I'll speak to her."

"Could you please ask her not to wake them? I really don't need her storming inside to scream at me."

"Inside? Where is she?"

"Having a party outside. They're quiet. That isn't the problem."

"Kate... you're being entirely... incompetent."

"I know. I have no idea how to handle this, which is why I called *you*."

"You're making a mountain out of a molehill. I'm sorry if your nose is out of joint because you weren't invited to the party but calling like this is entirely unacceptable."

"The party has nothing to do with anything!"

Even as I said it, I realized I was wasting my breath.

"Can I speak with Dad, please."

"Whatever for?"

"Because I don't know what to do! You aren't listening! I wish I could just drop this, but they're terrified!"

I hung up and called my father's phone directly.

"Kate, is Felicity sick again? Call Kenya or Grayson."

"Fell is fine. Well, not fine but she isn't sick. She and Wolf are both scared of Everly, so scared that they're hiding from her. I have no idea why because they wouldn't say. I can keep them with me, but something needs to be done."

"Slow down a second. All of the kids are fine?"

"They're all sleeping in the kiddo's room."

"So what's the problem?"

It's like talking to a wall.

I took a deep breath, forcing myself to release it slowly and to speak calmly.

"I don't know what the problem is between them, but I'm certain there is one and that it's serious or I wouldn't have called. I called Mom and she isn't listening. I don't know what to do, but I do know I can't just ignore this. The kids are scared. I'm scared they'll run away or something."

"They aren't going to run away," he said like that was the stupidest thing he'd ever heard or maybe that this was the stupidest phone call that he'd ever gotten. I felt like the stupidest person on earth because I'd *known* they wouldn't do a thing.

He said, "And you want me to do what?"

Be their fucking father!

"I have no idea. I guess tell Everly to leave them alone. Just make her leave them alone!"

Which I knew was impossible. The room blurred from my tears I was so angry because she'd *know* I was worried, which would make her treat them even worse. *I* was making things worse, not better.

"Is everyone safe for the evening?" he asked.

"Yes."

"Then I'll handle this when I get home."

He hung up on me.

I called Grayson.

"I'm making an awful mess of things! Everly is picking on the kids. She's got them terrified and I didn't realize it until today. They're scared to death of her! I called Mom and then Dad and they don't care or don't believe me. Not that they or anyone can make Everly stop whatever the hell she's doing! I can't leave them here with her!"

"Want me to come get you guys?"

"No. They're sleeping. I'll take them with me in the morning, which is probably the reason she's doing this, but it's seriously pissing me off! She didn't need to terrorize them! Now Mom will come home and yell at me for ruining her trip and Everly will know she got to me and up her game against them. And they won't even trust *me* anymore! And I don't blame them! I *am* making it all worse! But if I do nothing and they run away... so what the hell am I supposed to do?"

"I don't know either. I'll talk to the kids myself and explain that you were trying to help. There isn't a lot we can do, Kate. Honestly there isn't a lot Mom or Dad can do either."

"So she just gets to smack them around whenever she wants to?"

"She hits them?"

"I have no idea! I saw her smack Wolf. It wasn't a big deal, except that he acted like it was a usual sort of thing and he was afraid to complain about it. He ran around the fucking house to get to the car instead of walking past her!"

"We'll sort this out, sweetheart."

"I'm not going to sit by and let her do whatever she likes to them!"

"I'll come over tomorrow and take them to lunch. Maybe they'll tell me what the problem is? Because we really can't do anything until we know what needs fixing."

"You know it's Everly who's the problem!"

"We'll figure it out," he said again.

Everly was leaning on the closed bedroom door when I stepped into the hall.

She smirked at me then turned and sauntered toward her room, saying over her shoulder, "Nice job, Kate. Now they all see what a paranoid liar you are."

The kids were thrilled to go with their big brother. I took the kiddos to our grandmother and visited a while with her. My parents would pick them up on their way home that night and have dinner with his mother.

I was glad she and my mom had worked out whatever the problem was. Grandma seemed happier than normal to see us. She actually smiled at Hannah and offered to babysit the twins without once complaining about Felicity's allergies. She even asked me how I was and if I was enjoying my summer.

I dodged her questions on what I was doing, which made me feel sort of bad that she was making an effort and I wasn't willing to tell her what I was really up to. I was almost sad to go, but I made my excuses because I was dying to find out if Grayson had better luck than me finding out what was bothering the twins.

By the time the twins returned later that afternoon, I was a bundle of nerves.

Grayson gave me a quick worried glance as he said, "We're building a treehouse, Kate.

The four of us walked toward the garages as he told me their plans.

When we reached the first garage, he said to the kids, "Ask Howard if we can borrow the truck. Don't go in unless you're invited."

Wolfgang and Felicity ran for the far garage where the truck was parked.

They were excited about building a treehouse, but their smiles were too brittle, too forced, too desperate.

"Well?" I asked anxiously as soon as they were out of earshot.

"You're right, but they wouldn't budge..."

"Damn it!"

"It's a pickle," he agreed.

Howard stepped from the door of the far garage and waved.

The three of them stepped back inside.

I said, "I just want to pop in and say hi to Jace."

"You two are—serious?"

"Yes."

"I like him," Grayson said.

"Me too."

He snorted.

We stopped at the open garage door of the second building.

I think we were both shocked to see Everly there.

Neither she nor Jace noticed us.

He looked pissed.

I couldn't see her face. She was barefoot, wearing tight skimpy shorts and a bikini top, hanging off his arm.

He shook her off as we watched.

He said in exasperation, "Just stop already! I'm not interested. I'll never be interested!"

"You know she turned tricks all through high school, right? Ask anyone and they'll all tell you they paid her."

"You're disgusting."

She said cajolingly like he'd said maybe he'd go with her, "We could use the cot right upstairs. No one would ever know. Not even Kate if you want to keep stringing her along."

"Never speak to me again."

His face was bright red and his hands clenched—he was so furious that she had to be a moron not to see that she didn't have a prayer with him.

It made my heart expand even though I was just as furious as him.

She snapped, "Fine. Keep trying to get into Kate's pants. Not that she'll give you the time of day when you're fired, which you will be as soon as I tell my father you cornered me and I had to rip my shirt to get away from you."

"You..."

For a second I thought he was going to hit her but then he laughed.

"Go ahead. No one will believe you.

She laughed as she held out her shirt.

"Your handprint is on it, fool."

Still laughing she yanked on the neckline, ripping it.

Grayson yelled angrily, "Get up to the house right now!"

She whirled.

"He—"

"Would be within his rights to press charges! Which I'll advise him to do unless you get your lying ass to the house right this minute!"

She ran forward and slapped Grayson hard, shocking me.

I gaped at her in amazement as she ran up the drive laughing.

Grayson pulled out his phone and a moment later said, "Dad, I just caught Everly threatening to get one of the men here at the garage fired by claiming inappropriate sexual advances. She's out of control."

He listened for a minute, nodding grimly. Small lines by his eyes deepened. He didn't like what he was hearing.

"She slapped me when I sent her home. I hate to say this, but I think the man involved should make an official report just in case she tries again. He needs a record—"

He listened again.

"Yes. I can do that. What are you going to do?"

He pocketed his phone a moment later.

"I'm not pressing charges," Jace said flatly.

His angry tone made me suddenly sweaty. My family was turning into a real nightmare for him.

Grayson said, "Jace, you need to give a sworn statement. I'm calling a friend. He'll come with his notary."

"It isn't necessary."

"It fucking is!" I said angrily.

He shrugged at me.

Grayson said, "I'm going to insist. If you won't do it, I'll make a police report myself."

Jace snorted angrily.

Grayson said, "We both saw her threaten you. We'll both sign and get that notarized too. I'm *not* asking you to ignore this. If you want to call the police..."

Jace rolled his eyes at us.

I said, "What did she want?"

"My cousin's phone number. Not Crystal, Lloyd's. I don't know his number though. We don't speak. He's a douche bag. I have nothing to do with him. Plus she was being her usual skanky self. She's so stupid...which I don't get when the rest of you are so smart..."

Grayson laughed a bark of unhappy laughter.

"It's lucky for you she's an idiot," Grayson said over his shoulder as he headed to the truck.

I said, "I'm sorry."

"It's not your fault.

"I'm going to need to break our date for a few days to spend more time with the kids."

"I get that... I hate to think what she might have done to them. Lloyd has some very very bad friends."

"I'll make sure they're okay. Don't give up on us, Jace."

His eyes softened.

"I never would."

ELEVEN

I spent the next three weeks in my parent's backyard, working on my laptop, catching up on my video editing, working on my website, finishing some paintings, refinishing furniture, and doing some sewing while watching the kids and helping them finish the treehouse.

We'd gotten most of it up over the first weekend, but they were still adding small details—for the fun of it, I hoped, but I worried it was in the hopes of living there.

Over breakfast, I said, "We're going to an antique show today and won't be back until late, so bring pillows to sleep in the car. And run get the wagons."

"Antiques," Wolfgang said doubtfully.

"It's a flea market of old stuff. They'll have old games and toys and stuff."

"What are you looking for?"

"Candlesticks, blankets—"

"More blankets?"

I nodded as I continued, "Just pretty things that catch my eye and ideas for things I can make. Maybe some fabric."

They were their usual cheerful selves on the long ride there, which relieved me.

We walked through the large building quickly to get an idea of the sorts of things available then walked back slowly, pulling our carts, taking pictures of the furniture that caught my eye. I got some good ideas for making my own knock off decorations, a lot of which the kids could help with.

I stopped to admire a stall with quilts, holding a deep teal one with gold and silver stitching out to ask Felicity, "Is it elegant or gaudy?"

"It's beautiful."

"The color is perfect, and the price is great. Let's see if we can find at least five in my colors."

"The same colors we always look for?"

"Yeah. I need to be able to layer them and mix and match."

Wolfgang said, "Can I go to the next stall? I promise I won't wander off."

I nodded and watched him cross to the table displaying swords before turning back to the quilts. Felicity and I finally settled on the perfect six, which I bought with the last of the cash I'd brought, and we went to join Wolfgang who was still admiring the old weapons.

"Aren't these beautiful," he said.

"They are. I wish I brought more money."

He crouched, pulling me down with him to point out a large box of old hilts with cracked, pitted, rusted, or just plain gone blades.

I said, "I'm almost tempted to return my blankets. One of those swords would be perfect..."

"Don't you dare," Felicity said angrily.

"I can't because the blankets are perfect and I need them... but these would be so fun to make into a display. They're sort of creepy but in a good way."

Wolfgang nodded agreement. "We should buy one for our house, Fell."

I said, "Mom would never let you put one up."

He sighed wistfully.

"It would look cool," Felicity said thoughtfully. She marched up to the front table and said to the guy, "How much for the whole box?"

Wolfgang gaped at her.

The man laughed.

"More than you have, missy. And those are real knives, not toys."

"They're for my sister, not me. How much?"

"Four hundred."

"Two."

Three fifty.

"Three and I can't go higher. It's all she has."

I gaped at her.

"Three then."

"And it has to include a sword. Is there a sword in there?"

He pursed his lips at her then laughed, reaching under the table to pull out a badly welded set of crossed swords that he dropped into the box. With a little work they'd be perfect for the wall on the landing over the portrait of my grandfather that I planned to hang there.

"Is that a good deal, Kate?"

"It will be a month before I could pay you back unless any of my furniture flips sell."

She nodded.

The man said, "What do you want these old things for?"

"Wall art."

"Some of them have sharp blades. You be careful, missy."

Felicity nudged Wolfgang hard, "Wolf, pay the man for Kate."

He handed over his money.

We loaded the box onto her cart. They'd only bought themselves an old Boy Scout manual, which did my nerves no good at all, but I didn't say anything.

I said, "I'll pull this one. You take the blankets. And thanks, guys."

I took them out for dinner on our father's credit card.

They were sleeping by the time we got home.

I left my stuff in the car to carry their pillows and book bags and was glad I had when our father stepped from his office, saying, "You guys were out late."

I said, "Mom said it was okay. We went to an antique show."

"Antiques, *huh*. Did you buy anything?"

"Just a book," Felicity said. "And Kate got a blanket."

I felt bad that we were lying and was surprised he didn't notice something was afoot because Wolfgang was bright red, looking really nervous. I *knew* I should say something to set a good example, but I didn't want our father to know what we'd bought.

I said, "I took them out to eat on the credit card."

"Don't make a habit of it or I'll deduct it from your allowance."

"How much do you think a real nanny makes?"

I was sorry as soon as I said it, but he didn't respond, except for a slight narrowing of his eyes.

I said, "Come on guys, let's get to bed. We'll get some rope tomorrow and see if we can make the right knots with that book of yours to make a better ladder."

They both hugged our father before running up the stairs.

"Good night, Kate," he called after me, which surprised me.

I turned back to say, "Night, Dad," but he'd already stepped back into his office.

The next morning, I brought the box of knives upstairs and left it under the blankets in my closet because I was picking up Crystal's kids for a play date at the library and needed the back seat for it.

My father came into the kitchen while I was packing the lunches, and the kids were finishing their eggs.

I said, "Want some eggs? The pan's still hot and the coffee is fresh."

I regretted that the minute I said it because it might occur to him that I was drinking more of his coffee than he was.

He just nodded though and poured himself a cup while I started more eggs.

"Fell, want Jell-O or a fruit cup?"

"Can I have both?"

"Sure. Wolf, grab eight juice boxes and four of the small Cheerios and whatever snacks you want times two for you and Evan."

I served my dad his eggs, put their lunches in their bags, then wiped down the kiddos.

"Put your bags in the car and make sure you all have a clean sweatshirt."

They scampered out.

I wiped down the table and finished the dishes while eating my egg sandwich.

I offered my father a coffee refill before filling my thermos.

All four kids returned with sweatshirts.

"Where's your mother?" our father asked.

We all shrugged, which made me laugh.

"We've got to run or we'll be late."

"Where are you off to so early?"

"This isn't early... It's Saturday, Library Day and we're picking up friends."

"Say goodbye," I said to Harley who ran to give our father a hug.

I tried to see it through unbiased eyes because maybe it was my imagination that they all looked bewildered by his presence. Maybe it was just me who found him so disconcerting. I never knew what he wanted from me—what would earn me a smile and what a frown. I had no idea when it had happened, but I realized I liked it better when he wasn't around because when he was I was nervous, afraid I'd say or do something that he'd disprove of—that would make me feel insignificant.

He stood to hug the kids.

They seemed normal, which was disconcerting in its own way because I couldn't decide if they were faking their smiles and affection or if they honestly felt real affection.

I probably need therapy.

That thought made me laugh.

Hannah laughed too, saying, "I love library day! I love books. I love them! Don't you, Fell?"

"Yep."

Hannah gave her a hug, laughing over the joy of books, which was so her that it made my heart hurt.

I kissed her head then Felicity's.

She took my hand.

"Drive safely," he called after us.

"I always do."

TWELVE

Our mother was waiting and fuming mad when we returned that afternoon.

She said to Felicity, "Go outside to play and keep an eye on the kiddos."

Wolfgang gave me an anxious glance, taking Harley's hand and tugging him to the door.

When it was just us, she said, "What the hell are you playing at telling your father I don't make them breakfast!"

"I didn't."

You don't.

I knew better than to say it though.

She talked over me, "Telling him you should be paid what a nanny makes!"

Uh oh.

"Keep it up, missy, and you'll be out on your ear, cut off. No school, no allowance, no nothing!"

I gaped at her in astonishment. She said that before like a million times but usually after Everly had driven her nearly insane with a tantrum. I'd always thought she'd said it to pacify Everly, because it always *did* pacify her, but maybe I'd been wrong. The pain of that took my breath for a moment but then I was furious.

"Okay."

"Okay! Okay! What's that supposed to mean!"

"Toss me out. Oh wait, you can't, can you? At most you could ground me, if I bothered to listen, which, let's face it, I probably wouldn't do."

She gaped at me.

"Are you—defying me?"

"I think I am, yes. I didn't tell Dad you don't make them breakfast, but so what if I had? You *don't* make them breakfast! What's the big deal? No one cares. That nanny thing was true, but I was mad 'cause he was mad that I bought the kids dinner on the credit card. But how is it fair if I have to buy them dinner? It wasn't practical to pack dinner and I bought them lunch and it's not like a fifty-dollar meal is going to break us so, yeah, I was a little snarky. If you're going to kick me out over something so lame, then whatever."

"You're getting entirely too big for your britches."

"Did you buy a book of bad cliches?"

She turned red then white.

"Get out!"

"What's all the hullabaloo?" Everly asked cheerfully.

"I was just telling Kate to get out and check on the kids," My mother said calmly as if she hadn't nearly stroked herself out a second ago.

"Whatever."

I stomped out.

We made rope ladders for the rest of the afternoon.

The tension was thick enough to choke on.

It ratcheted up about a hundred degrees when both our parents joined us, but maybe that was just me. No one else seemed to notice that the twins kept their heads down, fussing unnecessarily with each knot, that they watched the book like it was the Holy Grail or a treasure map, which I thought it was to them. Every time I glimpsed the cover a cold chill crawled down my spine.

'How to Survive in the Wilderness'

Both of my parents saw it, but neither gave it more than a disinterested glance.

The kiddos relaxed and laughed like normal, flitting around, hugging us all with a sort of Christmas Day amazement that pissed me off all over again. They shouldn't be so amazed that their parents spent a few hours with them.

My parents smiled and laughed as if they were happy, which I couldn't imagine was the case if he was having an affair and she was doing god knew what. She was never around and brought home takeout for dinner more often than not now.

For something to do besides glare and make the kids nervous, I took out my sketch book and began drawing. I'd done about four decent ones and three crappy ones before my mother said, "Put that silly book down and come join us for once. We could use some help getting the rope rail nice and tight."

Fuming but not wanting to ruin their fun, I forced a smile and helped.

I was glad when it was finally late enough to take the kids in for dinner.

I gathered their sweatshirts and followed the laughing group slowly.

Everly was leaning on the rail of the back deck, watching with a sardonic smile and it occurred to me to wonder if she ever felt left out—except the distance was all her own doing. They'd love her too if she let them.

My thoughts had distracted me. I hurried to catch up, pausing again by the French doors to watch the kids happily setting the table.

"Sickening isn't it," Everly said.

She ran down the backsteps, disappearing into the dark before I could answer, not that I *had* an answer. Because I too found the hypocrisy of our parents sickening.

THIRTEEN

My phone vibrated notifying me of a text from Jace.

I hoped he wasn't about to cancel our date—not that it was a real date.

I climbed down from the treehouse before taking my phone out because I didn't want to wake the kids.

We still on?

I texted back, *the usual spot?*

I'm there now.

I climbed back into the treehouse to write, *I went out,* on the chalkboard and then climbed down again.

So far, the twins hadn't seemed to have noticed me leaving or coming back. I hadn't asked them to lie. I hadn't had to lie either. I wasn't sure if I would or not. It didn't seem worth lying about meeting Jace when I planned to tell my parents the truth anyway in just a few more days.

I jogged to the end of the road where Jace was waiting.

He leaned over to kiss me quickly before pulling away.

"I just saw Everly get into some guy's car. I thought she was grounded for lying about hitting that car?"

"She is but no one checks on us. My mom and grandmother just had one of their yearly rows and Everly is taking full advantage of it."

"Yearly rows?"

"My grandmother doesn't really like my mother and vice versa. They're coldly civil most of the time, then grandma loses it, and my mom will cry for a week or two until my father smooths it all over again by getting my grandmother to apologize."

"Your parents are nuts..."

"Are you complaining?"

"Hell no!"

I leaned closer to take his hand.

"We could catch a movie," he said.

I gaped at him then forced a smile.

"Sure. If you want."

"Kate..."

"A movie sounds great."

"No it doesn't!"

"Then why'd you say it!"

"Because we should go to a damned movie!"

I snorted with laughter.

He sighed hard, grinning and shaking his head at me.

"I love us, don't get me wrong, I just want more than this, Kate. We need more time together, which I know is unfair of me to say when it's me keeping us sneaking around like this..."

That was sort of true but only because I was always so busy with the kids.

I said, "They're getting better. School starts for the kids in just four more weeks, and I can officially move out in two."

"Is that still the plan?"

"God yes!"

We drove in silence until we reached my house. For the first time we didn't reach eagerly for each other.

It made my heart hurt.

I said, "Have you changed your mind about moving in? It's okay if you have..."

"I love you so damned much. I feel like I'm ruining us though with all this sneaking around."

He leaned over to embrace me. We hugged for a long time without speaking. I think we were both afraid to say or do anything that would tip us off the narrow path we were on.

I said, "We can tell my parents whenever you want. Mom has the kids Monday and Tuesday if you want to take a half day at work to go fishing or catch a movie. I don't care what we do, Jace. I just don't want you to get tired of me..."

"That could never ever happen. I worry you'll get tired of me... you should be pissed that I'm putting my job first... maybe I need to look for a new one..."

"Honestly, I don't think my dad would fire you over me. He's going to be pissed at me when I tell him that I'm not only not going to college but

I'm moving out to be an artist, so it'd be smart not to break it to him the day I leave or anything, but if we wait a week or so, he'll get over it and then he won't care."

He sat back to trace my lips with his thumb.

It sent a bolt of heat directly to my groin.

I jumped from his truck to run and unlock the door.

Laughing he followed me.

Thank God, I thought with heartfelt relief as he yanked his shirt off and dropped it on the porch.

It was going to kill me if he ever lost this passion.

Two hours later, he dropped me back off at home.

I said, "Drive home safely. Don't fall asleep or anything."

"We could both use some sleep. I should say let's skip tomorrow night but... maybe you could leave earlier? They'd be okay for a few hours out there on their own, wouldn't they? Maybe you could just say you're going out to buy paint or something?"

"Yeah. If I do it right, Everly wouldn't even know I'd done it. They're smart enough not show themselves to her if I'm not there."

"That pisses me off so damned much!"

"Me too."

"I seriously want to smack your stupid parents! I barely know the kids and I can see they're afraid of her. What the hell is wrong with them?"

"I guess they just don't want to see it or maybe they don't know what to do either and are hoping it'll just sort itself out."

"Which it's not going to do if they ground her then let her sneak out."

I shrugged.

He huffed in annoyance.

I said, "I'll text you when I can get away. What time will you be done at the shop?"

"I can leave any time after four. Don't forget to send me the link for your show. I can't wait to see it."

I said, "Only if you promise to give me honest feedback. I've got the knack of animating my cartoon drawings now so I can change that intro if you think it's too corny. I really hope you don't though because I just paid the sound guy a thousand bucks for that theme music but still tell me because I can rework the art to fit the music."

"I loved what I saw of it so far. Did you add the burglar sneaking in through a trap door on the porch?"

"Yeah, he reappears tip toeing across the roof with the green jeweled necklace a second later. Then he drops it and the camera pans on it as it unfurls into the drawing of the future back garden where my cartoon characters are having a fancy party. I just put in some quick teaser shots of the finished room in the first show. It mostly focuses on building the hearth stairs because I thought that was my strongest hook."

"I'm sure it will be great. I think you should put in an entire episode on painting those stairs though."

"Maybe I'll add it if I get enough requests. The stairs were a complicated project. I didn't want to cut any of the important safety parts out."

He snickered as he said, "Some dummy is sure to skip adding the joist supports but that won't be your fault."

"I'm going to add in a warning banner along the bottom reminding the viewer to follow all local building codes and not to skip any of the sensors that make sure it won't close on anyone, but it will be done and posted for a scheduled release tomorrow."

"Send me a copy," he repeated.

We kissed and I ran back to the treehouse.

Felicity was sitting up when I entered but she lay back down, turning away from me.

I whispered, "Do you need the bathroom?"

"No. We're good. Night, Kate."

FOURTEEN

The kids were quiet, exchanging worried glances over breakfast.

Felicity must've realized I'd snuck out. I should say something but didn't now what to say.

I sent Jace the intro and he sent me back an enthusiastic text a few minutes later saying he loved it.

Everly left as soon as my parents did. I had no idea where any of them had gone or when they'd be back, but it was a relief to not have her sulking about.

The kiddos seemed to feel it to because they were loud and running all over.

I worried about leaving the kids out there alone. I worried over what to say about sneaking away when I didn't want them to do it. I hoped they didn't think I'd abandoned them.

I spent the morning worrying over how to reassure them if I moved out in between running after the kiddos who were bundles of energy and uploading my first fifteen shows.

It felt as if I'd really accomplished something when I saw them all listed ready to air. I really hoped I could make this channel a success.

Before I could worry about it too long, the kiddos distracted me again by loudly proclaiming how boring it was to read books outside.

"How about we paint for a while on real canvases?"

They ran off eagerly to drag the easels and paint supplies outside.

I went to get a few of the hilts and some cleaning supplies.

I'd maybe paint some to make the edge glitter, I decided as I set them aside to take Harley's easel from him to set it up.

I said to him, "Fetch your painting smocks and you can use the oil paints."

Laughing in excitement he and Hannah ran back inside.

A few minutes later Hannah shrieked.

My heart immediately started pounding.

I'd never heard her scream like that before.

I knocked over the easels I'd just set out in my panic and ran through the back door into the front hall. My heart was already thudding, but when I saw Everly dangling my little sister over the railing sweat immediately coated me. Our ceilings were much too high for her to fall without a serious injury. Landing on the hard tile could kill her.

Everly looked wild with her eyes too wide, too dilated. She was pale and blotchy, glowering at Hannah then grinning when she saw me.

I yelled, "Don't you fucking dare drop her! She could die!"

Hannah shrieked again.

"Do it again and I *will* drop you," Everly said in a calm tone like she was offering her a cookie.

"Please put her down—on the floor."

"What are you going to say?" she asked Hannah sweetly.

"Kate did it."

I could barely make out her words she was crying so hard.

I said, "I'll call Mom right now and tell her I did whatever you want me to tell her. Or I can text her. "Please! Please, just don't hurt her."

"Help me, Kate!"

"I will sweetie. Please, Everly! She's your sister. Your little sister!"

Hannah shrieked again and kept screaming.

"You're hurting her!"

Everly laughed, shaking Hannah hard then flinging her away.

"Die bitch."

I screamed, running to catch her, hyperventilating, the air burning my throat but not reaching my lungs.

I tripped over a toy car, lunging forward awkwardly.

The weight of her pushed me back. I fell, cracking my head against the table in the center of the foyer hard enough to see stars, falling back, trying to cushion Hannah who was still screaming, which relieved me that she was at least alive. We hit the floor hard enough to make my ears ring and force the air from my lungs. I was terrified that she was stabbed or something, but I couldn't draw air in to ask.

My father bellowed, "Everly Avery!"

Everly laughed a high-pitched giggle.

He crouched beside me to take Hannah.

"Where's Harley? Kate! Where's Harley?"

"Don't know," I managed to gasp out.

"Don't move. Hannah, stay with Kate."

My breath again left me from Hannah clutching me.

I clutched her back.

"Kate. Kate."

She was sobbing too hard to say anything else.

The room swam but I lacked the strength to pry her arm off my neck.

"So kay," I mumbled.

She released me and I gulped in air for a moment until her piercing scream jerked my eyes open.

Her hands and face were covered with blood.

I fumbled for my phone, cursing internally over my clumsy fingers.

Our mother said, "What the hell is going on... Kate! Dear Lord! What happened?" She sounded bewildered.

Hannah's weight lifted from my chest, and I let the darkness take me.

When I opened my eyes, my mother was leaning over me, patting at my cheek while a stranger said, "Step away, ma'am."

"Where's Harley?" I asked.

"Dad has the kids."

"Hannah?"

"She's fine."

The man said again, "Ma'am, we really need you to move."

My mother moved away.

Two paramedics leaned over me.

The man said, "Can you see my finger?"

"I'm okay. I just fainted for a second. I've never been so scared..."

"How many fingers?"

"Three."

"I'm going to shine a light in your eyes for second." He shone his light in my face as he said, "Barb, get that neck brace on. My partner Barbara is going to tilt your head just a bit. If it hurts anywhere, holler out. Wiggle your toes for me. And your fingers. No, don't try to lift your arms."

"I'm okay," I said again although my head pounded in time with my heart. Adrenaline had left me feeling weak and shaky. The entire thing felt dreamlike.

"She was going to kill her," I said.

"Who was?"

"She doesn't know what she's saying," my mother said.

"Are you fucking kidding me? Everly almost fucking killed Hannah. Who's checking Hannah?"

"Hannah? There's another... patient?" he asked my mother.

"No. She's confused. Hannah is fine."

"Like hell she is!" I yelled.

"Hey, Ralph, we have a situation here!" Barbara yelled. She leaned over me to say, "What happened?"

"My sister Everly threw my little sister over the balcony."

"That isn't what happened," my mother said, sounding shocked I'd say something like that.

"How would you know? You weren't here. I was. I saw her do it! She dangled her over the side taunting me, said die bitch, and threw her! If I hadn't caught her..."

I closed my eyes because my head was hurting too much, and I was going to have to get up to punch my mother in the face if she didn't stop glaring at me.

I said, "Go check on Hannah please. I know she was hurt because she was all bloody. She's only four! Why the hell would Everly want to kill her?"

Imagining what might have had happened if I'd been slower scared me enough to make me hyperventilate again, which made the room blurry, and the sound all mumbled. It took me a few minutes to get myself under control enough to make out voices. My mother was arguing with someone, telling them to leave.

A few minutes later a different man said, "I want to see Hannah right now and no more bullshit! Produce her or I'm charging you with child endangerment!"

"And Harley," I said. "Check him too."

Barbara said, "How many kids and what ages are in the house?"

I said, "Hannah is four and Harley five. Felicity and Wolfgang are ten. They were out in their treehouse...oh my god. Oh my god, what if she murdered them... I told you they were terrified of her! I told you!" I tried to sit, got to my elbows, and vomited all over myself.

Stars bloomed in my vision, and I fell back again, caught by Barbara.

"Don't try to talk just breath. It'll pass in a second. The police went outside to check."

My father said, "Good lord, Kate!"

Barbara said, "Are you Harley, sweetie," and I began crying.

105

"Kate!" Harley yelled.

This proof that he was at least well enough to talk made my tears come harder.

I vomited again, choking on it.

The next thing I knew, I was in the back of an ambulance. Hannah was crying.

I held out my arm, which took Herculean effort.

Barbara tucked her close to me, wrapping my arm around her.

My father said, "Will she be okay?"

"She's concussed but the prognosis is good. Just try not to move around too much, Kate. Hannah has a broken arm, but we'll fix her right up good as new. Harley is fine just a bit scared. The twins are fine. They called for help.

I snorted.

"She's been terrorizing them for weeks now! They aren't fine! I told you she was!"

My father said, "You can yell at us later. Save your strength."

"Where is Everly?"

Barbara said, "In another ambulance. She's having a serious manic episode. Does she take medication?"

"She should..."

My father said, "We didn't realize she was sick."

"I'm so done with this bullshit."

Hannah whimpered.

I clamped my lips. Pissing him off would gain me nothing. I needed to be smart. *I needed Grayson.*

I waited until my father exited the ambulance to whisper to Barbara, "Please call my brother Grayson, but don't tell him I asked."

"You're father?"

"Don't tell him, please."

"Did he do this?"

"No."

Hannah started crying when Barbara tried to take her from me.

"Let me stay with her."

"You need a CT scan. Your injury is serious, Kate. You might need serious treatment for it. She's upset, but it isn't life threatening, I promise you."

"Don't let them leave with her."

"What the hell is going on there?"

I said to Hannah, "Banana, I'll be back as soon as I get my boo boo checked. Barbara will take good care of you. Please stop crying or I'll start too."

"Kate!" she shrieked.

I forced my eyes open to see my father had picked her up.

"Kate!"

I'm sorry, Hannah."

Her shrieks faded into the distance as he carried her away.

"Is my phone in my pocket?"

"No. The police took it."

"Grayson will take care of her. He'll know what to do. He's a lawyer."

"Your father..."

"Will take care of himself."

"Did he hurt them or you?"

"No. Except that I told him Everly was, and he ignored me. I'd never have left her with them, but I didn't know she was home! Are you sure Felicity and Wolfgang are okay?"

"Yes. They're with your mom."

"Jesus..."

"We're bringing you in now. Take nice slow breaths."

I tried to tell myself that the kids were fine, but I didn't trust my mother a whit. She'd been trying to cover it all up. I suddenly wondered what Everly had on her and how far my mother would go to keep whatever it was secret.

"I have no idea what to do."

"About what?"

I pretended I hadn't heard because I hadn't meant to say it aloud.

Exhaustion fell on me like a weighted blanket. The sounds of the nurses and people bustling about faded.

I'd worry about them when I woke, I decided. I couldn't do anything anyway and she wasn't going to hurt them physically. I could live with whatever lies she told as long as the kids were okay.

"Wake up!" Kenya yelled urgently right in my ear.

For a moment I'd thought I'd overslept and missed the bus but then I remembered.

"Ken?"

"You're scaring the wits from me," Jace said.

"Is that my superpower?"

I thought that was hysterical for some reason and laughed for a good minute,

His lips on neck made my breath catch.

"I love you," I said.

"Prove it by staying awake. Tell me what happened."

"Everly tried to kill Hannah."

"She wouldn't," Kenya said breathlessly.

"But she did. She dangled her by her arm over the fucking balcony and said die bitch when she let her go."

"Maybe she meant you."

"Jesus!" Jace yelled. "What is wrong with you people!"

"I didn't mean it like that. I just meant why would anyone want to hurt a little girl?"

"Why would anyone want to hurt Kate? You people are crazy!"

"I said I didn't mean it like that! I just meant we all know she hated Kate."

"You all knew and none of you did a thing about it!"

I said, "Stop yelling. My head hurts."

"I'm sorry but they piss me off so fucking much!"

Kenya said, "The police want a statement."

"Don't even bother asking me to lie to them. I'm not covering for her psycho ass. I don't care if she's sick and needs meds. She should've been helped a long time ago. Whatever shady shit she has on you all is your problem!"

"I wasn't going to ask you to lie and what do you mean?"

"I mean Mom's been covering for her, letting her get away with everything, go anywhere, do anything. It finally occurred to me to ask myself why. I don't think Everly was just terrorizing the kids. I think she had something on Mom too and probably Dad!"

My mother said, "That's true."

Kenya turned to glare at the door our mother had just entered, saying, "What is going on!"

"Let me speak to Kate privately, please.

"No fucking way!" Jace said. "You aren't threatening her or any bullshit."

"Who are you... you're the car guy."

Jace said angrily, "I'm her boyfriend and I have a name and it isn't car guy."

"This is family business."

I said tiredly, "Just say whatever you need to say."

"I wasn't going to threaten you," she said tightly.

I said, "Let me take the kids. Grayson said we can stay at his house."

"It isn't like that, Kate, although I can see why you think it is. I love the kids—all of you. Which is why when Everly found out I'd had an affair, I caved. I was afraid I'd lose all of you in a divorce."

"That's tragic and all, but I'm still not lying to placate that psycho."

"I honestly didn't realize she'd gotten so... out of control. I didn't realize she was in such a bad crowd or was having mental issues."

"Bullshit. But whatever. I just want the kids safe. Since I'm with them most of the time anyway, what difference does it make where they sleep? You could see them whenever you wanted just like you do now."

Which was never. She spoke to us for minutes—seconds—as she was heading out and maybe for thirty minutes or so for dinner—when it suited her. I'd no idea if I was making her angry or if she was grateful that I'd offered. Well, not grateful. She'd *never* be grateful. Maybe relieved. Or smug. Maybe this entire thing was just to get me to take the damned kids!

I tried to force my weighted eyelids open, but it was too much.

"Don't be ridiculous. I can take care of *my* children!"

I said, "If I hadn't caught her, her little head would've cracked like an egg! She was all bloody!" The images in my head made me vomit again.

"Nurse! Doctor!" Jace yelled.

Kenya said, "Now isn't a good time, Mom."

Our mother said, "She should've told me that Everly was doing drugs!"

Jace said angrily, "Seriously, you're going to blame Kate for that! If you can take care of the damned kids, then why does *she* need to tell you! And she did tell you! She told you there was a serious problem with Everly! She told all of you! And you let Everly almost fucking kill her!"

His voice had faded from the strength of the pain in my head but then I realized it was because they'd moved into the hall.

The vomiting had left me shaking and dizzy. I was confused over what the strangers around me were saying. Two seemed to be arguing on what I was doing there while two were throwing medical terms around and agreeing with each other, saying yes doctor, and talking numbers and medical terms that I couldn't make sense of, so I stopped trying and instead tried to hear Jace, but his voice was an indistinct angry murmur of sound now.

Someone took my hand and Kenya said, "They're taking you to surgery, Kate. I'll keep the kids with me. Just relax and feel better."

I was feeling much too shivery and weak to speak, which was terrifying if I thought about it, so I didn't think about that or surgery because that was ridiculous. No one got surgery for hitting their head. I'd be fine if they'd all just stop yelling. I strained to hear Jace, which worked like magic because he was suddenly whispering right in my ear, "I love you, Kate."

"Your superpower," I managed to whisper.

The pain and love in his laugh were a warm blanket that took me into the dark.

FIFTEEN

When I woke, I felt much better and only then realized how awful I had been feeling.

Jace was holding my hand.

Grayson said urgently, "Wake up, Kate."

"I'm awake."

"Can you open your eyes?" a stranger asked.

He'd said it like he wondered if I had the ability to, not like a request.

"I'm really tired," I said as I forced them open. "Who are you?"

The room was dark with just small pockets of light.

An older man with graying hair was leaning over me blocking the view of everyone else.

He examined my eyes as he said, "I'm Dr. Kennedy. You suffered a pretty serious head injury. You'll be fine if you follow my advice though. I want you to keep as still as you can. No trying to sit or turn your head or nodding. Am I making sense to you?"

"Yes."

He straightened and I could see Jace, who looked terrible. I realized I must be hurt way more than I'd thought for him to look so strained.

A monitor began to beep.

Kennedy said, "On a scale of one to ten, how bad does your head hurt?"

"Five, maybe six. I feel better. It was a ten before."

"I bet. If it starts to creep up to seven, you're going to press the button by your right hand."

While he was speaking the beeping slowed then stopped.

Grayson leaned over me to kiss my brow.

111

Kennedy said, "If everyone could step away from the bed a moment, I'm going to perform a simple exam to test your response. I just want you to say yes when you can feel me touching you. Can you do that?"

"Yes."

Jace released my hand.

The monitor beeped again.

Kennedy said, "Okay. I'm starting now. Can you feel this?"

"Yes."

It felt like he'd grabbed my big toe.

Jace inhaled sharply and I said, "Sorry, I was expecting the other toe. I felt you touch my ankle."

Kennedy said, "It's okay, just say yes and don't try to guess."

I said yes what felt like a hundred times then he had me wiggle my fingers and toes then move my arms and legs. I could do it, but it was exhausting.

Jace finally took my hand again.

The machine beeps slowed to a steady beep every few seconds.

Kennedy said, "It's all looking very good."

"Jesus, Kate..." Jace mumbled as he pressed my hands to his lips.

"Don't jostle her," Kennedy said warningly. "No food or drink for a few hours, Kate. If you feel thirsty, press the button by your right hand and the nurse can give you an ice chip. The nurse," he said again, I thought for Jace's benefit because he was looking at him.

"Don't cry. I'm fine," I said, which made his tears fall faster.

"You better be!"

Grayson said gruffly, "You scared us to death!"

Kennedy said, "Rest and try not to worry about anything. Don't get her upset. I'll be back in a bit to check on you."

"What happened?" I asked when he'd left the room.

Grayson said, "You don't remember?"

"I meant to my head. I know I hit it but..."

"You cracked your skull. It's just a tiny fracture and the doctor says you'll be fine, so don't even worry about it."

"Hannah?"

"Will be fine," Jace said angrily. "Her arm has been set and Kenya has her. She has all the kids."

Grayson said, "Family services is investigating. Mom and Dad agreed to let Ken and I watch them so they didn't need to go into care."

"Hannah... you're sure she's fine?"

Grayson said, "She's very upset and confused. But physically she's fine."

"Everly told her to say I'd done something. I told her to agree, to say whatever she wanted. If you're lying to me about the twins..."

Jace said, "I swear, they're all okay. I saw them all myself. You can see them, but they're really freaked out and we thought they'd try to hug you and we didn't want to scare them more by not letting them."

From the doorway, a man said, "Can we come in a minute, Miss Avery? I'm detective Reynolds and this is my partner, Detective Sandy."

A woman said, "Sandy Sandy. My parents have a lot to answer for too."

It made me laugh, which sent a bolt of pain through my head and made the beeps rise to fever pitch for a moment.

"I wish that thing would shut up," I muttered.

"Sorry," she said. "That was my bad. My friends call me Dee."

Another woman said, "Is everything okay in here? The doctor said you could speak with her if she's up to it, but I don't want you upsetting my patient!"

"I'm okay," I said.

Dee said, "We can leave anytime if this is too much. We'd very much appreciate you telling us what happened though."

She walked me through it slowly, asking questions like if I'd heard Harley yelling or had Hannah called out for him.

"But she never said what you were supposed to have done?"

"No. I told Everly I'd agree that I had done whatever it was. That I'd call Mom right then and admit I'd done it or text her. I was afraid to reach for my phone and call for help and make her drop her or worse. Hannah was screaming. Not in terror but in pain. I was terrified she'd stabbed her or something and then when I saw all the blood... and no one will tell me what she did to her, but I know it was more than her arm!"

The beeping was joined by buzzing.

Grayson said, "That was your blood, Kate."

"Mine?"

"You'd cut your head when you fell, and head wounds bleed a lot. There was blood everywhere."

"You're sure?"

"Yes," he said dryly.

"And he left me there bleeding?" I whispered.

I closed my eyes against the tears that threatened.

"I'm so sorry, Kate," Jace said.

"He left you?" Dee asked.

Jace said bitterly, "Her father took Hannah and left her."

I said, "I told him I was okay. He probably didn't realize I was bleeding either. I bet he thought it was Hannah's blood too."

Jace snorted.

"Not now," Grayson muttered.

I said, "He told me not to move and asked where Harley was."

"Did you know where he was?" Dee asked.

"I knew both kiddos had gone up to their rooms to get their painting smocks while I set up the easels and paints in the grass. They'd only been gone a few minutes when Hannah screamed."

"How many minutes?"

"Five or six. Not long. I wasn't worried about them because I knew it would take them a few minutes to find the smocks. I thought they'd need my help to do it because I couldn't recall putting them away, which meant Mom had and she could've put them anywhere or even tossed them. So they went to look."

Reynolds said, "How often do you paint with them?"

"All the time. Not every day, but it's our normal thing."

"And you always make them wear these smocks?"

"Yes. Or sometimes I'll take a garbage bag and cut a hole in it to wear like a poncho if their smocks are still damp or dirty or the project will be especially messy. I wish I had..."

The detectives exchanged glances.

Jace squeezed my hand.

Grayson said, "You couldn't know she'd do that."

"I didn't know she was home, or I wouldn't have left them."

Dee said, "You had reason to think she'd hurt them?"

"Not the kiddos, the twins, although it was stupid of me to think she wouldn't hurt the kiddos too."

"She'd hurt the twins in the past?"

"I have no idea. They wouldn't tell me, but I could see they were scared of her. It's why we were painting there. I could hear the twins working on the treehouse from there. I'd have been able to keep an eye on all of them."

Jace said, "She was afraid the kids were planning to run away."

Reynolds said, "Please let Kate tell this her own way."

Jace made a zipping motion over his mouth.

Reynolds said, "Where do you get the garbage bags?"

"The kitchen. I keep a box of really big ones in the paint supplies too that I cut open and use as drop clothes. Can I get some water, please."

Jace said, "I'll get the nurse."

He hurried out.

Dee said, "We found a few old knives out by the paint stuff."

"I was planning to clean them."

"They're yours?"

"Yes. I'd just bought an entire box."

"To do what?"

"Decorate with."

"Decorate?"

"A wall display and maybe lamps or my special effects."

"You weren't worried the kids would get into that in your room?"

"I'd only gotten them the day before. I'd have put them on the wall or moved them soon."

Jace returned with the nurse who offered me a spoonful of ice chips, saying, "Suck them slowly. Don't chew. Just let it dissolve."

She handed a small cup to Grayson. "One spoonful every minute or so. Pace it out."

She felt for my pulse, read the machines, pursed her lips at all of us then left.

Dee said, "If you don't mind my saying so, it doesn't seem to be the sort of thing to match the decor anywhere in your house—including your room."

"No, *my* house."

Grayson said, "She means her own house, not our parents' house."

"Oh. I thought she lived there with them?"

"I do."

"I'm confused."

"Me too."

Dee snorted with laughter.

Grayson said, "She plans to move out when she turns eighteen in a few weeks."

"I see."

Reynolds said, "And what about the kids?"

Guilt squeezed the air from my lungs. I began to cry.

"I don't know! I didn't know what to do. I hoped she'd chill when school started and maybe forget about them when I wasn't there to get a rise out of. They'd be in school, and I could take them on weekends, but

I was worried. Gray told me Mom would let them come over after school, but she might have been pissed when I left. Or not her but him."

"Him? Your father."

"Yeah. He was going to be angry when he realized I had no intention of going to college. I knew he'd cut me off. I thought it was a fifty-fifty chance, maybe seventy-thirty that he'd forbid me to see them. But I hoped that would be just temporary while he got over being mad, and if I wasn't watching them, *someone* would have to, so they'd have hired someone—I hoped. But it was a risk because they might've made Everly watch them and then what? But what was I supposed to do!"

Grayson said, "Kate had told us there was an issue. I'd spoken to the kids and saw there was something, but I never suspected... but I would've insisted that the kids be left with anyone else except Everly. I was certain Mom would let them go with Kate. I hadn't been worried about the kiddos either, except I didn't want them at Kate's house."

"Because?"

I said, "I didn't want them there either because it's a mess. They're too little and could get hurt if I wasn't watching them every second, and I have too much to do to watch them every second."

Grayson gave me another spoonful of ice.

I closed my eyes to savor it.

"She could really use some rest," Jace said.

Dee said, "So the knives and all the cleaners and things were to clean those knives?"

"Yes."

"Where did you get them from?"

"The flea market. I borrowed money from the kids to buy them."

I opened my eyes to see her nodding at Reynolds.

He said, "So Wolfgang wouldn't be wrong in saying he'd bought them?"

"He paid the guy, but I was going to pay Wolf back. I normally stick to my budget, but it was an unexpected opportunity. I'd already bought some great old blankets with my own money and then we saw the knife guy. He had some old swords that would've been perfect for the upstairs hall and a box of random hilts and broken blades that he gave me for a steal."

"Three hundred dollars isn't exactly a steal."

"It is if your boyfriend can work metal and maybe fix them up. But even broken, I could use them in art pieces."

Jace kissed my hand again then pressed it to his cheek.

Dee said, "Where did you keep the box when you brought it home?"

"The closet of my room covered by the blankets I'd bought. But the kiddos never go into my room, except at night if they have a nightmare or something. I'd never leave something like that laying around where they could get into it. Which is why I didn't want them at my house. I'd only brought a few of them outside to try some of the solvents on to see what it did to the metal because I'd read online that the cheap metals would discolor but the real stuff brightens."

Reynolds said, "We'd like permission to... see your home."

Grayson said, "I can show you around, but I don't see how it pertains."

"We're just following up on Everly's claims."

I snorted.

Jace said, "Everly lies more than she breathes."

Grayson said, "Kate has nothing to hide, but if this is going to be a search, then I want a list of what you're looking for."

Dee said, "Let's get back to the twins a moment. Had they ever given you a concrete reason, not a feeling or a hunch but an actual reason why they'd be afraid of Everly or anyone else?"

"My house had me all distracted. I hadn't realized they had any problems at all because I hadn't been spending much time with them."

Jace said, "That isn't exactly true. She spends a lot of time with them."

"Not like I used to. Normally I'd see them every day during the summer. This summer I saw them only on weekends and just once in a while for breakfast or bedtime."

Dee said, "So before today, when was the last time you spoke with them?"

"Every day for the last few weeks. I didn't let them out of my sight. I meant I hadn't seen them much before I realized they were scared of Everly."

"So what happened a few weeks ago?"

"I was making them breakfast when Everly came in. She slapped Wolfgang, not a hard hit. From someone else I'd have said it was a teasing sort of thing, but I could see it had upset him. She was supposed to be watching them that day. She'd told them they were going to stay inside and be quiet. Neither of them even looked at her. I could see it had scared them, but I might have just thought it was normal sort of Everly crap. I told them they could come to the flea market with me, and we all left.

The car had a flat and no spare, so I called for one. The kids went to get their money, which made me realize they'd been afraid I'd leave without them if they'd gone to get it, and when they returned, they had their book bags, which were packed with clothes. They'd only been gone for a few minutes. Later I realized they'd had the bags ready to go. At that moment I thought they really didn't want to have come back to the house because it rained or something and they needed their coats—they didn't want to be left with her. So, I decided to keep them until bedtime, and I sent Wolfgang for the bug spray.

Everly showed up and Wolf ran around the house to get back to the garage instead of walking past her. Then in the car he said something about buying a tent and Felicity shushed him, which was when I realized those bags were their go bags. I could see they were thinking of running away. Their little faces were just terrified when they looked at her!

"That night they hid in with the kiddos. So I called to tell my parents that they were frightened. I'd asked the kids about it, but neither would tell me anything, which hadn't surprised me because I know from personal experience Everly is a master at striking terror. So I had nothing much to say to my parents except the kids were afraid."

"She called me too," Grayson said.

"And me," Jace said. "I saw the kids that day and agree they were scared of her."

Grayson said, "I talked to them the next day and it was clear there was something going on. I thought they'd open up to Kate in time. I spoke to our mother about it because I thought they were maybe thinking of running away too."

"Did she do anything?" Reynolds asked.

"No," Grayson and I said at the same time.

He grimaced at me. "She told me she'd keep an eye on them and speak to Everly."

"She yelled at me for working everyone up."

Jace said, "So Kate began working from home or bringing them to the shop."

"What shop?"

"In the garage there," I said. "Dad has all sorts of tools and machines. We were building their treehouse. I hoped that getting out of babysitting had been Everly's plan all along because she left us all alone, except to smirk at us. She only came to the treehouse twice to make fun of it. The kids seemed happier. They spend all their time there when we're home. Mom let's them sleep out there."

Grayson said, "It's perfectly safe. They can pull the ladder up at night and I put an alarm out there they could press if they needed help or just got scared."

I said, "I sleep out there most nights with them."

Grayson shook his head at me. "You should've told me."

Jace said, "Told you what? There was nothing to say. Besides, your parents knew they were all out there. And the kids *did* seem happier. I think they were hoping Everly would forget about them too when school started again."

Grayson said, "Wolfgang asked me about boarding schools. He wanted to know how much they cost and how you got into one and if there were ones that take boys and girls. I began looking into it and spoke to Dad about it."

"What'd he say?" I asked. "And why didn't you tell me?"

"He said it was silly. I told him that the kids were obviously unhappy and that something needed to be done. That if they continued in this downward spiral, I'd have to take steps. He was pissed and said he was on top of things, and I wasn't to work everyone up with my idiotic notions. So I didn't mention it to you. But I did plan on keeping an eye on them and if their grades suffered or they still wouldn't return to the house as it got colder, I was going to insist he consider that school again."

Dee said, "And if he hadn't?"

"I have no idea because there wasn't anything illegal going on. There hadn't been reported incidents or injuries or anything at all. Insisting was about all I could do," he finished miserably.

I realized Grayson felt as bad as I did.

I said, "What's going to happen now?"

Dee said, "Child services will investigate and submit their recommendations to the court."

Grayson snorted.

He said, "They'll be returned to the care of our parents."

"Even Everly?"

"No. Or at least not for a while. She'll be in treatment and then maybe jail."

"Good."

"*Maybe* jail?" Jace asked angrily.

Grayson said, "She's sick, Jace. And while I'm horrified over what she did, maybe jail isn't the best option. Maybe treatment can help?"

"As long as she isn't allowed near them," I said.

Dee said, "As soon as possible, we'd like you to write out a statement. Meanwhile, do we have permission to search your house?"

Grayson said, "You never said what it is you're looking for."

"Everly claims that it was Kate who broke Hannah's arm and tied Harley up. That Kate was hurt while she was fighting with her over a knife. Your father's version of events matches yours. Hannah's version is...confused. She says Kate did it *and* that Everly said to say Kate did it."

"What did I supposedly do? Tie Harley?"

"Harley was found tied and gagged in your room, wrapped in an old blanket on trash bags that had been cut open and laid out with a few of your knives laid ready."

The room swam.

All kinds of buzzers and beeps sounded.

"She was going to murder him?"

Jace said, "Oh my God..."

"Did Hannah say what Everly intended?" Grayson asked as I said breathlessly, "She'd only had minutes! How could she have done all of that?"

Dee said, "Hannah says she went to the laundry room, and Harley went upstairs to look for their paint jackets. When she didn't find them, she went up. Everly was there waiting, and she had a knife. She grabbed Hannah by the hair, dragged her into the bedroom where Harley was tied, held the knife to his throat and said you'd done it."

A nurse came in followed by Doctor Kennedy while Dee was speaking. They began reading the machines and talking in low voices while Dee continued, "Hannah said you were outside and would call daddy. She was confused about the next sequence of events saying Everly had hit them both. She'd thought Everly had meant for her to get you when she was yelling it's Kate, I'm Kate and didn't understand why Everly was hitting her. Then she dragged her out of the room and held her over the rail and told her if she didn't say that you'd killed Harley and hurt her, she'd drop her over the side and stick her with every knife in the house. But Hannah also says Kate did it and cries."

"Jesus," Jace said again.

His grip on my hand was reassuringly tight.

"What's Harley say?" Grayson asked.

"The Everly did it. He claims she'd told him he was a dead little mouse. A ghoul for the house. A ghost for Kate. She sang it laughing. He says he wasn't that scared until she pulled Hannah out and he heard her screaming because he thought it was just like one of Kate's pictures, that Everly was just playing."

Vomit burned the back of my throat.

Jace moaned, grabbing my hand in both of his.

I could feel his hands trembling and heard it in his voice as he said, "This isn't your fault, Kate."

"What isn't?" Reynolds asked.

"None of this! Kate's making a haunted house. It's supposed to be a fun theme hotel, not a house of horrors! How Everly even knew about it I don't know!"

"My pictures," I said weakly. "I think I'm going to be sick. I made little coffins... they're just props for the game... I have a dungeon hidden in the basement. And ghosts and stuff. It was supposed to be fun..."

Grayson kissed my forehead, smoothing my hair back.

"Don't worry about this, Kate. I think that's enough now officers. Kate, I'll show them through the house."

"Is this my fault?"

"Of course not! She's sick is all. We'll get her help."

They all left, except for Jace.

"I never drew kids being hurt. Never!"

"It isn't your fault."

"What should I have done?"

"You did everything you could."

"I'm never going back to my parents. I hate that house!"

SIXTEEN

Three days later, my brother drove me home from the hospital.

I, of course, had to go back home, not to my house. I wasn't old enough to just leave as much as I wished I could, but even if I could've gone, I couldn't have because the kids were there, and they needed me.

Our mom was waiting with Kenya and all the kids.

She said, "I'd have come got you myself but didn't want to take them or leave them."

I shrugged.

Her frown deepened.

I said, "Hey, Hannah banana, can I get a hug?"

Hannah ran to me when I knelt, bursting into loud sobs.

Seeing her little arm in a cast made me furiously angry and wildly grateful that it was only her arm.

Wolfgang said angrily, "She feels bad about lying."

"I didn't lie," Hannah sobbed.

I said, "It doesn't matter. I know you love me, and I love you. Nothing but that matters. I'm just so glad you're okay."

"She's mean. I hate her."

"Me too."

"I hate her too," Harley said, sounding like he was fighting tears himself and I was sorry I'd said it.

I said, "I could use a Harley hug."

He ran to give me a hug. I hugged them both with Felicity hugging us and Wolfgang looking all worried and patting her back.

Kenya squatted beside us to pat backs too and offer soothing words.

I hadn't expected my mother to hug us so wasn't surprised she wasn't. She looked worried though and not angry when she took Hannah from me with a grunt of effort.

Grayson scooped up Harley, saying, "I could use a Harley hug myself."

Felicity said, "We should've said Everly was being so bad."

Our mother said, "None of this is your fault and you don't need to think about it anymore. Now, who wants hotdogs?"

Kenya heaved an exasperated sigh.

"Mother, they need to express themselves. Not talking about it isn't going to make it go away. Fell, no one blames you guys, but if you want to tell us, we won't judge."

Wolfgang said angrily, "Mom said we were lying. We didn't lie! Everly did so say she'd get Kate in big trouble if we said anything."

Grayson said, "Ken, take the kiddos to the kitchen and fix us all some ice cream."

He set Harley down, took Hannah from our mother and handed her to Kenya, saying, "I want bananas and chocolate sprinkles in a smiley face like always."

Hannah smiled nervously.

Grayson headed across the hall to the smaller formal living room.

Not a mark remained on the white tiles. It still gave me the shivers to cross them.

Wolfgang stomped after him.

Felicity took my hand, whispering, "We knew about your boyfriend and that you hadn't told Mom. Everly told us you'd been sneaking out and Dad would throw you out if he found out it was to see him. Then she said you'd go to jail for stealing the tools and stuff."

I was furious, but, like always, had no outlet. My anger would scare them. And it was pointless to be so angry because even if Everly was here to rage at, it would only delight her.

"What weren't you supposed to tell me," I said as I sat and pulled her into my lap.

"We had a kitten."

Tears trickled down her cheek.

Wolfgang said angrily, "I found it in a box by the river. There were three but two were dead. So we snuck it into our room and were taking care of it. I knew Mom wouldn't let us keep it..."

"We could've kept her hidden though," Felicity said guiltily like it was a familiar defense—one she felt bad about.

Wolfgang made a face at her as he said, "We were going to ask you to help once it got big enough to leave its box. But Everly found it and took it. She said we could have it back if we gave her our allowance. So we did, but she didn't give it back. She just laughed and said she meant forever and to prove that we would, she'd keep it a month. I said she'd never give it back and if we didn't have the kitten there was no point in paying for it. And she said she'd kill it if no one was paying.

Felicity said, "So I said I was going to tell, and she said she'd blame you, and that Mom would believe her, and Dad would throw you out. I wanted to pay her," she said angrily to Wolfgang.

"It's not my fault she's so mean! I didn't think she'd really do it, did I!"

Grayson said, "She killed the kitten?"

Wolfgang began to cry as he said, "She dropped it over the balcony and then stomped on it."

I thought I'd be sick and had to close my eyes and breathe deeply for a few moments.

Our mother said, "I wouldn't have let her do that."

The inaneness of that made me laugh a bitter bark of laughter.

Our father said from the doorway, "I'm glad you're home, Kate. We have some things to talk about. "Alise, take the children to the kitchen."

Grayson said, "She's only just gotten in."

My father surprised me by kissing Felicity on the head and mussing Wolfgang's hair as they passed him.

He and my mother exchanged cold glances.

She glanced back at me with a bewildered air that despite my anger at her I found heartbreaking. She was clearly out of her depth with all this.

My father sat in the chair across from me.

"I'm glad you're recovering."

"Well that's swell of you."

He was so glad that he'd visited me twice in three days for ten minutes total.

Grayson said, "Now probably isn't the best time, Dad."

"Best time for what?" I asked.

"To inform you that I'm not your father."

I was stunned speechless and could only gape at him.

124

"That is to say your biological father. I *am* your father and believe it or not, I do love you. I should've taken your warning seriously, but in my defense, your mother had been telling me that you were prone to flights of fancy and that the trouble between you girls was caused by you and wasn't at all serious. I should've been more involved..."

"Then why weren't you?"

"I was busy... and selfish, and frankly not interested in having more children. I didn't know you weren't my child until very recently though."

He smiled bitterly.

"Everly told us," Grayson said.

My not father said, "Again, in my defense, you all seemed happy enough with the attention I was willing to spare. And I know how that sounds but I think I owe you the truth."

"The kids deserve a real father."

"I know. I'll do better. Your mother and I are divorcing. I plan to ask for custody, which leads me to the kids."

"No. Absolutely not! I'm not agreeing to be their mother."

He shook his head at me.

"Of course not, but the transition would be smoother if you agreed to stay with us when you were home from college."

"No. For a few reasons, but let's start with how upset the kids will be not to see their mother. What makes you think they'd want to stay with you in the first place?"

"They won't have a choice. She clearly isn't up to the task of looking out for them."

"Neither are you."

"I'm at least willing to try and can be counted on to not let an obviously ill child cause such havoc."

"Except it *was* obvious and you did allow it."

"I told you that I was acting from misinformation. Years of it. I assure you, I'll be checking facts more carefully in the future."

I said, "I'm not an idiot. I know you were having an affair too."

He flushed dark red.

I continued, "This isn't all my mother's fault. If you'd been honest with her, maybe she'd have been honest with you."

Grayson said, "This isn't about whose fault it is, Kate, but recovering. Dad probably will get custody. He's going to hire a housekeeper to look after them. I thought you'd like to be involved with that. I think it's a terrible idea to keep this house and he's agreed to talk that over with Mom and look into finding a new place. The kids are just here today to pick some stuff out. They'll be staying with me and Ken a few days while Dad finds a rental. I haven't told him a thing about your plans, but I think you should, and not just because he's going to find out any day now from the police."

"What plans?" my not father asked.

I said, "I'm not going to college. I can take the kids after school but not the kiddos. The kids could stay over whenever they wanted to although I'm not sure now if I'm going to open the hotel..."

Grayson said, "Don't let her ruin your dream, Kate."

"What hotel?"

"Seriously? You don't remember me talking about it—asking for help?"

He looked so puzzled that I knew he really didn't remember it.

I laughed harshly at myself for thinking he would. It had meant everything to me and nothing at all to him.

I said, "So why did you keep having kids?"

"She wanted them, and I loved her. And I got used to the idea and love you guys. I really did think everyone was happy as we were."

"You really thought I was happy?"

He flushed again.

"Except you. I knew you were unhappy, but I thought it was because you were..."

Grayson snorted as he said, "Mom told him you were having trouble fitting in because you were unpopular in school when Everly was so popular."

My not father said, "I knew you'd grow up to be as beautiful as Alise and thought it was just a stage. I wasn't worried about you being unpopular because who cares about grammar school? I knew everything would change for you in college and it will, Kate. The world awaits and I was right. You're a beautiful girl and smart enough to do anything you want to."

Anger, hurt, confusion. I had no idea what I felt. *How could he have seriously thought it didn't matter if I'd been miserable my entire childhood, like those years meant nothing at all...he couldn't think that....it had to be a lie.*

"I'm an artist."

"You could be more than that."

"You...."

I was too angry to form words.

Grayson said, "Let's go for a ride, Dad. I think it's time to show him your house, Kate."

"*Her* house?"

I snickered. "Yeah. *My* house! I don't want to be more than an artist! It isn't a stupid hobby!"

"I... I guess I should have no opinion when I was probably told lies about that too. I think you'll need to bear with me while I get up to speed on what my children are really doing—who they really are."

"Then maybe you should go help them pick their toys! Hannah will want her pink horse and Harley will want his brown one even though he'll pretend he's too big. Fell and Wolf don't care about stuffed animals and things like that, but they'll want their crafts table and all their projects, which is going to take a pickup to move, so you need to help them pick just one thing to work on."

Grayson whispered, "Did you know about the kitten, Dad?"

"Not until all this. I wouldn't have cared if they kept one. I'd have backed whatever decision Alise had made about it."

He sounded so sad that I realized he really did love my mother and that he was really hurting from her betrayal, which was so hypocritical of him, but pain was pain.

I said grudgingly, "I'm sure she didn't think Everly was capable of this either.

A new thought occurred to me, and I said, "Is Everly your real daughter?"

He winced as he nodded.

"I believe so. *You're* my real daughter in all the ways that count."

Grayson said, "And she might have been mistaken, Dad."

He shrugged as he said, "I'm getting all of you tested. Not that it will matter a whit either way."

"To you maybe..."

He flushed again.

I said, "So who is my real father?"

"I'm not sure we'll ever know."

Grayson said, "Mom claims she went to a clinic but won't say which one or where. Everly says she found out by reading Mom's diary, but she won't tell us where it is now. She claims that Mom got pregnant from one of Dad's friends."

I laughed harshly as I said, "Oh my God! that's just like her to sow as much confusion and angst as she can. She wants you to mistrust all your friends! I bet it wasn't anyone you know at all. Can I sue Mom, Gray, to get the name?"

My hope that my mother had been honestly trying when she spoken to me earlier withered under this information. She'd been lying about the affair or the clinic and anything else that she wanted to lie about.

He said, "Yes. We can petition the court, but that doesn't mean they'll agree to make her or that she'd say when ordered to."

Hannah ran into the room, skidding to halt with a comical look of dismay on her face when she spotted our father.

"Your ice cream, Grayson, but we aren't allowed to eat in here."

He stood to take the bowl from her and give her a hug.

I followed them back to the kitchen where I accepted a bowl from an anxious-looking Harley.

My father said thoughtfully, "Maybe we all need a vacation. Go find your swimsuits and we'll find a hotel with a great pool."

They all brightened and dashed for the stairs.

He said, "Alise, you're welcome to come. I think it'd be good for them to see us acting civilized."

"One of us should be here to speak with the doctors."

"We won't go far."

She nodded and they both left the room.

Kenya muttered, "Good grief, he's going to take her back, I know it!"

Grayson shrugged.

"It's none of our business. If he can forgive that, more power to him."

I said angrily, "It is too our business! She can't be trusted with the kids."

"I thought you wanted her to get custody?"

"No. I want her to be able to see them like she does now, quickly with no real interaction. What I don't want is the kids plunked into a place they don't know, watched by strangers and the parent they think doesn't care a whit about them! Jesus, Gray, you saw Hannah's face just now. What's she going to do if she's having a problem? At least Mom would help her, not tell her that her arm won't itch in a few weeks so just don't scratch it now. Mom's help will be sending her to one of us, but it would still be help."

"They both suck," Kenya said.

Grayson said, "They were good parents to us. I didn't really realize how different he was with you guys until recently."

"Mom changed the most," Kenya said thoughtfully. "She used to be really hands-on—like Kate is now."

"I don't remember her like that at all. She was always too busy or too tired to do anything with Everly and I."

"Everly was always a brat even as a baby. God, I was so glad to get out of this house. No offense Kate but *she* was awful. Maybe Mom just couldn't handle her either?"

"Sure. I get that, but why have four more kids if you can't handle the ones you have already?"

"Because I love you all so much..."

We all turned to the door.

Our mother said, "I love our family. When Everly found out what I'd done to have that family, I was frightened to death that I was going to lose all of you. So I let her get away with things I shouldn't have, but I'd no idea how sick she was."

"That's so bullshit!"

"I didn't!"

I wanted to call her a liar again, but Hannah ran into the room trailing her blanket, clutching her pink horse, and I didn't have the heart to ruin the bright sparkle of her smile by yelling at my lying mother.

"Where's your stuff, Kate? Want me to get it?" Wolfgang asked as he came in lugging his and Felicity's bags.

Grayson said, "I'll drop Kate off later with her stuff. The doctor wanted her to nap when she got home. You get the kiddos all settled and tired out in the pool, and we'll all be there for dinner."

My mother pursed her lips at me. I wondered if she'd have the nerve to order me to come watch them, but she just nodded, turning away to take the blanket from Hannah, folding it as she said, "Bring the bags out to the car, darling."

Grayson picked up my mother's suitcase and took the blanket. Wolfgang and Hannah followed him. She stopped in the doorway, speaking with her back turned as she said, "Everly is lying about everything. I always knew she was lying. It was just easier. And in a way, I wanted it to be true."

She walked out, calling for Harley to bring their pillows.

Kenya said, "I have no idea what's going on with her."

"Maybe she's sick too," I said bitterly.

Kenya hugged me.

She said, "I'm sorry I've been such a crap sister."

"You aren't the problem."

"I wasn't the solution either. God, Kate, I had no idea how unhappy you were! Why didn't you tell me or ask *me* for help?"

"No offense or anything but we both know you wouldn't help me if it meant crossing him."

She flushed, looking guilty.

"Not lightly, no... but if I'd thought any of this was happening..."

"It wasn't. The kids *were* fine."

"That's what I mean. You *weren't* fine." She kissed my cheek then stepped away to search my face. Tears clouded her eyes when she smoothed my hair back, her fingers stilling as they brushed the small bandage covering the shaved spot and hole in my skull. It gave me the willies to think about it, so I put it out of my mind and gave her another quick kiss on the cheek.

Our father said, "Kenya, could you please keep an eye on the kids until I join you all in an hour or so? Kate and I still have things to discuss."

"Sure, Dad."

In the hall, Grayson said, "I called and made reservations. We can share a room like old times."

She laughed, which made me smile.

My father smiled too and sounded wistful as he said, "I missed so much. God what a fool I was..."

Before I could answer, not that it needed an answer when I thought he'd been worse than a fool, Harley ran in to hug him.

At least he loves *him*, I thought bitterly, surprised by how angry and jealous I was of the obvious love and affection he felt for his son.

He carried him out to the car.

I headed to my room to pack. I had no intention of spending another night here. I wasn't even sure I wanted to go to the hotel. Fighting about it though probably wasn't worth it.

Broken police tape fluttered from the doorways of the bedrooms. It made my heart flutter too to see it and a cold pit formed in my stomach as it did every time I contemplated how close we'd come to losing both the kiddos.

If my father hadn't come home when he had... I wondered why he had as I stomped into my room.

My room had been ransacked. Numbered yellow crime scene place cards had been left all over. The box of knives was gone. It again gave me the cold shivers to think she might have used them on my brother.

I began throwing my clothes onto my bed.

Grayson entered my room a few minutes later, saying, "We're going to stop by and show Dad your house. You can stay with me until you can move in there."

"Great. Then I can move in there today."

"I don't want to be an ass or anything. I can't imagine how difficult this all is for you, but the kids really do need you."

"I know. I was just thinking about that. I'll stay with the kids at the hotel for their sake for a few days, but I'm not living with either of our parents again."

"Fair enough."

"I think mom is sick like Everly is."

He surprised me by snorting angrily.

"I'm not convinced Everly's sick at all. Sure, she's strung out and messed up from drugs, and obviously she's a psychopath, but I just found books on psychology in her damned room! She could be faking."

"Then let's hope she has good doctors who will know it. Why were you in her room?"

"Dad. Well, Mom. She claimed she was packing clothes for Everly. I think she was looking for her diary. Dad saw her go in and followed to shoo her out. We all looked through her things quick."

"It isn't Everly's style to hide things in her own room. They'd be somewhere meant to cause trouble if it was found... like my room or his office."

He nodded as he said, "What are you doing with all this?"

"Taking it home."

"Leave it for now, Kate. Just grab whatever you need for a few days. I'll help you move it all later."

"I don't want to come back."

"Then I'll move it for you. Seriously, Kate. This is all too much. You need to rest."

"I want to go home."

His embrace was safety and love and almost made me bawl like a baby.

"You're the best brother."

"I'm glad you think so," he said bitterly.

"Don't let her do that to you."

He released me to grab my sketch bag.

I grabbed up some clothes at random and stuffed them into an old paint-stained tote, added my phone charger, laptop, and the purse I took when my sketch bag would be too big but I wanted to bring makeup along, which I'd just started doing when going out with Jace. It held my ID, cash, pictures of the kids, a note from Jace that said you're my superpower that he'd tucked under the door of my house, a comb, face powder, tiny eyeliner, lip gloss, and a small notebook and pen.

Grayson took the bag from me, so I grabbed my blanket and pillow. I never wanted to come back here.

EVENTEEN

When Grayson and I got out to the driveway, we found they'd all gone.

"I thought he wanted to see my house? Not that I'm surprised he changed his mind..."

I wished I could stop caring—I didn't want to care. I hated that my father had the power to hurt me. The best I could manage was to pretend disinterest as if his obvious unconcern for me didn't hurt. I wondered if he was lying, if he'd always known I wasn't his and hated me for it. If I wasn't his daughter, then his disinterest, his disapproval shouldn't hurt. *He shouldn't mean anything to me either.*

Grayson said, "He does. I gave him my key and told him we'd meet him there."

That made me angry for no reason I could pin down, so I didn't complain although I wanted to.

We drove to my house in silence.

To my surprise, my driveway was full of cars and Jace was waiting on the porch.

"He's upstairs poking around," he said as he hugged me.

I hugged him hard, savoring the warmth of his arms, the smell of the soap he used, and mostly the thought that he at least truly cared.

I wished I'd taken a second to fix my hair, but I hadn't expected to see him. I'd just clipped it back to hide the bandage so the kids wouldn't be scared. And I guess it didn't matter that I hadn't bothered to style it because I'd looked awful in the hospital and it hadn't sent him running.

Grayson entered the house, saying hello to someone.

"Who else is here?" I asked.

"Howard, Crystal—and you were right about them. They're perfect together. I've never seen her or him happier. My mom has her kids today,

133

but Howard is great with them. All the guys from work came to help get the bathroom finished so the kids could come if they wanted to."

I wasn't sure if I was pleased or horrified.

He chuckled as he kissed my temple, saying, "Don't worry, I made them stick exactly to the drawings."

Crystal rushed over followed by Howard.

"You gave us all a fright," she said as she kissed the air by my cheek. "You're lucky you didn't kill yourself falling down the stairs like that."

Howard was flushed and avoiding my eyes, smiling nervously.

I didn't correct her.

Everyone was super nice and super uncomfortable, and they all left within minutes of my arrival. I don't think it was me who was making them uncomfortable though, but my father, because he came downstairs to examine the room with us.

A cheap unpainted door had been hung across the hall leading to my rooms with a paper taped to it that said, 'temporarily here to keep out dust—keep closed! The wood floor of the little hall and the bedroom had been sanded and refinished.

My bedroom was full of furniture I'd made for it over the last few weeks, end tables, a padded bench, two lamps, and an upholstered chair. One of my paintings of the woods at night hung above the fireplace. Even the closet door was hung.

"Did you make the headboard? It's beautiful," I asked as I admired the wrought iron roses.

I'd intended to make it of wood, metal being out of my league for fashioning, but this was much better. He'd painted it a distressed white and gotten a mattress somewhere that he'd covered with one of my vintage quilts. White gauzy curtains framed the windows. Heavier felt-lined linen ones bracketed the newly installed French door that I'd thought I wouldn't be able to afford for at least another year.

It made me uncomfortable thinking about how much I was getting into debt with him—an uncomfortableness that grew when I saw he'd bought me the bathroom floor tile *despite* it not being on sale yet.

He followed my glance, saying, "Don't get mad. It didn't cost *that* much."

Which was a lie since I knew exactly how much it cost. I checked tile prices every week to see if my favorites went on sale or showed up in the returns or clearance.

He continued, "And we got the toilet and tub free, so it's right on budget."

"Who built the vanity?"

The tub was a huge old one, big enough for two if the two were cozy. I couldn't imagine anyone just giving such a great antique away. They'd switched the layout putting the vanity where the tub was supposed to go to fit it in, which made the vanity a bit smaller than I'd planned but the style of it was the same. It looked great as if it was meant to be.

"We did. I got that marble piece from remnants. If you hate it, I can switch it easily enough when you find one you like better."

Grayson said, "It looks great, guys. Are there any secrets in here?"

Jace shook his head.

"Secrets?" my father asked.

"Where'd the tub come from?" I asked, ignoring his question. The thought of trying to explain my idea made me feel sick with guilty nerves. And that made me angry because he had no right to ask. He had no right to even be here pretending interest.

Jace came to take my hand as he said, "My grandmother. It was Crystal's idea. Our grandmother is the queen of hoarders. I didn't even know it was back there behind the garage, but Crystal did. She'd seen it when she was a kid. So Howard and her went and dug it out and we lugged it to the shop along with about a hundred pounds of caked on dirt. I didn't think it could possibly look good again, but I figured what could it hurt to try the reglazing stuff? so we sanded it all down at the shop, then sprayed it, and it looks good as new. Just do me a favor and never tell my grandmother because then she'll be certain she's sitting on a heap of treasure instead of a heap of trash."

"She doesn't know you took it?"

"Sure, but she saw it as it was."

"I hope you recorded it!"

He rolled his eyes at me then gently smoothed my hair.

"Crystal did and now she thinks she's a superstar."

I snickered, which made him laugh in relief.

"She recorded the whole makeover. I even let her film me making another headboard, which I sort of cheated on because I bought a base and just added the vines and flowers."

"It's absolutely perfect. You're absolutely perfect!"

I stepped into the bathroom to open the cabinets to admire my towels and old glass jars, most of which were empty. A few held cotton balls, q-tips, small soaps, and such.

Brand new fluffy white towels were on a black metal shelf with the same roses worked into the brackets above the old-fashioned toilet. A ruffled white shower curtain that I'd made what felt like ages ago now was pulled back, revealing a tile table tray across the tub that held a few candles, a pink bar of soap shaped like a rose, and a white washcloth.

Two matching hooks, one with a white robe and the other a long-handled scrub brush were between the closets with a wicker laundry basket under them. He'd even gotten a fern to put into my antique copper pot for the corner by the tub.

He said, "I took a tiny liberty," as he opened the other closet.

"I can't afford that," I said in dismay.

A stacked washer and dryer filled what should've been my linen closet.

"I swear you can. I got it online for a steal. It only cost me a few bucks for some fittings and the parts to fix it. Howard has a buddy who owns a laundromat and can get us a used commercial size set for the basement that guests can use, so we're actually saving money from the budget."

My father leaned past my shoulder then examined the papers in his hand, which I realized were the drawings of these rooms.

I returned to the bedroom to see if my plan for the closet had been followed, which should've been relatively easy since I'd already cut most of the pieces—or if I was in for more surprises.

It was empty without even the stacked cut pieces.

He said, "We didn't finish the closet because I was thinking we could put bunk beds in here for the kids for now. It's either there or mats on the floor in here and I was thinking it'd be easier to keep clothes in boxes under the bed and let them keep their stuff in there for now. Once we get the big bedroom with the bunk beds done upstairs, we can use that when they come, which is why I took another tiny liberty."

"Jace, I can't afford the wood for that yet."

"I know, but think about it, I'd have to pay rent anyway and a two-month advance is perfectly normal."

"You're going to live here—with her?" my father asked with heavy disapproval.

Jace met my eyes over the bed. I could see that he could see that I was looking forward to using it with him and he was looking forward to using it with me. It made me feel a bit better, a little less angry, a little less hurt, and a lot more loved.

I smiled at him.

His return smile was full of relief.

"Yes."

"Did you know they were planning this?" he asked Grayson.

"No. But I'm not surprised. Frankly, I'm glad he wants to move in. I'll feel better if she isn't here alone."

"She's much too young to live with a man! She should be going to college!"

"I'm standing right here! I don't need your permission to do anything—or I won't in a few more days."

Jace said, "I know how this looks, sir, but I swear I love Kate."

"*Hmmph.*"

He stomped out.

Grayson winced apologetically and followed him.

Jace whispered, "The minute you turn eighteen, I'll move in, but I can't before then."

"Why is this a secret?"

"It isn't, I guess, it's just...I don't want to give him ideas. You're technically a minor and I'm not. I could get in big trouble if he decided to cause a scene. I should tell you—"

"Kate!" Grayson called.

"I'll tell you later."

I went to see what Grayson wanted.

He and our father were standing in front of the plastic-blocked door of the parlor. I could tell by the way the tape was sagging that it had been opened and closed a bunch of times.

"Can he go in?"

"Why not?"

My father tapped the drawing, "Is this how the room looked or will look?"

It made Jace and I laugh.

I said, "Those drawings are how the rooms will look. Most are based on styles of the period, but they aren't reproductions or anything. They're meant to have a...vibe. To be comfortable and fun, so I break style rules and mix art styles sometimes."

As I was speaking, Grayson had peeled the plastic back.

He said, "She did all this herself, Dad. She made most of the furniture in here, including the paneling on the wall and adding the windows and shelves by the fireplace, and check this out."

He pulled the candelabra, revealing the hearth stairs.

I followed them down the stairs.

Grayson knew the secret of opening the door in the small room at the bottom, so we didn't get trapped for more than a few seconds when the hearth slid closed.

We entered another small room that wasn't quite finished, and now I wasn't certain I wanted to finish it. The red light from the stairs faded slowly leaving us in darkness that Jace and Grayson lit with their phones.

The harsh light wasn't as creepy as candlelight, but it was creepy enough. The only other light was a very dull glow outlining the exit door.

"What is this?" my father asked, sounding shocked.

It made me giggle nervously.

Grayson rattled the chains on the wall as he said, "A dungeon. The idea is to figure out how to get out."

I crouched to press the hidden button to turn on the single bulb overhead, saying, "The plan calls for electric candles and the clues to open the door built into the props."

As I was speaking, the dull glow around the door was brightening and symbols began appearing on the wall. The symbols were on keypads that opening the door triggered to light up.

I said, "Within five minutes you'll be able to see the symbols clearly even if you couldn't fumble your way to a candle to light it."

"How's it work?"

He ran his hand over a lit symbol in the faux rock. The entire wall with the faux metal door was made to resemble rough rocks, an effect I'd achieved with plaster, glue, styrofoam and paint. Each rock had a symbol carved into it that could be pressed.

I said, "I can reset the code to any of symbols I want with the alarm app. That way you could come play again if you wanted. I leave the clues for which symbol, and you press the symbols, and the door opens."

"And if you do it wrong?"

"I was planning to add some creepy sound effects and pointy stakes to start coming out of the ceiling. I was thinking I'd add a false wall and door that could start to open and have a skeleton hand or something reach out, and maybe another door into another much smaller room to trap people in. I'd paint a 3D effect on the floor so it looks like a hole or maybe put in a real hole and fill it with water or something. They'd need to figure out how to get back into this room."

"Kate! You could kill someone with a spiked ceiling!"

"The stakes wouldn't fall out just slid out a little. The ceiling would lower a bit but there would be a camera in here. I could see if they were too scared and trigger the door or lights remotely."

I pressed the sequence to open the door and let us into the next room.

"This room isn't done at all, except for the wall that hides the door to the dungeon. The plan calls for bookshelves to line the wall with one blocking the door sliding out and over, so you'd need to find the lever to open that and then the switch to open the door."

He went to the open doorway to examine the paper there.

"A lab?"

"Yes. Not all games will progress the same way or have the same goal. This room will have a small office, a desk, filing cabinets, typewriter, a safe, all the usual office stuff, along with a lab counter with the chemicals, none of which will be dangerous. It'll just be stuff to make writing visible or the microscope to see the clues, that sort of thing."

He returned to step on the foot pedal that opened the door to the dungeon.

The door opened.

Jace said, "That's just temporary until the furnishings are here. We'll make it work remotely so we can move the opener as needed for the games."

We exited the room into a short hallway.

Jace said, "That will be a bathroom and that room is utilities and storage and off limits for the game. But those two will be for the guests."

I said, "The theater will have a huge tv, comfortable seats, small coffee tables and a bar. We'll show movies and sporting events, and they can come hang out, game or not. The wine cellar will be mostly props and much smaller. I plan to paint the back wall to look like the shelves and casks go off into the distance so the room seems bigger than it is. The ladder there now will be hidden and there'll be a hidden exit to the yard and another door into the theater. It will mostly be used for the games that require a secret meeting room between the players."

While I was speaking, he was examining the stack of drawings.

Grayson reached past his shoulder to flip the page, "There'll be an emergency exit down here, Dad, and she could tell someone how to open the hidden door from the intercoms."

"No ghouls just ghosts..."

I winced, suddenly exhausted.

"Let's go upstairs. I'm tired."

I headed for the stairs, which were just ordinary cellar stairs, not the wide elegant ones I would put in when I could afford to.

We returned to the parlor where I sat gratefully beside Jace on the couch.

Heat flushed me as I considered the last time we'd been in here.

My father headed right to the fireplace to examine the painting, which was one of my better ones.

"Is this a reproduction of a picture of my mother?" he asked.

"Sort of. It's her face how I imagined she looked when she was my age. That's her cat, Trixie, but the dress and background are made up."

My father examined the room again, playing with the safe and the window exit, then he and Grayson left the room.

"How's the head?" Jace asked.

"Fine. Creepy...I hate thinking about it."

"Have you been home?"

"I *am* home...but yeah. He's taking them all, and me, to a hotel for a few days as if they're going to forget in a few days... He told me he isn't my father."

"What!"

"I know, right?"

"Who is?"

"My mother won't say. Not that I asked her. Maybe she'd tell me if we were alone..."

I filled him in on what I'd learned.

"They better lock Everly up! She's a menace."

"My mom will lie for her. She tried to get the medics out. I think he'll lie for her too. Or not her exactly but to cover it up."

"They can't!"

"They already have or you'd have heard all this on the news. Crystal thought I fell..."

"I'm... worried."

"*Ha!*"

Before he could say what he was worried about, my father and Grayson returned. They'd brought the large painting that would hang in the dining room. It was a twilight scene of my mother in a long gown, sitting in flower-studded grass in the aisle of a hedge maze with an open picnic basket, five silver goblets scattered about, and the kids. She held a glass vial of purplish-black liquid that could've been anything. Her expression was cold or resolute—empty—but beautiful with just the smallest smile curving her lips. I'd been trying to capture her absent inpatient affection, but I'd liked the mysterious result of wondering if she'd been about to smile and serve juice, or poison herself or one of them, so had left it.

Four children based off my siblings but wearing period appropriately clothes and hairstyles were sitting beside her, Felicity with a book, reading peacefully, Wolfgang with a smudged cheek and dirty shirt tinkering with a wooden carriage, Harley laying back with his head on our mother's lap, grinning as he bit an apple, and Hannah facing away from everyone holding up a rag doll. Her hair and profile were haloed by the setting sun that lit the doll's black eye with just a hair of menace. Angel and demon. In the background, shaded by the maze was a faceless man.

"Is this finished?" he asked.

"Yes."

"You're going to think this is a lie or worse, but I had no idea you were so talented."

I snorted, closing my eyes, leaning my head on Jace's shoulder.

It occurred to me how much harder this would all be, how awful and alone I'd feel right now if he didn't love me.

I pressed our clasped hands to my cheek without opening my eyes.

Jace said, "That's one of my favorite paintings. There's something really mysterious about it. You're not sure if it's sad or menacing or if they're all having a marvelous time waiting for him to join them."

I laughed harshly. "I didn't realize I was painting the real us. I bet a psychologist would have a field day with my work."

"The faceless man in the background," my father said sadly.

I wondered if that tone was an act meant to manipulate me—to keep me sympathetic to him. Maybe to keep his failure as a parent secret, maybe because he hated being thought faceless by anyone—even me, maybe to agree to watch his children so he could continue to be the faceless man in the background. The one who liked everyone to think he was a good father with happy children.

I wondered if it mattered.

EIGHTEEN

My father said, "Would you sell me this painting?"

"What for?"

"Because I like it."

I thought it was more likely that he wanted to throw it out.

"It was made for this house. I have others of the kids and Mom you could have."

"I'd like to see all your work."

"Why? Or should I say why now? But I guess I don't need to really ask that, do I?"

His eyes widened.

"You think I'm… lying? Pretending interest? Why would I bother?"

"Exactly? Why would you?"

"I told you. I didn't realize—"

"Even if that we're true, which I find hard to believe when I painted *all* the time at home, it's hardly going to endear you to me that the only reason you want to see them *now* is because you think they're good—which is probably a lie anyway."

Jace said, "They *are* good."

I shrugged.

"I stopped caring ages ago if he liked my work or not. I can see my paintings are mostly good, but he doesn't like this sort of stuff. He likes abstract and modern art. I've never once heard him say any portrait art was good. So—he's lying."

Grayson took the painting from my father and leaned it against the wall—facing the wall, which was so symbolically apt that I laughed.

"You're right, Gray, it's a stupid thing to fight about. The paintings I'm not using here are in the basement at home. Take any you want."

Jace said, "Crystal wants one of her and her kids. I told her she couldn't afford it. You should offer to do custom work on the website but not cheap."

"I started one of Evan that she'll love. I was going to hang it in the theater, but I can make another one for there. It will be my thank you for filming."

"Evan... you really like him, don't you?"

"Yep."

"He likes you too and he doesn't like anyone, but that's your superpower."

I laughed in delight.

Grayson said, "Why don't you join us for dinner, Jace?"

I rolled my eyes at him as I said, "Why would he want too... It's going to be awful."

My father said, "There's no reason it should be awful. The kids will have fun if we don't ruin it for them."

Here we go.

"You mean if I don't."

"I mean if we tell them Everly is sick and they're safe, that she hadn't meant to hurt anyone..."

"Sure, but they were there and saw her stamp their kitten to death! You think that's not a memory that's going to stick a while? You think they'll be okay with us pretending it wasn't horrible and terrifying and gross? That she hadn't *meant* it..."

"I'm not saying we make light of what happened just maybe we let them think it's all over now and we're okay."

"We—as in you and me, or we as in you and Mom, or what?"

"Yes. All of that. We'll tell them your mother and I are divorcing but not today. Today we'll just talk about moving or maybe not even that. You can bring them over and show them around and let them get used to the idea of visiting you here. But I really would like you to think about staying home and not just for them but because you *are* too young to be on your own. You're too young for all of this. I'm not saying your plan isn't good or that you're not doing a good job, but you don't need to rush like this. You can go to school and explore your options."

"I don't want to go to school. I want to build this house."

Grayson said, "Maybe you can compromise and build it but live home?"

"No. I'm done being the nanny. They can come here, but I'm not living under her authority again—and I don't need his."

"You do need us though, Kate. Without your allowance—that I pay—you couldn't do any of this."

"That's not true at all. It's bullshit of you to say it!"

"Grayson can't support you indefinitely. It isn't fair to him."

My head began to throb. I knew my face would be red from the heat of my angry flush.

"He'll get most of what I owe him in a few weeks. I can start paying my loan back as soon as I get another tenant."

"Which you can't do without fixing the rooms."

"Do you really think I'm this stupid?"

Grayson said, "He didn't mean it like that, Kate. He just hasn't read your plan. I'm in no hurry for you to pay that loan back. We can wait the four years like we agreed and see where things are then. I'm sure the house will be worth at least twice what you paid for it, so you'll be able to get a real mortgage if you had to even if you decide a hotel isn't what you want anymore and you'd rather just flip houses. Or you could sell it outright. My point is, I still think you have a solid business plan. One I'm totally willing to help finance. If you need more money to finish the bedrooms and put in a kitchen, is all you need to do is ask me."

"We can afford it ourselves," Jace said challengingly.

I turned to see if he meant me, but he was glaring at my father who, by his return glare, I thought was debating firing him then and there.

Grayson said hurriedly, "I know you mean well, Jace, but it's a mistake to mesh your finances like that. You should pay rent if you live here but not for renovating stuff. Neither of you should feel beholden to the other." He said to me, "If he works on the house, he should be paid for his time like any other carpenter would be."

"I didn't ask him to."

"I want to help," Jace said.

"Then do the housework but leave the investment stuff to her."

"I agree," I said.

My father said, "We should go. They'll be wondering where we got to. You're welcome to join us for dinner."

I said to Jace, "Take a night off. And close up here for me, would you? I'll call you later."

He frowned uncertainly.

I said, "I'm going right to bed after dinner. I'll order the kids room service, ice cream or cake or something, and they can watch a movie, but I'm exhausted. You can see them tomorrow. I'll bring them by the shop to say hello and we can pick up the table legs and stuff and get them out of Howard's way."

"You're not in the way," he said as he nodded agreement and smoothed my hair, resting his fingertips lightly against my neck behind my ear for a few moments.

It was just a small caress, not even a caress really, but the love in it flowed through my entire body, soothing the heat of my anger. I expected my father to say I shouldn't bring the kids to the shop, but he didn't say anything. He'd probably just tell them not to let me in. I was going to be a few table legs short, but I could always rent a lathe or maybe buy one and then return it...

While I was musing on that, Jace stood and offered me a hand.

I let him pull me up.

The room swam alarmingly.

"You okay?" he asked anxiously.

"Yeah, just stood too fast."

He gave me a quick hug and kiss.

Grayson and my father left.

I said, "Stay here if you want. Move in if you want. Just turn the alarm on if you go out."

"We need to talk about the house finances."

"Can we do it tomorrow?"

"Sure. Get some rest, sweetheart. You don't need to call me later if you want to go right to bed. Text me at least though so I know you're safely in your room."

I didn't roll my eyes or ask what he expected to happen because god knew what *else* would happen. I didn't trust my mother one whit.

It made me think maybe it wasn't all Everly's fault. Maybe our mother had been lying to her too, encouraging her to hate me for her own reasons—

I suddenly wondered what she'd think of the painting.

NINETEEN

Jace picked me up from the hotel the next morning.

It felt weird to see him in the daylight—to boldly get into his truck.

It was weird to walk into the house without hurrying to drop our clothes or caring if my dad spotted us. I hoped the normalness of coming here wouldn't ruin the passion—*not that this was at all normal...*

I snorted a laugh at myself that earned me a confused look.

"How's the head?"

"Better than yesterday, I guess."

I was used to the headache now. Pain meds dulled it, but I thought it was a *bit* better.

"We need to talk."

My heart plummeted to my toes and tears blurred the room.

"Never think that, Kate!"

His embrace made me sob.

He said, "I'm sorry. I shouldn't have said it like that, but it shouldn't matter how I say it! You should trust me! I love you, Kate! All this bullshit isn't going to change that. Nothing is going to change that!"

I couldn't stop crying, which was pissing me off, making me cry harder.

His body relaxed and he stopped talking, just stroking my hair, kissing my cheek and neck, murmuring, it's okay, occasionally until my tears trailed off to shuddering breaths.

He led me to the couch and pulled me into his lap.

"I wish I could help... it makes me so damned mad that your parents are such assholes to you! I should've told you this ages ago but... at first I didn't because it didn't matter and then because it mattered too much,

146

and then it didn't matter again because I knew you'd believe me and understand. But now I'm worried."

"I've no idea what you're babbling about."

Except I had a sick feeling I did.

I'd cried myself out so had no tears left but my eyes began to burn. My hands became sweaty and shaky. My head began to throb. I wanted to believe that it didn't matter if he'd slept with Everly *before* he'd said he loved me, but it *did* matter.

He said, "The summer I was sixteen I had this girlfriend."

Relief left me lightheaded.

He continued, "She'd just moved in right down the street, and I thought I was in love. I didn't have a car that worked so we'd ride our bikes and walk, and I spent days trying to think of a place to take her where we could be alone because she'd made it really clear she wanted to have sex. I was a virgin but more than ready to change that. So, I finally gave in at the park, which was a crappy spot, but I couldn't think of a better one, and I knew other kids went there all the time and she seemed totally okay with it. So there we are, me with my pants down and her with her skirt up under those stupid bleachers by the basketball court and her dad arrives. He called the police, and I was arrested for rape."

"What!"

"She was only fourteen, which I hadn't known, I'd thought she was the same age as me. But her age wasn't really the problem. If she'd have admitted she'd wanted to go there... but she lied, said I'd forced her, that I'd been following her around, which of course I *had* been.

"*We* hadn't had sex, but *she* had and recently enough that there was evidence of rough sex. It was looking bad for me. I'd been talking a bit of trash how she was all hot for me and shit, and she hadn't mentioned me to any of her new friends at all—as a boyfriend, I mean. None of that matters except to point out that I was a fool. I probably would've been sent to prison if Frank hadn't helped me."

"Your stepfather?"

"Yeah. He wasn't my stepfather then though. He was just a cop who believed my story. Not that it mattered what he believed because I couldn't prove it—except he had an idea that saved my life."

He dug in his pocket and handed me a small metal square, closing my hand around it.

"He gave me this. Said to give it to one of my pals, someone she wouldn't know. Someone she'd think was hot. He made me swear I wouldn't tell anyone that he'd had a thing to do with it. Entrapment by a police officer would make anything she said inadmissible.

"I had a buddy who was in boot camp when all this went down. Dan was just eighteen and hugely popular. I begged him to help, and he agreed. He came back on his very first leave and of course was invited to every single party, a lot of which were thrown just because he'd come back. He trash talked me, made it seem like he was glad I'd be going down and got her on tape admitting she'd lied as well as talking about her other lovers. She'd also told him she was seventeen and a bunch of other really incriminating shit. Long story short the charges were dropped and I was free to go."

"Please tell me she got arrested for that..."

He shook his head, saying bitterly, "At the time I was just so grateful to get out of jail that I signed the papers I was offered. Later, I wished I'd gotten a lawyer myself and charged her, not so much for myself but to save some other poor jerk. Her family moved before school even started. I have no idea, nor do I care where she is now. I never saw her or spoke to her again. I spent three nights in jail because of her, and three weeks thinking I was going to prison, but she taught me a lesson I never forgot. I was much more careful picking my dates in the future."

"So you and Everly..."

"Never! If she said differently, she's a liar. Even before us I could see what a whore she was. Not that she ever tried anything until us. After she cornered me the first time, I started carrying that recorder again."

"The first time..."

I jumped from his lap to glare at him.

He stood to grab a water bottle from the table, handing that and the paper towels to me.

I accepted them absently.

"I didn't mention it because I thought it didn't matter. She just came to the shop and flirted, but she wasn't aggressive about it. I think she thought that if she was nice, I'd eventually give in. So when she was leaving and said she'd be back I told her bluntly I didn't like her, that I'd never like her, and she was wasting her time. So she told me you were a whore who turned tricks for money. The phrasing of that pissed me off so much. I know she'd done it purposefully because if I'd asked around your school people would've confirmed it thinking I meant magic tricks. She is such a fucking devious bitch! She told me that all you were interested in was money. That you hoarded it or had a drug habit or something, but she implied that your parents were on the verge of throwing you out and said straight out that you'd already been disinherited.

"I don't think she knew then about your house because she didn't know what you were spending your money on. She slapped me and left, and I figured that was that—but just in case, I began bringing the recorder with me."

"So you got her on tape that second time?"

"That was actually the third time, but yes."

"Third!"

"She came in a few days before that time wearing even less but she didn't speak to me, just went to the loft, and began removing her shirt. I left."

"Why the hell didn't you tell me!"

"What could you have done? I didn't want to cause any problems for you. Plus, I had no real idea how bad things were between you. I knew they were bad on her part, but I also knew how much you love your siblings. I thought she was just a stupid jealous kid, not a homicidal maniac. I didn't want to hurt your feelings..."

I handed him back the recorder.

He shook his head, closing my hand around it.

"That one's for you. It can record a hundred hours. Just press the end there. You can download it to a computer to listen to it. I think you should get your mom on tape and play it for your father and get him on tape and play it for her because I have no idea who's lying. I can't believe your dad *couldn't* have known how good your painting is... I believe he has no clue about Everly being so sick, but he *must* have known she was such a skank. And your mom must've known that too. Just because they didn't react to her coming in so late doesn't mean they didn't know she was. So ask them why but do it when they aren't together."

"I don't think it matters."

He shook his head at me, closing my hand around the recorder.

"It matters. What if whatever Everly has on them is huge? Every lie you catch them out in could help you. You don't have to tell anyone what you find out, but if they try to twist things..."

"It's probably too late for my mom to turn this on me... isn't it?"

"I have no idea. Maybe she could convince the kids to lie if given time. Just get her on tape telling you why she wanted the paramedics to leave and why she always takes Everly's side."

"How did you know about that?"

"I saw the ambulance and stuff arrive. I was there and you said it in the hospital—don't you remember?"

"It's all blurred."

"I bet."

He hugged me again.

I was suddenly worried that she'd try to hurt him to get to me, which was stupid—except it wasn't.

I said, "I have no idea what's really motivating my mother. All this time I'd thought it was Everly instigating everything. But maybe my mother was using her as an excuse?"

"What do you mean?"

"My mother would yell at me all the time about fighting with Everly. She never believed me when I told her what Everly had done or said. Everything was my fault, which used to piss me off so bad because the truth was always so obvious. She'd always end the lecture by saying she was going to throw me out without a cent. She'd lecture me on how hard living alone would be, that I'd have to turn tricks or sell drugs, and I'd probably be murdered or beaten every day because I had no skills, so I better shape up—stop being so stupid."

"She said that!"

"All the time. I never believed it though. I mean, I thought she was saying it to pacify Everly because it always quieted her right up. She'd be smug as shit for a few days and try to aggravate me into lashing out and getting yelled at again. I think it's why the twins were so worried because *they* believed it. They thought I'd be kicked out and die alone on the streets, which pisses me right the fuck off because I could've reassured them so easily.

"Even if I didn't have my house, Grayson and Kenya wouldn't let me starve to death. And sure, Kenya and Gray want to stay on Dad's good side because he's loaded and gives them expensive gifts and shit, but they're good people and they don't *need* his money. They make good livings on their own. The kids must be really messed up about money... I should tell them that grandpa left them money too..."

"You're sure he did?"

"Positive. I was at the reading of the will—by his request. He left us all equal shares of a trust. Gram inherited everything else. We get the money when we turn eighteen and I'm quoting gramps here when I say, follow your dream, no one else's. College, a business, a home, you choose, don't let your mother decide your future for you, which in light of all this I'm wondering if he knew something?"

"Was that message for all of you or just you?"

"I'm not sure. The lawyer was talking to me, but I'd thought he'd meant all of us. Gramps always encouraged my art. He was on my side about the whole college thing. It was him who'd showed me that house when I was little. He liked the mystery of it too. I sort of began drawing it for him, and it came alive to me. I had the first glimmer of an idea, but then he died... I'm sure he'd have backed my idea. I'm *sure* of it. He was really angry at my father, which is why he left my parents nothing at all."

"Why was he angry?"

"Gramps saw how he was with us kids and it pissed him off, so he stepped in. God, when he died... we were all so devastated. Even Everly..."

"She got along with your grandparents?"

"She was an angel with them. Gramps saw through her though... he used to say to me, you watch out for that one, she's just like your mother, which... now..."

"He didn't like your mom?"

"He was polite—but no. Grandma doesn't like her either, but she's a bit of a snob. My mom had no money or anything when she and my dad married. I've heard my grandmother call her a social-climbing gold digger who belonged in the gutter."

"Jesus! Right in front of you?"

"They didn't know I was there. I think I was like eleven or so. I don't even remember what brought it on. I just remember being shocked because until that moment I'd thought my grandma liked her or at least approved of her. Grandma isn't the sort to keep her opinions to herself and I'd never heard her say anything like that before. The most I'd ever heard her do was critique her clothing choices for us, and when my mother announced she was expecting Hannah she said, good grief, another one? But in a really annoyed tone. Not that that meant anything really. Against my mother, I mean. I think it was more that grandma wasn't thrilled with babysitting. She takes them overnight about twice a year. The rest of the time one of us has to go along to watch them. She never comes to our house. I bring them by her place every couple of weeks for a visit. She's always glad to see us—or at least she *acts* glad..."

"I'm sure she *is* happy to see you."

"I wish gramps was still here... but, I guess, maybe he isn't my grandpa anyway..."

"Don't be silly. He'd love you because of *you*."

"I like to think so."

He hugged me for a long minute before saying, "How are the kids doing?"

"They're thrilled with all the attention from their parents. Both of my parents are being super nice. I hope it's real, but I think it's for the child welfare people. I'm not sure if it matters or not—not like there's a thing I can do about it anyway..."

"Have you heard anything more about Everly? Will she be charged?"

"I have no idea. I'm staying out of it. My father is hiring a full-time nanny to live in the house. He told Grayson he was looking for a boarding school for Everly so Hannah won't have to see her for a while. Whether that means Everly's getting released from the hospital soon, I've no idea. But since there's nothing I can do about it anyway, and he's going to keep her away from the kids, I think it's the best that I can do."

"But they didn't talk to you about it?"

"No. To be fair though, he didn't really have the chance to. Kenya told me he was dealing with the police and stuff for the last few days. She said it's a lot of child services stuff that has to be done. None of that stuff can be put off and we can't talk about it in front of them. And last night I didn't give him a chance. I went right to bed. We're supposed to be meeting tonight."

"Record it."

"All of us are supposed to be there."

"Still... if they change their minds later about letting you see the kids or something, maybe the recording would help."

"I don't see how, but if it'll make you feel better..."

"Speaking of that, we need to talk about my rent. I asked around and the going rate for a place like this, and by like this I mean run down with no real amenities, is between four and eight hundred a month. So, I was thinking we could go with four hundred and that would include me fixing up the carriage house to be my garage. The outside of it, how it looks will be up to you, but I get to do whatever I want on the inside of it. Plus, I'd do five hours a week on this house and that doesn't include normal stuff like dishes and whatever. I mean construction stuff. Which puts my rent right in the normal range."

"Okay."

"Because that garage is for my use, and the house is getting nicer all the time, we'll discuss a new rent every year."

"Okay."

His eyes narrowed.

"I'm going to want to add some things to the house like a stove and refrigerator and stuff, so we can either buy the one you really want, and I subtract the difference in the cost of the one I'd pick from my work hours, or you find a temporary one and we split the cost straight up, or you just let me do whatever I want."

"Let me think about it."

He smiled, the tension easing from his face.

I wondered how much this was sucking for him, how close he was to washing his hands of this entire mess. I would if I were him. There were bound to be some legal court issues over this. My sister wasn't one to take the blame for anything. I was sure that she'd try to blame everyone else any way she could—including him, and he had to know that too.

While I was musing, he was saying, "Fair enough. I thought we could have a look around my grandmother's to see if there are any other hidden gems in there. Crystal said she thought there might be another tub or two out back and she thinks there was old sinks and stuff. I already asked my grandmother and she's thrilled with the idea that her crap is coming in handy now. She wants to come see the place."

"Sure."

"I don't think we should tell her about the mystery part because she's sort of getting confused and I'm afraid she might think there really are ghosts here."

"You like her a lot, don't you?"

"She's a crazy old lady but I love her. We all do. I wish she'd sell her heap... it can't be comfortable to live in it, but she won't hear of it."

"I can't wait to meet her. Does this mean I can meet your mother too?"

"Yes. As soon as you're up to it."

"Will she like me?"

"She'll love you because I do. Once she gets to know you, she'll love you for yourself."

"Does she even know about me?"

"I'll tell her tonight. I'll tell her I'm moving in here August sixteenth."

"At one a.m."

He laughed and kissed me.

When we broke from the kiss, he said, "Did they say you could move in?"

"No. Not that it matters."

"It matters. They could call the police and have you dragged home, and then Grayson would be in trouble for letting a minor live here unsupervised."

"Then I'll stay with him or Kenya until my birthday."

"I'm putting the alarm system in and no arguments. We can talk later about splitting the cost."

"It really doesn't need much, except for the door alarms. The smoke alarms and stuff I'm adding as the rooms get done, but there's already the battery powered kind you stick up on every floor. I need to have automatic sprinklers in the kitchen because this will be a hotel. I was debating putting sprinklers in the hallways too just because I plan to use real candles in this hall, not electric ones like in the rest of the house. When the water heater is installed, I was planning to put in the carbon monoxide detectors."

He nodded, saying, "We're getting security cameras. I need them anyway for my garage. But it's better to do it now before there's stuff worth stealing so when the local kids come around to see what's what they see there's alarms and stuff. And I was thinking, maybe we should put cameras in all of the rooms. You could use it now for your shows and later you could record the guests when they're playing, with their permission of course. I think people would watch it."

"Okay."

"You're being too... am I taking over too much?"

"No. It makes sense. I was just thinking I'm not at all prepared for crime. It didn't feel like something that could happen to me. I'm not sure how to prepare for it now."

"It won't happen here. This will be a safe place, Kate."

"I really thought she was going to kill Hannah, and then when she tried... and when I think she'd have used my knives on Harley..."

"She didn't," he said worriedly.

"I don't know why I'm talking about it. It's over..."

"It's okay to be frightened, Kate. God, I was terrified when I saw you there all bloody and your damned mother acting like you'd just stubbed your damned toe."

"I never got a chance to ask her why she wanted them to leave. I assumed it was to protect Everly, but why? She *must* have seen then that Everly needed help?"

"Ask her."

"I plan to."

My phone rang with Grayson's ring tone.

When I answered, he said, "Kate, I'm on my way to pick you up."

He sounded worried and my headache ratcheted up from a dull ache to a hard throb.

"What happened?"

"I'm not sure. The kids are all fine, but the police called, and they wanted you to come to the house. Howard called Dad a few minutes ago to say the police had come with a warrant to search it."

"For what?"

"I have no idea."

"Dad's on his way there now. He called to ask what was going on and they just said they wanted to speak with you."

"Am I in trouble?"

"I don't see how you could be," he said worriedly.

Jace said, "I can give you a ride there."

Grayson heard him because he said, "No, wait for me."

Butterflies danced in my stomach and the back of my neck suddenly felt tight and hot.

Jace took the phone from me and put it into his pocket. He hugged me for a minute then said, "Grab your sweatshirt. I'll lock up. I'm sure it's nothing, Kate."

Neither of us believed that.

TWENTY

The police made us wait two hours before they'd let us in. Tons of them went in and out of the house, all of them giving us weighing glances just this side of hostile.

A stream of them left and Detective Sandy came outside to greet me.

She said, "Thanks for coming. I'd like to speak to you privately for a moment."

Grayson said, "I'm her counsel."

Dee grimaced at him. "I'm afraid I have to insist as it would be a serious conflict of interest for you to be present. She can request council be present. I just thought seeing as she's just weeks shy of eighteen that we could cut out the red tape of getting a family service lawyer and just talk. But this isn't the sort of talk that she can have with family members present, especially ones who might influence what she says."

Grayson's eyes narrowed.

I said, "I'll be fine."

He said to me, "If you get uncomfortable, ask for a lawyer. Don't let them bully you."

Jace kissed me then whispered so low I almost didn't hear him, "Turn it on."

I nodded.

Grayson and Jace went to join my father who was speaking to another officer in the driveway.

Dee said, "Your sister is claiming your father and brother have been sexually abusing everyone."

"What! That's totally not true!"

"It has to be investigated, Kate. So here we are. So far, we haven't a found a thing to substantiate her claims—except this."

She handed me one of my photo albums, so I knew there would be pictures of Hannah and Harley naked in it.

I said, "I took these pictures years ago. It's just the kids in the bathtub. They were like two..."

She said, "Flip to the back."

I could feel the blood drain from my face when I did.

"I didn't take these."

The last few pages were naked shots of all of us, mostly me in the bathroom. There were a few of the kids naked in their rooms and more bathroom shots, two of Harley that almost made me vomit they were so explicit—so obscene.

I said, "I've never seen them before, and I didn't pose for any of them!"

I flipped through again slowly although it was making me flush with shame.

"I can date some of these. Hannah only owned that dress there on the floor for a day. She got it for her last birthday and ruined it that same night. Mom tossed it. I have real pictures in my newest album of her getting it. Dad couldn't have taken the picture of her because he wasn't home those days. He was gone that entire week on a business trip. I remember because Mom was so mad that he was missing her birthday party. Grayson was in town, and he was here for her birthday party, but he left early with Kenya to meet friends. This picture had to be taken that night. Hannah had an absolute fit about having to take the dress off, which is why she's crying and crossing her arms like that."

"You're sure?"

"Yes. You can ask anyone. Hannah was really upset she'd ruined the dress. She only wore it that one night. And this picture of Harley is photoshopped. I do a lot of video editing. See how the light from the door cuts off? It's his head but not his body."

The image was disgusting. I wondered where she'd gotten the picture to splice the head onto. There was another naked shot of both boys together about to get into the tub. The next few pages were all naked shots of me, which was infuriating because I *knew* she'd have shown them to all her skanky friends.

I pointed to a picture of me sitting on the edge of the tub. "This one of me was taken the first week of June."

"How do you know?"

"I'd just gotten that birth control implant and it made that swelling on my arm there, but it only lasted a few days. I have no idea where my father and brother were, but they didn't take the picture. I thought I was alone in the room. The door is closed when I shower, so how is she taking them? For the kids, I can see how it'd be easy because I still help the kiddos and will bring towels or whatever to the older ones. They wouldn't think a thing of the door opening, but I sure as shit would. So how did she do it?

"And did you notice how everyone except Everly and the photoshopped Harley shots are candid shots? We're all looking away. She's posing looking right at the camera, and might I just say—ick. *We're* all getting into or out of the bath. There's nothing sexy about any of them. I bet if you dust these for prints, it'll have hers on them. And since as far as I know she's never looked through these, that alone should prove she put them there."

"She claims you sleep at your brother's a lot. Your mother says that you go see him almost daily."

"That's true. I did always say that's where I was going. It wasn't technically a lie since Grayson owns my house until I'm eighteen. But he wasn't hardly ever there, and really, so what if he was? He's my brother, and he's never once done anything at all inappropriate with me or anyone else!"

"So you never had reason to think he was..."

"Never! That's just sick! I bet I know why she did this. Grayson and I caught her trying to seduce my boyfriend, and when he turned her down, she threatened to get him fired by claiming he'd sexually harassed her. Grayson called our father, and he grounded her and took her car away. I bet she was planning a little payback."

"No one reported it..."

"Jace didn't want to, but he made a notarized statement just in case she tried it again later."

"What can you tell me about the bathroom in the basement?"

"What's to tell? It's just a bathroom. All of the bathrooms have the same tub and wall color and all of them usually have the same shower curtain although the one down there isn't replaced as often. Every few months, Mom buys new ones, and we replace them all. I use that bathroom as my dark room, so it has a red lightbulb sometimes, which I might have left in although I try to remember to put it with my film stuff, which I keep in a locked cabinet in the garage because the chemicals can be dangerous."

"You develop your own film?"

"Yes, but I haven't done it in ages, which is why I think I must have removed that lightbulb or my mom would've said something by now, although, no one really uses that bathroom or the basement much since Grayson and Kenya moved out. I don't think anyone has touched that exercise equipment in years. Or at least not that I noticed. I suppose Mom or Everly could be using the bathroom when we're not home. The kids and I go down there to paint if the weather is crappy outside, but we aren't showering there."

"Does your father go down there?"

"Not that I ever saw. He isn't home much and when he is, he's in the office, the dining room, or his bedroom. Once in a great while he'll watch a movie with us in our playroom, or he and Mom will have a party with friends in their living room."

"What about at night?"

"You mean did I ever hear him creeping around?"

She nodded.

"No. I would've noticed. I check the kids every night when I go to bed and if I hear the alarm when Everly comes in just in case it's one of them wandering about. Wolfgang used to walk in his sleep, so he has a chime on his door that sounds similar. It hasn't gone off in a while, but I still always wake when she comes in, and then I check everyone. Plus, I check if I make a bathroom trip or hear them ask for water or something. The twins sometimes wake early, and I always hear that."

"How early?"

"Five or so. They'll go to the playroom and watch tv and work on one of their projects, so I usually get up when I hear them, but not always, it depends on what I think they might do."

"What do you mean?"

"If their project calls for something that needs adult supervision like if I think they might decide to use the iron to get veneer to stick or maybe paint inside or anything messy. So I keep track of what their plan is so I know if I can sleep in or not. They're good about telling me, and they wouldn't sneak it if I told them to wait, but they're also kids and kids sometimes don't think things through."

"How often is your brother alone with them?"

"He stops by a few times a week but doesn't usually stay long. The kids are never left alone, so Mom, Everly, or I would be here when he got here. He'll go play catch with them or take them swimming, normal brother stuff. I don't think he's ever really alone with them cause we're still around. He babysits all of them once in a while, or rarely Wolfgang alone. It's really bullshit that she can tarnish his name and reputation like this!"

"There's one more thing I think you should see and you're not going to like it."

I followed her into the house.

"You can't really believe her claims, can you?"

"She's obviously really troubled, which could mean she's lying, but maybe she's telling the truth, because abuse can cause kids to lash out. We have to investigate it, Kate."

"I swear, neither of them ever laid a hand on me or even made an inappropriate remark."

"I believe you, but we can't assume that because you weren't abused no one else was."

"It's just so unfair. Grayson will be so upset—so hurt, that anyone would think that of him."

"But not your father?"

"I don't care about his stupid feelings."

"What's going on between you two? The paramedic who picked you up reports you were scared of him."

"I'm not scared of him. I'm worried he won't take the kids' needs seriously. He can't be trusted to look out for them, not because he'd hurt them on purpose but because he doesn't care."

My father said from behind us, "That might have been true, but this has opened my eyes that I need to pay better attention. I've been taking everything for granted and just—coasting. I always cared but I thought your mother was doing a good job and didn't think there was anything to worry about."

Grayson, Jace, and the officer who I didn't know had followed us down.

My heart fluttered when I saw a crime scene tech taking pictures of the kids' toy box. Another two were stacking the boxes I'd kept my old paintings in.

The exercise equipment was untouched but little place cards surrounded the easels and my stacked boxes of finished paintings. Tears blurred my vision because I could see holes and gauges in the boxes.

Dee said to my father, "When were you down here last?"

"I have no idea. I don't recall coming down here in years. Maybe when Grayson was eighteen or so and there was a pool table down here... We'd play pool once in a great while."

I said, "He took it with him his second year of college."

He shrugged.

I wondered if he knew what Everly had accused him of.

She said to Grayson, "When were you down here last?"

"Last week with Harley and Wolfgang. Wolfgang wanted to use the weights, which are locked with a bicycle chain to keep them from playing with them, so I took out the one-pound weight for them. Hannah, Felicity, and Kate came in to get paint or something, then we all went swimming."

I said, "In the winter or crappy weather, we paint down here. Mom doesn't mind if we leave our projects spread out down here."

My father walked past us to examine the line of easels.

My easel was laying on its side with my half-finished paintings scattered.

"Whose is whose?" he asked.

My throat felt thick, too thick to talk.

Grayson said, "Harley painted the firetruck. Fell and Hannah the flowers. Wolfgang doesn't really like painting; he draws out the pictures for the girls sometimes but mostly he just tinkers on his latest project. The girls are losing interest in painting and bring their dolls down more often and play with them while Harley and Kate paint."

I took a breath and said, "What did she do to my paintings?"

Jace stepped closer to take my hand.

Dee said, "Someone defaced some."

I knelt to pick up the scattered pictures.

"Oh, Kate," Jace said as he took the picture of his mother's house from me.

I'd painted my vision of him laughing at the table in his mother's yard. Everly had slashed his face, stabbed about a hundred holes across it and cut out the woman that I'd painted leaning over to water the pansies, leaving just a pair of feet in the grass and a woman's hand holding a watering can.

"Who are the kids?" Dee asked as she handed me the picture of the kids on the bikes.

"I don't know. Just kids. I thought they were beautiful, interesting, that they were having a grand adventure together..."

There was a crease in the center, but she hadn't slashed it. I'd have to start over but probably wouldn't bother. It had taken hours and hours to sketch them all out.

Evan's picture was untouched. I'd perfectly captured his beautiful blue eyes narrowed in amused derision—the love of a good con, a boy with a man's hard eyes but still sweet.

I handed it to Jace. "Give it to Crystal."

"Is that a picture of someone you know?" Dee asked.

"Yes. A friend's son."

"What's with the clothes and stuff?"

"It was for my house."

My father said, "It's a beautiful picture, Kate."

"You painted all these?" Dee asked. "How long did it take you? You must be down here all the time?"

"I mostly do these outside and just put them here to dry. The time it takes varies. If my vision of the image is really clear, and it's just a portrait like the one of Evan with the cards, it takes about four to eight hours depending on how many layers the image needs. It can take me hundreds of hours for complicated pictures."

"You can paint that in a day?"

"No, drying time and stuff. I'll paint the shirt or something then add on the pockets and ruffles and all that once the shirt dries. It could take seconds or hours for each layer depending on my vision for it. There's no set amount of time. Sometimes I just stare at it deciding what to add or change. It's not really finished either..."

I could see they'd emptied the storage boxes and had piled the ruined pictures to one side.

My father flipped through them, his expression growing grimmer.

"I'm afraid to look," I said.

I was afraid my legs weren't going to support me much longer.

I turned back to the door.

Dee laid her hand on my arm. "I'm sorry to ask you to, but we need to know if you drew all of these."

Jace released me, saying, "I can look. I'd know her work."

Dee said, "We'd like to know what the missing bits were."

"Let's just get this over with," I said angrily.

My father held out a pristine portrait of my mother smiling at Everly who was holding up a cocktail dress. The dress was wildly inappropriate for a fifteen-year-old. My mother's smile had stayed with me because it was so loving, so clear that she hadn't given the dress a second thought. She'd just been happy Everly was happy. That smile had hurt because I couldn't remember her smiling like that at me since I was Felicity's age.

"Can I have this one?" my father asked.

I shrugged.

Dee crouched beside the ruined ones, taking out a notebook.

I said, "Wolfgang and his friend Tommy and Tommy's dog Hoot."

Wolfgang's eyes had been poked out and the dog had been stabbed so much it wasn't recognizable as a dog.

She made a note and flipped to the next.

Nausea made me feel cold and clammy.

"Hannah and her first baby doll."

Neither was recognizable.

"Felicity...I really don't want to see these."

Grayson said, "Go sit down a minute. I've seen them often enough to be able to tell."

I went to sit on the weight bench.

Jace crouched in front of me, taking my hands and rubbing them.

My father joined us a minute later.

"I don't know what to say... it's a horrible thing she did."

"It sucks," I agreed.

My voice cracked.

Jace winced, scooting closer.

"Sweetheart..."

The officer I didn't know said, "Dee, take a look at this."

He held out one of my first sketch books.

I said, "Those are really old."

Dee flipped through it for a few minutes.

"Who is the older man?"

"My grandfather. He'd just died. My house, not this one, *mine*, was our spot. I was just a kid and had gotten the idea for my house and then he died, so I put him everywhere as a ghost or creepy guy because I didn't have a really strong concept of a haunted house, except for the sort you see in movies, but then he started becoming a zombie, so I stopped drawing him because it was too scary. I started making the house beautiful instead and eventually it stopped hurting as much and I added my ghosts again but this time they were beautiful and fun. That's in my sketchbooks there."

My father said, "When you say your spot..."

"We liked it. It was mysterious and even run down it was beautiful. He used to say it had breeding and class that even age couldn't ruin it. It was a house for a great family and then he'd moan and complain because grandma wouldn't hear of living there. He'd tell me how it could be fixed up again.

"I think it made him sad to think someone might tear it down or ruin it with cheap ugly fixes.

"I liked to sketch it. We'd go sit in the grass there and he'd tell me about growing up in a house like that one while I sketched. We'd laugh over how we'd fix it and I'd make him drawings of how he wished it would be. We broke in a few times to walk around..."

The low murmur of Grayson and Dee was making my heart hurt.

Everly had destroyed all of the pictures with the kids and my mom unless she was in it too.

Grayson said, "Kate didn't paint these."

Dee said, "Kate?"

Jace helped me up, keeping his arm around me.

I examined the canvases, saying, "I assume that's supposed to be me in a coffin? No. I didn't paint these. I did the backgrounds on those three. They were meant for the wine cellar in my house. I'd been making a backdrop for a Pepper's Ghost. The goal was to have it look as if a ghost was flitting across the pictures into and out of the room, which is why it's a cemetery and an old wine cellar."

My father said, "This is horrible and all, but I don't see how it's a police matter."

You wouldn't, I thought bitterly, wondering if he'd feel the same if I'd smashed up *his* office or been painting *him* dead.

TWENTY-ONE

"So now what?" I asked.

"Now just take a look around and see if anything seems... off."

"Am I looking for anything in particular?"

"Just tell me what you see."

I turned to examine the rest of the room first.

"The machines have been slid around."

Grayson stepped past me to crouch beside the rowing machine.

Dee said, "Don't touch that," as he reached for the plug.

He turned to me and shrugged.

I scanned the room slowly, wondering what she saw that I didn't and why it mattered.

"My paints are out of order. There's a can there I didn't buy. I've never seen that brand before."

I stepped closer and she said, "Don't touch it."

The other officer said, "I'll call."

Dee nodded.

My father said, "Call who?"

"The bomb squad."

"What?" he asked incredulously.

She said, "Kate, I want you to come with me through the rest of the house."

My father grabbed my arm.

"Like hell she will if you think there's a bomb in here! And why the hell would you think that?"

"Because we found the plans for how to make one tucked into one the photograph albums."

"Is it something for your house, Kate?" Grayson asked.

"A bomb? No. Why would I make a bomb? I do have plans for pressure release doors and stuff and big jack-in-the-boxes."

Dee said, "We found that too in a blue notebook in your room."

I nodded.

She said, "This device was based on a similar premise, but it would send out shrapnel, specifically nails. We believe there's a good chance she made the device because die bitch was written across the page with a smiley face. We know the approximate size it needs to be, and we'll check everything, but it would help us if we had an idea."

Jace said, "What if it goes off while you're looking?"

"There's little chance of that."

"How do you know? What if she made different types?"

"It's possible but I doubt she'd leave something that could go off and hurt her."

"Maybe she wasn't planning on coming back? Maybe she hoped a bomb would kill the survivors?"

"She hadn't time that day. They must have been placed earlier. If the intent was to kill the kids, if she placed them anywhere except their room there was a chance she'd be hit too. We don't think it would be anywhere she might go, and since she was sent to get the kids and bring things to their rooms, it's more likely it's just in Kate's room or that it can't be set off by accident. Our techs went through Kate's room and searched it pretty thoroughly on the first visit. If there was a bomb in there that could be set off by moving things around, we'd have set it off."

She turned to me and said, "Don't touch anything, just look with your artist eyes."

My father said, "I still don't like this."

Dee said, "None of us like this. We'd like your wife and yourself to come down to the station and help us clear this all up."

Grayson said, "Call Martinson, Dad. This is getting out of hand."

I snorted.

He winced.

I said, "Gray, Everly is saying you and Dad are sexually abusing all of us."

He nodded like he wasn't surprised.

I said, "Why would she send the police back here if she intended me to open that can and blow myself up?"

"That's a good question," Dee said. "Maybe she's having second thoughts—or first ones even?"

I snorted with annoyed laughter.

Dee shrugged at me. "There's a good chance she doesn't actually want to kill anyone. She could have killed Harley or Hannah, and she didn't."

"Not from lack of trying," I said angrily.

"True, but even if you hadn't caught Hannah, she *might* have lived. I'm just saying, she had knives. She could've ensured her death."

Jace said, "But killing the kids isn't the point. Hurting Kate is. She wanted Kate to suffer. Part of the fun for her was flinging Hannah and having Kate be too late to save Harley, which she would've been even if she hadn't cracked her skull. Killing the kids was the bonus. I bet she sent you here just to make Kate scared in the house. The bonus is if you believe all the lies."

My father said, "Why does she hate you so much?"

Jace said angrily, "You have to be fucking kidding me! This isn't Kate's fault!"

I turned to hug him.

Dee said, "That's a good question."

I said, "I have no idea. She's always hated me. Honestly, I thought it was getting better between us until recently."

Jace said, "You mean me..."

"Not you exactly. She was ignoring me, and I was ignoring her. Then she started picking on the kids. Maybe if I hadn't butted in... but it got her angry at me again. Maybe she realized she wouldn't be able to keep the kids quiet about what she'd done much longer? As far as she knew, I was going away to school soon or more likely she thought I'd be kicked out for not going, but either way I'd be gone, and since that's the threat that was keeping them quiet..."

"What do you mean kicked out?" my father said.

I gaped at him.

Grayson said, "We all knew—or I guess I should say—we all believed that we have to go to college or get out."

"I've never once said that," he said indignantly.

Grayson said, "Mom says it all the time."

I said, "She says it in front of you, so don't pretend you don't know anything about it! Even you can't be that oblivious! I'm getting damned sick of you blaming her for everything that's going wrong here!"

"I've heard her say we won't support a lazy lay about, and I agree, but I've never heard her say it's college or you're out."

"Dad..." Grayson said.

I said, "Even Hannah and Harley know that's true. She has the twins terrified of getting bad grades. A terror Everly took full advantage of. Mom tells us stories about how awful it would be without your help, how we can't make it without a degree. They think it's a death sentence to be thrown out of the house. If gramps hadn't been telling us how he built his fortune after leaving home with nothing, I'd have been afraid to chase my dream too..."

"Kate, if you're not ready for college, that doesn't mean you have to leave home."

"I hate this house."

He looked stricken.

I *almost* felt bad.

Five men wearing black armored clothing and jackets that said bomb squad entered the room.

The other officer said, "Over here, guys."

Dee said, "Let's just take a quick walkthrough and then continue this at the station."

We walked through every room in the house, including the attic and garage.

Grayson insisted they search the treehouse.

I felt like a dummy for not thinking of it.

My father trailed us, making phone calls.

Back outside in the driveway, Dee said, "Is there anywhere you go that the kids never do?"

"The bathroom near my room. Everly and I share that one and she doesn't like them in her things, so they just stay out of it. I could give a crap if she doesn't like me using it, so I use it whenever I want to. She stopped complaining about it years ago, but the kids still don't go in it. The pump house for the pool is off limits for kids. I go in there once in a while if we lose a hair tie or something in the pool just to make sure it isn't clogging the filters up. The maintenance guys usually do the regular pool maintenance when they do the lawn. But if there's leaves or bugs or something in the pool, I'll go in for the pool vac or net."

"Does your mom or Everly go in?"

"I have no idea."

My father said, "How often do you use the pool?"

"It depends. Pretty often though."

Dee said, "Why do you ask?"

"I was just wondering why she didn't know if they use the pump room."

"We don't use it at the same time. The kiddos swim in their day camp. They go to that camp every weekday. The twins only go to the library Saturday and to their arts and crafts classes on Monday and Tuesday, so they swim at home. Before I realized there was a problem with Everly, I was only taking them if Mom and Everly were going out. Everly stayed with them days because she sleeps late and they're almost big enough to be alone. So I make breakfast for all of us and then drop off the kiddos, and Everly would be here for the twins. They know they're not allowed to swim without an adult, but she usually comes down by lunch. She takes them to the pool sometimes or at least I thought she was. Once I realized there was a problem, I stayed home to watch them, and we'd swim almost every day."

My father said, "You stopped working on your house?"

"There's always things I can do on my computer. I made stuff for the house here, tables, curtains, paintings, all sorts of things. I finished a bunch of my shows and got them posted. The kids come with me to check the prices and flea markets and stuff. And I could work on it while they were at their classes, not that I cared about falling behind. I know it will take me years to do. It's part of the plan."

"What about your mother?" he asked.

"What about her?"

"Where was she?"

"Working."

"Where?"

"What do you mean where? At the dealership."

"When did she leave for work?"

"Right after you."

"Every day?"

"Are you saying she wasn't going to work?"

"Of course she was," he said too heartily. "I just thought she came in later."

Dee said, "Interesting."

He flushed dark red.

Grayson said, "What difference does it make?"

She shrugged. "Maybe none. Maybe a lot. I guess it depends on what Everly got up to so unsupervised."

"She wasn't a child," my father said angrily. "She's seventeen for crying out loud. That's more than old enough to be alone or babysit two ten-year-olds."

"When your daughter told you there was a problem with Everly, what did you do?"

"Spoke with Alise. We both spoke with Everly. Everly seemed normal—and surprised. Maybe even amused. She said something like Kate was a worrywart and jealous that the kids liked her better now. Alise didn't think it was necessary to even speak with her. She thought Kate was jealous of them too."

"And what did you think?"

"That they were probably right. I spoke to the kids, and they *were* nervous. But I thought it was because they didn't want to hurt Kate's feelings or get her into trouble. I did ask them if there was a problem with Everly."

"Was Everly there when you asked?"

"No."

"What did they say?"

"That everything was fine."

"Did you believe them?"

"Not really, but I didn't think it was anything to worry about. I thought they were just worried about going to a new school. That they were growing up and were realizing that maybe Everly could be fun, and they felt bad about it. Every time I saw them together, Everly was smiling, sweet, being as nice as anyone could ask for. It wasn't like she was screaming at them or hitting them or anything."

I said, "We're they smiling and cheerful too?"

He flushed again.

Dee snorted softly.

"Kids are like that," he said defensively. "They get mad when they're asked to clean their rooms or get out of the pool. How was I supposed to know there was more too it?"

"I knew. Grayson knew."

He glowered at me a moment before smoothing his expression.

He said to Dee, "Our lawyer will be meeting us there at three. I assume we'll be informed if anything is found in the house?"

"I'm sure you will. Kate, if you can come to the station now, we can get your written statement out of the way."

Jace said, "I'm coming with her."

Dee shrugged. "You'll have to wait outside but suit yourself."

Grayson gave me a quick hug. "Hang in there, sweetheart. It has to be almost over. I'll met you at the station as your lawyer."

Dee 's eyes narrowed but she nodded.

My father said, "I really am sorry I let it come to this."

He stepped forward, hesitated, then gave me a quick hug too, which surprised me speechless.

"Mom and I will be there in a few minutes. If you want to wait for us..."

"It doesn't matter. I'd rather get it over with."

Dee said, "Shall we?"

Jace said, "I'll drive her."

We followed Dee to the station. Jace called his stepfather on the way there and filled him in. He listened for a few minutes and looked grim when he put his phone away.

"He's going to call me back. He said warrants are being issued but he's not sure for who. Dee seems friendly but she could be suckering you in. Be careful. Frank says she's one of the good ones, but that doesn't mean she'll be on your side. If she thinks you're lying..."

"I'm not though."

"They found an explosive device in the paint can and are now tearing the house apart. Frank says that device is going to bring in all kinds of people because whoever made it might have more."

"Whoever..."

"Exactly. They could think you did it."

"Why would I?"

"Because you make things."

"...I'm scared."

"Me too. Tell the truth. Leave your phone and the recorder with me. They'd need a warrant to take them that way."

His phone rang as we pulled into the police station.

He listened for a minute then hung up.

"They've got a warrant to search our house. That's not *necessarily* a bad thing. If there is anything there, we want it out of there."

"She doesn't know about our house."

He grinned at me.

I smiled back. It felt weird, forced even though it wasn't as if I'd had Novocain and couldn't really feel my face.

"We'll get through this, Kate."

I nodded.

"You better tell them we were sneaking out because Everly might have followed us. We have to remind them that she probably knew about the house if she sang that song to Harley or they're going to think anything found there is yours."

"This feels like a nightmare..."

"She's framing you—or trying to. And frankly, I'd rather have her be doing that than trying to murder you."

"I think she's doing both. I wonder if someone told her I wasn't planning to go back to my parents' house? Maybe that's why she sent the police?"

"You mean she figured if you weren't going to open that can then on to plan B? Yeah... although if you were going to hide something in a can, why not use one that was there already? Why buy a new one and a brand you don't use?"

"To make it obvious so the police could find it."

"Make sure you tell Dee that."

I said, "I will. You don't need to wait. I can get a ride with Grayson. I'd rather you went to *our* house to see what's going on there."

"Yeah, okay. But first I'm going to the store for those security cameras."

"They really better not let that bitch out!"

He hugged me for a long minute.

We were both afraid I was going to end up being the one they didn't let out.

TWENTY-TWO

Dee led me and Grayson directly to an interview room where she handed me a few sheets of paper.

"Write out what happened the day you hit your head. And then we can worry about today."

I told her what Jace and I had been talking about in the car.

"It's a valid theory. I get the feeling your mother isn't working the hours your father thinks she does. What's her schedule?"

"He leaves between seven and seven-thirty and she leaves ten minutes or so after him. She comes home at five. We eat dinner every night at six. She goes out some nights and stays in some nights."

"Where does she go?"

"Out with friends, school meetings, committee meetings, work. When she stays in, she likes to take a glass of wine and a book to the back porch. If it's a nice night, the kids will swim a bit but it's always bed by eight for them. They can read in bed if they want to."

"And you and Everly?"

"Can do what we want. We don't have a curfew or anything. I'm usually in by ten or eleven because I make breakfast for the kids.

"Mom takes off Mondays and Tuesdays from work and takes the kids to their classes. I have no idea where she goes after she drops them off. I assume shopping. Both of my parents usually take Sunday off."

"And your dad?"

"I have no idea. He comes home for dinner about three times a week. He sleeps late on weekends. Well, late for him anyway. He gets up around nine, nine-thirty. We're usually gone by then or heading out."

"And Everly?"

"She comes in around three in the morning and sleeps to noon at least and sometimes she's still in her pajamas for dinner."

"Where's she go?"

"Friends, parties, maybe bars. I've heard her talking about a place called The Den."

"I'm going to want a list of her friends' names."

"It's going to be a long list. She has about eight kids who are in the inner circle and fifty or more in the outer."

"An inner circle..." Dee said musingly.

"Yeah. The inner circle of Hell is what I used to call it. She's a grade behind me but she's the biggest bitch in the school. She's probably loved and hated about equally..."

Dee laughed. "I can imagine. What about you?"

"Neither loved nor hated. Everyone was afraid to talk to me because doing so made them a target for her insults. Our school was grades six through twelve. The younger kids were supposed to stay on their side, but she isn't one to let a rule stop her. I had one blissful year..."

"How'd you meet Jace?"

"He works for my dad at the shops there. I work in the shops on my woodworking projects sometimes and use the other tools. I've had a crush for over a year. We only just recently got together. I was sneaking out a few nights a week to see him because I couldn't leave the kids during the day to see him."

"Where did you two meet up?"

"Sometimes there at the shop, sometimes my house. Sometimes we'd just walk."

"Are the two of you... intimate?"

"That's none of your business."

"I only ask because you mentioned a birth control implant."

"Still not your business. Lots of women get that implant to help with their periods."

"How would you say your parents' marriage was?"

"Stupid."

She snorted with laughter.

Grayson patted my hand.

"Do they get along?" Dee asked.

"Yes."

I debated mentioning I thought my dad was having an affair, but since I wasn't a hundred percent certain and it made no difference, except to my mom, I didn't say anything.

"Do you like your mom?"

"I never really thought about it. I love her but I'm not sure if I like her."

"And him?"

"I don't know. He has a lot of good qualities. It's his parenting skills that are lacking. The kids don't seem to notice, so maybe that's just me. I tell myself I don't care about him, but that can't really be true if he can still hurt my feelings like he does. We get along fine because we never see each other."

"Do you get along with your mother?"

"Mostly. We had a fight the other day. Usually I just ignore people who annoy me because arguing gets me nowhere and makes them think they won or at least that's how Everly gets. She smirks and gloats when she gets me to yell at her because then Mom yells at me. If I yell back, I get sent to my room and she'd take my books and paints and if she was really mad, she'd take everything."

"Everything, everything?"

"She hasn't done that in a long time but when I was about seven, she emptied my room and kept me in there a week. It was the worst longest week of my life, so I learned to keep my mouth shut and not argue. It's easier to just let her yell."

"What sort of things does she yell about?"

"Not much actually. I don't want you to get the wrong idea. She doesn't go around screaming at us. Just once in a while Everly will start picking a fight. Sometimes she just yells for no reason and at no one in particular, but Mom always blames me like I'm the one making Everly lose her shit. So she'll yell why can't we get along and lecture me on how crap my life would be if she kicked me out. That it was my fault, and I was so stupid. I always thought she did it because it would make Everly smirk, which meant she stopped yelling."

"What set Everly off?"

"It could be anything. Her soda was too cold, too warm, someone drank some. She didn't have any clothes to wear, they'd been washed wrong, were stained by our grubby hands, weren't ironed because she had to watch the stupid kids. One of her biggest triggers was homework. She never did it, but she'd rant about it, blaming all of us for not having the time, or accusing us of taking it. My mom would blame me for not helping her do it or not watching the kids and letting them ruin it. It pissed me off so much..."

"You never told your dad?"

"He was there. He'd just leave…"

"What a shit…"

I nodded. "I started leaving too as soon as she kicked off. It was really tough there for a while because she'd get the kiddos screaming too. I'd take the twins with me. It became a sort of funny thing. We'd hear her yell where's my damned shoes or something and we'd all run to the door laughing, which in hindsight—my poor mother. She'd have the kiddos *and* Everly to deal with."

"Did she ever punish them?"

"Sure. She'd send us to our rooms or make us do dishes or other chores. She never beat us or anything. But by the age of thirteen, Everly just wouldn't do it. She wouldn't do any chores at all. The only thing she'd do was go to her room. She spent most of her time in there. By fifteen she spent most of her time out with friends."

Dee said, "I'll leave you to write your statement. Write down what happened as you remember it. Want a soda or anything?"

"No. I'm good."

I picked up the pen to write my name and couldn't do it. The pen shot off the page.

I must have exclaimed or something because Dee turned back at the door, saying, "Problems?"

I began to shake, which sent a shaky line across the page.

"Something's wrong with me. Really wrong."

"Kate?" Grayson asked worriedly.

I tried again and managed a crooked K.

I began to cry and couldn't stop. I didn't hear him or anyone and didn't realize I was scratching up the paper until a man lightly slapped my cheek.

"Kate! Look at me, Kate!" Dee said urgently.

"I can't do it! I can't do it!"

"Take a breath, honey. Someone give her a water." Dee crouched beside me to hand me a water bottle. "We have an ambulance coming. How's the head?"

"I can't write my fucking name!"

"Calm down before you burst a blood vessel or something." She wiped my face with a wet paper towel then handed me a wad of them.

I began to cry again.

Grayson hugged me, saying, "It's going to be fine or words to that affect, but I couldn't hear him really over my internal screaming that I couldn't write my own name.

The first man left and two new ones came into the room.

Dee said, "The medic wants to know if your feet or hands are numb or tingling."

"I can't write my name. I can't write! How am I going to draw if I can't write!"

The next thing I knew Barbara was leaning over me.

"I didn't want to see you again," she said.

Jace said, "Kate, you're scaring me to death."

He reached past her to take my traitorous hand.

"How can it feel so normal and not work? How! Why didn't they tell me it wouldn't work! I can't not write, Jace. I can't!"

"Calm down, sweetheart."

"I can't!"

Grayson said, "I called our parents. Please calm down, Kate, before you give yourself a stroke or something."

Barbara said, "I'm putting an IV in. I'm no doctor, but I do know it can take time to recover from a head injury. Your hands work, you can learn it again if you have to, but you might get better all on its own once the swelling goes down."

"They aren't swollen. They just don't work! What am I going to do?"

I started crying again.

My parents showed up at the hospital as I was being wheeled in for a CT scan.

Dr. Kennedy was with them when I was brought back.

He said to me, "I'm going to keep you here overnight for observation. I know this is scary, Kate, but I don't want you to panic. There's a good chance you'll be perfectly fine or have only mild impairment once the swelling in your head goes down. The nurse is going to give you a little something to relax you. Your father has told me you've had a really stressful day. I know you have a lot going on, but you can't get yourself all worked up. No more stressful days!"

"Tell that to my psycho sister!"

My father said, "Will she be able to paint again?"

Jace yelled, "Are you fucking retarded! Didn't you just hear him say no stress!"

He was so angry I thought he was going to punch him. I hoped he would. It was all my father's damned fault that Everly was so out of control.

"What do you care if I can or not! Just get out!"

My mother said, "Kate, darling, that's—"

"You too! Just leave me the hell alone! Get out! Get out!"

Kennedy said, "It would be best to let her rest. She'll be calmer in the morning."

His voice faded as he led them away.

Jace sat by the bed.

Neither of us said a word as the nurse puttered around, injecting my IV with something, taking my blood pressure, checking my eyes.

She said, "You have a slight fever, dear. I'm sure the doctor will prescribe something. I'll be right back. Can I bring you dinner or a snack or anything."

I shook my head. If I opened my mouth, I was going to start screaming again.

She *always* fucking won. She'd done worse than murder me. It was time I started fighting back. I had no idea how to though.

I cried myself to sleep.

When I woke up in the morning, my father was sitting by my bed.

"How do you feel?"

"How do you think I feel?" I asked bitterly.

"Your fever is up."

I shrugged.

"I'm really worried about you, Kate."

"Sorry to inconvenience you."

"I deserved that but I'm not going to let you use your energy fighting me."

"Just get out."

"I will but first hear me out. I want us to have a real relationship, which I know is asking a lot. You feel like you've lost everything, and I feel like I've gotten a second chance. When I saw you laying there on the floor at home—I thought you were dying. I've never been more terrified or sorry in my life. I can't tell you how grateful I was to find Harley alive and how horrified I was over his condition. I was even more horrified because I couldn't go back for you because I had to cut him free to be sure he wasn't stabbed, and then when he was free, I had to find the twins and all of that time I thought I'd left you to die alone. I swear on my soul, on your soul, it was the hardest most horrible thing I've ever done. But it made me realize how much I'd missed.

"Over the next few days, I realized I didn't know you and that it was my fault. We're strangers to each other and I don't even know how that happened. I thought I was being a good parent, absent a lot, but good, but I wasn't a parent at all... it's—my life is a fucking mess, but I swear to you that I *want* to be a good parent. Give us a chance, Kate."

"I'm not sure I want to."

"If I were you, I wouldn't want too either. I don't expect you to... do anything at all. I'd like you not to shut me out though. We can talk and get to know each other and maybe someday you'd want to."

"What do you imagine we have to talk about?"

He winced.

Dr. Kennedy and a nurse entered.

He said, "Kate, we want another CT scan and some more blood work. It's nothing to be alarmed about. I don't love your fever. What I think you need is a day of rest. So, I'm keeping you here another night. I'm sure your dad can bring you some clothes and anything else you need."

"Like what? I can't draw or read or anything. I have nothing..."

"You can't read?"

"It hurts my head, and the words are all blurry."

"Then don't try. Give your eyes a rest too."

My father said, "How's her blood pressure?"

"A bit high but we'll soon have it sorted."

"Can she have visitors? The kids will want to see her."

"I'm not sure that's a good idea. If they get upset and upset her... now we could use some privacy for my tests. We're doing the same ones we did before, Kate. I'm also going to have you walk some straight lines and try some stretches. Let see if we can work up a good appetite for lunch."

"She hasn't had breakfast."

"If the CT looks good, we'll feed her before my test. If not, we want an MRI, and the dyes are easier on an empty stomach.

My father said, "Your mom wanted to see you. So I'll go get you a change of clothes and she can drop it off. I'll be back later though."

He surprised me by kissing my forehead.

"I love you, Kate."

Tears burned my eyes.

I *hated* that I gave a shit.

Jace arrived as they were pumping dye into me.

"Not so good, *huh*?"

"They don't say much but my guess is it's not good seeing as they ordered a bunch more tests and I still can't read or write."

"Reading too... I'll be the smart one now."

"Ha!"

He kissed my cheek then rested his on mine because I was attached to too many wires to hug.

We didn't separate until the nurse said, "We're ready to go now, dearie."

He said, "I'll be here when you get back."

"You don't need to wait. I'm sure you have better things to do with your time."

"I love you so much, Kate."

"It's your superpower."

"I hope so."

TWENTY-THREE

When I returned to my room, Jace was gone, and my mother was waiting.

Before I could ask, she said, "I asked him to give us a minute. Besides, he has things to do. He's much too old for you, Kate. He has a real job—a job he's going to lose if he doesn't go in."

The nurse bustled about doing her checks, tucking me in.

I said, "Then his boss is an ass. And since *you're* his boss..."

The nurse turned, pursing her lips at my mother. She turned away quickly, but it was clear she thought my mom was an ass too.

Two small red patches appeared on my mother's cheeks and her eyes narrowed a tiny bit. A hint of a malicious smile played on her lips as she said, "It'd be best to keep that in mind."

I shrugged, saying, "You're going to do whatever you're going to do. Speaking of that, who's my father?"

"Now isn't the time, Kate."

The nurse said, "I'll be back shortly with your meal. The doctor will be by with your test results."

She hurried away.

"Stop playing around, Mom. Who is it?"

"I have no idea."

"What the hell does that mean?"

"It means I was working late one night when the store was robbed. The man raped me and nine months later you were born. I was too ashamed to tell anyone, so I lied, said I wanted more kids. I lied to myself too. I should never have had that baby, but he'd never have forgiven me. How could I..."

She glared at me.

"This is all your fault!"

181

"Me? What did I ever do?"

"You always screw everything up! Always!"

"You know that's bullshit."

She glanced at the door then leaned closer to almost whisper, "I've had about all I can take of you. He should be arrested! I should've said something right then! But I let him get away with it! I bet you made that bomb! I should tell. You're so stupid. It's such a stupid slutty thing to do. You're going to ruin your life! But you deserve it, don't you! All those lies! All those lies!"

I was too shocked to be angry.

"I never lied."

"Who do you think they'll believe? Not that it matters. You know what you are. I hate you so much!"

I gaped at her astounded, shocked she felt that way. I knew we had our issues, but I'd thought she loved me.

She said thoughtfully like she was thinking about it, not like she was angry, "Make yourself useful and you can stay. Keep being a pain and you can go and good riddance."

"I'm sorry a bad thing happened to you, but it wasn't my fault!"

She slapped me hard enough to make my ears ring. My head thunked the plastic headboard.

"A bad thing! How fucking dare you! You're ruining my life and say it's a bad thing! I hate you! You don't deserve—"

She lifted her hand to slap me again and the doctor walked in.

He was looking down at a folder in his hand.

She stepped back, clenching her hands the anger draining from her face, leaving her looking embarrassed and surprised as if she'd forgotten where we were. She looked really worried when she turned back to me.

"Kate!" she said as if surprised to see me there.

Kennedy said, "We're seeing a bit more swelling than we'd like—what happened to your face."

"My mother slapped me."

Her eyes narrowed and lips pursed.

Kennedy's opened in shock.

"She what!"

My mother said indignantly, "I did not!"

She stomped out.

"What happened?"

"Apparently I'm ruining her life, so she's going to ruin mine."

He pulled a little flashlight from his pocket and shone it into my eyes.

"That hurts," I said. "I feel sick."

"Sick, sick? Like you're going to vomit?"

"Yes. The room is spinning. Maybe I'm having a panic attack..."

He reached over and pressed the buzzer to call the nurse.

"How bad is the headache?" he asked grimly.

"About an eight."

"I think you have another little bleed in there that needs to be stopped."

"Another one... am I ever going to be able to draw again? Will I go blind?"

"Is the room getting blurry, Kate?"

I nodded.

"I can help. Don't panic. Take nice slow breaths."

He ran into the hall, yelling for a nurse to call his operating staff and get a theater ready.

I lay there in shock unable to really process that my mother hated me. *My house,* I suddenly thought. *If I wasn't his real granddaughter, maybe I had no right to that money...*

If she hated me so much, she'd never give me my college fund. How would I pay Grayson back?

The nurse ran into the room to turn off the shrilling monitors.

Jace returned as they were changing the bag of my IV.

"What's going on? What happened to your face?"

I kept my eyes closed because the haloes and shadows on everything were terrifying.

Kennedy said, "Her mother hit her and she's going into surgery now."

I said, "She said she'd get you fired and arrested. I'm so sorry, Jace. She said it was me who made that stupid bomb. I bet it was her..."

"Why the hell?"

"She said she was raped, and she hates me."

"Oh, Kate... sweetheart."

He took my hand and the world faded to black.

My father and Jace were there with a man I didn't know when I woke. Jace said, "Can you hear me?"

"Yes. Am I losing my hearing too?"

"You're not losing anything!"

Kennedy entered followed by a new nurse.

"Everyone out while I examine my patient."

They left and he performed his familiar exams.

When he was done, he sat beside the bed and took my hand.

"I'm not going to sugarcoat this, Kate. You need to stay calm and give yourself time to heal. I think you'll recover just fine—except you're an artist and that might take a bit of work to get back. Your reflexes are good. Your hands work. The muscle memory is impaired. You can retrain it. Once the swelling goes down, which is going to take a few weeks, we'll talk about therapy, but I promise you'll paint again if you're careful now. No more injuries! We're going to do the same thing we did before, keeping you nice and still for a day and gradually working up to walking around, but this time we're keeping you an extra day. If you're headache gets worse or your vision blurs or you start to get clumsy or anything feels off, you're going to call for the nurse right away."

"Will I die?"

"My patients don't die!"

"Will I?"

"Not if I have anything to say about it. Try not to worry. I know you have a lot going on, but you can't afford to worry now. Besides, as I understand it, your mother is having a mental issue, so there's nothing you could do anyway when she isn't able to really talk with you. Stress manifests itself in lots of ways, Kate. She'll probably be horrified later that she took her frustration out on you."

"Can you make sure she can't come back, at least for a few days."

"Yes. I can keep your father out too if necessary?"

"No. I want to know what's going on. What *is* going on?"

"That I don't know. The police asked to be notified when you're up to a visit by them. I'm keeping them out this time for at least twenty-four hours. What I want you to do is have a nice calm visit with your young man. No strenuous anything, fighting, kissing, laughing. In an hour or so the nurse will be in with a little something to keep you nice and calm, but we want you awake for a while, so talking is good."

"What are my chances of dying of this. Fifty-fifty? Eighty-twenty?"

"Anyone can drop dead, Kate. You can't dwell on it. If you follow my advice, you'll be fine. A hundred percent chance of being just fine."

"Is Everly here?"

"She's in the psychiatric facility. I'm not sure for how much longer. I expect she'll be transferred out soon. Your father will know."

"Is her kind of crazy hereditary?"

"Yes, but you don't have it."

"How do you know?"

"Because crazy people aren't calm like this when they're scared. They lash out."

Tears burned my eyes.

"I think my mom might be crazy."

"I think so too, but there's medicine and treatment that can help her. She's obviously highly functioning, so I think her prognosis would be good. And maybe I'm wrong and she's fine. I didn't examine her or anything. Just don't give up hope and be ready with forgiveness. Because sometime a little forgiveness and love is the best medicine."

"Everything is falling apart."

"Just hold on, Kate." He released me to pat my hand.

"I'll be back in a few hours. Hit that button if you need us."

"Thank you."

He left and Jace and my father entered five minutes later.

I said, "What did Mom say."

My father sat heavily, heaving a hard sigh.

Jace leaned over to kiss me, taking my hand, and kissing that as he closed it around the little recorder.

He said, "She said she'd confronted you about your bad behavior and you tried to hit her, so she slapped you but that she hadn't meant to hit you that hard."

"Well, it's at least partially true."

Jace smiled grimly. "I downloaded the recorder to my cloud account then gave it to Detective Sandy."

I sagged in relief that he'd left one going.

My father said, "What recorder?"

We both ignored him.

I said, "Did you listen to it?"

"Yeah."

"I feel like a jinx. First Everly and now her… unless… you think she puts Everly up to all this crap?"

"Who knows?"

My father said, "I have good news. You *are* my biological daughter."

I gaped at him.

A shivery feeling like hot tingles swept my entire body. I didn't know whether to laugh or cry. The machines hooked to me all began to beep and buzz.

My first thought was, *thank god, my house,* which I knew made me a horrible selfish person. My second was maybe he does love me if he's glad. My third was maybe he's just glad because it wasn't as embarrassing for him.

The nurse ran in, giving them angry glances as she flipped switches.

She said, "I don't know what's going on in here, but knock it off or I'm going to have to ask you to leave! She could use the company to keep her awake or I'd kick you out right now!"

I said, "Can I get a drink?"

"I'll be back in a minute with some ice."

She glared at them another moment before marching out.

He said, "Sorry, I didn't think... I'm thrilled, but I see you're upset..."

Jace said, "You can talk about all of that in a few days."

The machines beeped again.

"Sorry," I said to the nurse when she ran back in with her ice.

"They're being good. My life is just upsetting is all. While she's here just tell me what the test said."

My father said, "Hannah isn't mine. I'm petitioning the court to test your mother to make sure she's hers."

"What do you mean?"

"I never saw your mother during that pregnancy. She was sick and said it was high risk. We were fighting...For the last month or so she was in a private clinic. One she'd picked. One I can't find a record for."

"You never went to see her?"

"We all did but it isn't there now. Don't you remember?"

My memories of my mother when she was pregnant were all of her sleeping. She'd been bedridden with the twins. I wasn't surprised when she was with Hannah too.

"Not really. I remember being mad—and tired. I loved Hannah though when she came home. She was so perfect...she's still so perfect. What about Harley?"

"He's mine."

Jace murmured, "Stop worrying her." Then firmly to me, "Stop worrying, Kate."

I said, "What will we do for Hannah?"

My father said, "Ask Alise and see what she says. The police will run Hannah's DNA through their database if Alise isn't a genetic match."

"This can't be happening..."

The nurse said, "Any other bombshells you'd like to drop on my very fragile patient?"

Jace said firmly, "No. She'd have worried more if we hadn't told her though."

She sniffed and stomped out.

Jace said, "The man with me in the hall earlier was my stepfather. He wanted to meet you. My mom sends her best wishes. She's dying to meet you. I showed her your poor ruined painting and she cried... I wish... but let's not talk about that except to say Crystal loves her painting and so does Evan. They send their love."

"I hope he still likes me now that I can't do tricks with him..."

"Please don't worry about that now."

"Tricks?" my father asked.

"Not now," Jace said firmly. "My friend Dan will be in town next week. I was hoping you'd come fishing with us? I sent him a few pictures of our house and he had a good idea. What if we put a back entrance in to go to the carriage house? If we put a tiny parking lot behind the carriage house, we could connect that with the road behind there and maybe put up another gate? Then we put some hedges in and you won't even see it. That way my customers won't bother yours and it could be used for the wedding guest parking."

"Okay."

It made me feel sick to think I'd cost him his job too.

His eyes filled with tears.

"You're killing me..."

"I'm sorry. My head hurts so much... I really can't concentrate now. It *does* sound like a good idea. I can't wait to meet Dan. Is he still in... I have no idea what branch he was in..."

He told me about Dan and the rest of his friends.

I listened with my eyes closed.

My father held my hand, which hurt in a way I didn't have words for. I *wanted* to believe he and I could find each other—really find each other, but it didn't seem possible that he'd really want to. I thought he was maybe acting like he thought a father should act. I really wanted him to be that father, so I held his hand back, but I kept the recorder Jace had slipped me in my other hand—just in case.

TWENTY-FOUR

The doctor didn't let me sit up or have any other visitors for two days. So I was really surprised when my mother came in the morning of the third day.

I hit my little recorder.

She said, "It won't work, you know."

"What won't?"

"You won't get the money from his father. I've already spoken to Grayson. He'll sell it. And don't go thinking they'll take you in either. You'll be out on the street—exactly like a girl like you deserves."

"I'm so sorry you're hurting so much."

"No one cares about you, Alise."

A cold sweat broke out all over me.

She continued, "You think you can fool this boy? He'll see right through you eventually. You'll never be good enough for him, not really. The best thing to do is..."

The monitor attached to me began to beep.

She stopped talking, looking confused and then angry.

"What have you done to yourself now, Kate? I swear you're more trouble than ten kids!"

"What's the best thing to do?"

"I better go check the kiddos. Feel better."

She walked out.

I called Grayson.

"Mom was here talking crazy. Don't you dare leave her with the kids!"

"She was there?"

"I just said so, didn't I!"

"Are you okay?"

"She's sick, Gray. She called me Alise."

"We know. She's off her meds. She'll be better soon."

"You know!"

I was more than astounded. I was furiously astounded.

"We just found out," Grayson said.

"We? Did Dad know?"

"He says not."

"Do you believe that?"

"I'm not sure. I'm coming to see you after work. We can talk then. Don't get all worked about any of this."

"Ha!"

"I know…"

He sounded anguished, which made me realize I was being selfish. This was happening to him too.

I said, "Find me a good lawyer. A criminal lawyer. And we need to talk about the money."

"Don't worry about the stupid money! If you need money, then I can wait for the damn payments! I'd feel like a complete shit taking money from you now, Kate!"

"Don't be ridiculous. I don't expect you to buy me a house! Gramps bought it for me. He'd be so happy I was there."

"I know. You were always his favorite. I used to be jealous, now I'm so glad you had him."

It occurred to me that grandma hadn't even called.

I said, "Is grandma okay?"

"She's angry. She just found out what was going on."

"No one called her?"

"I thought Dad would've."

"Why didn't he?"

"He told her he was waiting to see what the doctors said, but I think he was waiting to be sure the state wasn't going to take the kids. She'd cut him off for sure if they did."

That cold shivery feeling swept me again.

"Does he love us, Gray?"

"That you have to ask…"

"…. Yeah."

He said firmly, but I knew it was the firmness of he *wanted* to believe, "I think he does, in his own way."

"Whatever."

Jace stopped in the doorway. He'd brought me roses and smiled uncertainly.

Grayson said, "I'm so sorry. *I* love you, Kate."

"I know. I don't have to ask... I love you too."

"I don't have to ask either. See you soon."

"Give the kids hugs for me."

"I will."

"Grayson?" Jake asked when I set the phone down.

I nodded.

He put the roses into a water jug and set it beside my bed.

"Thanks. They're beautiful."

"How's the head?"

"It has holes in it, and it freaks me out when I think my brain could fall out. How's yours?"

He winced, leaning down to kiss me.

He sat beside the bed, keeping my hand.

"My stepfather said the police will be by today. They know of the connection between us and him now so are keeping him out of the loop, but he thinks they're not going after you. Your mom got caught in some huge whoppers."

"She was here today."

"They let her in here!"

"She looks normal. Why would anyone stop her? She didn't do anything, except talk. She called me Alise, which is creepy as shit. I don't think it's personal, Jace. I think she just thinks I'm her sometimes and she hates herself."

"That's—disturbing."

"It sure as shit is. Grayson said she'll get better; that she was off her meds."

"They knew!"

His indignation made me feel better.

I relaxed against my pillows, closing my eyes.

"*He* didn't. Who knows if my dad did? Grayson said my grandmother just found out about all this and she's pissed."

"I certainly am!" my grandmother said angrily.

Jace and I both started nervously.

"Who is this?" she demanded.

Jace said, "Jace Blake, her fiancé."

I gaped at him.

She huffed.

"That's ridiculous. You're just a child."

"True. But I will be her fiancé in a few years and then her husband."

My grandmother said sneeringly, "Alise was like just like that. Had men devoted to her…" She grimaced apologetically, saying briskly with relief, "But you're nothing like your mother, thank God. What do you have to say about this engagement, Kate?"

She brushed passed Jace to kiss my cheek. Her eyes were worried behind the anger as she gently smoothed my dirty hair.

"I love him. I hope he really asks me one day."

Jace said, "I'm asking Thursday."

She said thoughtfully, "Thursday—her birthday… how old are you?"

"Twenty-two. I can take care of her though."

"What do you do for a living, Mr. Blake?"

I said, "He's a mechanic. He can make anything."

To my surprise a smile flit across her face.

"Your grandfather could make anything too. He was a mechanic when we met. Did you know that?"

"No."

She nodded. "He'd left home, which was brave or foolish depending on how you look at it. His family was very well to do. But he didn't like the life they'd planned for him, so he walked out with the shirt on his back and a few bucks in his pocket. He spent a year being a tramp, seeing the world. Then he found a job at a little garage. I think that might have been the happiest time in his life… we met and despite his prospects, I fell head over heels. I probably wouldn't have married him though if he hadn't made a fortune on the part he patented. I could see he'd do great things and I was right."

Jace said dryly, "I'm unlikely to make a fortune."

I said, "We don't *need* a fortune. We'll have that great house and a great life together."

My grandmother huffed.

She said, "Grayson told me you spent your inheritance on that wreck. Romantic claptrap… he had the *damndest* notions! I maybe should've let him have that house… but I was so angry."

Jace said, "We haven't told her."

"Told me what?" I asked.

She instantly looked furious, giving Jace her haughtiest cold glance, the one I'd seen very rarely when someone had insulted her to her face.

She released my hand to pull a chair closer then sat, folding her hands in her lap, glaring down at them as she said, "Kenya is my stepdaughter. Your mother had an affair with my husband."

"What!"

"I found out when Kenya was about four. The guilt got too much for him. He was going to tell your father. I wish now I hadn't dissuaded him... except if I had, the rest of you would never have been born."

"Why..."

"Why? God only knows. I should've kicked him out. I should've warned my son. I should've done a million things differently. I'd never really approved of Alise, but she'd grown on me as she lost her trashy ways—or pretended to. She stopped dressing like a slut and was a good mother. I confronted her, of course, and she was so sorry. They blamed each other, and I believed both of them. He *had* begun to drink heavily. And she *had* been a horrible flirt. It was entirely possible that he'd gotten drunk and forced her, but she'd put herself into that position with her revealing clothing, always flirting, always... trashy.

"Your father would've been beyond devastated. He adored Alise— was obsessed with her. He never saw her flaws just her beauty. He was happy and grew happier when his father gave him the dealership. Your grandfather signed the entire thing over.

"I had a bit of a rough time of it. It was a bit much having his bastard running around. It was easier when there were more of you and he could spread his attention around. Then as you grew, you looked just like her. At first, I was jealous of how much he loved you, but then I realized you were a love he could indulge without betraying me or himself. I grew to love Kenya for herself. After he died, I was glad of her. She was a secret piece of him who I could love and who loved me back without guilt, which had been a growing issue with us."

"Gram..."

She patted my hand.

"None of it was your fault, dear. I saw that you were having some problems at home that I attributed to Alise being jealous of you. She was always staring, always finding excuses to visit. She didn't flirt, and he ignored her as much as he could, but she'd follow the two of you sometimes. I thought at first that she was worried for you, but she followed *him*, would sit outside our house and just stare. And she'd begun yelling at you, calling you the names I'd called her.

"I hoped that after he'd passed, she'd stop being so... herself. She began following your father like she'd done my husband. I'd see her at the dealership on her days off just sitting in her car staring at his office. His eyes would light up when she came in and they'd giggle and run into the office and close the door. The two of them acted like teenagers. She was utterly besotted or so I thought.

"I had no idea Everly was suffering with her mother's sickness. When I heard about Hannah, I was genuinely shocked. I'd have bet my life that Alise was as obsessed with Brent as he was with her. When they married, I never once saw her flirt with my husband again. She just stared... Of course, the damage as they say, was done by then..."

"My father thinks she might have stolen Hannah."

"What! From who?"

"I have no idea."

Jace said, "Not stole—bought."

I said, "How did you find out about Kenya?"

"He told me. Alise wanted him to divorce me and marry her, and when he said he'd never do that, she seduced your father, my son, and claimed the baby was his. He married her. He was *thrilled* to marry her! To be fair, she was a good mother and she worked hard to build that dealership up. They made a success of it. I sometimes wish your grandfather had never told me, but then I think how much worse it would be to find out now. We fought—it hurt, God it hurt. But I also saw how much he loved me; how sorry he was. And we both loved you all so much...but now my son is suffering, really suffering, and I don't think he and Alise have the sort of love that can get past this because she has no depth. She's a shell of a person, and for that I hate myself because I saw it. What kind of a mother let's her son marry a shell of a woman?"

"How could you have stopped him?"

She huffed.

"I love my son, dear, but he'd have buckled if I told him we'd withhold his inheritance—she'd have run off forthwith."

Jace said, "Good lord—his daughter is really his sister!"

She grimaced, nodding.

"I'll see to Kenya in my will, but she won't be treated as my husband's daughter but my granddaughter because that's what she *is*."

"Does Kenya know?" I asked.

"Yes. She's angry at me, as well she should be, but I'm sure she'll come around in time."

Jace said, "Did Alise know you knew?"

"Oh yes. We fought about it frequently when I first learned. I told her I'd cut them out of the will completely if my son learned of it. Your grandfather had signed everything over to me, which everyone knew although no one but us knew why he had. Guilt was eating him up. She tried to talk your grandfather into leaving me again, said the money didn't matter, which we all knew was a lie, but he said no—emphatically. He told her he loved being a grandfather and we could be a happy family."

She grimaced as she said, "I think that's why your mother decided to have more children. Your grandfather spoiled her when she was pregnant and went around to the house often to see the babies. I loved the man dearly, but he could be *so* oblivious. He'd begun to think it was all water under the bridge. I think he almost convinced himself it hadn't happened, after all it *had* been ten years. He never seemed to notice her obsession, but perhaps I'm fooling myself..."

I wondered if my grandfather and mother had carried on their affair all that time—*maybe I'd just been an excuse for him to visit.*

I didn't remember anything odd, no lingering glances or whispers, no sneaking away or quick touches, but I hadn't been paying attention to them. My nose had always been deep in a sketch book.

The reminder felt like a slap.

She said, "Your mother is a whore and a liar who did what she did to get her hands on the family money. I hope my son has the sense to leave her now."

"He was lying too. This isn't all my mom's fault! He was having an affair with a woman down the street from my house. Someone he works with."

The machines began to beep and buzz.

"Oh dear," my grandmother said ruefully. "Are you certain?"

"Ninety percent."

Jace said, "Should I get the nurse?" But the machines were already settling down again.

"Then you shouldn't say such things!" She stood to kiss my cheek. "I'm sorry I'm upsetting you. I should go and let you rest. I want you to stay with me when you're released."

"I'm not sure what I'm doing. The kids..."

"I'm keeping all of the children with me. The granddaughter of one of my friends from a good family is with them now. If she works out, she's agreed to be a full-time nanny. Your father and I are discussing options. Grayson mentioned that Wolfgang and Felicity had expressed interest in attending a boarding school, which might be an ideal solution for the next year."

"I don't want them to think we don't want them. They can stay with me."

"What does your young man think of that?"

"We haven't talked about it," I said as Jace said, "He thinks they're family and that we should take care of our families."

She said, "Your father and I will discuss the options."

She kissed my cheek again. Jace escorted her out.

When he returned, he said, "She's... intense. Do you think your grandfather and mother continued their affair?"

"I was just thinking that."

He took my hand, slipping a ring on my finger then closing my hand while I gaped at him.

"I'm not asking. I'm begging you. I know it's a risk for me but it's a bigger one for you to be at your family's mercy. As your fiancé, I can get access to your room here. If your dad tries something shady like having you committed or ordering no visitors for you or something, I might be able to get you out if people know we're engaged."

"I'm...conflicted. I appreciate the gesture, but I hate it too."

"Me too. I don't want you to feel pressured."

"What *do* you want?"

"Our life in our house with the garage and a small fun hotel or maybe no hotel and just a wife who paints on the back porch and makes windows and beautiful furniture, and two kids of our own in about ten years. I'd thought we could take our time, live together there until we were both sure we were both sure, and then have a garden wedding when the house was done—the very first event at Briarwood."

"And if I can never paint again?"

"You will, Kate! You will!"

TWENTY-FIVE

My lawyer, Dwayne Getty, arrived with Grayson right after lunch. I'd met him before. He was Grayson's best friend since college.

Grayson kissed my cheek.

"I can't stay, Kate. I have to be in court for a client. Dwayne is a really good lawyer. You can trust him. Grandma is paying him, so you don't need to worry about that."

He tucked a pen into Dwayne's top pocket, then straightened his tie, saying, "And we're getting a good deal, right?"

Dwayne batted his hand away, loosening his tie with his other hand. "Beat it, dork. You'll pay cause I'm worth it."

They exchanged a quick guy hug. Grayson shook Jace's hand and left.

Dwayne said, "Our meetings should be confidential, Kate."

"Jace is my fiancé."

Jace beamed at me.

It made my chest feel hot.

Dwayne said, "I'm *your* lawyer, so what you say goes. If you want him present, he can stay, but client confidentiality doesn't extend to him. He could be subpoenaed and asked about this meeting."

"What if you were his lawyer too?"

"Being his lawyer as well will limit me. I'd be bound to protect him."

I said, "That's fine with me. I want you to protect him."

Jace nodded.

Dwayne shook his head. "In the same token, it would limit my defense of him."

"Can't you defend us both?"

"Unfortunately, that isn't quite how the law works. I'm not saying it's fair or right but if I can convince a jury of reasonable doubt by casting aspersions on someone else, planting a reasonable seed of doubt is my job. The seed doesn't need to grow into a full-blown tree. It could be enough for me to allude—to say that it's possible that Everly and Jace had an affair and that he agreed to retrieve nails and wood from your house for her to use. I don't have to prove that just prove that it was possible. I couldn't say anything like that if he was my client unless I knew it was true."

Jace said, "I'll come back later, Kate. Talk things over and then we can talk. I want you to do what's best for you."

"I'm not throwing you—or anyone else—under the bus to save myself."

"Just talk to him and really listen. We can talk later when we know what we're talking about."

He kissed my cheek and left the room.

"I'm not framing Jace or anyone else."

"I'm not advising you to. I was simply making a point."

"Will I be arrested for that bomb or the kids?"

"The kids—no. The bomb, maybe. It's a long shot for the DA. The evidence is circumstantial. The motive is solid if they can prove that you had it in for her *before* she tried to kill the kids—or they have to prove you have an accomplice."

"Jace," I said in dismay.

"Exactly. It might be smart for me to represent you both, but we should talk over your options first."

"Why do they think I did it?"

"I'm not certain they do. I'm not certain if your prints will be found on the device, but I have a hunch they will be."

"I swear I didn't put it there!"

"I believe you. I think it was meant to be found, which means it was prepared. You work with all of those materials as a regular thing. Your computer has the plans, granted not for that exact device but the base—the premise of that device, is something you have plans for. The changes are well within your skill set. Everly, on the other hand, has no such skill. I'm not saying she isn't smart enough to read your notes and figure it out.

I'm just saying a jury would be shown her grades and then yours. You have access to the machines—"

"So does she!"

"But it wouldn't arouse anyone's suspicion if you'd used them to make a bomb whereas people would remember she'd been in the shop. Again, I'm not saying it couldn't be proved she'd used them or that she had access to a friend's tools, I'm just pointing out the difficulties. The good news is that the DA will be taking all of this into account. Everly has been proven to be homicidal. If they can find one solid link that she did it, it will be placed on her doorstep. But, if all of the evidence points to you, he'll have no choice but to charge you, even if he *thinks* the evidence was planted. He can't go by what he *thinks*. He has to go by the *evidence*. And that's where I come in. It's my job to make the jury think it was planted too. That's it's much more likely that Everly framed you then you were trying to frame her. So, we actually want there to be a lot of evidence because no one would leave a lot. It would be an obvious frame."

"When will I know?"

"If they arrest you, they have to give me access to all of their information. If they arrest her, we'll hear the evidence in court or maybe the news. Until then, they'll keep the information need to know."

"This is so unfair. She's taking everything from me!"

"We'll talk about ways to take it all back, but for now let's concentrate on keeping you out of jail. Is there anything that she can use against you? Have you ever threatened her or done anything to her?"

"I hit her a few weeks ago after she hit Wolf, and I told her if she ever did it again, I'd beat her."

"Did anyone hear that?"

"No. I told Grayson, maybe more than once, I can't really remember how many times, that I wanted to smack her."

"How about your mother? Have you ever threatened her? Have you ever hit her?"

"Never."

"I'm aware that she hit you. Does she do that a lot?"

"No. I can't remember the last time she did. She doesn't hit us. She doesn't even yell that much."

"Did anyone tell you she was charged with assault for hitting you?"

"No...I wouldn't have pressed charges. Can I undo that?"

"No. And she's lucky it was only assault and not attempted murder. She might have killed you, Kate. I know that wasn't her intention, or at least I don't think it was, but if I was prosecuting her, I could make a good case that she was trying to kill you because that wasn't the only instance. She might have killed you by denying the medics access to you. Do you think she might have left that bomb in your stuff?"

"I have no idea. A week ago, I'd have said no, but she's been talking crazy."

"I heard the recording, and that could be a problem. It's great that you have it recorded but it could look like entrapment to a jury. They're going to want to know *why* you had a recorder handy."

"Jace gave it to me."

I told him why he had.

He said, "Let's hope we don't need to mention that."

"I really won't do anything that would hurt him."

"I'm sure he'd rather be embarrassed than to have you do time."

"Speaking of that, I don't want my sister Kenya embarrassed either."

"Kenya? Why would she be embarrassed?"

I told him what my grandmother had told me.

"Grayson and I are going to have a little talk about full disclosure. He never said a word about the paternity issues."

"He probably thought it didn't matter."

"Everything matters! No secrets, Kate. The worst thing that can happen for your case is that I'm blindsided. So, tell me your story. Don't try to protect anyone, not even Grayson. Just give me a rundown of your home life, your school life, even your sex life. I don't want the intimate details, but I do need to know if there are x-boyfriends, irate wannabe lovers, anything that could even remotely be used by Everly against you. Anything your mother could twist."

"It's going to take hours!"

"Days, but I need the full picture."

"Okay but... I don't want to do any time or anything but even if I had done it, would it be *that* serious? It never even went off!"

"Yes and no. That one incident is probably not enough to send you away long. But we know Everly is deadly dangerous. She'd have killed you all. Who's to say what else she did or will do? What if there's another bomb? We need to be able to prove it wasn't you. The best defense is a good offense, so I need to know everything so I have time to dig before she can convince her friends or your enemies to help her."

"I don't think I have any enemies, except for maybe my mom and dad."

"See! Now we're getting somewhere. Tell me why your dad might be an enemy."

"Because he loves my mom, and he doesn't love me. I think he'd sacrifice me for her. I think he'd sacrifice me for money. If my going away gives him my inheritance..."

"Will it?"

"I don't know."

"I'll find out."

TWENTY-SIX

The police didn't arrive that day.

My father visited me at dinner time with Felicity, Wolfgang, and Grayson. All of them carried bags. My father's was from my favorite restaurant.

I wondered if that was a lucky guess or if Jace, or more likely Grayson, had told him.

Felicity gave me a hug, saying, "I hate staying at grandma's! When are you coming home?"

Wolfgang said angrily, "She can't eat anything there, Kate! There's nuts in everything!"

"I'll speak to her," our father said to them, then to me, "It's not that bad. I bought her cereal and the bread she can eat."

Wolfgang scoffed, saying, "And she poured almond milk on it!"

Our father flushed. "I've spoken to the nanny already and she's checking everything. We'll keep Felicity approved food in its own cabinet."

I said to the kids, "Check everything yourselves. I'll be home in another day, two tops."

"What's wrong with you? You look okay."

Grayson said, "Her head, sillies, you know that."

I said, "I have high blood pressure in my head that medicine is fixing but the doctor needs to check it to be sure it's working right before they release me."

"I hate hospitals," Felicity said sympathetically and gave me another hug.

Wolfgang said, "We made you this."

He handed me the bag he carried.

Felicity said, "It was supposed to be for your birthday, but we thought you could use cheering up now."

The bag was surprisingly heavy.

Both kids watched eagerly, so I knew it would be one of their inventions.

They'd made me an art box, which made a pit form in my stomach.

I forced a smile.

Wolfgang said eagerly, "Fell painted all the little holders. We spaced them like that so you could leave the brushes pointing up and they wouldn't fall into each other so you can just set them down and the paint won't get all smeared with other paint."

She said, "And the back flips down and has clamps built in. It can hold the canvas or the pictures you're working with or your tablet. You put the paint tubes in the space between the cups with the matching color then you always know right where the color is without needing to read the tube. And there's room for extra and stuff in the drawer."

"The palette knife and palette go right in this little slot here so you can put it in there dirty and it wouldn't matter, or you could flip this spindle out to hold paper towels and wipe it off."

"This is amazing," I said.

My father took it from me to examine it.

"It's very well made," he said approvingly.

Grayson hugged me, murmuring, "Hang in there, Kate, it's going to be fine. You'll be painting again in no time."

Wolfgang said accusing to our father, "I told you she'd want her sketch bag!"

"I'm too tired to sketch," I said.

Grayson said, "We should let her get some rest. You guys are staying with me tonight to give Grandma a break. We can go for dinner."

He set his bag on the floor by the bed. "I brought you some clothes."

Felicity handed me hers, saying, "I brought your hair and makeup stuff and a present from Grandma. She sent you nice pajamas to wear for when your boyfriend comes to visit."

"She told you they met?"

"She said he was perfect for you. She seemed ... happy, I guess. She was really smiling..."

I laughed with Felicity because our grandma seldom smiled, except for her polite smile.

"She really said that?"

"Yeah," Wolfgang said. "I like him too. He's really nice. He fixed my bike and everything and painted Fell's for her so it isn't that stupid pink color."

"That was nice of him," I said.

Fell hugged me and whispered, "He told us you guys were getting married."

"Someday, I hope."

She cast a nervous glance at our father over her shoulder.

I said, "Jace and I are engaged," and held out my hand.

"Don't be ridiculous."

"I have to agree," Grayson said. "You're much too young."

"We know. It's going to be a long engagement. But he's the one, Gray. I know it. He knows it."

My father released a long slow breath of air, smiling wistfully, "I knew it too when I met your mother. She was just a year older than you are now... when I think what my father did to her..."

Grayson rolled his eyes at me.

I shrugged.

"What'd he do?" Wolfgang asked.

I said, "Grandma and Grandpa didn't always approve of Mom. They thought she was too young to get married too."

Felicity said, "Everyone says Mom is sick... no one will say with what or where she is."

I said, "She's sick like Everly is sick but not so bad."

Grayson said, "When she takes her medicine, she's fine. I think she'll be much better soon because she'll know she doesn't need to keep it secret from us anymore. She was afraid we'd find out and think she was bad like Everly is."

"There isn't enough medicine in the world to help Everly!" Wolfgang said angrily.

Jace knocked on the open door.

"Good, you're all here. I brought Kate an engagement present, but she'll need some help with it for a few days."

He grinned hopefully at me as he held out a box.

The box made goosebumps rise on my arms because it had holes poked all over.

"I hope you like her," he said anxiously, so I knew he'd seen my unease. "I have a cat—sort of. She lives under my house, and she brought me this the other day. She's wild, not a house cat at all. I feed her and stuff, but she never lets me pet her. I was shocked to see this little thing. I hope we can keep her..."

I lifted out a little black kitten that meowed soundlessly.

"*Aww*, she's so cute!" Felicity said.

Our father said, "She's probably diseased."

Jace rolled his eyes at me, "I brought her right to the vet. She's got a clean bill of health. She's just a bit undernourished and needs bottle feeding."

Wolfgang said, "Did you look around for more?"

"It didn't occur to me. Mamma cat brought her right to me and then ran off. I waited to see if she'd come back with another one, but she never did. She's still eating her food but there was no sign of another. You guys can come over and look if you want?"

"Can we, Gray?" Wolfgang asked anxiously as he took the kitten from me to cuddle.

"Sure. Just be careful picking any stray animals up."

Jace said, "I was hoping you'd volunteer to feed it for me because I have to work, and Kate can't have it in here and the vet said it needs to eat every few hours."

"Can we, Gray?"

"Sure.

Tears trickled down Felicity's cheeks as she hugged Grayson and then Jace.

"It's the best engagement present ever!" she said. She released him to hug me, "We'll take good care of her. I'll make her a nice bed and we'll get her toys and everything!"

Tears filled my own eyes as I said, "She really is the best present ever. She needs a good name." I hugged Felicity saying to Jace, "She's perfect. Thank you."

The kids cried over the kitten for a few moments before their happy plans to make her a bed distracted them from their tears.

Wolfgang said, "Will she be okay in the car a while if we stop to see if she has brothers or sisters?"

Jace said, "I'm sure she'd be fine. I just fed her. She sleeps most of the time still. I'll stop back later, Kate."

He grabbed the box from me and kissed my cheek. The four of them left.

I hoped they'd find more kittens.

My father said, "I'd thought of getting them one but was worried it would be too much of a reminder."

"It probably would've been. Let them take care of her a while and get over the jitters."

"I spoke to the doctor earlier on the phone and he assures me that you're doing really well. How are *you* though?"

"I don't know."

He nodded. "I don't know either. All of this…. It feels like it all came out of the blue but also like a weight finally crashed down."

"You didn't know Mom was sick?"

"I knew she had… episodes. I thought it was just women troubles. She'd get moody and irritable and sometimes cry… After she had Grayson, I made her see a doctor. He prescribed Xanax or something and she got better. We were happy, Kate. She wasn't faking that she loved me. I wasn't her second choice. She loves me, I'm sure of that."

"You think he raped her then?"

"Yes. And it makes me so goddamned mad! I wish she'd said something."

"Would you have believed her?"

"Hell yes! We were in love. I was only twenty and we'd only just met really but I knew she was the one for me. She wasn't the type of girl who'd sleep around. I was worried about that because I knew she wouldn't without being married and I knew getting married would piss off my parents."

"You never suspected?"

He snorted angrily.

"Who suspects something like that? I knew something was seriously bothering Alise, but I thought it was just her being worried I wouldn't be willing to wait for her. When she changed her mind… I should've suspected but I was just glad she had. And then she told me she was pregnant, and I knew she felt horrible about it—really guilty. So, we had no choice but to get married. Not to imply I didn't want to marry her, I did. I just would've waited and finished college and did it the right way to make my parents happy. I was completely shocked when my father gave me the dealership as a wedding present. That goddamned bastard felt guilty! I hate that she had to face him all those years!"

"Grandma told me she was stalking him."

"That's complete bullshit!"

"Where is she now?"

"Getting treatment. I won't divorce her, Kate. I'm sorry. I know she did and said some really terrible things to you, but it was my fault. If I'd taken better care of her…"

"I don't want you to divorce her—at least not for my sake. But she wasn't just saying mean things to me. She was warping Everly... she can't be trusted with the kids, Dad."

"I know. She knows she needs help. We'll hire a housekeeper and a live-in nanny. I'm cutting my work hours at the dealership to work from home more. She can stay home to be with the kids or just take time for herself. We'll both be around the house more. I want us all to be a *real* family."

"And Everly?"

"I'm trying to get her into psychiatric care instead of jail. I think the courts will agree."

"I want her to get help too, but I don't want the kids living in fear, which they *will* do if she moves back in."

"I know. I don't want Everly to think she's being discarded either though. I'm hoping she'll be okay with a boarding school or that she stays in care until she can go to college. I'd make sure she lived on campus."

"So she gets everything she wants..."

"I understand why you're so angry, I'm angry too, but it really wasn't all her fault."

"I'm angrier at you than her! You should've helped her before all of this!"

"You're right. But I really thought she was fine. Your mother, my mother, everyone except you and Grayson said she wasn't the problem."

"Why *was* I the problem? Why does Mom hate me?"

"She doesn't hate you. She hates herself. Her doctor, the one she's seeing right now says she has manic episodes brought on by stress. Everly acts up and in Mom's mind she isn't yelling at you, she's yelling at herself. You triggered it more than the others because you look just like her. She says she's looking into a mirror at the stupid girl she was. She thinks she belongs in the gutter, that she's nothing, that she doesn't deserve her home and family. And frankly, I blame my mother for that because she's been telling her that for years!"

"You let your mother speak to your wife that way?"

"No. They'd had a huge scene when I told my mom Alise was pregnant, and I told her if I ever heard her speak to Alise like that again, I'd never speak to *her* again. I'd cut her off from us. But Alise claims Olivia told her she was trash all the time. I knew they didn't really like each other but Alise never told me Olivia was still being mean to her. Maybe that was all in her head too..."

"It wasn't. I heard Olivia being mean to her. I saw her hit her. Poor Mom..."

He nodded.

"I'm trying to be...understanding with *my* mother too. I can't imagine how difficult it was for her all these years either because she wants to believe her husband would never have done that. She put all of the blame on Alise. She told me she was afraid to tell me and lose me and you kids..."

"Was grandpa capable of that?"

"Obviously he was! But he *had* been drinking heavily back then. I'm not saying that to excuse him. I'm just saying I think he was sincerely sorry and tried to make amends as best he could. He was always very kind if somewhat distant to Alise. I think he was trying to make it up to her. She does too... he'd apologized and begged her to let him come see Kenya. She was afraid he'd tell me, so she let him, but she also says he was good with her and that he loved all the children. She was a bit worried when he began singling you out but there'd never been any sign of anything inappropriate and she'd follow the pair of you on your walks. Did he ever..."

"No. He was a good grandfather—the best grandfather."

I was shocked to see tears on my father's cheeks.

"I'm so glad of that."

He turned away and I knew he was crying.

I didn't know what to say.

He finally cleared his throat and wiped his face, turning back to sit beside the bed and take my hand.

"When I heard what he'd done to Alise, is all I could think was what if he'd been abusing you all those years... I was sick over it. Afraid to ask Alise if she suspected because she can't take much more. Her doctor said that Alise's memory of him and you could be how she wishes things were, not how they actually were. He told me that Alise could be repressing more abuse at my father's hands. I hope to God you're telling me the truth, but if it isn't true, you don't need to be afraid to tell me. I'm not going to do anything, except get you the help you need."

"Gramps was good to me, Dad. I never saw him do anything to her either. They barely spoke. Gray or Kenya would take us over to their house. He never came to our house, except to pick us up or drop us off or for parties. He wasn't stopping in to see her unless he was doing it while we were at school."

"She was at work most weekdays. I never understood why she'd rather work than be home with you guys because I know she wanted to

207

be home... I think she was afraid to be there. I hate that he took that from her too... "

"Before you blame him for everything, you should find out why she chose as she did because she continued going to work *after* he died."

"She didn't. She'd cut her hours drastically when Hannah was born. I'd no idea she'd been leaving after me. I thought she was staying home with the kids."

I was shocked.

"Where does she go?"

"Nowhere. She walks for a few hours or does her shopping then goes home and waits for you all to come home."

"That can't be true. We're home all day in the summer."

"Only this summer. She came into the dealership more this summer. And she was around the house more, but she was afraid to change her habits and have me or one of the kids say something. So she just kept doing what she had been doing. She was growing worse, unable to manage her job and thought I'd leave her. The stress of Hannah was eating her. She couldn't face her either. She spent her time just watching from a distance because she felt as if she didn't deserve her life."

"Maybe... I'd want some proof of that if I were you..."

"What do you think she was doing?"

"I have no idea. Maybe she was having an affair—like you."

"That was a mistake. I've broken it off with Claire and told your mother. She knew though. I think that's what was making her so...unstable. She thought I was going to leave her."

"Where you?"

"No—maybe. I don't know. It's complicated."

"My poor mother..."

He winced.

"And Claire?"

"What do you mean?"

"Did she think you loved her?"

"Maybe... I never told her I did because I didn't. I love Alise, but Alise was growing distant and cold. I thought she'd fallen out of love with me. I was so hurt... Claire works at the dealership. She saw I was hurting. I'm not saying the affair was her fault, but she took every opportunity to flirt, and I fell for it."

You are such an ass.

I didn't say it, of course.

He continued, "I was an ass. I am an ass... I've let this entire mess build up."

"What about Hannah? Did Mom say who her father is?"

"She claims it was an anonymous sperm donor. That she was afraid of losing me and knew I'd stick around for another child."

"Then why not make one the old-fashioned way? I hate to say this, Dad, but I think she's lying."

"Maybe... the tests will be back any day now. It really worries me that the rape thing at work was real but with Hannah as the result, not you. I'm having a full panel run on Hannah because either way I'm sure she'll want to know everything she can about her biological father someday."

"You won't tell her?"

"Someday."

"Claire wasn't the first, was she?"

"Frankly, it's none of your business!"

"So, that's a no. God, Dad! How could you do that to her! No wonder she's crazy! I'd be crazy too if my husband who claimed to love me was having these stupid affairs!"

"Her mental Illness Isn't my fault!"

"Your neglect of her and us, is!"

"I'm trying to do better!"

My head began to throb.

I turned away to rub my temples.

He said, "Sorry. I shouldn't be yelling at you. None of this is your fault and you have every right to be angry. I hope you can forgive your mother though. She really does love you, Kate. She's so... confused and hurt. It's just breaking my heart."

"Mine too. Mom and I were never close, but I do love her. It wasn't my idea to press charges or anything."

"No. I know. The police had no choice. She doesn't remember the visit at all now. She barely remembers the entire incident. She thinks you fell."

"She wants to believe that..."

He nodded.

"What's she think happened to Everly?"

"That she overdosed. In her head, you and Everly where arguing and you ran down the stairs and fell and Hannah followed. Everly grabbed for her but missed and she fell. And Everly took some drugs and had a bad reaction. The doctor says to let it go for now, that when Alise lets herself remember the truth, we'll know she's truly getting better."

"So I'm supposed to lie and say that's what happened?"

"Not at all. He doesn't think she'll ask you about it until she's ready to face it. So tell her the truth just don't bring it up until she does."

"Okay."

"She doesn't remember making the bomb at all."

"Are they sure she did?"

"I don't know." He cleared his throat, leaning closer and not quite whispering as he said, "Did you do it to get Everly in trouble? I won't say anything, I swear. It's just Alise is so certain she didn't do it and the doctor thinks it's out of character for her."

"No. I didn't do it."

He nodded and sat back but I could see he didn't *really* believe me.

I said, "Why would I do it? How would I? When would I have had the chance? Do you really think I'd take the slightest chance and leave something like that where Wolfgang or Felicity might open it? They'd be much more likely to open it than Everly, like a million times more likely, and how would I have found"—I made air quotes on the word found—"it without opening it and killing myself?"

"True. She must have done it."

I didn't ask to which she that he was referring to.

"Are you staying at the house?"

"I'm still not sure. The kids seemed okay there. I'm more worried about Alise going back there. She used to love that house though, so I hate to urge her to sell it because I know she'd agree with me."

"Talk to Grayson before bringing them back to stay. He'll have a better idea then I would about how they're really holding up."

"I think I owe you another apology about that. I hadn't realized that you were so involved with their daily care—or Everly really."

"I love them."

He nodded.

He said, "I'd like to make amends and help myself by paying for their care retroactively."

"I didn't do it for money."

"I know but you could use money to finish the bedrooms in your house, which would help me. I'd feel better about letting the kids stay with you if they had a real room to sleep in. If you'd be willing to put some doors in on the downstairs rooms that aren't done to lock the kiddos out, they could even go there to visit. I'd hire a contractor to finish those rooms."

"I appreciate the thought, but I *want* to finish them, although maybe I can't now..."

"You'll get better, Kate."

The monitor began to beep.

He winced, surprising me again by kissing my forehead.

He said, "I'll get that bedroom upstairs done so you can have the twins over. We'll talk about the rest later. I wish I'd helped when you first came to me with your dream. I really do want to make it up to you. Grayson told me you'd hoped Mom would give you your college fund. We will. Just please, Kate, take your time and really think about your future."

"You don't like Jace?"

"He seems nice. He's hardworking and really talented, but that isn't the point. You're not even eighteen!"

"I will be in a few days."

"You know what I mean. You're a traumatized young woman who wants to escape from a cold house. I just don't want you latching onto the first man who comes along."

"He's special."

My father sighed hard.

"I'm not going to waste my breath because I thought the same about Alise. I'd have done anything to have her. It hadn't mattered what anyone said..."

He smiled sadly.

"We had some very good years and could've had more of them if I'd tried harder. Try hard, Kate."

He stood to kiss my forehead.

"I'll be back in the morning, hopefully to take you home."

He handed me the bag of food and left.

Jace returned at seven-thirty followed by a nurse who warned him he had to be out by eight.

He kissed my cheek then sat beside me, taking my hand, laughing a bit ruefully as he said, "I think we're going to end up with more than one cat. Crystal and Evan came over to help search and before I knew it there were like twenty kids there and we found three litters of kittens."

"Three!"

"The kids are thrilled—all twenty whatever of them. The parents are horrified.... Grayson seemed okay with taking all four of the bitty ones. I think they all have that same momma."

"That poor mamma cat, Jace. She's going to so sad to find all her babies gone."

"Don't tell the kids but I sort of lied about that. She did bring me the one. She left it by her food bowl yesterday, and when she didn't come back, I went to look for her. She'd gotten hit by a car. She wasn't coming back..."

"Oh... that poor thing."

"I considered giving them the kitten straight away but then thought it might be a bad idea if they can't have one in their new place or even if they could, so I asked my mom to look after it a few days. She only had it for the one night. Our engagement seemed like a good excuse to try. The kittens they just found might not make it. The vet is keeping them overnight and says if he can get them through one night and eating regularly that we can take them home and their chances will be good. The kids seemed to understand. They were upset but not tragically upset. I'd say they were properly optimistic, looking forward to helping them. But they aren't going to want to give them up if they all make it."

"Well, they can't have *my* kitten, but the others they can keep, or I could keep them for them if they don't want them at that house."

"They're going back there then?"

"Probably. My dad said he and my mom are staying together."

I filled him on what my father had told me.

"I don't like that he asked you if you'd made that bomb."

"Me either. I'm going to be so relieved when this is all over. Speaking of which, we never really talked about the kids."

"What's to talk about? They're your family. If you want them to live with us, then that's what we'll do. I like them. They don't seem like they'd be hard to get along with."

"I think my dad is an optimist thinking my mom is just going to bounce back from this. She's been repressing some real terrible shit, and then there's the whole Hannah thing... but I think if he hires competent help, the kids would be happier with them because they do love their parents. But I would like to have a room ready for them to visit, so I think I'll take my dad up on his offer to get that bedroom room sheet rocked. I'll worry about trimming it out later."

"I agree. I was planning to start it this weekend anyway, but if he's going to hire someone, I'll finish the security and get our closet installed."

"Keep track of your hours."

He kissed my forehead.

"I will. Not because I'm worried about it but because you are. I don't want you to ever feel obligated to stay with me. If you decide you need time or space, I can move back into my trailer or with mom anytime. You don't need to worry about it. I know I'm rushing us, but my intent isn't to trap you, to make you feel indebted or dependent on me. I just want to be there if you need me. I love you so damned much!"

"I love you too. I want you to stay because you love me, not because you've invested all your time and money into the project."

He laughed as he kissed me. We kissed for a long minute.

"Then I'll keep track. Speaking of keeping track, I've been checking the papers every day and there hasn't been a word about this. I'm not sure if that's good or bad news."

"What's Frank say?"

"That it either means they're treating it as a mental health issue or they're gearing up for big charges."

"Did he say which he thought it would be?"

"Mental health because of who your dad is. Except your grandmother came into the station demanding Alise be charged with attempted murder and she's a big supporter of the local police and friends with the mayor. Frank said she might have enough clout to put pressure on the DA."

"I'll tell my dad to talk to her."

He nodded. "If it weren't for Hannah, I'd say it was a good thing Everly is getting help but anyone who could do that..."

"I know. I want her to pay—for all of it!"

We hugged until the nurse came back to shoo him out.

Dwayne stopped by the next morning.

"I've spoken to the police. They still want an official written statement from you, so we're going to write it all out. Officer Sandy told me on the down low that your mom is going to be officially charged with making that bomb. She didn't come right out and say it, but she implied your statement about her behavior, especially when she hit you here will have a big impact on the final charges. I think Officer Sandy is worried that you're holding back either through fear or years of manipulation making you afraid that crossing your mother will leave the kids alone with her."

"She'd be right in a way. I never thought my mom would ever hurt anyone. But I *was* concerned she'd leave the kids with Everly because she never seemed to see anything bad that Everly ever did."

"I spoke to Alise's doctor, and he says it's a classic symptom. Alise can't handle the bad, so she just doesn't see it, or she internalizes it. If she didn't have the mental health issues that she has, it might not have been that big of a deal, but she does have those disorders, and to Alise, she wasn't yelling at you."

"I know. My dad explained."

"Do you believe it?"

"I guess so."

"Honestly, I think your dad is an ass, but he's stepping up now. If he follows through with her care and arranges for the live-in help, I think your mother and the kids will lead pretty normal happy lives."

"I think so too if he doesn't go and fuck it all up by driving her off the deep end with his women."

"I know he's working with Grayson to get your mom released. I'll speak to Grayson because that's a valid worry. But maybe we can make it clear to your father that he's going to be held responsible if he causes her to lose control because he's the one guaranteeing the court of her care. It won't stop him from having an affair, but it should be enough that he makes sure his children are safe—that you're safe from another psychotic outbreak from her."

"And Everly?"

"Is a different story. I checked into your grandfather's will. He'd left the trust with the intent that it be given to the children of Brent or Alise Avery in equal shares. The word or is purposeful so as not to cut Kenya out if the truth became known.

"He shifted everything else into a trust with your grandmother as the sole beneficiary. In the event that she was to die first, that trust would've been split equally between your father and Kenya. He'd made that will right after Kenya was born. There were no other grandchildren. When Grayson was born, he began putting money into a separate trust, the one he left to all you kids. Kenya's trust is larger than you kids get. It's about double because she's entitled to a share of the other trust as well. Those trusts are irrevocable.

"Your grandmother has just recently redone her will and left everything to her grandchildren with Kenya listed as an acknowledged grandchild. The trust stipulates that the shares won't be paid out to spouses, children, or dependents but that if one of the eight of you were to die, their share would remain in the trust and be split equally between the remaining children. The thing is, Everly had accompanied your grandmother to the lawyer when she made those changes three weeks ago."

"So you think Everly wanted to murder the kids to get their share?"

"It seems likely. I know your grandmother goes to see her in the hospital almost every day. I've spoken with Everly's doctors too and she was angry and ranting over the money being hers. That she was promised it. She's stopped ranting and is doing much better or at least acting much more civilized. I spoke with her briefly. In my opinion, she's a very sick girl. She's going to need treatment for a long time."

"Did my grandma leave anything to my dad?"

"A modest amount. She left small bequests to her housekeeper and church and individual bequests, things like her wedding rings to go to Hannah and her pearls to Felicity. Everyone in the family—except your mother, was mentioned personally. When I spoke to her, she mentioned redoing her will to put her son back into it. Which, again if I'm being honest, I think she did just to make him toe the line."

"What line?"

"She said it in front of him and then demanded the children be left in her care until they once more had a proper roof over their heads. She was—irate, for lack of a better word, to hear you planned to move out with no intention of attending college. They had a small argument over it, but she conceded that she was happy you'd met such an appropriate young man."

"Appropriate?"

"I think she's unaware of your health difficulties. Your father had said something like Jace was as artistically gifted as you were, and the match made sense to him."

"*Ahh*... she never really approved of my painting. Not that she ever said anything exactly. It was more a look and she never really let me do it at her house. I'm glad she likes Jace but it's surprising."

He snorted with laughter, nodding agreement. "I've met her before. The first thing she asked me was who my parents were. I *barely* passed muster as an appropriate friend for Grayson."

He took out a notebook, "Now, let's get this done."

We finished my statement that I signed in my kindergarten scrawl right as the police arrived.

Dee took the papers and flipped through it. She handed them to Reynolds saying, "I think you can rest easy that your part in this is done. Despite your fingerprints being all over the materials in that can, we're certain your mother made it. We found matching paint cans in the garage at your house."

"The carriage house you mean?"

She nodded.

"I haven't started that yet."

"That was apparent when compared with the condition of the rest of the place. The nails, wood, tools used to make that bomb were all from your workroom there. She made it there. And we know it wasn't you or Everly because she made one tiny mistake. Well, two actually. She couldn't have known you'd be unable to have written anything or have drawn a smiley face. There was also paint in the can, a unique color that would be almost impossible to match chemically speaking. The paint was too old to match modern paints. It isn't something you could go buy off the shelf. Your mother wiped off the tools, getting that paint on a rag. It was a quick cleanup because she wanted us to trace that can to your house. She'd tossed the rag she'd used into your trash there, but she hadn't bothered to look into the trash can. We found that paint on a newspaper in that trashcan dated the day after Everly attacked the kids.

"Your friend Crystal Remember tossing the paper and a few empty coffee cups that we also found in the trash. So we know when the bomb was made and that neither you or Everly could've made it because you were both in the hospital.

"We also know your mother had gone to your house. She was seen on your surveillance cameras having an argument with your grandmother in the driveway. They walked around the outside of the house and the cameras lost sight of them. Two men who work for your parents were there delivering sheetrock and some boards, so the doors were open. Neither saw her do it but she *was* inside for a few minutes looking around.

"Both men said Alise was very upset and that your grandmother was furious. They thought it was because they'd just learned of your house. Neither of the men really spoke to either woman. They unloaded the wood and left. Your mother left and then your grandmother. Your mother returned and sat outside for an hour or so, then the camera lost sight of her again when she walked around the house. She could've have gone back in if she'd left a door open.

She reappeared on the camera about twenty minutes later.

She denied making that later visit. When she was shown the recording, she thought it had been taken years ago. She said she used to follow you there to make sure you wouldn't be hurt. She'd look in all the windows to be sure he wasn't hurting you. I don't think she was lying; I think she had a real psychotic break."

"My poor mother..."

"Had your grandfather ever been inappropriate with you?"

"Never!"

Dwayne said, "Why would that be of interest to the police now that he's dead?"

"It's just a detail that might have a bearing on Everly's case."

"Is she saying he did?"

"No. Which is odd, right? I mean, she claimed your father and Grayson have been abusing her, but not him. Although she's retracted her statement that your father had been abusing her or the rest of you."

"And Grayson?"

"She won't say. She just says she's done talking about it for now. I think she's hedging her bets, leaving herself room to claim it again later."

"Did she admit to taking the pictures?"

"No. She's pretending she doesn't remember telling us that you were all abused."

"Pretending…"

"And doing a horrible job of it. We can see she's fighting laughter. Her doctor has told us that she admitted she lied about it to him— confidentially, of course. You aren't to say that to her!"

"I won't, but aren't her sessions supposed to be private?"

"Yes, but not when there is potential for further victims. Her doctor has a duty to warn the police if he thinks the abuse is ongoing. If he thought your father or Grayson were still hurting any of the children, he'd have to tell us. She probably thinks he can't say if the opposite is true, but she'd be wrong. Police resources aren't meant to be used on personal vendettas. Were she and your grandfather alone a lot?"

"No. She'd stay with grandma and I'd go with grandpa. Grandpa and I liked to walk and bike and explore and they liked to shop."

"Did your grandparents get along?"

"I always thought so. He was always really sweet to her. He'd pick her flowers and stuff when we were out. Not that she really liked them. She only really like expensive gifts. So he'd give her a bouquet he picked himself and she'd make some comment about how diamonds were a girl's best friend or how flowers just die, then the next day he'd bring her diamonds or a new flower pin. I used to tease him because he'd bought her all sorts of gem flowers, enough to make a garden I'd say, and he laugh but look sad and say it could never be enough…"

"And the other kids? Was he alone with them?"

"I've no idea. I don't remember any particular times. I'd always go over with them if I was around. It's possible he saw them while I was in school, but I don't think so. He was nice to the kids, but it was us older ones he spent time with. I don't think he really knew what to do with a baby. Harley was just a baby and Hannah hadn't even been born when he died. The kids visited but didn't spend time hanging out there like we did."

"Whose idea were the visits?"

"I don't know. I never really thought about it. Mom and Dad used to go out a lot back then and the grandparents would babysit us when Gray or Kenya were out, which happened more often the older they got. I can remember my grandparents coming over when I was really little to watch us at the house. My grandmother hated to watch us there, which now I understand why. So my dad would drop us off at their house and when I got older, I'd ride my bike over or Gray would drop us and visit, or Kenya would take us, but it was usually him."

"Grandpa would take the boys fishing and to games and all of us to the shop at the garages to teach us how to make stuff."

"So pretty normal grandparent type stuff..."

"I thought so. The only odd thing was Everly. She never went with us really. She stayed with Grandma. I'd always thought it was because Grandma loved to shop and would buy her stuff. I'd have said Everly was Grandma's favorite."

"And maybe it *was* as innocent as that," Dee agreed.

"It's such bullshit she can ruin everything like this! He wouldn't have done anything bad to any of us. He loved us!"

"He did a very bad thing to your mother. Even if it wasn't rape, she was just a young girl, and he was her boss and a married man."

"I know...I can't seem to get my head around that. But that doesn't make him a pedophile or mean he didn't love us!"

"No it doesn't."

Dwayne said, "Will you be needing anything more from Kate?"

"I don't think so."

She offered me her hand.

I shook it and she said, "I hope things get better for you, Kate. Your paintings are truly beautiful. Don't give that up even if takes you another eighteen years to regain it. I saw that painting you did of your mom. It's worth saving. I really hope you don't get rid of any of them, which I know you'll be tempted to do for lots of reasons. It would be a real shame though."

"I hadn't thought about the paintings at my house. I guess I should maybe rethink hanging my grandfather's portrait on the landing... "

"Maybe, but don't throw it out. Your mom could use some peace. Whether she'd done it consensually or not, it obviously took a huge toll on her and it's probably better for her not to have to face that every time she visits you, but *you* loved him, so keep it at least.

TWENTY-SEVEN

Jace called me the next morning.

"Your dad called me to say he spoke to the doctors, and you're being released today. I've been invited to your grandmother's for lunch with your family. Since he wanted to pick you up to sign papers and stuff, I thought I'd meet you there?"

"Sure. You don't have to go if you have stuff to do."

"I want to get more cameras up at our house."

"Imagine how terrifying it must be to do stuff like that and not remember doing it?"

"It's crazy...and I mean that she could do it at all. I wouldn't have thought she *could* do it never mind that she *would* do it."

"I don't think she meant it to go off... she *couldn't* have."

"Let me know if you hear anything."

"You too."

He snorted softly and disconnected.

Butterflies danced in my stomach. I just wanted my life to go back to normal, which was impossible if I couldn't paint or draw. I grabbed the pad and pencil the doctor had given me. It was lined paper like the kind little kids used with letters and numbers written in lighter dotted lines.

Contemplating eighteen years of trying to relearn it was daunting. Contemplating that I might never regain it was terrifying.

I painstakingly traced the letters, trying not to let the crooked wavering lines discourage me.

My father brought me to my grandmother's. Her smile was strained, which was perfectly understandable, especially considering her husband's illegitimate daughter was holding a box with four crying kittens in her living room.

The kids were thrilled to see me and even more thrilled to introduce me to the kittens. Mine was a hair plumper but the others looked healthy enough, which relieved me. There were two gray ones and two black ones. Their eyes were barely open, and they slept snuggled together in a ball.

I hugged Kenya who was remarkably poised.

Wolfgang showed me the feeding schedule, the bottles and canned milk while Felicity explained how they had to warm it and rub their bellies. Hannah and Harley both told me how they could feed them, how much they loved them, how they'd play with them when they could leave their box.

They spoke excitedly about the kittens until Jace arrived with flowers and wine for my grandmother, which made me a bit nervous that she'd embarrass him by snubbing his offerings, but she smiled and kissed his cheek.

Grayson exchanged an amazed glance with me that made me giggle.

The bell announcing dinner rang.

"Girls," grandmother said like she always did.

Kenya and I went to serve.

"How are you?" I asked as we set the platters grandmother's cook handed us onto the table.

"Having new appreciation for what you must've felt."

I said, "Honestly, I don't think it ever sank in for me..."

"Me either, yet. Grandma is so nice about it... poor Mom."

"Have you talked to her?"

"No. Dad said her doctors wanted to give her a few days for the meds to work."

I said, "She told me a different story every time she talked to me."

Kenya grimaced crookedly. "She' been telling herself different stories for so long that she probably doesn't remember what really happened. I can't believe grandpa would've raped her, drunk or not. We know she makes bad choices...I think she'd hate me, not you, if he really had raped her. It seems more likely to me that she made a bad decision, one they both really regretted." Kenya shrugged at me, "It's probably a mix of both of their stories. I hope now that it's all out in the open that she can heal."

She leaned closer to whisper, "I'm amazed at how well Grandma is taking all this."

"And Dad... I've been so caught up in my own worries, I didn't really consider them..."

"How are the hands?"

"Girls!"

"Coming," we chorused.

Kenya gave me a quick hug and we grabbed the rest of the platters.

I slept late the next day and then spent the day watching the kids watching the kittens.

I didn't think the kids really realized what was going on. They wanted to go home, which was understandable. Our grandmother had been out all day and even though she didn't say anything when she came home for the evening, except, "I hope you plan on picking this all up," it was clear we were getting on her nerves.

Over dinner, our father said, "I was thinking that after dinner we can take the kids to your house and show them around. Your mom should be home in time for a birthday celebration."

"So soon," our grandmother said with deep displeasure.

Our father nodded.

I was wondering if my mother knew she was expected to attend a birthday party for me.

"She'll be released Wednesday," my father said.

Wolfgang said, "You have a house? You're not coming home with us?"

Our father said, "Kate is going to open a hotel. She wanted it to be a surprise and wait to show you when it was done, but we've talked it over, and your mom and I agreed she could move in there Thursday. I thought we could go home tomorrow and get things ready for her. Ms. Maria will move into Kate's room."

"What about Everly?" Felicity asked angrily.

Hannah began to cry.

I stood to pick her up.

Our father said, "Everly won't be coming back to the house to stay. When she's released from the hospital, she can have supervised visits. Ms. Maria will use Everly's room as her sitting room. You're not to go in either room unless invited."

Kenya said, "Grayson and I will help pack everything up and you guys can help Kate unpack it."

I said to Hannah, "I'll be right down the street, Hannah banana. Ms. Maria will bring you to visit."

Our grandmother said, "It's time Hannah had a big girl bed. We can pick one out tomorrow. Perhaps one with a pink canopy?"

"Can I, daddy?" Hannah asked excitedly.

"Sure. Thanks, Mom. That sounds great."

"Would you like to come with us, Felicity? We can pick new bedding for you and maybe find you a desk to replace the toy box in your room? And we can start looking at furniture for the basement playroom."

Our father said, "Grayson is taking the exercise equipment so that room will be empty. I was thinking we could move your project table down there and make a real craft center that would be off limits to the kiddos unless Ms. Maria was with them. That way the two of you could leave your tools and projects out."

"Could we have real work benches and power tools?" Wolfgang asked eagerly.

"Benches, yes. We'll talk about the tools. You'll need chairs and maybe a couch and television down there."

I said, "They've been wanting a good microscope. Maybe you could put in a lab counter for them? Wolf could use some kind of storage cabinet for all his parts and pieces and Fell needs bookcases to display her projects."

Our grandmother said, "I think we can ask Ms. Maria to help find appropriate furniture."

Our father said, "I was thinking what the house needs is a puppy."

Wolfgang exclaimed excitedly.

Felicity said, "What about the kittens?"

"Kate will take hers with her, and we don't want it to be lonely, so maybe we can keep two and she can have two?"

Felicity said, "A puppy might hurt them."

Wolfgang said, "We can wait until they're bigger. Lots of people have dogs and cats together. We'll teach it not to."

I wondered what our mother thought about getting a dog *and* cats or if he'd even asked her.

Felicity said, "Mom won't like it."

He said, "She won't mind if you take good care of it."

I said, "If it upsets her, you can keep them at my place."

"One can be ours and one yours," Harley said to Felicity.

Hannah said, "I want the gray one! She loves me. I feed her and everything."

Our grandmother laughed, which silenced everyone.

We all gawked at her.

She said, "Then I suppose we'll need to pick up some cat supplies too on our shopping trip."

Kenya and I began clearing the table. Grandma's cook would wash the dishes, is all we needed to do was rinse and stack them in the sink.

Kenya handed me another stack to rinse.

I whispered, "Did he even ask her?"

She shrugged, whispering back, "I have no idea. Grandma's acting weird too with all this agreeing, it's creeping me out."

We giggled.

"Girls!"

Kenya rolled her eyes at me. Still laughing, we returned to the dining room.

"I'll be glad to get out of here," Kenya murmured. "This is exhausting."

It was exhausting. Everyone except the kids was worried and strained.

Three days until I could start my real life. I could hardly wait. I'd no idea what to do when Everly was released from the hospital. I knew she'd never stop trying to make me miserable but at least there I wouldn't have to see her. And I hoped with me being gone that would be enough to keep her from wanting to hurt the kids.

Felicity and Wolfgang were smart enough to call me or another adult if she was around, but Everly might be able to fool Harley into going with her.

I'd have to have a serious talk with him and maybe tell Felicity to keep an eye out although I hated to worry her more.

It was damned frustrating—terrifying really, knowing that Everly always got away with everything. She probably thought she could still get away with this and maybe she could if she were smarter in the next attempt.

I was certain she'd do something. Maybe not murder now that she knew she'd be a suspect but she'd do something.

Of course, I could do something too... if I was careful the police might believe that she'd hurt herself trying to make another bomb.

Is all I needed to do was have them catch her doing it. *I could set something off in her room*, I thought excitedly. She wouldn't even need to be there. They'd have to lock her up if they thought she was still dangerous, which I was certain she would be.

The trick would be to make it noticeable but not able to really hurt anyone, but not to seem like it wasn't meant to hurt anyone. Well that and getting into her room. I didn't know where she was going yet but she didn't know either. It would take her time to make her plan. At least I hoped it would.

It wouldn't take me any time at all to build something like my mom had. If I laid the can on its side like it had fallen over and set it on a timer, I could shoot the nails into the wall. And if I put it under the bed there was hardly any chance anyone who happened to be in the room would be seriously hurt. I'd need to work out some believable scenario for the timer to go off and make it loud enough that people would notice.

The minute I found out where she was being sent, I'd work out a way to sneak in. She wasn't getting away with it this time. I'd be damned if I let her hurt my kids!

TWENTY-EIGHT

The next morning, my grandmother joined me on her back porch as I drank so-so coffee prepared by her cook who'd shooed me from the kitchen. The kids were still sleeping. I'd taken the early morning kitten feeding so they could get some sleep.

She said, "I don't approve of farm animals in the house, but they do keep them busy and distracted. And, I suppose, they're cute little things."

I laughed to myself that these kittens were farm animals, but her pedigree cat wasn't.

I said, "The kids seem to be recovering..."

"Speaking of that, I'm not sure a birthday party is the best idea, but I suppose your father knows best. I shan't be attending it, which I think won't come as a surprise in the circumstances. Maybe the two of us could celebrate it with a nice dinner with just the two of us?"

"Sure, grams."

Her lips tightened the barest amount as they always did with that diminutive. She hated to be addressed informally. She preferred being called Grandmother or Gram. I made a mental note to make an effort for her. She didn't need any more stress even if I thought it snobby of her.

"What are your plans today?" she asked.

"I don't know. I'll probably visit Jace at work and maybe go see if my closet is done. He was going to work on that. Maybe I'll try to make something."

Cook brought her out of cup tea. She absently nodded her thanks to him as she said thoughtfully, "Please promise me you won't try any powered tools until we know better how you can handle things. You could kill yourself if you lost control of a saw like you do a pen."

"I'll be careful."

Cook said, "Would you like breakfast out here, madam?"

"No. We'll eat in the dining room."

Cook left us.

She said, "Leave your house key with me and I'll drop off your clothing."

"Gray said he'd do it."

"Ms. Maria can assist me. She needs to see the place anyway."

My grandmother dropped me off at the shop.

Everyone quieted when I walked in.

"Kate!" Jace exclaimed as he hurried to hug me.

Howard said, "Congratulations on your engagement, guys. How you feeling, Kate?"

"Better every day."

"Crystal wanted me to tell you that the two of you are invited for a celebratory dinner as soon as you're up to it."

"Sounds fun," I lied. I wasn't sure how to handle our fake engagement—if he'd truly meant it, which maybe he had if he was telling his friends and family. It made me breathless to think he might've and not to keep me safe from my crazy family but because he wanted to marry me.

I said, "I didn't mean to interrupt your work. I just popped in to say hello."

"Where are you off to in such a hurry?" Jace asked.

"I thought I'd go see about sanding some of my spindles."

"Don't try to ride your bike."

"Yes, Doctor."

"Don't drive either. I'll take you out in the Toyota later."

"The doctor didn't say anything about driving…"

"Because he thought you'd have enough sense not to try it alone."

"…I hate this."

"I know, sweetheart. I'd hate it too."

We hugged a long time. I finally released him and went to see if I could manage sanding.

He joined me a few hours later.

"How's it going?"

"Good, I guess. I can manage brute force. Nails, sanding, even the nail gun. I haven't tried saws yet."

He picked up one of the scrap pieces then tossed it back down.

I'd left a mangled mess of pieces that I'd tried to router. I could manage straight edges if I braced the outer edge but not curves.

"Let's go for lunch. You can try to drive on the driveway."

We drove up and down the driveway a few times. To my relief I had no problems with it. He grudgingly let me drive to the diner, keeping a white knuckled grip on the dashboard the entire time.

I didn't think I could manage backing in so circled the lot until I could pull in.

"Don't try this at night, Kate. And don't go far or fast."

"I did fine," I said.

"I didn't. I'd just feel better if you go slow. I'm worried your reaction time isn't quite up to what it should be yet."

"I'll be careful."

I spent the next day at the shop too, cautiously trying the hand saws. Jace came looking for me at noon.

He said, "Have you seen your mom yet? I saw your dad drop her off."

"No."

"I think your dad is crazy for encouraging her to have a party for you."

"I'm...conflicted. She loved birthday parties—any party really that included all of us. I like to think Dad checked all this with her doctor and her. Maybe she's well enough... I don't want to set her back by making her think I hate her now."

"I get that, but seeing you could make her snap again."

"Which is why I hope he cleared it with her doctor too."

"Maybe you should check? Or at least meet with her privately first."

"Dad wants me to come to the house after dinner tonight while Grayson and Grandma have the kids. Grandma took the girls again and Gray the boys so Dad could get Mom and settle her in. He assures me that she's happy making cake and stuff."

"Like it never happened...

"She doesn't remember a lot of it. I think he's suffering from wishful thinking. Mom was always a nervous baker so she's probably as nervous of seeing me as I am of her. He told me to treat her like normal. We're not to lie just not offer any information unless she asks. Mrs. Lane, the day nurse, will be on hand tomorrow for, as my father says, any unfortunate incidents."

"Just... be careful."

"I will. It still hasn't really sunk in that she'd try to really kill me. It just isn't something she'd do... she isn't cold like that. Planning and plotting are more Everly's style. If they hadn't found the paint on that newspaper, I'd never believe my mom did it."

Jace hugged me.

I said, "Have I said lately how much I love you—how grateful I am to have you in my life? I can't wait for us to live a normal life together. It feels like forever since we had a moment alone together. I miss us."

"We're always us."

His kiss was passionate and very reassuring as was the way he pressed against me. I was suddenly eager to be alone in our house for a different reason.

He broke away from me a minute later, laughing ruefully.

"It's probably a good thing I'm not spending the night with you. I'd be too tempted to break the doctor's orders."

"Good. I'd hate to think I've lost my—allure."

"It's your superpower.

Howard came into the shop, interrupting our kiss.

"Excuse me. I didn't know you were here."

"I was just going," I said. "I just stopped to borrow your house key again. Grandma still has mine."

He handed me his key.

"No power tools."

"I won't. Maybe I'll try a paint roller, but really, I just want to unpack. Dad has people coming next week to do the bedroom upstairs. If the kids want to come before the room is ready, they can sleep on the bedroom floor."

"We could use the chaperons," he agreed laughingly.

"When are you moving your stuff in?" I asked.

"Tonight."

"I love you."

"I love you too."

I said, "I know. You don't have to say it as much anymore. I feel it now."

His smile lit his eyes for the first time in days.

I turned back in the doorway to wave, knowing he'd be watching me.

I called back, "I have a checkup in four days."

He laughed.

His laugh made my head stop hurting or not my head really. My headache had faded but my neck and shoulders were always sore now. That soreness eased.

I took the Toyota, which reminded me I needed to put my car up for sale and buy something more practical—a truck or maybe an SUV. I was about halfway to the house when my watch vibrated, notifying me that the house alarm had gone off.

I expected it to stop and when it didn't, I pulled over to call Jace to see if he'd sent anyone there with a delivery because I didn't think my new clumsiness would allow for me to make a call and drive.

Kenya texted me before I could call him, saying she was at my house and needed the alarm code.

I sent her the code then called Jace because he'd have gotten the notifications on his cell although he might not notice them if he was working with power tools.

"Is everything okay? You shouldn't drive so fast!" he said accusingly.

"It wasn't me. Kenya must have borrowed the key to drop off my stuff. She texted for the code. And before you ask, I pulled over to use my phone."

"Sorry, Kate. I'm just worried."

"I know. I don't mean to be a bitch about it."

"You aren't. Call me when you get there though."

I laughed and disconnected.

My mother's Aston Martin was parked in my drive.

For a second I was uneasy but there was no way she'd be allowed to take her car out—I didn't think. *Kenya must've borrowed it.*

I parked at the head of the drive so I wouldn't block her in or have to turn the car because I still wasn't certain if I could back up.

"Ken! I called as I stepped inside the house.

My heart began to pound hard enough to leave me breathless.

My sister lay in the hall by the parlor in a puddle, bleeding from a head wound, gagged with one of my rags, and tied hand and foot with black zip ties.

The hall stank of paint thinner.

I ran forward, falling to my knees beside her to feel for a pulse and realized she lay in a puddle of the thinner.

Another unopened bottle was in my rag box that had been left beside her.

Kenya opened her eyes.

I tried to yank at the zip ties on her hands but couldn't budge them. I yanked the gag away then grabbed her under the arms and dragged her into the parlor.

She began to sob.

"Run. Get help!" she said, sounding terrified.

"And leave you to be murdered!"

I debated trying to drag her outside and into the car but was worried our mother would show up any second and the secret room was much closer and easier to get to.

Kenya wasn't that heavy, but she was awkward to maneuver. It took me a minute to open the door in the hearth and pull her down the stairs. Every second of that time I was expecting I'd need to fight off my mother.

I was a shaking mess by the time I got us onto the stairs.

I said, "This door opens if you press the rock above it and turn the handle."

I dragged her into the next room and set her down before taking out my phone and calling nine-one-one.

I said to her, "I don't think Mom knows about this room. We should be safe here."

"What's the nature of your emergency?" the woman on the phone asked.

Kenya said, "It wasn't Mom. It was Grandma."

I stared at Kenya in shock.

"What! She has the kids! Grandma did this?"

"What's the nature of your emergency?" the woman asked again.

"Kidnapping! Come quick!"

I pulled Kenya's shirt open to tuck the phone under her bra strap, saying, "The light by that door will turn red if anyone comes down the stairs. I have to go see about the kids. You should be safe here."

"Don't go out there!"

"I have too! You can get out by pressing the fish, the two triangles, and the pig tail."

"I didn't see the kids."

"The girls were with her."

I kissed her brow and ran to press the symbols, whispering to her, "the fish, the two triangles, and the pig tail."

Which was dumb when she couldn't move but I'd want to know if it were me tied like that.

The room was too dark to really see her, but I knew she had to be terrified to be left alone, tied, and helpless in this dark room. I was afraid to turn on the light though and have it seep under the door in the basement.

I whispered, "She might be able to hear you, so be quiet."

"Kate..."

"I love you too."

I left her in the dark room whispering to the woman on the phone and ran to the wine cellar to climb the ladder there into the library.

The click when I opened the closet door seemed explosively loud. I peeked into the room. It appeared empty. I ran to grab a long screwdriver, snatched a pair of wire cutters, and tiptoed to the hall.

The house was ominously silent, except for a faint tinkle of running water.

I ran through the kitchen and the dining room to check my rooms.

I found Hannah sleeping in my filling bathtub. At least I hoped she was sleeping. I couldn't wake her, but she was breathing normally and had no visible wounds. Her shoelace had stuck beneath the stopper, letting the water drain out a bit as it filled. It was up around her shoulders, just inches from her face.

I had to remove her shoe to get her from the tub. The water was cold, she was cold, which made my heart pound with dread and fear as I wrapped her in a towel then ran back to the parlor with her, back down the stairs and handed her to Kenya.

She said, "The police are on the way."

"Felicity... I can turn a light on in here, but I'm not sure if it can be seen."

As I was talking, I snipped the ties on Kenya's wrists and ankles.

I said, "I didn't see Olivia. Maybe she changed her mind and left?"

Kenya said, "Or maybe she's going to burn this place. She was crazed Kate! Why is Hannah all wet? It doesn't smell like gas, thank god. Come on sweetheart, open your eyes."

"She was in the tub."

"Dear God! She drowned her?"

"She tried. Let me go look for Felicity. If I'm not back in ten minutes, press the fish, triangles, the pig tail and take Hannah and run."

"I can't run. I think my ankle is broken."

"I can't leave Felicity!"

"Take Hannah out."

I debated taking her to my car, but I had no idea where our grandmother was. *If I ran into her while holding Hannah, I couldn't fight her for Felicity and Hannah was safe here.* That last thought decided me.

"I'll be back," I said as I let myself out again and climbed the ladder to the attic then ran down the attic stairs.

There was no sign of Felicity. I hoped it meant she had nothing against Felicity and had left her at home. I ran down the stairs to peek out the front window.

My mom's car was still there.

My grandmother must have made that bomb. Felicity might be in the carriage house.

I ran for the back door.

It was wide open.

My mother was in the back driveway talking to Claire.

Claire had her arms crossed and was shaking her head.

Kenya was wrong, I thought but then realized it wasn't my mother but my grandmother wearing a black wig and my mother's red coat.

I wondered if Claire knew who she was speaking with.

"Olivia!" I yelled.

She whirled to face me, and I saw she held a gun.

"Run!" Claire yelled.

Olivia shot her twice.

I stared stunned speechless for a moment then yelled furiously, "Stop! The police are on their way!"

I ducked back into the house, slamming the door closed as she turned to shoot at me.

Glass tinkled from her bullet. Shards from the window of the door fell around my feet. Despite finding Kenya and Hannah and seeing her shoot Claire it was still a shock that she'd actually shoot at me.

It made me furious.

I turned to run to the library and the nail gun there.

It wasn't where I'd left it. My hands were shaking so badly I kept dropping my screwdriver.

I stuck it into my waistband to use two hands to ransack my tool drawer.

My watch vibrated.

She'd come in the back door.

I ran for my room. *Jace had probably left it in my closet.*

She yelled, "Kate! It isn't what you think! She deserved to die. She was a lying gold-digging whore just like your mother! Did you want her to ruin your father and steal your inheritance!"

Jace had left the nail gun right outside the closet.

"Where the hell is Kenya!" she yelled from the hallway in a completely different tone.

I let myself out the patio door in my room and ran around the house to let myself in through the parlor window. I was really worried now that she intended to burn the house using the paint thinner and rags in the hallway.

My stomach squirmed with nausea as I considered she'd intended to burn Kenya.

My watch vibrated.

She'd gone out again or had at least opened the door.

My heart pounded hard enough to make me feel lightheaded.

This can't be good for my blood pressure, I thought, snickering in hysterical amusement as I crept to the front window to peek out.

She was dragging Felicity from the car.

Stupid! Stupid! You should've checked the damned car!

It was too late now though. She was likely to shoot Felicity right there—or maybe not because she was keeping her head down, hiding from the cameras.

I didn't know what to do.

I let myself onto the stairs under the hearth saying, "It's me! It's me!" as I ran down.

Kenya had picked Hannah up and sat against the wall by the door.

I said, "She shot Claire twice and has Felicity. I don't know what to do."

"Who's Claire?"

"The neighbor."

"Why... it doesn't matter. We have to get out! She's going to burn this place."

"If I take Hannah, can you crawl?"

"Yes."

"I can open the stairs on the hearth. There's a lamp in the corner of the room by the fireplace. Pull it like a handle and that window will open. You can get out and maybe she won't notice you crawl across the yard?"

Kenya started to cry.

Thinking of my sister reduced to crawling when she was covered in paint thinner, and that Olivia had a gun she was clearly willing to use gave me the cold shivers too.

I said, "Or maybe you can crawl up the basement stairs? If I could get her to chase me down here, she'd be trapped in this room. There's a ladder in the corner of the third room on the right. It comes out in the library—my work room. There's a regular window there. I'll take Hannah and put her outside then see if I can get Fell."

"Maybe we should wait?"

"I don't think we have time. I told her I called the police. Get up the stairs, Ken! I'll distract her." I opened the door for her, kissed her cheek, gave her the screwdriver, and grabbed Hannah.

I ran back to the ladder. It was much harder to climb it with Hannah's dead weight over my shoulder, but I managed it.

Worry for Kenya, Felicity, and the limp body of Hannah was a cold knot in my stomach.

I opened a window to lay Hannah outside, closed the window, and crept to the hallway door to peek out.

It was really worrying me that all this running around hadn't woken Hannah.

One of the fire alarms began to shrill. I thought it was the one in the main hall.

I cautiously peeked into the hall.

Water was pouring from a sprinkler system that I didn't even know that Jace had installed. Grandma was cursing with her back to me, leaning over a pile of soggy paper and a box of kitchen matches.

The box of rags was scorched as was the floor in a circle around it. Black smoke hung thick in the air.

Felicity lay on the floor by the front door. I imagined it had been difficult for my grandmother to get her that far. Felicity was too far for me to tell if she was alive or dead.

I crept closer, meaning to get to the parlor door before shooting at her with the nail gun. I didn't think it would do more than annoy her unless I got a lucky shot, but it would hopefully be enough to get her to chase me cautiously enough that I could open the hearth stairs and run down them before she shot me.

The front door opened.

"Run!" I screamed at Jace with a terrible feeling of *déjà vu*.

Olivia glanced over her shoulder at me as she fired at him.

I screamed as he fell back.

"You evil bitch!"

I emptied the nail gun at her.

She screamed, whirling toward me, firing blindly. Wood splintered from the doorway of the parlor as I ducked inside, throwing the empty gun at her over my shoulder. Her footsteps were weirdly loud as she ran. Sharp click clacks echoed against the floor. I expected to feel a bullet any second and almost didn't care, except I knew if she murdered me, she'd finish off my sisters next.

I yanked the candelabra to open the hearth and ran down the steps as she fired at me.

The gunshots echoed in my head.

"Kate!" Jace screamed.

This proof that he was alive—at least for the moment—gave me a burst of adrenaline. I half fell down the stairs in my haste.

Barbara was going to be pissed if she needed to pick me up again.

The thought was somehow comforting. Help would be on the way. If I could get to him...

Kate! There's no place to go," she said happily from the head of the hearth stairs.

"Why are you doing this?"

I didn't care why she was doing it. I just needed time to press the buttons to open the door.

"Why? Why? That whore thinks she can pawn off her sluts on my son! I think not! She can rot in jail. I hope she believes she did it! God, I should've killed her years ago! And you're just like her, fucking a boy you barely know! A boy from the trailer park for god's sake! Which is exactly what I'd expect from her spawn! You're all whores! Every one of you!"

A bullet sent pieces of wood into my face. The door at the bottom of the stairs opened, and I fell through the door as she screeched with rage and fired again—at the bookshelf I thought by the sound.

She realized there was nothing there except moving books or maybe it had been the lights flickering that had got her attention, but in those moments before she fired at me again I made it through the door and got to my feet, holding the door open with a foot, hiding behind the wall.

The next bullet hit the wall behind me. It would've killed me if I'd been in the doorway. My special effects on that shelf had saved my life— for the moment.

Sirens sounded in the distance.

Luckily for me she was firing in a rage, not aiming or having really shitty aim because I had to hold that door open until the hearth slid closed again. The wall hid my body, leaving my leg from the knee down exposed. The light on the stair from the opened door of the hearth stair was fading as the trap door closed.

It seemed to take forever. I didn't dare let this door close before I was certain she'd be trapped.

My grandmother was remarkably spry and had almost reached the bottom before the hearth door had closed enough that I didn't think she could make it back up before it closed completely. I pulled my foot away, letting the door close.

I yelled, "There's no way out of there!"

She shot another two rounds through the door.

I let myself from the room worried she'd be able to shoot her way out.

Kenya was at the top of the cellar steps talking on the phone, trying to crawl.

Her terror and pain was horrible to see. She was sobbing each time she lurched forward.

I said, "She's trapped for a minute, but she might be able to shoot her way free or set another fire."

I pulled her up, mumbling apologies. We were both crying. Kenya hissed on each step, moaning occasionally.

"I'm so sorry but we have to hurry."

The police reached the front door as we did.

Jace was leaning over Felicity who he'd dragged to the porch.

"Kate," he said, sounding exasperated.

He fell to the side in slow motion.

I released Kenya to crouch and feel for the pulse in Felicity's neck.

Oh thank God!" I crawled to Jace as I said to the policeman, "She's on the stairs under the hearth. You open it by pulling the candelabra on the right. Or she might have gotten that door open and be in the next room. It opens by a foot pedal in the basement."

Another two gunshots sounded in quick succession below us.

An ambulance pulled up right behind my mother's car.

One of the officers said, "How many weapons does she have?"

"I have no idea."

Jace was warm and breathing. Kenya sank to the floor beside me and handed me a wad of fabric. I pressed her hand to the wound in his thigh, realizing it was her shirt when I stood.

I said, "She has a gun. There's a shot woman out back."

"Another ambulance is on the way."

"I put my little sister outside. I need to go get her."

"No. Go to the police car. We'll get her."

I ignored them.

Two other police cars had arrived by the time I'd gotten Hannah and reached the front of the house. Kenya was sitting on the porch, crying on the phone, I think to our father because she said daddy twice, which was heartbreaking—she was still terrified. Jace and Felicity were gone.

Two of the new officers approached me with their guns out.

Two others ran past us and into the house.

I began to cry. I'd no idea if my sister was alive or dead—or Jace. Hannah was still cold but breathing.

I said, "She must have put Everly up to it."

Another ambulance pulled in and drove straight passed the house to the carriage house.

One of the officers crouched beside us to feel Hannah's pulse.

I said, "Hannah needs help."

He said, "You're sure there's only one woman in there armed with a gun?"

"Yes."

I told him where I'd last seen my grandmother.

"How many times did she fire?"

"I don't know. I lost count. A lot."

"Think hard."

"She shot Claire twice and then twice at me from the yard and three times in the hall at Jace, and twice more I think, no five more times on the stairs because she shot at the books—and then two more."

Another shot muffled by the house so it just sounded like a pop interrupted me.

"And that one."

Another ambulance pulled in followed by a fire truck.

Relief left me feeling dizzy. *Barbara was going to be seriously pissed.* A paramedic took Hannah from me.

Seeing her little arm in the soaked cast, her little body lying there so still, the feverish way the paramedics cut her clothing off, made me feel weak and shivery.

She could still die. Olivia had meant to murder her.

"How could she! How could she!"

"It's alright now. Take a deep breath!"

Kenya grabbed my face, yelling, "Kate!"

I stopped yelling and we hugged each other crying until another ambulance arrived a few minutes later.

Our parents arrived at the hospital a few minutes after us. The paramedics were still unloading Kenya from the back when my mother ran over, crying hard.

"I knew I'd never do anything like that! They told me I had but I knew I wouldn't!"

She hugged us both. I could feel her shivering.

I said to my father, "She shouldn't be here. This is too much. This is too much for anyone!"

"She wanted to come—for her children who she loves."

He kissed Kenya on the cheek. "God, when you called..."

He kept her hand, leaning to kiss my forehead.

I said, "I love you too, Mom."

My mother said, "I'm so sorry, Kate. I knew I needed help, but I was so scared... I'm so sorry!"

My father said, "Kenya, sweetheart, you need a doctor, and you should get your head looked at, Kate."

My father looked sick, shaky, and pale. It suddenly struck me how terrible all of this must be for him, his children, his wife, his crazy parents...

The hospital staff were all quiet, avoiding our eyes as we passed. They brought Kenya and me into one of the curtained off alcoves right in the main corridor.

It made me feel sick with dread that the girls or Jace had died.

My father said, "My daughters?"

"If you'd just come with us, sir," a nurse said worriedly.

I didn't like her tone or her expression.

"Jace Blake?" I asked.

"Is in surgery. The prognosis is good."

The nurse said to another nurse, "Cheryl, take this young lady to exam room four."

"No."

My father said, "Your face is bleeding, Kate, and someone should check your head and blood pressure."

"Later. I want to see my sisters!"

"We'll see to them. Go with the nurse."

"No!"

Cheryl said, "We'll *all* go to exam room four."

She led the way there.

I sat on the bed and let her check my blood pressure while my father told her I was recovering from a serious concussion that had needed two surgeries already. She left the room returning a minute later with a doctor.

Another doctor came in while the nurse was checking Kenya's blood pressure. He said, "Mr. and Mrs. Avery, I'm afraid I have some bad news."

"No!" I yelled as my mother sank weakly to the floor.

Kenya began to sob again.

Lines wavered across my vision.

My father crouched beside my mother.

The doctor continued, "It appears as if your daughter Everly has taken her own life."

"Everly?" my mother asked as if she didn't recognize the name.

"She's dead?" I asked, shocked and also relieved, which made me feel terrible. I *shouldn't* be relieved—but I was. Except, I didn't think she'd kill herself—on purpose anyway.

My father said, "Hannah and Felicity?"

"We don't know yet. I'm sorry. Both are being treated."

The room swam.

I said, "Did that evil bitch visit Everly today?"

My mother was sobbing so hard I feared she'd give herself a stroke.

I said to her, "This isn't your fault, Mom. Dad, get her help! Doctor, my mom needs her doctor! She needs her meds! This isn't your fault! None of this!"

The other doctor said to me, "I'm prescribing a mild sedative and a little something for your blood pressure. I see from your chart that you're Doctor Kennedy's patient. He'll be in shortly to re-examine you."

He gave the other doctor an exasperated glance as he crouched by my crying parents.

The doctor who'd told us the news left the room with Kenya.

The other doctor spoke to my parents, but the words were white noise lost in my pounding head and worried thoughts. *She'd obviously killed Everly...* I'd thought she'd loved Everly, that she'd loved us all.

I said, "Why now?"

No one answered me. There were more people in the small room now. Most of them were trying to get my mother off the floor. One was putting an IV in my arm while another woman handed me a pill and glass of water.

I took it then handed her the empty glass, saying, "She might've given whatever she gave to Everly to the girls."

One of the men by my mother said, "We're checking that now."

They got my mother loaded onto a stretcher and wheeled out.

My father kissed my forehead.

"I'll be back when I can. Try not to worry."

Deep lines creased his forehead. He looked haggard, aged—I wondered if he knew Claire had been shot too. I wondered if she was dead.

"Go take care of her!"

I waited until I couldn't hear them to say to the nurse who was taking my blood pressure again, "Did Claire make it?"

"Claire?"

"A blond woman. She was shot twice."

"I'm afraid not..."

"Someone should tell my father but *not* my mother."

"Put this gown on. The doctor wants an EEG."

I did as I was told.

The nurse had just finished the EEG and was taking blood when Dee and Reynolds entered.

She said, "Never a dull moment with you."

"Did they catch my grandmother—Olivia."

"Yes—she's claiming she was a prisoner in that room. That it was all your mother."

"Oh please!"

Dee snorted, nodding agreement.

"Still, you have to admire her chutzpah. We'd like a written statement from you as soon as possible, and we'll need all the clothes you're wearing. Your sister gave us your phone. Your father gave us permission to look through it. Someone should drop it off here in a few hours unless you'd rather we dropped it at your house?"

"Here's fine. My clothes are on that chair there. Someone will have to write my statement for me."

She nodded. "How's the head?"

"Hurts," I said shortly. "Have you heard anything about my sisters? Are my brothers okay? Did you check on Jace?"

"Your brothers are fine. Your sisters are being treated. I'm cautiously optimistic."

Reynolds said, "It's a good thing she was—squeamish."

Dee snorted angrily. "I don't think she was. I think she poisoned them to drown them to make it more believable that their mother had killed them."

"My mother had nothing to do with it!"

"It appears really unlikely," Dee agreed.

"Appears! You have to be kidding me! Why would I lie about that when that goddamned bitch was trying to kill me too?"

Reynolds said, "Her claims need to be investigated, Kate."

"What claims! What could she possibly say to excuse what she's done?"

"Nothing at all—if she did it."

"This is unbelievable!"

Dee gave him an exasperated glance, shaking her head at him, saying to me, "We don't believe her. My partner just means we can't take anyone's word—that we have to examine the evidence. Olivia's scrambling right now for a cover story, but we have hard evidence that is sure to put the blame squarely on her and her alone."

Reynolds said, "What we want to know is *why* she'd do it?"

"Cause she's a crazy psychotic bitch! Actually she isn't crazy, she's just jealous! I think she lied about when she found out about my mom and grandpa. My mom gets confused... I'm not sure she *can* tell you when grandma knew or not."

"Knew what?"

"That Kenya is my grandfather's daughter."

Dee gaped at me.

"Why would she shoot Clair?" Reynolds asked.

"My father was having an affair with her. I think that's my fault—not that he was having an affair, but that Olivia murdered her. I'd told her about it..."

"How did you know about it? Did your mother know?"

"I saw him go there. He didn't know about my house. He thought it was Grayson's house. I saw him at Clair's a few times a week. I have no idea if my mom knew."

"Still, why would Olivia kill her?"

"She was wearing my mom's coat and a black wig. I bet she hoped my mom would be blamed for just that reason—Olivia had no motive, and my mom did, although Olivia called Claire a gold-digging whore who'd ruin the family and steal my inheritance. So maybe that's why she killed her, but I really think she did it to frame my mom just like that stupid bomb. And Everly... did she give her whatever she gave the girls?"

"It looks like it. Both your mother and Olivia went to see Everly. Someone gave Everly the pills she took."

"Someone..."

"It's *possible* that it was another patient there who gave them to her. The staff does it's best to keep narcotics from the ward but visitors occasionally sneak stuff in. Your sister had been responding well to her treatment and was allowed to use the day room and come and go from her room as she liked. She had a few other visitors besides your family. We'll check them all because it's possible she had the pills for days before she took them."

Reynolds said, "Your sisters were dosed with the same stuff but a much lighter dose. My personal theory is Olivia hoped it would be overlooked in an autopsy."

Dee shook her head.

"I think she just ran out of it, or they didn't eat much of whatever she put it in. We have teams going through her house now."

"But you know what it is?"

"We have a good idea. The labs will confirm it shortly."

"Will they be okay?"

"We hope so."

Reynolds said, "We'd like you to call your lawyer to give us that statement."

"I don't know his number. It was on my phone. Kenya or Gray will know it. How's she doing?"

"Getting seen to. She's going to be fine. I can call your lawyer and ask him to come."

"Can you call Jace's mom?"

She was going to hate me. I couldn't blame her. I hoped he didn't hate me too.

TWENTY-NINE

It was late when Dwayne brought me clean clothes and my phone. Grayson had been sitting with me. He stood when Dwayne arrived.

"Gray," Dwayne said worriedly, giving him a quick hug.

I was worried over how haggard Grayson looked too.

He gave me a kiss on the cheek, Dwayne a harried glance, and left me to go check on the kids again. He'd been going from room-to-room for the last few hours, giving us all updates.

Dwayne said, "I'm sorry to see you again under these circumstances. How's the head?"

"The doctor changed my medicine because my blood pressure is too high, speaking of which, I'm officially eighteen in a few hours, so can I check myself out?"

"Yes. But I don't recommend it."

"I want to go see the kids and Jace, and the doctor won't let me leave the room, which is stupid. It's worse for my blood pressure to be stuck in here!"

"Still... blood pressure is nothing to take lightly."

I shrugged.

He sat beside me to take out a notebook.

"Let's get your statement done. Start with the morning when you left your grandmother's house. Just tell it to me like it happened. Did you think anything was out of the ordinary?"

I said, "I left while the kids were having breakfast. Olivia had let them eat in the living room in front of the television, which she'd never done before, but I thought it was just to keep them quiet and because the kittens were in there... good Lord, did she kill the kittens?"

"No. They're at your parents' house with the boys. And then what happened?"

"She was taking the girls shopping again and asked me if I needed anything. I said no and then she asked if Everly would want anything in particular because she planned on stopping in to see her. I said I didn't know but the kids shouldn't go there. She said Kenya was taking them for lunch. Hannah asked Olivia if she knew that Everly had been bad, and Olivia said that she did, but that Everly was sorry for being so bad.

"Felicity said something like Everly didn't deserve anything, and I could tell by her tone she was angry that Olivia was going to visit and bring her stuff.

"We were all angry about it, but none of us complained because we all knew Everly was Olivia's favorite. I thought she was being nicer to the kids than normal because she wanted to be nice to Everly.

Dwayne said, "Explain that."

"Dad had spoken to us older ones and Olivia the night before about how to handle talking about Everly to the kids. Olivia had said we needed to stress forgiveness, that people made mistakes, that it was Alise's mental illness that was the problem. She kept saying Dad should divorce her—that he should tell the kids now that he was going to. She wanted him to move in with her. Dad kept saying it wasn't anyone's business and he finally yelled at her to butt out. He said if she was going to tell the kids it was Alise's fault, he'd take them and not let her see them. He yelled at her about Everly too, saying it was time she faced the facts that Everly had a drug problem and she'd been lying.

"Olivia was angry but not furious. We all agreed we'd tell the kids that Everly had a drug problem and was getting treatment for it and that we'd let Dad handle talking about our mom's mental health issues. He planned to tell them she was upset over Everly's drug problem and Everly's actions because of it and wait and see how Mom was coping before saying anything else, which I thought made sense because my mom acts normal most of the time. I figured with medicine, the kids wouldn't notice anything, and they wouldn't need to worry about her. They could be told when they were older—when it wouldn't be so confusing. Mom was coming home the next day.

"Olivia offered to take the girls shopping again for school clothes to keep them busy—out of her hair, she said."

"Okay, so the next morning..."

"Was normal, except for the eating in the living room. I went to the shop at home to talk to Jace and see if I could use the machines. He took me out driving to see if I could do it then we went for lunch. After lunch I went to my house to unpack. Olivia had taken my key the day before to drop off my stuff. She, Kenya, and Grayson were emptying my room at my parents' house for Maria to use. I didn't want to go back there. I thought it was nice of her to offer..."

"So you didn't know she planned to go there that day?"

"No. On the way to my house, I got an alarm notification. Jace had installed door alarms that sent notifications when the doors are opened. Mine is set to make my smart watch vibrate. It sends the same notice if the alarm is tripped. So I pulled over to call him to see if he'd arranged for a delivery or anything, but Kenya texted me to say she was there and wanted the alarm code, so I texted it back. Jace told me to call him when I got there because he was nervous about me driving with the concussion.

"When I got there, I saw my mom's car but figured Kenya had borrowed it. I almost had a heart attack when I saw her tied on the floor..."

"Describe what you saw."

"She'd been tied with black zip ties exactly like the kind I keep in my toolbox. She had one around each hand and foot with another one connecting the two with one of my rags wrapped around her face. She was covered in paint thinner too. There was another unopened bottle of thinner in a box of rags that I normally keep in the library.

I thought my mom had done it and I didn't think I could get Kenya all the way to my car, and since I didn't know if my mom was there making a bomb or something, I figured the smartest thing to do would be to hide. So I dragged Kenya into the hidden room beneath the hearth and then she told me that it was Olivia, not mom. And I realized Olivia had taken the girls and she was nuts, so I went to look for the kids.

"I found Hannah in my bathroom in the tub half full of water. It would've been completely full of water if her shoelace hadn't gotten wrapped around the drain. So I brought her back to Kenya and went to look for Felicity.

"My mother's car was still there, so I figured Olivia was still there, maybe in the carriage house getting another paint can, so I went to look out the back window and saw Olivia wearing my mother's red jacket with a black wig, talking to the neighbor, Claire. There was no sign of Felicity, which I hoped meant Olivia had left her at home. So I called to Olivia.

"I thought if she saw me, she'd stop whatever craziness she was about. She turned to see me and then shot Claire twice. I was stunned and stood there a second staring in shock. She shot at me. So I ran. She shot at me twice. I wanted a weapon, so I went to see if I could find the nail gun. It wasn't in my tool room. I knew Jace had been planning to work on our closet, so I ran in there and sure enough it was on the floor. My watch beeped notifying me someone had opened the front or back door, so I ran to the front door to look out to see if she'd left.

"She was pulling Felicity from the car. Felicity was clearly unconscious. I couldn't tell if she was dead or alive. I didn't know what to do because Olivia had the gun and was clearly willing to use it, so I ran back to talk to Kenya.

"Kenya told me that Olivia planned to burn the house down, so I took Hannah, opened the door for Kenya, brought Hannah to my library using the secret ladder and placed her outside the window, and then went to see if I could get Olivia to chase me into that room because I didn't think she'd be able to get out of it—at least not quickly. I hoped I could trap her in there and then help Kenya to my car and get the girls.

"Olivia was in the front hall trying to start a fire but the sprinkler in the ceiling was making the paper too wet. Felicity was laying on the floor by the door. Jace walked in and I yelled for him to run. She shot at him twice right in a row. I knew at least one shot had hit him because he fell back.

"She chased me as I shot at her with the nail gun. She was shooting at me, yelling how she wanted to kill us all because we were sluts like my mother. My moving books or maybe the lights flickering startled her and she shot at them, which let me get through the door. I escaped through the dungeon room, leaving her trapped on the stairs. She shot a few more times, at the door, I thought. The police had arrived. I told them how to get into the stairs and the hidden room and I went back for Hannah.

"Jace and Felicity were gone when I got back. A paramedic took Hannah. Kenya and I went to the hospital in the back of another ambulance where we found out that Everly was dead, and my mom collapsed."

"Good, now give me descriptions of everyone's clothing."

I described their clothes and then read and signed the papers with my kindergarten scrawl.

I said, "I want her charged with everything from trespassing to damaging the damned house! And she better be charged with trying to murder us all!"

"I'll be speaking to the DA latter today. I'm sure he'll be gathering statements from everyone."

"Is she still denying it was her?"

247

"As far as I know."

"How can she deny it when we saw her do it?"

"It's going to your word against hers."

"My mother wasn't even there!"

"The police are busy gathering evidence, which includes video footage from your security cameras. I don't think you need to worry too much."

"Too much..."

"It's going to be a long, complicated process unless she admits it and enters a plea. And even then it won't be pleasant for any of you. Two people are dead, one shot, one fatally poisoned. Then there's the rest of you... I hope the girls make full recoveries. I hope the DA charges her with attempted murder, but every charge will need to be proved."

"My mom can't take much more."

He winced, nodding agreement.

"I'm sure the DA's office will be as kind as they can be given the circumstances."

"It must have been Olivia who planted that bomb."

"The police are looking into it."

"I fucking hate her! Looking into it! She did it! My mom shouldn't have to take the blame for that!"

"They *will* reinvestigate it, Kate, but I don't want you to get your hopes up because there's nothing the DA hates more than admitting he was wrong, so it's going to take pretty compelling evidence for him to change his verdict, especially when you consider the consequences. That wrong charge left Olivia free to murder. The DA is going to fight that because it leaves his office somewhat culpable in the deaths that followed."

"Will he try to frame my mom too?"

"No, but he's going to give Olivia more—leeway. Or at least I think he will. Hell, he might surprise me and admit he made a mistake and throw the book at her, but what I think will happen is he'll act as if he believes her claims and investigate them as if they were true because then he can say that it wasn't a mistake, that Olivia perpetuated a fraud that would've fooled anyone, that it was his office's good detective work that convicted her."

"It's all so unfair..."

"It is. Just hang in there, Kate. I'll keep you updated, and I'll make sure the DA knows we expect her to be charged with attempting to murder you. It will most likely mean you have to testify. I expect the DA to impose a gag order any time now."

"What's that mean?"

"You won't be allowed to talk about it to anyone."

"What about the kids? We have to tell them something!"

"As of this moment, there's no orders. You can tell them whatever you want. Your father's lawyer will be offering his advice about that. I want you to avoid the press. If pressed, just say no comment. Don't talk to anyone, except to me about it more than you need to."

"My dad will want to know what happened—and Jace."

"Like I said, as of this moment there's no order. I don't know your boyfriend, so I can't offer advice, except to say you shouldn't talk to anyone who's prone to gossiping. Plus, there's a real possibility that he sues you. His insurance will likely insist on it—even if he sues her, her insurance could sue you."

"That's crazy."

"That's the way things go."

"Still, he has a right to know what happened."

"I don't disagree, but my duty is to inform you of *your* legal risk. Anything you say to him, especially if you admit responsibility in any way, could be used against you. I don't think a suit against you would win, I'm just saying it's possible that you get sued by his insurance or hers."

"Will I be charged for shooting at her with the nail gun?"

He grinned crookedly, shaking his head. "Since she's denying she was the shooter, she can hardly say you shot her with the nail gun, can she?"

"Did I hit her?"

"A nick on her shoulder, which will hopefully be enough to place her in that hall upstairs if the techs can find the nail with her blood on it."

"How does she think she's going to get away with this!"

"She isn't."

"She better not!"

"I'll be in touch."

I went to get dressed and go find Jace.

THIRTY

"It's you," Jace said muzzily when he opened his eyes.

His mother leaned passed me to kiss his cheek and smooth his hair.

"Mom... what...oh... are you okay?" he asked me anxiously.

From the doorway, Dee said, "We'd like to hear what you recall, Mr. Blake."

Reynolds said, "Start with why you left work to go there."

His mother said angrily, "He just woke up!"

Dee said, "I know. But we need his unbiased statement."

Jace said, "Can I get some water?"

A nurse entered, saying, "Everyone out while I see to my patient!"

I gave him a quick hug, saying, "I'm fine. I'll be back as soon as they let me."

In the hall, Jace's mother said, "He needs his rest."

I wasn't sure if that were directed at me or not. It was a valid observation either way though.

She put her arm around me, saying, "He needs his family!"

Her kindness made tears fill my eyes.

Frank approached, saying, "Ginny—thank God. I heard he woke, darling."

She began to cry and ran to hug him.

"Why isn't my wife allowed in his room?" he asked angrily.

Dee said, "The nurse kicked us all out."

A doctor and another nurse entered the room.

We waited in tense silence to be readmitted to it.

I thought the police would make me leave but they let me follow his parents in.

He looked better, more awake with healthy color in his cheeks and was sitting up, propped by pillows.

I burst into tears when he held his hand out to me.

"Felicity?" he asked with a wealth of sorrow in his voice.

"Still out but we're hopeful."

Dee said, "Please let him tell us, Kate."

Jace said, "I went to the house because Kate didn't call me to say she'd arrived there. When I called her, her phone was busy. I tried for like five minutes and knew something was wrong when she didn't even text me to say she was on the phone."

Dee said, "That's a little... do you always insist she call and let you know where she'll be?"

"When I'm worried her concussion will make her have an accident—yes!"

Dee nodded.

He continued, "I almost had a heart attack when I saw Alise's car there. Then when I opened the door and saw Felicity... I thought she was dead. I thought they would both be dead!" he said accusingly to me.

His grip on my hand tightened.

"I was relieved when I saw her grandmother. Olivia looked pissed, which was understandable. I was pissed! But then Kate yelled run and Olivia shot me... I was shocked! I'm still shocked... I'd never have imagined... she's just a little old lady! Then she shot at Kate. By the time I got myself sitting, they were gone from the hall. I could hear Olivia yelling about Alise's daughters all being sluts like their mother—and shooting. I couldn't get up! I could see Fell was breathing, so I tried to drag her out. I hoped I could get us to the car.

My leg was bleeding pretty bad, making my head swim—I thought we were all going to die...

"The shots became muffled, and I hoped Kate had run into the secret room, which with any luck would trap her damned grandmother. I could hear sirens and knew help was close... it was maddening! I was actually relieved Olivia was still shooting. I hoped it meant Kate was still alive... I've never been so relieved to see anyone in my life!"

He kissed my hand, closing his eyes to add, "I guess Olivia wasn't so accepting of her husband's affair after all..."

"That lying crazy bitch!"

Unseen weight lifted with each slow pass of his hand over my hair.

"You really do have a superpower," I whispered.

THIRTY-ONE

Nurses, doctors, more police, all came and went. I went to check my sisters briefly before returning. I stayed sitting beside him, leaning forward to lay my head on his shoulder.

I don't remember falling asleep.

Jace's mother woke me when she came in.

"Have you been here all night, dear?"

"They let me stay."

"Are you sure your up to it? If you'll pardon my saying so, you look exhausted."

She leaned passed me to feel her son's forehead.

"Kate?" he said sleepily.

"No. It's Mom. Sorry to wake you. How are you feeling?"

"Good I guess."

He held a hand to me.

"Did you sleep here, fool?"

"I had nowhere else to go."

His eyes gained an anxious cast.

His mother said, "Don't be silly. You're always welcome at our house. Any time, day or night, the door is open to you.

I was embarrassed I'd said it even though it was true. I could feel my flush.

"Thanks. My brother would take me in. I just meant I couldn't go until I heard about my sisters, and they wouldn't let me stay in the waiting area."

"They released you?"

"I released myself."

"Kate!" he said in exasperation.

"Don't Kate me! What difference would it make if I sit there or here?"

"A nurse checking your blood pressure, fool!"

Tears clouded my eyes, which was stupid when I *knew* he wasn't really angry with me.

"Did you hear anything?" he asked anxiously.

"Fell woke up. They let me see her for a minute. She's still here, sleeping it off. They think she'll be fine."

His grip on my hand tightened.

His mother said firmly, "Hannah will be fine too! You'll see. You have to have faith."

Jace's eyes filled with tears as he brushed my cheek with his thumb.

I said angrily, "I hate her for what she did. I'll never forgive her! Not ever! How could she do that! Hannah is just a baby!"

"Did you see her?"

"They won't let me—or anyone, except Dad. She's still in intensive care. God, I wish I'd killed her..."

His mother glanced over her shoulder at the door, shaking her head at me, whispering, "I agree, but it isn't smart to say that where anyone can hear you."

Jace said, "Have the police charged your grandmother yet?"

"I have no idea."

His mother said, "I heard on the news that she was charged with murder and attempted murder but not how many counts."

I said, "I didn't tell him about Everly."

"What about her?" Jace asked.

His mother said, "She committed suicide."

I said, "No she didn't. Olivia murdered her too."

His mother gaped at me.

Jace said, "Are you kidding me?"

"She's claiming she had nothing to do with it. But I know it was her! It had to be her! She used the same stuff on the girls."

"The boys..."

"Are with Grayson. I'm going to stay with Kenya for a while. She'll need help seeing as how her ankle is broken. She said you could stay with us."

As I said it, I realized *we* had no house now. I wondered if there still was an us without that house. It made my head throb and my hands feel sweaty.

I was glad I was sitting.

His anxious expression deepened.

His mother said, "I'm sure your brother could use some help too. Give him my number, dear. I'd be happy to watch the children for him. Speaking of which, I've made some meals that I'd like to drop off for him."

"I've no idea if he's at his house or my parents."

She said, "Jace, darling, you're welcome to come home to recuperate. If you'd rather stay at your own place, I can drop off food for you. Crystal has offered to put you up, which is sweet of her, but I doubt you'd get a lick of sleep with her crew running about."

He said, "I hadn't thought about it. The doctor said I should be up and around in a day or so."

She tisked, saying, "He said you could *try* to get up in a day or so but that you needed to be careful that you don't rip the stitches or you could bleed to death."

Jace shrugged.

I said, "Kenya's boyfriend, Dennis, came to get her last night. She could stay with him or Gray if you don't want to stay with us. Grayson wouldn't mind you staying with him. Dad asked him not to say anything to the boys yet. I've no idea what he intends to tell them..."

"How's your mom?"

"Sedated. She totally lost it."

His mother said, "I don't blame her. I'd lose it too..."

"My dad is a wreck worried about everyone..."

He said, "I don't like that you're not getting your blood pressure checked."

"My head is fine—just the normal ache."

"I'll have Gianna pop in," his mother said.

Jace nodded.

He said to me, "My aunt Gianna is a nurse."

She said, "She wanted to stop by anyway. I told her to wait until this afternoon."

"Ask her to bring us some breakfast sandwiches or something too, Mom. And see if Crystal can run by my place and grab me a change of clothes. Tell her I threw all of my stuff into a few garbage bags so she'll have to sort through it."

She peered between us. Little frown lines appeared on her brow.

She said, "I suppose it isn't really my place but I'm going to just say it anyway. That house clearly meant a lot to you. I'm sure you could sell it and find an apartment to share, but you shouldn't let her chase you from your home. Jace told me your plans. It'd be a shame to let her ruin your dream. It isn't the house that was the problem."

Jace said, "We haven't had a chance to talk about it. We can do whatever you want, Kate. If you want to look for a new place, we can. I hope your plans still include me..."

"I can't ask you to go back there.... I don't know what I'm going to do now..."

She leaned down to hug me. "That's what I mean! Why let her take everything? She could just as easily have tried to murder you at your parents' place or her own house or your sister's place. *She's* sick."

She kissed Jace's cheek.

"I'll go call my sister and let you two talk. There's plenty of time to decide what you want to do. We're here for you."

She left.

Jace said, "I mean it, Kate. Whatever you decide is okay with me."

"How can I keep it? My sisters would be horrified...I fucking hate her!"

I began to cry, which made me feel worse.

"I'm so sorry! I'm the worst girlfriend."

"I knew I'd find you here!" Dr. Kennedy said in annoyance.

Jace and I both started nervously.

He continued, "What were you thinking, discharging yourself like that! You have a serious head injury, Kate! You aren't going to do yourself or your young man any good if you drop dead!"

His anger made me feel worse. I rubbed my face on my shirt.

"I'm fine."

"I'll be the judge of that!"

Jace said, "I'd feel better if you got checked out."

"I *have* been checked. I'm fine."

Kennedy said, "Your blood pressure is high and needs to be monitored. I'm glad you're feeling better, Kate, but until I'm sure the meds are working, you need to let us keep checking, and if your pressure is still high, you need another MRI. Please listen to me about this. You really can't afford to take this lightly."

"Go get it checked, Kate. I'll be here when you're done."

"You could've died, Jace..."

"I promise I'll be right here. My leg is getting better. It doesn't even hurt that much. Staring at it won't help. Go get your head checked."

"I really couldn't take it... I really couldn't."

"You won't have to."

He kissed my hand, saying to Kennedy, "Take good care of her, please."

Kennedy said, "It will only take an hour or so, three tops if you need another scan."

I kissed Jace and went with the doctor.

He brought me back to the emergency room where a nurse had me sign another paper while he took my blood pressure and checked my eyes with his little scope.

He said, "How's the vision?"

"Fine. I don't feel any worse."

"I'm ordering another round of blood tests. I hate to worry you because I'm certain all of this is the root of your rising blood pressure, but I really am concerned. The medication should've lowered it. I'm ordering another scan just to be on the safe side, and I'd like you to take a mild sedative. It won't put you to sleep. It should lessen your anxiety, which will hopefully help with your blood pressure. The nurse will page me the minute the MRI opens up. I know I'm asking a lot but try to rest. She'll be by in a few minutes with your medicine."

He left and a nurse came into the room a few minutes later.

I took the pills she handed me.

She made me get into a wheelchair to take me for the scan.

Kennedy was there, taking with the man who ran the machine.

When the test was over, Kennedy said, "It looks okay, Kate, but you need to keep getting that pressure checked for the next few days."

"Can I do it myself?"

"No. I don't want to admit you, but it needs to be done by a professional. I think we could compromise though. I want you to stop by my office around six tonight and then around nine in the morning. My staff can take your blood pressure. If between now and then your head starts to hurt, or your vision gets blurrier, or you get tingling or numbness anywhere, you're going to call me immediately and get yourself to the emergency room. No driving, heavy lifting, or strenuous activity. Try to get some sleep."

My father came into the room.

"Kate! You should've called me!"

"You have enough to worry about. How's Hannah?"

"She woke but she's sleeping again. A real sleep, we think. Kenya is with her."

"How's Mom and Felicity?"

"Felicity is responding well. She'll be released tomorrow. Grayson and Wolfgang are with her. Harley is with Ms. Maria. Your mother is... sick."

"Did they tell you about Claire?"

"Yes."

"I'm sorry, Dad."

"None of this is your fault. How are you? How is she, Doctor?"

"Her pressure is higher than I'd like. We were just discussing treatments. I want her to get it checked at least twice a day for the next few days."

"Mrs. Lane—Lacey the nurse we hired, can check it."

I said, "I'm not coming home."

"I know you don't want to, but it really would be best for everyone."

"Not for me or Jace. He'll need help."

"... Of course... I hadn't considered. They told me he should make a good recovery, that he'd likely need some therapy, but it wasn't life threatening. We could make up a bed for him in the playroom or basement and Lacey could see to him too."

"I was going to stay with Kenya to take care of her."

"She's agreed to come home for a few days. Grayson too. The kids... it's a circus. We thought it'd be easier on all of us to stay together."

"I'll talk to Jace."

He gave me a hug, saying, "You never said how you're doing?"

"I have no idea..."

He grimaced.

Kennedy said, "I prescribe plenty of rest for all of you. You can go home, Kate, but call in those pressure results to me. If your nurse can take your pressure, you don't need to come to my office. Get that script filled though and don't forget you're taking two of the pressure pills now, one with breakfast and one dinner."

He patted my shoulder and left.

The nurse wheeled me back to my room, which was silly when I walked out of it after signing the discharge papers that she handed me.

My father and I went to see Hannah.

The nurse on duty said, "She hasn't woken. Her stats are good. Sleep is the best thing for her. It'd be best to let her be. We'll call the minute she wakes."

My father said, "I'll be back to sit with her after I check my daughters."

I said, "I'll wait out here until you get back."

He kissed my cheek and hurried away.

"That poor man," the nurse murmured.

I said, "Do you know where my mom is?"

257

"Sixth floor but I don't know what room."

"Is Hannah really going to be okay?"

"I think she's out of the woods, but as to what damage was done... we'll have to wait and see."

"That goddamned bitch!"

"You had no idea she was so crazy?"

"No."

"Are you sure it wasn't your mother?"

"Positive."

Her questions made my hands sweat.

I said, "We saw her. There's no way I'm mistaken. I saw her shoot Claire and Jace. She'd have drowned Hannah if her shoelace hadn't blocked the drain. She meant to kill us all."

"Why on earth would she do that? That's so crazy..."

My stomach sank.

I said, "I'm not sure if I should say... Did she say why she did it?"

"She says she didn't do it. Of course, I'm hearing all of this second hand. The police have charged her with the murder of Claire McAllister and the attempted murder of Jace Blake."

"But not Hannah and Felicity? And what about Everly?"

"Not as far as I know."

"That's... what about me? She shot at me like ten times! And Kenya! She bashed her head!"

One of the lights over a nearby doorway lit.

The nurse said, "I have to get that. Please don't wake my patient."

She hurried away, leaving me fuming.

My father returned about forty minutes later.

I whispered, "She hasn't woken. I'll come back after I see Fell and talk to Jace."

"The doctor thinks it could help your mom to see you and Kenya. Could you wheel her over there for a quick visit?"

"Of course. I'm not mad at Mom. Or you. Or anyone, except your evil bitch of a mother!"

He winced, lifting a trembling hand to rub his temple.

"Sorry," I whispered. I gave him a hug and left.

Felicity greeted me with a relieved, "Kate!"

I hugged her then Kenya then Grayson and Wolfgang.

Kenya said, "Dad said the doctor has you on new meds?"

"Yeah. I'm fine. He's just a worrier. How's the ankle?"

"Hardly hurts at all."

Grayson snorted, saying, "They gave her pain meds for it."

I sat beside Felicity's bed and pulled Wolfgang into my lap.

He didn't complain he was too big, which sent a pang of angry worry through me.

I wasn't sure what the kids knew, what they'd been told, so I said, "How are you feeling, Fell?"

She looked terrible with bags under her eyes and bruises covering what I could see of her arms.

It made me angry and worried in equal measure.

"I want to go home," she said.

Grayson said, "Tomorrow morning. Wolf and I will pick you up."

I forced a smile and said, "I'll make you pancakes, and we can make orange juice like Ken likes it."

"Will Mom be home?"

"I don't think so."

Wolfgang said, "Dad says she's sick cause of Everly."

I kissed his temple, smoothing his hair.

He burst into tears, clutching me hard.

"It's not our fault!" Felicity yelled angrily. "Tell him he's being a stupid head, Kate! She got her stupid self sent to that hospital!"

Kenya said, "It really isn't your fault, Wolf. None of this is any of our faults."

I said, "I'm sorry she's dead but I didn't like her. Her being dead doesn't make me like her any better."

"Kate!" Kenya said disapprovingly.

Grayson shook his head at her, saying, "I'm sure it's confusing for them, Ken. She *was* scary. They have to sort of be relieved. Not that she's dead but that she can't hurt them again."

Kenya said, "She was sick…"

Wolfgang stopped crying, sniffling on my shoulder.

"I hated her," he whispered.

"Me too. But we didn't do a thing to her. And maybe Kenya is right. She was sick. Maybe with medicine she'd have been nicer, and we could've gotten to like her. But we never got the chance. You don't need to feel bad that you didn't like her."

Kenya said, "It's such a stupid tragedy!"

"This whole thing is stupid," I said angrily.

A knock on the door was immediately followed by Officer Sandy entering. A man and a woman accompanied her.

Dee said, "This is Mark Lionel from child protective services and Evelyn Frost. She's been assigned as counsel to Felicity."

Kenya said, "If Felicity needs a lawyer, she has me."

Evelyn offered her hand.

Grayson shook it, nudging Kenya who'd crossed her arms.

Dee said, "Evelyn will help Felicity with her statement. Since you're also involved, it'd be a conflict of interest for you to help her."

Kenya's lips pursed.

Grayson said, "Just let it go, Ken." He said to Evelyn, "Fell can talk to you, but I'm staying with her."

"Am I in trouble?" Felicity asked.

I could tell by her tone that she was scared.

Wolfgang jumped from my lap to yell, "You leave my sister alone! She don't need no stupid lawyer. We didn't do anything!"

Grayson said, "No one's in trouble. The police just want to talk to her."

I said, "Wolf, let's take Kenya to the cafeteria and see what they have for Fell to eat. Maybe they'll have something good."

Grayson said, "Go ahead, sport. I won't leave her, I promise. They just want to hear from her what she remembers."

"Fell?"

"Bring me an orange soda if they got it. And grapes."

I pushed Kenya from the room then let him push her.

"What do they think we did?" he asked.

Kenya said, "Nothing. They really do just want to hear her say what she remembers,"

"Then why are you so mad?"

"I shouldn't be, I guess. It just pisses—makes me mad that we have to answer all these questions. Hand me my purse. I need to make a few calls."

Wolf rolled his eyes at me, which was such a typical response it made me feel much better. I grinned back.

I said, "Want anything to eat, Ken? We'll get it for you—assuming you have money on you. I have none."

"I got ten bucks," Wolfgang said.

Kenya rooted in her purse a moment then handed me a couple of twenties, my credit cards and ID.

"Coffee and a sandwich. Anything but roast beef or tuna. Get Grayson one too."

We left her at the first empty table making calls and went to buy food.

They had lactose free ice cream, so we got one for Felicity as well as soda, grapes, and chicken soup. I wished I could grab something for Jace, but I didn't know if Wolfgang knew he was here, and I wasn't up to explaining.

I took the cardboard carrier for the coffees and the bags of food and let Wolfgang push Kenya back to the room.

She said, "I've called and arranged a lawyer for you too, Wolf, just in case they want a statement from you. He'll be stopping by later. You might remember him from last Fourth of July. Dennis Fuller—the guy who brought all those bottle rockets."

"Sure. He was cool."

"He's going to work with this Evelyn person and whoever they assign to Hannah."

"It's dumb we need lawyers when we didn't do anything."

"I agree but if you need one, then I want you to have a good one, and Dennis is good."

"When can we see Hannah?"

"She hasn't woken up yet, so probably not until tomorrow."

"Why'd gramma give *um* that medicine?"

"Dad will tell you later."

"Is Fell really sick. She don't have what Everly does, does she?"

"No. Fell isn't sick at all. It was just the medicine that made her sick."

"Was she allergic?"

"Not really. She didn't need medicine. Taking medicine when you don't need it can make you sick."

"Then why—"

I said, "Dad will explain. The police are probably asking her if she knew she'd taken it."

"Oh... she might've thought it was something else?"

"Don't ask her about it until after Dad talks to you. It's important that she tells the truth."

"You think she took it on purpose? Like drugs?" he said incredulously.

"No."

"That's stupid!"

Kenya said firmly, "We don't think that. We know Felicity is too smart to mess with drugs."

He glared at Kenya.

I said, "We know that, Wolf. The police might think differently. So it's super important she tells the truth. Don't tell her to lie or hide anything, even if that truth will get someone else in trouble. Just tell the truth and everything will be okay."

"Everly gave them to her...but how could she? Unless... did she put them in our candy stash or something?"

Kenya said, "You better tell me where that stash is."

"My mattress. Our money and stuff is in hers."

I wondered if the police had found it and what they'd thought of it if they had.

When we reached Felicity's room, I knocked on the door and brought in her food.

Grayson said, "You guys can come in. They're done here."

Kenya said, "I've arranged for counsel for Wolfgang, Hannah, and Felicity. He'll be in touch."

Evelyn nodded, offering her hand again.

This time Kenya shook it.

Evelyn said, "I'll be speaking with Hannah when she wakes. I don't think it will take long at all." She turned back to Felicity to say, "You can call me if you have questions or think of anything you'd like to add to what we talked about. Anything you tell me stays just between us."

Felicity shrugged.

She said to me, "I don't remember going to your house at all or seeing Jace."

"Where is he, anyway?" Wolfgang asked. "He didn't come see us at all and he said he would to check on your kitten."

Grayson said, "He's here in the hospital."

"Gray..." Kenya said worriedly.

Evelyn said, "I advise that you tell the children the truth because they're bound to hear all sorts of rumors as soon as they leave the house, but it's your call."

She and Mark left.

Felicity said, "What's going on?"

Kenya sat on the side of her bed and took her hand.

"Dad wanted to tell you, but I guess it won't really matter. Back before our mom and dad were married, Mom had an affair with our grandfather. She got pregnant and because Grandpa was already married, they couldn't get married. So she married our father and lied about him being my father, which was dumb of her."

"Why'd she do it then?" Felicity asked.

Grayson said, "Mom has a mental illness. Medicine can help her, but back then she wasn't taking medicine. Her memory from that time isn't reliable because of it. But that really isn't any of our business anyway. Whatever happened then had nothing to do with us. But when Grandma found out, she was angry, so angry that she wanted to punish everyone, especially our mom. So she decided to take us away from her."

Wolfgang frowned uncertainly.

"She was going to kidnap us or just Fell—No Fell and Hannah?" His eyes widened with a horrified look as he stared at Kenya. "She hurt you! It was her who hit you on the head!"

Grayson said, "She tried but she didn't succeed. We're all fine!"

"Mommy..."

"Will be okay. The doctors are looking after her. She's really upset about all of this even though it isn't her fault."

Felicity said, "It sort of is if she had affair with Grandpa when he was married to Grandma."

I said, "Mom was really young, and he should've known better because he was way older, but that one mistake doesn't give Grandma the right to try to hurt *us*. We didn't do anything!"

"She was going to hurt me?"

Grayson gave me an anguished glance.

I said, "I want to lie to you, Fell, and say of course not, but you're bound to hear all sorts of stuff at school. Grandma wasn't thinking about us. She was just thinking she wanted to hurt Mom, and she knew it would really hurt her if she killed us."

Wolfgang grabbed Felicity and began to cry again.

I said, "We're all fine, Fell, and Grandma is locked up."

"She was going to kill me," she asked through her sobs.

I hugged both of them.

Grayson said, "I'm so sorry we had to tell you. Don't say anything to Hannah and Harley."

Kenya said, "You don't have to say anything to anyone. Just tell people it's none of their business. If anyone bothers you, tell us and we'll handle it."

The twins eventually calmed, crying themselves to sleep, exhausted from the stress of knowing their own grandmother would have killed them.

It left me feeling sick. It left all of us feeling sick.

I said to Kenya, "I doubt they understand this. Neither of them really know what an affair is or how babies are made.

Grayson said, "When they have questions just answer honestly."

Kenya snorted angrily. "Honesty... it's not really a family trait."

I gave her a quick hug, saying, "Dad wanted us to go see Mom. I'd like to stop and check on Jace first because I told Dad I'd go sit with Hannah after."

Grayson said, "I'll stay with the twins. This shit turns my stomach!"

Kenya said, "I wish we could lie but they're bound to hear..."

I said, "I know but, God! How will they ever get over this! I always knew she was a snob and a bit cold but this... I thought under all that haughtiness that she loved us."

"She isn't capable of love!" Kenya said angrily. "I should've known something was up—I did know it. She was giving me the creeps with all her niceness!"

Felicity took a deep shuddering breath.

Kenya clamped her lips together.

I whispered, "We'll be back," and rolled her from the room.

Jace greeted me with a relieved smile that died as his gaze traveled us.

"Hannah?" he asked breathlessly.

"Sleeping."

I released the wheelchair to give him a kiss.

Kenya said, "How are you?"

"The doctor says I can go home tomorrow afternoon baring any complications. How's the head?"

Kenya said, "Mine's fine. Kate's thick headed enough to get through this."

I said, "I've got new medicine and have to get my pressure taken every few hours. The nurse my dad hired can do it. He wants me to come home for a few days."

Kenya said, "We're all going home a few days to make it easier to meet with the police and our lawyers. Speaking of which, I've arranged for one for you. He'll be by later. He's also representing the kids."

"The kids..."

I said, "We had to tell them. The police came for their statements with a court appointed lawyer. We didn't tell them about you or Claire yet or that she killed Everly."

"We don't know for a fact that she did," Kenya said.

"Oh come on!"

"I'm just saying we shouldn't tell them anything that we don't know is true."

I said to Jace, "My dad invited you to come to the house too. The nurse can look after you."

"What do you want to do?"

I said, "I thought we'd be together now... I want us to be together, but I know it will be awful for you..."

"Don't you dare cry! I want us to be together too, Kate! This hasn't changed a thing. Not one blessed thing! We could go home to our house."

Kenya said, "You could, but Fell and Wolf... they can't go there right now. The best thing for them is to have some normalcy. This next week is going to be brutal. We'll have to bury our sister and the press is swarming. It's absolutely swarming! The kids are going to have to stay inside. I hate to be a jerk, especially when I know you don't want a thing to do with that house, but they really do need all of us, Kate."

"I know."

Kenya said, "We have to go see our mom. She'll be back later and you guys can talk it over."

Jace said, "There's nothing to talk over. Kate and I are staying together. I wasn't moving in because it was convenient. I was moving in because I love her. We were starting our life together, not having a... fling. It wasn't about the house but being together. If she wants to move somewhere else, then we'll move—together."

I ran to hug him.

"I love you."

"Good. Then tell your dad I accept his offer. My mom will be by later with food and my clothes."

I nodded against his shoulder.

Kenya said, "I'll go call Grayson and tell him he has a roommate and give you guys a minute."

She wheeled herself from the room.

I said to Jace, "I really want you to stay with me, but I'd totally understand if you didn't want to."

"Neither of us want to stay there but it won't kill us—assuming there's no more bombs or lunatics..."

"No promises."

He snorted with laughter.

"My family is crazy."

"Just a few of them."

"Ha!"

"All families have a black sheep or two. You have a big family so of course you have a few of them."

"Will your mom be mad?"

"Of what? Me staying with you? God, no! She knows I'm serious about you. I wish I'd asked you the right way to marry me... I really meant it. I still mean it. I'll always mean it, but I wish I'd asked just for us."

"Me too... can you ask me again later so I really feel engaged?"

He laughed again, a soft light laugh full of love, his body relaxing.

"I love you so much, Kate. I'll never stop asking until we're officially married."

We held each other until Kenya returned a few minutes later.

I said, "I'm not sure when I can get back here. I want to sit with Hannah a while and if she wakes..."

"Take whatever time you need. I'm not going anywhere."

Kenya said, "Grayson told me to tell you that he'll pick you up and no arguments. Your mom doesn't need to fight her way through the press. Tell her she can come to the house whenever she likes and if she wants to avoid the press to park at the shop and Howard will drive her around back."

"Thanks."

"No, thank you. You probably saved Felicity's and Kate's lives. God knows what she'd have done if you hadn't arrived. She might've had time to set a fire, which would've killed me and Hannah too."

"I almost got Kate killed," he said bitterly.

Kenya said, "Kate was determined to get that bitch to chase her. I shudder to think what would've happened if she hadn't made that room." Her eyes grew thoughtful as she said, "It's sort of creepy when you think about it. It's like Grandpa knew you'd need that house. He left you enough money to buy it and encouraged you... if he hadn't, we'd probably all be dead."

She shook her head briskly. "Let's go see, Mom."

THIRTY-TWO

"Girls," our mother said in a quavering voice.

I was shocked by her appearance.

Her hair was lank with gray streaks, her cheeks sunken and pale with deep circles under her eyes.

When she held out a hand, I could see bruises the length of her arm and her nails were all chipped and broken.

She looked seventy, not the forty-eight she was.

"Mom," Kenya said, in deep dismay.

We took turns hugging her.

"The children?" she asked.

"The boys are perfectly fine. Hannah is still sleeping but we're hopeful. Felicity is physically fine but upset, of course. She'll feel better when she's home. When can you come home?"

"Soon, I hope."

Kenya sat beside her on the bed, having to jump awkwardly to do it.

Our mother said, "What happened to your ankle?"

"I broke it. It's nothing to worry about."

"Your head, Kate?"

"Is getting better."

"Dad told me you're having problems writing... is that temporary?"

Kenya said, "It's getting better too. She'll go to therapy for it and be good as new before you know it."

Tears clouded my mother's eyes.

"You didn't fall, did you? Not on your own. Something very bad happened."

I leaned past Kenya to kiss our mother again.

"It's over with now though and it wasn't your fault. I want you to feel better."

"Feel better?" she repeated as if she didn't know the meaning of the words.

Kenya winced.

I said, "You need to stop beating yourself up over things that happened in the past. You aren't that same person anymore. You're a good mother. We all love you."

"She's right, Mom. Everyone makes mistakes. We love you—the woman you are right now."

"I'm not a good person. I want to be... there's something wrong with me. I feel it inside. I can't remember why but I know you should hate me or will hate me or do hate me... is this a dream?"

I said, "It makes me so sad for you that we don't show you how much we love you enough for you to really feel it."

Kenya said, "Scared people do desperate things. I swear there's no reason to be scared of us. We really aren't judging you or holding the things that you did while you were so scared against you."

Our mother had begun to cry.

"I think I killed Everly."

"You didn't!" I said.

"I really think I did. It's my fault, I know it. They keep saying she took the drugs herself but... isn't that still my fault? It's my fault. It's my fault."

A nurse entered to give Alise a pill, by which I deduced she'd been listening.

She said briskly, "Take the medicine, Mrs. Avery. You're not responsible for other's actions only your own. The pill will make you feel better."

Our mother took the pill, saying through her tears. "They don't work but I have to try, don't I? I want to forget but I can't—I shouldn't. I should suffer for what I've done! My children... I should suffer!"

She began to sob too hard to speak.

The nurse said, "I think you should go and let her rest."

Kenya said angrily, "And leave her in this state? Kate, go call her doctor. I'll stay with her. She and I need to talk. I think she'll feel better if we do but she doesn't need us all. One problem at a time."

I kissed my mother's cheek.

"Please feel better. Everly was never your fault," I lied.

I went into the hall to call our father.

"Kate," he whispered worriedly.

"Mom is crying, really crying, and Kenya wants you to call her doctor. She's staying with her."

"I'll be right there.

"I'm coming to sit with Hannah."

I debated saying Jace was coming to stay but he didn't need any added stress right that second. *I'd tell him later.*

He was gone when I reached Hannah's room and a nurse was changing the dressing on a cut on her leg.

Like Felicity, Hannah was covered with bruises too, deep purple splotches went along her entire left side.

She had sensors wired to her chest, temple, neck, and thigh leading to a row of machines beeping and humming.

"Dear god," I said and began to cry.

The nurse said, "Please don't wake my patient."

"How..." I broke off to catch my breath. I hadn't realized how injured she was when I'd been running around with her and hoped I hadn't hurt her. I couldn't imagine what Olivia might've done to make those bruises.

I didn't want to imagine it.

The nurse said, "You need to get control of yourself or I'll have to ask you to leave. Children can get very upset when we fuss over their injuries. It's best not to mention them to her. Let her tell you what hurts. Don't ask."

"Will she be okay?"

"None of the cuts are infected and most are small shallow lacerations. The bruising should clear up in a week or so. She'll be sore, of course. I've already spoken to your father and the nurse he's hired about her after care. No hot baths. Swimming or better yet lounging in a pool will help with the soreness. Your father assures me you have a pool," she said in a tone that said she didn't believe a word he said.

"We do. We can heat it if warm water would be better?"

"Cool water would be best. Just wrap the cast good and make sure she wears a vest. No strenuous activities. We find if we cover the bruises, it won't worry her as much, so a lightweight long sleeve shirt over her bathing suit and when she isn't swimming a lightweight long robe or loose pants. If she complains of new pains, tell her nurse right away but do it calmly."

I nodded that I understood.

"But will she be okay?"

The nurse gently straightened Hannah's hospital gown, smoothing the wide sleeves around the cast on her arm and the IV in her other hand as she said, "The prognosis is good. She responded well when she woke earlier. It isn't unusual for children exposed to narcotics to have mood swings, excessive tiredness, or even hyperactivity. I expect she'll be cranky because of the bruising. It's impossible to say how she'll be mentally. Children can have a very hard time processing trauma. It can manifest in lots of different ways."

"Did she say anything?"

"About what happened to her, you mean?" the nurse gave me a weighing glance, shaking her head. "No. She wasn't that lucid. She asked for you, Felicity, and was worried her mother would be mad about a mess but she really wasn't clear."

"But you think she'll be okay?"

"We're very optimistic. Of course, if we knew exactly what was done to her..."

"That goddamned bitch!"

The nurse grimaced at me, nodding agreement.

"The police were able to fill us in on how some of the injuries occurred but there are gaps in the timeline when she was out of sight of your security cameras."

Bile rose in my throat. It hadn't occurred to me that Olivia might've hit Hannah like she had Kenya.

"Do they think Olivia beat her or..."

"The injuries appear accidental. Well, not accidental exactly but not done for the sake of hurting her. They were made from carelessness. I don't think she went out of her way to hurt her."

I grunted in annoyance.

The nurse huffed in aggravation. "I mean she meant to hurt her, but the bruises and cuts were caused by careless handling. Hannah was unconscious so she wouldn't have felt them."

"Thank God!"

The nurse nodded agreement. She eyed me speculatively, leaning closer and lowering her voice to say, "There were no signs of prior abuse on her X-rays. But if you suspect she was being abused by anyone..."

"She's the happiest sweetest kid. God, how could Olivia do this!"

As I was speaking, it occurred to me that the nurse meant abuse by my mom.

I said, "My mom would never! She loves us!"

Her gaze went to the bandage on my head and her lip curled in clear doubt.

I said angrily, "My mom doesn't hit us."

She nodded, clearly not believing me.

I didn't know what to say.

She said, "Children abused by their parents often don't see it as abuse. They think it's normal, that all families are like that, but it isn't normal for a parent to hurt their child."

Before I could respond a buzzer went off in the room next door and she hurried out.

I sat in the chair beside Hannah and dozed off, waking when Hannah said worriedly, "Kate, where are we? Am I sick?"

"Banana!" I gave her a hug as the nurse ran in followed a minute later by another one.

The original nurse left, saying, "I'll just fetch the doctor. It's nice to see you awake, sweetie."

I said, "You were sick but you're better now."

"Why are you crying? Are you sick too?"

"You scared me."

"I don't member being sick."

The nurse said, "What's the last thing you do remember?"

Getting into the car with Grandma. I fell asleep."

"Did she say anything to you?" the nurse asked.

Hannah said, "She was laughing but wouldn't say why. It made me mad cause I'm *not* a baby."

I said, "Did she call you a baby?"

"She said a bad word. I think she meant mommy. But maybe she was telling Fell a joke. It was a bad joke. We aren't allowed to say words like that. She gave us ice cream. I dropped it and she was really angry. My hands began to itch but I fell asleep."

"Do they itch now?"

"No. They hurt."

The nurse said, "The doctor will be in to look at them."

I made myself say calmly, "Do you have a headache?"

She didn't answer me. I could see by her face that she was angry and scared.

I said, "It isn't an allergy, banana."

"Then why'd my hands itch?"

The original nurse returned with the doctor.

I said to him, "Hannah is afraid she'll have allergies like Felicity has. She's seen Fell get examined a few times and I think she's scared to say what's wrong with her." I said to Hannah, "I promise it isn't an allergy to the food. You can still have ice cream and chocolate sauce."

271

"It's all we had. She let us have it for lunch in the car, but I dropped it. She was really really mad and yelled bad words at both of us! Maybe I'm allergic to the car. It smelt bad like the pool."

I said, "Maybe. Cleaning stuff is easy to avoid though. And it might not have been an allergy at all. Tell the doctor if your head hurts."

She nodded.

I said, "How bad?"

"Just a little."

"Can you show me where?" the doctor asked.

She pointed to the back of her head.

"Does your tummy hurt?"

"No... I think I'm hungry and I have to potty."

"I can take her," I said.

The nurse said, "You can accompany us."

She picked Hannah up, having to disconnect her and rearrange wires to do it. I followed them to an adjoining bathroom where she set Hannah on a plastic bowl covering the toilet.

Hannah exclaimed when she saw her bruised legs.

I crouched in front of her because I could see tears were imminent. All of this was scaring her.

"Where did all these boo boos come from?" she asked me sounding bewildered. "Did I fall off my bike or something?"

"I don't know. I wasn't with you. Bruises heal quick though. You'll be all better in no time."

Hannah shrugged like it was no big deal.

The nurse nodded at me approvingly.

I said, "Just go and get it over with. The bowl is so the lab can test it."

"Eww..."

"I agree. I wouldn't want that job. I wonder if Wolfgang knows that's what they do at laboratories?"

She giggled, which eased some of the tightness in my shoulders.

The nurse helped her wipe and carried her back to the bed where all three of them ran some tests on her.

She didn't cry when they took her blood although she looked horrified to see it. I don't think she realized what the bandage on her hand was until then.

I said to the doctor, "She said her hands hurt."

"We need the IV in for a few more hours. Try not to touch it. Now, how about some Jell-O and juice?"

She nodded. "Kate too?"

"Absolutely. Kate looks like she'd like green Jell-O."

"Orange is our favorite 'cept Grayson. He likes red."

"Orange it is."

"Where's mommy?"

I said, "We're taking turns sitting with you and it's my turn. No cutting."

She nodded as if that made perfect sense. It made my heart lighten that she believed we'd all be wanting to sit with her—that she felt our love.

The doctor said, "After your snack, I'd like to get you out of bed for a little walk. How's that sound?"

She shrugged.

I wanted to ask if she'd be all right. She *seemed* fine but I was worried about the pain in her hands and head. I didn't ask because I knew doing so would scare her no matter what the answer was.

Contemplating she wouldn't be okay made my chest feel tight. Tears continually burned my eyes. I had to pretend to cough and blow my nose every few minutes as an excuse to wipe them.

Our father returned while we were eating orange Jell-O.

"Daddy, want some?"

"Hannah... thank God!"

He picked her up to settle her in his lap, saying, "The doctor says we can go for a walk when you're done."

She didn't appear to notice the strain in his voice or on his face.

"It's Kate's turn. She says so."

I forced a laugh, saying, "Daddy's don't have to wait their turns. We can both walk with you, banana."

She shrugged and finished her Jell-O.

The doctor returned and we walked Hannah around the room and then down the hall, which left her breathless and me worried. When we returned to her room he said, "And what would you like for dinner, Ms. Hannah? Chicken soup or vegetable?"

I said, Any chance of tomato or plain broth? She doesn't like floating bits in her soup. She does like soup crackers though."

"And milk. I love milk. Can I have milk?"

I said, "How about ginger ale with a straw? I'll make us milkshakes when we go home."

"For Fell too?"

"Of course."

"We need sprinkles."

"And strawberries?" I asked.

She nodded happily. "Can we go home now?"

"One more night here," the doctor said.

Grayson and Ms. Maria entered.

She said, "It's nice to see you awake."

Grayson kissed Hannah on the forehead and handed her a pink gift bag.

"My favorite," she said happily as she pulled out a coloring book and new crayons.

It made tears cloud my vision again. Everything was her favorite. I stepped outside the room so she wouldn't see me cry.

Everyone who passed gawked at me, quickly averting there gazes.

I asked a passing nurse for a restroom.

It took me a few minutes to get control of myself.

When I returned to the room, Hannah was showing Maria how to color, saying the kitten had to be gray cause hers was. My father and the doctor were gone. Grayson gave me a worried glance.

I shrugged at him.

He smiled tightly.

I said, "I can stay."

Hannah said, "It's Grayson's turn. Daddy went to get me a book. He said he'd read the whole thing himself. Gray wants to hear it too, don't you?"

"I sure do."

Maria said, "I'll be back in the morning with clothes for you, Hannah. Felicity would like a turn to see you."

"And Wolf?"

"He'll be taking his turn feeding the kittens."

"Then I should get extra turns cause I'm missing mine!"

"We'll see."

Hannah pursed her lips, clearly considering arguing.

Grayson said, "Kenya will be taking her turn sitting with you later and she's bringing her tablet to show you the different types of puppies Dad's considering."

"I love puppies! I love them!"

He said, "You're all going to have to take turns walking and brushing it and cleaning any messes it makes."

"I will. I love them!"

I said, "We're only getting one. Everyone gets to pick their favorite and then we'll vote."

She nodded happily.

"Me and Fell want a fluffy one!"

Maria said, "I'll see you tomorrow. Sleep well."

She left.

Grayson said, "Kate, you need to get some rest too. I'm staying with our banana here. You go say goodnight to the kids and get some sleep, and don't forget to get your blood pressure checked again."

I said, "I love you, Hannah Banana."

She gave me a hug and a kiss.

"Don't forget the milkshakes."

"I won't."

Maria was with the twins when I got there.

Felicity said, "How's Hannah?"

"She lovvves puppies."

Felicity giggled. "Me too."

"We want the sheepdog," Wolfgang said.

"She wants a fluffy one, so you probably got another vote there."

Wolfgang said happily, "Harley don't care. He'll agree."

"Where is he?"

Maria said, "With Lacey—Mrs. Lane. She'll be by shortly to pick up Wolfgang. The boys are going to make the beds for us."

Wolfgang nodded. "Grayson, Harley, and I are sleeping downstairs so you can have my room."

"Jace is staying, so make him a bed too. He'll need help getting to the bathroom, so make sure there's room for a wheelchair."

"Kenya is staying in our playroom 'cause she can't do stairs neither."

"I'll stay with her, and Mrs. Lane can use your room for now."

I said to Maria, "Jace will need a real bed, not a mat on the floor. He can't do stairs either, so either he and Kenya need to share the playroom or put one of them in the living room. You better ask her."

"I'll see to it."

"Thanks."

Wolfgang looked worried.

I said, "His mom, Ginny, is going to be stopping by to drop off food and clothes for him. Make sure you're polite. Invite her in and make her tea with one of the pods. She's nice. You'll like her. Evan might come with her."

He brightened.

"Cool. I can show him our treehouse."

Felicity said, "I wanna go home too."

Maria said, "In the morning after we visit Hannah. She'll need some help bathing, but once we get her settled, we'll go home and make sure everything is arranged there for your sisters to come home."

I said, "I promised Hannah milkshakes with strawberries. I can order the groceries if someone will be home to get them."

"Either myself or Mrs. Lane will be there."

"Any requests, guys, before I put the order in?"

Wolfgang said, "I wanna go to the store to see what they got for our kittens."

"The doctor says I can't drive for a few days because of the blood pressure medicine, so it's going to have to wait."

He heaved a disappointed sigh.

Felicity said, "Grayson might take us?"

I said, "He's with Hannah and we want her to rest, so don't call him unless it's an emergency, which cat toys are not."

They both nodded.

"Text me any food requests. You can look for a good cat tree online but don't buy it. We'll make our own."

"That'll be cool!" Wolfgang said.

Felicity said, "And a doghouse!"

I nodded.

"Start designing one."

"We'll make one for your house too for when we visit," he said enthusiastically.

I forced a smile.

Maria said, "Don't forget you need to get your blood pressure checked, Kate. And you should get something hot to eat. You look all tuckered out."

I gave both kids a kiss.

"I love you guys."

"We love you too," Felicity said.

Maria said, "I'll be staying here all night. She's in good hands."

"Thanks."

I left the room reaching for my phone to call my father.

"Kate?" he said worriedly when he answered.

"How's Hannah really?"

He said, "I think she's going to be fine—it feels like a miracle. The doctor is running tests on her lungs to see why she's so breathless. He thinks it's probably strain, and she'll recover in time. He says I can take her home tomorrow—maybe in the afternoon if they get all the tests back, or the evening if they need more tests. I got her DNA results back and she *is* Alise's daughter, which is a huge weight off my mind."

"Did she ever say…"

"She's still claiming it was artificial insemination. I don't know if I believe that… it could just be what she wants to believe."

"What will we tell Hannah and the twins?"

"Nothing right now. Maybe your mom will recover enough to give her real answers when she's old enough to ask real questions."

"What are we telling her about all of this?"

"Nothing."

"She's going to need to be told something…"

"We'll tell her it was an accident for now. She has no need to know. We can keep her and Harley from hearing rumors. Maria can homeschool them for a year. Little kids don't gossip about this sort of thing…"

"I don't like lying to her, but I guess…"

"I don't like it either but she's much too little to understand any of this."

"We all are."

He huffed an annoyed laugh.

I said, "Jace is going to stay with us a few days until he's back on his feet."

"That's fine."

"I'm going to order groceries delivered. If you want anything in particular, text me."

"Thanks."

"The kids want to make a doghouse and a cat tree. I think it'll be a good project to keep them busy. Can I use the credit card to buy the wood?"

"Of course. Buy whatever you need for them and yourself. I trust that you'll be responsible."

Since when?

I, of course, didn't say that.

I said, "I'll ask Ms. Maria to see what they have to wear to a funeral. Will you or Mom need me to pick anything up?

"I… no."

"I'm sorry, Dad."

"I know. I'm sorry that I can't be there for you like I want to be."

"Take care of Hannah. She needs you now. And Mom. And yourself. Grayson and I will see to Kenya and the twins."

"Don't overdo. Let the help, help. Promise me you'll get some rest."

"I will."

"I love you, Kate."

I hesitated then said, "I love you too."

I knew we were both doubting that, but it was the best I could do.

I went to get my prescription filled at the hospital pharmacy and then to get my blood pressure taken before going to see Jace again.

Ginny and Frank were there when I arrived.

"Kate!"

"I can come back later."

"Don't be silly."

Frank stood, gesturing me to the chair.

"Sit! you look exhausted.

I sat as I said, "Hannah woke, and she seems fine. All her tests are coming back good. She's a little weak but the doctor said that was to be expected. They say she might be able to go home tomorrow afternoon or evening. Fell will be released in the morning."

"And you?"

"My pressure hasn't changed, and the doctor said I could go home. Speaking of which, when can you leave?"

"Tomorrow if I can stand on my own. One more day if I can't."

"How are you feeling?"

"Don't worry about me, Kate. This is nothing."

Frank said to him, "She has a right and a reason to worry." And then to me, "His doctor says it's looking good. They'll be some muscle damage but with therapy he can probably regain it. He might end up with a bit of limp. His pain is at a three now, so that's good."

"Frank..." Jace said in exasperation.

I said, "Thank you. That's exactly what I wanted to know."

Frank quirked an I-told-you-so eyebrow at Jace, which made Ginny laugh.

I said to her, "I told my brother Wolfgang that you'd be dropping off clothes for Jace and that Evan might be with you."

"That's a wonderful idea. I'm sure Wolfgang could use a distraction."

"He wants to show him his treehouse. Jace can call Crystal when we're home and we can plan a real playdate for all the kids."

"Playdates," Frank said in amusement.

Jace flushed.

"Don't tease him," his mother murmured.

"I ain't. It's just nice to see him living his life instead of working all the damned time. It's good to work hard but family—that's what counts. Crystal's kids could use some attention from their kin."

I said to Jace, "Playdates with Wolf and Fell are easy. I just have to feed them occasionally. You don't actually have to play with them."

"I wasn't worried about it," he said.

Not when there's so much else to worry about like being crippled for life...

I didn't say it, of course.

His parents left an hour later.

I lay carefully against his side, resting my head partially on his shoulder and partially on a bunched-up pillow.

"You're going to fall off," he said as I grabbed his hand to stop him from putting an arm around me.

"I won't. You won't be comfortable with your arm like that for too long. I'm hoping the nurse will take pity on us if we're asleep and just let me stay here, which she won't do if she thinks your arm will be sore."

"You should go home and get a good night's sleep."

"I don't want to. I wouldn't sleep anyway. I'd just lay there and worry."

Which was a lie. I could barely keep my eyes open.

"Kate... did you even have any dinner?"

"I ate with Hannah."

"Jell-O..."

"I'm fine—unless you want me to go to get some sleep yourself?"

"I... hate the thought of you being alone. Or me being alone. But I hate the thought that you fall out of bed and hurt yourself more."

"I won't."

I snuggled against the warmth of him, not his physical warmth although that made my muscles relax but the warmth of him—his presence—the knowing that he was alive and well.

It felt as if I'd barely closed my eyes when a nurse grasped my shoulder, waking me.

"Miss, you can't sleep here."

Jace was still sleeping. He'd turned more toward me to rest his head against mine and had scooted up a bit to put his arm around me.

I sat carefully so as not to wake him and left without arguing with her—I knew it wasn't a fight I could win and would only upset him.

A glance at my phone showed me it was just three in the morning.

Why the hell had she bothered, I thought irritably.

I headed to Hannah's room.

Grayson was sleeping, looking uncomfortably cramped in the chair beside her bed.

She looked comfortable without all of the wires of earlier. Only her hand was still bandaged.

I kissed Grayson's cheek, whispering, "You can go home if you want. I'll stay until Dad arrives."

"Kate?"

He sat and stretched, groaning as he glanced at his watch.

"You should be sleeping," he said accusingly as he stood. "Thanks. I'll see you tomorrow. The chair isn't half bad. It isn't half good either."

I took his seat, and he tucked the blanket around me, kissed my forehead and left.

I sent Jace a time delayed text so he'd know where I was when he woke.

I worried about where we'd live—how we'd live until sleep claimed me.

Hannah woke me in the morning by saying Kate happily as if of all the people in the world she was most pleased to see me.

How could her grandmother do this to her? Hannah loved everyone and everything...

"Good morning, Hannah Banana," I said as cheerfully as I could as I unfolded myself from the seat.

It had left a surprisingly painful crick in my neck.

I took her to the bathroom and used it myself.

She giggled over the soap suds dispenser, saying, "I love soap, don't you, Kate?"

"I sure do. I'd be all stinky without it."

"I love perfume too. Not all of them though. I love Kenya's perfume. She lets me wear it. It makes me smell beautiful too. I love Kenya!"

"Me too. Scoot over and we can watch cartoons until breakfast."

She happily obliged, letting me cuddle her, talking nonstop about how she loved cartoons while I fumed that my grandmother had put this child who loved so much here.

Maria and Felicity arrived before breakfast.

A nurse followed them in and removed the IV from Hannah's hand.

The girls chattered like normal, which was very relieving.

My father arrived with the breakfast.

"Kate, you're up early." He paused to kiss my temple then kissed both girls, picking Hannah up to sit with her.

"I love you, daddy!"

"And I love you. Now eat your pancakes like a good girl."

"They aren't as good as Kate's," she said as she eyed them.

"They're alright," Felicity said. "I had the same thing cept mine were gluten free with the icky butter."

I said, "They look alright to me. I think I'll go buy myself some. I'm starving."

Our father said, "I think they'll let me take them both home after breakfast."

He stood, placing Hannah in the seat. "I'll be right back. Let me see you out, Kate."

I kissed both girls who barely took any notice, being too interested in a movie that Maria had just put on.

In the hall, my father said, "Don't go see your mom alone. She's too easily confused. The doctor wants another day on these new meds before we try that because he's worried she'll think you're her again. It might be best to wait a few days to visit at all and then go with Grayson or Kenya. I'll bring the girls to see her before we go home."

"Is that a good idea? She didn't look so good."

He grimaced, nodding as he said, "She showered, and I had someone come in last night to fix her hair and nails and I brought her some of her own clothes. She looks much better. She says she feels much better... which is probably a lie but maybe she does feel better now that you older kids have been to see her and she knows you don't hate her. You don't hate her, do you?"

"No. I'm not even angry. I feel bad for her. I wish she'd said something. I can't imagine how bad she must have felt all these years..."

"I know. It kills me that I didn't see it. She was always so... I see it now. When I look back, I can't believe I missed all the signs! But I always misinterpreted them."

He shook his head briskly. "None of that matters, except as a life lesson. One I hope you all take to heart. I wanted to believe Alise was happy with me, so I ignored all of the little things that told a different story because I knew she loved me, so I let myself believe the lie of her smiles. I saw the brittleness..."

He shook his head again. "I'm sorry for my part in all of this, don't think I'm not or that I don't see it. We can talk more later. Go get your blood pressure checked, and please, Kate, really try to rest. You don't look at all well. At least go home and shower and change clothes."

"I will."

He kissed my cheek again and returned to Hannah's room.

I went to see Jace.

He was up, sitting on the edge of his bed wearing sweatpants, one of his sweatshirts, and the stupid hospital socks, eating his breakfast.

He was heart-stoppingly beautiful.

"Kate...I'd hoped you went home."

"I will after I get my pressure checked here. Want me to bring you anything when I come back?"

"*Nah*. My mom brought me everything I need—except you."

He slid the tray away to hug me.

I'd have hugged him longer, but I didn't want his coffee and eggs getting cold.

I stepped away after a minute to slide the tray table back.

"How's the leg? Did you walk?"

"Yep. The doctor says I can take a few steps every few hours. He's going to let me try crutches in a little while. No lifting or stairs for at least a week. Howard called me to say they put in a temporary ramp at your house last night for Kenya, so if I'm still invited..."

"Of course you are. Why wouldn't you be?"

"I got to thinking and worrying, I guess, that you felt guilty. I don't want you feeling like you have to invite me."

"I was thinking about that last night too. I don't want you feeling like you have to accept. Everything's changed and maybe you want to think about—"

"Nothing has changed for me. My life is with you, Kate. It doesn't matter where. If you don't want that house anymore, we can find a new one to flip."

"I'm not sure I can do it anymore..."

"Of course you can! You were fine with the nail gun. A paint sprayer is the same thing. I'll show you how to use that instead of a roller and brush. I can cut the boards that need cutting just until you can do it again. It's only the little details that need work. But we could add them in when you're able to do it again."

"I'm not sure I'd want to just flip an ordinary house. That house was special."

"I think so too. You don't have to give it up, Kate."

"I'm not sure I can face it again..."

"We can face it together, and if it's too much, we'll find another great old house somewhere."

"Your job..."

"Is just a job. Mechanics can find work anywhere."

"But you're not really a mechanic..."

"I can open a metal working shop anywhere, Kate."

A nurse stuck her head in the door, saying, "Did you need anything, Mr. Blake? Want me to take the tray?"

Her gaze at me was speculative, almost hostile.

She probably thought I'd done this to him... I had done this too him... if he'd never met me, he wouldn't be here right now, that last thought made my stomach squirm with guilty nerves.

I said, "He hasn't finished yet." I gave him a quick kiss and headed for the door, saying over my shoulder, "I'll come back after I shower and change."

"I love you," he called after me.

I turned to say, "I love you too."

I believed it was true and knew it might not be enough. It left me feeling weak and shaky.

I'd feel better when I'd rested and ate something, I told myself firmly and headed to the cafeteria to buy a sandwich to go while I called for an Uber.

I'd finished my sandwich by the time the driver arrived. I'd only taken an Uber twice before with Kenya, so was uncomfortable to begin with. His front seat was stacked with takeout boxes, so I sat in the back.

He kept glancing at me in the rearview, which was making me really uncomfortable, so I took out my phone to pretend to send a text, which reminded me that I needed to send in the grocery order.

We were almost at my parents' house when he said, "You're the Briarwood girl, aren't you?"

I was caught completely unprepared.

He continued, "I recognized you—man, my girlfriend is going to be pissed she missed this ride! We both do Uber after work and shit. Are you renting rooms out yet?"

"No."

"You should. I'd rent there. It'd be cool as shit even without running water. Did you know you'd need those secret passages and stuff—is all your family crazy?"

This conversation was so unexpected—so surreal—that I had no idea what to say.

He continued, "You look normal, better than I'd thought you'd look. In real life, I mean. You can't even tell you have a hole in your head and brain damage or anything."

Gee thanks.

He continued, "I knew your sister sort of. She was always a bitch. Sorry, I guess I shouldn't have said that. She shouldn't have killed herself or been knocked off like that. Did she kill herself?"

"No comment."

I felt dumb—even dumber—as soon as I said it, *but what was I supposed to say to that?*

He rolled his eyes at me.

He had to look back at the road and slow as he pulled onto my street because there was only a narrow lane left for traffic. News vans and cars were parked on both sides the full length of it.

Two policemen and a police barricade blocked my driveway.

Orange construction fencing had been erected in front of the shops and the parking lot there. Three police cars were parked in that lot.

I said hurriedly, "Thanks for the ride. I can get out here."

"No problem. It was cool meeting you. If you need a ride, you can call me direct."

He hollered his number after me, having to shout to be heard over the swell of crowd noise when I stepped out.

People rushed toward me, holding out microphones and yelling in a confusing cacophony.

I glanced back to see he was filming on his phone, which was infuriating, but since there wasn't anything I could do about any of this, I ran for the door to a chorus of men and women yelling my name and asking why I'd built the secret rooms.

Grayson let me in.

"Didn't you check your texts, fool? You should've called me for a ride. I'd have warned you."

"I saw them but never imagined... this is crazy. Have they been here all night?"

"Yeah. What they expect to see is beyond me."

"Where are the kids?"

"In the basement playing with the kittens. Howard and the guys are down there too helping them design the perfect cat tree and doghouse. Go get cleaned up and something to eat before you go see them.

"Ken?"

"Was resting in the playroom—or maybe working."

"Can we make them all leave before Hannah comes home?"

"No."

"This is such bullshit!"

I ran up the stairs and realized I had no clean clothes there when I saw my room had been repainted and the furniture rearranged, my desk removed, and a small table and chair added.

I went to borrow something from my mom's closet.

She and I had completely different styles in clothing. She preferred suits and dresses like Kenya did and never wore jeans. So I borrowed some of her workout clothes and underwear so I could throw all of mine into the washer.

I used my parents' shower because I didn't trust that there weren't hidden cameras in mine, which made me angry all over again as I considered how many people had probably seen those pictures.

I texted Dwayne when I got out of the shower asking him if there was anything we could do to keep those pictures confidential because I didn't want even the police gawking at them.

When I went downstairs, I found Grayson had left with Lacey, the day nurse. Maria was with Harley, Wolfgang, and Howard, who was measuring out a square with painter tape on the carpeting.

The room had been emptied and blowup mattresses placed on the floor along with a new television that was plugged in and leaning against a freshly painted wall.

Maria was hanging empty picture frames that had clothes hooks in the center, a few of which already held art drawn by the kids.

"Kate!" Felicity said with relief.

She and Harley ran to give me a hug.

"No lifting," Maria said. "Why don't you show her your designs. I'm sure she'd love to see them."

"Come see, Kate," Wolfgang said happily.

I stopped to peek into the box of sleeping kittens then joined him, sitting beside him on the floor to take his notebook and flip through the pages.

He said, "The smaller cat tree is for upstairs. The bigger one is for down here. It'll have a platform in front of the patio door so they can look outside and another in front of the small window. We want Mom to like the one upstairs, so we'll sand it to stain it like the wood there already and put the scratching post inside the little house on the bottom and put a nice pillow on the top so they can see out and stuff but we can wash it. That way we can put a pillowcase on it to match whatever furniture she wants. Dad said we can have that old furniture down here."

Maria said, "We've ordered them a few tables, some cabinets, and a toolbox. "

Felicity said, "Dad said we don't need to worry about the carpet down here cause he's having tile put down so we can clean our sawdust and stuff."

I said, "Just make sure you don't track a mess into the rest of the house or leave anything around that the kiddos or pets can get hurt on."

Maria nodded agreement, saying, "I'll be down here every day with the kiddos. We'll have lessons down here."

Wolfgang said, "Dad says we can redo the playroom so it isn't so babyish."

"I like it," Harley said.

Wolfgang said, "The new stuff will be way cooler. We can pick out some movie posters and have a snack machine. Sides, our old stuff will be down here and that will be cooler to cause you can put your easel up and paint and stuff while Fell and I work on the benches. Maria can watch Hannah so she don't get hurt. We can make her a little painting spot too, a table so she can finger paint."

Felicity said, "She'll want her dolls."

Both boys snorted, which made me laugh.

I said, "There's plenty of room for all of you. She can share her doll space with the pets. A little playpen would be good for a puppy. She wouldn't mind sharing. You could bring her little kitchen down here and she could feed the dog and cats in it just make sure you're checking to see she gave them enough and not too much."

"Let's go get it now," Wolfgang said, and the kids ran upstairs.

Howard said, "The guys will be back after lunch to move the furniture down here so there's more room around the beds up there. Crystal told me to tell you to call if you need anything. She dropped off a lasagna already that just needs heating up."

"You two are getting along then?"

"She's great. I can't believe my luck... how someone as sweet and beautiful as her isn't already married..."

I wondered why he'd never married but didn't ask.

I said, "I like her a lot too."

"She brought Evan with her, but they didn't stay long because of that media circus out there."

"I don't blame them. Are the shops closed?"

"Yeah. The dealership too. I don't know if or when we'll reopen."

"He's closing it?"

"I was hoping you'd know..."

"I'll ask. You could ask..."

"We didn't want to bother him with all the kids so sick. Are they going to be all right?"

"I think so. Hannah's a bit weak. The doctor says it's too soon to tell if the damage is permanent or not. Fell seems fine but the doctor warned us her allergies could act up. We have to be careful what we give her and that includes cleaning products and laundry detergent. So if you're painting or staining things for the kids, make sure it's aired out good before bringing it in here."

"I was going to cut the pieces and bring them here for the kids to assemble, but maybe I better wait?"

"They can do it just have the boys paint it outside. We can leave it under the porch out there with a tarp or something."

Maria said, "When you get a minute, Kate, I'd like you to look over the furniture we picked for down here."

"I can do it now."

"Let me grab my tablet."

She hurried away.

I whispered to Howard, "How is she with the kids when the family isn't around?"

"She seems nice. I really couldn't say."

I could see I'd made him uncomfortable.

"She does seem nice. I guess I'm just a bit paranoid..."

"I can see why. I'd never have imagined..."

Loud thumping on the stairs warned the kids were on the way back.

Howard flushed, turning away to fiddle with the tape again.

I was probably flushed too—from anger.

It made me furious to think about what she'd done.

The boys had brought armfuls of toys from the toy boxes.

I said, "Get the laundry baskets but don't overfill them with heavy stuff. And get a garbage bag to throw away the broken stuff."

"I can fix it."

"You *can*, but will you? Wouldn't you rather spend your time making new stuff than repairing stuff no one plays with anymore? Put all the broken stuff aside and when Hannah gets home, you can go through it

287

and decide what to keep and what to toss. And maybe you can get rid of the stuff you guys don't play with or the old books you already read?"

"Can I give the little microscope to Evan? He don't have one and we're getting a new one."

"Sure. I bet he'd like those books you and Fell have already read to the kiddos to read to his own kiddos. Maybe we can swap the books you're reading now? Give him a call and see if he'd be interested."

"Later. Come on, Harley, let's find the laundry baskets and load up our stuff. Maybe we can think of something cool to make with the broken things?"

They ran back up the stairs.

"*Ahh*, the energy of youth," Howard said laughingly. He handed me the tape. "We're laying out the size of the doghouse. I'll go make sure they can carry the books."

I examined the drawing of the doghouse and adjusted the tape, hoping Hannah was on board for a big dog because the doghouse had clearly been designed for a sheepdog-sized dog.

I used my phone to Google the necessary size house for that type of dog.

Maria returned and handed me her tablet. I flipped through her choices.

"This looks great. I think it can really grow with them. My only suggestion is to switch out those two cabinets for the IKEA closets. I looked at them for my house but decided to build my own. But I think they'd be perfect for down here because they can change out the shelves for drawers. If we put four in the corner, they'd each have their own and you could put the hanging bar in Harley's to hang his art to dry so the cats don't walk over it."

We designed the system while the kids made a bunch of trips bringing down their toys.

The men returned from their lunch break and began bringing down the furniture. Howard went to pick up the cabinets, tables, chairs, and lights we'd just ordered.

I'd expected Grayson to be back by now so called Jace to tell him I was still waiting and was informed that he'd been discharged.

It felt like a punch—as unreal as seeing my grandmother shoot Claire.

I sat weakly on the carpet.

Maria said, "Kate, are you okay? You've come over all pale."

"He didn't even call me."

"Who didn't? What's wrong?"

"Nothing. I just need a minute."

"Is it your head? When's the last time you checked your blood pressure?"

I scrambled to me feet and ran to the bathroom, saying, "It's fine. I just need a minute."

In the bathroom I splashed water on my hot face, too stunned to cry. The pain hung over me like an avalanche about to smother me.

"What's wrong with you?" I asked my reflection bitterly. "Of course he wants away from this madhouse. You're so fucking stupid!"

I realized I was yelling at myself the same way my mother yelled at herself, which made my stomach jump with nausea. Contemplating I was going crazy like she was an entirely new level of terror that left me a shaking heap on the bathroom floor.

Maria knocked a few minutes later.

"Kate, you okay in there?"

"Yes. No. Maybe you better see about checking my blood pressure."

I got up to let her in.

She held a blood pressure cuff like the doctor used and a larger one with a plug.

She said, "I'm not sure I can do the real one right, but your dad had me buy this one. Sit here a sec before you fall down. You look terrible. Maybe I should call an ambulance?"

"No. Just check it. If it's high, someone can bring me back to the hospital."

"Kate..."

She slid the cuff on my arm and handed me the instructions, saying, "I'm not sure how accurate this is. Lacey should be back soon to take a real one, but I don't think we should wait.

As she was speaking, she'd pressed the button to turn on the machine.

My panic had faded leaving me feeling disconnected. I didn't care if it was high. It was too much effort to care about anything.

She said, "I think it's okay... I don't know, Kate. You need a real nurse to check this!"

"I'm going to go lay down. I think I'm just tired."

"I'd feel better if you went to have this checked by a professional."

She followed me up the stairs still arguing.

Tears clogged my throat when I realized I had nowhere to go lay down. This wasn't my house. I had no house. I had nothing. She'd taken everything from me.

I sank to my knees crying.

"That's it. I'm calling for an ambulance."

She'd lifted her phone when the front door opened.

"Oh thank goodness. Lacey is here!"

Hannah was saying happily, "We're home. We're home. We're home!"

I wanted to stop crying, to get up and hide so I wouldn't scare her, but I couldn't catch my breath enough to stand.

"Kate!" my father said, sounding shocked.

"Kate," Jace said, sounding scared.

Blackness rushed toward me, knocking me over.

THIRTY-THREE

When I opened my eyes, Jace was leaning over me on one side and Barbara on the other.

"Nice of you to join us," she said sarcastically. "I almost think you're stalking me. What have you been up to this time, Kate? Your pressure is through the roof."

She continued to talk as she hooked an IV to my arm.

"I'm okay."

Which was a lie when I couldn't stop shivering.

Jace said, "What the hell! You scared ten years off my life! Stop doing that!"

Barbara snickered.

"She's what I'd call high maintenance. I like her. She's keeping me in business. Now, how many fingers am I holding up."

"Three."

"Are they blurry?"

"No."

"Did something happen to give you a shock?"

"I...no."

"Out with it, kiddo."

"I yelled at myself and it scared me. My mom does that..."

"We all do that. It's nothing to worry about. Hand me that blanket there, Mr. Boyfriend, and let's see if we can get her nice and warm."

To my embarrassment, I began to cry again.

Barbara patted my hand then felt my pulse.

"Cry if you want. There's no need to be embarrassed. I ain't judging. Stress can do some shitty things to us. It's best to just cry and release it that way. One time I ate an entire box of Oreos followed by a gallon of ice cream and an entire liter of soda. Not the recommended approach to stress. I vomited for a day—which led me to this career, so it wasn't an altogether loss. Silver lining and all that. So the next time I was feeling like complete shit—yelling at myself, throwing shit, and all that, I tried the alcohol approach. Which was a worse disaster than the food."

My shivering eased as she spoke. By the time we arrived at the hospital I was shiver free and much calmer.

"Thank you," I said as she and her partner lifted my stretcher from the back.

"No problem, just try not to call me for a ride again for at least a week or I'll be firmly convinced you're stalking me."

She clasped my hand as two hospital orderlies appeared to take the stretcher. "Take care of yourself, Kate. The world needs your talent. I'll bring Mr. Boyfriend in when I round him up a wheelchair."

"Don't let him walk."

She saluted me.

Jace called after me, "I'll be right in!"

My father said, "I'm here, Kate."

I was shocked that he'd come and that he sounded so worried, which made me really ponder what I'd imagined he'd do.

I had no idea.

It made me sad we were such strangers to each other.

The orderlies brought me right to the MRI room.

I said to my father, "This must be costing a fortune..."

"We have insurance, good insurance, but I'd pay a fortune to keep you safe, Kate."

Doctor Kennedy arrived as they were doing the scan.

He said, "Your fiancé is waiting in the hall. We spoke briefly. I'm looking at the scans and I think it was just stress related but I'm going to admit you so I can monitor your blood pressure for a few hours."

"No. I want to go home."

"Too bad. You're staying where I can keep an eye on you. I've ordered another blood panel. We're waiting until that comes back to release you. No bullshit, Kate. You're staying and that's the end of it! I'm not having you ruin my perfect record by dropping dead of a stroke. You need rest. So like it or not, I'm going to ensure you get that rest!"

My father said, "Don't argue, Kate. It's just one night. I'll bring Jace back to the house and make sure he gets a good night rest too."

Kennedy said, "Now, let's finish this scan and then I'll arrange for your tests. Your fiancé can join you for dinner but then he has to go so you can get some sleep."

I wondered if they could see my headache on the scan. My head was throbbing in time with my heartbeat, which kept speeding up every time I considered how angry—or not angry—but upset Jace was going to be to be alone at my parents' house.

I began to cry again.

She keeps doing that," my father said worriedly.

"She's had a bad few days and she's exhausted. Sleep is going to fix her right up. It isn't a sign of insanity or anything, Kate. It's just stress. Trying to hold it in will just make it worse. What you need is sleep. I'm prescribing an extra of the sedative pills just to help you sleep. I promise, you're not going crazy."

He and my father spoke for a few minutes, but I couldn't hear what they were saying because music was now playing while the machine hummed around me.

They wheeled me out a few minutes later.

Barbara was there with Jace.

She pushed him after us while my father told him my scan looked good, but I was being admitted for more tests and I needed to get some sleep.

I'd stopped crying by the time we reached my room and was wildly embarrassed and angry with myself for breaking down like that.

Barbara left us.

Jace wheeled himself close enough to take my hand.

My father kissed my brow.

"I'll get back to the kids and let you rest. Jace, Grayson will pick you up at seven."

"I'm sorry about all this," I said.

"Don't be silly," Jace said.

My father said, "Get some rest, Kate, and you'll feel better."

A nurse came in to take blood and check my IV. She gave me a pill to take then checked my blood pressure again. When she left, Kennedy came in pulling a light-board.

He said, "I think you should see these scans, Kate, so you understand better why I'm concerned."

He put a picture up on the screen.

"This is your head. That black shape there is bleeding. That was the first scan and this the second and this the third."

293

They looked like growing ink blots with a jagged white line, except for the last one which was a smaller blot with a white circle and the white line.

He showed me all of the scans. My latest one had a lighter discoloration of a larger area with two small circles and a jagged line.

"Your head is bleeding again. We can tell by the coloration that it's a slow bleed with a recent harder bleed but that the bleeding has mostly stopped. Too much blood puts pressure on the brain, causing headaches and potentially damaging your brain. High blood pressure will make the blood pump faster, so even a tiny bleed will put pressure on the brain. So we need you nice and calm. I'm prescribing two days of bed rest when you go home. Lay around and do absolutely nothing. You're young so should heal quickly, but we need to keep an eye on this. From what your fiancé said, I think you scared yourself, causing your blood pressure to spike suddenly, so really try not to do that. But if you felt the pain in your head building, you can't wait to come in. You have to come in right away.

"What I want to do is schedule another scan in five days, which will hopefully show that spot growing smaller, but don't wait those five days if you have any symptoms at all. Relieving the pressure is a dangerous procedure but not as dangerous as letting it build up. I promise you those tiny holes I made won't be noticeable at all in a few months on the outside. Your hair will cover them."

Jace said, "And that crack there?"

"Will heal eventually. It's small and very thin, so that's good news. We need to keep the cut clean and bandaged so it doesn't get infected. So keep using that ointment and make sure you're keeping the bandage dry. Change it immediately after a shower after patting the cut dry with clean cotton. If you get a fever or it gets red or sore call me right away."

"I'll take good care of her," Jace said.

Kennedy nodded briskly and left the room with his slide show.

I said, "I'm sorry for being such a pain..."

"Stop it already!"

"I mean about being here and leaving you there."

"Oh... it's no big deal, Kate."

"I'd be pissed if I were you and you left me alone with your crazy family—if you had a crazy family. Your parents seem really normal, but I'm a shitty judge of character, so what do I know? Maybe they're both crazy too."

"There's a lot to unpack there, Kate. Let's start with the first bit. I won't be alone. Grayson is a friend now and I like the kids. Kenya seems

294

okay. I think we'll be friends too eventually. She reminds me a lot of you—how you'd be if you were career orientated. I don't love your dad, but I don't hate him either. He probably feels the same way about me. I bet he's worried I'm taking advantage of you, which I know I am, but my intentions are good. It isn't to get your house or anything, which is what I'm sure he's thinking. I don't blame him for that. He has to think that. He loves you and I'm a poor kid with a record of sexual abuse."

"They dropped the charges."

"Still—if he heard about it... and who can blame him? I'd be worried too if our daughter was dating a guy like me. I'll win him over in time when he sees that I'm not using you.

"My parents *are* nice and normal. You're not a shitty judge of character. Anyone would be blindsided by the level of... evil your grandmother showed. I don't think that woman has ever had a real smile or emotion in her life."

"I thought she loved us. Especially Everly."

"Her life was a show. She was playing the part of a lady and she fooled everyone, not just you. I think if you're honest with yourself though, you'd admit that you knew she didn't really love you and you probably didn't really love her. You wanted to, so told yourself you did. I did that too with my sister. I guess I still do... if someone were to ask me, I'd say of course I love her, but I don't even know her. It's the idea of her or how I wish we were that I love. We all make excuses for the people we want to love so that we can love them."

I said, "I look back now and wonder why I let the kids go there at all. She was constantly screwing up Felicity's food—maybe she was hoping to kill her right along. If it had been anyone else doing that, I'd never have let her go there to eat. But I told myself grandma loved us, and it was just a mistake even though it happened a lot. What kind of idiot does that?"

"One who sees the best in people. Don't lose that, Kate. Without that, you wouldn't have given me a second glance."

I pondered that for a few minutes.

"I can't imagine not giving you a second glance," I finally said. "I've always thought you were beautiful. I'm trying to remember when I first noticed you. You were making something. I'm not sure what it was meant to be, but the metal was alive for you. It was beautiful. I could watch you for hours. Talent like that... I really admired it. I still admire it. I didn't know a thing about you, so I wasn't seeing the best or worst, I was just seeing your amazing talent—the grace and beauty of you, and suddenly I noticed you as a guy, a guy I wanted to notice me."

"I wish you'd said something sooner."

"I wish you had..."

"I wouldn't have dared, which now I think was one of the most cowardly things ever, but it wasn't that I was scared of rejection. I fully expected to be rejected, but I would've asked for a date if you weren't my bosses daughter. I didn't though because I didn't think you'd ever say yes and didn't want to make it uncomfortable for you—assuming you didn't get me fired on the spot.

"I wasn't sure about you. You seemed nice but I'd also heard all about Everly. She was the type I'd cross the street to avoid, and I didn't want to take a chance I was wrong about you being nice. It just didn't seem like a situation I could win."

"That's how I feel now."

"Don't say that. We can get through this, Kate."

"I don't see how. I have no job now and no idea what I can do to support myself. I can't let you support me for lots of reasons. It was one thing to let you pay a higher rent than you were paying when I knew the house would be yours too one day. It's another to ask you to delay your dream by putting money into a rent for my house—one I might never be able to finish. You'd grow to resent me. We'd both be unhappy."

He said, "You could stay in my crappy trailer with me, and it wouldn't cost me anything extra. I could get us a better one seeing as how it's my uncle's place. We could move anywhere you wanted, even into one of our parents' homes while we figure out what we want to do. But if you're turning your back on our house for me, don't. I still love that house. In fact, I love it more now. It saved our lives. It isn't the bad guy in the story but the hero. If it were up to me, I'd say we bandage it up like a hero deserves and live happily ever after there. But like I said earlier, there's other houses. We could find one. I have a bit of money set aside. We could afford a big down payment and get a loan. I could open my own garage and fix cars on the side while we fixed a place up together. I really love that idea, Kate."

"It's all just so... impossible."

"It just feels that way because you're so tired. Our options are limitless. There isn't anything we can't do together."

"I thought you'd changed your mind and left the hospital without telling me—that you'd just left..."

He looked stricken and then angry.

"I never would! Not ever! I'm mad you even thought it for a second! Even if we'd had a massive fight, I'd never just walk away."

"This is such a nightmare; I wouldn't blame you if you wanted to."

"There's no denying it's bad but *we're* good. We'll get through this week, and it'll all seem better."

"That's just it. Dwayne told me Olivia is denying she did anything. She's blaming my mom, and he warned me the DA is going to treat her claims as true because he can't afford not to seeing as how he charged my mom for that bomb. He thinks Olivia will eventually be found guilty but warned me it was going to be a long fight. She's rich and plays dirty. She wouldn't scruple to threaten us any way she can to get us to change our story."

"Dwayne said that the DA is going to charge your mom!"

"He said the DA could be in trouble for charging my mom for that bomb. They never even looked at Olivia. So they might want my mom to be guilty of the bomb because it looks super bad for them that they charged the wrong person and then Olivia went on to murder two more people. He said they'd need inconvertible proof that Olivia murdered those people."

"Don't they have that with our eyewitness testimony?"

"I have no idea. I'd have thought so, but Dwayne said it would be our word against hers. There's physical proof though, so I'm hoping she just enters a plea so we can avoid a trial. There's a real possibility she tries to dig up dirt on all of us."

"Me you mean..."

"And me. I'm sure she can find a ton of dirt on Everly. How hard do you think it'd be for her to find people from my school who'd say I was turning tricks for money? And god knows what bullshit Everly's friends will say about me. I didn't tell you because I hadn't had time but when the police searched the house, they found naked pictures of me taken while I was in the shower."

"What!"

"I'm sure she took them for god knows what purpose, but I think it's a safe bet they're online on some skanky site somewhere."

"That's... Kate! You should've told me!"

"I *am* telling you. It's bound to be horrible—I'm embarrassed just thinking about it. I'm glad that bitch is dead, but I wish I could punch her in the face."

A nurse entered pushing a cart with our dinner.

I snapped my mouth closed, blushing in a mix of anger and fear that she'd overheard me.

Jace released my hand to roll away to make room for her to place the tray.

We didn't speak until she'd left, after taking my blood pressure and filling in the chart at the foot of the bed.

"I don't know what to say about that... it's horrible for you and I'm pissed as shit she did that. Let's hope we never have to see them again, but if we do—you have to know I'd be supportive."

"I'm trying not to let it bother me because there isn't anything I can do about it."

"Maybe there is. I'll call Dwayne when I get back to the house and ask him to see if the police can search her laptop and all the computers to see if she sent the pictures anywhere. We can get a court order to take them down."

"I'm not sure I want to know what she did with them..."

"I can handle it for us, Kate."

"I hate her so much! Which makes me feel bad but..."

"I agree but I think we better pretend we don't—at least until your grandmother is sentenced."

"I hate her too."

"Let's not worry about any of that. Our wilted salads can't stand much more."

I forced a smile and stabbed the lettuce.

THIRTY-FOUR

The doctor let me go home after breakfast the next day with renewed warnings about bed rest.

Reporters were still camped outside our house. There were fewer of them, and they seemed less frenzied though.

Grayson said, "Have you watched any of the news?"

"No. You?"

"Yeah. It's not worth watching."

The police had gone, except for one car parked down by the big garage near the shops.

"Is Dad reopening?"

"Next week, I think. Maybe longer. He was talking about doing some upgrades now while the dealership is closed."

"But he will reopen?"

"Yes. We all talked about it last night and decided we weren't going to let her scare us away. All of this is *her* problem, not ours. None of us, not even Mom really, are at fault. Even if Mom had an affair, it doesn't make her responsible for any of this. All of that, her decisions to lie to Dad about Hannah and Kenya, are personal problems between her and Dad and no one else's business."

"That's great in theory and all, but we're the ones having to face this gauntlet."

He drove past the house.

"It's annoying," he agreed. "I gave up on worrying about what reporters say years ago. I had to or I'd never be effective counsel. You should hear some of the crap that gets yelled at me as I go in or out of court. Half the time it isn't even my case. People get heated, Kate. You can't worry about it because they're also stupid and rude. The police will keep them off the property because fools *will* try shit."

"Have there been break ins at the shops?"

"It's nothing we can't handle."

I wondered if there were police parked at my house—and if it mattered.

We pulled into the big garage. The van that was usually at the other garage was parked beside the rear door. It had black glass tint on the windows now.

Grayson drove us out the back door across the lawn to the back of the house, parking between the pool and the garage.

"Is this necessary?" I asked worriedly.

"*Nah*. It's just fun to aggravate them."

"It's more likely to aggravate Mom if you ruin the grass," I said as we hurried into the house through the basement door.

He snorted with laughter.

"Kate!" the kids all exclaimed, rushing to greet me, except for Wolfgang who continued screwing one of the white cabinets together.

"Look what we're making!" he said happily to me.

"I'm watching kittens," Hannah said happily. "They sleep in my house. Come see!"

Jace smiled a greeting.

He and Howard were sitting on rolling stools behind the couch with crutches laying on the ground beside him, putting together a long counter that sat on drawer units.

Four other stools were shoved under the finished section of counter that ran the length of the back wall, minus where the closets system would be.

To the left of the couch near the stairs, they'd already assembled a round table that had six chairs around it with colorful cushions.

Harley had clearly been using it because his crayons and drawing pad were spread out.

I let Hannah pull me to the corner where her playhouse had been set up. It was one of the folding kind with the house printed on the side.

A new portable playpen was outside of it with her old doll bed and the kitchen from the playroom, her little rocking chair, a new small table with four white chairs on a colorful rug, and her bookshelf from upstairs that held some books and her favorite dolls and toys.

A new cube shelf that held four different colors of cubes lined the wall beside it.

I admired the kittens with her and Harley while Felicity told me whose cubes were whose and what was in them and how she and Wolfgang were going to make more spots for the kittens to hang out above it and more of the frames like Ms. Maria had but bigger to put their stuff in, and Harley pointed out his artwork with pride, and Hannah told me how much she loved kittens and making cat trees and putting shelves together.

They were all so happy and normal—so themselves that it made tears burn my eyes.

Grayson said, "Kate can lay on the couch and watch if you all promise to keep quiet if she falls asleep. Otherwise she has to go upstairs to rest."

"We will," they chorused.

I went to give Jace a hug.

He followed me back to the couch, using the crouches.

"How's the leg?" I asked.

"At a two mostly now. The doc has agreed I can use crutches for longer stretches if I keep it infrequent." He sat, putting a couch pillow over his bad leg, and patting the seat beside him.

I said to Grayson, "Where's the boys' beds?"

"They decided to sleep in the girls' room tonight. Lacey can sleep in Maria's sitting room since we got a small pullout couch for it now. She's only staying tonight to take care of you guys. She can stay longer if we need her, but I think we'll be fine with her just coming in days. The boys could go back to their own rooms anytime; they just want to campout with the kittens. I might sleep in Wolfgang's bed tonight.

"Kenya is working upstairs in the dining room, speaking of which, I have to go get some work done myself. I'll be back for dinner."

He kissed my cheek.

"Thanks for picking me up."

"Don't try to drive. Wait for me."

Jace said, "Lay down, Kate. Hannah, can we use one of your blankets?"

As he was speaking, he reclined the seat.

I lay beside him with my head in his lap. Hannah tucked us both in with blankets she took from her playhouse. She brought me a book and one of her bears.

"We don't have no books for you," she said to Jace. "Unless maybe you like this one."

She scampered off and returned a minute later with the kids' Boy Scout manual.

"Nice, thanks Hannah. What one did you get, Kate?"

"*The House at Pooh Corner*. She loves that book," Hannah assured him.

She brought him back a stuffed rabbit then brought us both fake tea.

Howard finished with the long counter, which distracted her from offering us fake food to putting her coloring books and pencils away in her drawers with the rest of the kids.

Maria came downstairs with drinks for everyone and helped them decide where to put what.

I dozed off, waking when I heard my father say, "It's good to see her sleeping. How's the leg, Jace?"

"Hannah is an excellent nurse, sir."

Lacey said, "Let her sleep. I can take her pressure when she wakes."

My father said, "The room looks great. Really practical. Thank the men for me, Howard. You've all gone above and beyond, and I really appreciate it. I'm closing the shops for two weeks. Tell the men it's a paid vacation that won't count against their real vacation time. Offer one of them time and a half to swing by the shops every day to be sure the doors are locked and nothing was messed with. You and I can meet there tomorrow to discuss getting that new lift installed while we're all out of there. If there's any other improvements or repairs that need to be done, we can talk about it tomorrow."

"Yes, sir. We're happy to help, sir."

Jace said, "Tell Crystal to send more food."

Howard laughed. "She's got a huge pot of soup going for tomorrow and bread—the woman makes her own bread. She's a bloody miracle. Her house always smells amazing."

"My grandmother was a great cook too. It runs in the family."

I sat to say, "You don't cook."

While I'd been sleeping, they'd brought in a large wooden workbench and two rolling toolboxes for under it that they'd placed along the wall by the door.

Jace said, "I can, I just don't have a good spot to and it's no fun cooking for one."

Hannah said, "I'm a good cook too. I can make bread. Want some bread, Kate?"

"Not right now, banana. I need a bathroom."

"Me too," Jace said.

He wrinkled his nose at me, saying, "You first. By the time I get there, you'll be done." His eyes softened and he shook his head at me.

"I really am getting better, Kate. You don't need to worry about me. I'm just being careful, following doctor's orders like you should be doing."

Lacey laughed agreement, saying, "I can take her pressure when she's done."

Jace went into the bathroom when I exited.

Lacey took my blood pressure, which all the kids seemed to find fascinating.

They all gathered around to watch.

She said, "It's good, Kate, getting lower. Don't take that second pill until I speak with the doctor. Maybe we can skip it. Dinner is almost ready, guys, so upstairs and wash up."

My father went with the kids.

Jace exited the bathroom and Lacey pointed at the wheelchair.

"I'll wheel you around, but first, let's check that leg."

I realized Jace's sweatpants snapped down the side when he sat in the wheelchair and unsnapped them to let her peel away the bandage.

His leg was bruised from the knee up with a massive dark purple and green bruise with a crusty red center with painful looking stitches on the inner thigh.

He said, "It looks worse than it feels."

Lacey took a picture of the wound as she said, "It's healing well. Tomorrow, I think we can leave the bandage off to let some air get at it."

She sprayed antibiotic spray followed by smearing a clear gel on a fresh bandage that she gently placed and taped down.

"Keep weight off it and absolutely no straining. We'll ice it again after dinner for thirty minutes."

She took his temperature and blood pressure, nodding happily, which was a huge relief.

"Go ahead upstairs, Kate. I'll bring him up."

She handed Jace a sweatshirt jacket and donned one herself. They both put the hoods up.

I said, "It's such bullshit they can camp out and harass us like this."

She shrugged. "I don't know why they bother but we'll only be in view a few minutes. There's a handicap ramp in the garage. He can't do stairs. Absolutely no stairs for at least another week! You need that ultrasound before you do anything that could make that vein burst again."

"Yes, ma'am," he said cheerfully.

I said, "What do we do if it does burst?"

"Call nine-one-one and put pressure on it and a tourniquet above it."

He could die! my heart screamed.

Jace said, "It isn't going to burst. I'm being really careful."

I wanted Olivia to pay for what she'd done. It was wildly frustrating knowing there wasn't a thing I could do to her.

Three hospital beds with blankets hanging between them for privacy had been set up in the empty playroom. The kids had obviously made the beds because every bed had piles of stuffed animals.

Folding tray tables had been set up beside each bed and each had a small cheap-looking desk light on it. Three folding chairs had been left at the foot beside cardboard boxes. The bed nearest the door had one of Kenya's suitcases on an overturned box and her white bathrobe laying across the bed.

Jace and I both had the same sort of clothes in our boxes, jeans, t-shirts, flannel shirts, and sweat clothes.

I headed to the dining room where I could hear Kenya talking to the kids.

Our father was placing a meatloaf on the table. I wondered who'd made the potatoes and sides. It all smelled and looked delicious.

Hannah said happily, "I love mashed potatoes! Don't you, Kate?"

"Yep."

"Kenya let me help mash them. I did it good. That bowl there is for Felicity. It has the butter she likes and that green stuff."

I kissed the top of her head and took my seat.

Felicity said, "Jace can sit here by you. I'll sit in...over there."

I wondered if she were relieved or sad—or maybe terrified that Everly was dead.

I didn't ask. It gave me a new appreciation for my mother's penchant for avoiding painful conversations. *I would ask her though*, just not until I spoke to her doctor.

Dinner was a weird mix of normal and oddness. The kids were thrilled to have their older brother and sister there and I think a bit confused by their father who was talking to them, or maybe that was just me. He'd never really talked to us while we ate—or anytime really. He talked at us sometimes but never *to* us.

Usually he and Mom would talk about work or whatever family things that were coming up that she wanted him to attend— that he seldom did.

The kids would tell our parents what was happening in school, but he'd usually be on his phone, not usually talking but texting or checking his emails—not paying attention. But tonight he was engaged, asking them about their lives.

The kids returned downstairs after dinner with promises of milkshakes in an hour, leaving us with our coffee while Grayson and Maria cleared the table.

Our father said, "The coroner will release Everly's body in two days. I've spoken with the funeral home and church. We'll have the funeral next Sunday. It will be a service at the church followed by a burial. The police recommended that we return to the house instead of a restaurant for the wake. I thought we could have a caterer serve a buffet at the church for her friends."

Kenya said, "Will Mom be up for it?"

"I have no idea... this isn't something I have any experience with. I never imagined... She wants to attend it. She'll be home Wednesday, I think. We'll all go to the church and if she isn't up to going to the cemetery, she can come home with the kiddos."

"What about the twins?" I asked.

"They can go or come home, whichever they want. Lacey will stay with your mother and Maria with them. I'm renting a van so we can fit the two wheelchairs."

"I can use crutches, sir," Jace said.

"We'll see. The police warned me to expect a bunch of gawkers. I don't want Kenya knocked over in a crowd. It would probably be smarter for you to use a chair too."

I said, "You don't need to go either."

"And let you face that alone? I don't think so."

My father nodded approvingly.

He said, "If you'd like to arrange a meal for your friends, Kate, I can rent a hall, somewhere private to keep out the strangers."

What friends? I didn't say.

Kenya said, "I've spoken to my friends and coworkers and told them it was going to be a private ceremony. Grayson and I think we should put an announcement in the paper saying that and asking that donations be made to NAMI in lieu of flowers."

Our father nodded agreement.

"I'll see to it," Grayson said. "Ken picked an outfit for her. I'll drop that and the pictures off at the church. I'll contact her school and let them know in case they feel they should post it on the school website or anything."

Kenya said, "Gray and I will handle everything, Dad. You just take care of Mom."

THIRTY-FIVE

Jace's watch vibrated after dinner as my phone rang with my alarm ringtone right as I handed Hannah her milkshake.

"That's the house alarm," I said.

Jace grimaced, not looking up from his phone as he said, "I guess I should've taken Frank up on his offer." A few seconds later, while I was opening the alarm app, he said, "Frank, can you swing by my house? The house alarm is going off."

I was surprised by the number of cameras now on the list.

"We're all these cameras working Wednesday?"

"Yeah," he said absently. "I hadn't yet set any to send notifications though."

The notification panel told me that it was garage camera one that had gone off followed by the camera labeled back door. A minute or so later the back door had opened. The app was asking for the alarm code.

I clicked for a live view and saw a police officer was standing in the open back door.

My phone rang as I was looking for the setting to see the camera history.

"This is officer Michael Dowe. May I speak with Kate Avery, please?"

"Speaking."

"I'm just calling to inform you that there was a minor incident here at your home."

"I can turn off the alarm and check the locks from here."

"Thank you. You'll need to leave it off for say an hour. Or better yet, until I text you. We'd also like your permission to search the house just in case someone used the commotion here to sneak in."

"Sure. Thanks. What commotion? What happened?"

"Someone threw a rock wrapped in burning paper through a window in the backdoor. The backyard security lights came on and we were back there pretty quickly, but it's possible someone got in."

Jace whispered, "I'll open it."

I said, "It's open."

Dowe said, "I reached through the broken window to open it to put the fire out. It barely scorched the floor. I don't think anyone had time to run in, still—I think we should check it."

"Thanks."

"Kate!" Hannah said impatiently.

I shook the whipped cream and topped her up.

She scampered away.

Jace said, "Have them check the secret room."

I said, "My fiancé reminded me that if someone *has* gotten in, they're probably going to try to look in the secret stairs. You pull the right candelabra in the parlor to open the stairs and then press the stone in the center above the door while turning the handle to open the door. Hitting the fish, the two triangles, and the pig tail will open the next door."

The officer stepped into the house.

I got a notification on my phone that Jace had turned off the house alarm remotely.

The officer said, "We know. We've been inside before. Are there other secret rooms in here?"

"There's a secret exit from the parlor where the hearth stairs are. If you pull the floor lamp in the corner, the window will open. You can open it from the outside by pressing the trim pieces along the left edge in the right order."

"Is that alarmed?"

"No but no one except us knows the order."

Jace said, "Tell him we'll get it alarmed ASAP."

"I'll get it alarmed though."

"What's the order?"

"Top, bottom, one up from the bottom, and then top again. I can change those though. Should I?"

"No leave it for now. Are there any others?"

"There's a ladder in the library closet that goes to the attic and the basement. The lights and books in the parlor will flicker and move unless she broke that when she shot it and there's a hidden safe in there but it's empty."

"This place is cool as hell."

It made me laugh ruefully.

"I used to think so..."

"I'm walking through it now with my partner and it all looks good."

Muffled by distance, a man said, "Wow! Look at all these."

Dowe said, "Ma'am, I think you should move all these paintings to a more secure location. We're going to be called off guard duty here any day now and god forbid they try more successfully with the fire."

"I will. Thanks."

Jace said, "Warn them the front porch isn't really safe."

I said, "The front porch has rotten spots so be careful on it."

"How about the upper floors?"

"The floors inside are all good. There's hardly any walls upstairs and I probably missed some nails during the demo. The lights work though. There's a switch right at the head of the stairs and a few others where the doors were for the rooms. Those lights go on and off randomly."

"Yeah. We noticed."

"You can get into the attic from the stairs on the left down the short hall. There's lights there too. The attic floors are safe but there's a hole where the basement ladder comes out. I hadn't gotten around to making the trap doors for it yet."

"When you get this place finished. I want to stay for a weekend. When do you think it'll be done?"

"I don't know that it ever will be now..."

"Man—I'm tempted to buy it myself. Are you going to sell?"

"I have no idea what we're doing..."

"I should let you go. I'll text when we're done. A detective is on his way, so this might take a little longer than we thought. We're going to go through the garage too. Does that need to be unlocked?"

"I can do it from here. Only the people door works. The others are padlocked and rusted shut. I'm not sure the lights work in there and it's still full of junk."

"I just noticed the room sketches. This place is going to be so fun. You're really doing a great job. It'd be a shame to quit. I know it's none of my business, but damn... and it's not the house's fault. She *had* to be nuts."

The man in the background said something, sounding irate.

Dowe said, "Sorry. I shouldn't have said that. You have a nice night. I'll call if we find anything and send you a text if we don't."

He disconnected.

"See?" Jace said.

"See what? How dangerous that house is?" my father asked dryly.

"That kind of stuff can happen anywhere," Jace said.

He'd no sooner said it than one of the shop alarms began to shrill.

We all rushed to the front of the house to peer from the windows.

One of the police sirens whirred twice. Red and blue lights lit the street as the other two cars turned their lights on too.

Reporters bubbled from the vehicles like ants running from a disturbed hill.

My father said, "I should go see what's going on and turn that alarm off. Stay inside and away from the windows."

None of us moved away.

He let himself out.

Grayson said, "I should probably go with him, but I hate to leave you all alone…"

Kenya snorted. "We aren't alone. Besides, nothing is going to happen. It's just assholes causing trouble."

"Still…you're all crippled… and the kids."

I said, "Maybe you should run downstairs and make sure the door there is locked."

He nodded, turning to go when glass broke in the kitchen.

"Stay here!" he shouted as he ran toward the sound.

"Kids! Come up here right now!" I yelled. "Maria, Lacey, get them upstairs!"

I could hear the kids running on the stairs and Grayson cursing in the kitchen. He sounded annoyed, not scared, which was some comfort.

I grabbed Jace's arm.

"Stay here."

Kenya said worriedly, "Move away from the windows though. Gray! You okay?"

"Yeah. Stay there!"

A hint of smoke wafted to me.

"Is there a fire?" I called as I grabbed Hannah.

I took Wolfgang's hand for a second, releasing him to say to him, "You help Jace out if we need to go outside. Fell, you help Kenya."

Maria had Harley's hand. He looked confused as though he didn't know if he should be scared or if this was a game. She looked shocked.

As I was speaking, Grayson said, "It's out. It was nothing to worry about. I'm just cleaning the glass for little feet."

Kenya said, "Leave it, Gray. The police will want to see it anyway."

Maria said, "Let me take Hannah, Miss."

"Call me Kate," I said absently.

"I think we should all sit down," Lacey said.

She led the way into the living room.

Kenya said, "Keep the lights off in here. Fell, sit with me and Hannah."

Maria put Harley down beside Kenya then took Hannah from me.

Grayson entered, saying, "I'm just going to step out quick and tell them we got a rock too."

Maria said, "Should we go to the garage?"

"Let's not panic."

He left through the front door.

"Please sit," I said to Jace.

"You too. This can't be good for your blood pressure..."

"I'll check it," Lacey said.

"It can wait a few minutes. I feel fine and don't think you should go anywhere alone."

"What's going on?" Wolfgang asked.

Kenya said, "I'm not sure. A window broke in the kitchen."

"We heard the alarm," Felicity said worriedly.

She jumped to her feet to take Wolfgang's hand.

"Dad went to check it," I said. "It was probably just someone messing around."

"Probably one of the stupid reporters," Wolfgang said angrily."

Felicity said, "The kittens..."

Maria said, "I'll get them. You wait right here!"

Lacey said, "I'll go with you. My bag is down there."

"Lock the doors down there," Jace said.

Kenya said, "Gray, get my wheelchair. It would be faster than my hobbling."

I said, "Bring Jace's too."

Felicity released Wolfgang to hug me and started to cry, which made Hannah and then Harley cry.

Wolfgang sat beside Harley to hug him.

"Don't cry, stupid. She's just being a silly head. Stop it, Fell! You're scaring the kids!"

"It's okay, sweetheart. It scared me too," I said and kissed her head. "Leave her alone, Wolf. They've had a rough couple of days. It's okay for them to cry. Nothing's wrong, Harley. Come give us a hug and she'll feel better."

Sniffling and breathing in shuddering breaths, Harley hugged us both, letting me pick him up to cuddle him.

Wolfgang went to hug Hannah.

He didn't complain when Kenya hugged him too.

Jace said, "Did you name your kitten yet?"

Wolfgang said, "I want to name him Stormy."

Jace said, "Mine's going to be Igor."

Hannah stopped crying to say, "Ours is a girl."

Maria and Lacey returned.

Harley said, "We want to name ours Stormy too."

Wolfgang shook his head. "You can't. How about Sky or Lightning?"

I said, "How about Gracie because she's gray?"

Lacey slid the pressure cuff onto my arm and pumped it up.

"Or Foggy or Mist?" Kenya asked.

"What will you name yours?" Jace asked me.

"Boo."

"Misty..." Hannah said thoughtfully.

Felicity continued to sniffle on my shoulder.

Harley said, "I guess Mist is a cool name."

"She'll be cool like mist, creeping around all quiet," Wolfgang said approvingly.

Grayson and a police officer entered the house. They both headed into the kitchen.

Lacey said, "Your pressure is up just a hair."

She handed me one of my pills and a bottled water that she took from her bag.

I took the pill with a sip of water, then offered Felicity the water.

She shook her head, clutching me tightly. I handed it to Jace who shared it with the boys and Hannah.

Grayson returned a few minutes later looking strained.

"Maria, why don't you and Lacey nip upstairs and pack the kids an overnight bag. The police are going to be in and out and I'd rather go somewhere quieter. Harley, can you help Kenya to the garage? Wolf, let's go grab the cat food and stuff. We'll be right back."

"Jesus Christ," Jace muttered.

He forced a smile when he caught my eye.

I pushed his chair, trailed by Kenya who was still holding Hannah, trying to roll herself with one hand while being pushed by Harley.

He was laughing and Hannah giggling. Kenya's laugh sounded forced to me as she set Hannah down to let her help push.

We had to go through the kitchen to reach the garage door.

The patio door was broken. A charred rock as big as my head lay on the floor amid glass shards and scraps of burned newspaper beside a damp, soot-stained, kitchen towel.

The officer dropped a dry towel over it but not before I read the words Die Bitch on the side written in red paint.

"Think it has a smiley face?" Jace whispered as I rolled him onto the chair lift.

The officer rolled Kenya out a moment later. He and I buckled the kids in while she got into the passenger seat.

The officer said, "We'll escort you. There's nothing at all to worry about."

"I'll get your crutches," I said.

I went back to the living room and peeked outside.

There were more blue and red lights now and a bigger crowd of reporters. I wondered if they slept in their vans or took turns just sitting in there waiting for something to happen. It made me wonder how anyone had known about the Die Bitch—if it had been in the papers, which I hadn't been reading at all.

Wolfgang and Grayson came upstairs. Grayson went up to hurry Maria and Lacey along while I took Wolfgang and the kittens to the van. I returned to the house to get Kenya's bag and grabbed Jace and I change of clothes too.

When I got back to the garage, Maria and Lacey were there. They handed me the kids' bags.

I began stowing the bags and Kenya's wheelchair in the small compartment in the back.

Maria took two of the bags back, saying, "We'll follow in Lacey's car."

An alarm shrilled in the distance.

The officer said, "Wait here."

He ran from the room.

Jace said, "Get in the car. I'm talking to Frank, and he says the fire trucks are enroute and more police. There's a fire at the trailer park that he thinks could be my place."

I folded down the jump seat to sit beside him.

"Your mom!"

"He's taking her to his brothers. They're fine."

"Should we call Crystal?"

"It couldn't hurt, I guess. No one has any reason to mess with her though."

"They don't have any reason to mess with us either..."

"True." He spoke on the phone for a moment telling Frank to call.

"Frank said he'd call her and send a car there. He's sent some of his buddies to our house."

"Thank him for me."

"Everyone's fine, Kate."

"It makes me glad I have no friends..."

Kenya said, "Dennis, I can't talk now. I'm sending you a text. Read it right away. Love you."

Grayson turned to examine us all with worried eyes. He stepped from the car to make a phone call.

Jace made another call, to Howard I thought by the conversation. He made a few more quick calls before Grayson returned.

Grayson said, "Dad says he'll catch up to us."

Very faintly in the distance two pops sounded in quick succession.

"Get in the car, Gray," Kenya said tightly.

I said, "I don't know about you guys, but I want a hotel with room service. We can order pizza and stay up late to feed the kittens. I get first dibs cause I called it."

Wolfgang said happily, "We can feed them all at the same time. We've got four bottles now. Stormy licks a bit now too."

"Misty does too," Hannah said stoutly. "She's almost as big as Boo now. I bet she gets bigger!"

"It's my turn to feed her," Harley said.

"You can feed Igor for me and show me how," Jace said.

"I can show you," Hannah said eagerly.

"He asked me!"

Before that could become a full-blown fight, the officer returned.

"We're leaving now. Just follow the police car."

I wished I hadn't mentioned pizza now since I had no idea where we were going.

Felicity hadn't made a peep. I couldn't see her well in the dark garage but could tell she was huddled against the side of the van.

I said, "Wolf, switch seats with me and you can explain to Jace how to care for the kittens so when the kiddos show him, he knows what he's doing."

We switched and I hugged Felicity, meeting Grayson's worried eyes in the rearview as he opened the garage door and the lights came on.

It somehow helped to see he was as angry and worried as I was.

"Duck down," he muttered to Kenya.

I slouched lower, pulling Felicity with me, saying, "Lay down, Fell, and get some rest."

There were two black-tinted windows in the back. I thought the four of us back here were pretty safe unless they had an Uzi or something and just shot up the sides. It'd have to be a very unlucky shot to get past the seat in front of us—which would hit my little brother or Jace.

Jace said, "Dang, I dropped my phone by your feet, Wolf. Can you grab it for me?"

He leaned over Wolf as we pulled into the driveway, having to release the clamp holding his chair to do it.

The light from the reporters' cameras seemed blindly bright after the dark of the garage.

Jace sat up when we reached the next street, saying, "Don't worry about it. I'll get it when we get there."

He reclamped his chair to the floor.

Kenya turned in her seat to say, "Fell, you good?"

Felicity shook her head, clutching me hard enough to bruise.

I said, "She's just tired."

Hannah said happily, "I'm not tired! I love going for rides at night!"

"Me too," Harley said.

"Not me. It's boring." Wolfgang leaned over again, looking for the phone.

Jace said, "Here it is." He held it to Wolfgang, "I was watching NASCAR on Fubo. My buddies have a pool."

"A pool?"

"A bet—but I guess I shouldn't tell you about that..."

Wolfgang snickered. "Dad bets on football. He showed me how, but I don't really remember. Do you, Fell?"

She shook her head again.

I said, "She's dozing." I leaned down to whisper, "It's okay, sweetheart. Everyone is fine, I promise."

"Daddy?"

She started to cry again.

"Is Mommy dead? Did she kill Mommy?"

"No, honey! Of course not! We'd never lie about something like that! Mommy is getting better. The doctor is just keeping her there to make sure her medicine works. She needs more tests than Lacey can do like she does for me and Jace."

Grayson said, "She really is fine, guys. Daddy stayed home to turn off the alarms."

"Why'd they go off?" Wolfgang asked worriedly.

Hannah said, "Why you crying, Fell? Are you sick? Did the ice cream hurt your tummy? I hate being sick! I hate it! Poor Fell..."

Kenya said, "We left because someone threw a rock through the window."

"Probably a reporter to make us come out. They're so dumb! They already got a billion pictures! Who cares about stupid pictures like that?"

"Not me," Jace said. "Man, look at those cars go! Now that would be a cool picture. If I were a reporter, I'd go there to film that."

"Can I see?" Harley asked.

Jace passed his phone back.

I handed it to Harley.

"Careful."

"Yeah," he said absently.

"Look, Hannah! I bet I could drive like that! Vrooom."

The two of them made car noises for a minute.

Felicity continued to cry but she was doing it mostly quietly.

Hannah said, "Poor Fell. We should call Mommy and tell her Fell has a tummy ache."

Wolfgang sighed hard, which made Jace laugh.

I said, "Pass back the phone, squirt. And keep it down. We don't want to wake the kittens."

I handed Jace back his phone. "Hand it out at your own risk."

Wolfgang said indignantly, "I ain't going to drop it!"

"*You* probably won't," I agreed.

"I won't!"

Kenya said, "How about some music, Gray."

All of the kids were asleep by the time we arrived t a Hilton forty minutes later.

One of the policemen went inside. The other got out of his car but didn't approach.

Kenya said, "I don't know how you do it, Kate. I haven't the patience."

"It's easy. I don't take them on car rides all together like this for longer than ten minutes..."

Jace snorted with laughter.

Grayson said, "I'll get Harley. Maria can take Hannah."

I said, "I hate to wake Felicity."

"I'll come back down for her, or should I take her first?"

"No. Take Hannah. I don't want her to wake alone. Kenya can go up with Hannah and Harley. We'll wait here."

Wolfgang woke when Grayson opened the sliding door.

"We there?"

"Yeah. Can you help Kenya?"

"Sure."

He climbed out through the front while Grayson was putting the lift down.

Maria took Hannah and Lacey grabbed a few of the bags.

I wasn't sure if Felicity was really asleep or just unwilling to let me go.

"Fell, honey, are you awake?"

She shook her head.

I kissed her temple, smoothing her hair back as I whispered, "You and I can share a bed, okay?"

She nodded.

"Mom really is okay, sweetheart. I promise."

"Why does Grandma still want to kill us? Why would she hurt us? Doesn't she love us anymore?"

Her scared confusion was heartbreaking.

I said, "Some people go sort of crazy when they get mad."

"Like Everly..."

"Yeah. And some people let themselves get really mad and don't try to control themselves. Like you know when you and Wolfgang fight, you can sometimes say things you don't mean and you see it hurts his feelings, so you stop yourself from saying mean things? Well, some people see that and don't stop because they don't really care how anyone else feels. They like to yell and hurt feelings. Grandma is one of those people. Someday, when she gets over being mad, she'll be sorry for what she did."

Felicity shook her head.

I said, "I doubt I can forgive her because what she did was so awful, but even if I did forgive her, I'd never ever trust her again. You should never believe that sort of person. Once you see someone is mean like that, you know they'll eventually be mean to you. Even if they say they're sorry, you can't trust that won't be mean like that again unless you've seen them get really angry and not be mean. Angry people say and do dumb things. It's best to stay away from them."

She said all sniffly, "I don't think I could forgive her either."

"You should think about it and make up your own mind. But you're still learning, so don't make it up now."

"Will the police arrest her for throwing rocks?"

"Yes. The police will arrest whoever threw the rocks. I'm not sure if it was her though. Grandma is already in jail for what she did to all of us."

Felicity's grip tightened. I could feel her shaking.

Jace let himself out using the chair lift.

I said, "I'll get the kittens."

She continued to sniffle but released me and climbed out.

Jace said, "I can get a few of these bags."

"Grayson and I can get them."

"You're not supposed to be lifting things either."

"Everyone is hurt," Felicity said worriedly.

"We're all getting better," I said.

We went up in the elevator with the second police officer.

We'd gotten four rooms. Two of them were adjoining rooms with two queen sized beds in each.

I said to Grayson and Kenya, "Jace, Wolfgang, and Harley can have the room adjoining this. Me and Fell can share a bed and Hannah can sleep on the couch. Trust me, Ken, you don't want to share with her unless you have to."

Wolfgang laughed in agreement. "She kicks and squirms. Harley does too sometimes."

"If he bugs you, you can sleep on the couch in your room."

Jace said, "We're taking the kittens. You need to get some sleep or you'll end up in the hospital again. Wolf and I can see to them."

"Thanks. I *am* bushed. We can have our pizza party tomorrow, guys."

Felicity said worriedly, "If grandma is in jail, who's taking care of Trixie?"

"Trixie..." Wolfgang, said worriedly.

Kenya said, "I'll go call right now and make sure someone is, Fell."

I went to kiss Harley who was already tucked in still wearing his clothes. He didn't stir.

I kissed Wolfgang's cheeks, stroked Boo's nose, and then kissed Jace, whispering, "I'm sorry about all of this."

"I adore you. Get some rest, darling."

"Did you hear from Frank?"

"Yes. Everyone we love is safe and sound. The houses and your dad's store are fine and being watched."

"The store too?" I asked in dismay.

"Is fine," he said firmly.

I forced a smile and kissed his cheek.

"Night."

"Sleep well, guys."

I helped Fell find her pajamas and we both went into our bathroom to change.

The boys had turned the television on. The low sound lulled me to sleep.

THIRTY-SIX

We spent the next two days hanging out at the hotel, which, despite the awfulness of why we were there, I enjoyed because Jace and I spent it together, hanging out in his bed during the day, watching old movies while the kids played with the kittens and Trixie, who a nice officer had dropped off. We dozed together when the kids went to the hotel pool or restaurant with the adults.

Jace's parents stopped by to visit both days.

On the third morning Frank arrived with Dee in tow.

Maria took the kids to the pool.

"Any news?" I asked.

"Yes. Richard Wiess, the DA will be by in a moment with your father and sister."

"Should I call my lawyer?"

Jace was already reaching for his phone.

"That's up to you, but we aren't here to question you or anything just to fill you in."

I reached for mine to call Dwayne.

"Hey, Kate, how's the head?" he said as a greeting.

"Much better. It hardly hurts at all. The police are here at the hotel and want to talk to me. Officer Sandy says they aren't here to question me just to fill me in. She says the DA will be by in a few minutes."

"I'm coming. If Grayson is allowed in, you don't need to wait for me. If they keep him out, say no comment until I arrive."

"Thanks."

"It's probably nothing to worry about. For you, legally speaking, I mean."

"Probably," I agreed.

"See you soon."

I called Lacey.

"I think I should get my blood pressure checked again. I feel fine but maybe I should take one of the pills just in case?"

"I'll be right up. Wait for me."

I lay my phone down, saying to Dee. "She's my nurse and I skipped one of my pressure pills this morning because I was doing so good."

"I'm really glad you're feeling better, Kate."

Frank said, "There hasn't been another incident at your house. My pals are camping in your backyard."

"They can stay inside the house."

"We walk through it." He turned to Jace to say, "Your mom and I stayed in the finished bedroom room last night and now she wants to redo the bedroom and our bathroom. I might've finally found the key to getting her to move."

Jace laughed a quick huff of laughter.

"I don't think new tile is going to pry her from the family—unless... is she unhappy there? Worried?"

"No."

"Are you?"

Frank shrugged, saying, "Not more than usual. I want her to move into one of the condos now while we're still young enough to make friends there so when we're old we can sit out with our friends in a nice quiet safe courtyard. It scares me to death that I'll die and she'll stay and let the place fall apart..."

"I'd never let that happen."

"She's the stubbornest woman," Frank said like he admired that even though he found it aggravating.

Jace nodded agreement saying, "She'd never let her house go either."

I said, "There'd always be a place for Ginny with us."

Frank grimaced wryly at me as he said, "I might take you up on that. I was a looking at the houses in that neighborhood. There's a few that might do nicely for us if they ever came up for sale or maybe we should buy one of the fixer upper ones. There's four right on the street behind you. If I could entice you to help us redo it, the lure of that and being so close might just do the trick."

"Of course," I said while wondering why he really wanted them to leave their home.

Jace said, "What's really going on, Frank?"

Before Frank could answer, someone else knocked on the door.

I let my father, Kenya, Grayson, a man I assumed was Richard Wiess, and a woman in.

The man offered me his hand.

"I'm Richard Wiess, the district attorney, and this is my top assistant, Lona Henson. We'll be prosecuting the case against Olivia Avery."

I shook her hand.

Lona looked like a supermodel with her red hair in a perfect bun, wearing a maroon color suit just like one my sister had.

Wiess was older with graying sideburns. He had a competent yet kind expression, one I wasn't sure was real or something he'd practiced. I imagined it was helpful for him in his line of work. I'd have liked to draw him, which made me angry that I couldn't.

She said, "And a few other people in connection. But, please, have a seat."

I returned to the bed and Jace, scooting over so Kenya could sit on the side. My father sat in the upholstered chair near the window beside the bed. Grayson sat on the foot of the bed to leave the small table and two chairs there for the lawyers.

They both set their briefcases down.

My father said, "I could get us a conference room?"

Wiess said, "We won't be here long on this visit. My office is still gathering information. There's a lot of evidence that needs to be processed, so I'm sure we'll eventually need to meet and go over it all, but for now I thought you'd just like an update."

"Yes."

"Let's start by saying we believe we know who was responsible for the rock incident. We've made an arrest and expect more of them to follow shortly."

Lona said, "It's going to take us a bit of time because we have to be absolutely certain of our facts. The damage to your trailer, Mr. Blake, was total. The fire there was a serious safety hazard. We believe that fire wasn't intended to get so out of control, but we could be wrong."

I said, "Someone could've been trying to kill him?"

Wiess said, "We don't *think* so."

I didn't at all like the way he stressed the word think.

He continued, "It's our belief that the person who threw that burning rock, who we believe was Margo Russell, meant to burn the building down, not kill you. We only have hearsay evidence to go by right now, but two separate people confirm that she said, and I'm quoting here, 'It would be doing the world a favor to get rid of that eye sore and teach that bitch Kate not to fuck with us.'"

Lona said, "From what we can gather, the plan was to scare the two of you into saying you'd doctored the recordings from the house cameras. Which brings me to the next point. Olivia was claiming she was a captive in that room, not a participant but a victim.

"When we confronted her with the video evidence, she changed her story to say she was trying to escape. We didn't show her all of our evidence, wanting to see how far down the rabbit hole she'd bolt."

My father snorted softly.

She wrinkled her nose at him.

"I'm sorry. I know this must be difficult. This new incident complicates things for us because it was meant to. We're certain she asked Margo to do it and told her what to write on the rocks, but so far Margo is holding firm and denying involvement. We caught one of her friends literally red handed thanks to a tip and he's spilling his guts. We're questioning all of the suspects and gathering evidence but there's a lot of them—six more that we know of for sure and potentially twelve others. But that investigation led us to a very serious criminal enterprise. One we can't really talk about at the moment, except to say that we don't believe Olivia was actively involved."

Wiess said, "I'm not convinced of that yet. This entire thing with the rocks could've been staged to make us think that. It wouldn't have taken a criminal mastermind to think of the idea of sacrificing one of her pawns to distance herself from it. Shane Marsh, the boy we have in custody, could be telling the truth as he knows it, but that doesn't mean it really is the truth."

Lona said, "Margo will crack. If Olivia is involved, she's going to tell us to save herself."

"Involved with what?" Kenya asked.

"We really aren't at liberty to say at this stage. I think we can keep our speculation and investigation out of the press. If we have reason to believe that isn't the case, we'll get in touch to give you time to brace yourselves."

"That bad, *huh*?" Grayson asked dryly.

She grimaced at him, nodding.

Lona said, "We've gotten two completely different stories from Olivia so far. I'm betting she has more ideas that she'll try. What we'd like from you, Mr. Avery, is for you to stop by and ask her to accept a plea deal."

"No fucking way!" Kenya said angrily.

Wiess said, "The deal is we take execution off the table. She's going to be found guilty. There's simply too much evidence for her not to be. The law will require a life sentence for Claire McAllister's death since it was premeditated malice murder. When you add in what Olivia's entire plan was and the other victims... even if we can't pin Everly on her, she'd still get life, and if we ask for the death penalty, which the case is overqualified for, we'll get that too."

"Then why plea?" my father asked.

Grayson said, "The cost of the trial, and they probably want her to cooperate in this other investigation."

Wiess nodded. "It's going to take us a lot of man hours to prosecute. That's time that could be better spent elsewhere. I don't mean to belittle what she did at all. I'm just saying a trial is pointless when we're so certain of her guilt. But that trial is her right, which she has to willingly waive. But the time isn't our only issue. My office feels that a death sentence although justified isn't... palatable. Olivia is an old woman who's likely to die in prison before her execution date could arrive, but the fact that she *is* an old woman is going to outrage the public. It could lead to all sorts of problems with picketers and press. Problems we'd like to avoid if we can."

Lona said, "We can't afford to just take it off the table though because that sends a message that we give elderly offenders a pass."

My father said, "I'll go speak with her."

Lona said, "We'd like you to try as well, Grayson. The two of you seem to be the only ones she really cares about at all, not that she cares much..."

I said, "She didn't say she was sorry at all?"

She shook her head. "I've never spoken to such a cold person before. She gives me the shivers."

Wiess said, "The investigation is ongoing, and as I said, complicated. Officer Sandy is going to be asking you to go over that list of Everly's friends again."

"Did Margo kill Everly?" I asked.

"It's a possibility, but if she did, the drug used was supplied by Olivia."

My father buried his face in his hands.

Kenya stood awkwardly and hobbled over to hug him.

Lona said, "I'm sorry we need to ask these things and talk about it. We think Everly was involved in some bad things, but there's no point in us speculating on the depth of her involvement until we know more. It's sure to be very distressing for all of you. Which brings me to my next question. Is the plan still for Alise to return home on Wednesday?"

My father said, "Yes. If the doctor thinks she can. She's doing really well. The doctor has her medication sorted. She's herself again although still very upset over all of this."

"I can imagine. We've given Margo a restraining order. I don't think she'd attempt to break it by attending the funeral or approaching but we're absolutely certain she has a serious drug problem and people who do drugs aren't always predictable. If you see her, call the police immediately. That goes for all of you. We believe it was her who fired the shots at your house."

"Why not arrest her?" Jace asked.

"We will when we get evidence. Our witnesses aren't at all credible legally speaking. Any lawyer could get her off with them as the sole evidence. We've done what we can legally by issuing that restraining order. She isn't to come anywhere near you. She isn't allowed on your streets, by the kids schools, the park, the library, the dealership or even the grocery store you use. If she happens to run into you at the movies or whatever, she's supposed to leave without engaging with you, but be smart. It's my personal belief that she's as unstable as Everly was. If you see her, leave."

Jace said, "Does that cover Kate's house?"

"Yes."

"Can we get it to cover the home improvement store where Kate always shops?"

"Yes. If there's any other place any of you frequent just let me know and I can issue a warning."

My father said, "How concerned should I be that she'll be in the woods taking potshots at the family?"

Wiess said, "I don't *think* she will."

Again, I didn't like the way he stressed the word think.

Jace said, "You need some security cameras out back. Get the kids some smart watches and we can set the tone and tell them if they hear it, they're to run into the house or one of the shops, whichever is closest."

Lona nodded agreement.

Lona said, "I think just basic precautions are all that's necessary. If we have any reason to think that's changed, we'll contact you at once."

My father said worriedly, "The kids are due to start school... I'm not sure if we should let them or not."

"That's up to you but we've heightened security at the local schools. Not that we think she's going to go shoot one up, but there were lots of kids involved and it just seemed prudent not to take chances that one of them decides suicide by cop is the answer."

Someone knocked on the door.

Grayson let in Dwayne, made introductions and gave him a quick recap.

"This is a nightmare," I said.

She grimaced at me. "It's going to get worse before it gets better."

"Worse..."

Wiess offered his hand to each of us, saying, "Lona and officer Sandy can take your statements. I'll be in touch."

Officer Sandy asked us a million questions about Everly's friends and what we recalled about her schedule.

I could see that Lona's questions were making my father angry—not so much the questions but that they revealed his bad parenting.

Of all of us present, I knew the most about Everly's schedule, which wasn't saying much.

Lona said, "Take me through a school day one more time, Kate."

"I'd get up when my dad leaves for work and get the kids breakfast and do whatever still needs doing for them. Mom usually has their book bags ready to go, but I'll make sure they have homework and signed papers and stuff. Mom grabs coffee and takes all the kids.

"I leave for school. Everly has lunch before me. I usually see her, but we don't talk or anything."

"Who's she with?"

I gave her the list of names again.

"Most of the kids she hung out with were rich. All of them are popular sort of."

Sort of?"

"They aren't popular like the jocks are popular. People don't like them or maybe that's just my perception. Everly's crew is known as the party crowd. Almost everyone in the school wants to be invited to their parties or maybe I should say they're afraid not to be. Kids who get on their shit list have shitty things happen to them, everything from nasty rumors to being beat up. Kids Everly liked got treated nicely. They got rides places, seats saved, free food, booze, smokes, and rumor has it, drugs."

My father said, "She was dealing?"

"Not that I ever saw. But it was common knowledge that if you needed anything at all her crew could get it for you from term papers to a fake ID. They always had concert tickets and club invites. They traveled—the beach, skiing, Disney, you name it, and if they really liked you, you were invited along."

Which he knew because Everly was always going somewhere.

I continued, "There was always lots of older kids even some much older people around at their parties, picking them up and taking them places."

"But you don't know names?" Dee asked.

"No. I didn't like them. I left her alone and she left me alone. It had taken us years to reach that point. From seventh to tenth grade she was brutal to me and anyone who was nice to me. People learned to leave me alone. I learned to leave her alone. I know she skipped a lot of classes and even entire days, but I wasn't checking up on her. I spent my time in school in my classes, not watching for what she was doing."

Dee asked, "Did your mother know she was skipping school?"

"Yes. I was sent home with notes for my mom all the time."

"What did the teachers say to you about it?"

"Mr. Williams, my computer teacher, was also Everly's home room monitor. He'd ask me occasionally if Everly was going to deign to show up today? and if I said I didn't know, he'd say tell my mom to call and he'd need a doctor's note. Mom would sometimes give me a note for him. He was the only one who ever asked me. I always got the feeling that the teachers were afraid of her crew too."

"How come?"

"Mostly because all of Everly's friends were passing. They were getting Cs and Ds, but still passing, which shouldn't have been possible when they mostly slept in class when they bothered to show at all. I know that for a fact because I could see Margo in her English class and she was always laying with her head on her desk more often than not on the days she went."

"How could you see her?"

"The computer room was across the quad directly across from her room and I worked at a standing desk. I could see Spencer Robbins and Todd Hall both sleeping in their English classes across the quad while I was in drafting."

"Was it the same teacher?"

Yes. Ms. Darcey's room. But rumor had it they all did it a lot in all their classes. They'd sometimes be playing poker in the lunchroom when I went in, and I know none of them should've still been there. No one ever made them leave, except Mr. Williams. He'd write them up and send them to get a pass, and they'd laugh and toss it into the trash as soon as he left."

I answered a million more questions before Dee put her notebook away.

Lona turned off the recorder.

My father said, "Were their teachers involved in whatever was going on?"

"We'll find out. It's clear the kids have some kind of hold on the teachers there, but it could just be old fashioned indifference."

I said, "It's more likely to have been fear. No one wants their tires slashed every day, which began happening to Mr. Williams. It happened the year before to Miss Scott. She finally quit."

Lona said, "Make me a list of every teacher you remember quitting, please. You can text it to me. If you think of anything you think I should know, call me. I'm going to speak with you again, probably more than once. I'll call your lawyer to arrange it."

Grayson and Dwayne didn't look particularly worried about that, which was a relief.

Grayson escorted my father, Kenya, Lona, and Dee out, leaving Frank with us.

He said, "Turn it off, Jace."

Jace placed his little recorder on the bedside table.

Frank said, "You didn't hear this from me, and don't repeat it or anything, but we're pretty sure Everly was involved with sex trafficking."

I gaped at him.

"Sex trafficking—as in forced prostitution?"

"Yes. Borderline pedophilia. It's early days, so I can't say how young the victims were, but we know for sure they were hunting at your school, so it's possible, even likely there's some underage kids involved."

Jace said, "Was Olivia involved?"

"They'll find out."

"My dad is going to freak."

Frank said, "He had to know Everly was getting up to no good. No one is that oblivious."

Jace nodded agreement, leaning forward to whisper, "She must've had something on him too."

"Probably his stupid affairs," I said.

Jace said, "Maybe. Don't mention this to him though, Kate."

"I won't—it isn't a conversation I want to have with my father."

Frank said, "Talk your dad into staying here a few more days. Let this unravel a bit more before leaving. Margo appears to be the only one with any sort of grudge against you, a grudge we're certain is inspired by Olivia.

"Shane, the boy we have in custody from the burning rocks incident, told us that Margo said that Olivia had promised her half a million dollars if she could discredit you. She'd given her five thousand in cash and some jewelry, which was really clever on Olivia's part because she's locked up, so it's going to be easy for her to set Margo up by claiming the jewels are stolen."

"Was her house robbed?"

"The alarm went off and the place was tossed but we don't think it was a real robbery because most of her things weren't touched. If you were really robbing her house, why would you just take a few pins and leave the rest of the jewelry behind? Nothing else was taken, no silver, no electronics, none of her designer clothing, shoes, or purses. The desk wasn't rifled. The pin box was the only thing reported missing and it was sitting right next to a glass box holding about a hundred grand in watches. That box is being dusted for prints as is a gold pen found on the floor there. The box had been dumped out. My bet is we'll find Margo's prints on the pen and that Olivia's lawyer will argue that Margo thought the watches were fakes so left them."

I said, "Everly borrowed Olivia's jewelry all the time and lent stuff to Margo. I've seen Margo wearing Olivia's pins before. They both wore Olivia's jewelry to the junior prom."

"I'll let Dee know. Do you have pictures?"

"No. Mom took some though and I bet there's a billion on social media."

Frank said, "Make a list of any jewels you remember Everly borrowing and when she did. Jace, your mom will stop by later. I've got a night shift myself, but don't hesitate to call me."

He surprised me by kissing my cheek.

When the door closed behind Frank, Jace slumped back on the pillows, throwing an arm over his eyes muttering, "Oh man, a teenage prostitution ring... the reporters are going to freak. This is going be so bad for your parents."

"For my mom..."

"For both of them. Child services is going to be all over them."

"Will the court give me custody?"

"I have no idea—maybe if your parents approve it. Grayson or Kenya probably have a better chance."

"I don't think Kenya would want custody..."

"Grayson would do it."

"Yeah..."

"We won't let them be taken away, Kate."

Like we could stop it.

He said, "We should get going for our checkups."

I headed to the bathroom.

When I returned, he was dressed in his clean sweats.

"I can drive us," he said.

"Don't be silly. I can drive us."

"You don't be silly. Call Grayson and get the keys."

Grayson, of course, insisted on driving us.

"Alone at last," Jace said as he closed the hotel door.

It had only been a few hours since we'd left the hotel, but it had been a crammed couple of hours.

Everywhere we went, reporters followed us, yelling questions. I hadn't expected how pushy they'd be. It was a real relief to finally be alone again.

His kiss was passionate, not the quick chaste ones I'd been getting. It made my chest feel tight.

"I wish we could be alone..."

He glanced at the adjoining door then tugged me to the bathroom where he closed and locked the door before putting the bathroom seat down and dropping his pants then tugging my shorts down.

He sat on the closed toilet, groaning deeply when I straddled him.

"God, Kate..."

We held each other unmoving for a few minutes just relearning the feel, the connectedness we'd been missing—or at least I was.

"Is your leg—"

"Someone could cut it off right now and I wouldn't care. I missed us so much. It feels like it's been years..."

He stood suddenly, surprising a squeak from me that changed to a moan as he turned me to thrust hard.

It wasn't at all romantic, except it was. His urgency matched my own.

I hoped no one entered the bedroom because we were being loud.

"Kate," he said hoarsely, then, again and his warmth filled my soul.

We sat weakly on the toilet again, kissing and breathing hard.

"I need you like I need air," he whispered in such an emotion laden tone it made tears blur my vision.

"I love you so much, Jace."

A knock on the hotel room door interrupted us.

I scrambled from his lap, grabbing at my shorts.

He was flushed and flustered looking and I worried he'd hurt himself.

"I'll get it," I said as I yanked my shorts on.

He followed me slowly, buttoning his jeans. I glanced back at him as I opened the door.

His expression made my breasts ache.

I really wished we could cuddle naked.

His gaze left mine as his cheeks flushed.

"Mom."

He stepped close, pressing against my back to open the door wider, his free hand going around my waist against the bare skin of my stomach.

Without thinking I turned to kiss him.

His hand drifted up.

"It's nice seeing you up and about," Ginny, said.

I laughed nervously as I jerked away from him.

His flush deepened.

"Come in," I said.

I think he'd forgotten her for a moment too.

As she walked past him, she said, "We just left the kids at the pool."

Crystal carried an enormous bag and looked strained.

It occurred to me that she could be worried for her own family, leaving me feeling like a selfish ass.

"Chris," Jace said in dismay when he saw her, stepping past me to hug her.

She burst into tears.

"Why are men such assholes? I thought he was different. I really did, but he's just like the rest of them!"

"What he do?" I asked as I closed the door.

Ginny said, "Chris, honey..."

Crystal said tearfully, "Why is it if a woman stops at a bar to talk to friends, she's a lying whore, but when a man does it and stays for hours, it's perfectly fine? How come we have to call and say where we'll be every second? I'll tell you why, it's because they're all a bunch of lying cheating assholes who assume we are too!"

Ginny said, "I'm sure if you explained..."

"I shouldn't have to explain! He should trust me! I'm glad I know what he really thinks of me!"

She pushed away from Jace to stomp to the small table where she opened her enormous bag to place a few foil-wrapped packages.

Ginny said to me, "How did the doctor visit go?"

Jace said, "We're both doing great. I can forgo the crutches whenever I want and even do stairs now."

"Short flights and walks," I interjected.

"Kate's latest scan shows a lot of improvement."

"My writing is almost readable."

Crystal winced. "I'm sure it'll improve as you do."

Ginny said, "Practice makes perfect. Speaking of that, you should see how good Evan is getting with his slight-of-hand."

Crystal said, "Speaking of *that*, I should go check on Kenya. God bless her, she already looked a bit overwhelmed even with Maria and Lacey there."

I said, "Ken will retreat to her room when it gets too much for her, and Maria and Lacey are perfectly competent."

"Let them play," Jace said. "We'll all get dinner together. I have a favor to ask Evan and wanted to clear it with you first."

"What sort of favor?" she asked suspiciously but with humor.

He said, "If the twins go back to school next week, would he be able to tell if they were catching shit from the other kids?"

"Probably, but he ain't no rat..."

Jace huffed in amusement.

"I don't intend to do anything to the other kids just take ours out of school."

"He still might see that as snitching."

"Sometimes you got to snitch..."

"You don't need to tell me that!" she yelled.

He looked shocked.

Red climbed her cheeks and she turned away to rummage in her bag again.

Ginny said, "It can't hurt to explain a bit and ask him. I would think that the twins are too little to get too much attention. Kids their age aren't paying any attention to the news. At most someone might ask why their sister died. Just tell them to say she was in the hospital. "

Crystal nodded agreement, grimacing apologetically at Jace. "If they're asked for details, tell them to say they don't know, but kids that age won't be asking for details. Send them with some extra snacks to share with friends, something good, and maybe some pencils with the animal erasers. Giving those to his pals got Evan through a rough patch when his damned father got released. You just need something that the kids can talk about instead."

Jace said worriedly, "Has Stephan been around?"

"No."

She began unwrapping the foil-wrapped food she'd brought.

Ginny cocked her head meaningfully at her as she said to us, "I promised the kids to watch them dive. You have a nice visit until dinner."

She hurried out.

Crystal scoffed, turning to roll her eyes at Jace who laughed.

She said, "He really hasn't been by. I know she thinks it's why Howard and I... but it wasn't one of my ex's."

"What really happened?"

"You've got to promise not to tell—both of you. And I mean never ever!"

"You know I won't," Jace said worriedly.

I held up my right hand.

She pursed her lips at me.

Jace said, "You can trust Kate's word, Chris."

She slumped onto the chair.

"Lloyd called me. He told me the girl who'd burned your trailer down was dating a kid called Shane Marsh and that he was at the Den shooting his mouth off. Lloyd said he couldn't be involved—that no one could know he snitched. Is all I needed to do was go in there pretending to look for Lisa while Shane was there and claim I heard the kid talking about it. Lloyd said the kid would fold like a cheap suit once the police found the evidence on him. He wouldn't say what the evidence was and made me swear not to tell. He told me to say I'd heard the kid say Margo had paid him a hundred bucks and sucked him off on camera, which knowing Lloyd..."

"Is she one of his girls?"

"She must be, right?"

Jace shrugged.

Crystal said, "Lloyd told me she was bad news, really crazy, and he didn't want anything to do with her or her crazy friends anymore. I knew he didn't really want to help *us*, that this must somehow help him, but I figured the worst that could happen was the police found nothing. Even if Lloyd had set the kid up, I could always come forward and say that latter, but I didn't think he was lying. He knew all sorts of details. He might have been involved himself. So I went when he called me, and Howard didn't believe I'd stopped in to see Lisa, which *was* a lie, but it *could've* been true. I was only there for like fifteen minutes. I had one drink and talked to a few people I knew. And, yeah, all but one of them was a guy, but so what! I wasn't flirting or anything. I should be able to go anywhere and talk to anyone—I really thought he loved me, really loved me... which I know makes me the biggest fool of all fools!"

She started to cry again.

I said, "He just walked out—just like that?"

"I went to the police station, and it took me a few hours. He left without even talking to me... he just walked away."

"That goddamned bastard!" Jace snatched his phone from his pocket.

Crystal jumped up and tried to grab it.

He held her off easily with one hand, holding the phone up and yelling into it, "You fucking asshole! How fucking dare you break her heart!"

"Me! She broke mine! I knew she was too good to be true! And then she goes and disappears for three hours and when I ask her where she was, she says the bar!"

He wasn't on speaker but was yelling loudly enough that we could hear him.

"She can go where she wants!"

"Yeah... I'm not going to be her chump though."

"She doesn't need your permission to go out or have friends!"

"I never said she did! It's none of your business anyway!"

"It sure as hell is when you made her cry!"

Crystal tried again to snatch his phone.

Jace said angrily, "Walking out on her without a word is a dick move!"

Crystal crossed her arms, glaring.

Jace hit the speaker button.

Howard said, "She walked out on me first. She got a call, and I knew something was up because she was all nervous. She told me she was running to the store for milk and comes back three hours later with no phone call or nothing. So what was I supposed to do?"

"You've got me there. That was really dumb, Chris."

"It wasn't like I meant to be late, was it!"

Jace said, "She was only at the bar for a few minutes to say hi to a friend, but she overheard a conversation. A guy there was bragging about burning my trailer down, so she went to report it and it took the police a while."

"Then why the hell didn't she say that!"

"You didn't give me a chance too!"

"You should've called me right away. God, Crystal, he might have hurt you to keep you quiet!"

"Not in that bar. I know them all."

Jace said, "Come to dinner with us. You two should talk. Neither one of you idiots know how to have a real relationship."

"You should talk," Crystal said, then shot me a guilty glance that made Jace snicker.

He handed her his phone then took it back to press it against his chest and whisper, "Howard's a good guy but don't tell him. He'd fold like a cheap suit too if he thought it was the right thing to do—even if it really hurt him to do it."

She rolled her eyes at him, holding her hand out.

He dropped the phone into it.

She took it into the bathroom and closed the door.

I whispered, "Was Lloyd setting that kid up? Is it all a pack of lies they concocted?"

"Who knows. We're pretending we know nothing about it. Margo's a bitch. I'm not going to lose any sleep over her. Lloyd is trouble. His dad is doing hard time and Lloyd's well on the way to joining him."

"Trouble..."

"He's been dealing since he was twelve and been in and out of juvie for everything from car theft to selling fake IDs to check fraud. Our grandmother washed her hands of him when he did two years for pimping out his girlfriend. My grandmother will put up with a lot of crap from us, but any kind of domestic abuse sets her right off. She's the one who turned Stephen, Evan's dad, in."

"He beat her?"

"Yeah. Just the once—or at least just the one time we all knew about, but grandma didn't turn him in for that. She always knows what's what and wanted him to go away for good. So she called the cops on him, and he was caught robbing a convenience store across town, which he'd been doing as a regular side hustle for months. He was armed with a pistol, which was linked to a murder—whether she knew about that or not, I've no idea."

"And he's out now?"

"He did eight years and I think he's still on probation. Chris was just fifteen when he knocked her up..."

I whispered, "Does she still love him?"

"I doubt it. They haven't spoken in all that time. He married in prison. God knows if that's still on or not, but it makes me think he won't bother with her."

"Poor Evan…"

"Yeah… Stephan doesn't bother with him either. I tell myself that's probably a good thing, but it must hurt the kid."

"And her…"

"I really hope she and Howard work this out. She could really use a break."

"She needs to smarten up."

"I know, but it's hard when you've got no one. When my mom first met Frank, it was rough for me. There was a time when I felt really alone, and I wasn't even close to being alone. They were always right there. She's been alone her whole life, except for her kids. Mom and I try, but it isn't the same as having someone who's all yours."

I hugged him hard.

He kissed the top of my head, whispering, "I thank God every day for us. Every day, Kate."

I believed him but I also knew there were some hard days ahead. I hoped it remained true.

THIRTY-SEVEN

After dinner and everyone had left, I put on a Disney movie as an excuse to snuggled beside Jace in my pajamas.

Felicity lay beside me snuggling Trixie, which was worrying because it always made her cry a bit. I wasn't sure why she was crying—because she was worried over the cat or because the cat reminded her of Olivia.

I was hoping she'd start feeling better soon, which I knew wasn't at all likely.

I'd tell Dad and Grayson in the morning, I decided.

I pretended to be asleep when the movie ended, hoping Kenya wouldn't want to wake me and would just take Felicity to their room, which she did.

Jace laughed a soft breath of laughter, whispering, "Mission accomplished."

Wolfgang said sleepily, "You say something, Jace?"

"Nah. I'll get the kittens tonight. You can take the early feeding."

"Alright."

"Mind if I watch a movie?"

"Go ahead."

Jace turned on an old western while I contented myself with resting my lips against his neck. That small touch built a fire in my stomach that sent a wave of heat from head to my feet. He turned toward me to cup my breast and kiss me.

"Kate," he said breathlessly.

He caressed my breasts a moment before withdrawing his hand and pulling the blanket up tighter around me, whispering ruefully, "I haven't the willpower to stop. I was thinking, what if we move back home when we leave here?"

"Our home?"

"Yeah… your mom will be home for the kids. We can go visit, but I think it'd be less confusing for them—less traumatic, if we go home when Kenya and Grayson do. If we don't make a big deal of leaving…"

"Are you sure you want to live there?"

"We can always change our minds if it gets to be too much, but Frank says no one has been by, not even reporters for a few days."

"They're bound to show up again when we move in…"

"So what? There or your parents—it's all the same thing. But we can be *us* there, Kate. Plus, it'll be a place the kids can come if your mom needs a break—without them feeling like she's sending them away or *her* feeling like she can't handle them. They can come and help out after school, even the kiddos could come for a few hours after school. We can arrange our schedule around that so we're doing something they could do too—like grocery shopping or going to the hardware store or cleaning our room or anything where they can't get hurt doing it."

"Shopping is out—at least with all of them. But it would give my mom a nice break if I take them twice a week after school for a few hours."

"I'm planning to ask your dad to cut my hours. I'm hoping he'd be okay if I do a forty-hour week in four days so I can take either Monday or Friday off to work on the garage at home. If he says no to that, I'll still do just forty hours over five days, which shouldn't be a problem because he never used to insist on overtime. If he does, I'll quit and go to work at Garret's Garage. He's been after me for years to come to work there, and he'd be thrilled to get me part time."

He kissed me before I could respond.

We kissed for a long time.

When he finally pulled away, he whispered, "I know this is all making you nervous. It wasn't my plan to rush you, but it just seems so stupid for me to hold back—for *you* to hold back. Let's just go all in and stop worrying about breaking up in the future. It won't matter a bit to me about who gets what because I'm going to be miserable no matter what—even if you gave me the house and garage it wouldn't be enough. Nothing would make up for the loss of us. If we lose that, I think I'd lose my mind…"

"All in…"

"Yes. We share everything, our time, our trouble, our money, the decisions on where we live and how we take care of our families and other responsibilities. There's no more my stuff and your stuff—it's all our stuff."

"My stuff sucks…"

He laughed soundlessly as he kissed my temple.

"My family isn't peopled with saints either… Lloyd's entire side of the family, except his mom, my Aunt Laurie, are awful. I must have ten or more relations in jail for one stupid reason or another. Most of them are petty criminals. Lots of drunk and disorderly and that sort of stuff. My grandfather's brother had a ton of kids and took care of none of them. My grandmother took them all under her wing with limited success.

"My dad's brother John was the black sheep in our family. Lloyd's older brother is doing hard time just like his old man was. We don't really speak to that branch of the family much. My uncle Roger used to give them the family discount when they lived in the trailer park, but he stopped that when Lloyd's brother Jared got nicked for pimping, pandering, and selling drugs. He kicked the lot of them out."

"So why would Lloyd help us now?"

"I don't know that he is, but maybe for Crystal's sake. She still feeds him once in a while. I wouldn't say they were close, but she does try to reach him. She's bailed him out a time or two. I think he gives her money occasionally. She's the reason me and Lloyd are even civil to each other. He *might* be motivated to help her. He's probably using her though."

"What's in it for him?"

"Getting rid of Margo would be enough for me."

That made me laugh.

He said, "I don't like Chris being involved with all this. I'm tempted to talk her into telling the police how she really heard, but I'm afraid it'll make it worse for her. I wish she'd called me *before* she listened to him."

"It's going to make all three of us look guilty if the police find out later she lied and we knew it."

"She won't say anything."

"How do you know? The DA told us this was going to be a huge case—with sex trafficking. She might feel bad enough for getting Margo involved that she confesses it was a setup."

"I'll talk to her tomorrow. It won't matter if she confesses though as long as she doesn't say she told us, which she wouldn't do. I'm certain of it. She loves me like you love Grayson. She wouldn't do anything that would hurt me unless there was a really compelling reason, which telling that she'd told us wouldn't be."

"What if she told Howard?"

"I'll ask her. If she told him she told us, we'll call the DA ourselves and tell him."

I said, "I'm telling Dwayne that I want him to represent you too."

"I'm still conflicted about that. I don't want to limit your defense."

"I haven't been charged with anything..."

"True. I guess I'm just being paranoid..."

I said, "I'll have to talk to Grayson about paying him. I have no idea what lawyers cost. I should budget for that."

"We have my savings. I wanted to spend some on appliances. We have my job too. What I'd like to do is get that garage fixed up ASAP so I can do some side work there until I get enough steady work to quit my day job. If Grayson could wait until after the trial and we have a better idea of how much we need for a lawyer, you could spend all your grandfather's money on that and I could pay our bills. I might be able to get a mortgage to cover the house or maybe Grayson would be willing to let us pay him over time?"

"My dad said he'd give me my collage fund."

"See—we have lots of options. Besides, you probably won't need a lawyer at all and even if you did and had no money at all you have two of them in the family."

"Let's find out the projected expenses of that. I'll talk to Grayson tomorrow about worst-case scenario and see what he's willing to do about the mortgage."

"*We'll* talk to him."

I nodded agreement.

Harley said, "Kate? I gotta potty. And it's my turn to feed the kitties!"

Jace laughed quietly, throwing back his covers as I got up to take care of Harley.

He said, "I got him. You get the bottles ready."

I didn't get a chance to speak with Grayson until he joined us at the pool after dinner, which was our nightly ritual when we were home.

We'd usually hang out on the back deck in nice weather and swim or play in the backyard while Mom sat on the deck with her wine and book.

Now it was Dad who sat beside the hotel pool with his wine and laptop, which he mostly left closed. He even joined the kids occasionally in the pool. Kenya would work at her own table in the pool courtyard most of the day. It was a nice room with tall glass walls and ceilings, huge potted trees and colorful planters, lounge chairs, and tables with colorful umbrellas.

Jace and I came and went. Neither of us could get our stitches wet so we'd sit at our own table until the stares or kitten feedings drove us away.

Few people used the pool besides our family. There was always a few people sitting watching though.

I was getting used to the whispers and stares that followed us whenever we came in. There were only four other people in the pool room tonight. Two couples sitting at a table across from us.

I stopped at my dad's table to say, "Felicity cries a lot over Trixie. I'm not sure what's worrying her, if I should talk about things with her or not. I don't want to put ideas into her head when she just might be worried about the cat."

"I'll speak to Lacey. She's arranging for a therapist. And I'll assure Felicity that Trixie can live with us."

"Thanks, Dad."

"You don't need to thank me, Kate, for taking care of my own kids."

I shrugged and headed to Jace who was sitting at the other end of the courtyard where it was shaded. Kenya sat at the next table working on her laptop.

Grayson joined us at our table and listened attentively as I laid out my concerns.

Jace said, "I make enough to pay the bills. I'm not sure how big of a mortgage I could get but I swear I'd be good for it if you let me take over the payments. I'd sign a contract and everything."

I said, "That's just worst-case scenario too. I still intend to pay you back just like we talked about. Dwayne says I should have grandpa's money by the end of September if not sooner."

Grayson said, "I'm okay with waiting the four years, Kate. I'm okay with carrying the mortgage for the entire twenty years if it comes down to that. I don't want you worrying about needing a damned lawyer though! You aren't going to need one!"

"Still... I'll sleep better at night if I know I could afford one."

"Olivia paid Dwayne a retainer, which he accepted in good faith. She'd have to sue him to get it back and she wouldn't win."

"Why would she have done that?" Jace asked.

Grayson snorted angrily. "To make herself look good. For the same reason she left the jewelry to the kids in her will. It makes it harder to prove premeditation. You can bet your life that she's going to say in court that she left them jewelry and paid your bills. Her lawyers are going to argue that those things prove she had no intent of harming any of you.

I'm hopeful for the kids' sake that she'll feel compelled to keep them in her will…"

That made me realize that he and Kenya would be seriously hurt financially if they were disinherited. I'd never really considered what my share of her estate would be. I'd assumed she'd leave everything to our father and maybe Grayson and Kenya because they were her favorites.

Grayson continued, "She's going to have to sue you to get that money back. I doubt she'll try that now while the case is pending, but even if she does, I wouldn't worry about it. Dad would pay for your lawyer and we're going to sue her for all the expenses anyway."

"I want to pay my own way."

He heaved an exasperated sigh, which made me feel bad. He was trying to help, and I was always being a pain.

He said, "I'll text you the going rates. He's my best friend, Kate. He isn't going to be worried about the damned money! If she sues any of us, Kenya will be handling that. Dwayne and I will handle any criminal charges. You really don't need to worry, but if it'll make you feel better, put ten thousand aside, which should be more than you'd possibly need."

"You're sure that's enough?"

"Yes."

"I'll call him and tell him he's to bill me, not her, from now on."

"Gray! Come watch me dive!" Harley called.

Grayson kissed my forehead. "Don't worry about this, Kate."

He headed to the other end of the pool.

The two couples sitting at another table across from us watched him cross the room.

"Probably reporters," Jace said angrily as one of the women lifted her phone.

I whispered, "I should tell him what Frank said."

"He's no dummy, Kate. And he has contacts. I'm sure he already knows. It could compromise him if you say anything…"

Which reminded me that we were compromised.

"What did Crystal say?"

"That she's sorry she put us into this position and that she'd call the officer tomorrow and confess. She promised she wouldn't say she'd told us, and I believe she won't."

"I feel like this is spiraling out of control…"

"That's because you're a control freak. Speaking of that, we're buying the appliances. I called my buddy Pauly and asked him to send me a list of the brands and models we want. He repairs ovens and refrigerators for restaurants and does some HVAC on the side. He told me he knows a place we can get some really nice used commercial equipment and offered to come see the space to help lay it out. He's coming over Tuesday after work. We'll show him the idea for the house, and we can figure out how to incorporate everything a modern kitchen needs for catering while still keeping it looking like it should."

"Sounds great."

The lines in his face relaxed and his smile gained depth.

"I want us to be us too," I said.

The smile reached his eyes.

I loved his smile.

The woman across from us took our picture when he half stood to lean over the table and kiss me.

From her table two down from us, Kenya called to the woman, "This hotel pool is not a public property. It's privately owned and pictures aren't permitted. I *will* sue you if that picture is ever published. Georgia law prohibits the filming or videoing of minors, except by their parents or with parental permission. That was an official notification of law, which means if you persist, you're in flagrant violation of child protection statuettes."

The two couples got up and left.

Jace snickered.

Kenya grimaced at us then returned to the paperwork spread across her table.

I called Dwayne.

"Hey, Kate. I was just going to call you."

"Did you speak to Grayson?"

"About what?"

"Billing me, not Olivia."

"*Ahh*... no. Her retainer is still covering you. You don't owe me a thing if that's worrying you."

"I should pay that back."

"Hell no! Let her sue! But we do need to talk."

"That doesn't sound good."

"Put it on speaker phone," Jace said worriedly.

Dwayne said, "I just became aware of your website."

"Oh my God. I totally forgot I'd scheduled releases."

"Put it on speaker," Jace said again.

I said, "Jace is here, and we want you to be his lawyer too."

"That's fine but we need to talk about that site."

I put my phone on speaker and set it on the table.

"Am I in trouble for it? It has nothing to do with all of this really."

"You're not in trouble. But the potential for trouble is there. The site is getting a lot of traffic. The DA contacted me to ask how many episodes there are. They didn't ask you to take it down because they know they haven't the legal right, but they weren't pleased. I was told pointedly that public perception would be that you intend to profit from this situation—which will make you look bad and could make his case harder. They aren't wrong, Kate. About a third of the comments people are leaving are negative ones. Some of them are really vile vicious stuff. Things I don't think it will do your blood pressure any good to read."

I said, "I can delete the really bad stuff."

"I've already requested the DA to trace the IP for a few of the more hateful commenters. Don't engage with anyone about anything that could remotely be linked to the case. It'd be best not to engage at all. How many shows did you post?"

"Fifteen, I think. I'll have to check. I have almost forty of them done but I was waiting to see if people liked the intro or if it needs work before posting, although now maybe I can't really change it much since I won't be able to draw new animations. I have at least another fifteen half done."

"I only saw two."

"It's set to release one a week. The first one went out on my birthday and the rest will be every Friday."

Jace said, "She should be able to release them. It's how she planned to finance the repairs! And even if it wasn't, she shouldn't give that evil bitch the satisfaction of taking them down!"

I said, "I'm not taking it down. I'll add a short video explaining that I scheduled the posts before all of this."

Dwayne said, "Have you been checking your email?"

"I haven't even looked at it."

"You probably have some advertisement offers in there. Don't accept any without speaking to me first. I'll set up a meeting with the DA. Can you send me the videos? I'm sure he'll want to see them."

Jace said, "What about future videos? We planned to release one a week for the life of the project."

"I'll get back to you on that, but I assume the DA won't want anything about the crime shown until after the trial, which is going to include clean up and, of course, commentary."

I said, "We're planning on moving back in on Saturday. I hadn't really thought about recording the cleanup, but now that you mention it, I think I should."

"Promise me you won't show it though without talking to me first. I really think you need to think long and hard about this though, Kate. Olivia is scheduled to make her arraignment September fifth. She was denied bail again when she faced the judge this morning to hear the new charges."

"New charges?" Jace asked.

"She's been officially charged with attempting to murder Kenya. We expect further murder charges when the lab results are back with the kids' bloodwork, which won't happen for another week at least because the samples are being sent to three different labs for analysis. With four maybe five attempted murders... she isn't getting out again even if they don't charge her for the kids."

"What about Everly?" I asked.

"Her blood samples are still being checked too. Linking Olivia to her is going to be harder. I can't swear they'll charge her."

Jace said, "Have they withdrawn the bomb charge on Alise?"

"Not yet. You have to be patient. I know it feels like it's going slowly but it really hasn't been that long."

"She should be charged with attempted murder for that bomb! It isn't fair that she gets away with murdering Everly. I didn't like my sister, but she didn't deserve to be murdered."

"If it's any consolation, the murder of Claire is premeditated with malice, which has an automatic life sentence attached. That means she'll serve a minimum of thirty years even if the DA offers her a plea with parole."

"Will he offer that?"

"I don't know. Anything is possible. But even if he does, she'll be too old to hurt anyone when she gets out."

"If she still has money, she can hurt people," Jace said.

"We're going to talk about that once she's sentenced. Grayson, Kenya, and I spoke really briefly about it because that worries them too. We can sue her. We can ask the court to put her on an allowance and track her expenditures. There are options that we can talk about once we know what she's facing."

Jace said, "And meanwhile we need to worry about all the bills she's racking up for us."

"It's unfair. There's no doubt about it. Keep track of it all."

"She'll drop dead for spite before we can sue her ass."

"It wouldn't matter. We can sue the estate."

I said, "The estate... what about Dad? I'm sure he was counting on that..."

"He could try to sue for it. And who knows, she might leave it all to him anyway."

Jace said, "I wouldn't want it if I were him..."

I said, "He has expenses too—lots of them, all caused by her! and it's his by right. Grandpa never would've cut him off! He talked all the time about how family money should stay in the family no matter what. His family left all of their money to him despite the fact that they hadn't spoken in years. He always said that was his biggest regret..."

"You'd think it would've been Kenya..."

"No. He loved her. I'm sure he regretted how she came about but I doubt it was something he'd have changed because then Kenya wouldn't have been born. Although maybe he regretted keeping her a secret because he used to say he regretted not speaking out. I thought he'd meant talking to his folks, but he'd thought he had time. We'd sit there staring at our house and he'd say, 'I should've gone back to make it up, but I was too young and stupid to realize they were mortal. In my head they were ageless, living in their grand home—a home just like this one. I'm not sorry I left to make my own way, but I'm sorrier than I can say that I didn't try harder with them. Brent's doing it right—all you kids. A happy loving family. You all have each other. I did that right at least.' He gave Kenya to us and us to her."

"How did your grandparents die?" Jace asked.

"Car accident right after my dad was born. Grandpa had been planning a huge party intending to invite them to show them how well he was doing. He wasn't as rich as them, but he was heading there. His reply to the invitation came from their lawyer. They'd left him everything."

"That's so sad," Jace said.

"I always thought so. When Grandpa went to close up their house, he found out his mom had ordered his favorite meal cooked every day on the anniversary that he'd left home. She'd wait all day for him to return, then cry the next day. But then she'd say next year he'll come home to me."

Dwayne said, "I don't know if that would be a comfort or make me feel worse. Did he ever say why he'd left?"

"His father told him he had to work managing the family mills or get out—so he left. He wanted to prove he was as good as his great grandfather—that he didn't need them. It was such a stupid tragedy for all of them. I'm glad he knew though that his mother always loved him. He'd miss her either way but that means something."

Jace said, "Your mom loves you too, Kate."

"I know."

Dwayne said, "I'll be in touch."

I turned off my phone.

Jace said, "Let's go back to the room and lay down."

I nodded agreement.

"Kenya's never going to believe I'm sleeping when they come in."

He scoffed, putting an arm around me.

"She won't make you leave. Neither will your dad if we're watching a movie. He'll just kiss the kids goodnight and go.

Which is exactly what he did.

I wondered if my father went to his room or if he went out looking for company. He'd be crazy to with all the reporters about, *but maybe he had another mistress or two tucked away somewhere...*

Felicity and Wolfgang lay in the bed beside ours to watch the western Jace had picked out. Hannah and Harley went with Kendra, happy with the promised treat of her reading their bedtime story.

She tiptoed in fifteen minutes later dressed to go out.

She said, "They're sound asleep already. I won't be back until morning. You can reach me on my cell if you need me."

I glanced over but couldn't tell if the twins were sleeping or not. I assumed they were because neither asked where she was going.

"We'll be fine. You be careful."

She grimaced at me.

"I keep telling myself nothing's really changed. It's the same world it's always been."

"Are you listening though?"

Jace said, "It's the same world but you've changed. How people see you has changed. Don't tell yourself things are okay when you feel they aren't."

She nodded.

"Night, guys."

She left.

I kissed his neck then whispered, "Four days but it feels like four years."

"We should rent our own room tomorrow."

"My parents would freak. Besides, I can't leave them in a hotel room alone. Kenya needs time with her guy too…"

"I meant for an hour or two. We could sneak away when they go to the pool and say we went for a walk if we were missed."

I contemplated that.

He said worriedly, "It isn't just for sex. I mean it is, but it isn't. I just want us to be really together with nothing between us. I miss that…"

"I miss it too. Take your shirt off."

He tossed his shirt onto the floor. I lifted mine to lay against him."

"This would be better except it's really stretching my willpower, Kate."

I reached to fondle him.

"Kate…" he said in a mixture of exasperation and pleading.

"Fell isn't a very deep sleeper," I said warningly.

When I woke in the morning, he and Wolfgang were gone, and Felicity was feeding kittens.

"The kiddos?"

"Still sleeping. Jace went to get us breakfast cause we're starving. Daddy said we can go with him to pick up Mom. Is she going to hate us, Kate?"

"No. She'd never hated you or anyone. She isn't mean. She'd never hurt anyone."

Except herself.

I didn't say that, of course.

"What about the kittens and Trixie?"

"I have no idea, but she'd never hurt them. If she doesn't want them in the house, they can live at my house."

"Daddy says it's okay, but I'm not sure he really knows."

"I'm not sure either."

"Why are we still at the hotel?"

"Because the police are still investigating the rocks. We'll be going home soon. Jace and I will be going to our home though."

"You really love him, don't you?"

"I really do."

"Me too. He's nice. I like Grayson's boyfriend too. I'm not sure if I like Kenya's or not. He seems nice but he's never around."

I gaped at her. I was afraid to ask because if I'd misunderstood it was going to be a conversation I really didn't want to have with her.

She didn't seem to notice my shock.

She continued, "I want a boyfriend like Jace. He knows how to make everything! He said he'd let us try bending metal. We want to make glass like you did but we want to make the frame too."

"I'd like to learn how too."

"I watched some videos. Simple frames don't look that hard to do. But we want to make a cat shape. Maybe we could trace out a mold?"

"Maybe but metal is really hot. What could you use to hold it?"

"I'll Google it later with Maria."

"Do you like her?"

"Yeah, I guess."

"Promise me you'll tell me right away if she does anything mean to anyone."

"I will. I'm sorry, Kate. I should've told..."

"Me too. Neither of us meant any harm though. I'm not at all mad at you. I think we both just need to forgive ourselves."

Jace and Wolfgang returned with breakfast, which I think relieved her.

Wolfgang said, "Daddy said we can go with Jace after lunch if we want."

Jace said, "I want to drop by the house. Your dad thought it'd be good to let Alise take a nap and rest before dinner, so I offered to take the kids with me. But I have an ulterior motive."

"What's that?" Wolfgang asked.

"The real reason," Felicity said.

Jace nodded agreement. "I thought maybe I could hire you guys to help me clean out the garage. There's lots of junk in there, but also lots of things I think Kate could use. We'd need to sort it all out. You'd know better than I would the sorts of things she uses in her art."

"Can we, Kate?" Wolfgang asked eagerly.

"Sure. As long as you wear gloves and are careful of broken glass and nails and stuff."

Jace said, "I thought we could just look today. I'll order a dumpster—"

I said, "It's cheaper to go to the dump yourself, a lot cheaper. Speaking of that, what kind of car should I get? I was thinking a truck but maybe a van would be better?"

Felicity began going through the bags and setting out our food.

Jace said, "We have a truck. I'd say an SUV with a seat you can fold down because taking seats out of a van can be a pain in the neck. But maybe a car would be better? If we got something with good gas mileage for running around... how often do you need to haul stuff?"

"A lot," Felicity said. "We're always picking up trash."

"Not trash," Wolfgang said in such an affronted tone that it made me laugh.

I said, "We pick up furniture at tag sales and stuff. I don't know if I'm still going to do that though..."

"Of course you are. We should shop for an SUV. Do you have a color preference?"

"No. I don't love red but if the price were right, I could live with it."

"Make, model, year?"

"I don't really care. I'd like something I could fit the four kids in but that I can easily fold the seats out of the way or take them out."

"New or used?"

"Used. I was going to go through a dealer though for the warranty."

"You won't need one since I can fix it if it breaks. Besides you can buy those warranties direct. What's the budget?"

"As cheap as I can get it."

"How much did you think you'd spend?"

"I was hoping to find something in the twenties. It needs to last at least four years with no major repairs."

"You sure the make and model don't matter?"

"I was until I saw that glint in your eye..."

He snickered.

Felicity handed me a breakfast burrito, taking one for herself that she nibbled for a moment before passing it to Wolfgang.

He ate his then hers while staring over Jace's shoulder at his phone.

I fixed her hair while the boys talked cars.

It was worrying me how nervous she was about seeing our mother or maybe it was the idea of visiting the hospital.

I said, "You don't have to go if you don't want to. Mom would completely understand that you didn't want to go back to the hospital."

She shrugged.

"Wolf wouldn't be mad either."

"Yes he would. I should go... everything is so scary now."

"I know, sweetheart."

I hugged her until Jace knocked on the open door.

"You ready to go, Fell? I can bring them to your dad's room while you dress, Kate."

I kissed her forehead, whispering, "It'll get better. I promise."

Wolfgang called from the other room, "Come on! The kids are up!"

She ran out and took his hand.

I was worried he'd brush her off, but he just laughed and tugged her from the room.

Jace gave me a worried glance over his shoulder as he hurried after them.

I went to feed and dress the kiddos.

Maria arrived and they happily accompanied her to the pool.

I dressed myself, grabbed my laptop bag, a stack of towels, and headed down myself, stopping at the front desk to get two pitchers of iced tea and a fruit platter sent to the patio.

I set myself up in the farthest corner, leaving a stack of towels on a nearby table.

Two men, a lady and a little boy were in the pool. None of them gave us more than a cursory glance.

I opened my laptop, logged Into my YouTube account, and stared in shocked at the number of messages. I had almost a half a million subscribers. I didn't know if I should be thrilled or horrified.

"What's so funny, Kate?" Hannah asked.

"My life."

"Can you swim yet?"

"Not yet, sweetie. Soon."

"When is soon?"

"When the doctor says so."

"Can't you wrap it in plastic like me?"

Harley said, "Don't be stupid. You can't wrap your head in plastic."

"I'm not stupid!"

Maria said, "Let's see who can grab two rings fastest."

She tossed a handful of weighted rings into the pool.

Hannah said to the little boy, "Wanna play?"

I turned my attention back to my messages, forwarding a bunch to Dwayne. I couldn't believe how many people wanted to buy ad time or we're offering free materials for a mention.

Jace joined me there, leaning over my shoulder, whistling softly as he read with me.

"Should I be happy or horrified?" he asked, which made me laugh again.

"It's bound to peter out soon."

"Then we should accept these ads before it does and they withdraw the offers."

"Is that ethical?"

"We didn't approach them."

"No, I mean to take the money when it's offered because of what happened."

"You might have gotten some of these sponsors anyway."

"You know what I mean."

"We have no choice with all the bad. It just seems fair that we can salvage some good from it. I think you should pick the brands that you really like and treat it like you would've if all this hadn't happened. Speaking of that, can you give me moderator privileges or access so I can start going through the comments?"

"Sure. Make a list of the sorts of things they want to see. If there's lots of questions on the build, I'll put in another video answering them. If it's just a few, I'll answer them right in the comments."

We worked on that until my dad returned with my mom and the twins.

I was glad to see Felicity looked normal and a lot less strained.

I stood to greet my mother and was surprised when she hugged me.

"Kate. It's so good to see you, especially looking so well. Dad has been keeping me informed on your health issues... I really am so sorry."

"I don't want you to worry about it."

"And I don't want you to worry about me. I'm doing much better. I know I have a ways to go but I truly am handling my thoughts better.

She smiled down at Felicity, saying ruefully, "I let my own ideas scare me for too long. I should've talked them over with someone but the idea that I'd scare people away from me stopped me. Talking things out can really help."

"Mommy!" Hannah yelled happily.

"We can dive now," Harley said. "Hannah don't do it so good yet, but I do."

She released Felicity's hand to grab a towel and kneel by the pool.

"How about a hug first?"

Wolfgang and Felicity took off their shorts and jumped in.

My father sat beside us wearing the first genuine smile I'd seen on him in ages.

My mother took off her sundress and kicked off her shoes to swim with the kids.

The two men who'd been paying no attention at all were now staring. I didn't think they knew who we were. I thought it was just my mother's beauty.

The woman and little boy had left unnoticed by me while I was busy on my laptop.

My father said, "It's nice to see them all smiling. She's so happy to see you all. I appreciate you staying, Kate. It means a lot to her."

"We're going home Saturday."

"I know. Jace told me. He asked if I thought the kids would be okay. I agree it's a good idea to get things as normal as they can be as soon as possible. We spoke briefly about the kids visiting there. I want to wait and see what Alise wants. I don't want her sitting alone at home waiting for her family. We've been discussing different options. She doesn't want to work in sales anymore but was interested in taking over the ad campaigns. We could work together like we used to, but she misses the kids too, so we're seriously considering home schooling. The school allows part time students and even online classes since so many people work from home now."

"The twins love school. Taking them out is going to worry them."

Jace said, "I have a cousin their age who's friends with them. His mom will be asking him how the twins are really doing with the other kids. If we all keep paying attention, I think we can pull them out if they begin to have problems before the problem can get serious."

The woman and little boy returned.

Hannah greeted him like a lifelong friend.

The two of them joined my mom and Maria in the pool.

I said, "We shouldn't pull them out unless the problem is serious. Fell is nervous about people now. We can really screw her up if we aren't careful."

"Alise and I have already made appointments for them to speak with a therapist. She's going to be stopping by the house. I think you should speak to her as well, Kate. Or if not her, someone."

"I have someone."

Jace kissed my temple.

"I love you too. But your dad is right. I'm not a trained therapist. We should probably both see one. I think we're both handling all of this really well, but this is huge. What could it hurt to get some help now before we need it?"

That he asked really worried me that he was feeling much worse than he was letting on.

"Okay."

"Your dad has agreed to let me get my forty hours in a four-day work week. I was thinking we could arrange our doctor visits together. You can get therapy for your hands and me for my leg and we speak to a therapist and just have a day to do what needs to be done but together."

"I don't think therapy will help my hands but okay."

"Kate…"

"I'll really try it; I'm just saying it isn't my hands that aren't working right. It's my head."

My father said, "Your head can relearn though."

"Art isn't like that… it isn't something you can do because you want to do it. It just is… there's no movement to learn, no button to press or anything like learning to dial a phone."

"You'll get better, Kate," Jace said firmly.

My father said, "We'll all get better." His expression darkened as his gaze traveled to the door.

I followed his glance to Detective Sandy.

She and Reynolds were making their way around the pool to us.

"They can't even give her one damned day of peace."

He forced a smile. "Better to get it all over with, I guess."

Like it would ever be over with…

THIRTY-EIGHT

Dee took the seat beside me.

None of the other pool patrons gave us a second glance.

Reynolds remained standing, which I thought was rude of him because he was staring at my mother who was playing with the kids in the pool and hadn't yet noticed their arrival.

Dee said, "We just dropped by to tell you that we think it's safe for you to return home. The reporters have cleared out too. I expect they'll return for the funeral and maybe the deposition."

Kenya hobbled over to our table.

Reynolds' shifted his gaze to her.

She said, "My mom could use a break. If you'd like to speak with her, call for a visit, please. We need time to arrange for childcare."

"No problem," Dee said. "She can come in and make her formal statement when it's convenient for her."

Reynolds handed Kenya his card.

"Call and make an appointment. It's nice to see the kids are doing so well. We were all really concerned."

My anger at him faded.

My father said, "They're thrilled to see their mom and she them. Hannah still gets a bit breathless. She's scheduled for more tests on Monday. We hope therapy will help..."

I said, "Felicity is still terrified. I don't think anything will ever help..."

My father winced.

Jace stood to kiss the top of my head and remained standing behind me, resting his hands on my shoulders.

Dee said to me, "We'd like you to come in and go over everything again."

"Now?"

Kenya shook her head, laying her hand on my arm.

"Not now," she said firmly. "Our mom just got home. Kate will call and make an appointment for tomorrow."

Reynolds said, "We'll need to speak with you as well, and you, Mr. Blake."

Jace said, "I have nothing new to say."

"We have some questions about your cousin."

Jace shrugged. His grip on my shoulder tightened for a second then relaxed.

Dee said, "I actually stopped by to ask for a favor, Kate. We have some pictures we'd like you to look at. We think you could help us identify the people."

"Sure."

"Before you agree, I should tell you that the reason that we need help is that the pictures are naked shots. Mostly back views or with the face covered in some way. I was hoping your artist eye and familiarity with the kids from your school could help us identify them."

"I'm willing to try, I guess."

I was angry and embarrassed for the poor kids who had the misfortune to meet Everly and her skanky friends and hoped I wouldn't see myself in any of these new pictures.

She said, "I'll drop them off. This is for your eyes only. Take a look and then we'll go through them together."

Kenya said, "Is that all you wanted to speak with her about?"

"I think you can expect us to have lots of additional questions. This is turning into a complicated case."

She stood, offering her hand to each of us.

"Keep us appraised of any changes of address, please."

Jace said, "We're moving home Friday night."

I said to my father, "Jace and I will take the kids Saturday. We'll go to the library like normal and then show them around the house—assuming we can go in the house?" I asked Dee.

Dee nodded. "Our crime scene team is done there. Thanks for sending us all of your recordings. Your shows are really good."

"Shows?" my dad asked.

"She means her You Tube channel," Jace said.

My father nodded as if he knew what Jace was talking about—I was pretty certain he'd forgotten. It reminded me how much must be weighing on his mind right now.

I reached across the table to clasp his hand.

"We're all going to be okay, Dad."

It made tears come to his eyes.

I felt like a fool because as much as I'd despised Everly, he'd lost a daughter, which would never be okay.

From behind us, my mom said anxiously, "Brent?"

"It's okay, darling, they just stopped by to say we can go home whenever we want. I'm enjoying this pool though, so we'll stay a few more days."

The kids began clambering for their mother's attention again, telling her what they could do here in happy excited tones, except for Felicity who watched us with a worried anxious expression.

Dee and Reynolds left.

Jace took out his phone and a minute later said, "Frank, I have a favor to ask. We're bringing the kids over Saturday and need to be sure the inside of the house is... you did? Thanks. I really appreciate it." He listened for a few minutes then said, "that sounds great. Thanks again. I'll call mom later."

He set his phone down, saying, "Frank had a crime scene cleanup crew go through the house. There's still some bullet holes but none that they're likely to notice. Everything else is all cleaned up. He's going to replace the scorched flooring with new plywood tomorrow morning. Mom rented a storage unit to put all of your paintings in. If it's okay with you, I'll ask her to take down all of the ones in the parlor, except the landscape."

"Yeah... I should've thought of it."

Kenya said, "I never got a chance to tell you how much I loved what you were doing there. I was really impressed."

"It's going to be great," Jace said.

She said, "If you need help—financial help—I don't do painting or anything, just ask."

It made me snort with laughter.

Kenya laughed too, which made the anxious expression on Felicity's face ease a bit.

I called to her, "Ken says she'll help on the house. Should we ask her to help garden?"

It made Felicity giggle.

Wolfgang called, "Do you have a garden tractor?"

"Not yet. You can help me pick one."

"Can I drive it?"

"Me too!" Harley said.

"I can drive it! I love to drive!"

I said, "We'll see. Maybe we can get a small one for you. No one drives anything or uses any tools without asking first every time!"

Jace whispered, "I'll get a door on the library that we can lock ASAP."

"Let's go shopping for it now," Wolfgang said as he climbed from the pool.

In moments they were all leaning over me.

Kenya laughed as she handed out towels, saying, "Use my tablet, Wolf. Let's see if we can find some garden tools for little hands."

Jace and I finished hanging the new door on the library and I turned the camera off.

"Should you be filming all of this?"

"Yes. I can always leave it out, but I'm sure my viewers will want to see the damage and how I fixed it."

"I'm sure they will too, but is that smart?"

"I don't know... it makes me so fucking mad that she did this!"

I stomped to the stairs.

Jace followed me back to the dungeon room where we surveyed the broken keypads. She'd shot the door then smashed all of the keypads. The police had broken the door in to get to her, which was super annoying because the door on the stairs was intact, except for the latch that had bullet holes.

I said, "She had to know smashing the keypads wouldn't work. She did it for spite! To ruin it for me!"

"We can fix it, Kate."

"That isn't the point!"

He said, "Let's not show the kids the hearth stairs or this room until we fix it."

"I'm not sure I want to fix it."

He followed me back upstairs.

I stopped on the landing on the basement steps to say, "Imagine how scared Kenya must have been when that fire alarm went off? She wouldn't have made it outside on her own, Jace. She'd have been trapped... thank God you put that sprinkler in."

"We're finishing that first thing just in case more of Everly's friends have rocks to throw."

"Why the hell would they? That doesn't make any sense to me."

"I'm sure it was Margo's idea."

"But why? I get she hates me, but I had nothing to do with Everly's death. And why throw rocks at my parents' house and burn down yours?"

"Because she's an asshole."

"Still—she's always been an asshole and never did anything like that before."

"You think it was my cousin? He has even less motive to do it than she did."

"Unless he did it to frame her or one of her scummy friends."

"Now that I'd believe. But if so, mission accomplished as far as he's concerned. He has no further reason to throw more."

"He burned down your house, Jace...."

He snorted.

"He burnt a piece of shit camper. It's no great loss."

"What if you'd been in at the time?"

"Then I'd have put the fire out. But he wouldn't have lit it on fire with someone in it, especially family."

"So maybe it wasn't him..."

"Please stop worrying about this."

"It would just kill me if anything happened to you."

"I know sweetheart... let's say we go take a bath."

We headed to our room.

Ginny had left us flowers on the nightstand with a note that said, 'You need a refrigerator. I made your favorite meatloaf and had nowhere to leave it. Stop by and pick it up.'

Boxes had been stacked to the side of the French door. All of them had yellow crime scene stickers across them.

I said, "Why would they bother...it's just my clothes?"

"I'm glad they bothered. God knows what your grandmother might have left inside of them."

I opened the closet door to see how much work still needed to be done before it was useable.

"I think it'll take me a day. Maybe a bit more for the paint to dry."

He shrugged, saying, "I don't have much to put in it. Take your time. The boxes don't bother me."

"I want them out of here. We can go shopping tomorrow for you if you want?"

I began emptying the boxes, stacking the clothes in piles according to type.

They'd packed everything in my room, the contents of my desk, my shelves, and even the pictures from my walls.

"Most of this is junk," I said as I tossed random school crap into one of the empty clothes boxes.

"My mom will be bringing me some stuff that I had sent to her house. And knowing her, I'm sure she bought me some stuff too."

I tossed all the paints and drawing things into another box. Jace ripped the yellow police sticker off a box of books.

"Leave it for later, Kate. You don't need to do everything tonight."

"I just don't want the kids to see the police stuff."

I sorted through a box of shoes, tossing a lot of them. The next box held old toys and cameras.

"Man, I didn't realize what a hoarder I was. I haven't cleaned my closet out in years."

He took the box from me, saying, "I'll put it downstairs. We can go through it when the closet is done."

"Take the painting stuff too."

He heaved a sigh.

I ignored it to begin stuffing my underwear into the nightstand.

He watched for a minute then brought the books, paints, and boxes of random stuff downstairs while I sorted through my winter clothes looking for my heavy robe.

I'd undressed and was wearing it when he returned from his last trip.

I said, "Want me to throw your clothes in the wash with mine?"

"Sure."

He followed me into the bathroom, leaning over my shoulder to read the dials on the machine with me.

We had it sorted in a few minutes, and he turned to the tub.

"I'm glad I didn't see Hannah here but it's just a tub, Kate. This one—another one, the location doesn't matter." He turned the water on and added a dollop of liquid soap.

The smell of roses permeated the room.

He continued, "It isn't the tub's fault. And this is a great old thing. Imagine someone tossed it out? Evan and Wolfgang are sure there's more back there. I told them we had to wait for winter to kill off the grass so we could see what was there. Crystal thinks we should put a goat back there..."

"A goat?"

"To eat the scrub. She might be onto something. Maybe we should get a herd of them for here."

I snorted with laughter.

His shoulders relaxed and his eyes smiled when he offered me his hand.

The place wasn't the problem. And I couldn't blame myself for not realizing what an evil woman Olivia was. She'd fooled everyone. No one sane could do what she'd done. I'd be smarter in the future about who I trusted though because I'd always known she was cold.

Jace said, "If you want to go..."

I shook my head. "I'd wanted to believe that she loved us even though she never acted like she did. But even if I'd admitted that hard truth to myself, I'd never have imagined she'd try to murder anyone. No wonder Felicity is a wreck. She's probably worried about everyone now..."

"You don't need to be worried, sweetheart. Olivia's never getting out of jail. The chances of running into another psycho like her have to be a billion to one. People just don't do what she did. Felicity is too little to judge people by their actions, to notice when things are off, but you're not. Not that there was anything to really notice. She was a bitch, but I never imagined she could be a murderer..."

"Who could've... my poor father... and Kenya, god, she must be a wreck too..."

"Your entire family will need help dealing with this. Anyone would. Normal people just don't do what she did."

"We'll see that therapist together."

He stepped closer to smooth my hair back, saying, "We'll all just have to work hard at making sure Felicity feels our love."

I let the robe drift to the floor.

The bedroom was dark with only a sliver of moonlight crossing the floor from a gap in the curtain covering the French windows.

I thought Jace had fallen asleep until he whispered, "This is the first night of my life, Kate. The first one that really mattered."

We didn't get much sleep that night.

THIRTY-NINE

Howard drove Jace, Grayson, and I to Everly's funeral so that my mom and dad could take the kids and Kenya, which in my opinion was going way above and beyond for his boss. My dad had rented a limo, but even a limo would be cramped with all of us. The van would've been better, except my father despised it even though it was a really nice van. So, to make him happy, we took his Jaguar.

A police barricade kept the crowd back and a lane of traffic open.

Two distinct groups of kids were shouting at each other in the street in front of the church. One was made up of Everly's friends and the other group was everyone else. There had to be over five hundred kids there and they all looked angry or happy to be yelling. I was completely shocked at the turnout—and the hostility that the two groups were displaying.

What they were yelling I couldn't make out because of crowd noises—mostly from the parents trying to get their kids to go home, but a lot of reporters were yelling to. I figured rumors must be circulating about the pictures and suddenly felt bad. It wasn't just my life my crazy sister had messed up.

The police made us wait in the car for thirty minutes until the kids had been cleared away.

I'd have liked to go in through the basement like my parents did, but Kenya couldn't manage those stairs, so Jace and I accompanied Grayson who pushed her up the handicapped ramp.

Jace's parents, Crystal, and an old woman I just knew was his grandmother were already there when we arrived. Jace and I sat in the pew with them directly behind my parents. Kenya sat beside Wolfgang. Grayson sat in front of us by Hannah.

Jace's grandmother stood with the help of a cane to hug him and then me, thrusting an embroidered handkerchief into my hand and closing hers around it.

He said, "This is Kate, Gram, and I'm going to marry her someday."

"Don't you be waiting too long, boy."

She patted my hand, saying to me, "He's a good one, Kate. Just like my Edward."

"The best," I agreed.

I leaned over the pew to kiss Hannah and Harley on the cheek. Wolfgang smiled wanly. Felicity didn't pick her head up from our mother's shoulder.

I kissed my father's cheek too because I felt bad for him.

"Kate," my mother said in a shaky voice.

I kissed her too.

"I love you, mom."

Tears began to trickle down her cheeks.

I hastily sat; sorry I'd said anything.

Organ music began to play, and the crowd quieted.

Jace brought our clasped hands to his lips.

Every seat in the church was full and both of the side aisles. I wondered who'd decided who got admitted. I recognized people from my parents' business and a few police officers, a couple teachers, and surprisingly a few friends of my grandmother.

It felt as if everyone was staring, so I hastily turned back to the front.

Flowers lined the altar, their scent cloyingly strong.

There were only two pictures of Everly on display on top of a white coffin covered with a white silk cloth, a school photo taken a year ago and one of her as a little girl. She'd looked a lot like Felicity with lighter hair. Everly's smile was never as sweet though. She was smiling in the picture, but it was a cold smile—the smile she always had when she'd gotten someone else into trouble. I wondered if I was the only one who saw that smile that way.

Maybe everyone else saw a girl as sweet as Felicity.

I wondered who'd picked the picture.

The priest spoke the typical passages, which I thought didn't really apply to her or us. I couldn't see how she'd be with God—I didn't think she'd want to be even if he'd have her. She'd always enjoyed being bad too much.

Felicity kept her face pressed against our mother's shoulder the entire time. Wolfgang went from looking bewildered to worried as his gaze scanned the crowd and coffin and then his sister. The kiddos sat quietly beside our father; Hannah was turned away from the pictures of Everly toward Grayson, hugging her pink horse. He kept his arm around her, which I thought was brave of him when there were bound to be rumors that he was abusing her. It made me furious at Everly all over again.

I hoped people mistook my grimace as pain not anger because I was having a hard time keeping a neutral expression.

Harley fiddled with the buttons of his jacket, clearly bored or maybe nervous because his mother was crying. He kept glancing at her and away.

He finally tugged on our father's arm, whispering loudly, "Mommy's crying, Daddy."

It made someone behind us sob.

My father leaned over to hug her.

The kids probably hadn't a clue what was going on, I thought gratefully.

Hannah began to cry so I picked her up to cuddle her, whispering, "We can go home soon. Mommy will feel much better at home. She doesn't like all these people staring at her."

"Me neither."

"Kate?" Harley said uncertainly in the tone that warned crying was imminent.

I handed Hannah to Jace and picked up Harley.

"We're going soon. Mommy just doesn't like all these people staring."

"Let's go now. I don't like it either."

"*Shh.* We can't until the service is over. When we go home, we'll make Mommy cookies."

He leaned over to say to Crystal, "Can Bobby come over?"

She nodded, holding a finger to her lips.

He nodded back, frowning but no longer on the verge of tears, which was a relief because he was a loud crier, which was sure to make my mother hysterical.

The service finally ended with the priest inviting everyone to a buffet downstairs.

Crystal said, "I can take the kids home, Kate, if you want to go the cemetery."

I really didn't want to go but of course I couldn't say that.

Hannah said, "You said we can make Mommy cookies!"

Crystal took her from Jace, saying, "And we can. We can make Kate special cookies, unicorns with pink and white icing."

"I love unicorn cookies!"

It made tears fill my eyes.

"Thanks, Crystal."

"It's no problem."

"Maria is at the house. She can show you where everything is."

"We'll stop and pick up my kids. Howard can bring the twins home if they'd rather make cookies with us..."

Jace hugged her and Hannah.

"Do you like unicorn cookies, Jace?" Hannah asked.

He ruffled her hair as he said, "I love them. Make lots!"

He kissed Crystal on the cheek, "Thanks, Chris."

"It gets better," she said, grimacing ruefully at my crying parents who'd followed the casket and were now standing in the doorway of the church with my brothers and sisters.

Jace and I went to join them.

The crowd outside was surprisingly quiet, letting us pass without yelling any questions. Hundreds of flashes followed our progress, which was really pissing me off.

My father was carrying Felicity. Wolfgang was crying by the time we reached the rented limo.

I said to my father, "If the kids want to go home..."

"Can we, Daddy," Wolfgang asked pleadingly.

Jace said, "I'll take them, sir."

I said, "Fell, honey..."

She sobbed. "Kate!"

"I'm here, honey. Let me have her, Dad. Take care of Mom.

Kenya stood, leaning awkwardly on the car.

"Use my chair, Kate. You're not supposed to pick up anything heavy."

I sat and cuddled Felicity in my lap.

I said, "Jace and I will catch up if we can."

Our father said, "Just get her out of here. This is too much."

Jace said to Kenya, "One of the guys will bring the chair to the cemetery for you."

She nodded.

Grayson reached passed me to hug Wolfgang.

"Everyone is fine, pal. We'll all be home soon, and Mommy and Daddy will feel much better. Help Jace get Kate and Fell to the car. We won't be long."

"Text Lacey," I said.

He grimaced and nodded.

Felicity was shaking, crying in fear not sadness. I was angry at my parents now for subjecting her to this. I was even angrier at myself for not taking her out when I'd arrived and seen how upset she was.

"It's okay, sweetheart. All these reporters are just working everyone up. It has nothing at all to do with us. It's all just politics."

Two police officers and three men from the funeral home, or at least that's who I thought they were, escorted us to Crystal's car where Howard was waiting. Two police cars escorted us out.

I said to Howard, "Crystal has the kiddos and is picking up her kids to bring them all to our house to make cookies. You're welcome to come over too..."

"She texted me and took the Jag in case the kids wanted to go... I could take the kids..." he trailed off doubtfully, likely cursing himself for agreeing to this at all.

"Thanks but Jace and I want to make cookies too and maybe take a nap. There's so much noise here it's exhausting. We could use some peace and quiet."

The kids had mostly stopped crying by the time we reached our street. Felicity was still shivering though and clutching me. Her tears returned full force when we saw the mob of people filling the street.

Howard had to slow to a crawl, which let people press right up to the glass to take pictures.

Felicity screamed as a flash went off.

Wolfgang yelled, "Get away from her, you! Get away!"

Jace took off his jacket and draped it over us, forcing a laugh as he said, "It's nothing Fell, just idiots with cameras. It's just pictures, honey. Just nosy neighbors with nothing better to do."

She screamed again when the car stopped.

"Felicity! There's nothing to be scared of. I promise!"

Jace said "Howard, just drive across the lawn.

"Kate!"

"I'm right here! Nothing is going to hurt you! I promise!"

"I hate them!" Wolfgang yelled. "It's just dummies, Fell!"

"Kate!" she yelled again then was crying too hard to say anything.

The car lurched forward over the curb.

Howard honked the horn a few times then we picked up speed.

A minute later he'd pulled up by the basement door.

She vomited when I opened it, moaning piteously.

"Don't worry about it," I said as reassuringly as I could as I rubbed her back.

Lacey ran out and wrapped her in a blanket then picked her up, grunting with the effort.

Wolfgang chased after them.

"Sorry," I said to Howard. "Thank you."

I ran after the kids.

Lacey brought her upstairs to her bathroom where she gave her a pill and a glass of water.

"How about a nice bath?" she asked.

I said, "We can take one together like we used to."

I helped her undress.

Lacey said, "I'll be right outside the door if you need me. A nice warm bath and a little nap is just the thing for a bad case of nerves."

"Thanks. Check on Wolf, would you? He'll be worried. Tell him to make us some soup and we can have lunch in bed."

Lacey nodded and hurried away.

I closed the door to undressed and we took a shower, I washed her hair then my own and then filled the tub with bubbles.

"It's okay to be afraid. All those people scare me too. I wish they'd all go."

"What if they throw more rocks!"

"The police won't let them, but they aren't here to throw rocks. They're here to make money."

"Money..."

"Yeah. Pictures sell for lots of money."

"Pictures of us?"

"Pictures of anything really. Whatever people find interesting. Our grandmother did such a bad thing that people find it interesting. They want to know why a grandmother would do something like that, especially when they see how sweet and cute you and Wolf are. It makes them mad that anyone would do anything bad to you. So they want pictures to see that you're okay. They don't mean to frighten you. They're just really nosy."

I wish they'd go," she said again.

"Me too. I think they'll be around now for a while though because grandmas just don't do what ours did."

"Why did she do it?"

"I don't really know. I think it's because she was mean like Everly. She was just better at pretending."

"Not better. Everly pretended really good."

"When she wanted to," I agreed.

"How do you know when someone's pretending?"

"You watch them and see if what they say matches what they do. You see how they treat people—all people, not just ones they want things from."

"Grandma was never very nice, but she was never really mean either."

I was thinking about that when she whispered, "Daddy's like that."

That made me shiver with apprehension.

I said, "Grandma wasn't much of anything to anyone. Daddy isn't like that. He loves mommy and you guys, but work became—not more important but more his priority. He got caught up in it and forgot the things he really loves kind of like I do when I get busy painting and forget to pay attention to you guys. It doesn't mean I don't love you or anything, it just means I was distracted. He got really distracted for a long time and he's sorry for it now."

I really hoped that was true.

"Maybe," she said.

"Daddy never gets really angry like Everly did. He keeps his temper when he gets mad, and he says something right away."

"True," she said with relief.

I wanted to tell her she didn't need to be afraid of him, to reassure her that of course he loved her and would never hurt her—but I didn't a hundred percent believe that either.

I didn't think he'd snap and try to murder her, but I thought he could easily remain distracted—which was a different sort of pain, but it *was* pain.

I said, "He isn't a violent man, Fell. Mommy isn't violent either. Neither of them would ever ever want anyone to hurt you."

"No... they let Everly though... she was always bad."

That stymied me for a moment because it was true.

I finally said, "She was but she hid it from them."

She shrugged.

"Mommy was sick and needed medicine and Daddy wasn't around much."

"You won't be around either..."

"I will. You can come over after school and help with my house or hang out there. It's just a few minutes away. In a few years you and Wolf will be able to ride your bikes there. Meanwhile, you can just call me or Jace for a ride or ask Mom."

She stood to turn the water on and rinsed off.

I rinsed too, glad to see she'd stopped shivering.

I wrapped us both in towels then dried our hair.

She was yawning by the time I was done.

Lacey had laid out sweat suits for us on Hannah's bed.

She came in with a tray with soup followed by Wolfgang who had Trixie.

He climbed onto the bed beside us, saying anxiously, "Do you feel better now?"

She nodded.

"Evan made the soup. I had some. It's good. Crystal said she'd show us how to make it later. She made real bread and said she'd try to make you some that you can have. It's really good. I wish you could have some…"

Felicity began eating the soup.

Lacey felt the pulse in her wrist then took her temperature with the forehead thermometer.

I said, "We'll make sundaes that she can have after her nap. Run down and show Crystal where we keep the stuff Fell can eat and ask her if she has any ideas for a good snack."

"She and Maria are already making her cookies."

Lacey nodded reassuringly to me.

I said, "Tell the kiddos to keep it down or play downstairs so we can nap."

"You're sure you're okay?" he asked her again.

"Yeah."

"I didn't like it either," he said as he headed for the door.

Lacey followed him, half closing the door behind her.

I ate my soup then set the tray on the floor.

Trixie curled up on Felicity's pillow.

They were both sleeping within minutes.

I waited fifteen minutes before easing from the bed and bringing the tray downstairs.

Jace had showered and changed too. The kids were all downstairs, with Maria I assumed, because only he and Crystal were in the kitchen.

"How is she?" Jace asked.

"Sleeping."

Lacey said, "She's going to be fine."

"What was in the pill?"

"Just a mild sedative. The same one you took but a much smaller dose."

Jace said worriedly, "I've never seen a kid so terrified before..."

"We talked. I think she's feeling better about it. She was afraid they'd throw rocks at us..."

Crystal said, "The purple unicorns are made with Felicity safe ingredients."

"I really appreciate you coming over like this. I hope it didn't scare your kids too..."

"They thought it was a street party, except for Evan. He's worried about her."

"I'm sorry we're worrying him," I said.

"I'll have a talk with him," Jace said. "Both boys are probably confused. I don't think we should try to keep this from them because they're bound to hear things at school and on TV and we don't want them to start thinking they need to worry about everyone. I'll remind them that Everly was never nice. She was always mean and that none of us really knew Olivia but we all knew she wasn't nice either."

I knew he'd said that for my benefit.

Crystal nodded. "That poor kid..."

I knew she meant that for me too by the way she flushed and looked away.

I said, "I never made much of an effort to get to know Olivia."

Jace snorted.

"She never made any effort to get to know any of you."

"I bet she's done other horrible things," Crystal said. "Maybe not murder but I bet she was always bitch."

Jace gave her a quick hug and me a longer one as he said, "Let's not think about her. She doesn't matter at all. Besides we have better things to talk about. Kate's show is doing really well. I was thinking you could work with us on that, Chris. You did a great job filming me making that bed. What do you think about doing some more filming?"

Crystal's eyes lit.

"Really?"

I said, "We've got a few sponsors already. It won't be a huge paycheck but if the numbers keep climbing..."

"I'm in," she said excitedly. "When do we start?"

"Tomorrow," Jace said. "We're going to have so much fun doing this."

I snickered at him, saying to Crystal, "Making the shows is hard work. I'll show you how to edit the recordings and make the captions and stuff. If this does well, I'll make you a partner."

"I'm in," she said again as Evan called, "Mom, can we go out to the treehouse?"

"I'll go with them," Jace said. He kissed my temple then whispered, *"We're* partners, Kate. I'm so glad we have each other. I never imagined I could be this happy. It isn't true what they say—you can pick your family."

He kissed me quickly then headed to the stairs, calling for the boys to wait for him.

"I've never seen him this happy," Crystal said. "This bad patch will blow over, Kate. I know it can be hard to see through all the darkness, but I promise, it does get better. Once all this legal stuff is behind you... Look at me, there were times when I wanted to just curl up and die. Not that I'd change any of my past even if I could. It gave me four great kids and made me the person I am today. I never imagined I could be as happy as I am with Howard, but you have to let yourself be happy. You can't wallow in your mistakes or the shitty things that life throws at you."

The oven dinged and she hurried to it, saying, "Life is what you make it."

That was true, I mused. Jace and I could be happy. There was no reason I couldn't enjoy working on the house just like I'd planned—and I had a new friend to do it with.

I said, "Let's bring the cookies out to the kids. You can bring yours over to my house and we'll set up a room for the kiddos and set some ground rules for the kids."

"I can't wait!"

"Me either," I said.

Her smile made my heart feel light. The home of my dreams waited.

PART TWO

FORTY

FOUR MONTHS LATER

Our doorbell chimed out Jingle Bells.

Jace laughed ruefully as he set the nail gun aside, saying, "Maybe that was a mistake..."

"I'm sorry we had such a shitty first Christmas..."

I hadn't wanted to decorate because I hadn't wanted the kids here while we were still cleaning up all the damage and I'd known putting up a tree would make them want to sleep over, which my father didn't want them to do until an upstairs bedroom was finished, which it was now.

Greyson had called minutes ago to say he and our father were almost there.

This was the first time my father had been here since we'd moved in months ago.

I wasn't sure if he'd been trying to give us space, pretend to the kids that everything was normal, or just hadn't cared. His worried hesitant manner when he'd called me yesterday to ask to come made me think that maybe he'd been waiting for an invitation. I felt sort of bad for not asking, but I'd been keeping busy trying to keep all of our minds off everything—trying to pretend everything was okay.

I wasn't exactly avoiding him, but I wasn't up to a long heartfelt talk either because I wasn't sure how I felt about him.

Grayson yelled, "You guys upstairs?"

"Yep! we're still at it!" Jace yelled back.

373

I set the camera down to greet them.

Jace and I were filming the installation of a trap door in the hallway upstairs, which was taking days longer than planned because we had so little time to devote to it.

We had to fit in repairs between what felt like countless meetings with lawyers who endlessly asked the same questions. Then there was my endless therapy and all the work adding my paid advertisements to the shows I'd already done and the new shows I was planning.

"It's freezing in here!" Grayson said while he leaned over my shoulder to peer through the hole in the floor.

My father poked his head into the second bedroom, which now had paneled walls, refinished floors, and a bed Jace had made. A pile of plaster pieces was waiting to be glued to the ceiling and around the windows.

"It's looking good."

It hadn't done much in there in the last month. I'd been too busy getting videos together from my existing footage to do much new work.

The cleanup was mostly finished now. I'd wanted good before and after comparison shots—and I wanted it all done so I didn't ever have to think about it again.

I said, "Anyone want tea or coffee? We've got a real working stove now to boil water on."

"You started the kitchen?"

"No. We have appliances and a plywood counter on a few sawhorses, but we do have a coffee machine and Mom gave us a bag of the good beans."

We all trooped down to the kitchen where I made coffee.

The kitchen walls were still bare studs with insulation now but no sheetrock. It was just as cold in this room as the rest of the house.

We all kept our jackets and gloves on as we sipped the coffee.

I said, "Not that you aren't welcome to drop by, but what brings you here?"

My father said, "The DA called to let me know they got the recordings admitted into evidence, but he warned us that the defense will be claiming that you faked the footage. He's also concerned with the public perception of how you make your money, specifically he's worried that Jace will be angry after your testimony and be tempted to bait Olivia because if it.

"He wouldn't be wrong," Jace said.

His tone was normal, but I could see he hated all of this.

I said, "Jace can say whatever he likes, however he likes."

"That's what I told the DA. I just thought you'd like a heads up before he springs it on you. I was a bit worried he was counting on Jace being really mad by the time you're through testifying and that he'd act on it without thinking. Because it *would* piss Olivia off if he says he's able to build his shop from the channels popularity, but that's just a momentary pleasure. The long-range repercussions of having everyone think you're doing this for a buck or adding fuel to the conspiracy fire probably aren't worth the few minutes of angst you can cause Olivia."

Jace said, "Doing this...marrying Kate? Or the house—both I guess..." he shrugged, smiling crookedly at me as he said, "Anyone with eyes can see why I'm with you. I always knew your family's money would make me look bad to lots of people and since there's nothing I can do to change that..."

"Their money, not mine."

"I know. We can make our own money and the jokes on her if she's giving us the audience to do that!"

"That's what I mean," Grayson said. "You're angry—rightfully so. Just think before saying anything."

I nodded agreement as I said, "He's right. We've already taken so much from you."

My father said, "In that vein, I also wanted to discuss an idea your sister had. I plan to sue Olivia in civil court to make her pay all of the medical and court expenses. Olivia's lawyer approached me today to show me her newest will, which names me as sole beneficiary. He mentioned that she was considering an irrevocable trust to ensure you and Kenya couldn't get your hands on it. He blathered on about how much good I could do for my family now that I wouldn't have to keep supporting such obviously greedy children. He didn't come right out and say it, but the bribe was clear. He wanted me to say I thought the two of you were motivated by her money and lying about what happened.

"Kenya thinks, and I agree, that all of us should state a public intention of putting anything that she leaves us into a fund earmarked for NAMI, which would hopefully sway the jury that we aren't prosecuting her from greed."

Grayson snorted in annoyance, "She's a fool if she thinks we'd turn on each other for her promises. She's more likely to spend it all at the rate she's going. I hope she tries to spite us by donating it right now while she's alive to see how we react."

"It's fine—"

My father shook his head, interrupting me by saying hurriedly, "Talk it over with Jace. Grayson is right and she might decide to donate the majority *before* we can sue her in civil court. Before Jace can sue her.

"My father's will stipulated that the trust he left for her had to be passed down to a family member. She can spend the money while she's alive however she likes but she can't leave it to a charity or anything. Kenya is going to petition the court to put her on an allowance. I'm not sure if the court will take my father's wishes into account or not."

"I don't want her money," Jace said again.

Grayson said, "You can't think of it like that. She has a financial responsibility just like anyone else. It's only fair that she pays to repair the things she broke, including home repairs and medical expenses. What you do with any remainder is up to you.

My father said, "This could potentially affect him financially, so the two of you should talk about it. It's going to take Kenya a few days to draw up the paperwork anyway."

Grayson said, "Take your time and think about what you want to do because it'd be just like her to leave you money if she thinks you won't get it just to mess with your head."

Jace said, "There's nothing to talk about. I never wanted any of that bitch's money. I wasn't even going to sue her."

I said angrily, "Like hell you aren't! Money is the only thing she loves. We're suing her ass! Speaking of that, Dad, I've got hundreds of thousands of requests for an interview with you and Mom. I think we can make quite a lot if you agree. I'd like to set up a live question and answer interview for after the trial. I'd give you the questions in advance and let you choose which ones to answer during the live stream."

"I'll think about it."

I said, "I'd planned to ask all of you. We'd do an hour show for each of us, even the kiddos. I think it would help people to see how the kids feel about all of this, how hiding these types of family problems, mental health problems, affects even the kids. It'll give them a safe space to say what's really on their minds about all of the media that's always around. I'd put any proceeds from their show into a trust for them. It's just a bonus that it'll piss Olivia off."

Jace said, "We can run a go-fund-me for the mental health charity at the same time."

I nodded agreement. "I mainly want to do it as payback to Olivia, but it's also for me. I want my side out there, unfiltered by all the lawyer bullshit. I was tempted to accept one of the interview requests, but why should I make some random reporter rich when I can sell my own interview?"

Grayson said, "Is it still your plan to close down the You Tube channel when Briarwood is done?"

"Unless we decide to flip another house. But even if I keep my channel, I'm not going to keep talking about Olivia. I'll air the repairs show and my trial recaps and our interviews and that's it, except for maybe a follow up show when she's executed."

My father paled and I immediately felt bad.

"Not that I think they *will* execute her," I added hurriedly.

He said, "I can't argue that she doesn't deserve it. I despise what she did but she's still my mother... it's the worst feeling knowing my children hate her—that she isn't worthy of love. My father has to be turning over in his grave because if there's one thing I'm a hundred percent sure of is that he loved all of us."

Grayson clasped his shoulder.

My father said, "I'll call if I hear anything further from the DA. He kissed my cheek and he and Grayson left.

Jace said, "Let's call it a night."

We headed to our room, which had a space heater keeping it warm.

We both headed right to the bathroom. Our on-demand hot water would be nice and toasty. Sharing a bath had become our nightly ritual.

He dropped his clothes and settled into the tub with a sigh of contentment.

He said, "I was thinking about what you said earlier."

"Which part?"

I began brushing my teeth.

"About us not knowing what we're doing, and it occurred to me that we're still letting that evil bitch control us. I'm not letting her, or anyone, run us from our home. I love this house, Kate. And so what if the show does so well because of her? That money is ours. We should spend it how we want to. Who cares what anyone thinks about it!

"I think we should get the pool put in this spring. We can work on the garden with the kids. If you sell a few paintings, which I think you should do now while interest is so high, plus I want her pictures out of here, we could afford to buy the property on the road behind us. We can get that wall rebuilt and add in the security and put in the parking lot like we talked about. If we make the carriage house have just one pass through bay and keep the rest of the garage doors on the side facing away from the house, we could put in a nice, cobbled courtyard in the center there to use for weddings and parties with paths connecting it to the pool area, the house, and the woods. If we can't make enough selling the pictures, maybe I can get a loan to put in the conservatory, which I think we should do now before we plant the gardens so we don't mess them all up."

"I hate to invest all our savings before we know what's going to happen."

"We do know what's going to happen. The reporters are going to lurk about until the trial is over. It doesn't matter if we win or lose. Either way there's going to be people who are sure we're liars—but not many of them will be showing up here. It's all going to be trolls online."

"Everly's friends..."

"Will all be going away to school soon or starting families of their own. I think most of them will be glad to see the last of us. If someone causes us trouble, we'll handle it then. I'm not letting her scumbag friends, or my scumbag cousin run us from our home."

I set my toothbrush into the holder then sorted our clothes and tossed in a load of laundry.

He offered a hand to help me step into the tub, flicking the plug with his toes to release the water in preparation for adding more hot water.

The glug glug of the water still occasionally gave me the willies, which I knew would be true no matter what bathtub we used.

This bathtub had more nice memories than bad ones now, I thought as I leaned back against him.

"Has Lloyd contacted you?"

"No. His mom called mine."

"Oh no..."

"It's nothing to worry about. My mom set her straight. Lloyd's been arrested before and he will be again. I should probably go see him..."

"Don't. If you want to talk to him, do it through our lawyer. Is all we need is a charge of witness tampering."

He snorted in amusement, reaching for the soap and washcloth on the tub tray.

"I have the cleanest breasts in the world," I said laughingly.

He continued to kiss my neck.

I turned to kiss his lips, laughing in approval as he hit the plug with his toes again so we wouldn't splash too much water out.

When we were cuddling together in our bed latter that night, I said, "Hire us the pool contractors and start looking for a company to build the conservatory. I'll look around for used bricks. We should rent a little backhoe to put our tunnels in."

"We'll have to hire a contractor for that so we're sure it's safe."

"I guess we should get some estimates then. It might be too expensive to bother with."

"Maybe. But maybe not if we put them directly under the paths and laid our own forms with the paths as the roof. I have some buddies who do construction. I'll ask around and get us some numbers."

"I'll call Grayson's godmother tomorrow and ask her to talk to her friend about selling my paintings. Esmeralda has all sorts of connections. She'll know who I should list them with."

"I didn't mean all of them."

"I'm no dummy. If I can sell them for good prices, I should."

"Not the one for the dining room. It's still my favorite. The one you did of Evan is a close second."

"Let's have them over this weekend and do something fun."

Jace laughed, nodding agreement, kissing my bare shoulder before saying, "The kids love coming here to play. They always think it's fun to run around here but maybe we could take them to see the panda cubs at the zoo? Felicity's been asking. Now is probably a good time when it won't be busy."

"Sounds good. If Crystal and Howard want us to take the kids so they can have a day out, they could just meet up for dinner or something, or we could keep them all here overnight and meet for brunch."

"Sounds good," he said absently.

His fingertips glided along my side, barely grazing the skin.

It made my chest feel hot, a heat that spread until it consumed us both.

FORTY-ONE

SIX MONTHS LATER

Mid-June

My mother laughed as she plucked Hannah from a huge mound of dirt, one of the piles left over from excavating the pool.

Piles of dirt covered the backyard.

As usual, I had a dozen projects in progress at once.

The frames for the wall footings that would hold up the new brick wall on three sides of the house, the pool framing, and the conservatory basement frames were up in preparation for being poured tomorrow.

Using our new utility tractor, we'd scraped years' worth of weeds and brush away to clear the future paths and courtyards.

It had taken a month to clear the scrub and larger weeds.

The local fire department had helpfully burned the back field, which was a sooty mess to the tree line. The entire field needed to be tilled after we dug out the bigger root masses, which we planned to do this week.

Our new rototiller would be delivered tomorrow along with the attachments for our ride on mower. The tiller was small and meant for keeping up the flowerbeds. We'd bought a cart that the lawn mower could pull, two weed whackers, a wheelbarrow, which the kids were playing with now, and assorted hand tools.

My dad had bought the kids a junior gas-powered tractor with a cart attachment and two battery powered ones for the kiddos.

We'd torn out the weeds and scrub in the yard the old-fashioned way, leaving holes and clumps with large dirt patches.

The kids thought it huge fun to play in the mud of the yard, which was extra muddy today due to a heavy rain yesterday.

My mother didn't appear to mind the mess. She was as dirty as the rest of us.

I'd never imagined she could enjoy yard work or would wear jeans, yet here she was, and she came often.

I hoped this was the real her, not something she was forcing herself to do because she felt that she owed me or that she needed to watch the kids, but she seemed genuinely happy—it worried me though.

She set Hannah on her feet, saying, "Don't you dare go in the house, but go see if Evan and Wolfgang need help laying out the pipes. If they're ready for us to start connecting them, come get me."

"Come on, Lady!" Hannah called happily.

"Don't go in the house!" I called after her.

Lady clambered over the mud pile followed by Crystal's mud-coated kids and Harley.

They all ran after Hannah.

"That dog," my mother said laughingly as Lady stopped to roll in a mud puddle.

Lady shook herself, sprinkling the kids who all shrieked with laughter and began jumping in the puddle to the delight of Lady who ran in circles around them barking and wagging her tail.

My mom said, "I'll go see if they have the pipes in place."

She handed me the level and hurried off.

I finished checking to be sure the heights of the forms were all correct and level, then headed to the front yard where Crystal was filming the kids laying out the irrigation pipes while Jace dug out the trenches for it.

Orange spray paint marked out the gardens, yellow paint the driveway and paths, and white the irrigation.

The kids were playing some game they'd made up, jumping and skipping between the different colored markings.

The front was almost ready for planting. A quick pass with the tiller and we could start laying out the shrubs and flower beds.

I couldn't wait.

My mom was kneeling beside the boys, looking like a teenager in her jeans, dirty shirt, and ponytail.

Crystal was filming Jace, *likely admiring him*, I thought in amusement. He was shirtless and swinging a pickax like he meant it, cutting through the overgrown grass where we meant to make the driveway circle around, which is how it had been originally, but someone had planted raspberry bushes or let them take root. That entire corner of the front yard had been a brambly mess. We'd yanked it all out but there were still patches of matted roots and grass.

He was sweaty, dirty, tanned, and utterly beautiful.

I said, "Leave that until I get it tilled."

He stopped to wipe his brow and grin at me.

"I will once I get this line done. I want this all in before they come and pour tomorrow."

"I can hardly wait to start on the wall. This is better than Christmas!"

Which was true of all my Christmases, not just this last one which had been stressful for everyone. I hoped it would get easier in time. In just a few more months it would be a year since it happened. But I knew we wouldn't really begin to heal until after the trial.

This garden was just what we needed. A chance to show the kids something beautiful could come from a mess.

Crystal laughed as she said, "I don't know about that. I *am* looking forward to seeing it all done though."

I stopped to kiss Jace, meaning it to be a quick peck, but his sun-warmed skin pulled me closer.

I hugged him for a long minute before reluctantly stepping away.

"I better get started then," I said.

My heart thudded as he pulled me back for another kiss. The warmth of his palm on my back through my shirt filled my soul. His smile, his eyes, the merest brush of his hand could captivate me.

"I love you desperately," I said when we parted.

His eyes lit.

"Kate!" Harley called.

"Bad dog," Felicity said anxiously.

I tuned as my mom said, "Come, Lady!"

Harley said, "Drop it, girl. Kate!"

He sounded really panicked now.

Jace and I both ran to see what had him so upset.

My mother had grabbed Lady by the collar.

I beat Jace there because he limped.

Felicity said, "I don't think she ate any but maybe we should take her to the vet anyway."

She'd taken Hannah's hand. Crystal's kids looked confused—Felicity looked terrified.

"Harley, come here, darling," my mom called.

The older boys had both stopped laying out pipe and were watching worriedly.

"Damn," Jace muttered as we saw what had alarmed Harley.

I picked Harley up.

A dead cat was covered by flies so thickly it was hard to make out what it was.

I said, "It isn't Boo or Igor. Mom, take Fell and my car. The keys are in it. Don't worry about getting it dirty. I'll call and tell them you're coming. We'll bag a piece up so they can test it. Wolf, run get a plastic bag and the barbecue tongs. Evan take the kiddos to the backyard."

"Come on, guys," Evan said.

I said, "You guys can spray out the irrigation line with the white spray paint. I'll be right there."

My mom and Felicity followed the kids.

I said to Crystal, "Get some shots of this."

"You can't include this, Kate."

"It's for the police."

Jace was already on the phone, to Frank I assumed. He said, "Kate, did you get shots of this side of the yard yesterday?"

Crystal said, "I did. I walked around the entire perimeter filming the wall footings."

Jace leaned over the broken wall, which we hadn't removed yet. The new wall would be set back to make room for hedges and a sidewalk along the front of the house.

He said, "There's footprints here. Small ones—a woman, not a man, I think."

I said, "Stay back. Maybe they can find more if we don't muck it up."

Lady's prints circled the dead cat. Her paw prints were clear in the mud around the fly-coated hunks of meat too, which I hoped meant she hadn't sampled any.

My mom pulled up in my car as Wolfgang ran out the front door with the plastic bag and tongs.

"Did she eat any?" he asked me worriedly as he handed them to me.

"I don't know. She seems fine..."

I plucked one of the gobs up and dropped it into the bag that I sealed and handed to him.

"Don't open it. Give it to the doctor."

He ran for the car with it.

I called the vet to tell him they were on their way in.

When I hung up, Jace said, "I called it in. The police are on their way."

Crystal said, "What kind of asshole does something like this!"

"Margo," I said angrily.

Jace shook his head, saying, "Who knows. Maybe it's unrelated to us. We should go warn the neighbors to check their yards."

I snorted softly.

Jace said, "I'll hang those dummy cameras we talked about on the broken wall and put up a few signs saying the house is monitored."

I said, "It was Margo or one of scumbag friends—or do you think it's just a coincidence that they graduated last night?"

"Son of a bitch!" Jace said angrily.

"I guess we should be thankful she didn't shoot at the house or try to burn it down as her celebration..."

Crystal said, "Did they say when the trial is going to start?"

"No."

Jace said, "It's going to be months, maybe a year or more, I think, by the time they finish all the pretrial discovery."

"A year..."

I said, "Olivia's going to do everything she can to drag it out because when she's found guilty, she'll be put in with the death row inmates."

"They wouldn't really execute her, would they?"

I said, "I doubt it, but she'd hate being there, which is all I've got to make her pay."

I stomped away to the pipes laid out beside the small trenches.

Jace returned to cutting the trench to bury the irrigation pipes.

Crystal watched us worriedly for a minute then set the camera on a tripod and headed to the backyard.

I called after her, "I'll call Maria and my dad just in case Lady ate any of it."

Crystal turned to say, "What will I tell them..."

"That we sent her to the vet as a precaution because we don't know what killed the cat, which is perfectly true."

I called my dad.

"You ready for the big pour tomorrow?" he asked cheerfully when he answered.

"Someone threw poisoned meat into the yard. Mom took Lady to the vet with the twins. We don't know if she ate any or not. It killed a neighbor's cat, which the kids saw. Can you call Maria and maybe Lacey just in case Lady..."

"Jesus! Did you call the police?"

"Yeah."

"Call your lawyer too. I'll call Grayson and Maria. Is your mother..."

"She was mad but seemed okay. Lady seemed okay too, but it only just happened. The cat appeared to have died quick. It died right by one of the clumps, which I hope means Lady didn't eat it. My neighbors are going to freak!"

"It isn't your fault, Kate."

"Tell that to the people whose cat just died."

"Call me if you hear anything. Tell the kids I'm on the way but it's going to be at least thirty minutes."

"I can handle the kids."

"If that dog dies..."

"I can't bear thinking about it."

I disconnected to call Dwayne, getting his voice mail. I left a message telling him what had happened and that I'd call when I knew more.

I went to check on the kids.

Dwayne called me back minutes after the police arrived.

We hadn't heard anything yet about Lady.

"What's my liability with the cat?" I asked him.

"None. Unless, of course, the police say you poisoned it."

"I'm sure it was Margo."

"Unfortunately the law doesn't share your certainty. Do your house cameras cover the spot where the cat was?"

"No. Jace is going to put in some dummy cameras along the broken fence. I'll get started on installing the real ones. We'd intended to wait until the planting was done to start the wall, but I'll start it this week and hire some help to get it done quicker."

"Keep records of the costs."

"What do I do about the cat? Should I go door-to-door or what?"

"Not yet. Let the police handle it. I'm sure they're going to check to see if any neighbors were also targeted."

"It's such bullshit that she's going to get away with this."

I disconnected and went to begin connecting the pipes.

My mom called thirty minutes later.

"We think Lady is fine. The vet sent the sample out to a lab for analysis but she's showing no symptoms at all, and he says that if the cat was laying right there it would've had to be fast acting because she'd have eaten her fill and run off, and if she'd started to feel ill while eating, she'd have run off. We're going to leave Lady here for a few hours just in case because she's a lot bigger than the cat, but I don't think she ate any, thank God."

"That's great news. I'm not sure if I should tell the kids or not though in case you're wrong."

"Tell them what I told you. They're old enough to understand the reasoning."

"Are you coming back here or taking the twins home?"

"Wolf wants to come back. I thought I'd drop him and take all the kiddos home. They can help me get a picnic ready for this evening. Tell Crystal she and Howard are invited as well. The pool should be nice and warm for a late swim after dinner, so bring suits."

"We won't be able to stay long, Mom. We have an early day tomorrow and we still have a ton to do."

"I wish I could help more..."

"You help plenty!"

"I'm really looking forward to planting."

"Me too. I've got to run. We'll be there for dinner."

I disconnected and jogged over to the police. I knew most of them by name now and they all knew us.

I said, "Hi, Brian. Thanks for coming so quick. I just spoke to my mom. The vet thinks Lady will be okay."

I told Brian what the vet had said.

Brian said, "We're taking samples too. We'll probably want the footage you took last night. We're going to take the cat. Leave the scene as is until we get back to you, which should be in an hour or so. We want to check the neighborhood before we mess with it."

Jace said, "They want us to check the entire property."

"My mom is coming to take the kids. Can it wait until they're gone?"

"Sure."

"I'm going to go hose them off. Call me if you need me."

I gave Jace a quick kiss on the cheek and ran for the backyard.

I said to the kids, "Lady is fine. Mom is coming to pick you guys up."

"Can we swim?" Hannah asked.

"Mom says we're having a picnic and the pool will be nice and warm for a night swim. You'll have to help her cook."

They started chattering excitedly, seeming to have forgotten the cat.

Except for Evan. He crossed his arms, glaring at me.

I said to Crystal, "You and Howard are invited too. You can go with her now or hang out with us and get a break. Hose them off. I'll get towels. Ev, you want to go with them or stay here?"

"Stay."

"Then come help me get some towels."

I headed to the carriage house where we kept the outdoor towels, seeing as how filthy kids who needed hosing off was a regular thing here.

When we were out of earshot of the kids I said, "Thanks. You handled that great."

"Will she really be okay?"

I told him what my mom had said.

"Wolf is coming back. The police want us to check the property. I thought I'd wait until the kids are gone. They don't seem that upset though."

"They don't realize someone did it on purpose."

"We're adding more cameras and lights."

"They might've killed Igor."

I crouched to hug him.

He let me for a minute before pulling away and saying briskly, "I'll go get some garbage bags in case we see anything."

"If you see anything just lay a bag over it. Don't touch it until the police see it."

He nodded and ran for the house.

I grabbed the towels and headed back to Crystal who was spraying the kids off using the hose at the front of the carriage house, which had a graveled driveway.

I handed her the towels and went to see if there were footprints in the mud by the gate.

Jace had put the front of the garage facing the street in the back, not the yard. We'd bought a piece of property behind us that we intended to use as parking. It had a tiny ramshackle house on it that would be Jace's metal shop someday if we could get the permits. If not, we'd make it into a garage with an apartment and use the carriage house for our own cars.

The downstairs of the carriage house was almost finished. Jace and I had done most of the work ourselves over the last few months.

It had three large bays with the one in the middle being a pass through with double doors on the back wall that opened to the future courtyard. Large roll up garage doors opened to the parking lot that connected to the side road. A cheap gate blocked the entrance to the parking lot that we planned to cobble and landscape, adding bushes to block the view of the street and the parking lot from the yard.

The brick wall that surrounded the house would end fifteen feet past the entrance. A much cheaper palisade fence would go from that wall to the edge of the woods were it grew too steep to walk. The rocky ledge there could be climbed. The woods at the bottom was owned by the town. No one ever used it. I hadn't intended to do anything security wise there, but I was rethinking that now.

Maybe a fence along the bottom?

I walked around the outside of the building to the new stairs along the outside wall of the garage that led to an unfinished apartment upstairs. There weren't any muddy footprints on the stairs.

The outside of the building was painted but lacked any trim yet, except for a balcony that ran the length of the back wall that faced the future courtyard. It had two security cameras already, one facing the back of the house and one facing the parking lot.

I'd add another two, I decided. One on the wall that faced the woods and one facing the pool. The kind with security lights. And one on the gate.

I took out my phone to order them.

Evan returned with the bags and garden gloves.

I said to Crystal, "We're going to go check things. Maria and my dad will be with the kids if you want to stay here and hang out."

When we were out of earshot again, I said to him, "Keep your eyes peeled for flies and watch out for footprints."

When we reached the steep edge I said, "The dog can't get down this, but a person could climb up. You think I should put a fence on the bottom?"

"What about the paths on the nice hill?"

"I don't know. A fence would ruin the view there when you were walking on it as well as being really unneighborly. That's public land it adjoins to. No one uses it much but sometimes people cut through our land to reach the lake."

"There's no power down there," he said thoughtfully. "Maybe a few of those solar powered cameras like my friend Tim has on his house. They beep on his dad's phone just like yours do on yours. He has lights that come on when you walk by. Could you put some in the woods with the solar power things and maybe add a warning? It'd be cool if it said something like you're entering a minefield."

I snickered.

"Let's go see how many we'd need."

His eyes lit.

I really loved this kid.

Jace joined us a few hours later.

"If he were older, I'd be nervous," he said as he leaned in to kiss me.

"I do love him."

I stepped closer to really kiss him.

From the overgrown field that abutted our woods, Evan called, "Two signs here, Kate. They're old ones but they're all rusty, and you can't read it."

Wolfgang hollered, "Another should go here cause there's a small path. It hasn't been used in a while, but it looks like it goes into our woods."

Jace and I headed toward them.

When we reached Evan, I said, "Want to help me get the signs up next Saturday? We'll have to climb a few trees to put the lights in."

"Sure."

We followed the path Wolfgang had found. It cut only a tiny way into our woods in the opposite direction of the lake.

"We'll have to see where it goes one day but not today. I'm starving. Let's go eat."

"How many lights do we need?" Evan asked.

"I'm buying ten for now. We'll hang four real cameras and ten fakes. It's the signs I need to think about. We should have some that say this way to the lake. The ones on the path that lead to the house should be official posted signs. The ones off the path in the woods will need some thinking."

Jace said, "We can't just post it?"

"Sure but what fun is that? We want it to say something like you've entered a restricted area. And then maybe something like active minefield but we don't want anyone having a heart attack or calling for help either."

Wolfgang said, "How about game in progress and just having the sign all shot up."

I snickered.

Evan said, "Can we add sound effects?"

"If we can figure out how to."

They immediately began throwing ideas around.

I said, "Research it. It needs to be affordable, low maintenance, and hard to steal, scary but in a fun way."

Jace said, "But not so fun they continue."

I said, "I'll have the camera on the top of the path send a notification. The rest of them we won't bother with. They're just for checking."

"Maybe we can think of game that would use them?"

"I'm going to call around tomorrow and hire some help to get the wall done and the alarms on it installed. I want everyone, even Lady, safe here."

Evan said, "Did the police find any more?"

"No."

"So just us then," Wolfgang said.

"It looks like it. Kate's probably right and it was Margo just being an ass."

I said, "She'll need to get a job now that school is done because I can't imagine she's going to college. I bet soon she's too busy to worry about us."

Jace said, "She's just a dumb kid. Now that they're all graduated, they'll have better things to do than harass us."

"Fell is scared of her," Wolfgang said.

Which I knew meant he was scared of her too.

Evan looked worried.

When we reached the house he said, "Someone should stay here in case she tries fire rocks again. You and Fell wanna sleep over tonight? We can go to my grams in the morning and see if there's anything good in the shed."

Jace said, "I think he's right, Kate. I'll stay. Bring me back a hamburger or something."

"I won't be long."

I didn't bother change from my dirty clothes or hose them off. The inside of my car was filthy. Our dirt wouldn't make it any worse.

When we arrived at my parents, I pulled Crystal aside to say, "Fell is scared of Margo and the boys are worried. Evan asked them to sleep over. I hate to ask for another favor when you already do so much, but if she wants to, could they? I already told Evan he can come over next Saturday to help me hang lights in the trees. I'd keep them overnight as payback."

"Of course. She's always welcome. The poor thing..."

I gave Crystal a quick hug.

"Thanks. I'll clear it with my parents."

"Where's Jace?" my mom asked when we entered the kitchen.

"Home in case Margo isn't done having fun at our expense. Can I take some burgers to go?"

"Yes... do you think... I suppose we should assume she would. Excuse me, I think I should speak with your father."

I said, "Crystal is going to take the twins tonight. Fell really doesn't need any more stress. I don't think Margo will try another flaming rock here, but just in case, keep the extinguishers handy."

She nodded and hurried out to the back deck.

I began loading two plates with salads. Crystal put together two hamburger buns with all the toppings and then one hotdog with beans and one with cheese.

I thanked her and headed out to snag the burgers and dogs from the grill.

Evan had stripped off his dirty clothes and hosed himself off. He sat on the side of the pool with his arm around Felicity.

He really loves her, I thought as I watched them.

Crystal handed me tinfoil to wrap the plates.

I said, "That has to count for something, right?"

She followed my gaze to the kids. Wolfgang had joined them, sitting on the other side of her.

I continued, "She's seen the worst but also the best. That *has* to count for something. I'd have given anything for a friend like him at her age—hell, at any age! He's my best friend too..."

Crystal snorted with laughter. "He's an old soul. I was worried for him but is all he needed was to find a kindred spirit and now he has three of them."

"This trial is going to hurt him because it's going to hurt her. No matter how it plays out there's no good ending for her—or any of us. There can never be justice for what Olivia did, or forgiveness. At most we can ignore it. I sometimes wish she'd at least pretended to be sorry for Felicity's sake. It'd have made it harder on the rest of us—and I guess on Fell really. At least this way she can't be confused, or more confused about what she feels.

"Oh, that reminds me. Evan wanted to go see his grandmother to raid her junk. It'd be good for the twins to see there are good grandmothers out there. But maybe you could warn her Fell is a little sensitive..."

Crystal snorted in amusement, nodding agreement.

I gave her another quick hug.

"I don't say it often enough or show it either. Too many years of having to hide how I feel about people, I guess. I love your cousin for lots of reasons, especially giving me you."

She looked surprised, which made me feel bad that I hadn't been showing her that I liked her for herself, not her babysitting or because she worked for me filming, or our relationship with Jace.

I hurried away to say goodbye to the kids.

Howard arrived, which let me sneak away without embarrassing myself more.

When I got home Jace was in the basement hanging our enormous television.

I handed him one of the plates and flopped on the ratty couch we'd bought at a church sale for fifty dollars to eat my own dinner.

He set his plate on a console table that I'd planned to redo someday that held the kids game system.

The room was completely unfinished still. We'd bought the used couch, which was huge with two lounges, one on each end, and had gotten some free hand me downs from his family: three chairs, four little tables, a big coffee table, and a bunch of old blankets. There were a few cardboard boxes of toys and the first cat tree the kids had made. Their latter attempts had been much better, so it had gotten relegated to the junk heap as we called this room, seeing as how everything in it, except for the tv and console was destined for the dump.

"What's the occasion?"

"Dan's coming for a visit. He's going to stay a few weeks. So I thought we could watch some games or movies."

"Did you call him and ask him to come?"

"No. Well, yes, but not because of this. It was just a friendly invitation. He's got some leave he has to use it or lose it, so he's coming home and took me up on the offer. He can have the bedroom upstairs. The kids won't mind sleeping down here."

I nodded agreement. They crashed down here more than they did in the bedroom.

He sat beside me to eat while flipping through the channels, putting on a Jimmy Stewart movie.

I browsed on my phone to see what sort of solar powered cameras and lights I could get.

When he was done eating, he grabbed a handful of blankets, removing his sweatpants to lay beside me naked.

"I should go shower," I said.

"Later."

I giggled when he plucked my phone from me and tossed it to the couch.

Loud banging on the door woke me.

"I'll get it," he said as he reached for his discarded sweats.

I hunted for my clothing, which had gotten lost in the blanket pile.

He was upstairs, talking to Brian in our kitchen when I finally found them.

The kitchen was still unfinished and dirtier than normal from the kids running inside to grab snacks.

Jace was making coffee so whatever had brought Brian here so early couldn't be too urgent, I thought in relief as I took down three coffee mugs from the plywood shelf above the coffee pot.

Jace said, "Someone graffitied the fence. I'll go paint over it before the kids come, but maybe see if your Mom can keep them home today?"

"They've been excited about seeing the pool poured... is it dangerous for them here?"

Brian shook his head.

"*Nah*... I don't think so. It's probably just some crackpot. Jace tells me you're planning to get more cameras up. That should take care of it."

I said to Jace, "I'll call my mom and tell her I'll call when the concrete guy gets here. If she thinks it's okay, she can bring them by to see it. They'll probably lose interest quick anyway."

Jace said, "I'll call and warn Crystal."

"They're going to your grandmas today to steal stuff for their projects." I laughed as I added, "It worries me how much they like her place."

Brian laughed too. "Martha Blake is one of a kind, that's for sure. I'll let you guys know if I hear anything."

"Thanks, Brian."

I went to shower.

Jace was outside laying pipe when I was dressed.

I made us both egg sandwiches and thermoses of fresh coffee before joining him.

We sat on the front steps to eat.

He said, "I'm going to take next week off. Dan and I can get the cinderblocks in for the wall and the posts for the cameras and lights."

"We can't ask your friend to do heavy labor on his vacation. Besides, I can hire that done."

"I think Pauly's cousin does stuff like that. I'll call him later. I can finish these pipes this morning. You go order the blocks and wire and whatever else we need to get the wall up."

He kissed the top of my head and went to finish setting the pipes for the irrigation system.

I went to grab my laptop and notebook.

The first thing I did was check my current balance, which was a healthy one because the channel was so popular. I knew that income wasn't one we could count on, but it was enough to pay for the help and materials to get the wall up and I might be able to recoup that expense by suing Olivia—*it was her fault we needed the wall and security, after all.*

By the time the cement truck arrived I'd arranged for the cement blocks to be delivered on Wednesday with cement, a mixer, and the hand tools I'd need. I bought extra trowels and gloves because the twins would be out of school so would be around to help.

I'd ordered the lights and cameras for the wall because I had them picked out already but the ones for the woods would have to wait another day or so because I needed to research it.

I placed a pickup order for another wheelbarrow, the posted signs and the posts and wood to make my own signs.

The guy at the masonry store assured me the thin bricks for the facing would be in by Friday at the latest. The plan was to use panels that just needed to be glued up then grouted for the walls. I'd set the thin brick myself for the columns. I'd been planning to make a cement topper and two big planters to match for outside the gate, so I knew just what I needed for that already, so I ordered all of that too.

I ordered the gravel for the front drive but told him it'd be at least a month maybe two before I could have it delivered.

I went to grab the camera to film them pouring the foundation for the conservatory.

The man driving the cement truck waved when I appeared. His four helpers didn't stop working. I filmed for an hour then left the camera with Jace to go make us lunch.

I brought out a stack of sandwiches and a cooler of soda.

The cement truck driver said, "We'll be done with this load in ten more minutes or so. The crew with the gunite for the pool should be arriving any minute. We'll be back with the cement for the wall footings in an hour or so."

I called my mom to tell her the cement was on the way, then went to make sure the graffiti had been painted over.

Jace followed me.

You couldn't read it. I hadn't asked what it said because I knew.

He said, "I'll get this bit of wall down after work this week. Don't let it worry you, Kate."

"It worries me on a lot of levels. Olivia could be instigating this— maybe to say someone else had put her up to what she did or forced her or something or maybe just to make us miserable. But she has a lot of money—she could decide to hire someone to finish the job for her."

"It's more likely Margo."

"That doesn't make me feel much better. She and Everly were two peas in a pod. Everly would've murdered Hannah and Harley and probably me too."

"But Margo won't have money as a motivation like Everly did. She's just being a petty spiteful jerk."

"My grandmother could leave her money like she promised Everly."

"The courts wouldn't let her, would they?"

I shrugged, saying, "What if this is Lloyd?"

"It isn't. We aren't close but we *are* family. He has absolutely no reason to do this."

"Except we got him arrested."

"He got himself arrested. We didn't ask him to set that guy up. Besides, he's out already."

"Crystal..."

"She claims he wasn't mad. I'm not saying that's true, but *she* believes it and she knows him better than I do."

Neither of us mentioned the random strangers who left us hate comments and nasty emails. None of them used the phrase die bitch with a smiley face though. The police had managed to keep that information quiet so far—or maybe not. Maybe it had finally made the papers and this graffiti was the result.

"Don't worry about this, Kate. Let's go get the sprinklers working."

I followed him back into the yard.

Those words, *die bitch*, even though I couldn't read them, had stolen the joy from this day, which was infuriating because I *knew* that was

Margo and Olivia's intent. I thought they were likely working together. I wondered what Margo had done to piss Lloyd off because Crystal had told me he'd been smug when she'd told him she was going to tell the police the truth.

He was playing his own game.

I wished they'd all just leave us the hell alone.

I couldn't wait for that wall to be done.

FORTY-TWO

ONE MONTH LATER

The new front wall shaded the garden more than I anticipated.

I'd have to rearrange some of the plantings, I thought in annoyance and headed for the porch steps and my notebook to make notes on what needed to be done.

"Problems?" Jace called, which made me start in surprise.

I hadn't heard him coming from the backyard.

I pasted a smile on my face, shaking my head.

His smile changed to a frown.

"It's nothing I can't handle. I just need to replant some of the gardens since the wall shades them so much."

His frown faded into a pleased grin.

"Good. The planting shows do really well. I was meaning to talk to you about it anyway. We should put in the plantings by the pool while there's so much interest. We even have some sponsors interested. I think we can get the plants we need free or at least at cost."

"That would be awesome."

Take that you bitch, I thought in satisfaction like I did every time we profited from her evilness.

I never said it though, except to Jace.

I'd almost stopped feeling guilty about it because it was the only revenge I had.

I'd just stood to hug him when the house phone rang.

We both stopped to stare at the house.

"Gimme your phone," he said gruffly.

I shook my head, pulling my phone out right as it rang—the house phone transferring to my cell.

"Hello?"

"Die bitch," a woman said breathily.

I hung up.

"Another one?" Jace asked grimly.

"Let's go pick out the plants we want."

His expression grew angry before he heaved an exasperated sigh.

"We should call it in, Kate."

"Why bother when we know they won't do anything?"

"Still..."

"Be my guest."

We'd called the first few times and the police had taken the reports but nothing came of it.

He grimaced and walked away, making a quick call before returning.

I didn't ask if he'd called the station or his stepfather, neither could do anything, except tell me to change the number again.

"Let's go order our plants," he said gruffly.

It pissed me off that Olivia was still sucking the joy from our life. I knew that was her intent, so tried to forget her and just enjoy browsing the plants, which wasn't fooling Jace at all.

He finally slid his laptop aside, saying, "I'm going out to pick up the grocery order. I'll bring back dinner and we can eat by the pool and talk over the design again there."

"Sounds good."

"We'll get through this, Kate. Don't let her ruin it."

I forced a smile.

He kissed me and left, reaching for his cell.

This time I was certain he'd be calling his stepfather. I hoped he'd have advice or comfort to offer because I had none.

I puttered around cleaning up our makeshift kitchen and had just made myself tea when the phone rang again.

I debated, my hand hovering over the phone but left it unanswered. No businesses would be calling this late, and we weren't taking bookings. It had to be her again and I didn't want to give her the satisfaction.

I headed into the future library intending to draw out new plantings for the front when my cell beeped, notifying me that an alarm on the back path had tripped.

I opened the app to see what had set it off, expecting to see a deer or something when the fire alarm on the carriage house began to ring.

I reached for my cell, jumping to my feet to run for the door, pausing by the back door to grab one of the fire extinguishers, trying to balance it while scrolling through the cameras in the alarm app.

Wisps of smoke by the carriage house made my pulse accelerate.

The grass at the head of the path had barely begun to burn. The grass was too green and short to catch despite whatever accelerant had been sprayed. I was sure there was an accelerant by the way the fire was burning in a twisting line headed to the side of the garage.

I got it out before it could do more than singe the siding.

My pulse thudded madly. I was terrified that whoever it was was still here, that the fire had been set to lure me out.

I didn't know if I should run for the house, the street or to hide in the garage.

I burst into angry tears that she was managing to make me so scared in my own home as I ran for the apartment steps, fumbling for my phone while slinging the strap of the fire extinguisher over my shoulder.

The woman who answered said, "Nine, one, one. What's your emergency."

"Someone just set fire to my backyard, and I'm scared they're still here."

By the time she got my name and address, my tears had stopped.

I was coldly furious.

Officer Sandy arrived minutes behind the fire trucks.

I was annoyed that the trucks had come since I'd told the operator that I'd put the fire out.

My annoyance vanished as three firefighters took samples with reassuring competence under Dee's watchful gaze.

She and the three men walked around the entire place, inside and out before she rejoined me.

"I need you to come in and make a formal statement."

My head began to pound.

"I should call Jace."

It suddenly occurred to me that I should've called my parents.

Panic made my hands shake as I grabbed for my phone to call my father.

"Dad, someone set another fire here."

He heaved an annoyed sigh. "I'll call home and make sure they're okay."

"Sorry to bother you."

He sighed again, sounding exasperated this time.

"It's no bother, Kate. I'm just worried. Are you okay?"

"Yes and there was hardly any damage. I'll feel better when I know the kids are okay though."

"Me too. I'll call you right back."

"The police want me to come in and give a statement."

"I'll call your brother."

He hung up before I could say it wasn't necessary, which was probably good because it was necessary.

"I'll meet you there," I said to Dee.

She nodded tightly and escorted me to my car.

I called Dwayne as I left my yard.

"There was another fire at the house and the police want me to make a statement. I'm on my way there now."

"I'll be there as soon as I can. Wait for me."

I snorted.

"It's going to be fine, Kate. Just wait. Don't let them pressure you."

"See you in a few."

"Hang in there," he said and disconnected.

I called Jace.

"Hey sweetheart," he said as a greeting.

"We got another call that I didn't answer, and they set fire to the yard."

"Jesus Christ! Are you okay?"

"I'm fine. Pissed, but fine. There's hardly any damage. I got it out quick. I'm headed to the police station now to make a statement."

"Jesus Christ," he said softly and worriedly.

"I already called Dwayne and my Dad. Dwayne is meeting me. Just finish whatever you were doing. I got this."

He snorted angrily.

"We're adding more alarms."

"I'm not going to argue."

"I love you, Kate. This makes me so goddamned mad!"

"I love you too. I've got to go though. My dad will be calling back."

"Call me and let me know."

"I'm sure they're fine."

The road blurred from my tears.

"Please don't worry, sweetheart."

He disconnected.

I wiped my face on my sleeve, angry all over again that she was still hurting us.

Frank was waiting when I arrived. He escorted me to an interview room and brought me a cup of tea, sitting beside me while I drank it.

"Jace called. I've spoken to his mom and Crystal, and we have cars at all five houses."

I knew he meant my parents' house and the store.

Dee said with strained patience, "We need to get her statement, Frank."

"My lawyer told me to wait for him."

Her eyes hardened.

Frank clasped my hand quickly, saying briskly, "That's smart with all this shit going on. Let's do everything by the book."

I knew the words were intended for Dee, not me, and smiled gratefully.

He patted my hand.

My father finally called me back and I couldn't stop my tears of relief when he said everyone was safe and sound."

"Let me speak to Jace," he said worriedly.

Frank handed me a box of tissues and I blew my nose before saying, "He isn't here. I'm at the station."

"I'm on my way."

"I'm fine."

"I'm coming."

He disconnected before I could argue.

I wasn't sure if I wanted him to come or not.

"Where is Jace?" Dee asked.

"Grocery shopping."

Frank tightened his grip on my hand a moment before releasing me to stand.

He headed to the door saying, "Let me warm up your tea. Take a minute, Kate, to catch your breath. There's a bathroom right down the hall here."

I took the hint.

Dee escorted me to the bathroom where I used the facilities and then splashed cold water on my face for a few minutes.

Frank was waiting with fresh tea when I exited the bathroom.

Reynolds had joined Dee. They were conferring quietly down the hall.

She joined me as I sat back down at the metal table.

"Can we look at your surveillance tapes, Kate?"

"Sure."

I turned on the app and slid her my phone.

"We'll want copies of these. Can I take your phone and make them?"

Frank shook his head at me.

"Wait for your lawyer, Kate."

Dee frowned at him then forced a smile at me.

He shook his head at me a tiny bit.

I was really worried now that I'd screwed up by showing her my phone although I couldn't see how it would be bad for me, but Frank's demeanor made me think it was.

I grew more anxious as Dee scrolled slowly, making notes while Reynolds peered over her shoulder.

By the time Dwayne arrived I was close to tears again from stress.

My father arrived as I was telling Dee about the second phone call for the second time. I only knew that he had because an irate officer stuck his head into the room to say, "Mr. Avery is here demanding he be allowed to speak to his daughter."

"Send him in," Dee said tiredly.

Dwayne stood and offered his hand to my father, saying, "Mr. Avery." They shook briskly and both sat.

Dee said, "Why did you grab the extinguisher, Kate?"

"To put out a fire."

She snorted, rolling her eyes at me as she said, "How did you know there would be one?"

"Because the fire alarm went off. We had another fire last week too. It just seemed smart to go prepared."

Her eyebrows rose.

"You didn't report it."

"It seemed like more trouble than it was worth. It was just the grass by the road. Besides, no one ever does anything."

Her eyes narrowed.

Reynolds said, "You mean about the phone calls? There isn't a lot we can do about hang up calls or even prank calls. You really should change your number."

"What's the point when it's a business number and anyone can find it?"

He shrugged, shaking his head at Dee as if to say you convince her.

Dee said, "Tell me about the other fire."

"I got a phone call just like these. The first one said die bitch. The second I didn't answer and about thirty minutes later the alarm at the front of the house tripped. Someone had thrown a glass bottle that landed in the rocks right by the porch. I put it out."

"Why didn't you call?"

"What would be the point? I could see from my security tapes that the bottle was thrown from the road. It could've been anyone. I know it's Margo... I was hoping she'd get over it and leave us alone."

Frank said, "Did Jace know?"

"I didn't want to worry him."

Reynolds and Dee exchanged quick glances.

"He wasn't home?" she asked too casually.

I could see where this was going and was furious.

"No. The second time it happened we'd just left to go to my parents for dinner. My house phone sends the calls to my cell but I didn't answer because it was after business hours. I was worried though, so I told him I'd forgotten something, I don't remember what now, but we went back to the house and we got there right as our alarm went off. This time it was the carriage house alarm. Two people ran out as we pulled in."

Reynolds said, "You called that one in. I remember it. There wasn't a fire though."

I shrugged. "We'd only just left. I think they meant to start one."

"You think... Do you have anything concrete to base it on?"

"Margo's a bitch who likes fire."

She sighed in annoyance.

Reynolds said, "Where there any other incidents?"

"We get a call every few days, which you know. I was answering them because I thought if I didn't there might be another fire and I was right! She's casing my damned house!"

Dee said, "There's absolute no proof of that."

"You have to be fucking kidding me!"

Dwayne took my hand, squeezing it as he said, "She's right, Kate. There's no proof it's Margo. There's no proof that the calls are connected but it seems likely."

My father said angrily, "What are you going to do about this! This is more than prank calls! She could be in danger from this lunatic!"

"I agree," Dee said. "Unfortunately, there isn't much that we can do. We traced all of the calls that she reported. None of them gave us any information we can use since all of the calls were made from a pay-as-you-go phones."

"Then fucking search that bitch!"

"You're not helping, sir," Dwayne said softly.

My father pinched the bridge of his nose, speaking in a voice of forced calm as he said, "You must be able to pull her in for questioning. You bring us in often enough."

Dee winced.

Reynolds said, "Without evidence, we can't accuse her. She *has* been questioned about this and has an alibi for all of the calls." He turned to me to say, "Was anyone with you when you got these calls?"

"You think I'm lying about it?" Why would I?"

Dee shook her head, giving him an irate glance, saying to me, "We know you're not lying about getting calls. There's corroborating records on your phone. We know which towers pinged to send the message, the length of the calls, the times, and whatnot."

Frank said bitterly, "You think Jace is doing it? That's ridiculous!"

I said, "He can't be doing it because he's usually with me. They only call me twice in the same day after he leaves."

"Now we're getting somewhere," Dee said.

She shot a Frank a glance that said shut up as she continued, "How soon after he leaves do the calls come in?"

"It isn't him!"

Dwayne said, "They know that, Kate. They're trying to determine where the person is watching the house from."

"Dear lord," my father said breathlessly.

Butterflies danced in my stomach at the reminder that someone was watching us. Someone who was setting my house on fire was watching to see when I was alone. Before that thought could really grab hold and make me panic, Dee said to him, "It's probable they're calling to see if anyone is home. It's unlikely they mean to hurt anyone if they're calling first."

"Not necessarily," Dwayne said. "They're probably calling to see if the coast is clear. We can't count on them caring if anyone is hurt or not. Especially when you consider they've spread poison that did kill."

"A cat," Reynolds said as if it were of no consequence.

Dee said, "This is a serious situation. There's no arguing that. Kate, you need to call us and report all of these calls."

"Then I'll be calling every day..."

She winced again.

I wasn't sure if she was annoyed or worried.

"Excuse us a minute," Reynolds said.

He and Dee left the room.

"This isn't Jace!" I said angrily as soon as the door shut.

"Of course not. They're just being thorough," Dwayne said. "This room is being recorded, Kate, so keep your cool."

"So fucking what! I can see how they're twisting this! We didn't do anything wrong! I can't be expected to call about every hang up call I receive!"

"I want you to make a log of them. All of them."

My father said, "You should've told us, Kate."

That pissed me off even more because I had told him. I'd told everyone because I was worried that Margo was still at large and being such a bitch.

We glared at each other until Dee and Reynolds returned a few minutes later.

A tech in a white coat followed them in.

"We'd like to take some swabs from your hands."

Dwayne's lips tightened.

"Fine, but keep in mind that she was fighting that fire."

Dee nodded at him, gesturing the lab tech forward.

I let him take his swabs.

"We'd like your clothing."

"Again, she was fighting that fire," Dwayne said.

He escorted me to the bathroom with the tech where I traded my clothes for an orange coverall.

My stomach was flipping and squirming. I didn't think they could arrest me but here I was wearing an orange coverall. My breath began to come faster as we returned to the small room. I was practically a prisoner right now.

Dee said, "Change your number and leave it unlisted for a month. Let's see if that stops all this. Add a few more cameras. Make sure all the driveways are covered and that back path. Call me if you get a call making threats but just make a note of the hang up calls. I'll be checking in at least once a week."

"That's it?" my father asked angrily.

"I'd like permission to copy your phone so we can go over the security footage in more depth. If we can link anyone at all, we can take more swabs and maybe get lucky with a chemical match. Speaking of which, we want to send a tech to your house to see if any of the thinners or things there are a match."

Dwayne said, "I assume you want Jace to come in and get swabbed?"

She nodded, shooting me an apologetic glance.

"It's my job, Kate, to be check all of the facts."

I huffed angrily too terrified to get words past the lump in my throat. I was afraid to yell at her like I wanted to. I thought Dee really did like me but maybe I was wrong. I could see how making her an enemy would be a mistake. Yelling wouldn't help even if I could manage it. I hoped she wasn't taking my silence and tears as guilt.

Dwayne stood, pulling me up with him.

"Call me if you have more questions for my client. You can have her phone for a reasonable amount of time."

"I'll drop it off when we're done with it," Dee said.

"I can't fucking believe this!" my father said angrily. "You're treating us as the suspects, which is just ridiculous! She needs help, not platitudes and empty promises!"

"We really are doing everything that we can."

"Thank you for your time," Dwayne said firmly. "I'll call Jace and have him come right here."

Reynolds said, "I'll escort Kate home and check the house again before I go."

My father stomped from the room.

Dee took my hand, "Trust the system, Kate. We'll get to the bottom of this. Meanwhile, use your common sense. "

I must've grimaced or looked more worried because her worried expression deepened.

"Honestly, Kate, I'm not sure what to advise. I think it's just Margo being a bitch too, but she's playing with some heavy hitters. It probably isn't smart to run to put a fire out when that fire could've been set to draw you out. On the other hand, not running to put it out could lead to serious property damage or get you hurt from the fire. You need better security cameras so you can see if anyone is around and hopefully ones that warn you before they can reach your house to set a fire."

"I'll see to it," Dwayne said.

He pulled my hand from her grasp, putting his arm around me to lead me out.

My legs were trembling enough to make me unsteady.

We said nothing until we reached my car where I burst into tears as soon as I sat.

He let me cry while he called Jace and arranged for him to come in.

When he was done with his calls, he crouched to hug me.

Grayson arrived fifteen minutes later or so and he looked worried and pissed.

They exchanged a quick hug as they traded places.

"Let me take you home, Kate," Grayson said worriedly.

"I'm waiting for Jace."

His worried look intensified.

"He didn't do anything!" I yelled.

"I know. I'm just worried that she made it look as if he had. We know that bitch likes to plant evidence."

"You're not helping," Dwayne murmured.

"This is my family!"

Dwayne hugged him again, whispering something too low to hear.

Grayson wiped his eyes when he stepped away.

"I'm sorry, Kate. Dwayne is right. I'm not helping. It's probably just Margo being a bitch. Get some hidden cameras up and we'll catch her in the act."

I nodded, trying to project that I believed him.

"Dwayne, can you stay with her? I need to go make sure my dad is upping the security at the house too."

"Of course. Do what you have to. We can catch up later."

They hugged again.

Grayson said, "I'm coming over later, Kate, and staying the night."

"You're both welcome to stay," I said.

Grayson flushed.

Dwayne squeezed his shoulder quickly.

"I need a rain check. I have court in the morning."

Grayson nodded and hurried away.

I wasn't sure if I should apologize, make an excuse to pretend I hadn't meant to imply anything, or ignore it.

Before I could decide, Dwayne said, "He isn't out yet."

I flushed to my toes.

"I'm sorry."

"Don't be. This has him so…. I don't know, afraid of disappointing everyone. He's really worrying me."

"It doesn't matter to me, except I'm glad that he has you."

Dwayne smiled crookedly. "I'm not sure telling him that would help… just leave it alone for now, Kate."

"I will. I love him so much. We all do. It wouldn't matter to the kids or Ken."

"She knows. She pretends she doesn't, but we know she does. He was thinking of coming out when all this happened and now he's worried that it will make people think he was abusing the kids."

"That's stupid!"

"Is it? You see how the police go for the easy route. What's easier to believe, that a gay man abuses the kids he has access to or that an elderly grandmother does?"

"They weren't abused.... were they? They never said a thing! I never saw a sign of it!"

"No, they weren't, but some kids were, and it's all connected. And does it matter if he's never charged with it if it's a rumor that he can never get out from under? He's just *destroyed* by this. He loved that crazy old bitch! He loves you guys and is terrified that his love will hurt them because they'd be exposed to those same damned rumors."

"I'm so sorry. This must be hell for you too."

"It is. I'd never abandon him though. I love him, Kate. If we need to sneak around for the next ten years, so be it."

"Ten years..."

"It takes a long time for the rumors to die but eventually people stop giving a shit. Don't worry about us. We're fine."

"I wouldn't be."

He huffed. "I'll admit, I'd prefer if we didn't need to hide it, but it isn't so bad really. Our apartments are right next door to each other..."

"Still..."

"Don't worry about us. I can take care of us. I'll take care of him too. And you and Jace. It won't matter if he has traces on him. Not that I think he will. I don't think Margo is smart enough to plan that far ahead. Just get the security under control. I'll handle all of this."

I nodded and we waited unspeaking until Jace arrived.

"Don't touch her," Dwayne said as Jace exited his truck.

"Let's not take a chance you contaminate him."

He looked confused.

"They think I'm lying, that we're setting the fires."

"Fires?"

"Talk later, guys. Let's get this over with."

He led Jace away.

Imagining how angry and scared he was going to be made me cry again.

I was still sniffling an hour later when he exited wearing an orange suit like mine.

We hugged for a long time.

"Next time tell me," he finally said.

"I will."

"Let's go home. I'll have Howard drop me tomorrow to get your car."

I got into his truck.

"We'll update everything."

I nodded.

"I love you," he said as he brought our clasped hands to his lips.

I wanted to apologize but knew it would worry him.

I said nothing.

What was there to say when we both knew my grandmother was ruthless and would do anything to hurt us.

FORTY-THREE

LATE JULY

"Dan!" I said in surprise when I opened the door and found him standing there. "Come on in. What brings you here? Not that you're not welcome anytime, I'm just surprised to see you. I thought you were in Iraq."

"I was. But they gave me a medical discharge and sent me home, the fuckers."

"Medical! What happened?"

"I got shot in the leg. I hardly even limp and they tossed me out!"

"Come in and sit down."

"Where's Jace?"

"Work. He'll be back at five."

"I see you got the wall done."

"It's not done. I figure by the end of September. The pools done though if you want to see it. Drop your stuff. You can sleep in the parlor if the stairs are too much."

"About that. I have a favor to ask."

"The answer is yes."

He smiled crookedly. "Wait till you hear it."

"Jace would be in prison if you hadn't helped him. The answer is yes, no matter what it is."

"I was glad to help, and it was nothing. It pisses me right the fuck off she never got arrested for that."

"I'm just glad they let him go."

"Have you guys finished the apartment over the carriage house?"

"No. Between the wall, the pool, and garden, we haven't had a second. That's a winter project."

"Perfect. I was thinking I could stay there and instead of rent, I'd put the sheetrock up and paint it and stuff while this leg heals up and I find something to do with the rest of my life. Jace told me a while ago I could help out in the garage if he gets some repairs. I have a buddy who wants his sixty-nine Camaro restored. He's got some parts but no idea what to do. If Jace is interested, we can do that as partners here in his garage. I've got my own tools and stuff."

"It's fine with me, except you should stay here in the house while you make that livable." I headed for the kitchen when I had a thought.

I said casually, "Did Jace put you up to this?"

"Up to what?"

"Staying here?"

"What do you mean?"

"Nothing."

"What's going on, Kate?"

I began taking sandwich stuff from the fridge.

"He didn't tell you about our vandal?"

"He said you had some graffiti a while back."

"They stay away from the new wall because it has cameras and lights but now they come in from the woods and set fires and twice now they came into the backyard at night."

"They set fires!"

"To the woods. They can't reach the house anymore before alarms go off. Or I should say they don't have time to do anything. I think they were trying to see how far into the yard they can get before the alarms go on because they always trigger a different camera. We never leave the house unattended because we get hang up calls on the house line pretty much daily. If we don't answer, the alarms trip in the back or by the garage ten minutes later."

"Jesus, Kate...."

"I think it's just Margo being a bitch... if you changed your mind about staying though, I'd understand."

"Hell, no! He should've said something. We'd have taken turns watching the place."

"It's our problem. We're handling it. We've got a trial date now, so that's something anyway. Get a swimsuit on and meet me outside by the pool. I'll make us a snack and drinks. I could use a break."

"What are you working on?"

"Gardening. I have fifty rose bushes, another fifty boxwoods, twenty-five lilacs, and some holly coming tomorrow. I just finished putting the trellis up along the wall outside on the front. Did you see them?"

"Yeah. They looked good."

"We decided to add some climbing roses. The thorny old-fashioned kind to keep people away from the walls. I embedded barbed wire into the toppers of the fence along the side in the back behind the pool, which will hopefully deter anyone from trying to climb over. Roses are friendlier though. Plus they'll look nice along the sidewalk.

"The front gardens look great. Are they done?"

"I don't think they'll ever be done, but all the perennial stuff is in. It's always going to need maintenance, trimming and replanting the annuals. Plus, we keep thinking of things we want to try."

"You sure it's okay if I stay?"

"Of course. Fair warning though, there's kids around a lot."

He laughed as he headed back into the hall.

I finished making a stack of sandwiches and put four beers into the cooler along with the leftover fruit cup I'd made the day before and the potato salad. I grabbed a bag of chips and headed out to the pool.

A wrought iron fence surrounded the pool patio. Jace planned to add decorative elements to it someday, maybe remake it completely.

It was a large space.

A small pool house was built against the back wall. It had a changing room with a bunch of lockable cubbies that I'd made, and a small bathroom. Against the back wall, four pillars held up a copper roof that covered the outdoor kitchen and bar area. Right beside that there was a three-sided room that had two shower heads and two benches with blue curtains if you wanted privacy to change.

Four metal tables with four chairs each were between the bar and the pool. The pool stairs ran half the width of the pool with a Baja shelf with two lounge chairs on one side. We'd left empty space for the baby to play when she visited with Crystal. A net could be stretched across the ledge to keep the baby from falling down the stairs into the deeper water, but we almost never used it.

A built-in spa with a wide rim meant for seating trickled water into the pool. It could be heated and the water recirculated into the spa when the weather grew cold enough to want warm water or trickle into the pool to heat that.

Behind the spa to the right, a fire pit with cushioned seating was shaded by a trellis on one side and one of the original dogwoods on the other. I'd planted privet along the yard side of the fence and boxwood on the house side.

There were four lounge chairs on each side of the pool with a small table between them, a few planters of flowers here and there, and a few umbrellas on wheeled stands that I'd made myself. I'd made the cushions too. They were all navy blue or white or a combination of both.

On the right of the pool, behind the lounge chairs, we'd put in a step to make a raised area for the pergolas to overlook the pool. Cypress trees lined the inside of the fence behind them.

I'd built two small pergolas in the same style as the one over the bar. Each had white curtains and netting that could be closed to keep out the bugs. I'd also built the double wide lounges that were under the pergolas. Each had a small towel rack and small side tables to hold drinks and snacks.

Jace and I spent quite a few nights out here.

Thinking about it made me flush. I'd have to add an alarm to the pool gate with an automatic light if Dan was going to be staying so he didn't come upon us unawares.

I rolled one of the umbrellas to the lounge chairs closest to the pool stairs and set the food out then went to grab myself a soda from the refrigerator at the bar, then texted Jace to tell him Dan was staying.

He called me right back.

"How long can he stay? Maybe I can get out early."

"He's here indefinitely. He was shot in the leg, and they discharged him. I think he's pissed. He wants to stay in the apartment. He said he'd finish it in lieu of rent. I told him to stay in the house until it's done."

"How bad?"

"He's walking, so it can't be too bad..."

"He never called..."

"You never called him either. He had no idea about our vandal. Make sure you make it clear we won't be offended if our drama is too much for him."

He snorted.

I said, "Stop at the store for burgers and some sides and something for dessert and you're almost out of beer."

"Love you," he said and disconnected.

I checked my email until Dan joined me.

"Man—this is gorgeous!"

"It will be once the plants grow a bit. We're shopping for fountains for the entranceway. I think I'll end up making them. I made the small one in the front yard. But I wanted big ones for here. I'm not sure I can make them the size I want, although I guess we could rent a forklift or something to lift the pieces."

I handed him a beer from the cooler.

"We don't keep beer in the outdoor fridge because of the kids. Not that I think they'd take it but Child Protective Services pops in unannounced once in a while and my lawyer says I can't have alcohol out here unless there's a drinking age adult present."

"I forget you're just a baby..."

"Yeah, maybe to an old geezer like you. Speaking of which, if you want to have some of your old geezer friends over, feel free. The only rules are if you mess it up, you clean it. Jace will bring home burgers and we can cook out here tonight. There's a working bathroom and shower out here. Remind me to send you the plans. It'll show you where all the switches are and stuff. The jacuzzi has a built-in timer. It takes it about ten minutes or so to drain and refill with hot water. It'll turn itself off, so don't think it broke or something if you're using it and it turns off. Just hit the switch again. Jace uses it a lot for his leg."

"I thought his leg was better?"

"It's good but it still hurts him; mostly when he's on his feet all day. It aches. You can tell because he starts limping. You seem to be getting around okay..."

"I am. I had the knee replaced and have metal screws and a plate. It hurts a bit, but I can run and shit. It's just bullshit they kicked me out!"

"How'd it happen?"

"That's bullshit too and probably why I got the heave ho. My CO was drunk as shit and shooting up spiders in his tent. I was two tents over and caught a ricochet in the leg. It smashed my kneecap. I thought I was going to lose the leg it hurt so fucking bad. But I woke up from surgery and they'd fixed me right up. I was up and walking in a few days. They let me think I'd be back with my squad, then when I was off the crutches, they sent me home."

"It's not all bad—it's not Iraq."

He snorted with laughter.

My phone rang with the house phone ringtone.

"Let's see," I said.

It rang eight times before they gave up.

I started my stopwatch app.

He said, "Maybe you should change the number?"

"The only reason I have a house number is for the business. It's going to be a public number so there's no point in changing it. I could cancel it altogether, but I don't like giving the delivery people my real number."

"*Ahh*... Should we hide and try to catch whoever it is?"

"And do what with them?"

"I don't know—hold them for the police?"

"I doubt they're going to let themselves be held. Margo had a gun—it just doesn't seem worth it."

"She has a gun... do you?"

"No."

"You're sitting out here defenseless?"

"As opposed to cowering in my house when I get a phone call?"

"Kate..."

"I'm not letting her drive me out of my house!"

"If she's armed when she breaks in here and you're not..."

"If I go around shooting intruders, it'll be me going to prison."

"You have a right to protect yourself."

"Do I? You wouldn't believe the questioning I've gone through. If the alarm trips, I'll just go the opposite way and call the cops to handle it. My app will tell me which alarm it was. I could lock myself in the bathroom here and wait for help."

I held out my phone to show him the app, which was currently displaying the view from the camera at the head of the path leading into the woods.

He said, "How is Jace not crazy? That's the stupidest thing I've ever heard! You should have some way to protect yourself, Kate. A taser or at least mace."

"That would look great for DCS. Imagine if Hannah or Harley tased themselves while hugging me or something?"

"You're killing me."

"Nope. I'm a pacifist."

He snorted with annoyed laughter.

"How about a compromise? We could put a locked box out here and one in the kitchen or something."

"We have mace in the bedroom—and the nail gun."

"You should have a real gun."

"I wasn't kidding about that. If I'd had a real gun and had shot Olivia, I'd be in prison. I know it. She almost has me there now and there's video of her killing Claire."

"No way. You must be mistaken."

"No one wants to believe a grandmother could do what she did. It's much easier to believe I tried to kill her for her money."

"They didn't charge you though..."

"I don't think they will. I'm just saying it's going to be a hard sell to a jury. Maybe an impossible one if I'd shot her with an actual gun."

"No offense or anything but it probably would've made all of your lives easier if you'd had a gun and killed her."

"Not mine. My dad wouldn't have forgiven me—sometimes I think he doesn't forgive me now even though I had nothing to do with any of it."

My watch beeped.

I clicked the camera that had sent the notification and then the mic.

The trees shaded the path too much for me to see who was there. I didn't know if they could hear me or not. I flicked off the alarm, saying, "Hi. I thought you'd drop by."

"Die bitch!"

"That old line? Look, can't we just be adults about this?"

Dan ran from the pool—with an awkward gait that told me it was hurting him to do it, which was infuriating.

I said, "Why waste all of our time like this? You break in, we add more cameras. The police get more annoyed. Eventually you'll be caught and what's the point?"

"Your death."

I couldn't tell if it was a man or a woman. I wished I could turn the camera.

"Why kill me though? What would be the point? When you were caught, you'd spend years in prison. It hardly seems worth it to me."

"You can't hide in there forever."

"I'm not hiding."

"Soon."

Tree branches crackled and snapped. I hit the icon for the lake trail camera.

Was that Margo?

I wasn't sure. The person running away down the path was wearing jeans and a navy-blue hoody. They had to be sweltering. They were too hunched for me to be certain of the height.

I called Jace.

It went right to voice mail.

The house phone rang with an unknown caller.

I debated a second then picked it up.

A breathy voice said, "We're coming, Kate. You testify and you're dead. But maybe you have memory problems from that hole in your head or maybe you need another hole."

They hung up.

I called Kendra.

"I just got a call warning me if I testify that I'd be killed. Did you get any?"

"One."

"Why the hell didn't you tell me!"

"It happened yesterday."

"Did you report it to the police?"

"Of course. Are you alone at the house?"

"Sort of. Jace's friend Dan was here but he chased after the person who set off the alarm."

"Jesus, Kate! They were at the house! Call the damned police!"

"Jace will have. And why yell at me? I didn't do anything!"

"Sorry. I'm just freaked."

On my phone, Dan ran past the first camera.

I hit the mic button to say, "They're long gone down the lake trail. You might as well come back and it's not smart to chase someone who could be armed."

"Who are you talking to?"

"Dan. On the camera.

"Which way is the lake?" Dan asked.

He sounded farther than the voice had.

I said, "I'll take you for a walk later and point out the cameras and stuff. Don't go near it now though. I think she was close to it."

"Was it her?"

"I have no idea. Just come back."

My house phone rang again.

I said to Kendra, "They're calling me again. Should I answer?"

"No. Decline the call."

The camera showed Dan heading back up the trail.

I said to Kendra. "I'm going to try to call Jace again."

"First write down exactly what they said so you don't forget it. If you can't reach him, call the police yourself."

I opened the notes app and made a quick note then called Jace.

He said angrily, "I'm almost home. The police are on the way. I was watching the camera and heard you guys."

"She's long gone. But I got a phone call."

I told him what they'd said.

"Did it sound like her?"

"Not really. It sounded like a man trying to sound like a woman whispering or maybe it was woman trying to sound like a man or maybe it was a voice changer thing. It was creepy. I'm glad the kids weren't here."

"They never are... which means they're watching, right?"

"Not necessarily. The kids have a pretty set schedule."

"It's good they try to avoid them. It probably means they don't want to scare them. It must be Margo!"

"Don't go looking for her. Did you see the person on the lake cam?"

"No."

"I'm going to make copies of today's recordings. Maybe we got lucky and got her coming to the house."

"Where are you?"

"The pool."

"Turn on everything except the pool."

"Dan will set off the yard cams."

"Just do it."

I tapped the alarm all icon then disarm for the pool.

It asked for my password.

I typed that in.

My screen showed a clock counting down to zero then the app said, *System Armed.*

I wished it was really armed. It would be comforting to have a gun.

I went shopping for another nail gun.

FORTY-FOUR

Brian, his partner Cassidy, and Detective Sandy showed up a few minutes after Jace.

Jace introduced Dan to the officers.

I said to Dee, "I already emailed you copies of today's recordings." I slid her my phone. "I called my sister, and she told me to write down what I remember of the phone call. She said she's gotten a call too. How come no one told me?"

"We didn't think you needed to know. She didn't want to worry you. Jace, have you gotten any calls on your cell?"

"No. Howard told me that Crystal got a hang up call yesterday. It's probably unrelated but now I'm worried."

My phone dinged, warning me someone had pulled into the driveway. It dinged again a moment later telling me someone was in the front.

Jace said, "We need to do the gate next."

Dan said, "You should get a dog."

"Lady was almost killed."

"Lady?"

"The kids' dog," Jace said.

"Better the dog than you, Kate."

Dee said, "Did you look through the recordings?"

"Not yet."

Dan said, "The brush by the tree where the camera is was trampled behind the tree. I think they were planning to smash it."

I said, "I'm putting another one in. The kind you can turn around. I'll hang it from the bottom of a branch."

Jace said, "Let's put a few game cams in on the state property."

Dee said, "How many days were you alone here this week, Kate?"

"Only today. Mom had to work, so I took the kids an extra day this week. I won't have them again until next Wednesday though because they're going away for the weekend. Crystal and Howard are taking them camping.

Dee said, "You're usually alone Thursdays?"

"Wednesday and Thursday usually. Jace has Fridays off so he's usually here working in his garage. And I have the kids on Mondays and Tuesdays. They have their science camp Wednesday and Thursday, and sometimes Tuesday's they go to the library to help with the little kids, so I pick them up when they finish, which can be anytime from twelve to three. They call me. Saturday morning is always the library unless they go away. Maria takes them and then drops all four of them here, usually with Crystal's kids, except for the baby. Sunday, I go to my parents for dinner. Jace only comes if we have someone stay here at the house. We try not to leave it unattended for too long."

"Who stays?"

"Frank and his mom mostly. Crystal sometimes with Howard. They don't mind cause they can use the pool while we're out. Crystal comes over a lot with her kids. She works from home three days a week and can work here while the kids play together."

"Does she come on set days?"

"Mostly she comes when she knows the kids will be here because she knows if they aren't here that I'll probably be doing something loud and maybe dangerous for kids like using the saws. But she helps with film projects too, so we coordinate that in the calendar. I'll post a project and she'll put it on a day she can come film."

"Where do you post it?"

Jace said, "Kate posts on our family calendar what her plan for the week is. All of our family use it, even the kids. They post where they plan to be or want to go like a friend's house."

I said, "My mom and I make sure they list all their friends' numbers and addresses there because we carpool a lot with the other moms, so we're always working out who can take them or pick them up, which changes in the calendar as things are changed around.

Dee said, "Have you gotten any other calls where the caller made any sort of threat?"

"No. They usually just hang up. I answer them because when I don't someone shows up to set the alarm off, which is annoying. But every few weeks I let one go unanswered just to see if they're still doing it."

"Do they always show up to set the alarm off if you don't answer?"

"About ninety percent of the time."

Jace said, "Honestly, we thought it was Margo because she's stupid enough to call and believe that means we're home when we answer like she's never heard of call forwarding."

He turned to me to say, "We're getting the house calls forwarded to me from now on."

"We can't. I'm the one who's here and ordering the stuff. I'm the one they need to talk to."

Dee said, "He could get a number for you to call right back."

"And disrupt his work and day? Why bother? Answering the caller unknown or blocked calls isn't any big deal."

"I don't want you dealing with them," Jace said.

"And I don't want you dealing with it. I'm not doing it, Jace."

Dan said, "Can you track these calls now that they've made actual threats?"

"Yes. We'll get the phone records and then warrants to search for the phones. The die bitch comments will get a judge to sign off for the searches on Margo and her crew. I'll need you to come into the station, Kate, and give us your written statement."

Jace said, "I'll fill Dan in on how to use the alarms and stuff and we'll have dinner waiting when you get back."

When I returned home three hours later, I found Jace making burgers for four guys I didn't know and Dan.

Dan introduced me as Jace handed me a plate.

Jace said, "We're going away for the weekend."

"I can't. My plants."

Dan said, "I can take care of them until you get back."

"I have a delivery of pavers scheduled for Saturday. I was supposed to be getting more brick too. I have to check that the color is right."

"Is it the same brick you already have?"

"Yeah."

"Then I can check it."

"The pavers need to be checked for color too."

Jace said, "He can handle it, Kate. Just leave him the sample pieces and the order sheet."

"I hate to impose like this."

"It's no imposition. I'm looking forward to it."

Jace said firmly. "I could really use a vacation. I'm going to take a few days off. We can come back next Wednesday. Five days, Kate..."

"You're sure you don't mind watching the house for five days? The cats will need food and stuff."

"Not at all. Go have fun."

I went to pack and left Dan directions on the cats, the alarms, the deliveries, and the pool, realizing as I did it that I was a serious control freak, but I did it anyway.

More people had arrived while I was packing and writing my notes.

Dan was saying to Jace, "I can get us a few more gigs. Nothing cool like the Camaro but it's money all the same."

Jace smiled an excited smile at me as he said, "Dan and I are going to try a partnership. He does most of the grunt work and we supply the garage and shit. He's going to move his tools into the third bay."

"It's fine with me but we need to contact our insurance carrier."

"I'll handle it when we get back."

I must've looked worried because Dan said, "Relax, Kate. Nothing is going to happen to me and even if it did, your homeowners would cover it."

Jace laughed as he said, "She's not going to be happy until it's done right. I think it comes from having so many lawyers in the family... don't worry, I'll talk to Grayson, and we'll write up a real contract and get real insurance and everything."

He tossed Dan his truck keys.

"You can use it until we get back. And stay in our room. I don't want the police in there."

I said, "If the police need to check the house or anything, make sure no one lets the cats out accidentally."

"Have fun, guys. And thanks for letting me stay."

Barry, one of the new guys, said, "This pool is great. Do you need another partner? I can change tires."

They all laughed.

Dan and Jace bumped fists.

Jace was excited about a vacation, which made me realize he needed more fun in his life, less work, less stress, less babysitting, more friends.

As we drove away, I said, "Maybe we should work on the theater room next?"

"*Nah*. He won't care if it's a mess. Besides, we have to get the garden done before fall. Then we'll finish the bedrooms like we planned, then the kitchen and the other rooms on the main floor."

"Maybe we should stop on the house and do your real garage next?"

"Maybe... but let's not talk about work or any of that. It's probably too late to get a great hotel on the beach but call around and see if you can get us a room with an ocean view."

I scrolled on my phone for a few minutes.

"What's the budget?"

"Five hundred a night max, and that better have an ocean view."

I found one that looked good way under budget and called to see if they had any ocean view rooms.

"Nice," Jace said as we entered our room. He went right to the balcony and stepped out. "What a view!"

"How come I never met any of your friends before?"

"Because they're Dan's friends. I know most of them and like them, but they were too far ahead of me in school. Barry is Dan's brother's best friend. He's a cop in Atlanta and doesn't get home much. It's nice he made time to come visit Dan."

"Was his brother there?"

"No Dave is in the service too. A few of those guys were service friends. I told Dan they could crash at the house, which is why I told him to use our room."

"How upset is he about the medical discharged?"

"Very... he'd intended to make it his career. He was a drone operator. There's not much call for that in civilian life. He's a good mechanic and enjoys it but I don't think he'd really want to do that full time."

"Have him film the project. Get the Camaro guy to sign a release. I'll show Dan how I do the video editing. He can take some drone footage of the car racing down the road and we'll add some affects and stuff. People love car shows and we have a huge audience. I'm sure I can get my dad to let you guys use the equipment at the shop. Trick that car out like I do the house with the plans so the viewer can do it themselves. You need to find a hook, something you do that no one else does, so maybe you make some fancy metal trim work? Or one of those hood things or even a cool looking muffler, or maybe custom door handles would be cool?"

"I love those ideas!"

"If we can sell the first few shows, you'll get some sponsors. We'll take a loan and build your shop and use this situation to our advantage for once."

"If I'm going to do it, I think I need to take a risk and really do it."

"Quit your job, you mean?"

"Yeah..."

"Go for it. I'm making enough to pay the bills. And we're ahead of schedule with the house. Not that I'm in a hurry to finish when filming the work there is paying the bills. There's plenty for me to do that won't cost us much, so we can use the extra income getting your business going. We should design the building you need and get prices for all the machines and stuff so we know our budget and can plan the best way to spend our money."

"We should plan as if we aren't getting any of the money we've spent on security back."

I nodded agreement.

"We could up our income if we finish the bedrooms and rent them like I'd planned too if I needed money."

He frowned at me.

"Maybe. That's still a last resort though. Dan will have income from his severance pay and disability to live on, so he'd probably be on board with rolling any profits back into the business."

"You guys have a lot to talk over."

"You're sure you're on board with this? It would mean I'd be working on my own project more than the house."

"Sure."

"Not that I don't think the house is an important project."

"It's fine, Jace. I want you to have your own things—to do things you want to do. I really do think this is a great idea. You can make the kind of custom cars *you* want to make."

"I'm excited about it but I don't want you to think I'm glad of how we got here..."

"She has nothing to do with us! I hope she sees how well we're doing and chokes on it!"

His grip on me tightened.

"Can you design me a cool intro like you did for your website?"

"...not really. Maybe we can find an artist though."

"You should find more time to practice."

"Want to get room service? I could go for an ice cream."

"I mean it, Kate. If you won't do it for yourself, do it for me."

"It's just so pointless—and it makes me so damned angry!"

"It isn't pointless, and it makes me furious. One hour a day is all I'm asking. Just do the exercises the therapist recommended and sketch the shapes. You're already better at it than you were."

"If you think kindergarten art is good..."

"I think you should take an art class."

"What for?"

"For fun. And who knows, you might learn something. And it'll be good for you to see how other artists have to work at their craft."

"I... it's just so... I don't want to try and suck at it. I'd rather forget I could ever do it. It's so frustrating! I see what I want it to be and can't make it be how I want it!"

"I feel that too when the job is too hard for me but trying to do it makes me better at it and after enough tries, I eventually get it."

"My brain could be so damaged I never get it. I could try forever and never do it again."

"Not forever—try for a year and if you don't see any improvement, I promise I won't nag you again. But you might find that you like doing it even when it doesn't look like you want it to. Maybe the journey could be fun?"

"I know what would be fun," I said as I reached for his belt buckle.

"Now you're talking."

FORTY-FIVE

Jace's phone rang, waking me from a sound sleep.

I picked mine up to check the time.

A call at two a.m. couldn't be good, I thought in rising dismay.

"I knew it would work!" Jace said excitedly.

He listened for a minute then said, "No. I don't know the name. Let me ask Kate. Do you know a guy called Leonard Gould?"

"Leonard... Frenchy... Yeah, he was a grade lower than Everly and a real loser; the type who'd shoot up the school and no one would be surprised. Why? What he'd do? Did he break in?"

"He sure as shit did! He's the caller!"

"What? Why would he?"

"Who cares. We got his ass!"

"How... you set him up. You set me up!"

"For your own good. Dan, do the police want us back there?"

He listened for another minute, then said, "Good. Tell them all I say thanks and I owe them one! Kate and I really appreciate it—more than we can say. I hope you're giving the idea of a show real consideration."

He laughed a happy laugh that I seldom heard from him, which eased some of my anger—but only some.

I got up to use the bathroom and when I returned, he was sitting against the headboard with his light on.

"You're the most beautiful woman I've ever seen," he said.

The *non sequitur* threw me for a moment.

He laughed as he said, "That was a sincere compliment. Sometimes when I see you, it just hits me how perfect you are, how lucky I am. And sometimes some little thing will remind me how close I came to losing you. And then sometimes there's this huge thing that I can't overlook. I'd do just about anything to keep you, Kate, including murder if it came down to it. So Leonard is lucky it was Dan and not me who caught his ass. And yes, I lied to get you to go because I know you. You'd never have agreed even though it was a simple plan."

"Dan could've been hurt! This wasn't some stupid fourteen-year-old kid!"

"He isn't stupid. He didn't need to do much either. Is all he did was go to the bar and invite everyone he knew back to the house where he pretended to hook up with a girl, or maybe he really did, but whatever. He partied there until Sunday while loudly and frequently saying he had to go visit his family a few days and having the new girlfriend loudly and frequently say he better be back to meet her there Tuesday night for another private date in the jacuzzi before we came home Wednesday.

Then they just sat back and waited. Dee was there waiting with them. They caught that bastard red handed. He jumped the wall by the gazebo and nailed a camera up. The police have him in custody and now I don't need to worry that some asshole is going to terrorize you or worse."

"You should've told me, not tricked me."

He shrugged, crossing his arms.

"I guess it's better you know now that I'm going to do anything, whether you like it or not, to keep you safe. There's no law, no rule, no anything that's going to stop me."

"If you go to jail..."

"I'm not stupid, Kate. I'll let the law handle it but if they fuck it up, if Olivia gets off on some technicality or by buying her way clear, I'm not going to sit back and let her try again—and that includes letting her pay these stupid kids to do whatever stupid things she wants."

"I can't see how she could've paid him. He must have just wanted a camera there for whatever scummy reason."

"Or he's working with Margo."

"No way. She hated him. It was her who gave him his nickname."

"Who cares why he did it. He's caught and won't be doing it again. Dan has a buddy of his coming over to look over our security."

"You guys and your buddies..."

He shrugged at me again, extending a hand.

I headed back to the bathroom.

He followed saying, "Jeff did security in the army. Real high-tech shit. He recommended we put in a live feed screen so we can see all of the cameras at a glance. I told Dan to have him go ahead. We'll put one in the walk-in closet, which he thinks we should make into a real safe room, and one in the garage."

"That sounds expensive."

"It's necessary for my peace of mind if nothing else."

He followed me into the shower.

"You don't get to be mad about this," he said gruffly.

That made me laugh in annoyance.

"I love you so much, Kate...just let this go, please. For me..."

"Don't make a habit of it."

He began kissing my neck.

FORTY-SIX

When we returned home, we went directly to the police station as requested by Dee.

Dwayne met us there and the five of us Dee, Reynolds, Jace, Dwayne, and I all took seats in one of the interview rooms.

Dee had us all state our names and the date for the camera.

She said to me, "Have you ever had any prior encounters of any kind with Leonard Gould?"

"No. I don't recall ever even speaking to him."

"But you knew of him?"

"Everyone did. He was one of Margo's prime victims."

"Explain that."

"She used to pick a kid, one who wasn't popular for whatever reason. She liked to pick on the kids who'd just moved into the area, but she'd pick anyone really. She'd date them once or twice then break up with them publicly and as humiliatingly as she could. In Leonard's case she called him *La Nerd*, said he couldn't kiss worth a damn. The whole school started calling him Frenchy. He never seemed to get that it was an insult though or maybe he was just pretending that it didn't bother him."

"So he and Margo dated?"

"She was crystal clear that she didn't like him. She loudly and often turned him away."

"So he still liked her even after she dumped him?"

"He was always on the fringes of that group laughing at their dumb jokes even when he was the butt of them. I wasn't paying enough attention to know if it was her that he was interested in or one of the other girls."

"What about Everly? Did he date her?"

"Not to my knowledge."

"Did you ever see them together?"

"Not kissing or anything like that. I saw her pat his cheek and insult him a few times. But she did that to a lot of people."

"How about other friends of his?"

"I don't think he had any. But, like I said, I wasn't paying him much attention. Our paths seldom crossed. Mostly I saw them at school events like pep rallies and stuff that everyone had to go to and a few times he'd be hanging around while they played poker in the cafeteria or by their cars after school."

"Did he have his own car?"

"I have no idea."

"Did he ever approach you?"

"Not that I can remember."

"So you never saw him in classes?"

"He might've been in one of the computer classes. I used to help out Mr. Williams once in a while and babysit the freshman beginner classes. A few of us did that. The kids who were doing good in his class could use the room and equipment for our own projects if we answered questions while we were in there. I don't remember him, but he could've been in those classes."

She said to Jace, "Had you ever met him?"

"No."

She slid a picture across the table.

Jace said, "I saw him at Kate's graduation. He was sitting right behind Everly. I thought they were friends because he was leaning forward laughing with her when she yelled at Kate."

"What did she yell?"

Jace shook his head.

I said, "She called me a loser."

He said, "It surprised me she'd be friends with him because he was dressed so weird."

"In what way?"

"He was wearing a black turtleneck—in June. And his hair was slicked back. I thought he was one of those poser assholes who think they're cool. But now that I think about it, I think he was going for a French vibe—and failing badly."

I snickered.

"Yeah, he wore that black turtleneck a lot... actually I remember the first time I saw him in it. He'd come into the lunchroom where the kids were playing cards and Margo said something like look at Frenchy now! And she got up to kiss him. It was a long gropey kiss.

They all were laughing, and she sat in his lap at the table.

The next day she made fun of him for wearing it again, but he kept wearing it. It reeked of awful cologne... He only wore black after that and usually a turtleneck."

Reynolds said, "So not what you'd call a stable personality..."

"He was smart. He just missed social cues. I used to think he was on the spectrum and maybe had Asperger's."

"So it's possible that he believes he and Margo are friends—lovers even?"

"I guess... there's a good chance they were lovers for the days she dated him."

Jace said, "You think she put him up to it?"

Dee said, "It's a good possibility. One we're investigating. She had an almost identical camera in her possession."

Dwayne said, "That's hardly a credible link."

"I should've clarified. The camera contained the same sort of footage. We'd like to show you the recording from the camera Leonard was caught with and hear your thoughts on it."

I could tell by her tone I wouldn't like it.

Jace took my hand, saying angrily, "If that fucker filmed us at the pool..."

My flush felt like fire.

Reynolds said, "We don't believe the actors are you."

He angled his laptop screen to show us.

The angle was bad to see faces, which I'm sure was intentional. Two people were fucking in the leaves beneath a pine with lots of moaning and grunting with the girl saying give it to me Jace in a breathless shout.

I was already too flushed to flush more.

I said, "That isn't Jace—or me."

Reynolds fast forwarded to when they were done, laying side-by-side with the man's body blocking the woman's body with his back to the camera.

The woman whispered, "We'll get everything. Is all we need to do is stick to the story."

He whispered back, "We'll have to kill the old lady too, Kate. I told you framing her wouldn't be enough."

The woman said, "As soon as she's found guilty, we can kill them all and everyone will blame her. Your cousin knows someone who can shank her ass."

"Jesus Christ! She's going to hire a hitman and blame me!"

Jace said angrily, "That isn't us! Look he has no scar!"

Dwayne said, "What's the time stamp on this?"

"June twenty-ninth of this year at three in the afternoon."

Dwayne said, "Kate, send me all of the recordings taken in June."

Dee said, "That was from the camera taken from Margo Russell. This is the one from Leonard's."

She turned her laptop so we could see it and we watched two sets of leg and a man's ass humping for a few minutes. This time they were laying in grass at night with a brick wall behind them. Running water muffled their moans.

I said, "That could be my wall, except there is no grassy patch on the other side of the fence by the pool and I doubt they could get over the fence without tripping an alarm."

Dee said, "We think they built their own wall."

"He isn't admitting it's fake?" Jace asked.

"He's denying he put it up even though we have him on camera doing just that and five people including myself can testify to it."

The man sat back on his heels saying, "When we get all the money, Kate, we'll sell this heap of shit house, but we're putting in another pool like this."

"We're moving away as soon as I kill them all."

Kids laughed in the distance and the two stood and ran off laughing.

The water had made them hard to hear.

Dee said, "We already know that the sound of the voices was added after, so we know the words are fake."

"It wasn't us," Jace said tightly. "I have a scar on the back of my leg from the bullet."

Reynolds said, "We're going to want pictures."

Jace said, "And they aren't as tan as us."

I said, "Plus there's no grass like that. We have new baby grass just beginning to grow by the pool. There's none anywhere else yet, except by the sidewalk out front, but that strip of grass isn't wide enough on the inside edge and the outside edge would show the sidewalk even if they'd dared to do that on a public road."

Dwayne said, "So you don't know if Olivia put them up to it or if this was just their idea?"

"Margo is saying the camera was planted on her. We haven't yet confronted either of them with the contents of the cameras. Our forensic teams are still going over them. Once we have our ducks in a row, we'll confront them with the facts and the repercussions of lying in such a serious matter. She's going to do hard time for this unless she's smart enough to say it was meant to be a practical joke and convince you of it."

I snorted.

Jace said, "Do you know how they intended the police to find the cameras?"

Dee shook her head, looking angry. "My guess would be they'd commit a serious enough crime that the police would confiscate and search all cameras."

Reynolds said, "They might've been counting on the alarm they'd triggered initiating that search. The camera would've been found by an investigating officer and check for pertinent footage as standard procedure."

"Except it wasn't a camera in my network."

"But it's the same sort of game camera you use in your woods and along the bottom part of the public trail."

"Why would I use a game camera where I have real cameras and even if I did, why would I have sex under it!"

Dee said, "We know that isn't you, Kate."

"If this is shown in court... I bet that's why that bitch did it! She wants to humiliate us! And god, the kids will be terrified! Felicity can't take this! You can't let her know about this!"

Jace leaned closer to hug me.

Dwayne said, "I'll apply to the judge that this evidence be watched in closed quarters because of the intended inflammatory nature."

Jace said, "What are you doing to be sure Olivia or Margo aren't planning to hire people to murder Kate's family?"

Dwayne said, "The judge will be shown the recordings, and I can request an audit of her finances. I assume Margo and Leonard's finances are being audited?"

Dee nodded.

Dwayne continued, "The judge will ensure that Olivia doesn't have access to her money to pay for a hitman. All of her expenditures will be audited by the court."

"So now what?" Jace asked.

Dee said, "First we need to track down who bought the cameras and who the people are in the film. I think once Margo realizes the seriousness of the charges she's facing that she'll cooperate but that will have drawbacks."

Dwayne said, "Even if Margo admits Olivia put her up to it, Olivia's defense team will claim that she's lying. Unless Margo has proof, it's going to be her word against Olivia's."

"They're both liars!" Jace said.

Dwayne nodded agreement.

Dee said, "That's a problem for the court and their lawyers to settle."

I said bitterly, "Except it's our problem too if we don't know who to guard against."

Dee said, "No one does something like that for the hell of it. There's plenty of things Margo could've done—even legal things, to make your life miserable. The recordings are clearly intended to introduce doubt into the mind of the jury, which if they'd been done better and planted correctly, it might have done. As it is, I think they help your case, unless of course, her team can make a case that you had Margo and Leonard plant the cameras for just that reason."

"Then why would I have called the police before they were set up?"

"Exactly. Which is why I think this helps the case against her."

"But she almost got us," Jace said worriedly.

Dee said, "It will be much harder for her to manufacture that kind of shit now and have it believed."

Not impossible though...

Jace said, "So she can just do whatever the hell she wants..."

Dee shrugged uncomfortably. "We can charge her but she's already facing the death penalty. She's not likely to care about additional charges."

Dwayne said, "We want her charged. I plan on petitioning the court for the cost of the needed security so they freeze her assets before she can give it away."

Reynolds said, "Her visitor privileges have been revoked. Her lawyers can still see her though and they're a shady bunch."

Dee said, "She's going to be found guilty. Once that happens, she won't have motivation to frame anyone else. After the civil suits against her and she has no money she won't be able to do anything even if she still wanted to."

"So what are we supposed to do for the next six months?" Jace asked bitterly.

FORTY-SEVEN

Dwayne accompanied us back to the house where we found Dan, his friend Jeff Jansen, and my brother Grayson waiting at the pool.

Grayson set a plate with a hamburger in front of me then handed Jace a beer.

Dwayne said, "A hot dog for me, please, and two scoops of macaroni salad."

Grayson poured him a glass of red wine before heading back to the grill.

It made me sad for them that they didn't hug or acknowledge each other in a more meaningful way.

Olivia had so much to answer for and was answering for none of it!

I said, "Thanks for all your help."

Jeff said, "You're welcome. You have a good system for a civilian, but you need a better one. Especially seeing as we only caught one guy and he inferred there were others."

Jace said, "They caught two."

He told them what the police had found out.

Dan said, "Then I agree with Jeff. You need a better system."

"It's going to cost you though," Jeff said warningly.

Grayson said, "How much?"

Jace shrugged, saying, "It doesn't matter how much. Tell us what we need. We can always sell the car or tractor if we have to."

Grayson said, "I meant I'd help pay for it and I'm sure Dad would too seeing as how the kids are targets and they're here a lot."

I ate my burger and then sipped Jace's beer as the men discussed the best way to secure the house.

I said, "I like how the alarm vibrates my watch now. I don't want to have to run see a screen."

"We can do both," Jeff said absently without looking up from the diagram he was drawing.

I finished two beers over the next few hours.

Dwayne and Grayson left when the talk shifted to car design.

I kissed Jace on the cheek.

"I'm heading in. Night all and thanks."

They all said goodnight.

Jace didn't come in until late.

He was still up before me and had left me a note on the refrigerator saying he was making breakfast at the pool.

I made a batch of brownies then cleaned my room and did some laundry while they were cooking.

The house phone rang as I was heading out the door.

It made my breath catch and a pit form in my stomach.

"Hello?"

"This is Todd from Favors. You asked us to call when we got the white rhododendrons in stock?"

"Right."

Relief made me giggle.

"Well, we got 'um. Three different varieties. The boss says he can get you those candytufts too, but you'd need to take the whole batch of fifty."

"Thanks. I need to see if I can use them all. I'll call back by tomorrow."

"Sure thing. Just call the store. Not this phone. It's my wife's and I ain't supposed to use it for business."

"Thanks," I said again and hung up.

Jace startled an exclamation from me when I turned.

"Sorry. I heard it ring. Who was it?"

"The landscape guy."

To my embarrassment I began to cry. My tears stopped quickly, soothed by the warmth of his embrace. He held me a long time.

"Those brownies smell amazing," he said when he finally stepped away.

He took the plate from me, saying, "Grab your notebooks and laptop."

I ran back to our room to grab them.

He had the coffee pot and the canister of the expensive coffee under his arm when I returned.

Grayson, Dwayne, Barry Shae, Dan, Jeff Jansen, and Mike Hunt were already at the pool when we arrived.

Jace made me eggs on the griddle while I made coffee.

Jace said, "Jeff has the estimates worked out and that's with us doing most of the work. It's going to take us three or four days to do it, maybe five or six because you're going to be showing Dan how you line up the shots and he's going to be showing you how his drone works so you can decide if you want drone footage for the show."

Jeff handed me a stack of paper.

"We can sell some of the cameras you have and repurpose some."

While I was flipping through his sketches, Jace said, "Once we're done with that, we're moving ahead on my garage. Grayson agreed to co-sign for a loan for it if I can't get one."

Dan said, "We're going today to see if we can get the permits we need. Mike here is a general contractor and he's agreed to whip us up the plans."

He slid his notebook closer.

"If we expand the building to the left, we can put parking from your driveway to the right all the way to the property line."

I examined it a few minutes before saying, "That's going to be a huge apartment on top. No one is going to rent such a big place above a busy garage. It'd be too expensive. But I guess we could put it in two or three small apartments..."

"That space will be offices and the sewing room, not apartments."

"Do we need so many offices?"

"You need one, and Dan will need one, and our future secretary will need one. We'll need storage space for the wedding venue and catering stuff and for our parts."

He continued to lay out his dream with the others chiming in excitedly.

Crystal and the kids arrived.

By noon there were thirty or so people there. All were friends of Dan's who all seemed to know his plans and were excited to help. By evening, they'd staked out the outline of the building with surveyor marks and string.

Dan, Crystal, and I spent the next week talking video editing. I taught him how to use the equipment and programs and we roughed out an idea for an intro to the new channel.

I said, "That first show needs to be awesome and you should have a few done in advance so you never miss a post. I like to keep a few ready to go and I always save all the footage in case the viewers ask to see more. So make sure you label the clips by date and content. For long clips I add in my time stamps and sometimes I'll make notes, so I'll put that info right in the file name like: Office Desk build 8/2 CT 9/12, N-4, which I know means it was taken on august second and continued on September twelfth and the notes are in the fourth notebook. I used to write out all my notes and then read them into OneNote but now I just take all voice notes. I'm not sure how I'll handle making new sketches now, but you don't want to skip having some sort of resources for the viewers.

"I get a lot of traffic to my webpage with people downloading the blueprints or directions. And don't forget to keep track of your shopping list. I keep them with the build info, and I add in my own comments on what I liked or didn't like about the product just make sure you clear that with any sponsors first."

Crystal said, "Don't sponsor crap. It will ruin your show. Kate is making some good money from her sponsors because she's so choosy."

"I can contact my sponsors and ask if they want to buy ads from you too, so check my list and see if you like any. I think we should plan to release your intro on my site, which should give it a huge boost."

Crystal said, "How long will it take you to finish project one?"

"Not long at all."

"What's project one?" I asked.

Dan said, "We decided to use numbers to make it easier to keep track. We have three car builds going on right now. The Camaro is a straight restoration with no embellishments. He wants it as factory original as we can make it look but without paying the crazy prices for original parts, which I think will bring in lots of viewers because Jace is fabricating lots of them."

Crystal said, "Your dad is letting them use the sewing machine at the shop, but they'll need their own. I think you should wait though and send out a request once we get some numbers for the show and maybe you can get one donated."

Dan nodded agreement.

I eyed them suspiciously.

Neither had answered the question.

Two months later I posted that I was making a live announcement on a spin off show.

Crystal, Dan, Jace and I gathered in the unfinished basement of what would one day be Briar Metals, which was the only part of the building done. All of the shows ready to go on the Briar Metals channel had been filmed at the carriage house garage.

I'd sold ad time for this live show so needed it be popular.

The three of them watched on Crystal's laptop as I walked through the construction site, filming it while saying, "Hi. Thanks for joining me, everyone. You've met Jace briefly on my channel and you'll be seeing more of him there as the shows catch up to real time. For those of you who don't know, my fiancé, Jace Blake, is a mechanic with an artistic flair that's truly unmatched when it comes to metal work. He fabricates all sorts of parts and decorative metal work, which he'll be showing you on his channel Briar Metals. There's a link below for his very first post. We're both hoping Briar Metals will be as successful as Briarwood. I'll be helping to turn this building lot into his dream garage. You'll be seeing those posts starting in January.

I pointed out what would be where, ending in the basement where I introduced the Briar crew.

I turned the camera on myself as I said, "I expect most of you were brought here because of the trial that will be happening then. Because of legal reasons, I can't talk about any of that now, but I would like to thank you all for your kind wishes and support.

"And now, on with the show."

Crystal played the intro for the Briar Metals channel, and we watched the visitor number climb and read the comments, which were mostly good ones.

"One million and climbing," Crystal said excitedly.

Jace said, "Let's watch too."

We'd all seen the intro a hundred times, but it was still a thrill to watch it. Dan had done an amazing job getting the footage with his drones and splicing it together.

We'd hired out a few animated characters in the same style I'd used for my intro and for a soundtrack.

I was shocked when the show started in the front driveway with Jace standing in front of a new metal gate—the one I'd drawn ages ago with Briarwood in fancy script entwined with thorny roses.

"Is that really there?"

He laughed and the three of them bumped fists.

"It's beautiful—when did you do that?"

"Whenever I got a chance. Your dad let me build it at his shop for you—for us. We'll be safe here, Kate."

I wondered if he'd heard anything new about the case but didn't want to ruin this moment by asking.

Crystal said what we were all thinking.

"Let's see who sticks around."

We all knew these numbers didn't mean anything. We wouldn't really know if his show was a success until after all of the trial drama was over.

But meanwhile we were making bank.

We all bumped fists.

FORTY-EIGHT

Olivia was wheeled into court in an old-fashioned wheelchair. A hand knitted afghan covered her legs leaving just her feet visible. She wore sensible flats unlike anything I'd ever see her wear before. Her flowered dress was a size too big and her hair stark white instead of the salt and pepper she'd had as long as I could remember, arranged in a loose bun. She also wore a lot of her expensive jewelry.

I was certain everything she wore was chosen to give the impression of a rich little old lady—a helpless victim of her scheming family.

I really wanted to smack her.

Richard Wiess, the lead prosecutor, said to the jury, "I want you to meet the Averys."

The television at the front of the courthouse displayed a picture of our family that Olivia had arranged to be taken by a professional photographer three Christmases ago. She'd chosen our outfits and arranged us.

We all wore black and white except for Hannah who wore a red dress with white crinolines, black stockings and black shoes, and Harley who wore a red bow tie with his little black tuxedo. My grandmother wore a sleek, black, sequined gown with a slit up the left leg, revealing her four-inch stiletto heels, a white fur stole, and the same diamond necklace she wore today with matching teardrop diamond earrings and long elegant black gloves with a wide diamond bracelet.

The kiddos stood to either side of her with my father on her left and Grayson on her right, looking very handsome in their tuxedos. Everly and Kenya stood to either side of them, both wearing pretty black cocktail dresses with my mom and me behind them. My mother and I wore black pant suits with white shirts, but you couldn't see much of us.

441

The photographer had taken a bunch of different poses, but they all featured Olivia, and she always wore the same haughty not quite smile. Most of them also starred my father or Grayson. None of them featured my mother, except in the background mostly hidden.

I'd never really noticed before how Olivia had pushed me to the background too. I wondered now if that's why my grandfather had made such an effort for me. If he'd seen that she disliked me because I resembled my mom so much. I wondered if he'd known she hated my mom to the degree she had—*maybe Olivia had suspected that he was falling in love with her.*

Wiess paused the slideshow on an image of Hannah and Felicity smiling at each other over Harley's head as he knelt on one knee to tie his shiny black shoe.

Their smiles were bright and excited, full of love for each other. My grandmother stood behind them straightening her gloves, admiring her bracelet, not paying any attention at all to the children.

How did I not see her shallowness?

Not once during that entire evening had she spent a moment on the kids, except to tell them to sit or smile. She hadn't laughed with them or admired them or even said a kind word. Her only compliments had been to my father and Grayson.

I'd seen it but had lied to myself, made excuses for her, telling myself she just didn't like the messes kids could make. I'd been completely unwilling to see that she just didn't like the kids.

I hoped the jury was more willing to see the truth than I had been.

Wiess continued, "The prosecution will show that Olivia Avery planned and carried out the murder of her granddaughter Everly Avery. A plan she concocted right around the time she asked Everly to murder her siblings.

Olivia went on to murder Claire McAllister. She attempted to murder Kenya, Kate, Felicity, and Hannah Avery—her granddaughters, shooting Jace Blake with the intent of murdering him, all because she hoped that Alise Avery, her daughter-in-law, a woman she hated, would be blamed.

"Everly was just seventeen, suffering from mental health issues that Olivia took full advantage of. The prosecution will prove that Olivia attempted to pay Everly to murder her sisters and when that first attempt failed, Olivia then planted an explosive device in the hopes that it would kill her grandchildren. When Everly inadvertently foiled that attempt too, Olivia murdered Everly by purposefully supplying a lethal dose of drugs that she stole from Maureen Hilfiger, a woman who Olivia knew had been prescribed the drug because she was dying of cancer.

"The formulation of that drug has a unique chemical makeup that included fentanyl among other things—things that had been customized for the intended recipient that couldn't be in anyone else's prescription. All of the drugs that Maureen took were contained in a customized capsule formulated with custom herbal supplements that were intended to be taken in a sequence. Monday for relaxation, Tuesday revitalization, Friday for pain, that sort of thing. So we know exactly when the pills were formulated and when they were stolen.

"Maureen's video testimony, a death bed recording, will tell you that Olivia visited her home in June where the women discussed her worsening health. Maureen believed in homeopathic remedies and had mentioned how much she disliked the necessity of taking the pills that contained the fentanyl, not only because they were a manmade drug but because they were so strong.

"Maureen had told Olivia that she had to be very careful never to exceed the dosage because it could be fatal. Friday pills had a higher fentanyl content because the therapy she did on Thursday's always left her very sore. Her bones break easily. Her level of pain was severe, which took strong drugs to counteract.

"Olivia visited Maureen twice more over the summer. One day after Olivia's last visit, which was the day before Everly was murdered and the children poisoned with that very same drug, Maureen realized her Friday pills were missing.

"The defense will show that Olivia used her computer to research the most common ways that maternal filicide is accomplished. She clicked on numerous links that said poisoning and drowning were often associated with the murder of young children by their mothers while the murders of older adult children were more commonly violent. So Olivia hatched a plan.

It took her a few days to gather the needed elements—the poison, the disguise she intended to wear. A disguise chosen so that security cameras that Olivia knew were on her granddaughter's house would show Alise Avery arriving. We have proof that only two days prior she ordered the shoes she wore during the murders. Shoes chosen because Alise Avery had the exact same pair. It's our contention that Olivia intended to swap the shoes with Alise's pair after she'd committed the murders when there would be blood and the paint thinner used in the fire on them.

During the days she planned this murder spree, she'd been setting up her alibi by taking her youngest granddaughter's shopping. By offering to help her granddaughter Kate move, conveniently getting the keys to the house to make copies of that she then planted in a coat she'd stolen from Alise's room during those oh so helpful visits. We know exactly when those keys were made. Not only because of the stamp on the key. A date and time when Alise Avery was in a hospital and unable to have them made but the man who copied them remembers seeing Olivia.

"She stole a gardening hat Alise wore and a pair of black pants and a white shirt. All articles of clothing that no one was likely to notice missing. She'd cased Kate's house, learning her home security—at least she thought she had. She knew after she'd made the bomb in Kate's workshop that there weren't any cameras on the back of the house. There was just one doorbell camera on the front door.

"But unbeknownst to her, Jace Blake had installed additional security the day after the bomb was found. So Olivia made her plan and gathered her weapons and disguise. Now all she needed to do was wait for Alise to be released from the hospital.

"Here's where her plan becomes diabolical. She'd arranged for her son, Brent, to be away from home by convincing one of Brent's better clients to insist he attend him personally.

"Henry Karn will testify that Olivia was insistent when she called and rudely demanded that he call at once and demand Brent attend him. She'd never before asked for anything in such a manner, and he had no idea why she'd asked then. He just knew that he better do as she wanted if he expected her to continue to support the firehouse—so he did.

"As soon as Brent left Alise at the house, Olivia arrived to borrow Alise's car on the pretext that her own wasn't working and she didn't want to disappoint the girls with the treat they'd been promised.

"The girls will testify via recorded testimony that they were confused on why their grandmother had parked on a side street just feet from their own street until their father drove past.

"Both girls had waved. He hadn't notice them parked there—which is heartbreaking when you consider she was on her way to murder his children."

My father's breath caught loudly.

Wiess continued, "That phone call to Henry was one of the evilest, most diabolical calls anyone has ever made. Its sole purpose was to let her take those children to murder them in such a way that their own mother would be blamed. Olivia stole Alise's cell phone to call Kenya, her oldest granddaughter, her husband John's illegitimate child, and asked her to meet her at once at her sister Kate's house, telling her that she had new information that the two women needed to discuss at once, privately.

"She left the Avery garage with the girls wearing a wig and hat on pulled down low over her face and drove directly to a local ice cream parlor where she sent Felicity inside to buy them ice cream with a stern warning that she wasn't to eat it until Olivia had inspected it.

"Felicity did as she was told and gave her grandmother the cones. She told her that their mother didn't allow them to eat in the car. Olivia told her to get in the back. She then dosed both cones with one of the stolen capsules and handed one to each child. Felicity saw her do it, but it hadn't worried her because Felicity suffers from severe allergies. She assumed her grandmother was putting allergy medicine on the ice cream. And when she asked her grandmother if that's what it was, her grandmother had agreed. She'd smiled as she handed her the poisoned cone.

"Hannah took only one bite before dropping her cone. Felicity handed her cone to Hannah to try to clean the mess. She and Olivia argued over it with Olivia saying to leave it and that the two girls could share the remaining cone and Felicity saying her mother would be mad if she did.

Hannah was crying and refused to eat her sister's cone. Felicity ate a few bites but was worried about the spill and the fact that Hannah was crying. She didn't eat much before she fell asleep. The small amount that the children ingested was enough to keep them unconscious for a full day. A full day! If they'd finished that ice cream, they'd have been dead before they reached Kate's house.

"With both children sleeping in the back seat, Olivia went to meet Kenya Avery at her sister Kate's house. She arrived before Kenya did. Olivia brought Hannah inside where she dropped her on the floor and went to gather the paint thinner, zip ties, and a steel pipe. The home alarm went off, which would have foiled her plan if Kenya hadn't arrived because Kate had received notification on her phone and would have called the police had the alarm continued to ring. But Kate had to pull over to check the alarm app, which gave Olivia enough time to act.

"When Kenya entered, she saw Hannah and was immediately concerned. While Kenya was leaning over the child, Olivia struck Kenya over the head with a lead pipe. Luckily for Kenya, she'd worn her hair up that day, using a foam insert to plump her bun. It cushioned the blow enough so the blow didn't kill her outright. It knocked her out long enough for Olivia to tie her hands with zip ties, and take out her phone, pressing her thumb to it to send a text to Kate asking for the house alarm code that she then entered and continued with her plan.

"She returned to Kenya who was awake again. Kenya resisted being tied, so Olivia smashed her leg with the pipe hard enough to break the bone. She finished tying her, doing it as painfully and cruelly as she could, calling her vile names as she was dousing Kenya with paint thinner in preparation to burning her alive. She wanted her to die painfully and in terror. She'd said as much. It was caught on the home security footage.

"Next, she placed her youngest granddaughter, Hannah Avery who was just four years old at the time, into the bathtub. The little girl had failed to ingest a lethal quantity of the same substance that had killed her sister Everly, so Olivia left the tub running with ice cold water and continued her destructive rampage by luring a neighbor into the yard and shooting her dead.

"She'd chosen to murder Claire in cold blood knowing her son was having an affair with her and hoping that the police would believe it to be the motive—the trigger that started Alise Avery's murder spree.

"Olivia murdered Claire for the crime of having an affair that her son Brent had ended when he realized his daughter Kate knew about it. But really her motivation doesn't matter. There can't be any justification for Olivia's actions.

"It was only pure luck that foiled the attempts to murder her other granddaughters. If Kate Avery had arrived home even three minutes later it would've been too late for her to save her sisters. Hannah would've drowned and Kenya burned. We can only surmise what she intended to do with the unconscious Felicity before Kate arrived, but we know Olivia intended murder because she brought the little girl into the house, a house she attempted to set on fire, even after her plan began to go awry again with the early arrival of her granddaughter Kate.

"Olivia Avery has led a life of privilege that made her think she could do whatever she wanted—that her money could get her out of any trouble that she caused. No one and nothing means a thing to her, except her own selfish desires—not even the lives of her own family. It won't take you any time at all to see the real Olivia, and I guarantee you won't like her. This is going to a be a long trying trial because we have so much evidence to present on so many separate charges. I ask for your patience, and it will take patience as we plod through the legal hoops crossing all of our I's and dotting our T's. We have to be slow and methodical so we don't leave any legal loopholes that she can latter crawl through. She's guilty of everything she's been charged with. As difficult as it will be to see and hear the evidence, it'll be impossible to believe that she doesn't deserve to be found guilty."

He tapped the picture on the easel.

"Kate tried to stop Olivia from murdering Claire, warning Olivia the police were coming, which had no effect other than upping Olivia's deadly rampage. She shot at Kate, who managed to get away and hide and then Olivia proceeded to drag Felicity into the house that she then set on fire.

"Luckily Kate's home wasn't just a home but would one day be a hotel, so as part of the security, they'd begun installing a sprinkler system. It was only working in the hall and Kate's workroom, but it was enough to foil that attempt at murder.

"Olivia then shot Jace Blake when he arrived and again attempted to shoot Kate when she tried to warn him to run. If Olivia hadn't got trapped in a locked room during the chase that ensued—if the police hadn't arrived, she'd have certainly murdered the children who laid helpless unable to run away. You see her now, pretending to be a weak helpless woman—but we want you to remember this image."

He changed the image on the television to show a close up of Olivia as she turned to face the back door after just shooting Claire. Her expression was pure hate—evil—a snarl of fury. Her gloved hand held the still smoking gun pointing at the door. Her black wig was a hair askew allowing a bit of her salt and pepper locks to show.

"Objection, it hasn't been proven that is Olivia Avery."

"Sustained."

The prosecutor said, "The woman in this picture is the murderer of Claire McAllister. You can use your own eyes, which surely show you beyond any doubt who that woman is."

"Objection. The providence of the picture hasn't yet been verified."

"Overruled."

"Your honor may we approach the bench?"

The judge waved them forward where the two lawyers argued for a moment.

The judge said, "The court stipulates that the image was taken from the security camera at Fourteen Briarwood on August fifteenth but will allow the defense to present evidence as to what the images show."

Wiess said, "Olivia will claim that this is all a conspiracy perpetuated by Kenya, Kate, the police, relatives of Jace Blake, and anyone else she can think of. I'll prove that from her prison cell she conspired to have her granddaughters Kenya and Kate Avery silenced as well as to plant false evidence in the home of Kate Avery and in her son's home. We'll show you those devices and let you listen to the testimony of the people she'd tried to engage for the murders, some of whom deny involvement and some of whom have cooperated fully."

A spate of whispering broke out at the defense table.

Wiess said, "We have hours of video we intend to show you. Some of it was taken at twenty-two Briarwood from security cameras, some from police cams, some from neighbor's security cameras, and some from the home of Hannah and Felicity.

"We'll also be showing you the police interviews where Olivia changes her story three times on what happened—each time swearing it to be the true account. We trust that your eyes and ears, your common sense, will show you the horrible truth. Olivia hated her daughter-in-law. She never thought Alise was good enough to marry into her family. She was jealous of her beauty and the fact that her son had dared defy her to marry—that he loved someone more than her.

"Numerous witnesses can testify to the fact that Olivia raged at her husband, blaming him for letting their son marry such an inappropriate woman. Those are Olivia's words. An inappropriate woman. One of the milder epithets she threw at her new daughter-in-law. When John Avery not only supported the marriage but gave their son a flourishing car dealership and a large chunk of capitol to expand it, she suddenly changed her tune and to the public she pretended acceptance because her son threatened to cut her off from his life completely if she didn't. But she fumed and took every opportunity to belittle Alise.

"When Olivia found out that her husband had sired a daughter with this hated woman, she planned her revenge. It was her intent to take everything that Alise valued. To rid herself of a woman she hated, but in a way intended to make her suffer. It would've been much easier for her to just murder Alise than to murder four children—her own grandchildren, but she wanted to hurt Alise, to murder the children and have Alise be blamed for it. For her son to turn his back on his wife. To leave Alise knowing her surviving children were at Olivia's nonexistent mercy."

He continued laying out the case, walking the jury through the crimes from the moment my mother had told Olivia the truth, to the moment Olivia had changed her story for the third time.

When he was finished, he resumed his seat to let the defense speak.

Weldon Terry, the lead defense attorney, stood and said, "That's a sensational riveting yarn, but the simple truth is that Olivia Avery has the misfortune to have a brilliant, conniving, evil granddaughter. Kate Avery set her sights on her grandmother's money and convinced her sister Kenya to help her in a plan to force Olivia to make them the sole heirs. Three days before the bomb was found, Kate Avery had approached her grandmother, demanding she be given two million dollars or she'd call the police with false claims that her older brother had been sexually abusing her for years. As proof of those claims, Kate had shown Olivia lewd photos of herself and her siblings.

"Olivia refused to be swayed. But because she loved her granddaughter, she didn't call the police herself. She called a lawyer to ask for advice.

"When their blackmail scheme didn't work, Kate and Kenya decided to murder Olivia, framing their parents, using that opportunity to rid themselves of the siblings who'd have a claim on Olivia's money. We'll show that it was Kate who planted the bomb intending to murder her siblings. It was Kate who lured her grandmother to her house. It was Kate who threw Olivia into a room she'd prepared in her basement. It was Kate who put the faked images on her home security with the help of her lover Jace Blake's stepfather, Frank Calhoun, a man who'd used his position on the police force in the past to get Jace off of a rape charge—the rape of a fourteen-year-old girl."

"Objection. Jace Blake was completely exonerated on that charge. The girl recanted her story."

"Sustained. The jury will disregard that allegation."

Terry smirked as he continued speaking. We all knew he'd just wanted to get that information into the minds of the jury.

Even though I'd *known* he'd bring it up, it still made me furious to hear him say it. Jace didn't react but it must have made him furious too—and embarrassed.

Terry continued, "It was Kate who murdered Everly with the help of her boyfriend, Jace Blake. The two of them colluded with Kenya, poisoning Hannah and Felicity, even going so far as to shoot himself in the leg and murdering an innocent woman who just happened to be walking by."

Jace's grip on my hand tightened.

My father leaned past my mother to clasp my arm for a moment. My mother's hands shook as she patted me.

I released Jace to grasp her hands in mine.

My father put an arm around her, giving me an anguished glance.

The jury was staring at us with thoughtful weighing glances.

I figured it was much more believable that I'd try to murder Olivia for money than she'd try to murder me to hurt my mother, but I also thought there was too much evidence for her to get away with her lies—at least I hoped there was.

Terry spoke for three hours, laying out a complicated web of lies, implicating not only me, Jace, and Kenya, but Jace's cousin Lloyd, his stepfather, my mother, my father as the patsy and Everly as unwitting dupe.

I'd supposedly tried to seduce Grayson to get him disinherited or maybe arrested. Terry wasn't really clear on what my motive was just that I'd done it with evil intent and with a further goal of blackmail but had told Everly he was abusing me and the kids to discredit her and had somehow gotten Lloyd to get Everly hooked on drugs—how I'd gotten those drugs to her to kill her wasn't made clear. Olivia, through her lawyer, claimed Everly had confided in her the day she died that I planned to go the police with my claims against Grayson if Olivia wouldn't pay. Olivia claimed that Everly had been afraid for her life because I'd gotten Lloyd to threaten her—that she'd been so frightened she'd performed sexual acts with Lloyd's friends, which had led to her mental breakdown.

I bet there was some truth in that, except I doubted it was threats that had gotten her to put out but the promise of drugs. I wondered how Terry intended to connect me to Lloyd when I'd never spoken with him.

He wove a complicated web trying to account for all of Olivia's lies in the interviews she'd given. I knew most of the people he mentioned and was still having a hard time following his logic.

Terry kept talking until half past four, ending by saying, "We don't have to prove Olivia is innocent. The prosecution needs to prove she's guilty—that a seventy-six-year-old grandmother was capable of doing any of the things she's been accused of. Could she have carried a child up a set of stairs, run down an eighteen-year-old who regularly bikes miles, beat up a twenty-eight-year-old who runs marathons, built explosives with no knowledge of building anything at all? Found a drug dealer? A gun? And most importantly why would she have done it when she'd known for almost thirty years the truth of Kenya's parentage—when she'd loved her all of those years. The prosecution wants you to believe she was motivated by hate when these tragic murders where clearly motivated by greed. This trial will have serious life or death repercussions. The prosecutor wants you to find Olivia Avery guilty, for you to impose the death penalty on a seventy-six-year-old woman. He says use your common sense; we agree."

The judge admonished the jury then dismissed court.

As soon as the jury cleared the room and the judge left, I said to my mother, "She's trying to wreck you, Mom. You can't give her the satisfaction. If she sees you're all calm and collected, she's going to blow her sweet grandmother routine. So no more tears. We all know she's lying. Everything that happened—everything—is on her, not you."

Grayson said, "Kate's right, Mom. She knows she isn't going to get away with it. This trial isn't about that. What she's trying to do is hurt you as much as she can. She's going to try to hurt us because it hurts you—or maybe she's decided she hates us all now or maybe she always did... I have no idea how that woman's mind works, except I'm certain if we keep our cool, we can make her lose hers, and since the only punishment that will mean anything at all to her is her image and maybe Dad's opinion..."

My father said, "If she cared about my opinion, she'd have taken the plea deal."

Kenya said, "I bet she hopes we cave—that we'll feel bad and lie so she doesn't get convicted and executed, which is stupid of her! She won't be executed. She'll die of old age before all of her appeals are up!"

Jace said, "Maybe she's decided notoriety is better than going quietly?"

I said, "I don't care what's motivating her. I wouldn't even bother come listen to these lies if the prosecutor didn't want us here."

Jace said, "I think we should go out there and tell the reporters it's all a pack of lies and we can't be bothered wasting our time listening to it."

Grayson said, "If we only had to worry about public opinion, I'd agree, but the jury could see it as we don't want to face the truth or that we don't care what happens. It's going to be a hard sell for them to find her guilty. Not because they'll think she's innocent but because finding her guilty will make *them* responsible for her death. If we aren't here, they could convince themselves that finding her innocent is the easier thing. They'll tell themselves it's better all-around because she *is* so old and if we don't really care or want her put to death, why should they?"

"I don't want her put to death," I said. "I want her to live a long time behind bars, hating every minute of it."

"This is all so awful," my mother murmured.

I wondered if my mother wanted to see her executed— I couldn't blame her if she did.

The next morning Jace woke me with a kiss.

"It's freezing in here," I mumbled as I cuddled closer. The light seeping through the curtains was dim enough I knew it was early.

His hand on my bare thigh heated me enough that I didn't complain when the blanket slipped down.

"Who needs a heater," he said as he kissed his way to my breasts.

The sun had lightened the room considerably before I finally left the warm cocoon of our bed, which I didn't do until he'd exited our bathroom.

He said cheerfully, "It's nice and toasty in there. What are you wearing today?"

"The dress my mom bought me for Christmas with my blue sweater and my brown boots."

I made a dash for the bathroom.

I'd gone to sleep with damp hair, so it was a bit wild, but a bit of hair gel soon tamed it into a presentable bun. I curled a few wisps and did my makeup while Jace shaved.

He'd dressed in khakis and a dark blue sweater with his brown boots too.

We stopped to buy coffee and breakfast sandwiches.

The girl at the takeout window recognized Jace, or at least I thought she did, but maybe she just thought he was really cute and had called her friends to see for themselves, but I thought it more likely she'd called them to tell them that Jace Blake was at her window.

I hoped it was because of his car show but thought it was because of the trial.

She didn't do anything except giggle though, which was a mild reaction compared to some we'd gotten.

He thanked her politely and we drove away.

The crowd of reporters was even thicker when we arrived than it had been the day before.

I stopped on the top step to say, "I don't know why you bother. The judge has ordered us not to speak about the case, so we couldn't comment even if we wanted to. I can say this though, I wouldn't bother come here at all if the prosecutor hadn't insisted. I don't care what Olivia says because I know the truth and I know the only reason she's telling her lies, despite the overwhelming evidence that they *are* lies, is to hurt my mom. So, if coming here every day and listening to it helps the jury see how much we don't want her to get away with what she did, then I'll come and listen."

Someone yelled out, "You want your own grandmother to be executed!"

"No. I want her found guilty because she *is* guilty. I want her to sit in jail for the rest of her life being sorry for what she did although I think she'll only be sorry for herself."

"Will you ask the judge for leniency if she's found guilty?"

"Will you drop your charges against her?"

"How much money did you think you'd get from her?"

"How much money are you making off of this?"

I headed inside, leaving them shouting their questions behind us.

"How much do you think we could make?" I asked Jace as we passed through the metal detectors.

He gaped at me.

I said, "We haven't tried to leverage this on the channel, but I could..."

"No you can't! The judge would have a fit!"

"Only if I talked about the case though... how could he stop me from saying I hate her or anything else?"

"That's asking for trouble, Kate. The channels are risky enough."

I shrugged.

We headed to the elevator, passing three girls from Everly's outer circle who all stopped speaking when we appeared. I ignored them.

I bet they were sweating, worrying about what the lawyers knew and the world would find out about what they'd been getting up to with Everly. The pictures that the police had given me to help identify the people had shown me that it was more than Everly's inner circle involved with the hidden cameras. I'd been able to identify about forty kids and had a good idea that the little kids who I didn't know were their younger siblings. Only one of them had a younger sister that I knew that there'd been pictures of. There'd been hundreds of pictures though.

I was betting all three of these girls were involved and worried it would be found out.

We entered the courtroom where we sat in the front row beside Claire's parents.

Her mother clasped my hand, giving me a worried smile. Her smile died as her gaze shifted to the door.

I knew my parents had entered.

She leaned toward me to whisper, "We'll all get through this."

She patted my hand again and turned away.

Claire's father gave me a cold glance.

I didn't think it was personal. I thought he was just really hurting, and who could blame him. I'd hate us all too if I were him.

Grayson, Dwayne, Kenya, and her boyfriend Dennis sat directly behind us. My mother sat beside Jace with my father beside her.

A surprising number of my former classmates had showed up. I turned to face the front because I wasn't sure how I was supposed to greet anyone. None of the kids Everly and I had gone to school with knew me well enough to expect a smile or even a greeting. I wasn't sure if they'd showed in support for or against me or maybe they'd come for Jace.

I could see Sherry and Kaylee hoping to give him a sympathetic ear in the hopes it'd turn into a sympathy fuck. They'd been on the outer fringes of Everly's inner circle, looking to find a way in, which to them meant screwing their way into the in crowd. Both were only children, which was lucky for them because I was certain they'd have been cool with taking naked shots of their siblings without their knowledge or consent.

Jace whispered, "I'm giving ten to one odds that those girls are going to lie their heads off."

"That's a suckers bet."

"We've got her on film, Kate."

It didn't reassure either of us.

The prosecution entered the video the police had recorded of Olivia's first interview and the defense immediately objected.

The judge called them to the bench.

Grayson whispered worriedly, "If she manages to convince the jury that the police recordings are faked then it's just a small step to saying all of the evidence they gathered was planted."

"How can she possibly do that?" Jace asked angrily.

"The judge could declare a mistrial and make them go through pretrial again to stop this nonsense. It's one thing to question the validity of a home security tape supplied by the person the defense is claiming did the crime, it's another to say the police are lying. Unless they have compelling evidence, I can't see them getting away with it."

Court didn't reconvene for four days.

Reporters surrounded my house. A group of Everly's friends picketed outside with signs that said things like Kate Avery murdered Everly, and Kate Avery is a liar. One of them said I was a gold-digging whore, but the police made them take that one away.

The day after the picketers showed up, another group of them showed up with signs that said things like Everly Avery sold drugs. Everly Avery used drugs. Everly Avery was a liar. Everly Avery was the Queen of Mean, which I admit made me laugh.

The two groups spent the afternoon shouting at each other to the delight of the reporters.

"How many of them do you think are here just to get on tv?" Jace asked me.

"All of them."

It gave me an idea.

I spent the afternoon filming myself.

When court finally reconvened, the judge said, "Both parties stipulate to the veracity of exhibitions one through two hundred as being unmanipulated images and recordings taken at the times and places stipulated. What the recordings show is for the jury to decide. Carry on."

We spent the next two days watching Olivia lie in the interview room, looking smug and haughty, talking to the police as if they were beneath contempt, as if the lies she was dishing out couldn't possibly be lies because *she* was saying it. A different lawyer represented her in every recording. Her image and lies changed drastically when Weldon Terry began representing her.

I wondered if the jury was as sick of her as I was. If I were them, I'd be angry she was wasting my time like this, wasting the court's time.

They mostly appeared interested though—amused even.

Their interest sharpened when the police interviews had been shown and Wiess laid a new picture on the easel in front of the room.

He said, "Exhibit one is a picture taken by Sergeant Ricardo of the backyard of twenty-two Briarwood Lane on August fifteenth at four o'clock in the afternoon. This picture shows the layout of the backyard, including the locations of surveillance devices, which we've numbered for your convenience. Camera One refers to the camera located on the eve above the door that leads into the kitchen area. Camera Two is located on the side of the carriage house."

He continued to name the locations of all the cameras, entering five further images that showed the area that each camera covered, including the only one installed inside that covered the front hall.

The defense objected to that camera, saying they hadn't been supplied with any footage from it.

Both lawyers approached the bench. The defense walked away fuming.

The prosecutor said, "Now, let's talk about exhibit ten. This recording was taken by camera two at one twenty in the afternoon of August fifteenth."

Claire's mother began to cry.

Seeing Claire being pulled into the yard made tears fill my eyes too.

I didn't dare glance at my parents.

The prosecutor stopped the recording to say, "Two days before the time of this recording there were only two security cameras at this house. If that had still been the case, this incident wouldn't have been captured. We'll show you the footage from those two cameras, the cameras that Olivia knew about."

"Objection."

"Sustained."

"We'll show you close up images of every camera and tell you when and why all of them were installed. What I'm going to show you now is graphic and disturbing. I apologize for that. I think this recording is going to stay clearly in your mind so that when we finally show you where those cameras are and what each one could see, you'll be able to place this image there without needing to be subjected to it again. Claire and her killer are standing right on the corner of the building here."

The judge said, "Excuse me, Mr. Wiess. We're going to take a small break."

He waited for the jury to exit the room to say, "I'm going to remind the spectators that outbursts won't be tolerated. This will be disturbing. I urge anyone who feels they won't be able to control themselves to step out. Mr. and Mrs. McAllister, I'm understanding of your need to see justice done for your daughter. I can't order you out as much as I wish to spare you from this, but I can warn you that I'll be forced to ban you from the rest of the proceedings for any outbursts. I highly recommend you go now. These recordings can be made available for you to watch privately if you feel it's necessary. The trial in its entirety is being shown live but the court isn't allowing certain portions of footage to be seen, this being one of them. I truly do feel for you. But my job is to ensure no prejudicial outbursts can sway the jury."

He left the podium.

My parents walked out.

Her parents were both crying.

Kenya leaned over us to whisper, "Come with me, Celia. Don't put yourself through this. God knows I wouldn't want my mother to watch me be murdered.

Jace said, "That evil bitch would've laughed if she managed it—it would thrill her to make Alise suffer, which she is. We're all truly horrified over Claire."

"You fucking should be!" her father said angrily. "We want nothing to do with you loons!"

"It isn't their fault, Joe," Claire's mother said.

"Not the kids, no..."

He stood and helped his wife up. Kenya followed them.

Jace said, "We should go."

"Why? I saw her do it already. I kind of hope I puke and get banned..."

"I'm afraid I will and then you'll be alone here..."

"Close your eyes," Grayson said. "As long as you're quiet, the judge won't kick you out. It's good for the jury to see how sickened we are."

He came to sit beside me.

A girl in the back of the room said loudly, "Brother fucker!"

The bailiff said, "That's it! Out you go!"

"You can't do that!"

I turned to see who'd said it, catching Olivia's eye as she turned to. For one second she looked stricken as her gaze flit past me to Grayson. I turned away from her to take his hand.

The bailiff said, "I can. If I have to ask you again, I'll arrest you. You're now banned from these proceedings. This is a court of law. No one in it is above the law. There'll be no yelled insults, no threats, no rudeness of any sort! Have I made myself clear?"

The bailiff removed Sherry who began yelling once she was in the hall, but I couldn't make out what she was saying. I hoped she got arrested.

Jace said loudly, "She's an idiot. Even Margo stopped harassing us once she realized what a liar Olivia was. Why anyone would think publicly admitting you were dumb enough to believe her was going to impress people, is beyond me."

The bailiff pointedly cleared his throat.

Jace gave me a quick hug. None of us said anything else.

Court reconvened a few minutes later.

The three of us held hands while we watched Olivia murder Claire in cold blood. It was almost worse seeing it on the screen. In person I'd been too shocked to take in the detail and hadn't known she was dead. Watching her last moments was horrifying. In person, I'd run into the house. The camera had continued to record, had captured Claire's

457

terrified face, her hands clutching the wound then falling lax. I was so glad her parents hadn't seen it. Her eyes would haunt me forever.

Wiess pointed to exhibit one with a laser pointer.

"The carriage house is blocking the view from the street behind it as are the overgrown bushes. They're effectively hidden from sight—or so the killer thinks."

The recording had picked up Olivia taunting her, calling her a gold-digging slut, telling her Alise would be blamed and that her son would curse her name, curse the day he'd met her, that the world would see what a whore she was.

The angle was bad to see their faces, but the angry body language and gun were clear.

"You're crazy," Claire said, sounding more shocked than scared. "I'll quit and never see him again. He already broke it off. This isn't necessary. I don't want to see your son again now that I know how nuts his family is!"

She'd begun to turn away when I'd yelled Olivia.

The angle was perfect to show me, and I looked shocked.

"Die bitch," Olivia said, shooting Claire twice and then whirling to shoot at me.

I hadn't realized I'd stared in shock for so long. The first bullet hit the door frame before I turned to run.

Wiess let the recording play out of Olivia running to the door and me running away.

He said, "I have nothing further to say about this recording. I think it speaks for itself. We'll return to this camera in exhibits thirty-two and eight-seven because it catches some further incidents."

The defense called an expert witness who tried to convince the jury that the shots came from the house, not the gun in Olivia's hand.

When asked if he wanted to re-examine, the prosecutor said, "No. It's too ridiculous."

"Objection."

"Sustained."

Wiess said, "Then I guess we can watch it again in slow motion."

He played the recording again in super slow motion where you could clearly see the gunfire—or at least I thought it was clear.

He entered his next exhibit, the same incident but from camera one, stopping the recording when Olivia turned. It was the same image he'd shown in his opening statement.

He said, "The new cameras are showing you the face of the killer. The face of Olivia Avery. A woman so consumed with hatred that she murdered a woman for having the audacity to sleep with her son. Claire didn't name her killer by name, but she clearly says your son—I'll stay away from your son. I'll quit. Claire worked with Brent Avery, and they'd been having an affair for four months. An affair that Olivia had only just found out about."

"Objection."

"Sustained."

He took his seat to allow the defense to speak.

Terry said, "The murder of that poor woman was heinous, but Olivia Avery isn't the woman under that wig. The woman who pulled the trigger is Kenya Avery made up to resemble her grandmother."

"Objection."

The judge said, "I'll allow proof of that claim to be submitted."

Terry said, "When it's my turn to present evidence, I'll call Professor Blainwer as an expert witness on facial recognition. He can explain how we know this disguised woman isn't Olivia Avery."

"Counsel, please approach the bench."

A few minutes later Terry said, "The defense stipulates that their expert can't confirm the identity of the woman as being Kenya Avery."

"Objection, assuming facts not in evidence. The defense hasn't proven that it isn't Olivia under that wig."

"Sustained. This court will hear Professor Blainwer's credentials tomorrow. Court is adjourned for the night."

The jury left. Olivia was led away, then the judge left.

"She can't be serious!" Jace said angrily.

Wiess turned to us to say, "We knew she intended to try this. I honestly expect we'll get a mistrial any day now. Her counsel is skating the edge too hard. We have evidence of a large payoff to this so-called expert. Our expert is certain the person in the picture is Olivia.

"You see what she's doing with these videos. She'll have experts willing to say whatever she wants them to say about every single piece of evidence we supply. It's going to be a long hard haul. We're going to win it, but she's going to make us work for it."

He shook Grayson's hand, nodded at us, and left with his swarm of underlings.

Grayson said, "She's trying to spend all of her money on this to piss Dad off. I think she's counting on outspending the state. If she does this a few times—if she makes a big enough pest of herself, the DA will be ordered to give her a better deal for her plea. A nicer prison—or maybe even the chance for parole. It would be career suicide though for the DA to offer her parole even though she'd most likely be dead before she'd be eligible for it, so he'll probably stick it out even if he gets pressured."

Jace said angrily, "She's just doing this to bug us."

Another group of reporters was outside our house. We came in through the back street, past the partially built Briar Metals shop.

An electric gate was now across across the back driveway made of eight-foot panels of corrugated metal with a camera on each side.

Our home security was state-of-the-art. The yard was completely fenced in now with cameras facing in and out. Every one of them was independently powered and recorded direct to USB as well as sending to a cloud and our monitors. We'd also added cat fencing and a dog door so Dan's dog, Shadow, a retired bomb sniffing dog from Dan's old platoon, could patrol the yard.

Shadow greeted us with happy barking.

Dan had dinner waiting in our still unfinished kitchen. We hadn't done a thing inside the house. I'd spent all of my time over the last few months working on the new shop. Jace, Dan, and our friends helped with the heavy lifting, but they'd spent most of their time working on the cars.

Jace had taken an old wreck of a SUV and tricked it out for me, customizing everything from the grill to the hubcaps, putting in a new engine, and totally redoing the interior. He'd done a beautiful job. We'd had offers to buy it for a hundred times what he'd paid for it, including parts and materials.

He had enough jobs lined up to keep ten people busy for a year. Briar Metals was a success and it wasn't even built yet.

He and Dan began talking over their applicants. I excused myself to go make another video.

I wanted the world to hate Olivia as much as I did.

The entire next day was spent with expert witnesses for the defense and prosecution analyzing Olivia's disguise. The next day was spent examining close-ups of the clothing that Olivia had been wearing when she was arrested, which had specs of Claire's blood on them and matched what the disguised person was wearing.

It was so clear that Olivia was the woman in the video and so frustrating to have sit through all of these people making ridiculous claims. The prosecutor even had pictures of Olivia wearing the same outfit on the morning taken from the shop security camera's when she'd dropped me off.

The defense objected to the picture being admitted and the judge overruled it. He called for a sidebar. The defense walked away looking angry.

For his next rebuttal witness, Terry called on another expert who opened with a statement saying my film making skills were adequate to seamlessly splice images, which the prosecution objected to, which made the judge call for another much longer sidebar.

On rebuttal, the prosecutor got the man to admit that he had never examined a video that I had made of a moving image that had the head of one person on the body of another or had taken the entire body out of a live image to place it into another live background.

Mr. Williams, my graphic design teacher was called to testify about my grades and skill in photo manipulation.

Wiess said, "Did any of the classes that Kate took teach the process of filming on a green screen?"

Uh oh, I thought. I'd been studying just that on my own to learn how to put my animated ghost on the windows and walls.

"Not moving images, no."

"How about acting? Did she study that?"

"Not to my knowledge."

"How long would it take someone to put a clip like that together?"

"Days, maybe months."

"Objection. Speculation."

"Sustained."

"Describe the process as you understand it to make a video clip like that."

"Well, you'd need actors. You'd film them and then overlay that film against the background. But it's more complicated than just layering two images because the background needs to match—the lights, the motions of the leaves and stuff needs to match the motion of the actors' hair and stuff. When things fall, like footsteps and it crushes the grass, that needs to be added in or clipped out."

"How would you then get the film onto the camera?"

"Objection. Witness lacks the technical expertise to describe that process."

The judge said, "I'm going to allow him to answer as he's the one who mainly taught Kate Avery her computer skills."

"Objection. Kate could've looked up the answer on her own."

The judge said, "Overruled. That's speculation without any foundation at all. The jury will disregard that comment and you won't make a further comment on this. My ruling stands. The jury can hear what Mr. Williams has to say about what he believes the process would be to get a security camera to record a recording. You may answer the question, Mr. Williams."

"I don't think it could be done. I think you'd have to hack the cloud somehow."

"Objection."

"Overruled. The question was what he thought—not how it really could be done."

Wiess called an IT man from the alarm company followed by an IT expert, both of whom claimed it could only be done by inserting the image into the files, not by showing the camera a recording.

The defense expert claimed if the film was recorded at the correct perspective, it could be shown to the camera and get into the cloud files that way. The defense entered a few of my animated clips along with a picture I'd painted of the backyard as it would be and then tried to say I'd painted and animated the entire film sequence, which got them a long lecture by the judge and a stern warning about hearsay and speculation.

The jury was ordered to disregard that idea, which everyone knew they wouldn't. I hoped it was as clear to the jury as it was to me that it wasn't true.

The prosecutor reminded the jury that Olivia had been seen wearing the clothing before the crime was committed. He admitted pictures taken from the shop cameras and then later by the police of Hannah, Felicity, Kenya, Jace, and me all wearing the clothing seen in the house camera footage.

Terry argued we were wearing that clothing because this was planned, so I knew exactly what to paint and have my actors wear.

He claimed I'd asked her to wear that exact outfit, which the prosecution objected to as hearsay. It was sustained and the jury ordered to disregard it.

The prosecutor entered receipts for the shoes Olivia had been wearing in the recordings and when she'd been arrested, which had

Claire's blood on them. They'd been purchased using Olivia's credit card two days after Everly had tried to kill Hannah—two hours after Kenya had bought the same pair for our mother while she'd been visiting Olivia, which would've given me only days to forge the film—days in which I'd been injured and in the hospital or with witnesses who could say I hadn't even had a laptop with me.

It was such an obvious attempt to lie again. No one could do what they were claiming I'd done. It would take a team of experts years to do it—but they only needed one juror to believe it. It was maddening.

The prosecutor entered Olivia's and Kenya's phone records next. Both of their phones had logged into the site selling the shoes. Kenya had been at deposition for a client when Olivia had logged in on her home Wi-Fi.

When he went to sit, Olivia turned to smirk at me.

Jace was furious when we left and ranted all the way home.

I said, "I'm so damned tired of her. She's stealing all of this time from us. I should be working on our house. I swear she's just dragging this out to keep me from doing it!"

I went to make another video.

FORTY-NINE

We returned to the courthouse the next day.

Another long morning of boring expert testimony followed with the real experts trying to patiently explain how incredibly difficult it would be for me to insert Olivia's face into a video in such a way that it wouldn't immediately be noticeable.

The defense expert compared my work to Star Wars citing how fantastical things could be done with a camera—how lifelike and real it looked.

The judge had it stricken from the record and issued another warning to the defense team before he dismissed the jury for the lunch and called for a sidebar with the lawyers.

About a million flashes went off when Jace, Kenya, and I appeared on the courthouse steps.

A small group of teenagers began yelling, "Justice for Everly!"

I'd no idea if they meant that against me or Olivia.

Kenya left with Dennis. My parents and Claire's parent's hurried away.

I waited on the stairs and could see by their eager grins that the reporters knew I'd say something.

Someone yelled out, "What did you think of today's proceedings, Kate!"

A woman yelled, "Shut up, fool, and let her talk!"

I said, "I wish my grandmother had been the woman she was pretending to be. It didn't matter to any of us that she didn't have the sort of family name my grandfather did. We just wanted a grandmother— even one as distant as she was... My grandfather was a beautiful man in every way. We all miss him so terribly."

"Even your mother?" someone yelled.

"You'd have to ask her, but my guess would be yes. She loves my father, and he loves his father. She'd want her husband to be happy. John and Alise had worked out their differences ages ago. They were always polite, kind even, to each other. Their mutual love for their family was something they'll always have in common. I feel so bad for my grandfather—imagine being married to such a cold woman? He tried his best to reach her, but she has no soul to reach. She spurned all of his gifts, except those of money.

"My mother is nothing like Olivia. My mother adores her family, has always adored them, and never once placed material belongings over any of us. She's a kind, good woman who made one mistake when she was just nineteen and that mistake wasn't her brief affair, but the lie of Kenya's parentage, which who knows if she even knew it was a lie at the time? But none of that matters to any of us. My parents' marriage is their own business, and we know they love us regardless. You ask me what I think of these proceedings—I think everyone finds it a tedious bore to have to listen to the paid lies of these so-called experts. Anyone with eyes can see that the footage wasn't staged. Olivia doesn't care about wasting your time or how much it must hurt Claire's parents for Claire's brutal murder to be shown again and again, for every moment of it to be picked apart for Olivia's sick amusement because Olivia knows the evidence is irrefutable. She isn't doing this to prove her innocence but to spite us—she's desperate to hurt us any way she can and if that means she has to resort to paying people to say in court that my art is awful, then that's what she'll do, which is so ironic when she's also paying them to say it's so good that you can't tell it from real life."

I began walking and they immediately began yelling questions.

I stopped at our car to say, "No, I won't be back to the courthouse today.

"Will you be posting on your channel?"

"Yes, I intend to post daily recaps of the trial. I'll continuing posting on the Briarwood site and taking the requests of my subscribers there into account when filming the posts, which will be released the day the verdict is served.

We got into the car that Howard was driving.

Jace said, "What posts?"

"Exactly what I just said. I put together clips from the live feed with my reaction to it. I've only just started but I intend to ask my family and you for some small clips of your reactions, not daily ones because nothing much happens each day but just overall on the process."

"The DA will freak!"

"I could care less. I want that bitch to see it! For her to see how everyone thinks she's an evil monster! She doesn't care about the sentence. She doesn't care about much of anything, but she'll hate knowing there's thousands of people talking smack about her. I hope she chokes on it!"

Jace's worried look intensified.

There were thousands of people talking smack about me too.

I said, "This is no worse than high school. I've learned not to give a shit about what people who I don't know or like say about me. Besides, Everly's friends are bound to be brutal when that phase of the trial starts."

Dwayne called me as we were pulling into a restaurant.

"You have to stop giving interviews, Kate," he said sounding exasperated.

"Have to, have to? Like it's illegal or just you want me to?"

"Both. You have a gag order. If you piss the DA off, he's going to charge you. Even if you don't, the defense might be able to use it. Just stop. It isn't worth going to jail for or giving her more ammunition."

"No promises, but I've said all I wanted to for now. I'm going to be posting the shows of the remodel just like I'd originally planned, which includes the cleanup from the damage to the house."

"Please don't do that. Promise me you'll at least speak to me before posting any of that new stuff. I think we can compromise, and you could post the bedroom makeovers upstairs and the kitchen stuff and leave the cleanup for when the trial ends."

"I'll consider it. I'm just so done with letting her dictate my life. From now on, when the defense is blathering on, I'm leaving."

"If you do that too often, the judge could revoke your seat because it could be construed as prejudicial to the jury."

"Ha! They wish they could leave too. I see how angry they get when they have to listen to some idiot lie to them."

"I have some good news about that. The judge has issued an order that all experts must have been certified as an expert *and* have appeared in court as one previously and at a reasonable rate, which he decreed had to be within the ballpark of what other experts charge for their time and not in excess of four thousand dollars a day and he wants to see time sheets. The judge wants fact, not opinion, and has issued a warning that he's not going to put up with any more nonsensical theories told to the jury as if they were fact. If they don't have hard data to back a claim up the witness will be dismissed forthwith. Olivia's going to need to hire new experts for a good portion of the exhibits if she intends to keep going this way."

"Will that mean a new trial?"

"It depends on how many she wants to replace. The judge has granted her time to replace them but hasn't seen fit to halt the trial. He's asked the DA to press forward with the exhibits with undisputed experts."

"How will that affect the case?"

"I can't say it won't affect it, but I think he can link all of the parts up in his closing argument. He'll be shifting to the physical evidence tomorrow. The defense is expected to stipulate the evidence is true. By that I mean they haven't listed any rebuttal witness who are expected to say the evidence was planted or that the tests done on it are invalid."

"That doesn't seem like her."

"We expect her to claim that Kenya was wearing the same clothes and that she forced Olivia to don them."

"Can we prove that isn't what happened?"

"We can show that there was no DNA evidence inside her clothing suggesting anyone else wore them. Kenya's blood is on the sleeve but that should be explainable from the head injury. The hall and porch camera have time stamps. The medical evidence of Kenya's injury is indisputable. The timing just isn't there for her to have hobbled downstairs as Olivia, stripped to make Olivia wear that clothing, dressed herself again in her original clothing and hobbled out all without leaving any DNA evidence inside the clothing and no traces of paint thinner inside the clothing. There was paint thinner on Olivia's legs and cuffs exactly like one would expect if you'd been splashing it around but none on her shirt as there should be if Kenya had taken off her saturated clothing to put on Olivia's shirt."

"How the hell does she think she's going to get anyone to believe Kenya poured that thinner on herself when she's clearly visible on the floor with Olivia standing over her?"

"My guess is they'll say it's you posing as Olivia or Kenya."

"Except I'm on that same video."

"I guess we'll have to wait and see."

The next day the defense called their first witness and the judge said, "Excuse me. I think your forgetting Mr. Nolan, your video expert. He hasn't finished his testimony."

Terry, said, "He has, your honor."

"The jury is excused while I speak to council," the judge said angrily.

As soon as the jury had left the room the judge said, "Are you telling me that you have no evidence of tampering to present just speculation that such things can be done?"

"They can be."

"In my office, now!"

All of the lawyers headed to the judge's chambers.

Grayson said, "Wow... this is going to be a mistrial for sure."

"You mean we have to do this all over again?" I asked in dismay.

My grandmother laughed, which made me flush with anger.

Grayson said, "Expert witnesses are allowed to tell the jury how things are done but only if they believe that thing has been done. They can't just blather on putting ideas into the jury's head. There has to be some evidence to support their allegations. It's day one law school stuff. The fact that they'd listed all of those video experts means they should have something for those experts to say—something relevant to this case. I can't see how this could be anything but a mistrial if the defense just drops it here with just the lead up to how it could be done without the follow through showing the evidence that supports that."

As he was speaking I was watching Olivia who was smirking at my mother in a hateful way. My mother didn't notice her. Her attention was on Grayson.

I said, "But we knew there was none."

Olivia's smirk deepened.

I'd never wanted to hurt someone so badly in my life.

Kenya said, "It was their job to show the scientific evidence on the equipment and the servers that held the pictures to prove that there was evidence of tampering. The court can't check all of that. It's what the trial is for. The opposing sides gather the evidence and shows it all. What they just did was illegal."

"Damn it!" Claire's father exclaimed.

His wife grabbed his arm, saying, "We knew it wasn't these kids, honey."

"I fucking know that! I just thought this was almost over! This court is a fucking joke!"

He stormed out.

She grimaced at us and followed him.

I said, "So now what?"

"The judge will listen to their explanation and probably demand he be shown any supporting evidence. The good news is that his findings will be taken into account for the next trial and she won't be allowed to do this again. Those lawyers will probably all be disbarred or at least sanctioned."

My father said, "Why wasn't all of this discovered in pretrial?"

Grayson shrugged.

"The court takes the word of court officers, which is what we lawyers are. He has to assume that we're acting within the law. The lawyer is supposed to know how to proceed. It's common practice to question the validity of the evidence. The judge has to let both sides do it, but they're only supposed to ask real questions, never complete supposition. He probably assumed that facts had come to light."

"This is ridiculous."

I said, "Meh, she's ridiculous. I don't care if we do this again. It's giving me good ratings.

Olivia flushed, her eyes narrowing on me.

I smirked at her as I said, "It's just more people to see what a stupid evil bitch she is. I have so many fans. So many in all walks of life. I bet she can't escape them even from her prison cell.

She turned away.

The back of her neck was red.

I said loudly, "Was it worth it, Olivia? Are you loving your new place?"

The bailiff said, "Miss..."

Grayson shook his head at me.

Kenya muttered, "That stupid woman..." she stood to hug our father, which made me feel bad for a moment but only a moment. I wanted to hurt her, to make her sorry for what she'd done, which I knew was impossible. She'd never be sorry for that but maybe I could make her sorry for herself.

We waited an hour and then the bailiff told us court wouldn't reconvene until the morning.

On the ride home with Jace, I said, "She couldn't care less about any of this. It's amusing her, if anything."

"It's a hollow victory for her. She has to hate it in there."

"I want her to hate it more."

"Meaning?"

"What can we do to make her miserable in there?"

"Not much—legally at least. But maybe we can hire someone? I have family inside. I bet I could find someone who knows someone in her cell block."

"No. Don't do that. She isn't worth you going to jail."

"Or you either."

"Did you see her face when she heard I had fans?"

He nodded.

I continued, "She wants everyone to hate us..."

"*Ahh..*" he said thoughtfully. "You want her to see people hate her."

"More than that. I want her to see that they like us because of her. That she accomplished the exact opposite of what she was going for."

"Sure but how?"

"I'm an expert at photo manipulation. I could put together a clip to show her. She'd have no way to see if it were true or not. At most she could ask her lawyers..."

"How would you get her to watch it?"

"Go visit her?"

She isn't going to agree to see you and we probably can't anyway until the trial is over."

"Yeah... forget I said anything. She isn't going to care about anything that I do or say."

"Then get the people she does care about to say it."

"Like who?"

"Her friends, maybe? You've been filming your reactions why not film their's?"

"That's brilliant! Do you think they'd do it?"

"It can't hurt to ask."

As soon as we got home, I started making calls.

I worked until three a.m. putting the footage of the dead cat with other images featuring her with my mother.

I had lots of great shots of Lady because people really liked her, so I always filmed her and added her and our cats in. Boo and Igor had their own fan page and everything.

I hadn't been trying to sway my fans but if that's all I had to hurt her with I was going to do my best to make them hate her. And who knows, maybe I'd get lucky and one of my fans would end up in her prison.

The next morning the judge addressed the jury saying, "You've heard testimony from the defense experts speaking about photo manipulation and while it's true those things are possible I want you to understand that there has been no evidence presented that it happened in this case. Both parties stipulate that the recordings you've been shown are unedited images. The court apologizes for wasting your time listening to unfounded conjecture. You're to treat those recordings as factual, using your own judgement as to what they portray. The recordings haven't been altered, replaced, or in any way manipulated. They are true depictions of the events that transpired. The only questions that the defense can ask about are the actions and people in the images. They aren't allowed to question the validity of the images themselves. Now, Mr. Weiss, call your next witness, please."

"I call Kate Avery to the stand."

FIFTY

The recording of Kenya being attacked made me cry. Seeing her terror was terrifying.

It didn't take me long to say what I'd seen and done.

On the cross examination, Terry said, "You mentioned you sustained an injury that affects your ability to paint. Did it have any other affects?"

"I had high blood pressure for a while and headaches."

"An injury to your hands caused headaches?"

"It was a head injury that caused damage to the part of my brain that controls muscle memory. Small motor control specifically."

"So you have brain damage?"

"Yes. On anyone who wasn't an artist they probably wouldn't notice it."

He smirked at me as he said, "Objection. That calls for speculation."

"That's what the doctor told me."

The judge said, "Please wait until your asked a question and only answer that question."

Terry said, "Do you like your grandmother?"

"No."

"Do you think she likes you?"

"No."

Someone in the audience laughed, quickly stifling it.

He continued, "How much of the trust that your grandfather left you have you spent?"

"None of it."

"None? How did you buy that house then?"

"Grayson bought it for me."

"He just bought it—with no promises on your part?"

"Objection."

The judge said, "Mr. Weldon please ask the witness a question."

"What was the deal you'd worked out with your brother for the purchase of the house?"

"I showed him my prospectus, which had a breakdown of the expenses—"

"Objection," Terry said.

"Overruled. The witness can continue to answer the question."

"I'd drawn up a complete budget and timeline of my purposed restoration that included comparable comps of the building both as it was and as it would be, and Grayson agreed it was a good investment. He would buy it and I would pay the mortgage and all the rest of the bills beginning when I was eighteen. I would have four years to pay him back in full, including all expenses that he'd invested in the house, the roof repair, the taxes, and the mortgage that he'd paid until I was old enough to take over. As surety for the debt, but not payment for it, I signed a contract. That contract specified my assets, which included the trust from my grandfather, but I don't have to use those funds to pay it back. I can pay it any way I want to. If I don't pay it within the specified time frame, he gets the house free and clear. I'd get no repayment for improvements or the money I'd put into it for the mortgage and taxes and stuff."

"So you're saying that you never promised him the money from that trust?"

"Objection. Asked and answered."

"Objection sustained."

"How much money have you invested into the house as of this moment."

"Objection. Relevance."

"Objection sustained."

"I can show relevance, your honor. It's our contention that Kate framed Olivia for—"

"Objection."

"Objection sustained."

I spent the rest of the afternoon listening to the lawyers object.

Olivia slowly lost her smug smile; I think because I was amused and not bothering to hide it. I didn't care if the jury thought I was after her money because even if I was, that wasn't proof I'd done anything at all.

Terry didn't ask me one question about the recording.

On readdress, Wiess asked me, "What did you think would happen to your grandmother's money when she died?"

"That it would go to my father. I didn't know a thing about her will until Everly tried to kill Hannah.

Olivia changed her will—"

"Objection," Terry snapped.

"Sustained."

Wiess said, "What do you know about your grandmother's will?"

I told him what Dwayne had told me and when he'd told me.

The prosecutor entered my prospectus into evidence, and I spent the next day telling the jury how I intended to make my living with the house and how I'd made the films of the renovation and had posted them before Everly had attacked Hannah.

Wiess said, "Is that still your plan?"

"I'm not sure. I can't paint like I used to."

We had to sit through another round of objections before I was allowed to continue.

"I'm relearning it and it isn't a crucial part of my hotel. I can hire the needed art pieces out. I'm just not sure how much I'd enjoy that hotel if I couldn't do it myself. Plus, I don't really need to open the hotel anymore. I've been offered large sums for some of my original art pieces and my online store is doing really well as is my YouTube channel.

"My fiancé and I are discussing if we should pay Grayson back right now or invest in the improvements that we'd thought would need to wait a few years. Our plans for the house have changed a bit. Some of the changes will take more money than I originally budgeted for, but we aren't certain if we want to invest here or not."

Olivia glared daggers. I had to fight not to smile.

Weiss said, "Just to be clear, at any time did your financial plans rely on money from your grandmother?"

"No."

"Thank you. Your witness."

Terry said, "Do your financial plans rely on Olivia now?"

"I guess that depends on how you look at it. There's no denying that I get a lot more traffic to my website now, but since it isn't anything that I can control..."

"So you're admitting that you're using this situation for financial gain?"

"This situation is all Olivia's doing. She could've taken a plea deal and saved everyone—"

"Objection."

Another long round of objections followed.

I was finally allowed to say that my website and You Tube channel had launched on schedule and that I'd followed my plan, which I'd made before any of this happened. I knew he'd twist that in his closing argument to be proof that I'd planned it all.

"Is it true you put in an Olympic size pool, a jacuzzi, a bar, and an outdoor kitchen?" he asked as if it was the worst thing that he could imagine someone doing.

"Yes."

"How did you pay for it?"

"With money."

Two of the jurors laughed.

"We'd like to enter a copy of Kate Avery's latest financial statement."

"Objection. Relevance."

"Sustained."

Terry said, "Would you agree that a large part of your earnings come from your You Tube channel."

"Yes."

"Would you agree that this trial has boosted your viewership numbers?"

"Objection. Calls for speculation."

"Sustained."

"How many days a week do you have friends at your home?"

"Almost never. I can't think of one time."

"Never? Isn't it true that you host parties at your extravagant pool every weekend?"

"My family comes over if that's what you mean."

"Your family... you never have friends over?"

"No."

"You don't consider Crystal Blake a friend?"

"She's family. I like her a lot if that's what you're asking."

"What about Howard Carson?"

"He's Crystal's boyfriend, so he comes over sometimes when she'll be there. I like him but he's more Jace's friend than mine."

"And Dan Boyte? He isn't a friend?"

"He lives there. I don't have him over."

"How about Barry Shae or Jeff Jansen?"

"They're Dan's friends. I don't invite them."

"Objection. Relevance."

Terry said, "I'm trying to show that Kate does invite people, many more people than her family over for parties."

"Objection. She's clearly said that she wasn't the one inviting them over."

The judge said, "I'll allow it but please be clear in your questions."

Terry said, "Do you cook for these weekend parties?"

"I cook when I'm expecting my family to be there. I don't care if they bring friends, which they do often, so I always make extra."

"Please just answer the questions. How often do you see your brother Grayson?"

"It varies."

"Once a week? once a day? Overnight?"

"Objection."

"Sustained."

"Does your brother Grayson visit your house as often as your brother Harley?"

"No."

"Do you visit your brother Grayson's house?"

"He has a condo, not a house. I don't go there much, maybe once a month or so and usually it's just to drop off or pick up the kids."

"Your honor, please instruct the witness to confine her answers to the questions, not to elaborate."

"Objection."

"Sustained. The witness answered the question. Move on."

"Let's talk about the room where Olivia was found."

Jace rolled his eyes at me.

It almost made me laugh.

"Let's," I said cheerfully.

I woke to my blaring alarm and irritably slapped it off.

Jace was already up and dressed for the day, which I knew without seeing him because he'd never leave the room without dressing in this weather.

I got up to get ready, taking extra care with my hair and makeup because I knew the cameras would be on me all damned day.

He brought me eggs and coffee as I was buckling my shoe.

"Nice," he said as he set the food on my bedside table.

"I borrowed it from Kenya. Actually, she insisted I wear it. I had to buy the shoes because hers don't fit me. I'm not sure the suit fits either..."

Her skirt was shorter on me. The blazer was a little loose. I wore my own button-down white shirt so that fit me perfectly.

"You look amazing. Very librarian sexy."

I rolled my eyes at him, which he didn't see because he was in the bathroom throwing the laundry into the dryer.

I ate my breakfast while he puttered around the room, making the bed and pulling out clothes for later.

"This does have its compensations, I suppose," I said as I watched him.

"*Hmm?*"

"It's nice spending all of this time with you."

He grinned at me then grimaced, shaking his head.

"It's going to be so much better when we can spend all of our days doing what *we* want to do. Don't go thinking this is as good as it gets. This is just temporary bullshit. I want our time together to be us talking and building and just laying around watching tv, not listening to her stupid lies."

"Let's get it over with."

I left my dishes In the temporary sink, and we headed to the courthouse. An even bigger mob of reporters than usual had gathered outside.

"This is what happens when you feed the trolls," he muttered as he plowed through them, tugging me along with him.

It took me three days of testimony, most of which I had to sit there on the stand while listening to the defense argue or listen to stupid rebuttal witnesses who had nothing at all relevant to say.

And I knew I'd be recalled when the rest of the recordings were played, which was infuriating. It made me flush just thinking about it, which pissed me off even more because I *knew* that's why she done it—that and hoping it had worked of course.

I really wished I had some way to hurt her back. She had to know she'd be found guilty for Claire at the least and that would put her away from the rest of her life. She wasn't afraid of a death penalty because we all knew she could stall that for years with appeals. No one was going to execute a ninety-year-old woman no matter how much they deserved it. The most I could hope for was that she spent her remaining years hating her life behind bars, but I was afraid she could bribe her way to a cushy cell and special treatment.

The only thing I had to fight her with was a cool demeanor as if I were certain of and happy about the outcome, which years of living with Everly had taught me to project without half trying. I pasted on my bland expression and returned to the witness chair for another long day.

The next day Weiss showed the jury the footage of Olivia arriving at the house. She'd carried Hannah inside, but once inside the doorway she'd dropped her.

Everyone in the courtroom exclaimed.

It was terrifying to watch even though I knew Hannah had mostly recovered.

I thought I'd vomit.

She'd dragged Hannah by her arm down the hall, not caring at all that she was banging into walls and dragging her over the patched floor until the camera lost sight of her when she turned into the dining room.

He showed us pictures of Hannah's shoulders that both had two clear handprints from where she'd grabbed her to dump her into the tub. I hadn't seen those bruises, hadn't known she'd had them hidden under her clothing, hadn't imagined anyone in the world could be so evil.

The judge had to dismiss the jury to give them and the spectators time to stop crying.

My mother collapsed in the hall and the bailiff there called for an ambulance.

Jace and I returned to the courtroom where Weiss spent the rest of the afternoon speaking with experts who showed the jury how those handprints exactly matched Olivia's grip.

Olivia's lips stayed pursed the entire time and the back of her neck remained flushed.

When it was his turn to speak, Terry didn't reshow the video. He said, "The person in the video can't be identified with any certainty. The clothing and hair obscure facial features. There are millions of people the same size as Olivia Avery. If you can't say with certainty that it was her, that is reasonable doubt."

He resumed his seat.

"Redirect?" the judge asked.

"No. I'd like to admit states exhibit thirty-two, which is footage taken from the home of Hannah Avery."

The judge allowed it, and Weiss played the video, saying, "You can clearly see Olivia Avery getting into the car. The time stamp will show that the same car arrives at Briarwood home twenty minutes later, which is confirmed by time stamps. During that time, the car made at stop at the ice cream parlor, which we'll show you in exhibit thirty-nine. Hannah and Felicity testify it was their grandmother in the car."

He showed the relevant recordings and diagrams, then called me to testify about finding Hannah.

Speaking about it made me feel shaky.

Olivia whispered to Terry before he did his recross, and I could tell by his expression that he didn't like whatever she was saying.

He said to me, "You testified that Hannah was unconscious when you found her."

"Yes."

"Yet you didn't try to get her help."

"Objection."

"Sustained."

"Why didn't you leave with her? Take her to your car and bring her to a hospital?"

"I hadn't found Felicity yet."

"Did you think Hannah would die?"

"I hoped she wouldn't."

"Your honor, please direct the witness to answer the question with a simple yes or no."

The judge said to me, "Did you think Hannah would die?"

"I didn't know."

The judge said to Terry, "Proceed with the questioning."

"How much more money did you stand to inherit if Hannah had died."

"Objection."

"Sustained. Counsel, please approach the bench."

The judge whispered angrily for a moment and then Terry said, "No further questions."

FIFTY-ONE

I was careful not to show any relief and left the stand with my head high.

I was dismissed, but warned I was still under caution.

Wiess called Jace to the stand.

The judge dismissed us for the night.

The next morning, Jace's mother, stepfather, grandmother, and a woman I didn't know were in the courtroom when we arrived.

Jace testified to what he'd seen and thought was happening the day he'd been shot. The jury again got to watch the hallway footage.

Terry grinned cockily as he approached for his cross examination.

He faced the jury, not Jace when he said, "Let's go over the timing and your very convenient arrival. Why did you leave the shop only minutes after Kate did? Why not go to the house together?"

"I hadn't intended to go at all. She was supposed to call me when she arrived there. When she didn't call and didn't answer her phone, I was worried that she'd had an accident because of her recent concussion, so I went to check on her."

"And yet you left twelve minutes after her."

"Objection. Asked and answered."

"How long does it normally take her to get to the house?"

"About six minutes."

"So what took you that extra six minutes?"

"I'd asked her to drive slowly. She'd pulled over to call me when the house alarm went off and had only been gone a few minutes, so I knew she had to be almost there."

"And yet you wanted her to call again, even though you knew she was almost there and not experiencing any difficulty driving."

"Yes."

"Why?"

"Because I love her and was worried about her driving."

"Then why let her drive at all? Why not take her yourself?"

"I wish I had."

"But why didn't you?"

"I don't *let* her do anything. She isn't my property. We'd gone driving together on the previous day and spoken about her driving alone. She hadn't had any issues driving, except she hadn't felt confident enough to back into a parking spot. Her head injury impaired her muscle memory. Her hands and feet work fine but her instinctive reactions are off. She can't control big and small movements well—the kind of movements that take practice to master. If she drives slow on a simple road, it isn't a problem. But if something were to startle her while driving, it's possible she'd lose control of the car by overcorrecting. So, I was worried that an animal or something had darted into the road, and she'd had an accident. I honestly didn't analyze why I was worried. I just was, so I went to check on her."

"Leaving your work in the middle of the day after trying to call only three times in three minutes."

"It was five minutes away. But five minutes could make all the difference to her if she'd had an accident. I could go and be back within fifteen minutes. Wouldn't you go to check on someone you loved instead of waiting?"

"Objection."

"Sustained. The jury will disregard that last question. Please just answer the questions, Mr. Blake."

"Why didn't you call the police as soon as you saw Alise's car there?"

"Why would I call?"

"You claim you were worried. That didn't worry you?"

"That her mother was visiting?"

"That her mother who'd just been arrested for assault and then for making a bomb intending to kill Kate was there."

"I'd never believed Alise had made that bomb."

"Objection."

"Overruled. The witness can continue to answer."

"Alise had slapped Kate while in a manic state. Even then she hadn't meant to hurt her. I thought Alise was safe since she was on medication and had been released from both the hospital and police custody. I wasn't worried about her attacking Kate."

"How often do you see your cousin, Lloyd Blake?"

"Never on purpose. I see him around town occasionally."

"Do you meet him at the bar?"

"I see him there, but we don't go to meet."

"But you talk to him when you just happen to run into him?"

"Sometimes."

"Are you friends?"

"No."

"Yet you stop and chat occasionally?"

"We say hello. We aren't friends but we aren't enemies either, and we have relatives in common. If he asks how our grandmother is, or our aunts and uncles, I answer."

"Do you argue with him?"

"Sometimes."

"Objection. Relevance."

Terry said, "I can show relevance, your honor. Lloyd Blake is a known drug dealer and I have witnesses who will testify they saw Lloyd and Jace Blake fighting over Everly Avery and drugs."

"I'll allow it."

"Had you ever purchased drugs from your cousin."

"No."

"Had you ever attended a party with him?"

"I'd attended parties he was at, mostly family or neighborhood parties. We didn't arrive or leave together."

Someone in the audience laughed.

Terry said, "Did you ever date one of his girlfriends?"

"I have no idea. I doubt it though. He's a lot older than me."

"Did you ever date Margo Russell?"

"No."

"Did you ever have sex with her?"

"No."

"Did you ever give her money or drugs?"

"No."

"So why we're you heard arguing with your cousin Lloyd about Everly Avery and Margo Russell?"

"Because I didn't want him anywhere near Kate's family."

"Did you ask him to give you drugs intended for her?"

"I yelled at him to keep away from Everly's house—to keep his scumbag friends away and he said—"

"Stick to the questions."

"Objection."

The lawyers argued for a moment.

Terry said, "Have you ever been arrested for rape?"

"Objection. Prejudicial."

"Sustained. The jury will disregard the question."

"May we approach your honor? The question and answer are pivotal to our case."

"No you may not. My ruling stands."

Terry said, "No further questions."

"Redirect?" the judge asked.

Wiess stood to say, "How soon after you opened the door and saw Felicity did you realize that Alise wasn't there?"

"Immediately. Olivia was right in front of me. I recognized her right away. I realized immediately that her black wig was meant to be a disguise."

"What did you think was going on?"

"I thought she intended to burn the house down. I wasn't sure what was wrong with Felicity. I didn't know if she was alive or dead or why she was lying there, but I was certain Olivia's intent was arson because she was trying to light a pile of rags when I opened the door. I didn't notice Kate until she yelled for me to run."

"But you never thought it was Alise you were facing?"

"No. Never. It was clearly Olivia."

"The night you argued with Lloyd at the bar and mentioned Everly, can you recall exactly what you said?"

"I said, if you have to give that skank and her friend Everly drugs, do it away from the fucking kids!"

"So you knew he was supplying her drugs?"

"No. I assumed it because I saw Lloyd and Margo exchanging money right before—"

"Objection."

"Overruled. I think we can hear what this witness thought as long as the jury keeps in mind that this is only Mr. Blake's opinion. It hasn't been proven what the other people were doing. You may continue."

"I saw Lloyd talking to Margo. She was at the Avery's enough that I knew who she was. She went right to Lloyd's table. I got up to follow her meaning to tell her to get out because I knew she wasn't old enough to be there. I was just feet away when she handed him a wad of bills."

"Did she say anything?"

"Objection, hearsay."

"Overruled. You'll have your chance to call your witnesses to dispute his account. Continue."

"She said something like I'll see you later. Lloyd saw me standing there and waved her away."

"Did he say anything to her?"

"No. Martin Jensen, one of the men with him followed her out. I yelled at Lloyd and left myself."

"Why did you say, do it away from the kids?"

"Because Margo went to the Avery's every night Kate's parents would be out, which I knew they planned to be that night. I didn't want Lloyd or his friends dropping by, and not just because of the drugs, but because they were much too old to be hanging around those girls."

"Were Margo or Marty in the parking lot when you left?"

"He was leaning in her car window. I couldn't hear them or see what they were doing. I left."

"Thank you. No further questions."

"Recross?"

Terry said, "Did you go to the Avery's that night?"

"I picked Kate up at the top of the street around one and dropped her off at three."

"So she snuck out to see you?"

"Yes."

"How often did she sneak out to see you?"

"Almost every day."

"So she lied to her parents every day?"

"Objection."

"Sustained."

"Let me rephrase. Do you think she was lying to her parents to sneak out and see you?"

"No."

"No?"

"No."

"Then why do you call it sneaking?"

"She wasn't sneaking from her parents. She was sneaking away so as not to wake the twins."

"So your testimony is that her parents knew and approved of her leaving at one in the morning with you?"

"No."

"Did they know?"

"I have no idea."

"Did they approve of you?"

"How do you mean?"

"Did her parents like you?"

"I assume so. Mr. Avery was always nice. I'd never spoken to Mrs. Avery."

"You'd never spoken to your fiancés mother?"

"Kate wasn't my fiancé then."

"Were you hiding your relationship?"

"Yes."

"No further questions."

"Recross?" the judge asked.

Wiess said, "Why were you hiding your relationship?"

"We planned to tell her parents about us when she moved out at the end of August. It was my idea to wait because I didn't want to get fired. She agreed even though she didn't think her dad would fire me. But just in case he did, she didn't want to fight with him about it in front of the kids. We thought if there was going to a scene, it'd be easier on everyone if she didn't have to stay home and listen to it, not a scene from her parents, from her sister Everly."

"Did Kate tell you her sister Everly would cause a scene?"

"Objection. Leading."

"What did Kate say would happen if you were fired?"

"She didn't think I would be fired. We never really talked about that. She thought Everly would tease her about dating me and she didn't want to have to listen to her. She avoided confrontations with Everly whenever she could."

"Did Everly find out about the two of you?"

"I'm not sure. I think so, but maybe she just thought Kate was flirting with me or I was flirting with her. She showed up at the shop when Kate was there to make fun of her, saying her crush on me was pathetic. When that didn't get a reaction from Kate, Everly began making fun of me. Everly showed up a few times when Kate wasn't there and tried to seduce me."

Someone in the audience sniggered.

Wiess said, "Seduce you how?"

"She offered sex."

Hearing him say it made me furious for him—he had to be embarrassed to say it in front of everyone, especially his mother.

Wiess said, "Can you recall her exact words?"

"She said we could use the bed in the loft, and no one would ever know, not even Kate if I wanted to keep screwing her too. She called me some names and threatened to get me fired when I turned her down. The second time she went up to the loft and began undressing without even talking to me, so I left."

"So you and Kate decided to keep your relationship private?"

"Yes. Kate told me Everly had driven every friend she'd had away by teasing them or spreading lies about them. Everly would get her friends to pick on anyone being nice to Kate, and Kate didn't want her to do that to me. She didn't want Everly to try to get me fired. We both agreed it was smarter for us to wait and see if our relationship became serious before telling anyone."

"What had Kate told you about where she said was going at night?"

"She told me her parents hadn't asked, that she didn't have a curfew, and they didn't care where she went."

"And you believed that?"

"I believed that they hadn't asked her. I'd seen Everly coming and going very late all the time for years. I didn't think they'd really not care. I thought if they noticed her gone that they'd be worried and angry at both of us. Kate told me that if they asked, she'd tell them the truth."

"Did they ever ask her?"

"Not to my knowledge."

"Thank you. That will be all for now."

Wiess waited for Jace to leave the stand to say, "Permission to recall Kate Avery?"

When I'd been sworn in again and taken the witness chair, Wiess said, "Did either of your parents ever ask you where you were going?"

"Sometimes."

"Did you ever say you were going to meet Jace Blake?"

"I never was when they asked."

"No further questions."

"Recross?" the judge asked.

"Not at this time."

The judge said to Wiess, "Are you ready to call your next witness?"

"We call Lloyd Blake to the stand."

"Then we'll break for the evening and hear from Lloyd Blake in the morning."

486

Jace's stepfather, Frank, was waiting with our car to bring us home.

Jace said, "Thanks."

Frank said, "It's a relief to not have to listen to all those quacks try to say the recordings were all fake again. I think you can expect bigger crowds now that the recordings are all admitted, and the pace has picked up."

I exchanged a worried glance with Jace.

He said, "How's mom?"

"Angry on your behalf."

"And Aunt Laurie?"

"Honestly, I'm not sure if she was more embarrassed or angry."

"The other lady was your aunt?" I asked.

"By marriage. She's Lloyd's mother and divorced his father, my uncle Stan, years ago. She's a nice lady—way too good for Stan."

"I think you're off her Christmas list now, kiddo," Frank said.

Jace laughed harshly. "She's always been in denial that Lloyd is just like his old man. He's destined to spend his life in prison too."

"Lloyd is smarter than you think. He got himself a plea deal, but you didn't hear that from me."

I said, "There's more recordings. Awful ones Olivia had made that star a naked couple calling each other Kate and Jace screwing and planning to murder my family."

"What!"

Jace said, "We're hoping the DA doesn't need to enter it but maybe you better warn Mom."

"Are they believable?"

Jace said bitterly, "You mean will the jury buy it? I doubt it, but who the hell knows. Terry's bound to bring up my narrow escape from that rape charge again. The people in the recording aren't us. There's some evidence of that but it's weak."

I said, "No it isn't. The man didn't have your scar."

Jace shrugged. "People will believe what they want to believe. If Terry can convince them I'm a sexual predator with a cop in my pocket..."

"It isn't going to happen!"

He kissed my hand.

Frank looked worried.

We were all worried.

Margo was sure to lie, and God knew what Lloyd would say—not that anything he said would matter if he didn't have proof, but even if the jury saw the recordings for the lie they were, there'd be people out there who'd want to believe it. Our reputations would be tarnished forever—and there wasn't anything I could do about it.

Or was there... They weren't wrong, I did have the skill to fake footage.

FIFTY-TWO

"What are you doing?" Jace asked.

I jumped, grabbing for my beating heart.

"Sorry. I didn't mean to startle you," he said.

My pulse settled but I knew I was flushed from guilty nerves as I flicked the program closed, forcing a smile as I turned to face him.

"I thought you were sleeping," I said.

"What's going on, Kate?"

"Just catching up on work."

"Kate... that wasn't work. Did Weiss or Dee tell you there were more pictures of you there or something?"

He reached past me to grab my mouse.

"Let's just go to bed," I said.

He withdrew his hand but looked really upset.

I could feel the strain on my own face.

I didn't want to lie to him or involve him.

"How bad is it?" he asked.

"As bad as I can make it," I said angrily. "This has nothing to do with those stupid pictures Everly took of me. I'm going to make her pay, Jace. She isn't wrong, I could make her look bad if I try."

"Sweetheart..."

"She deserves it!"

"She does but we shouldn't do anything that could mess up whatever Weiss is planning."

"I'm not going to let her get away with it!"

"Me neither. I swear I'll do whatever it takes to protect us, but she isn't going to get away with it. No one could possibly believe her pack of lies!"

"You see how they look us."

"They might not like us but that doesn't mean they believe her either."

"I should've waited to post my shows..."

"Don't be silly. It doesn't matter if some of the jurors think you're making money off of this. We *are* making money off of it, but we're also spending way more than we'd have had to on security. None of this was our fault."

"You see what they're saying online."

"Most of the comments are in our favor."

"Most..."

"We both know there'll always be trolls online. It doesn't mean the jury will feel the same way. Even if they think you're happy to be making money that doesn't mean that Olivia isn't guilty. You're not on trial, Kate."

"She doesn't care about the damned trial! She's using it to hurt us!"

"I know, but now isn't the time to hurt her back. Trust me sweetheart. You can post all the pictures and whatever else you want the minute she's found guilty—which she will be."

"Lloyd and Margo—"

"Then let's compromise at least. If after we hear what they have to say we think she's going to skate, we'll do whatever we need to."

"I need time to do this."

"What are you doing?"

"We know Everly was involved with sex trafficking. The jury would never find Olivia innocent if they thought she was behind that or even involved."

"Kate..."

"I can put Olivia in a picture with a naked kid."

"Are you crazy! What if the police find that sort of picture on your computer!"

"I didn't mean kid kid. I meant one of the school kids. The police gave me the pictures, so it won't matter if they find them on my computer. Not that they will. I know how to destroy a file completely. I'll take one of the pictures and crop it so you can't see the man's face and put her in it."

"How the hell... unless she's naked, it isn't going to work."

I turned my screen back on.

I'd already made a picture of Olivia apparently kneeling in front of man with him ejaculating on her face.

"Good lord!"

I snickered as I said, "Kenya took that picture three years ago at the lake. Olivia was so pissed that she'd fallen and even angrier that Kenya had gotten pictures of it."

"She'll know where it's from."

"So. How could she prove it? But I doubt she'll know. This is the original."

I flicked to a picture of my grandmother kneeling at the edge of the water. She'd been wearing a sarong over a bikini that had gotten tangled around her leg, leaving her other leg bare to the hip.

Her hat had fallen off, leaving her hair in disarray. The furious grimace on her face could be mistaken for passion and the water droplets for semen.

In the picture I'd made, I'd airbrushed her bikini top out, replacing it with the saggiest pair of boobs I could find and positioned the naked man blocking half her body so that her naked leg was visible. I'd replaced the shore with a blanket, using a similar striped one that had been in one of the photographs the police had given me and changed the background to a plain beige wall.

I said, "I can use the picture of her sitting on the beach to make another one. She's naked there from the shoulders up and I can use this picture of the man leaning over to block her dress out. I think as long as I don't mess with her face, people will really believe it's her."

"Would this fool an expert?"

"I doubt it. But no one believes her experts."

"Weiss would know it was a lie."

"I was planning to take some of the pictures of her and add in some small clues like maybe one of those pill bottles Margo always used or even putting Lloyd in the background or some dirty magazines with the other ones."

"I don't know, Kate. She'd know you did it and maybe she can make them get a warrant to search your computer."

"They wouldn't be able to prove I did it. I'll get rid of the pictures and my files as soon as the image is finished. I can put it on a flash drive and use a public computer to upload it to the web."

"Where?"

"I was thinking Lloyd's site or any of the forums that are talking about this trial. Or maybe I just break into Margo's and leave it there or maybe both..."

"I hate this idea. There's too much chance that it leads to you."

"I hate the idea that she thinks she can do whatever she wants to us!"

"Kate, she must be miserable in there. She has to be!"

"It isn't enough!"

He searched my face a moment before saying decisively, "One picture a night and you give me the flash drive. Make sure you destroy any files that could link the pictures to you."

"One a night," I agreed.

"I'll see if I can get some pictures for you to use. Mike has a buddy with a huge porn collection. I can borrow some without him noticing it's missing."

"Do I want to know how you know that?"

He snorted in exasperation. "Everyone knows it. He brags about it all the time. He literally has six-foot high stacks of magazines and DVDs in his garage. There's boxes of shit in there. He's got an old Camaro too. No one would think it weird if we go see it."

"The younger, the better. No little kids or anything but young."

He grimaced at me.

I said, "I'm not using any of the pictures I have of the kids."

"You should give those files back to the police."

"I will."

"Please be really careful not to leave any proof that you did it."

"I will be."

I set back to work with a lighter heart.

Jace watched over my shoulder as I adjusted the shadows, making tiny corrections for the next hour and then spending thirty minutes to be sure I'd erased the metadata and all my files.

I handed him the flash drive when I was done.

"You're sure they can't link the file to you at all?" he asked.

"Yes. My plan was to upload it at the library or school then put it through one of the digital imaging programs there so it would have that metadata on it."

"I have no idea what that means."

"Hide it for now. When it comes time to use it, I'll do it. You never had a thing to do with this, Jace."

"We won't need to use it," he said. "Get some sleep. I'll take care of this."

He kissed me hard then hurried out.

I went to shower.

I was going to use it. I was going to use anything I had to hurt her.

FIFTY-THREE

Margo was in the courtroom when we arrived the next day.

Jace said, "Six months for arson—that's a hell of a deal."

"Maybe they just let her out because she's going to testify?"

He shrugged.

She barely glanced at us too busy glaring at the back of Olivia's head, which I thought might be a good sign.

Lloyd took the stand wearing an over-sized white t-shirt, baggy jeans, sneakers, and wearing a thick gold chain that might as well have had the word pimp on it. He looked like a meaner, colder, older version of Jace. He had a tattoo of a thorny rose on his neck that ended behind his ear and wound down his right arm ending in a broken heart on the inside of his wrist. His other arm had a tattoo of a crown encircling it.

So he wasn't the man in the video.

"The prosecutor said, "Mr. Blake, can I call you Lloyd? I think it would be less confusing for the jury."

"Whatever, man."

"Can you please tell the court how you knew Everly Avery."

"She worked for me."

"You bastard!" Margo yelled.

"Bailiff," the judge said unnecessarily.

The bailiff was already heading to the back where Everly's friends sat.

Lloyd laughed and blew her a kiss.

"You're such a fucking liar!" Margo yelled.

Two of her friends were trying to shut her up. The rest of them left.

She continued to yell that Lloyd was a liar even when two police officers entered to drag her out.

When the room was quiet again and the judge had stopped speaking to the jury, Wiess said to Lloyd, "You were saying?"

"Everly worked for me as an extra in our latest movie."

"As an actress?"

"Yeah. And a fluffer."

My mother moaned.

The judge cleared his throat.

Olivia glanced at us. She looked angry until her gaze landed on my mother and then her frown turned into a smirk.

I'd never wanted to hit someone so badly in my life.

Wiess said, "Tell us about this movie."

"Objection. Relevance."

"Sustained."

"Did you know Everly personally?"

"Did I fuck her you mean? Yeah. We all had a go."

The judge said, "I'm going to remind you to speak respectfully."

Lloyd shrugged.

Wiess said, "Where you aware she was underage?"

"*Nah*. She was seventeen. Which was why she was just an extra. She didn't have sex for the movie or nothing. She didn't want to. Her friend Margo was the star."

"How much did Everly make at this job?"

"She was working on spec. She'd get a percent of the sales."

Wiess said, "We'd like to enter her contract with Hard High into the record."

"When the contract had been entered and passed to the jury, Wiess said, "Did Everly receive any other forms of compensation?"

"I gave all my girls ecstasy and a little blow when they showed up for work. They could earn more by fluffing or cleaning and shit. She liked to fluff for Margo."

"When you say fluffing, can you tell the court what that is?"

"Objection. Relevance."

"Overruled, but keep the answer respectful."

Lloyd rolled his eyes but said respectfully enough, "A fluffer gets a man ready to have sex."

Wiess said, "In your opinion, did Everly have a drug habit."

"Absolutely."

"Did her friend Margo supply her with drugs?"

"I've seen them do lines together of Margo's coke, but I don't know if Everly paid for it or if it was just a friendly gesture."

"Had you ever been to Everly's house?"

"Yeah. She invited me and my crew to parties there. We'd been talking about filming a few scenes there."

"Objection. Hearsay."

"Overruled. You may continue."

Lloyd shrugged.

Wiess said, "Who else was at these parties?"

"Kids from her school and shit. We never hung around long. It was boring as fuck—sorry, your honor. It was boring 'cause she always had to be quiet 'cause of the kids in the house."

"Tell us about the party you went to there following the argument you'd had with your cousin."

"We never went again after that argument. We knew it was playing with fire. Everly's old man could cause us real problems. It wasn't worth the hassle. Everly was pissed—really pissed. She brought a chainsaw to the set and asked Marty to cut down the tree with the kids' treehouse in it—while they were sleeping. That shit was sick, and we told her so!"

"Objection. Hearsay!"

Lloyd sniggered, saying, "You don't got to take my word for it. We got that shit on tape."

Terry said, "Objection. We were never shown or told of this recording."

Wiess said, "We're just hearing about it ourselves."

The judge said, "The recording is to be surrendered to the court by the end of the day. My ruling on whether it's admissible or not will follow. Continue."

Wiess said, "During that conversation, did Everly say she wanted the kids to be hurt or killed when the tree fell?"

"She said she hoped they'd die."

"Did she say why?"

"She asked me to whack her sister. I told her I didn't do that sort of shit and she offered me a million bucks. Said I could keep all her sisters. That I should make a snuff film. I thought she was just talking trash. She was high as shit. I asked her where she'd get a million bucks. She never had any money, which was why she'd fluff for her fix. She told us her grandmother had promised to make her the sole heir if she'd kill her sisters."

"Objection!"

"Overruled. Continue."

"That's all there was. She asked and we said no. Marty told her something like she was a sick bitch 'cause they were just kids and shit and there was no way she'd ever pay up. So she said she'd do the kids herself. She wanted help with her older sisters. She was really into the idea of a snuff film.

"She started talking about how she could kill her father and get his dough too. She said something about how she could make it look like her mom had done it and she'd be left to care for the boys. She'd get the insurance, the house, all of it. But like I said, we all thought it was all just bullshit."

"Did she ever mention it again after you'd turned her down?"

"Not to me. I overheard her saying to Marty they'd need to take out the old lady too. I asked Marty about it later because if he was going to do that shit, I'd kick him off the crew. And he said it was all just her thing. It got her hot to talk about it. He didn't think she really meant it either. I warned him we didn't want any of that sort of bullshit. Everly was stupid and she had a big mouth."

He snickered like he didn't mean she talked a lot.

"She never knew when to shut up, but she was hot as shit..."

"When you'd heard she'd hurt her sister, did you do anything?"

"Yeah. We fired her. Sent a certified letter and everything. We didn't need her kind of trouble."

"You didn't think you should report her to the police?"

"No. I didn't think I'd needed to since she'd been caught doing it. Besides they'd never fucking believe me. Her family is too rich. I was more likely to be arrested for giving her drugs or encouraging her or some shit."

"But you had the recording..."

"I didn't know we had it until a few days ago. We finished filming the sequel and we're doing the edits, adding in some footage we'd taken for the first film."

"Why didn't you tell me about it right away?"

Lloyd looked at Jace as he said, "I wasn't sure I wanted too. That shit is prejudicial as hell against us. But then I reconsidered 'cause the terms of our deal say if I don't fully disclose everything I know than my deal is void."

"Your witness," he said to Terry.

Terry said, "Tell us about the deal you made with the DA."

Lloyd shrugged. "What's to tell? It's the standard shit. I tell what I know, and I get time off for my crimes."

"How much time off?"

"I get three years' probation for the drugs."

"You mentioned you gave Everly ecstasy and coke but what about fentanyl?"

"We did heroin occasionally, but Margo gave us that shit. We don't use much neither. That shit is for the girls, not us. We smoke a bit of weed and drink, but we keep our partying to a minimum."

"Did you ever go see Everly at the hospital?"

"No."

"Did Margo?"

He shrugged.

The judge said, "Speak up for the record."

"I don't know."

Terry returned to his seat.

The judge said, "Would you like to redirect?"

Wiess said, "How would you say the relationship between Margo and Everly was?"

"They were real tight."

"Were they lovers?"

"Maybe. I've seen them hug and kiss, but I never saw them have sex with each other even though I've seen them have sex in the same room and with the same man. They shared men a lot."

"Did Everly have female lovers?"

"No. I'd only ever seen her kiss Margo."

"Did Margo have female lovers?"

"She fu—had sex with women for the movie. I have no idea if she was really bi or not."

"To your knowledge, did Margo ever visit Olivia?"

"Yes."

"Objection. Hearsay."

Lloyd shrugged, saying, "There's pictures on her phone and webpage of the three of them."

"Did Everly talk about her grandmother?"

"She bragged a lot about how Olivia bought them everything."

"Who is them?"

"Her and Margo. Margo didn't like the old lady though."

"Objection. Hearsay."

"What made you think Margo didn't like her?"

"The names she called her. The things she said."

"Can you give us an example?"

"Objection. Relevance."

"It's very relevant as it shows the relationship between Margo and Olivia."

"Overruled. You may continue."

"She and Everly called her the chump frump."

Olivia leaned over to whisper to her lawyer. I couldn't make out the words, but the tone was angry and her face red.

Terry stood, saying, "Objection. He can't know to who that nickname was referring. It was unlikely Olivia since by all testimony so far Everly admired her."

Lloyd leaned forward into the mic.

"Everly didn't admire her. She said all the time that her grandmother was stupid."

"Objection!"

The judge said, "Please only answer the questions asked of you."

Weiss said, "What did Everly call her grandmother when she told you that she'd pay you to murder her sisters?"

"She said, my grandmother, the chump frump, is leaving me everything. Is all I've got to do is get rid of my stupid sisters."

"Did she ever tell you why she thought Olivia wanted them dead?"

"Objection! Hearsay,"

The judge said, "I'll allow it with the reminder to the jury that this is testimony of conversation between Everly and Olivia as Lloyd recalls it, so it can't be construed to what Olivia had actually said only what Everly had interpreted it as."

Lloyd said, "Everly said that the chump frump hated looking so frumpy. She said that gargoyle, which was another nickname she used for her grandmother, was pissed that her son was wasting money on all the stupid charities that her mother was involved in. Everly was pissed about it too, but she was angrier over all the time and money her parents spent on her sister's special diet. I'd heard Olivia and Everly both complaining about that."

"Let's talk about that a second. Tell us the occasion and what was said."

"Olivia was dropping Everly and Margo off at the set. They'd brought dinner for everyone, and me and two of the guys came out to help them bring it in. Everly thanked her, and Olivia said it was a pleasure buying food fit for decent people. Then Margo said something like, and it's cheaper than that soy shit you buy for your grandbitches. Olivia said, believe me, I won't be buying it much longer and Everly laughed and said defective runts should be put down."

"And what did Olivia say to that?"

"Nothing. She opened the trunk and handed Everly the chainsaw. Then she laughed and got back into her car. She said something like you my darling are the only beautiful thing Alise has ever done. And that was the day Everly first asked us to whack them."

Olivia had a tight grasp of her lawyer's arm and was glaring as angrily as I'd ever seen her.

Wiess said, "To your knowledge, did Margo go see Olivia after Everly was hospitalized?"

"I have no idea. We were done filming and the sequel was put on hold for a while because of all of this."

"Why?"

"Most of the actors were friends of Everly and most of them were doing it on the down low. No one uses their real names or anything and we avoid face shots of the guys, but we were waiting to see how all this played out."

"Have you released this movie?"

"You bet your ass! It's getting thousands of views. I think it's mostly the kids from her school but I'm betting it'll be getting millions of views now."

Someone on the jury or maybe the audience huffed a quick laugh and a few others gasped.

"Do something," Olivia said angrily.

Her lawyers shushed her.

The judge said, "I think this is a good time to break for the evening. We'll reconvene tomorrow."

Jace and I waited for the courtroom to clear before trying to leave. I was hoping to avoid my parents who were both glowering as if it was my fault that Everly had been such a ho.

My father pushed through the crowd to reach us. He waited for the room to mostly clear to say, "Did you know that's what she was doing?"

"No."

"You didn't suspect?"

"No—why would I? I knew she had a lot of boyfriends and a reputation as being easy, but I never even heard rumors of porn movies. But I didn't hang out with her crowd or any crowd. I had no real friends."

Jace said angrily, "This isn't Kate's fault."

"I'm not happy with you either... sneaking out at one... you had up to know we'd never have allowed that!"

Jace said, "We weren't happy about it either, but Everly was being a bitch when she didn't even really know about us. God knows what she'd have done if she knew we were in love. Kate didn't want to deal with it and neither did I! And we couldn't meet earlier because she couldn't leave the kids! Your kids! Believe me, I'd have rather gone for dinner like a normal person and gotten more than a few hours of sleep a night!"

"I handled it all badly," I said.

My father heaved a heavy sigh.

"We all did... I heard her come in late more than once..."

"It's my fault," my mother said tightly. "I was afraid to say anything..." She began to cry, burying her face in her hands. "It's all my fault."

Jace said, "We shouldn't be talking about any of this. We all made mistakes, Alise. Kate and I don't hold any of yours against you."

"We don't, Mom. God knows I made enough of my own..."

FIFTY--FOUR

The ride home was silent. I think we were both shocked. Our cats greeted us as if we'd been gone years. It was cold in the house, which made me feel bad for them. A shiver I'd been fighting since Lloyd had mentioned snuff films overtook me.

Jace went to feed them a snack, saying, "I'm starving."

"Nothing for me, thanks. I'm going to go to bed early."

"Are you sick?"

"No. Just tired. It was a shock, which is stupid, right?"

"*Had* you heard rumors?"

"No. It doesn't surprise me, but it's still a shock. I never imagined there was stuff like that going on around here."

"Stuff like that happens everywhere, I guess. I was surprised too. Lloyd always had a few strung-out chicks hanging off him. I suspected he was pimping them out. I didn't think he'd be able to talk Everly into it though seeing as she had her own sources of money. I'm shocked he got her as involved as he did. I'd have thought she'd be afraid of your dad finding out. He'd have kicked her out for sure."

"Would he if she knew about his affair?"

"You think she did?"

"Probably. It would explain why he never said anything to her."

"You never asked?"

"No. I'm not sure if I'd believe him if he denied it. My mom feels terrible about letting her get so out of control. But he was her parent too and equally responsible. I'm sure they were both thinking it didn't matter if they did nothing because the other one would."

"Then they probably suspected that Everly had something on them both. But I also bet that he never thought for a minute she was getting into shit like that. They probably hoped she'd finish school and go to college and outgrow all of that."

I shrugged and headed for the bathroom where I took a quick shower and then went right to bed.

Jace brought me tea, and the cats, saying worriedly, "How about a cup of soup, Kate?"

"I'm not hungry."

"Sweetheart..."

"I'm just tired. You don't need to stay in. God knows you deserve a night off."

"You aren't a job," he said in exasperation.

"I just meant we don't need to work on the house every minute. I can make something if I get hungry."

"Kate... I don't want to leave you like this."

"I just need some sleep."

He kissed my brow, stroking my hair. I could feel his indecision.

I wished he'd just go so I could cry without worrying him.

Both cats seemed to sense my distress too. They both were trying to cuddle on me, purring loudly.

I hugged Boo. Igor began kneading my shoulder.

Jace forced a laugh as he said, "I'll leave you to enjoy your cat massage. Get some sleep, sweetheart, and feel better. I won't be long."

"Take as long as you like."

He kissed my brow again and left.

I cried myself to sleep.

The low buzz of the door opening on my phone app woke me. He was trying to be quiet because it was so late. He took a shower before sliding into bed.

I turned to hug him.

He smelled of whisky despite his shower. I was worried he'd driven home drunk but wasn't up to arguing about it.

We fell asleep without speaking.

The next morning while I was dressing, he said, "I had to call for an Uber home. Don't call for one, sweetheart, or if you do, give them an address on the next street. The dude who picked me up was seriously annoying."

"I'm glad you didn't try to drive home."

He grimaced at me.

"It was stupid... I meant to just grab a drink and see if any of the guys were around. A bunch of kids from my school were there and all of them bought me a shot or two. We were watching the game and talking cars and time just got away from me."

"You should get out more or have them over. Maybe we should work on the theater room next?"

"It can be our rainy-day project once we get that second bedroom done. I've got a few contractors stopping by over the next week. We're putting in the heat and air. And before you argue we can't afford it. I can afford it. My savings will more than cover it."

"I wasn't going to argue, and we don't need to use your savings. We can use the money from the shows. It's what's it's for."

"I know, but I don't want to wait."

"We won't have to."

I handed him my laptop, leaning over his shoulder to sign into my accounts.

"Holy shit! That can't be right!"

"We're up to ten million views per show."

"Good grief!"

"I *was* thrilled but Lloyd's right. He's going to get millions of views too."

"She wasn't in the movie."

"My pictures are somewhere..."

"Son of a bitch!"

"I don't want to go surfing his site, but I think I should."

"Fuck no!"

"I don't want you to do it!"

He laughed an annoyed laugh.

I said, "The police must've looked. Especially since he admits he used high school kids. Which, man is that stupid. I'm sure they wouldn't give him a pass on using minors in porn...would they?"

He said, "I don't see how they could. But they have to know he's grooming those kids with drugs, and they gave him a pass for that—although he's probably smart enough not to be the guy giving the drugs to the minors. It makes me so fucking mad! He should be in jail!"

"Do you think he'd agreed to murder Kenya and me?"

"No. He's an ass, but not, I don't think, a murderer. His friends on the other hand... I have no idea what those assholes would do..."

We headed out to the car where he said thoughtfully, "But I don't think they'd have done it either because they knew Everly had asked too many people. Someone was bound to talk. Maybe one of them decided to shut her up?"

"How could they? None of them had access to her."

"Margo... or maybe another patient and got them to pass it on?"

"Except they know it was Mrs. Hilfiger's medication."

"True..."

I said, "But the defense is going to say that very thing..."

"Wiess will remind the jury just like you reminded me that there can be no doubt the drug used was the exact same thing as the missing drugs stolen from Maureen and that's a rare prescription formula with a distinct chemical makeup. It isn't something the average drug dealer is going to have."

"I wonder if Olivia suspected Everly was thinking of killing Dad and Grayson too and that's why she killed her?"

"He didn't mention Grayson."

I said, "She'd have had to kill him because he'd have gotten custody of the boys. She'd have only gotten a fourth of Olivia's estate and maybe none of our dad's because I'm sure that would be used on the boys, wouldn't it? She was going to steal it from them. Grayson would've put any insurance money in a trust for them. He'd have used it on their housing and education like our parents intended."

He said, "Good lord, imagine what she'd have done to those boys if she got custody of them...Those pictures she took of them are going to give me nightmares now..."

Contemplating that she'd have put my little brothers in porn films made me feel sick.

He said, "She probably would've murdered Olivia too once all of you were dead. But there's no way she'd have gotten away with it all. She wasn't smart enough, and like you said, too many people knew it was her plan. Someone would've said something. At the least, they'd have blackmailed her. She wouldn't have profited from it."

"Which makes me think she couldn't have really meant it. She couldn't! She wasn't stupid. Not really. She was a fool and made bad choices. The drugs messed her up and she was mentally ill, but not dumb. She *had* to know she'd be caught. I think she was just running her mouth, talking like an idiot to fit in with them. She was on drugs when she hurt Hannah. She *must* have regretted it..."

"Jesus, Kate... I've become so used to thinking Olivia wanted you dead that the horror of that doesn't horrify me anymore..."

He pulled to side of the road where he parked to bury his face in his hands, taking hard breaths for a moment while I patted his back.

"I'm an insensitive ass," he finally mumbled.

His eyes were shiny with tears when he turned to hug me.

"You must've been terrified. God! I'm terrified! They have no reason to hurt you now though, Kate."

He released me a second later to pull back onto the road.

"That bastard. That goddamned fucking bastard!"

He punched the dashboard and continued to mutter until we arrived.

He plowed past the reporters on the stairs to ask the policeman at the door if Lloyd had checked in yet.

"Haven't seen him," the man said.

Jace released my hand, nudging me forward.

"Go ahead. I want to talk to that fucker!"

He ran back outside. I went to follow him and the police officer, a man I recognized as one of Frank's friends but couldn't recall his name, grabbed my arm, shaking his head. "You don't need to be involved in this, Miss. Go on up. I'll take care of it."

He called for backup on his radio as he headed out the door. The other officer who was manning the metal detector said, "What's going on?

"Nothing."

The reporters had begun to yell Jace's name.

I peered through the window of the door to see the first officer was speaking with Jace. They both returned inside. The officer followed us through the metal detector, saying, "You have to keep it together, man. You start causing trouble and it'll be you in the slammer. Maybe you should go home? take a day off."

I said, "We can go home, Jace."

He stomped to the elevator.

"I want to see what that fucker has to say!"

I heaved an exasperated sigh, throwing my hands in the air, saying, "What do you think he's gonna say? He's never going to admit it! Besides, like you said, he probably wasn't even going to do it to begin with."

"Still! he could have said something! What kind of asshole hears somebody spouting that shit and doesn't warn the victims? If Hannah had died, he should be held accountable for that! She could have died, Kate! You could have died! Your whole fucking family might have been murdered by that whore and he knew it!"

The officer grabbed Jace's arm and pulled him into an empty conference room right beside the elevator.

"You're pissed. Hell, anyone would be. But you can't go in there like this. The judge would have to kick you out. And if you yell at his stupid ass or threaten him or anything, you could cause a mistrial. Stay away from him! Don't go looking for him. You've just got to suck it up until it's over."

He shook his arm hard before releasing him. "You're the one who's going to end up in jail if you do anything. I probably shouldn't say anything, but seeing as your Frank's kid, your cousin Lloyd is turning states evidence on a few big cases. The DA isn't going to tolerate anyone fucking with him."

"Me fucking with him! You have to be fucking kidding me! He admitted he knew there was a plot to murder her and not just murder her! If Everly hadn't been as high as shit—if she'd have managed to murder Hannah... God! I can't even think about it! And she took pictures of Kate that are probably on that scumbags website right now!"

"They aren't... the DA didn't talk to you about this?"

"About what."

"I probably shouldn't say anything then..."

"Like fucking hell!"

The officer winced. "Wait here a minute. And that's an order! Do not leave this room!"

He thumped Jace on the chest with his finger then left.

I wasn't sure what to do or say.

Jace stomped around the room.

I finally said, "Thanks."

"Ha! For what!"

"For this. I never know how to express my anger. It pisses me off too..."

"Kate," he said as if he was going to burst into tears—as if my name was painful to say.

He returned to hug me, and we remained in an embrace until the DA and his hoard of minions entered a few minutes later.

Wiess said, "I was planning to speak with you when you arrived. We have a two-hour delay while the defense confers."

"Confers about what?"

"The plea deal we offered, which is the same one we originally offered. The recording Lloyd had was very damning. I'm certain we can win this, but I'd prefer to skip right to the end and not just to save everyone's time but because we can't move on the rest of the information we have until this trial is over because it's going to seriously affect this entire city, which is sure to affect the jury. Plus, none of us want to see a little old lady, even such an evil one, face the chair. It would be better for everyone if she'll take the damned deal."

I said, "She isn't going to. Not when she wants to see us suffer."

"She might because if we release those recordings in court, it's going to make her look very bad."

Jace said, "And he just gets to walk even when he knew she planned to murder her sisters?"

"Yes. It isn't fair but prosecuting him for that wouldn't do nearly the good that we can do with the information that he's traded for his freedom. If it's any consolation, he knows that he can't afford to screw up again because life in prison for him will be a death sentence. He's going to need to keep a low profile for the rest of his life."

"Witness protection?"

"Yes."

"That's such bullshit! What about his stupid movie that he said he released?"

Wiess winced.

"We couldn't stop the release. He hadn't broken any laws making that movie."

"Like hell he didn't! She wasn't old enough to sign a contract!"

"She wasn't in the movie, except in the background, which was filmed in a public place. Your parents could sue him to get her taken out. I'm not sure they could win or that it would matter if they did because there's certain to be bootleg copies of it. Which brings me to Kate. He did have pictures and video of you, but he hadn't used any in the movie. We took them all down, but it's possible that his clients had made illegal copies. He didn't have many visitors until recently and your pictures were off the site by then. That site is still closed for the pending investigation because you weren't the only victim. It seems there was quite a side business in your high school with that group of kids taking pictures of their friends and siblings without their knowledge."

"And he gets to walk!" Jace yelled.

"He's giving us some very dangerous men in return. What he was doing was heinous but these men... believe me, it's better this way. As we speak, over a hundred warrants are being served across the US and we expect to serve hundreds more. We'll clean up an entire pedophile ring that reaches around the globe. He wasn't lying when he said he had no intention of producing snuff films, but he *had* been contacted. Honestly, I think he's grateful to get out of this now before he got in even further. I don't think he realized the sort of slime that would ooze from the woodwork once he started posting those candid shots of the kids.

"He'd taken most of them down, leaving just the pictures of the older girls up, but the damage to him was already done. He was getting contacted and pressured. A bigger operation was muscling in. He'd have been dead in a year or sooner if he hadn't backed down and let them take his girls. His buddy Martin has disappeared. We're certain the two of them colluded in that disappearance and that it's Martin whose handling that film. But seeing as we have nothing to charge Martin with, we aren't even looking for him."

"How can you have nothing on him?" I asked.

"They really do have contracts to make that film. None of the main actors are underage. Lloyd has taken all of the blame for all of the illegal activities. Martin *had* heard Everly as had about ten other people, including a few other kids from your school. Because so many people were present, it would make it very difficult to prove that Martin had conspired with her. Everyone is claiming they thought it was just stupid talk—a drug induced sex fantasy, not an actual plan or something she'd really do.

"Martin disappeared right around the time Everly went to the hospital. We know he was in Switzerland, which is where the film was uploaded. We can infer that Everly's actions were why he ran, but that's all it is—conjecture. We can't prove it. He's likely to claim that he had no idea that any of that happened until the trial, which puts him in the clear. We'd have to prove that he knew there was danger, which we can't do. We can't prosecute people for saying I want to kill someone because people say that all the time. It has to be a credible threat. Since none of them are saying she offered money but only promises that they didn't believe and that her ideas on how to do it were farfetched sex fantasies..."

"That is such bullshit!" Jace said angrily.

"I agree. The ironic thing is that she frequently claimed Olivia had put her up to it, which made her claims unbelievable to them. None of them believed she'd be the sole heir. They all said they thought her grandmother was more likely to disinherit her even if she wasn't charged because any investigation would show the sort of shit Everly was into. If I had Martin speaking on the recording agreeing to her plan—but I don't. It would be his word against the rest of his crew. And all of them are saying they didn't believe her and that they were all high and they all thought she'd really gone crazy when she attacked Hannah—that Everly had begun to believe her own fantasy.

"They're all saying that they thought she was no threat because everyone who knew her plan knew that she was in the hospital, and they didn't think they needed to do anything or tell anyone because the police already knew.

"I don't think we could win a case against any of them. I think Martin will just move around Europe, collecting his royalties from the film. *Hard Cock High* is making millions thanks to this trial. The longer this trial stays in the public eye, the more views it's going to get. I think your cousin is a fool if he believes his partner is really going to share the profits. I think all of the kids who participated are never going to see one cent from it. I hope it's a learning experience for them."

"Olivia isn't going to care about the stupid movie," I said bitterly.

"She's in it. So I think she will."

"What!"

I was so stunned I wasn't sure what I was feeling.

He snickered.

"Lloyd has a contract and everything. There's a chance it's a forgery and even if it isn't, she's sure to claim it is. She's welcome to sue Martin and Lloyd. But meanwhile, she's in the film. Margo and Everly had filmed her shopping with them, buying them dresses and underwear that they wore in the film. There's some shots of her dropping the girls off in her fancy car and even a few suggestive shots of her walking through the doors then the scene shifts to a body double and Martin. The voice over is horrible but there's people online—a whole chat room—arguing over whether she was really involved or not. The consensus was she had to be or why'd she buy them such sexy clothing."

I laughed, immediately feeling bad about it but not able to stop even when I pressed my hands to my face.

"Serves her fucking right," Jace said as he hugged me again.

"My poor parents," I said but I continued to giggle. "I don't know why I'm laughing when it isn't funny. It's horrible. Poor Everly... that witch really screwed her up!"

Wiess said, "If she declines the plea, we'll show the film today. We're asking your family to take today off if the trial reconvenes. The jury wouldn't expect you to want to see that. I think it will take a few days for all the questions and experts. Margo will be recalled and probably the rest of the cast. I'm going to try to get us back on track before we're too far down this rabbit hole, but the defense will be fighting me because each time we go off on a tangent, they're getting billable hours and Olivia is in a nice comfy cell with lots of visitors. My office will be in touch when we're ready to call our real next witness, your sister Kenya. But I think it will be at least a week because we'll introduce the recordings Margo and Leonard were going to plant next while the jury has the other images of Martin and Margo fresh in their heads."

"It was them in the recordings?"

Wiess nodded. "We're absolutely certain Martin was playing Jace. His passport records confirm the dates he came and went into the States. We're ninety percent certain the woman is Margo. She admitted as much but Leonard swears it couldn't be her, that he hired actors and planted the tapes. He's seriously deranged about her, not at all credible but it does leave room for doubt."

He shook our hands and left, followed by his minions.

I said to Jace, "Olivia's not going to go for a plea because that film is already out there. You mark my words; she's going to blame me for this somehow."

My family joined us in the conference room, waiting to hear if she'd accepted the plea.

None of us were surprised when she declined it.

I said, "Have you given any more thought to my interview idea?"

Jace said, "I can't believe how much the webcast is making. And Kate is right; why let some other reporter or tv show get rich off of this?"

"Taking money for this doesn't feel right," my mother said.

Jace said, "Our plans for a hotel might be totally screwed and we'll always need higher security now, which is going to take us money to do. Plus, there's the repairs on the house from the damage Olivia caused and the fact that Kate needs therapy for her hands. It just seems smart to me that we put away as much as we can now. I want to preserve Kate's dream. I don't want her to feel like she has to become an accountant or lawyer or something. If she can make money by setting the record straight, I'm all for that! Plus, I want it crystal clear that she was never involved with any of that shady shit. I don't want any of those assholes contacting her."

Grayson said, "Responding only encourages interest."

I said, "Which we have right now whether we want it or not. I don't plan on trying to prolong that interest just take advantage of it. I'm making a video diary of my thoughts and stuff about the trial. I do a little recap every day, which I plan to release when the trial ends. I'd like to release a weeks' worth of shows—an hour or so from each of you. If you wanted to do a small recap now about how this new information affects you, I can add it to your hour or even release it now."

My mother said, "Let me speak with my doctor and see if he'd be willing to speak with us on camera because I think you're right and we could take advantage of this to help others who suffer from the same condition."

I said, "That's a great idea, Mom. I'd be willing to give him the profits from that show or split them with the mental health charity."

Kenya snorted. "I'll write us up a real contract, Kate. We'll make a corporation that owns the rights to joint interviews and keep that income separate, which means posting to its own channel."

Grayson nodded approval.

Jace said, "We're sending letters out to our sponsors since we figure they deserve a heads up, but we'll also offer them a promo for a price."

I said, "Money is the only thing she ever loved. I want her to know she's making me rich—it's the only thing I can do and it's not nearly enough for all the pain she's caused us."

I checked my email and missed calls on the way home and was happy to see that Grayson's godmother, Esmerelda, had left me a voice mail. I returned her call as soon as I got home.

"Kate, darling, we've been following the trial and are just appalled at what that woman is putting you all through."

"That's actually why I called. I know this is a lot to ask but I was hoping you'd considered the interview. Olivia doesn't care about the trial. She could've taken a plea deal and avoided all of this, but she wants to hurt us all—or ruin us. Today was the first time she really looked at all upset. I think she was embarrassed, and it got me thinking, I don't have the power to hurt her because she doesn't care what I think, but she might care what you think. If you were to publicly say that you'd always thought she was a horrible person...

"I know it's petty of me but it's just killing me that she thinks she can do this to us with no repercussions. If the only thing I can do is make her see that none of the people who she wanted to impress were never impressed by her..."

"My darling, I can do better than that. I was calling you to say I'd do the interview. That woman has been a thorn in my side for years. She's been a thorn to so many people that I'm certain I can round up a slew of her old acquaintances willing to share their grievances. I'll be on the very next plane."

"Thank you so much."

"It's my distinct pleasure, darling. Ta."

I grinned as I ran downstairs to make my next picture.

FIFTY-FIVE

Margo marched into court, glaring at everyone. She wore a low-cut black dress and silver high heels. She was beautiful but completely inappropriately dressed.

I'd have felt like a fool, but she sat with confidence.

Wiess said, "Tell us about your relationship with Lloyd Blake."

"I don't have a relationship with him."

"How do you know him?"

"He was the producer of a film I was in."

"Have you ever had sex with him?"

"Yes."

"For money?"

"Sort of. We filmed it and it put it online and it made us both money."

"But you say you're not in a relationship?"

"No."

"Are you friends?"

"Not anymore."

"Why not?"

"He lied to me. A huge lie!"

"Tell us about that lie."

"He promised to never tell anyone my real name. It was supposed to remain secret."

"You mean for that sex film he posted of the two of you?"

"Yes and the others I did."

"You didn't want anyone to know you'd done them?"

"No."

"How come?"

513

"Because I was still living at home and my parents would freak and kick me out, and Everly was still living at home, and she couldn't leave for another year at least. If her parents had gotten wind of it, they'd have likely sent her away or something. We just didn't want anyone to know. We didn't want men to hassle us online or call or us or anything."

"So you were planning to do more movies?"

"Yes. It's easy and there's good money in it. And it was fun... Everly and I had so much fun together. I miss her so much...."

She began to cry.

Wiess entered pictures of the rocks that had been thrown through the windows of the houses and the footage of Jace's trailer burning down that had been taken by the fire department when they'd arrived to put it out.

She'd stopped crying by the time the recordings had played.

Despite what a bitch I thought her, I felt sorry for her. She was obviously really stupid, but I might've done something similar if I'd thought someone had murdered Jace.

Wiess said, "Ms. Russell, you admit that you were the mastermind behind these attacks?"

"I asked my friends for help doing it if that's what you mean, but it wasn't my idea."

Wiess said, "Why did you vandalize the Avery properties?"

"Olivia offered me half a million dollars if I could get Kate and Kenya not to testify."

"So Olivia asked you to throw rocks?"

"Objection! Leading!"

"Sustained. Rephrase your question, please."

"Wiess said, "What did Olivia ask you to do?"

"She didn't specifically say to throw rocks. That was my idea. She told me Kate and Kenya needed to pay for murdering Everly, and I agreed. She said they needed to be stopped permanently and that I must know someone who could help. I asked her if she meant for me to kill them and she said not me personally. She said I should think about it and when I decided what needed to be done, she'd help if she could. Then we talked about how unfair it was that Kate was getting away with everything and that she'd end up getting Olivia's money. I thought if I scared Kate and Kenya a little, they'd run away and Olivia would be released because it was just their word against hers and I knew how much Olivia loved Everly, so I really thought she was telling me the truth.

"So I arranged for some friends to throw rocks all on the same night so that they'd think there were a lot of us, and we were organized. No one was meant to get hurt though."

"Then why did you continue after one of the fires that you started got out of control and burned Jace Blake's house to the ground, which spread to a nearby residence?"

"No one got hurt and it was just a stupid trailer, not a real house. But it did scare me, and I quit. I told Olivia I wasn't going to help her anymore."

"Then why did you fake the footage trying to implicate Kate and Jace?"

"Olivia told me she'd leave me everything if I could plant the camera. It was just a camera. It wasn't like I was going to hurt anyone."

"So you did it for money?"

"No. I did it because I loved Everly. The men meant nothing to either of us. It was just sex. She and I had a real connection. She meant everything to me and me to her. Olivia told me Kate had killed her and I believed her. She told me the police—Kate's boyfriend's father, was framing her and I believed that too. All of the Blake's are connected in one way or another. Everyone knows that.

"Olivia told me that Kate and Kenya had set the whole thing up. Olivia, she loved Everly—or at least I thought she had until you arrested me. I believed her and wanted Kate to pay. But then you showed me the recording of her doing it! I was shocked. I still can't hardly believe it!"

Margo began to cry, glaring at Olivia. "And you had those lab reports about how Everly had died. I hadn't realized the kids had been poisoned too, which if I'd have known, I'd have known Kate couldn't have been involved because she loved those stupid kids. Everly used to go on and on about how Kate never had a nice word for her but she shit sugar for those kids. Everly was always jealous. Kate wouldn't have done anything to them, so I knew Olivia had been lying to me the entire time."

"Objection!"

"Overruled. The witness can say what she thought. Continue, Ms. Russell."

I was shocked both that Margo would admit she'd been suckered and that Everly had been jealous that I'd loved the kids.

Wiess said, "What did you imagine would happen to Kate if the police believed the people on the recordings were actually her and Jace?"

"Nothing because no one would believe it."

"So why do it then?"

"Is all I had to do was follow the directions and plant it. I was paid twenty grand up front and promised a hundred thousand more when the police found it, but the real payoff was Olivia would make me her heir when she was acquitted. I didn't think anyone would believe it was Kate in a million years. Kate's too much of a goody two-shoes to have sex outside, never mind kill those kids she's always gushing about. I told Olivia that and she said they would, that Kate was a whore. So I said I'd do it but made her pay me the twenty upfront."

"Why?"

"Why what?"

"Why make her pay for that?"

Margo flushed bright red, and I knew it was from anger by the way she glared and crossed her arms.

"I don't fuck men for free—any man, ever. If they want to fuck me, they pay for the privilege. I never make exceptions. It's the golden rule."

"Did Everly follow that rule?"

"Yes. It doesn't always need to be money though that they pay with."

"Let's get back to the planted cameras. Did you have a plan in case Kate was arrested for conspiracy?"

"No. I hoped she would be, but I thought Frank—Jace's father, would get her out of it again."

"Would you have come forward?"

She hesitated then muttered, "No."

"Where and with who did you film it?"

"On one of the closed sets with Martin Jensen. We set up the cameras ourselves and did a few takes. We had to make sure you couldn't tell it was us, but we were trying not to make it look like we were trying to hide our faces."

"Where is this set."

"A storage locker. Hard High rents a few of them that we use to film in and store our props and stuff."

Wiess introduced pictures of the locker and props, which she agreed had been used.

He said, "How did you know what to say and what set to use?"

"Olivia told me what to say. She told me to find a secluded spot where someone might sneak away for a tryst."

Margo rolled her eyes like she thought it was stupid.

"Did she use that word—tryst?"

"Yes. She said I should pick a place that wasn't too noticeable but that police would find in a search. I was supposed to plant the cameras and fu, er, sleep with him there but we couldn't get onto the property. Alarms always went off no matter where we tried. It was easy to make the films at her parents' place, but Olivia wanted them at Kate's place too. She said it'd be more believable."

I was seriously pissed that Wiess hadn't shown me the films made at my parents.

Margo continued, "So I decided we'd make a set that looked like her property and then we could just jump the wall and hang the dumb camera. It would only take us a few seconds to hang it. We could do that while the alarm was going off and then do something to make the police show up to search."

"Do what?"

"Anything."

"What did you plan to do?"

"I don't know. Maybe throw a few flaming rocks or something."

"Something like what?"

"Maybe shoot at the house. I really hadn't planned it that far ahead."

Jace snorted softly.

Wiess said, "Where did you get the cameras?"

"That guy."

She pointed to Terry's assistant.

Terry jumped to his feet. "Objection! That's extremely prejudicial! I'm calling for a mistrial!"

The judge said dryly, "This is her sworn testimony. You can present evidence to refute it. The jury is free to believe or disbelieve the same way they're free to form opinions about any evidence. Continue."

Wiess said, "Do you have any proof, any witnesses to that?"

"Leonard Gould was there."

"Why did you choose him as your partner for this?"

"He was the only one who didn't bail after Shane got arrested and turned us all in for the rocks."

Olivia said, "I'd like to request new counsel."

The judge said, "The court will hear your request."

He dismissed the jury for the remainder of the day.

"You may speak," he said to Olivia when the jurors had exited.

"My lawyer advised me to hire Margo—"

"Stop. Before you continue, please be aware that anything you say here and now will be entered into evidence."

"I'm willing to plead guilty to asking Margo to help me, but that's all I did. I didn't supply her with anything or make any promises for her help.

I simply asked her to show the world what a scheming slut my granddaughter is. She's just like her mother. Alise could lead men around by their—"

"Objection!" Wiess said.

The judge said, "Mrs. Avery, keep your personal comments to yourself. What the court would like to know is whose idea it was that you pay Margo Russell to plant faked footage?"

Franklin Hinton said, "I had nothing at all to do with it. I never heard Mr. Terry even allude to something like that."

Terry said, "We were shown the recordings taken from those cameras and conducted our investigation. Neither Margo nor Leonard are credible. Leonard is mentally challenged; newly diagnosed with Asperger's, and Margo has lied numerous times under oath to say nothing of her drug problem."

Jace snorted, muttering, "Pot calling the kettle black."

Wiess glared over his shoulder.

The judge ignored the byplay although I was pretty sure he'd heard it judging by the flush spreading across his cheeks.

He said, "Mrs. Avery, is it your testimony that Mr. Terry advised you to frame your granddaughter?"

"No. It was Franklin Hinton. And it wasn't a frame. It was just showing the world who she really is. He said they needed to see, and he could help make that happen. I paid him for his time. There's a record of it. Separate billable hours that Mr. Terry didn't receive because he wasn't there."

The judge said, "Motion to dismiss council is allowed. You may fire one or both of them. The court will grant a recess to allow your new council to catch up. Court will resume Monday at nine. Mr. Wiess, I expect your office to look into this matter and that appropriate charges will be brought against all involved parties."

He lectured them both for another twenty minutes then dismissed us.

Olivia laughed when she turned to us, calling, "Your daughters are all whores just like you, and the world will see that!"

Two officers pulled her from the room.

My mother slumped and began to sob.

Wiess said, "They won't see the recordings. I'll file a motion to keep the press out. I think it very likely the judge will agree seeing as how she just admitted that's why she had them made in the first place."

He stomped out.

Grayson said, "I can smell the mistrial in the air."

"She's really getting on my last nerve," Kenya said angrily as she leaned over to hug our mother.

On Monday, the judge ordered the jury to be sequestered for the remainder of the trial. He closed the court to onlookers, except for the injured parties, letting my family and Claire's parents stay.

Olivia had fired Hinton, but Terry remained, and he had a new assistant with him. She didn't look old enough to have graduated from law school.

I felt sorry for her. Olivia was going to ruin her life.

The judge advised the jury that Olivia had admitted to asking Margo to making recordings meant to be prejudicial against Jace and I by pretending to be us performing lewd acts. He handed them a printed transcript of what was said on the recordings and said that they were to treat that information as a true fact proved in court.

"This matter is closed, except that it can be referred to in the closing arguments, but no further witnesses need be called as the facts of the matter aren't in debate. Olivia did knowingly, willingly, and with malice attempt to perpetuate a fraud on this court. You may, however, call Leonard Gould and Margo Russell to testify in any other matter that pertains to this case.

FIFTY-SIX

"Oh. Excuse me," Jace said as he entered the parlor. "I didn't realize you had company."

I hit the remote to stop the recording, standing to say, "Jace, this is Lady Esmerelda Winthrop, Grayson and Kenya's godmother. Esmerelda, this is Jace Blake my fiancé."

"It's a pleasure," Esmerelda said as she shook his hand. "I'm a huge fan of your show as is my husband."

His gaze went to the camera equipment I had set up, but he didn't ask.

He said, "Thank you. Can I get you ladies anything? Tea perhaps?"

She laughed a low delighted laugh, taking his hand again to squeeze it a moment. She turned to me when she released him to say, "The accent crept up on me. I've been living in England so long now I don't even hear it."

We both resumed our seats.

She said to him, "I'd like to speak with you before I go to discuss a business proposition."

I said to Jace, "Esmeralda's husband wants some custom work done. A lot of work."

Esmerelda said, "We can discuss all of that later. You and your fiancé can join us for dinner at the hotel."

"We'd love to," I said. "I can't thank you enough for coming."

Tears filled her eyes as she clasped my hand. "It's the least I could do. Your grandfather was my very best friend. I shouldn't have abandoned him when he married Olivia, but I despised the woman."

I gestured to the cameras.

"Do you mind?"

"Not at all."

I said to Jace, "You can join us if you want or stay out of the shot. Your call."

He took a seat on the couch behind the cameras out of the shot.

I said to Esmerelda, "We're rolling."

She turned a bit so her face would be clearly visible and said, "Your grandfather was my dearest friend. The two of us were inseparable as children. I was one of the only people he kept in touch with when he left home to make his own way.

"I was proud of him and scared for him in about equal measure. You have to understand that our lives had been ones of wealth. I didn't think he was prepared for the real world and in some ways I was right and in others he proved me wrong.

"He had no problems fitting in, finding work, making his way. In fact, he flourished. He made friends wherever he went. His life was on track to be what he'd envisioned it to be until he met Olivia.

"Olivia was always a schemer. She'd been engaged to the man who owned the garage where your grandfather worked part time, which he did to pay bills while he worked on designing machine parts.

Benjamin Gafferty the owner of the garage had rented John a small falling down shack of a tool shed where he lived and worked from.

"Ben was aware that John had submitted more than one good idea to the patent office. He knew it was just a matter of time until those ideas paid off and had mentioned that to his fiancé, Olivia.

"Ben and your grandfather were friends and had been discussing a partnership for one of his designs. Some sort of valve thing. I'm sure you could look up the details of that as it made him quite a bit of money, but I digress.

"Most of those patents were in your grandfather's name. I'm certain he only put Ben's name on that patent because he liked him the same way he put mine on the patent for the jewelry clasp he designed. He wanted his good friends to be financially secure but also to have a link to them.

"It was his way of taking care of us, of keeping us in his life, or I should say it was his way of saying the money doesn't mean anything to me, you do. Not that those patents made money right away. It was the thought behind them. He knew they'd make money. He was saying he didn't want the money to matter.

"Well anyway, after Ben died, Olivia married your grandfather. I have my suspicions in light of all of this that she might have arranged things so he'd marry her."

"Do you think she killed Ben?"

"I think it's possible. He died in a boating accident. The two of them had gone on a picnic, which wasn't at all something she'd normally do. Olivia didn't like the outdoors. She liked fancy luncheons and attending events. Boating just wasn't her style, but who knows what really happened. She claimed he'd stood to offer her a glass of wine, lost his balance and toppled over, hitting his head on the side of the boat and falling into the water.

"I've no idea if there was any sort of investigation or if the police just took her word for it. But a month later she'd married your grandfather and seven and half months later your father was born."

"Grandpa might not be his father?"

"I'm almost certain he wasn't. I came to see him when the baby was born and caught John and Olivia arguing over the baby's name. He'd wanted to call the child Ben and was saying to her that it didn't matter to him who knew because he loved his son.

"She said in that icy cold way she has that it mattered to her and if he loved her, he'd never embarrass her like that. Then her tone got all sweet and she said, we'll name him Brent, but we'll never tell him. I won't have my son shamed.

"I was sure it was herself she was worried of shaming but even then it never occurred to me that she might have murdered Ben. I'd thought she'd just used the situation—her pregnancy and his death—to manipulate your grandfather into marrying her. Not that it took much manipulation. He'd always admired her. Olivia was a beautiful woman and I think John was impressed by her, thinking she was like him because she had very refined manners but had friends from the lower social circles.

"But Olivia was nothing like him. Her manners were a sham, and frankly, embarrassing because she never quite learned to fake it. It was always cold and overbearing, never gracious and classy. She was trying to climb out of the lower social circles into the higher ones. The moment she had the money and no longer needed those old friends, she pretended they didn't exist.

"Your grandparents bought a house as far from that town as your grandfather would go. He let her have her way in everything. She, on the other hand, was always a manipulative bitch. She wanted to be a great lady and was afraid his friends who'd grown up with money would realize she hadn't. I'm certain she's the reason that your grandfather never went home again.

"Your grandfather knew that Olivia lied to everyone about her family, but she was afraid that lie wouldn't hold up with his old friends, so she did everything she could to keep us away from him.

"It wasn't that difficult for her to manage because John was consumed with his work and his son. It wasn't until Brent got married himself that John slowed down and began reaching out to his old friends. I'm ashamed to say that I'd made myself scarce when he married because I despised Olivia.

"She was a rude cold woman who didn't even bother hide the fact that she was willing to do whatever it took to keep her current social position. She had the most demeaning way of speaking to everyone who she thought beneath her, which was everyone she thought she could bully. She was only nice to people she could use.

"When Brent asked me to be Kenya's godmother, Olivia was delighted. But by the time Grayson was born, Olivia realized I wasn't going to let her use my social connections. After Grayson's baptism, she and I had a showdown. A week or so prior to Grayson's baptism, I'd caught Olivia in Kenneth Holland's study going through his papers. He was a friend of my husband's that we did business with. The day of the baptism, I caught her speaking with Ken about divorcing his wife.

"Olivia said something like you can't afford me, unless she dies, of course."

"I confronted them immediately and they both claimed it had been a joke, but I'd seen them sneaking away more than once. I told them it wasn't a funny joke and that I was sure their respective spouses wouldn't be amused, and she said cold as you please that if I said a word to her husband that she'd ruin him, that she'd take everything that mattered from him, and it would be my fault.

"I was furious and stormed out. She followed and said the only things that really mattered to John was Brent and the kids. I didn't realize that had been a threat to them at first, but then she said in the sweet way she has when she's trying to be charming that Alise wasn't well that she suffered from depression and that since I was the godmother I must want John to be able to look after the kids, which he wouldn't have time for in a divorce. She told me kids got hurt all the time, they drowned in pools and fell downstairs.

"I knew it was a threat then but didn't know how serious of a one it was. I mean, I never believed she'd really do it. She went on to say how she loved her family and how I'd misunderstood the conversation I'd overheard.

"I told her I thought she was a lying whore and that if anything happened to those kids or Ken's wife I was going right to the police.

"I went to John and told him, but he was convinced I'd misunderstood. I've no idea what the two of them said about it, if anything, but I stopped getting invited to birthday parties and such.

"I could see John wasn't happy with Olivia, but he was thrilled with his son and grandchildren. I left it alone because what could I do? If he was content in that loveless marriage with his shrew of a wife then it wasn't my business to cause problems.

"I'd kept in touch with Brent who was my very first god child, but I was busy with my own family and had let the relationship fade.

"I heard on the grapevine as one does of petty indiscretions of Olivia's. Just stupid things like her penchant for leaving the bill for her dinner partners to pay, or the way she always bragged about attending art shows and lied about buying a new piece. She liked people to think they were richer than they were, which was silly when they were very well to do. She was always changing her service staff and I was constantly hearing stories from my friends about how badly she treated them.

"Olivia was finding it harder and harder to keep the invitations coming in. She was just too rude—too unlikeable. The only people interested in keeping up relationships with her were other social climbers or people who depended on her for their charitable contributions.

"John was a supporter of a number of charities, which he'd gradually let her take over. The very last conversation I had with him, in fact, was about how he no longer knew where his money was being spent and how he'd lost sight of his plans. We'd spoken briefly about how he planned to take that over again or at least insist that she include more of his choices."

I said, "Did he ever talk about divorcing her?"

"No. It wasn't something he would do. The one time we spoke of it was when I'd told him what Olivia had said about the children being hurt. He'd told me that he'd never leave his family for any reason that they were the only thing that mattered to him. He was firmly opposed to divorce and said he'd just had to try harder that he'd made mistakes, big ones that he needed to make up for."

I said, "Did Ken's wife ever find out?"

"In a way. Ken went on to have an affair with another woman. I forget her name now, but I'm sure you can find it as it made the papers at the time. He and she were caught in *flagrante delicto* by Olivia and a reporter. Everyone was certain that Olivia had arranged to have the reporter there. Public perception at the time had been that she'd done it for the wife's sake because she'd been a major supporter of that charity and on the board with Olivia. I'd always thought she'd done it out of spite. It was a huge scandal at the time, one that cost the woman and Ken their positions on numerous boards and led to an investigation that ended with Ken in prison for embezzling funds and the wife nearly destitute. I think the other woman involved killed herself. Threw herself from a bridge if I remember right."

"I wonder where Olivia was that day..."

Esmerelda eyes widened. "It never occurred to me..."

I said, "That's all just speculation but I'd be interested to know if there was ever an investigation."

Esmerelda said thoughtfully, "I'll put you in touch with Janice Harding. Janice was my prime source of information on the doings here once I left the states. She might remember more than me. I remember Janice telling me more than once that people who crossed Olivia came to a bad end, but she never inferred that it was an an actual end... still, she might have some insights into how Olivia ended up like this. And there's a girl, I forget her name now, but I'll call around and see if anyone remembers her. She was one of Olivia's friends back when Olivia was engaged to Ben."

I said, "Speaking of that, do you think Olivia was having an affair with my grandfather before Ben died?"

"I doubt it. It's possible, of course, but stealing another man's fiancé just wasn't done in our circles. An engagement was as good as a marriage back then. If she'd broken off the engagement, societal norms would have been she'd need to wait at least a year before stepping out again. If the man left the woman, the time she'd be expected to wait would be much shorter. Everyone was shocked they'd married so soon but it was understood that they were comforting each other and then when Brent was born, it was thought he'd done the right thing by her, the noble thing—stepping in for his friend, which is why I think Olivia might have murdered Ben.

"John was a gentleman. He wouldn't have pursued her for at least a few years even if he'd been wildly in love, or I should say, he wouldn't have done it publicly. He might have dated her if he could've kept the relationship hidden, but that wouldn't have worked for Olivia. She wanted to go out. She loved to be seen, to make a dramatic entrance, but what I'm certain she wanted was his money. John's patents had started bringing in large checks and then there was his parents' wealth.

"The girl I mentioned would have a better idea what happened between them because she was part of that foursome. I don't know if John dated her or if she was just accompanying her friends. I do know that John remained friends with her until Olivia put her foot down, which she did publicly enough that I heard rumors of it across the pond."

"What sort of rumors?"

"A very public fight at the opera of all places. Apparently Olivia and this woman screamed at each other from their opposing balconies. The next day lawyers were engaged on both sides. I've no idea what came out of it only that it was said to be very heated. But my sources weren't really interested. It was all comments of the sort like you know how Olivia gets, by which I deduced Olivia was trying to ruin the girl because it had become her known MO.

"Everyone knew that Olivia would persist in a vendetta until she felt that she'd won. She'd been known to take over a charity completely to roust a rival or have one disbanded; investigations into finances being her favorite weapon. One of her opening moves on a rival was always digging up dirt on their children. She'd be sure to mention publicly and often that so-and-so was in rehab again or had been arrested or was doing poorly in school. That reporter who caught Ken was in her pocket and would post pictures of her enemies' children doing embarrassing or questionable things... it got to be ridiculous, but she stopped all of that or a least stopped doing it so blatantly when Kenya was born.

"She seemed to have mellowed. They'd moved here and lived a much quieter lifestyle in a much smaller apartment. She still did charity work but stopped attending the big events that had been the mainstay of her life.

"Her reputation took an upswing. I hardly ever heard any disparaging remarks. I'd thought she was just finally content with what she had as well she should've been seeing as she had a devoted husband, a lovely family, and anything else she desired."

I said, "It doesn't seem to be her nature to be content. I wonder what really prompted her withdrawal from her society contacts?"

Esmeralda huffed a sound of dark amusement.

"My guess would be someone caught her doing something shady and demanded she retire. My bet is she's making huge payoffs because she lives well below her old means. I know for a fact that your grandfather's patents still pull in big money because of my royalty checks. So where is it going? If I were you, I'd see if I could get those patent records and see who owns them now. It's possible John sold some, but I think she's hiding that income somehow."

I said, "Money seems to be the only thing she ever cared about. I can't see her giving it up without a fight and we all see how dirty she fights."

"It's possible she grew tired of her reputation or that it became too difficult to overcome it, so she just changed her persona. She always wanted everyone to believe she was a lady of refinement, which was getting really difficult for her to pull off when she was making so many enemies.

"It was one thing for her to make enemies of the lower classes because they lacked the means to fight back, but quite another for her to make them with people with political or social connections. I think she stopped receiving invitations because people were afraid to become her target. No one wanted her around to cause problems for their children and themselves. Polite people just don't throw your child's drug problem in your face. They don't use that information to get tickets or a good seat or any of the millions of petty things she used things like that for. But it took time for people to realize she was doing it to everyone.

"She tried it with me a week after I'd caught her and Ken. She stopped by our hotel and handed me a picture of my husband kissing our daughter. It was a sweet picture with her squeezing his cheeks and kissing him on the lips. Our daughter couldn't have been more than three.

"I wasn't sure why she was showing it to me. It had been taken as he was leaving the hotel. I was there but not in the picture.

"Olivia smirked at me as she held out another picture, this one of a naked man from the back holding up a naked girl.

"I was shocked, horrified. I didn't even hear what she was saying so great was my distress. I knew it wasn't my husband or my daughter. I knew she meant me to think it was. I think she believed that I was listening to her, believing her or at least believing others would believe her, but I was in pure shock. When I finally gathered my wits, I ran for the phone and called the police, which shocked her.

"She tried to run out, so I blocked the door, and we fought over the picture.

"I lost.

"She actually ate it to destroy the evidence. I had nothing to show the police. My husband and I went directly to John who assured us he'd handle things. He was furious. We were furious. She was pretending that this was all my idea, that she hadn't done a thing. In the end, we just went our separate ways. In the back of my head I was always a bit concerned that she'd try again with a better fake, but she never did."

"Who was the man and little girl?"

"I hadn't recognized either of them. The man resembled my husband in height, weight, hair color and even hair style. But my husband has a distinct pattern of moles on his shoulder, which she wouldn't have known as he never even swims without a shirt on. The little girl had brown hair like my daughter, but it wasn't her. For all I know it was a perfectly innocent picture. The man could've been bathing her or swimming or any number of innocent things. The fact that she destroyed it the way she did made me think it was a real pornographic image, one that she didn't want to answer questions about."

"Did the police question her?"

"Yes. I was quite vocal. They searched their home and John's office, which did nothing to endear me to him, but I couldn't let it go. Not that he said anything to me. He was all apologies to me and furious with Olivia. Maybe that's what changed her mind about things like that..."

"You mean he put his foot down?"

"He was a brilliant man. He had to see what she was doing. Maybe he hid that money to keep her under control?"

I said, "When the trial is over, I plan to air this and ask people who might know anything to come forward."

Esmeralda nodded, saying, "It's past time for all of her lies to be revealed. She's affected too many lives and gotten away with it for too long. Everyone is afraid to expose her because we all know there'll always be rumors. I know that some people will choose to believe that I'm lying, that it was my husband and daughter in that picture. But giving in, keeping silent let's her continue. I'd thought at the time that I'd done all that I could for that little girl, but I knew I was lying to myself. I was afraid to do more because I was afraid of the rumors that would surely follow. I'm ashamed I waited so long..."

"What else could you have done?"

"Made it more public. My husband had insisted that the police keep it all quiet and they'd agreed. It hadn't been difficult to do seeing as all of the people involved were happy to keep it quiet and there hadn't been any proof of my allegations. I was happy to keep it quiet myself, but I could've gone to the press or even my friends. I did neither even though I suspected that Olivia had done that and worse to others."

I said, "I plan on getting my own hotline number and launching a go-fund-me page to pay for it and a team of private investigators so that hopefully if there's anyone who has information of that little girl or any others who Olivia might've been using to blackmail people that they'll come forward with their information." I turned to face the camera directly as I said, "All reports will be kept as confidential as possible. I'm not trying to find out who she blackmailed or why she blackmailed them just who the victims were in those pictures that she arranged. But if you'd like a forum to tell your Olivia story, you can leave me a message there.

"It will be probably reassuring for lots of people to know that the court has restricted her access to her funds. She won't be able to continue any of her schemes. Her days of tyranny are done."

"Unless they acquit her," Esmerelda said.

"It seems impossible to me that they can. The video evidence is overwhelming. There hasn't been one spec of proof that the images were tampered with only speculation. The judge has ordered that the recordings are to be considered true and unaltered. She can continue to say it isn't her in the images but it's just not true. The evidence is right in front of them. My sisters and I are in the same shots as she is. There's no way it's either of us pretending to be her.

"The exterior video cameras at my home and the shop saw all of us coming and going. I couldn't have been there doing anything if I was home."

Esmerelda said, "She's been getting away with things for so long that it worries me that she'll get away with this too."

It worried me to, but I smiled as though I was confident as I said, "She'll spend the rest of her life in prison, which really isn't punishment enough for what she did and what she attempted to do. Hannah's injuries alone... it was so evil what she did. It was all so senseless. There was no point in doing any of it. I think she's been holding herself back, fighting her true nature for so long that when she finally let it go she did everything she'd always dreamed of doing. I think she didn't care anymore about getting caught because nothing mattered to her. I don't think she cares what the verdict is, which is so wildly frustrating knowing she isn't the least bit sorry, that nothing that anyone says will make her sorry. I hope the judge doesn't let her access her money to make her life more comfortable in prison seeing as the few years she has left in there is the only punishment she'll ever receive for what she did."

Esmerelda said, "It's a small consolation to me to know that she never enjoyed her life even though she had everything anyone could want, but still, it *is* so unfair that no matter what the verdict is there won't be justice. She'll continue to be haughty and smug because she got what she wanted."

"Not totally. She managed to murder my sister, but she made my mother famous, which has to grate, seeing as her goal had been to hurt my mom. People hate Olivia. My mom on the other hand has become an international spokesperson for mental health, which wouldn't have happened if Olivia hadn't done what she did. My mother is really making a difference in so many lives.

"She was so young when she got pregnant with Kenya. Hiding her inner turmoil over that for all those years took a serious toll on her. It's so amazing that she can not only help herself but help so many others. The only person Olivia can really hurt now is her son, which is tragic because I think he's the only person she ever really cared about, not that she cared much..."

Esmerelda said, "She'd always wanted Brent's good opinion. I thought that maybe that's why she'd mellowed because she'd been afraid it would blow back on him, not that he ever seemed to care about that social scene. I'd always thought he was perfectly happy with his family and career. I wonder if she began this as a way to murder Everly? It seems to me that Everly was a lot like Olivia, not just in looks but in temperament. Maybe she snapped when she saw herself..."

I faced the camera again as I said, "Thank you, Lady Winthrop, for sharing your insights into the mind of Olivia."

I turned off the camera to say to her, "I'll send you a list of the sponsors for this episode and if there are any on there you'd like removed just let me know."

"I'd be happy to speak with you again. It would surely drive Olivia crazy if you did a show at one of her old stomping grounds with her old cronies."

"I love it. I'll see what I can arrange."

She winked at me as she stood to hug me.

"Leave it to me, darling. I'll line up a dinner party in support of your mother's charity that will make Olivia simply sick with envy. Dinner tonight, darlings. Jace, it was lovely to meet you."

He escorted her to the door.

When he returned he said, "Why didn't you tell me about this?"

"I wasn't sure she'd have anything good to say—good for annoying that bitch," I clarified, making Jace snicker.

He gave me a hug as he said, "Make sure you clear this stuff with Kenya."

"I could give a shit if Olivia sue's me."

"Still...."

"Fine."

I released him to make a copy of the interview.

"I already have ten of Olivia's old friends lined up to do interviews. I hope they're all as good as this one."

He snickered again.

FIFTY-SEVEN

The first witness that Terry called was Leonard Gould.

He took the stand wearing his signature black turtleneck.

After he'd been sworn in, Terry said, "Leonard, has Kate Avery every asked you to do anything illegal?"

"Yes. She asked me to lie about seeing her brother Grayson molesting her."

"Is that the only thing she asked you to do?"

"She gave me money to buy her sister Everly drugs."

"Do you know why she didn't buy them herself or give her sister the money?"

"She told me she didn't want anyone to know they were from her."

"Did you do it?"

"Yes."

"Did Kenya Avery ever ask you to do anything illegal?"

"Yes. She asked me to put a camera in Kate's yard."

"Do you know why?"

"I guess to see what was going on."

"Did she ever do or say anything else illegal to you?"

"She said she'd be my girlfriend if I helped her get rid of her grandmother."

"Get rid of her how?"

"She said is all I needed to do was get her to Kate's house."

"Did she say what she'd do when her grandmother was there?"

"No."

"You didn't ask?"

"No."

"Did you agree to do it?"

Leonard hesitated, finally shaking his head.

The judge said, "You have to answer out loud."

"No." Leonard said loudly.

He was flushed and sweaty. If he wasn't being such an ass, I'd have felt sorry for him.

Terry said, "No further questions."

"Cross examination?" the judge asked.

Wiess said, "Where did Kate ask you to lie about her brother?"

"School."

"What day and where were you?"

"I don't remember the day."

"What month?"

"June."

"And where did the conversation take place at the school?"

"The parking lot."

"Did she ever give you a ride?"

"Yes."

"How often?"

"A few times a week."

"What kind of car does Kate have?"

"Objection. Relevance."

"I'll allow it."

Wiess said again, "What kind of car does Kate have?"

"I don't know."

"What color was it then?"

"I... blue?"

"How about the seats, were they leather or cloth?"

"...Leather."

"What color leather?"

"I don't know."

"You remember they were leather but not what color they were?"

"I don't remember."

"Did this conversation happen before or after school?"

"After."

"Right after?"

He hesitated again then nodded, adding hurriedly, "Yes."

"Who else was there?"

"No one."

"No one else was in the parking lot?"

"I don't remember."

Wiess questioned him for twenty minutes on that with Leonard not being able to recall one detail.

Wiess finally said, "Is there anyone at all who could corroborate your story? Did anyone ever see you speak with Kate anywhere at anytime or see you get into her car?"

"I don't have to prove it. I just have to tell you."

Wiess said, "Is Kate Avery in the audience today?"

"Yes."

"Can you point her out?"

He pointed at me.

"Is Grayson Avery in the audience today?"

He hesitated then shrugged.

"Is Kenya Avery in the audience today?

He flushed bright red.

Wiess repeated his question.

Leonard said, "I don't know."

"What does Kenya look like?"

"I don't remember."

"You don't remember?"

"She has brown hair like Kate."

"Are you sure about that?"

Olivia huffed in annoyance, earning a hard look from the judge.

Leonard said hurriedly, "No I mean its blond like Everly's."

"Where did you speak with Kenya?"

"I don't remember."

"You don't remember where the conversation about the camera took place?"

"No."

"What was illegal about putting a camera in Kate's yard?"

"What do you mean?"

"You said Kenya asked you to put a camera in Kate's yard and that it was illegal. Why did you think putting a camera in Kate's yard was illegal?"

"I don't know."

"How did you meet Kenya?"

"What do you mean?"

"When did you and Kenya meet for the first time?"

"I don't remember."

'How long ago?"

"I don't remember."

"Where did you meet?"

I don't remember.

"I'm guessing it's pointless to question you about any of your statements..."

"Objection!" Terry said.

"Sustained," the judge said.

"Do you have a girlfriend now, Leonard?"

"Yes."

"Who is she?"

"Objection."

"Overruled. I'll allow it. You can answer the question."

"It's a secret."

"Did she tell you it was secret?"

"Yes."

"How long has Margo Russell been your girlfriend?"

"Objection!"

"Three years," Leonard said at the same time.

"Does your girlfriend love you?"

"Yes."

"Do you love her?"

"Yes."

"Does Margo have other boyfriends?"

"Yes but that's just work. She loves me."

"What about Everly? Was she your girlfriend too?"

"No."

"Was she Margo's girlfriend?"

"They were best friends. Margo was really mad when Everly died."

"How did Everly die?"

"Her sister murdered her."

"Who told you that?"

"... I don't remember."

"No further questions at this time," Wiess said.

"Recross?" the judge asked.

Terry said, "Can you have more than one girlfriend or boyfriend at time?"

"Yes."

"Has Margo ever asked you to do anything illegal?"

"No. Never."

"Your witness," he said to Wiess.

Wiess remained seated as he said, "What kind of car does Margo have?"

"A Camry."

"What color is it?"

"White."

"What color are the seats?"

"Black."

"Are they leather or cloth?"

"Leather."

"When did you meet Margo?"

"My first day of school here. She parked in front of my bus and the driver yelled at her. We walked into school together."

"No further questions."

The judge dismissed Leonard.

FIFTY-EIGHT

A parade of my old schoolmates came through, Everly's friends testifying that I was a mean-spirited trickster, and my classmates saying I was just a prankster.

Every one of them were asked the same question by the DA—had I ever hurt anyone. The answer was always no. I wasn't sure what the jury thought about it all. They mostly looked amused.

I was furious but practiced at hiding it, smiling at all of them the same way I had for the last six years.

I realized as Margo spoke, trying to make out I was the worst sister on earth that I really didn't care what any of them thought of me and wondered when that had happened.

Jace. He made everything better.

I smiled at him, shrugging a bit, which made him have to hide a laugh with a cough.

Terry recalled me to ask if I thought the proceedings were amusing.

I said, "I find it laughable that anyone would care what a girl that I never said two words to would think of me or I of her."

"Did you like your sister Everly?"

"Objection. Outside the scope."

"I'll allow it."

"No. She was mean to everyone, and lazy, and I didn't like any of her scummy friends."

"Objection," Terry said angrily.

"Overruled. The witness can answer the question."

I continued, "If given the chance, I might've grown to like her. I didn't know she was mentally ill. If I *had* known, it would've colored how I saw her, but more importantly she'd have gotten the help she needed and then maybe people like Margo wouldn't have used her to fund their own drug habits."

"Objection."

"Sustained. You can't allege facts not in evidence."

"Sorry, your honor. I just meant that I thought Everly's friends, the older ones mostly were using her and encouraging her to use drugs so they could use them too."

"Objection."

"Overruled. She can say what she thought."

Terry said, "Do you have any proof that Everly was doing drugs."

"No. It was all rumors to me—and the rest of the school."

"Had you ever seen her take drugs?"

"Only aspirin, which she took almost every morning with a glass of tomato juice."

"Had you ever seen her drink alcohol?"

"Yes."

"And you did nothing to stop her?"

"Objection."

"Let me rephrase. What did you do when you saw your *younger* sister drink alcohol?"

"Nothing. My grandmother was there and saw it too."

He paused, glancing back at Olivia. I thought my answer had surprised him.

"How much did she drink?"

"Objection too broad."

"Sustained. Narrow the question to a specific day."

My grandmother glowered at me.

I smirked back.

Take that you evil bitch!

"Let's move on. How often did you see your sister drink?"

"A few times a year. Olivia always let her have wine with dinner, but I didn't go there much when she was there, so I can't say if that was just when I was there or not."

"But you never saw her drinking with friends or at your parents' house?"

"With friends, no. I never hung out with her and her friends. She'd finish my mother's wine sometimes when we were cleaning the table."

"A couple of glasses of wine doesn't constitute a drinking problem."

I said nothing.

The DA said, "Is that a question or an observation?"

A few members of the jury tittered.

Terry said, "Did you think Everly had a drinking problem?"

"Yes."

"What did you do about it?"

"Nothing. What could I do about it?"

"Objection."

"Sustained. Keep your responses limited to the question."

"Did you ever tell your parents you thought she had a problem?"

"Yes."

"More than once?"

"Yes."

"More than three times?"

"No."

"So you ignored it?"

"Yes."

"Do you consider yourself to be a good sister?"

"Yes."

"To all of your siblings, even Everly?"

"Yes."

"So it was good of you to ignore her problems?"

"Objection."

"Sustained. Get to the point, please."

"I'm trying to clarify why she thought she was a good sister."

"I helped Everly whenever she asked me for help—with her homework, with the kids, even with her chores."

"But you never tried to help her with her supposed drug or alcohol problem."

"I told my mother. I told Everly she was mixing with a bad crowd. I told Olivia."

"Objection."

"Overruled. You may continue."

"The week before Everly tried to murder Hannah—"

"Objection. Facts not in evidence."

"Sustained."

I rolled my eyes at Terry as I said, "The week before Everly dropped Hannah over the balcony, I'd called my grandmother to remind her that Everly had been grounded for backing into one of the cars when she'd come in after three in the morning. Everly had lied about doing it, but it was seen by the home security camera, so my father grounded her. I'd told Olivia that it was my opinion that Everly had been driving drunk. I'd asked Olivia if taking Everly out shopping was the best way to get her to straighten up. I was told to mind my own business."

"Olivia said that exactly?"

"She said it has nothing to do with you, Kate. And hung up."

"A perfectly reasonable response."

"Objection."

"Sustained. This is your last warning. Refrain from personal comments."

"Let's get back to Everly and school. Did the two of you ever fight in school?"

I heaved an annoyed sigh. It was going to be another long day.

FIFTY-SIX

The crowds around the courtyard grew daily as the kids from the school testified. The tone had changed from amusement to hostility. No one wanted their kid involved. Now that it could be personal, people were showing up demanding the reporters and film crews be banned from the trial.

The judge denied the motion.

"I'll say again what I said at the start of this trial. Every person deserves their day in court and the public, their fellows, deserve to see justice done. The community can't be a community without a fair law that pertains to everyone equally. Our community is too large to fit in this courtroom but with modern technology the courtroom can come to you. Minors who speak to this court via video, and photographic evidence that has no evidentiary merit or would be harmful for said community to witness shall be restricted to the jury's eyes only. Now. Let's get on with this. Call your next witness."

Wiess said, "I submit exhibition two hundred and nine, your honor, the testimony of Felicity Avery."

The judge again let us stay but kicked everyone else out. Only the audio was played for the viewers.

Every juror appeared to be watching closely without the amusement they'd shown for Margo's testimony.

Hannah's testimony made a few of the jurors cry. I didn't think it was what she said so much as her sunny smile that changed to fear and confusion when asked about that day.

I was so grateful she didn't remember anything after eating that damned ice cream.

Wiess entered their medical records into evidence and then rested.

Terry spent three days calling witnesses who had nothing pertinent to say. He called in three x-police officers who never got to utter a word because he couldn't prove relevance.

I think everyone in the courtroom, even Olivia, heaved a sigh of relief when he rested.

I went to see Olivia.

Her haughty expression was firmly in place when she picked up her phone to speak to me.

I said, "I'm surprised you agreed to talk to me. You must be bored as shit in there."

"What did you want?"

"Just to say I hope there's a retrial. You're doing amazing things for my bank account. The day the verdict is read, I'll be launching another online channel." I held up my phone showing the interview with Esmerelda.

Olivia's eyes narrowed and she leaned closer.

I said, "Lady Winthrop gave me a great interview—great for me, I mean. Bad for you. She told me all about what a scheming whore *you* were. I've interviewed over twenty of your old friends and none of them had anything nice to say. They all thought maybe Esmerelda was right, that you'd murdered Everly because she reminded you of yourself, which is so pathetic.

"My mom has over five million likes—she's a celebrity now, did you know that?"

"Liar!"

It made me laugh.

"You're a celebrity too—on the porn sites. You should see the footage Lloyd posted."

She slammed her phone down.

I knew she couldn't hear me, but I said, "I won't be back."

She snatched the phone back up.

I said, "I have millions of fans. I hope some of them make your acquaintance in here."

Her eyes widened and her empty hand went to her throat.

I grinned at her as I said, "I have the money now to do anything I like—anything. Sleep well."

I hung up and went home to try to sketch that expression.

I'd finally reached her. I hoped she remained terrified.

FIFTY-NINE

Wiess stood to give his closing argument.

The jury gave no real clues to how they were leaning. I'd caught them glaring at me and my grandmother in almost equal measure.

He said, "You've seen the recordings and heard the defense try to claim they were all lies by hiring their own liars to say it. The defense wanted you to focus on the impossible claim that Kate can somehow manufacture a video that shows just what she wants it too. But they knew there wasn't any evidence to support that, so they went on to plan B—unknown people hired by Kate in disguises. But why would Kate have made her disguise be Olivia? Why not just use Alise as the disguise as the defense contests they meant to murder Olivia. Why put her face on the model if they were trying to frame their mother? It's all just so preposterous. But let's forget the recordings for a minute, there's still a mountain of physical evidence, the clothing Olivia wore, her injuries, eyewitness testimony of the police. And most damning of all the testimony of the granddaughter who she murdered, caught on tape. And the equally damning testimony of the two children she poisoned who lived.

"You'll be asking yourself why this case even made it to court. Why, with this mountain of evidence didn't she just plead guilty. And the answer to that is she still hates her grandchildren because they're Alise's children. She was offered a plea more than once and turned it down because she wanted to humiliate Alise. She wanted to hurt her by hurting her children, which the testimony of Margo Russel should make clear. Which the footage from the cameras recovered from Leonard Gould should show with no doubt whatsoever. Only someone consumed with hatred would forge something as heinous as that recording for the sole purpose of being able to say it in court—to put that thought into the heads of millions. To make her grandchildren have to live with the weighing glances and titters of ignorant people." He pointed to the picture of Olivia snarling with the gun raised. He changed the picture to show Felicity—a picture I'd taken of her grinning at me as she'd held up a birdhouse that she'd made of popsicle sticks. He changed the picture to show her lying unconscious in a hospital bed.

"Olivia Avery put her there on purpose. She'd meant to murder her."

He showed Hannah next with a dirty face and her mischievous smile, hugging a book, followed by her in the bed with our father crying and holding her hand then he and I holding her hands and helping her walk.

He said, "That Hannah lived was a miracle. She'd been poisoned and left to drown. She lived but now has damage to her lungs that leave her breathless when she laughs, when she runs, when she plays."

Two of the jurors wiped their eyes.

Olivia scoffed, which earned her disapproving looks from the jury.

Wiess continued, "And let's not forgot the wounds Olivia inflicted on Kenya. A bashed skull, an ankle shattered. The dousing in paint thinner and cruel taunting. Imagine how terrifying that was—to be told that you were about to be burned alive and to have no doubt that she'd meant it. Imagine how painful that blow was that shattered her ankle. Imagine how shocked Kenya was that the person doing those unimaginable things to her was a grandmother she loved. And then the shooting of Jace Blake and the numerous attempts to shoot Kate."

He showed pictures of all of us with our injuries then pointed at Olivia.

"That woman is a menace. A murderer twice over."

He changed the picture to show a slideshow of Everly.

"Everly Avery had issues, but she was just seventeen—just starting her life. She didn't deserve to be murdered. She didn't deserve to be used like she was."

He changed the picture again to show a slideshow of Claire.

Claire's mother began to cry.

Wiess said, "Claire was a beautiful young woman. She was thirty-two and a free spirit who spent her free time working at the local Red Cross. She spent her vacations volunteering, building houses in Africa, farming in Ethiopia, and teaching children in Honduras how to read and speak English.

As he was speaking, he showed pictures of Claire in all of those places.

"Olivia's reason for murdering this beautiful woman—to frame someone else for murder—is one of the most despicable things I've ever heard. She didn't happen upon her. She planned and hunted her down. No excuse, no reason, nothing anyone says will change the cold hard fact that Olivia Avery murdered her in cold blood."

Don't let her hurt them anymore. Find her guilty on all charges.

Terry stood to say, "Olivia Avery was a good mother and grandmother who was angry at her husband as anyone would be if he'd sired a bastard on a woman half his age. She was angry at Alise, but even the prosecution admits that she acted civilly for years. She'd have continued to act civilly. She'd have continued to be a loving grandmother who doted on the children.

But her granddaughter's weren't content to wait for her to die to get their inheritance. Kenya knew she'd stood a chance of being cut from the will completely. I don't think we'll ever know which of the girls proposed the plan. That there was a plan can't be in doubt. We heard the recording of Everly talking about that very thing. She planned to cut her sisters out, but they struck first.

They wanted to frame Olivia and succeeded; except they didn't quite finish the job. If Olivia had died as intended, there'd be no one to dispute their claims. The disguised woman in those recordings would certainly have been believed to have been Olivia. They'd have gotten rid of everyone in the way of their fortune, their mother, their sisters, and most importantly their grandmother.

"Kate and Kenya continue to attempt to shift the blame onto Olivia by convincing Kate's friends to lie. They lied to them too, offering money they don't have for those lies."

"Objection."

"Sustained. The jury will disregard that claim."

"Kate is making a fortune from this trial. She's celebrating her win every weekend, laughing at the chumps who believe her."

"Objection."

"Sustained. The jury will disregard that claim."

"Kate Avery's finances speak for themselves. Would an innocent person, a good person, seek to profit when their sister was murdered? Isn't it reasonable to think she was involved with the murder that *she's* profiting from? By all accounts Kate is brilliant and talented and also aloof with no friends, a prankster who the teachers never suspected, but *we're* onto her now. This was her plan from the beginning, and she used everyone, even her little sister, getting her involved with drugs, with her boyfriend's family's porn company, urging her to murder her siblings. You saw her hit her sister, hit her so hard it shattered her ankle. Will you let her fool you too? Will you let her continue to profit?"

He took his seat with confidence.

Wiess remained seated when he said, "The truth is evident in the images, in the lies Olivia tells that she expects her money to buy her out of. If she hires enough people with long enough fancy titles after their name to say the sky is green, she thinks she can convince you to believe that lie instead of the evidence of your own eyes because she knows that we don't want to believe that a grandmother could do such things. It's almost impossible to believe it when we remember how much our own grandmothers loved us, how they'd bake our favorite treats and play our favorite games and give us hugs, especially when life was hard and we'd failed in our expectations. Olivia never did any of those things. She expected her grandchildren to always look good. To sit quietly without speaking. To get good grades and socialize with the correct people and wasn't shy about showing her displeasure when they were loud or boisterous or got a bad grade. You've heard the testimony of how she was downright rude to anyone she felt was inferior to her, which was most people. But Olivia isn't on trial for being a bad grandmother or a snob. She's on trial for murder.

"Remember the face of the woman who murdered Claire in cold blood. Remember the sound of that pipe hitting Kenya. The fear in Kate's voice as she screamed when Jace fell. Remember the recorded testimony of Felicity Avery—the confusion in her voice when she said grandma gave us ice cream and wouldn't let me clean the car. Ice cream that tested positive for Maureen Hilfiger's medicine and left those children unconscious for a day and would have killed them if they hadn't gotten medical intervention.

"Remember the testimony of the kids she tried to manipulate into murder to stop her grandchildren from testifying here. The cameras that she admitted to paying the kids to plant and the really horribly faked footage on them—the sexual acts that she paid those kids to perform. And then remember that she doesn't expect to get away with this, she just wanted to hurt them more."

SIXTY

We returned to my house to sit in the parlor so I could record us talking about the trial. I'd positioned cameras to capture every angle of the room so that everyone could just talk naturally and I could edit the footage later.

"Thank God that's over with," my father said.

"I'm so very sorry," my mother said. "For so many things."

Grayson said, "I hope it's over, Dad, but knowing her..."

Kenya said angrily, "No one would believe that pack of lies Leonard spouted! It's absurd!"

"She'll appeal," Grayson said. "She'll think of more horrible lies to tell, more ways to hurt us all."

"There must be something we can do!" our mother said angrily. "I can't bear the thought that she spews that vileness on the children next! There must be something we can do!"

Kenya said, "We'll sue her. Money was always the only thing she ever cared about."

Grayson stood to crouch in front of our mother and take her hands.

"She won't be allowed to say anything about the children because she could have nothing to say. The law protects from character attacks without foundation."

Jace said, "Everyone knows now that she doesn't have access to her money to pay anyone to say or do anything. There won't be more gullible fools trying anything stupid."

"Not for money, anyway," my father murmured.

I said, "And if she's found innocent?"

"Impossible!"

Kenya jumped to her feet and began to pace.

"If they let her go, she'll murder us all the first chance she gets! They can't let her go! They can't!"

Jace stood to hug her, and she burst into tears.

Our father said, "If she's found innocent, then we'll sell everything and hide."

"Screw that!" Jace said angrily. "I'm not running from her or anyone. This is my home, and I won't be chased from it!"

Kenya pushed away from him to sit beside our mother, covering her face with her hands as she said, "Felicity will never get over this. I'd hoped Hannah wouldn't realize, wouldn't know to be afraid until she was old enough that we could assure her there wasn't anything to be afraid of, but if we have to run, to change their names, to change ours—and do what? And how do we leave our friends, our lives? It's so unfair!"

Our father said, "She can't possibly be found innocent."

Jace said, "This is exactly why she wanted that trial. Look how badly she's making you all feel! I was thinking about that porn movie. I wonder if she made that contract look fake on purpose so she could deny it if she ever needed to. Maybe Lloyd wasn't lying about that? Olivia is obviously really sick. It's possible she got off on that, a sort of fuck you to the Avery name. Everly was always her favorite. Olivia probably put her up to everything she did. All of those lies, Everly trying to get Kate into trouble and turning her friends against her. Olivia was buying Everly's affection for years—since the day she was born. She was grooming her to be just like she was."

I said, "I wonder how different all of this would've been if Everly hadn't resembled Olivia? I wonder if her mother was a scheming bitch just like her?"

My father said, "I never knew my grandparents. They died when I was really young. My father never liked them. I think he felt sorry for Olivia. He used to say he'd saved her although he never said exactly from what. She'd get angry in her politely cold way. I always thought he'd meant from the cold boring life of social teas, but she *likes* that. Not that any of that matters..."

I said, "When I look back, I can see how cold she was, but I never really noticed it, or maybe not noticed. I noticed but I hadn't cared because grandpa wasn't at all cold. I hadn't felt much for her until he died and then I felt sorry for her when I thought of her at all, which I'll admit, I didn't do often until I was older and realized the kids should have what

I'd had, so I'd bring them to see her, which was so stupid of me because she could never give them what I'd had..."

I turned to my mother to say, "You feel bad about what happened because you never told Dad the truth and you think if you had this all might never have happened. It's horrible to say, but I'm glad you never said anything about him, Mom, because then I'd never have had a grandfather to love. Olivia still would've done something horrible because that's the person she is. If you'd told her back then, she'd probably have murdered me, you, him... God knows where it would've stopped."

My mother said, "I'm honestly not sure what happened between John and I. I have no clear memories of that time just small glimpses that could be how I wished things were or were afraid they were. I've been pretending and repressing for so long... and then Everly found out about Hannah, and I was terrified and confused because I thought she knew about Kenya or maybe I was just afraid she'd say something about Hannah. If Brent had believed her and tested Hannah, it's possible he'd test you all and my secret would be revealed. I was terrified he'd leave me... I'm still terrified of that..."

"I never will, Alise. I'm sorry I've been such a crap husband. I don't know how it happened. I'm not blaming you, but I felt you withdrawing, and I just wanted to brace myself, to tell myself I could go on without you, that I didn't need you or the kids...I was a coward and selfish and I blame myself for letting Everly get so sick. I should've noticed. When I saw how difficult the kiddos were with all her tantrums, I should've stepped in to help..."

He kissed her hand.

I wasn't sure if she was a fool for believing him or not.

My phone rang, followed by Kenya's, Jace's, and then my mother's.

"They can't have reached a decision so soon," Jace said worriedly.

Grayson said, "Three hours for all of the charges—they have to have found her guilty."

I said, "Will they charge me or Kenya if she's found innocent?"

"It isn't going to happen."

I looked at the camera to say, "No verdict will ever be enough for what she did and is still doing."

I turned the camera off.

Dan ran into the hall from the kitchen when we all came out.

"I've made coffee if anyone wants some."

"The court called. The jury is in."

His mouth dropped open.

"Seriously?"

The reporters were in an absolute frenzy outside the courthouse shouting questions as our van passed them.

We were let in through a back entrance and brought to the courtroom, which was already almost full of people.

We took our usual seats.

Claire's parents arrived about fifteen minutes later and the bailiff closed the doors.

Nerves kept my mind spinning. A million what ifs ran through my mind. I was terrified she'd managed to sway them, that what to me had seemed clear was just wishful thinking on my part. I didn't hear much of the judge's admonishments.

Tingles raced over me as the jury entered.

Jace had to help me up.

He embraced me whispering, "Look at them, Kate. They found her guilty."

The judge said something that was lost in the wild beating of my heart.

"Guilty," the foreman said, and sound resumed, making the low gasps of relief explosively loud or maybe they really were loud.

I began to cry.

Jace kissed my cheek, squeezing my hand as the judge said, "On the charge of the murder of Claire McAllister by the defendant Olivia Avery, how do you find?"

"Guilty."

"On the charge of attempted murder of Kenya Avery by the defendant Olivia Avery, how do you find?"

"Guilty."

"On the charge of the attempted murder of Kate Avery by the defendant Olivia Avery, how do you find?"

"Guilty."

"On the charge of the attempted murder of Jace Blake by the defendant Olivia Avery, how do you find?"

"Guilty."

The judge continued to read the list of charges.

I hoped Olivia felt at least a tenth as bad as I had when I'd come into the room.

She was found guilty on all charges.

The judge dismissed the jury and the room erupted into sound.

I wondered if Olivia was the first grandmother in history to get the death penalty for trying to murder her grandchildren.

I bawled like a baby on Jace's shoulder.

"We're free, Kate. It's over."

The judge finally banged for order and finished giving his admonishments to Olivia who listened with pursed lips and her nose in the air.

He left the courtroom and again the people began exclaiming.

I said to Claire's mother, "I know you probably want nothing to do with us, and I don't blame you, but if there's ever anything I can do for you..."

She surprised me by giving me a hug.

"We never blamed you kids. I think you're a good person, Kate. I hope you regain your art. She should have to pay for murdering that too."

"Let's go," her husband said angrily.

She smiled sadly and followed him.

We all headed back to the van. I think we were all stunned by this sudden conclusion.

Kenya said happily, "I'm filing our civil suit tomorrow."

Grayson patted my knee. "I'll handle it, Kate. You should take a break. Maybe go away for a few days and relax."

"That's a great idea," Jace said. "Dan can watch the house. We can go to the beach."

SIXTY-ONE

It wasn't over, I thought in dismay when the crowds of people surrounding my house woke me the next morning.

Jace had left without me noticing.

He'd left me a note on the fridge saying he was in the garage with Dan.

I dressed in jeans and my favorite blue shirt, did my hair and makeup and headed to the basement studio I used to make my recordings.

I'd already made all the arrangements to air the footage I'd been filming. I'd been meaning to just upload it, but the crowd had changed my mind.

I typed up a quick banner and uploaded that instead alongside a meme of a ticking alarm clock.

By the time I returned with tea and pop tarts, there were already ten thousand people online waiting for me to sign in, which I did immediately.

"Hi everyone. Thanks for stopping in and your kind thoughts and words."

The volume of the crowd outside grew as I spoke.

"I'd hoped this could all be behind us, that my family could move on to a more normal life—or as normal as it's possible to be after living through something so horrible."

The comments were scrolling by too fast for me to read many. I caught only small sentences, most wishing us well or saying things like I hope they hang the bitch.

I said, "I think my grandmother was worse than I'd ever imagined even after I saw her try to murder us. I have no proof at all except hearsay, but I think she murdered her first fiancé and maybe even my grandfather's parents—maybe even my grandfather. I'll be uploading some interviews after this from people Olivia knew in the past and they all have horrible stories to tell about her.

"I admit, my lawyer isn't happy with this. My parents aren't happy I'm doing it either. I was sort of conflicted about it myself because I can see how this looks. But then I realized it doesn't matter what I do or say. People are going to think what they want to think about me, and I can't worry about what random strangers think of me.

"I know I might regret this someday but I'm so goddamned mad at her for what she did! My sisters are terrified! My brothers... my mom and dad! and Olivia is happy about that. I want her to know that I'm not afraid of her. That I see her clearly now. That everyone will see her and know her for the lying, murdering, nothing of a woman that she is.

"She always tried to force people to respect her. She liked to make people afraid. To make them think she could hurt them with impunity. She liked people to feel small so she could feel important. I hope she feels a bit of what she put everyone else through although I doubt she has the depth to feel anything at all except anger and jealousy.

"I know you all have a million questions and I'll try to answer some. Allison G, I see you want to know when I suspected that Olivia was behind everything. I'm ashamed to say I didn't suspect her until I saw her murder Claire. I never thought my mom had it in her to hurt her kids or anyone else. That bomb in our house confused me. I thought Everly must have done it somehow despite the evidence that said she couldn't have.

"Biglaugh2, I had no idea there was a porn industry of any kind in town never mind my school. I knew Everly's friends were all liars and jerks. They were always mean to everyone, but I was keeping my distance from them, which wasn't hard to do because I was also studying hard. I hated school and couldn't wait to be done with it."

"Melissaroo, I had no friends, and it did suck. I found the trick was to stay busy, and I had my family to love. I hope you have family to love too. Having them got me through some really rough years. I have good friends now and Jace. You'll meet your own Jace someday. There's so many kind caring people out there. We just have to find each other."

I stopped for a commercial break, playing a prerecorded three-minute blurb then answered questions on it for a few minutes before playing an excerpt from my interview with Esmerelda and then talking about what Esmeralda had told me to hopefully build hype for the release of those interviews.

I played another commercial and then talked for thirty minutes about the things that Olivia had especially hated. I knew it was petty, but I was really hoping her fellow inmates would make her miserable by touching her food or playing Spanish music or calling her Olive. I hoped they'd make fun of her hair, her figure, her fake manners. I mentioned everything I could think of that might annoy her in between my prerecorded commercials.

I was careful to say it all in the most passive aggressive way I could though.

I was still answering questions I picked at random three hours later when Jace came downstairs looking for me.

The crowd outside reacted to his arrival with clapping and yelling we could hear in the basement.

He and Dan answered questions while I made us all lunch. We talked with our fans another few hours.

I finally said, "Thanks for taking the day to let me vent. I really can't express what your continued support means to us. I'm begging all of you though to respect my family's privacy. They didn't choose any of this. They never wanted to be even a minor internet celebrity. I know no one will believe this, but I didn't want that either really. I'd hoped to build a small following of like-minded people interested in the same sort of things I was. I'd hoped I could make friends and trade ideas. This channel grew so quickly that I never got a chance to get to know anyone really. I hope some of you at least are honestly interested in what I'm building here and will stick around.

"I don't plan on talking about Olivia again. She's dead to me, although, I suppose that could change depending on what the police find when they investigate because I think they'll find she has many more victims.

"Jace and I will be monitoring the site where people can come tell their Olivia stories. There's over fifty hours of stories on that channel already. I might do more interviews if the mood strikes me, but moderators will be running the site on a day-to-day basis. It will be live at midnight tonight. The link is in the description here. I expect that police will be monitoring that site. Our rules for posting on it require you to leave your real name and address and contact information, including two valid forms of ID to make their job easier if they feel they need to follow up. That info remains private from the viewers, but we need it. Proceeds from that go-fund-me page will be paying for private investigators.

"We'll be asking for volunteers to oversee that. There'll be a link on the site if you're interested. That site is going to be a serious attempt to get the people who Olivia wronged the justice they deserve."

Jace leaned past my shoulder to say, "The proceeds from the interview with Kate's parents are all going to the National Alliance of Mental Illness. We all hope that public awareness can help people like Alise who are afraid to face their illness. No one should be afraid to get the help they need. Help is out there. Call the numbers linked in the description. Call your doctor or a friend. Don't suffer alone in fear and silence. Be good to each other. Good night all and God bless."

I said, "Thanks again and I hope I see you at Briarwood. We'll be putting the dumbwaiter in this week with the Scooby Doo panels."

I disconnected.

"Take that you evil bitch," I said and Jace and Dan laughed.

Dan said, "The crowd outside is dispersing."

"Good," I said absently.

"What are you doing?" Jace asked.

"Just checking the balance."

I flipped my laptop closed.

Jace kissed the top of my head.

"Come upstair, Kate, and forget her. We never need to think about her again."

Dan gave me a quick hug.

"You guys need a vacation. I can handle everything here."

"A vacation sounds great," Jace said hopefully.

"Sure, wherever you want to go."

"Let's go tonight."

"Maybe we can stop at a library?"

His eyes widened then narrowed. They softened as he placed his hand on my cheek and nodded.

"I'm going to go pack then."

I hoped the rumors of jailhouse justice were true and that there were women in there who's kids were involved with Hard High. The images I planned to upload should convince at least some people that Olivia was behind that movie.

Crystal and Lloyd were waiting for us in the garage when we returned home a week later.

"Hear him out," Crystal said hurriedly.

Lloyd said to Jace, "I didn't know she was your girl until after all the shit went down or I'd have warned you because believe it or not family still means something to me."

"Is she in danger?" Jace asked tightly.

"No. I did everything I could to get her pictures back and cleared off when I'd found out."

"You fucking bastard!"

"He's trying to make it up," Crystal said as she grabbed Jace's arm.

Lloyd said, "I can't fix the past, but if you want me to, I can put the footage we took of Olivia online."

Crystal said hurriedly, "The police confiscated all of his tapes and stuff, but Marty has copies and Lloyd can get him to put it out there. He asked him to hold off even though it would make them money, Jace. He really is trying to make it up."

I said, "Do it. The more humiliating it will be for her, the better."

"Was she involved?" Jace asked.

"Part of my plea deal was I can't say who the guys behind the scenes were. So you didn't hear this from me. She gave Everly money and knew Everly was investing in the film. The feds are looking at her as being involved because she's connected to some of the people we knew were involved. But she never passed us money directly or contacted us. Our original funding, the script, and Margo's name as the lead were all given to me anonymously. There's a good chance it was her. That bitch is a wolf in a grandma suit.

"There's a group, really hardcore. Wolf industries. They're into everything and I mean everything. If it's dirty or shady they got a hand in it, but no one, not even the feds knows who the head guy is. He's just called the wolf and you cross him you die. I got a warning when I went looking for him, telling me to stay out of the woods, which I knew was the only warning I was going to get.

"Me and Marty knew we couldn't go into those woods or we weren't ever coming out.

"I really did think Everly was talking out her ass about murdering her family. When she attacked those kids, I knew we were in over our heads. She had to be a complete moron not to see that old bitch was going to kill her too. For a while there I thought Olivia might even be the wolf, but I'm pretty sure she isn't. She wants to be though..."

"But you didn't turn her in even then."

Lloyd snorted.

Crystal said anxiously, "He couldn't. He needed that deal first, and really Everly wasn't any threat, and you know no one would've believed him."

"He could've warned me."

Lloyd nodded.

"I should've. I was debating it, but I was pissed you came at me like that in the bar. You should've talked to me like family too if you had a problem. I'm telling you, man, I didn't know you had a thing to do with any of it until that day."

"Will you call if you hear anything?"

"Damn straight I will. Chris can reach me. I'll reach out if I hear anything I think you need to know. It has to be on the real down low though cause of my deal."

He offered his hand.

Jace hesitated then took it.

Crystal hugged Jace then Lloyd.

"Gramma will be happy you two are mending your fences."

Jace snorted softly and Lloyd laughed.

"You keep being you, Chris," Lloyd said with real affection.

I thought he really did love her in his own way.

Jace said gruffly, "Keep her out of whatever you've got going on."

"You know it."

Lloyd got into the backseat of Crystal's car. She waved, smiling hopefully at Jace before driving out.

He said, "I'll fucking kill him if he gets her involved with his messed-up life."

"You didn't believe him?"

"I believe him, but I know he's a reckless ass. He wouldn't mean to get her hurt, but who the hell knows what his scumbag friends would do! She'd try to help him, and he knows it."

"He won't be around though—will he?"

"Knowing him, he'll sneak back to see the family, but hopefully he'll stay sober while he's here. I'll talk to her…"

"It didn't occur to me until now that Weiss had never asked Lloyd a thing about how he paid for all that."

"I bet Olivia did set it up. I bet she was doing sick shit like that… I wonder if your grandpa knew and that's why they moved here."

"No way. He'd never have tried to make up with her like he did if he knew. I'm not saying he would've divorced her, but he'd never have been so nice to her."

"Someone somewhere knows."

"Then let's hope our go-fund-me is a success."

"Maybe she'd tell you now?"

"Ha! She'd tell me any lie she thought would hurt me. But I do want to talk to that crazy old bitch."

"You can't tell her it was us who posted those pics."

"It wasn't us. It was me. You don't know a thing."

He snorted.

I was sorry I hadn't been more careful making the pictures. I never should've let him find out what I planned. I wouldn't make that mistake again.

SIXTY-TWO

She looks old and unhappy, I thought happily as Olivia was led into the visitor's room.

A guard shackled her to the table, not being gentle about it.

"I know you did it," Olivia said in the tone she'd used when I was a child and she'd wanted to scare me.

I shrugged. "I could give a shit about what you know."

Her eyes widened then narrowed.

It made me laugh.

"What, you think I came to beg you not to sue me? Or press charges, or whatever lame ass threat you thought you could make? You're not at all scary. You're not the wolf you think you are—that you imagined you were. You're just a stupid woman who threw away everything good she ever had because you always knew deep down that you didn't deserve anything good. But I didn't come to talk about what a horrible waste of a soul I think you are either."

"I'm going to—"

"Save it. I couldn't care less. I'd rather be surprised. It's better for my ratings. I hope you do sue or blame me publicly. Every time you open your mouth, my ratings soar. Every complaint, every time you cry wolf, we get more donations to pay more detectives. Of course there's a limit to my patience too. All of these petty annoyances are getting boring." I winked and she jerked back. I leaned closer and said, "I came to tell you—don't wander into the forest."

She paled and I laughed.

"Who's the wolf now," I said as I stood and headed to the door.

The guard there opened it.

"Thanks, Red," I said.

The guard laughed.

I glanced back to see Olivia staring after me.

Two bright red patches flamed on her pale cheeks.

I waved then pointed as if my finger were a gun, pretending to shoot.

I wished I really did have contacts here I could use although maybe I could get some... Red was a fan of the show after all and had talked Olivia into granting this visit. There was bound to be more.

I knew she'd recognized the name, maybe she even knew the wolf's true identity. But maybe not. Either way she had to be nervous.

Jace was waiting at the car.

"How'd it go?"

"Good, I guess."

He hugged me then we got into the car. We didn't speak again until we reached the highway.

"You have to let this go, Kate. Not for her sake but yours. She doesn't deserve a minute of your thoughts. We won. We have everything anyone could possibly want—jobs we love, family we love, our health, enough money and free time to do whatever we want to do. And we have each other."

"You're right."

"Then let's say we set a date?"

"To go where?"

"No silly. A date for the wedding. I was thinking the first weekend in June, the first June after the house is done."

"That sounds perfect. You're perfect."

"You'll stop making pictures now?"

"I haven't made one in weeks."

"But you'll stop?"

"Yes. "

I didn't mention my plan to hire people from the prison as moderators. We paid the moderators a percentage of the gross. New stories and pictures of Olivia always boosted our ratings.

I could pay them legally—it wouldn't be my fault if they encouraged the inmates to beat her ass so that more people visited the site.

"We're going to be so happy together, have the best life," Jace said.

"Just like a fairy tale," I said and laughed.

EPILOGUE

Azaleas added bright pops of color to dark green hedges surrounding the pool. The hedges continued around the perimeter of the estate, softening the tall brick walls until they reached the steeply wooded section, which had been left to grow wild with only enough clearing and trimming to give a view of the distant river valley.

The hedge was still small having been planted only three years ago. It would take years and years to become nice and thick.

Lilacs lined the far wall, perfuming the air.

A stretch of grass separated the house from the pool area. Two fountains bordered the entrance to the pool patio, which was opposite the carriage house. Violin music almost drowned the soft tinkle of water.

A wedding tent was set up in the grass on a low rise that overlooked the river valley.

I walked the cobbled path from the house with my father, through the chairs on the cobbled courtyard to the arbor where Jace waited while an orchestra played softly.

Sprigs of lilac and lily of the valley picked just this morning from the garden where in the bouquets that I and my sisters carried, mingling their scents with the softer scents of the roses that decorated the tables and climbed the wall surrounding the estate.

Jace and I loved to garden, and our yard showed it. Flowerpots of white begonias, grown in our conservatory, lined a blue carpet leading to the arbor and Jace, who was so handsome it made my eyes blur with tears.

We were going to get a million likes, I thought in amusement and pride as his eyes met mine and fifty flashes went off.

A professional film crew was recording this. It would be my last official building Briarwood post; the happy ending that my family deserved.

The garden and lawns looked beautiful, the perfect backdrop to Briarwood Manor.

It had taken us almost four years to finish it, mostly because we'd been in no hurry. Our You Tube channel was a huge success. We recorded all of the repairs, the improvements, the climb from depression and fear into light and love.

We loved our life here—a life we'd built together.

I'd regained my art, which if I hadn't had Jace, I don't think I could've done. But I *did* have him. His encouragement and faith that I could do it if I didn't give up had given me the incentive—the strength—to keep trying.

The new art I'd painted to replace my original pictures weren't nearly as good, but it was getting there.

I'd sold all of the pictures of my grandmother for whopping amounts but had kept the one of my grandfather. I didn't display it though for my mother's sake.

She looked beautiful, smiling with happy tears when my father and I appeared.

Jace stood with my brothers, his stepfather, and our friend Dan beneath the arbor I'd built just for this occasion. Purple wisteria dripped from it, some of which was fake to fill in the gaps from the immature trees, but it looked real.

Jace's show, Briar Metal, was a raging success—more successful than my own really because the viewers who turned in were honestly interested, not watching because of Olivia. Every show we posted got millions of views. My grandmother's trial had seen to that. Her intent had been murder—to take everything from me, and instead she'd made Briarwood a success. I hoped she got to see this and choked on her rage as we'd had to choke on ours all through her trial.

She'd begun calling me and sending me letters and even getting fellow inmates to post online asking me to visit. I declined all of her phone calls and burned her letters unread, showing it online just to further aggravate her. It was petty of me, but I truly enjoyed knowing it annoyed her and there wasn't anything she could do about it.

I knew she was furious and embarrassed over the interviews her friends had given me. More than a few of her guards and fellow inmates posted regularly on my forums, keeping the world abreast of what was happening in prison, posting pictures of her, recounting tales of prison justice.

Olivia lived in isolation because leaving her cell always ended with her in a fight. Her fellows hated her. Not so much for what she'd done to her own family but what she'd been accused of doing to the children of Everly's classmates.

Lloyd had made good on his promise. The six pictures I'd released had merely confirmed his story. I'd no idea if Olivia had really been involved with a pedophile ring or not. It sounded plausible to me though and everyone thought it was true. I didn't care if it was true or not, I was just glad she was getting beaten up regularly—that her life in there was hell. I hoped she never got a good night sleep again.

In a recent jailhouse interview, she'd claimed the stories told about her were all lies but she hadn't blamed me in particular for forging the pictures. When asked if she planned to plead guilty for any of the new charges being brought against her for the crimes she'd committed years ago she'd only glared.

It had made me laugh. The extra time wouldn't matter at all, but her embarrassment was priceless to me. I hoped she'd have the decency to admit what she'd done but doubted she would. I didn't think she'd every admit to any of the murders she was now suspected of.

She'd had the nerve to cry over Everly in the interview as if anyone would believe her crocodile tears.

I'd cried over Everly too, not because I was sad that she was gone, but because I wouldn't have wished her death on anyone. I felt bad for not feeling as bad as the rest of the family.

Only Jace knew how relieved I was that Everly was dead. Everyone else in my family spoke as if her murder was a tragedy, as if they thought she could've been cured. I didn't believe that. Everly had been hateful before the promise of money. She *was* sick but she'd always enjoyed being mean.

I wasn't glad she'd been murdered, but I *was* undeniably relieved that I'd never have to see her again, which had sent me to therapy for a few years because I used to feel guilty for that relief as well as stupid for not seeing that my grandmother had hated me, which she must have done; she must've hated all of us if she'd been willing to murder us to keep a secret that wasn't even a secret anymore.

The therapist had helped me see or maybe come to terms with the fact that people lie—even about important things—even or maybe especially to their families.

Olivia still stuck to her story that my mother had seduced my grandfather. She told the reporter that she'd thought my father would be happier without us, without the stigma of raising his wife's bastards. Anyone could see that was a lie because she'd brought more shame to the family name than any bastard could ever do. She'd only wanted to hurt my mother—she still wanted that. It was clear in every vicious word she said about us.

I couldn't blame my grandfather for looking for affection elsewhere.

In my heart, he remained a kind man who'd made a terrible mistake by having an affair with his son's girlfriend—not an evil man who'd raped and then stalked my mother.

Jace held his hand to me as I approached on my father's arm.

I dismissed thoughts of Olivia. Now was for us. For love.

I said to Jace, "I don't have to ask. I feel your love. It's your superpower."

His smile was light and air. I breathed him in.

He was my happily ever after.

THE END

C.M. Conney, a *nom de plume* for S.M. Savoy, lives and works on the family farm in New England alongside her husband and two grown children. She loves animals and owns more than she'd like to admit. Most days, when she isn't baking or planting, she spends her time writing. An avid reader since childhood, she appreciates work in all genres and likes to mix it up a bit in her own work.

Books by C.M. CONNEY

The Real Deal
Take the Shot
Ms. Denali
The Enemy at Home

C.M. Conny's Realms of Man
(Paranormal Stories)
Moon Caught
Heaven Scent
Pack Mates
Qarahpyr
Seethe
Lord Blackwood
Anima Whispers

Books by S.M. Savoy
(Science Fiction and Fantasy)

Valor

A Warrior's Fury

A Sun Priest's Magic

Beyond Valor

A Rogue's Passion

Hidden Nature

A Vow Unbroken

A Valorous Fight

RELATED SERIES

Return of the Fae

Enter the Frey

Danu's Children

COMING SOON

Realms Protector

NEW SERIES

Dusted

Hifis

ESSENCE OF THE STORM
STORM WROUGHT

www.ingramcontent.com/pod-product-compliance
Lightning Source LLC
Chambersburg PA
CBHW031021030726
47497CB00004B/949